Library of America, a nonprofit organization,
champions our nation's cultural heritage
by publishing America's greatest writing in
authoritative new editions and providing resources
for readers to explore this rich, living legacy.

KURT VONNEGUT

KURT VONNEGUT

NOVELS 1987–1997

Bluebeard
Hocus Pocus
Timequake

Sidney Offit, editor

THE LIBRARY OF AMERICA

Contents

BLUEBEARD

"We are here to help each other get through this thing, whatever it is."

—Dr. Mark Vonnegut, M.D.
Letter to Author, 1985

AUTHOR'S NOTE

This is a novel, and a hoax autobiography at that. It is not to be taken as a responsible history of the Abstract Expressionist school of painting, the first major art movement to originate in the United States of America. It is a history of nothing but my own idiosyncratic responses to this or that.

Rabo Karabekian never lived, and neither did Terry Kitchen or Circe Berman or Paul Slazinger or Dan Gregory or Edith Taft or Marilee Kemp or any of the other major characters in this book. As for real and famous persons I mention: I have them do nothing that they did not actually do when tested on this proving ground.

May I say, too, that much of what I put in this book was inspired by the grotesque prices paid for works of art during the past century. Tremendous concentrations of paper wealth have made it possible for a few persons or institutions to endow certain sorts of human playfulness with inappropriate and hence distressing seriousness. I think not only of the mudpies of art, but of children's games as well—running, jumping, catching, throwing.

Or dancing.

Or singing songs.

K.V.

BLUEBEARD

THE AUTOBIOGRAPHY OF RABO KARABEKIAN (1916–1988)

This book is for Circe Berman. What else can I say?

—R.K.

1

Having written "The End" to this story of my life, I find it prudent to scamper back here to before the beginning, to my front door, so to speak, and to make this apology to arriving guests: "I promised you an autobiography, but something went wrong in the kitchen. It turns out to be a *diary* of this past troubled summer, too! We can always send out for pizzas if necessary. Come *in*, come *in*."

• • •

I am the erstwhile American painter Rabo Karabekian, a one-eyed man. I was born of immigrant parents in San Ignacio, California, in 1916. I begin this autobiography seventy-one years later. To those unfamiliar with the ancient mysteries of arithmetic, that makes this year 1987.

I was not born a cyclops. I was deprived of my left eye while commanding a platoon of Army Engineers, curiously enough artists of one sort or another in civilian life, in Luxembourg near the end of World War Two. We were specialists in camouflage, but at that time were fighting for our lives as ordinary infantry. The unit was composed of artists, since it was the theory of someone in the Army that we would be especially good at camouflage.

And so we were! And we were! What hallucinations we gave the Germans as to what was dangerous to them behind our lines, and what was not. Yes, and we were allowed to live like artists, too, hilariously careless in matters of dress and military courtesy. We were never attached to a unit as quotidian as a division or even a corps. We were under orders which came directly from the Supreme Headquarters of the Allied Expeditionary Force, which assigned us temporarily to this or that general, who had heard of our astonishing illusions. He was our patron for just a little while, permissive and fascinated and finally grateful.

Then off we went again.

Since I had joined the regular Army and become a lieutenant two years before the United States backed into the war, I might have attained the rank of lieutenant colonel at least by the end of the war. But I refused all promotions beyond captain in order to remain with my happy family of thirty-six men. That was my first experience with a family that large. My second came after the war, when I found myself a friend and seeming peer of those American painters who have now entered art history as founders of the Abstract Expressionist school.

•   •   •

My mother and father had families bigger than those two of mine back in the Old World—and of course their relatives back there were *blood* relatives. They lost their blood relatives to a massacre by the Turkish Empire of about one million of its Armenian citizens, who were thought to be treacherous for two reasons: first because they were clever and educated, and second because so many of them had relatives on the other side of Turkey's border with its enemy, the Russian Empire.

It was an age of Empires. So is this one, not all that well disguised.

•   •   •

The German Empire, allied with the Turks, sent impassive military observers to evaluate this century's first genocide, a word which did not exist in any language then. The word is now understood everywhere to mean a carefully planned effort to kill every member, be it man, woman, or child, of a perceived subfamily of the human race.

The problems presented by such ambitious projects are purely industrial: how to kill that many big, resourceful animals cheaply and quickly, make sure that nobody gets away, and dispose of mountains of meat and bones afterwards. The Turks, in their pioneering effort, had neither the aptitude for really big business nor the specialized machinery required. The Germans would exhibit both par excellence only one quarter of a century later. The Turks simply took all the Armenians they could find in their homes or places of work or refreshment or play or worship or education or whatever, marched them out into the countryside, and kept them away from food and water and shelter, and shot and bashed them and so on until they all appeared to be dead. It was up to dogs and vultures and rodents and so on, and finally worms, to clean up the mess afterwards.

My mother, who wasn't yet my mother, only pretended to be dead among the corpses.

My father, who wasn't yet her husband, hid in the shit and piss of a privy behind the schoolhouse where he was a teacher when the soldiers came. The school day was over, and my father-to-be was all alone in the schoolhouse writing poetry, he told me one time. Then he heard the soldiers coming and understood what they meant to do. Father never saw or heard the actual killing. For him, the stillness of the village, of which he was the only inhabitant at nightfall, all covered with shit and piss, was his most terrible memory of the massacre.

• • •

Although my mother's memories from the Old World were more gruesome than my father's, since she was right there in the killing fields, she somehow managed to put the massacre behind her and find much to like in the United States, and to daydream about a family future here.

My father *never* did.

• • •

I am a widower. My wife, née Edith Taft, who was my second such, died two years ago. She left me this nineteen-room house on the waterfront of East Hampton, Long Island, which had been in her Anglo-Saxon family from Cincinnati, Ohio, for three generations. Her ancestors surely never expected it to fall into the hands of a man with a name as exotic as Rabo Karabekian.

If they haunt this place, they do it with such Episcopalian good manners that no one has so far noticed them. If I were to come upon the spook of one of them on the grand staircase, and he or she indicated that I had no rights to this house, I would say this to him or her: "Blame the Statue of Liberty."

• • •

Dear Edith and I were happily married for twenty years. She was a grandniece of William Howard Taft, the twenty-seventh president of the United States and the tenth chief justice of the Supreme Court. She was the widow of a Cincinnati sportsman and investment banker named Richard Fairbanks, Jr., himself descended from Charles Warren Fairbanks, a United States senator from Indiana and then vice-president under Theodore Roosevelt.

We came to know each other long before her husband died when I persuaded her, and him, too, although this was her property, not his, to rent their unused potato barn to me for a studio. They had never been potato farmers, of course. They had simply bought land from a farmer next door, to the north, away from the beach, in order to keep it from being developed. With it had come the potato barn.

Edith and I did not come to know each other well until after her husband died and my first wife, Dorothy, and our two sons, Terry and Henri, moved out on me. I sold our house, which was in the village of Springs, six miles north of here, and made Edith's barn not only my studio but my home.

That improbable dwelling, incidentally, is invisible from the main house, where I am writing now.

•   •   •

Edith had no children by her first husband, and she was past childbearing when I transmogrified her from being Mrs. Richard Fairbanks, Jr., into being Mrs. Rabo Karabekian instead.

So we were a very tiny family indeed in this great big house, with its two tennis courts and swimming pool, and its carriage house and its potato barn—and its three hundred yards of private beach on the open Atlantic Ocean.

One might think that my two sons, Terry and Henri Karabekian, whom I named in honor of my closest friend, the late Terry Kitchen, and the artist Terry and I most envied, Henri Matisse, might enjoy coming here with their families. Terry has two sons of his own now. Henri has a daughter.

But they do not speak to me.

"So be it! So be it!" I cry in this manicured wilderness. "Who gives a damn!" Excuse this outburst.

•   •   •

Dear Edith, like all great Earth Mothers, was a multitude. Even when there were only the two of us and the servants here, she filled this Victorian ark with love and merriment and hands-on domesticity. As privileged as she had been all her life, she cooked with the cook, gardened with the gardener, did all our food shopping, fed the pets and birds, and made personal friends of wild rabbits and squirrels and raccoons.

But we used to have a lot of parties, too, and guests who sometimes stayed for weeks—*her* friends and relatives, mostly. I have already said how matters stood and stand with my own few blood relatives, alienated descendants all. As for my synthetic relatives in the Army: some were killed in the little battle in which I was taken prisoner, and which cost me one eye. Those who survived I have never seen or heard from since. It may be that they were not as fond of me as I was of them.

These things happen.

The members of my other big synthetic family, the Abstract Expressionists, are mostly dead now, having been killed by everything from mere old age to suicide. The few survivors, like my blood relatives, no longer speak to me.

"So be it! So be it!" I cry in this manicured wilderness. "Who gives a damn!" Excuse this outburst.

•   •   •

All of our servants quit soon after Edith died. They said it had simply become too lonely here. So I hired some new ones, paying them a great deal of money to put up with me and all the loneliness. When Edith was alive, and the house was alive, the gardener and the two maids and the cook all lived here. Now only the cook, and, as I say, a different cook, lives in, and has the entire servants' quarters on the third floor of the ell to herself and her fifteen-year-old daughter. She is a divorced woman, a native of East Hampton, about forty, I would say. Her daughter, Celeste, does no work for me, but simply lives here and eats my food, and entertains her loud and willfully ignorant friends on my tennis courts and in my swimming pool and on my private oceanfront.

She and her friends ignore me, as though I were a senile veteran from some forgotten war, daydreaming away what little remains of his life as a museum guard. Why should I be offended? This house, in addition to being a home, shelters what is the most important collection of Abstract Expressionist paintings still in private hands. Since I have done no useful work for decades, what else am I, really, but a museum guard?

And, just as a paid museum guard would have to do, I answer as best I can the question put to me by visitor after visitor, stated in various ways, of course: "What are these pictures supposed to *mean*?"

•   •   •

These paintings, which are about absolutely nothing but themselves, were my own property long before I married Edith. They are worth at least as much as all the real estate and stocks and bonds, including a one-quarter share in the Cincinnati Bengals professional football team, which Edith left to me. So I cannot be stigmatized as an American fortune-hunter.

I may have been a lousy painter, but what a *collector* I turned out to be!

2

I T HAS BEEN very lonely here since Edith died. The friends we had were hers, not mine. Painters shun me, since the ridicule my own paintings attracted and deserved encouraged Philistines to argue that *most* painters were charlatans or fools. But I can stand loneliness, if I have to.

I stood it when a boy. I stood it for several years in New York City during the Great Depression. And after my first wife and my two sons left me in 1956, and I gave up on myself as a painter, I actually went looking for loneliness and found it. I was a hermit for eight years. How is that for a full-time job for a wounded vet?

•   •   •

And I *do* have a friend who is mine, all mine. He is the novelist Paul Slazinger, a wounded World War Two geezer like myself. He sleeps alone in a house next door to *my* old house in Springs.

I say he *sleeps* there, because he comes over *here* almost every day, and is probably on the property somewhere at this very moment, watching a tennis game, or sitting on the beach, staring out to sea, or playing cards with the cook in the kitchen, or hiding from everybody and everything, and reading a book where practically nobody ever goes, on the far side of the potato barn.

I don't think he writes much anymore. And, as I say, I don't paint at *all* anymore. I won't even doodle on the memo pad next to the downstairs telephone. A couple of weeks ago, I caught myself doing exactly that, and I deliberately snapped the point off the pencil, broke the pencil in two, and I threw its broken body into a wastebasket, like a baby rattlesnake which had wanted to *poison* me.

•   •   •

Paul has no money. He eats supper with me here four or five times a week, and gobbles directly from my refrigerator and fruit bowls during the daytime, so I am surely his primary source of nutriment. I have said to him many times after supper,

13

"Paul—why don't you sell your house and get a little walking-around money, and move in here? Look at all the *room* I've got. And I'm never going to have a wife or a lady friend again, and neither are you. Jesus! Who would have us? We look like a couple of gutshot iguanas! So move in! I won't bother you, and you won't bother me. What could make more sense?"

His answer never varies much from this one: "I can only write at home." Some home, with a busted refrigerator and nobody ever there but him.

One time he said about this house: "Who could write in a museum?"

Well—I am now finding out if that can be done or not. I am *writing* in this museum.

Yes, it's true: I, old Rabo Karabekian, having disgraced myself in the visual arts, am now having a go at literature. A true child of the Great Depression, though, playing it safe, I am hanging on to my job as a museum guard.

What has inspired this amazing career change by one so old? *Cherchez la femme!*

Uninvited, as nearly as I can remember, an energetic and opinionated and voluptuous and relatively young woman has moved in with me!

She said she couldn't bear seeing and hearing me do absolutely nothing all day long—so why didn't I *do* something, do *anything*? If I couldn't think of anything else to do, why didn't I write my autobiography?

Why not, indeed?

She is so *authoritative*!

I find myself doing whatever she says I must do. During our twenty years of marriage, my dear Edith never *once* thought of something for me to do. In the Army, I knew several colonels and generals like this new woman in my life, but they were *men*, and we were a nation at war.

Is this woman a friend? I don't know what the hell she is. All I know is that she isn't going to leave again until she's good and ready, and that she scares the *pants* off me.

Help.

Her name is Circe Berman.

• • •

She is a widow. Her husband was a brain surgeon in Baltimore, where she still has a house as big and empty as this one.
Her husband Abe died of a brain hemorrhage six months ago.
She is forty-three years old, and she has selected this house as
a nice place to live and work while she writes her husband's
biography.

There is nothing erotic about our relationship. I am twenty-
eight years Mrs. Berman's senior, and have become too ugly for
anyone but a dog to love. I really do look like a gutshot iguana,
and am one-eyed besides. Enough is enough.

Here is how we met: she wandered onto my private beach
alone one afternoon, not knowing it was private. She had never
heard of me, since she hates modern art. She didn't know a soul
in the Hamptons, and was staying in the Maidstone Inn in the
village about a mile and a half from here. She had walked from
there to the public beach, and then across my border.

I went down for my afternoon dip, and there she was, fully
dressed, and doing what Paul Slazinger does so much of: sitting on sand and staring out to sea. The only reason I minded
her being there, or anybody's being there, was my ludicrous
physique and the fact I would have to take off my eye patch
before I went in. There's quite a mess under there, not unlike a
scrambled egg. I was embarrassed to be seen up close.

Paul Slazinger says, incidentally, that the human condition
can be summed up in just one word, and this is the word:
Embarrassment.

•   •   •

So I elected not to swim, but to sunbathe some distance away
from her.

I did, however, come close enough to say, "Hello."

This was her curious reply: "Tell me how your parents died."

What a spooky woman! She could be a *witch*. Who but a witch
could have persuaded me to write my autobiography?

She has just stuck her head in the room to say that it was time
I went to New York City, where I haven't been since Edith died.
I've hardly been out of this house since Edith died.

New York City, here I come. This is terrible!

•   •   •

"Tell me how your parents died," she said. I couldn't believe my ears.

"I beg your pardon?" I said.

"What good is 'Hello'?" she said.

She had stopped me in my tracks. "I've always thought it was better than nothing," I said, "but I could be wrong."

"What does 'Hello' mean?" she said.

And I said, "I had always understood it to mean 'Hello.' "

"Well it doesn't," she said. "It means, 'Don't talk about anything important.' It means, 'I'm smiling but not listening, so just go away.' "

She went on to avow that she was tired of just pretending to meet people. "So sit down here," she said, "and tell Mama how your parents died."

"Tell *Mama*!" Can you *beat* it?

She had straight black hair and large brown eyes like my mother—but she was much taller than my mother, and a little bit taller than me, for that matter. She was also much shapelier than my mother, who let herself become quite heavy, and who didn't care much what her hair looked like, either, or her clothes. Mother didn't care because Father didn't care.

And I told Mrs. Berman this about my mother: "She died when I was twelve—of a tetanus infection she evidently picked up while working in a cannery in California. The cannery was built on the site of an old livery stable, and tetanus bacteria often colonize the intestines of horses without hurting them, and then become durable spores, armored little seeds, when excreted. One of them lurking in the dirt around and under the cannery was somehow exhumed and sent traveling. After a long, long sleep it awakened in Paradise, something we would all like to do. Paradise was a cut in my mother's hand."

"So long, Mama," said Circe Berman.

There was that word *Mama* again.

"At least she didn't have to endure the Great Depression, which was only one year away," I said.

And at least she didn't have to see her only child come home a cyclops from World War Two.

"And how did your father die?" she said.

"In the Bijou Theater in San Ignacio in 1938," I said. "He went to the movie alone. He never even considered remarrying."

He still lived over the little store in California where he had got his first foothold in the economy of the United States of America. I had been living in Manhattan for five years then— and was working as an artist for an advertising agency. When the movie was over, the lights came on, and everybody went home but Father.

"What was the movie?" she asked.

And I said, "*Captains Courageous*, starring Spencer Tracy and Freddie Bartholomew."

•   •   •

What Father might have made of that movie, which was about cod fishermen in the North Atlantic, God only knows. Maybe he didn't see any of it before he died. If he did see some of it, he must have gotten rueful satisfaction from its having absolutely nothing to do with anything he had ever seen or anybody he had ever known. He welcomed all proofs that the planet he had known and loved during his boyhood had disappeared entirely.

That was *his* way of honoring all the friends and relatives he had lost in the massacre.

•   •   •

You *could* say that he became his own Turk over here, knocking himself down and spitting on himself. He could have studied English and become a respected teacher there in San Ignacio, and started writing poetry again, or maybe translated the Armenian poets he loved so much into English. But that wasn't *humiliating* enough. Nothing would do but that he, with all his education, become what his father and grandfather had been, which was a cobbler.

He was good at that craft, which he had learned as a boy, and which I would learn as a boy. But how he *complained*! At least he pitied himself in Armenian, which only Mother and I could understand. There weren't any other Armenians within a hundred miles of San Ignacio.

"*I am looking for William Shakespeare, your greatest poet*," he might say as he worked. "*Have you ever heard of him?*" He knew Shakespeare backwards and forwards in Armenian, and would often quote him. "To be or not to be . . ." for example, as far as he was concerned, was, "*Linel kam chlinel . . .*"

"Tear out my tongue if you catch me speaking Armenian," he might say. That was the penalty the Turks set in the seventeenth century for speaking any language but Turkish: a ripped-out tongue.

"Who are those people and what am I doing here?" he might say, with cowboys and Chinese and Indians passing by outside.

"When is San Ignacio going to erect a statue of Mesrob Mashtots?" he might say. Mesrob Mashtots was the inventor of the Armenian alphabet, unlike any other, about four hundred years before the birth of Christ. Armenians, incidentally, were the first people to make Christianity their national religion.

"One million, one million, one million," he might say. This is the generally accepted figure for the number of Armenians killed by the Turks in the massacre from which my parents escaped. That was two thirds of Turkey's Armenians, and about half the Armenians in the whole wide world. There are about six million of us now, including my two sons and three grandchildren, who know nothing and care nothing about Mesrob Mashtots.

"Musa Dagh!" he might say. This was the name of a place in Turkey where a small band of Armenian civilians fought Turkish militiamen to a standstill for forty days and forty nights before being exterminated—about the time my parents, with me in my mother's belly, arrived safe and sound in San Ignacio.

•   •   •

"Thank you, Vartan Mamigonian," he might say. This was the name of a great Armenian national hero, who led a losing army against the Persians in the fifth century. The Vartan Mamigonian Father had in mind, however, was an Armenian shoe manufacturer in Cairo, Egypt, to which polyglot metropolis my parents escaped after the massacre. It was he, a survivor of an earlier massacre, who persuaded my naive parents, who had met on a road to Cairo, that they would find the streets paved with gold, if only they could find their way to, of all places, San Ignacio, California. But that is a story I will tell at another time.

"If anybody has discovered what life is all about," Father might say, *"it is too late. I am no longer interested."*

"Never is heard a discouraging word, and the skies are not cloudy all day," he might say. These, of course, are words from the

American song "Home on the Range," which he had translated into Armenian. He found them idiotic.

"*Tolstoi made shoes*," he might say. This was a fact, of course: the greatest of Russian writers and idealists had, in an effort to do work that mattered, made shoes for a little while. May I say that I, too, could make shoes if I had to.

•   •   •

Circe Berman says she can make *pants* if she has to. As she would tell me when we met on the beach, her father had a pants factory in Lackawanna, New York, until he went bankrupt and hanged himself.

•   •   •

If my father had managed to survive *Captains Courageous*, starring Spencer Tracy and Freddie Bartholomew, and had lived to see the paintings I did after the war, several of which drew serious critical attention, and a few of which I sold for what was quite a bit of money back then, he surely would have been among the great American majority which snorted and jeered at them. He wouldn't have razzed just me. He would have razzed my Abstract Expressionist pals, too, Jackson Pollock and Mark Rothko and Terry Kitchen and so on, painters who are now, unlike myself, acknowledged to be some of the most brilliant artists ever to have been produced not just by the United States but by the whole damn world. But what sticks in my mind like a thorn now, and I haven't thought about this for years: he would have had no hesitation in razzing his own son, in razzing me.

So, thanks to the conversation Mrs. Berman struck up with me on the beach only two weeks ago, I am in a frenzy of ado-lescent resentment against a father who was buried almost fifty years ago! Let me off this hellish time machine!

But there is no getting off this hellish time machine. I have to think now, even though it is the last I would ever want to think about, if I had a choice, that my own father would have laughed as hard as anybody when my paintings, thanks to unforeseen chemical reactions between the sizing of my canvases and the acrylic wall-paint and colored tapes I had applied to them, all destroyed themselves.

I mean—people who had paid fifteen- or twenty- or even thirty thousand dollars for a picture of mine found themselves gazing at a blank canvas, all ready for a new picture, and ringlets of colored tapes and what looked like moldy Rice Krispies on the floor.

• • •

It was a postwar miracle that did me in. I had better explain to my young readers, if any, that the Second World War had many of the promised characteristics of Armageddon, a final war between good and evil, so that nothing would do but that it be followed by miracles. Instant coffee was one. DDT was another. It was going to kill all the bugs, and almost did. Nuclear energy was going to make electricity so cheap that it might not even be metered. It would also make another war unthinkable. Talk about loaves and fishes! Antibiotics would defeat all diseases. Lazarus would never die: How was that for a scheme to make the Son of God obsolete?

Yes, and there were miraculous breakfast foods and would soon be helicopters for every family. There were miraculous new fibers which could be washed in cold water and need no ironing afterwards! Talk about a war well worth fighting!

During that war we had a word for extreme manmade disorder which was *fubar*, an acronym for "fucked up beyond all recognition." Well—the whole planet is now fubar with postwar miracles, but, back in the early 1960s, I was one of the first persons to be totally wrecked by one—an acrylic wall-paint whose colors, according to advertisements of the day, would ". . . outlive the smile on the 'Mona Lisa.' "

The name of the paint was Sateen Dura-Luxe. Mona Lisa is still smiling. And your local paint dealer, if he has been in the business any length of time, will laugh in your face if you ask for Sateen Dura-Luxe.

• • •

"Your father had the Survivor's Syndrome," said Circe Berman to me on my beach that day. "He was ashamed not to be dead like all his friends and relatives."

"He was ashamed that I wasn't dead, too," I said.

"Think of it as a noble emotion gone wrong," she said.

"He was a very upsetting father," I said. "I'm sorry now that you've made me remember him."

"As long as we've brought him back," she said, "why don't you forgive him now?"

"I've done it a hundred times already," I said. "This time I'm going to be smart and get a receipt." I went on to assert that Mother was more entitled to Survivor's Syndrome than Father, since she had been right in the middle of the killing, pretending to be dead with people lying on top of her, and with screams and blood everywhere. She wasn't all that much older then than the cook's daughter, Celeste.

While Mother was lying there, she was looking right into the face of the corpse of an old woman who had no teeth, only inches away. The old woman's mouth was open, and inside it and on the ground below it was a fortune in unset jewels.

"If it weren't for those jewels," I told Mrs. Berman, "I would not be a citizen of this great country, and would be in no position to tell you that you are now trespassing on my private property. That's my house there, on the other side of the dunes. Would you be offended if a lonely and harmless old widower invited you thence for a drink, if you drink, and then supper with an equally harmless old friend of mine?" I meant Paul Slazinger.

She accepted. And after supper I heard myself saying, "If you'd rather stay here instead of the inn, you're certainly welcome." And I made her the same guarantee I made many times to Slazinger: "I promise not to bother you."

So let's be honest. I said a little earlier that I had no idea how she had come to share this house with me. Let's be honest. I *invited* her.

•

3

S HE HAS TURNED me and this household upside down! I should have known how manipulative she was from the very first words she ever said to me: "Tell me how your parents died." I mean—those were the words of a woman who was quite used to turning people in any direction she chose, as though they were machine bolts and she were a monkey wrench.

And if I had missed the warning signals on the beach, there were plenty more at supper. She behaved as though she were a paying customer in a fancy restaurant, screwing up her face after tasting a wine which I myself had sipped and declared potable, and declaring the veal to be overcooked and ordering Slazinger to send his serving back to the kitchen along with hers, and saying that she was going to plan the meals while she was here, since Paul's and my circulatory systems were obviously, since our complexions were so pasty and our gestures so listless, clogged up with cholesterol.

• • •

She was outrageous! She sat across from a Jackson Pollock for which I had just been offered two million dollars by an anonymous collector in Switzerland, and she said, "I wouldn't give that houseroom!"

So I asked her tartly, after a wink in Slazinger's direction, what sort of picture might please her more.

She replied that she wasn't on Earth to be pleased but to be instructed. "I need information the way I need vitamins and minerals," she said. "Judging from your pictures, you hate facts like poison."

"I suppose you would be happier looking at George Washington crossing the Delaware," I said.

"Who wouldn't?" she said. "But I tell you what I'd really like to see there since our talk on the beach."

"Which is—?" I said, arching my eyebrows and then winking at Slazinger again.

"I'd like a picture with some grass and dirt at the bottom," she said.

"Brown and green," I suggested.

"Fine," she said. "And sky at the top."

"Blue," I said.

"Maybe with clouds," she said.

"Easily supplied," I said.

"And in between the sky and the ground—" she said.

"A duck?" I said. "An organ-grinder with his monkey? A sailor and his girl on a park bench?"

"Not a duck and not an organ-grinder and not a sailor and his girl," she said. "A whole lot of dead bodies lying every which way on the ground. And very close to us is the face of a beautiful girl, maybe sixteen or seventeen. She is pinned under the corpse of a man, but she is still alive, and she is staring into the open mouth of a dead old woman whose face is only inches from hers. Out of that toothless mouth are spilling diamonds and emeralds and rubies."

There was a silence.

And then she said, "You could build a whole new religion, and a much needed one, too, on a picture like that." She nodded in the direction of the Pollock. "All anybody could do with a picture like that is illustrate an advertisement for a hangover remedy or seasick pills."

• • •

Slazinger asked her what had brought her to the Hamptons, since she didn't know anybody here. She replied that she hoped to find some peace and quiet so she could devote her full attention to writing a biography of her husband, the Baltimore brain surgeon.

Slazinger preened himself as a man who had published eleven novels and he patronized her as an amateur.

"Everybody thinks he or she can be a writer," he said with airy irony.

"Don't tell me it's a crime to try," she said.

"It's a crime to think it's easy," he said. "But if you're really serious, you'll find out quick enough that it's the hardest thing there is."

"Particularly so, if you have absolutely nothing to say," she said. "Don't you think that's the main reason people find it so difficult? If they can write complete sentences and can use a dictionary, isn't that the *only* reason they find writing hard: they don't know or care about anything?"

Here Slazinger stole a line from the writer Truman Capote, who died five years ago, and who had a house only a few miles west of here. "I think you're talking about *typing* instead of *writing*," he said.

She promptly identified the source of his witticism: "Truman Capote," she said.

Slazinger covered himself nicely. "As everyone knows," he said.

"If you didn't have such a kind face," she said, "I would suspect that you were making fun of me."

But listen to this, which she only told me at breakfast this morning. Just listen to this and then tell me who was toying with whom at that supper, which is now two weeks ago: Mrs. Berman is *not* an amateur writing a biography of her late husband. That was just a story to cover her true identity and purpose for being here. She swore me to secrecy, and then confessed that she was really in the Hamptons to research and write a novel about working-class adolescents living in a resort community teeming in the summer time with the sons and daughters of multimillionaires.

And this wasn't going to be her first novel either. It would be the twenty-first in a series of shockingly frank and enormously popular novels for young readers, several of which had been made into motion pictures. She had written them under the name of "Polly Madison."

•   •   •

I certainly *will* keep this a secret, too, if only to save the life of Paul Slazinger. If he finds out who she really is now, after all his posturing as a professional writer, he will do what Terry Kitchen, the only other best friend I ever had, did. He will commit suicide.

In terms of commercial importance in the literary marketplace, Circe Berman is to Paul Slazinger what General Motors is to a bicycle factory in Albania!

Mum's the word!

•   •   •

She said that first night that she collected pictures, too.

I asked her what kind, and she said, "Victorian chromos of little girls on swings." She said she had more than a hundred of them, all different, but all of little girls on swings.

"I suppose you think that's terrible," she said.

"Not at all," I said, "just as long as you keep them safely caged in Baltimore."

•   •   •

That first night, I remember, too, she asked Slazinger and me, and then the cook and her daughter, too, if we knew any true stories about local girls from relatively poor families who had married the sons of rich people.

Slazinger said, "I don't think you'll even see that in the *movies* anymore."

Celeste told her, "The rich marry the rich. Where have you *been* all your life?"

•   •   •

To get back to the past, which is what this book is supposed to be all about: My mother gathered up the jewels that had fallen from the dead woman's mouth, but not the ones still inside there. Whenever she told the story, she was emphatic about that: she hadn't fished anything from the woman's mouth. Whatever had stayed in there was still the woman's very personal property.

And Mother crawled away after nightfall, after the killers had all gone home. She wasn't from my father's village, and she would not meet him until they both crossed the lightly guarded border with Persia, about seventy miles from the scene of the massacre.

Persian Armenians took them in. After they decided to go together to Egypt. My father did most of the talking, since Mother had a mouthful of jewels. When they got to the Persian Gulf, mother sold the first of those compact treasures in order to buy them passage on a small freighter to Cairo, via the Red Sea. And it was in Cairo that they met the criminal Vartan Mamigonian, a survivor of an earlier massacre.

"Never trust a survivor," my father used to warn me, with Vartan Mamigonian in mind, "until you find out what he did to stay alive."

• • •

This Mamigonian had grown rich manufacturing military boots for the British Army and the German Army, which would soon be fighting each other in World War One. He offered my parents low-paid work of the dirtiest kind. They were fools enough to tell him, since he was a fellow Armenian survivor, about Mother's jewels and their plans to marry and go to Paris to join the large and highly cultivated Armenian colony there.

Mamigonian became their most ardent advisor and protector, eager to find them a safe place for the jewels in a city notorious for its heartless thieves. But they had already put them in a bank.

So Mamigonian constructed a fantasy which he proposed to trade for the jewels. He must have found San Ignacio, California, in an atlas, since no Armenian had ever been there, and since no news of that sleepy farming town could have reached the Near East in any form. Mamigonian said he had a brother in San Ignacio. He forged letters from the brother to prove it. The letters said, moreover, that the brother had become extremely rich in a short time there. There were many other Armenians there, all doing well. They were looking for a teacher for their children who was fluent in Armenian and familiar with the great literature in that language.

As an inducement to such a teacher, they would sell him a house and twenty acres of fruit trees at a fraction of their true value. Mamigonian's "rich brother" enclosed a photo of the house, and a deed to it as well.

If Mamigonian knew a good teacher in Cairo who might be interested, this nonexistent brother wrote, Mamigonian was authorized to sell him the deed. This would secure the teaching job for Father, and make him one of the larger property owners in idyllic San Ignacio.

4

I HAVE BEEN in the art business, the picture business, so long now that I can daydream about the past as though it were a vista through a series of galleries like the Louvre, perhaps— home of the "Mona Lisa," whose smile has now outlived by three decades the postwar miracle of Sateen Dura-Luxe. The pictures in what must be the final gallery of my life are real. I can touch them, if I like, or, following the recommendations of the widow Berman, a.k.a. "Polly Madison," sell them to the highest bidder or in some other way, in her thoughtful words, "Get them the hell out of here."

In the imaginary galleries in the distance are my own Abstract Expressionist paintings, miraculously resurrected by the Great Critic for Judgment Day, and then pictures by Europeans, which I bought for a few dollars or chocolate bars or nylon stockings when a soldier, and then advertisements of the sort I had been laying out and illustrating before I joined the Army—at about the time news of my father's death in the Bijou Theater in San Ignacio came.

Still farther away are the magazine illustrations of Dan Gregory, whose apprentice I was from the time I was seventeen until he threw me out. I was one month short of being twenty when he threw me out. I was one of the Dan Gregory Gallery are unframed works I made in my boyhood, as the only artist of any age or sort ever to inhabit San Ignacio.

The gallery at the farthest remove from me in my dotage, though, just inside the door I entered in 1916, is devoted to a photograph, not a painting. Its subject is a noble white house with a long winding driveway and porte-cochère, supposedly in San Ignacio, which Vartan Mamigonian in Cairo told my parents they were buying with most of Mother's jewelry.

That picture, along with a bogus deed, crawling with signatures and spattered with sealing wax, was in my parents' bedside table for many years—in the tiny apartment over Father's shoe repair shop. I assumed that he had thrown them out with so many other mementos after Mother died. But as I was about to board a railroad train in 1933, to seek my fortune in New York City during the depths of the Great Depression, Father made me a present of the photograph. "If you happen to come across this house," he said in Armenian, "let me know where it is. Wherever it is, it belongs to me."

• • •

I don't own that picture anymore. Coming back to New York City after having been one of three persons at Father's funeral in San Ignacio, which I hadn't seen for five years, I ripped the photograph to bits. I did that because I was angry at my dead father. It was my conclusion that he had cheated himself and my mother a lot worse than they had been cheated by Vartan Mamigonian. It wasn't Mamigonian who made my parents stay in San Ignacio instead of moving to Fresno, say, where there really *was* an Armenian colony, whose members supported each other and kept the old language and customs and religion alive, and at the same time became happier and happier to be in California. Father could have become a beloved teacher again!

Oh, no—it wasn't Mamigonian who tricked him into being the unhappiest and loneliest of all the world's cobblers.

• • •

Armenians have done brilliantly in this country during the short time they've been here. My neighbor to the west is F. Donald Kasabian, executive vice-president of Metropolitan Life—so that right here in exclusive East Hampton, and right on the beach, too, we have *two* Armenians side by side. What used to be J. P. Morgan's estate in Southampton is now the property of Kevork Hovanessian, who also owned Twentieth Century–Fox until he sold it last week.

And Armenians haven't succeeded only in business here. The great writer William Saroyan was an Armenian, and so is Dr. George Mintouchian, the new president of the University of Chicago. Dr. Mintouchian is a renowned Shakespeare scholar, something my father could have been.

And Circe Berman has just come into the room and read what is in my typewriter, which is ten of the lines above. She is gone again. She said again that my father *obviously* suffered from Survivor's Syndrome.

"Everybody who is alive is a survivor, and everybody who is dead isn't," I said. "So everybody alive must have the Survivor's Syndrome. It's that or death. I am so damn sick of people telling me proudly that they are survivors! Nine times out of ten it's a cannibal or billionaire!"

"You still haven't forgiven your father for being what he had to be," she said. "That's why you're yelling now."

"I wasn't yelling," I said.

"They can hear you in Portugal," she said. That's where you wind up if you put out to sea from my private beach and sail due east, as she had figured out from the globe in the library. You wind up in Oporto, Portugal.

"You envy your father's ordeal," she said.

"I had an ordeal of my own!" I said. "In case you haven't noticed, I'm a one-eyed man."

"You told me yourself that there was almost no pain, and that it healed right away," she said, which was true. I don't remember being hit, but only the approach of a white German tank and German soldiers all in white across a snow-covered meadow in Luxembourg. I was unconscious when I was taken prisoner, and was kept that way by morphine until I woke up in a German military hospital in a church across the border, in Germany. She was right: I had to endure no more pain in the war than a civilian experiences in a dentist's chair.

The wound healed so quickly that I was soon shipped off to a camp as just another unremarkable prisoner.

• • •

Still, I insisted that I was as entitled to a Survivor's Syndrome as my father, so she asked me two questions. The first one was this: "Do you believe sometimes that you are a good person in a world where almost all of the other good people are dead?"

"No," I said.

"Do you sometimes believe that you must be wicked, since all the good people are dead, and that the only way to clear your name is to be dead, too?"

"No," I said.

"You may be entitled to the Survivor's Syndrome, but you didn't get it," she said. "Would you like to try for tuberculosis instead?"

•   •   •

"How do you know so much about the Survivor's Syndrome?"
I asked her. This wasn't a boorish question to ask her, since she
had told me during our first meeting on the beach that she and
her husband, although both Jewish, had had no knowledge of
relatives they might have had in Europe and who might have
been killed during the Holocaust. They were both from families
which had been in the United States for several generations, and
which had lost all contact with European relatives.

"I wrote a book about it," she said. "Rather—I wrote about
people like you: children of a parent who had survived some
sort of mass killing. It's called *The Underground*."

Needless to say, I have not read that or any of the Polly Madison books, although they seem, now that I have started looking
around for them, as available as packs of chewing gum.

•   •   •

Not that I would need to leave the house to get a copy of *The
Underground* or any other Polly Madison book, Mrs. Berman
informs me. The cook's daughter Celeste has every one of them.

Mrs. Berman, the most ferocious enemy of privacy I ever
knew, has also discovered that Celeste, although only *fifteen*,
already takes birth-control pills.

•   •   •

The formidable widow Berman told me the plot of *The
Underground*, which is this: Three girls, one black, one Jewish
and one Japanese, feel drawn together and separate from the rest
of their classmates for reasons they can't explain. They form a
little club which they call, again for reasons they can't explain,
"The Underground."

But then it turns out that all three have a parent or grandpar-
ent who has survived some manmade catastrophe, and who,
without meaning to, passed on to them the idea that the wicked
were the living and that the good were dead.

The black is descended from a survivor of the massacre of
Ibos in Nigeria. The Japanese is a descendant of a survivor of
the atom-bombing of Nagasaki. The Jew is a descendant of a
survivor of the Nazi Holocaust.

• • •

"*The Underground* is a wonderful title for a book like that,"
I said.

"You bet it is," she said. "I am very proud of my titles." She
really thinks that she is the cat's pajamas, and that everybody
else is dumb, dumb, dumb!

• • •

She said that painters should hire writers to name their pictures for them. The names of the pictures on my walls here are
"Opus Nine" and "Blue and Burnt Orange" and so on. My own
most famous painting, which no longer exists, and which was
sixty-four feet long and eight feet high, and used to grace the
entrance lobby of the GEFFCo headquarters on Park Avenue,
was called simply, "Windsor Blue Number Seventeen." Windsor
Blue was a shade of Sateen Dura-Luxe, straight from the can.

"The titles are *meant* to be uncommunicative," I said.

"What's the point of being alive," she said, "if you're not
going to *communicate?*"

She still has no respect for my art collection, although, during
the five weeks she has now been in residence, she has seen
immensely respectable people from as far away as Switzerland
and Japan worship some of them as though the pictures were
gods almost. She was here when I sold a Rothko right off the
wall to a man from the Getty Museum for a million and a half
dollars.

What she said about that was this: "Good riddance of bad
rubbish. It was rotting your brain because it was about absolutely nothing. Now give the rest of them the old heave-ho!"

• • •

She asked me just now, while we were talking about the Survivor's Syndrome, if my father wanted to see the Turks punished
for what they had done to the Armenians.

"I asked him the same thing when I was about eight years old,
I guess, and thinking maybe life would be spicier if we wanted
revenge of some kind," I said.

"Father put down his tools there in his little shop, and he
stared out the window," I went on, "and I looked out the

window, too. There were a couple of Luma Indian men out
there, I remember. The Luma reservation was only five miles
away, and sometimes people passing through town would mistake me for a Luma boy. I liked that a lot. At the time I thought
it certainly beat being an Armenian.

"Father finally answered my question this way: 'All I want
from the Turks is an admission that their country is an uglier
and even more joyless place, now that *we* are gone.' "

• • •

I went for a manly tramp around my boundaries after lunch
today, and encountered my neighbor to the north on our mutual
border, which runs about twenty feet north of my potato barn.
His name is John Karpinski. He is a native. He is a potato
farmer like his father, although his fields must now be worth
about eighty thousand dollars an acre, since the second-story
windows of houses built on them would have an ocean view.
Three generations of Karpinskis have been raised on all that
property, so that to them, in an Armenian manner of speaking, it is their own sacred ancestral bit of ground at the foot of
Mount Ararat.

Karpinski is a huge man, almost always in bib-overalls, and
everybody calls him "Big John." Big John is a wounded war
veteran like Paul Slazinger and me, but he is younger than us,
so his war was a different war. His war was the Korean War.

And then his only son "Little John" was killed by a land mine
in the Vietnam War.

One war to a customer.

• • •

My potato barn and the six acres that came with it used to
belong to Big John's father, who sold them to Dear Edith and
her first husband.

Big John expressed curiosity about Mrs. Berman. I promised
him that our relationship was platonic, and that she had more or
less invited herself, and that I would be glad when she returned
to Baltimore.

"She sounds like a bear," he said. "If a bear gets in your house,
you had better go to a motel until the bear is ready to leave
again."

There used to be lots of bears on Long Island, but there certainly aren't bears anymore. He said his knowledge of bears came from his father, who, at the age of sixty, was treed by a grizzly in Yellowstone Park. After that, John's father read every book about bears he could get his hands on.

"I'll say this for that bear—" said John, "it got the old man reading books again."

•   •   •

Mrs. Berman is so God damn nosy! I mean—she comes in here and reads what is in my typewriter without feeling the need to ask permission first.

"How come you never use semicolons?" she'll say. Or: "How come you chop it all up into little sections instead of letting it flow and flow?" *That* sort of thing.

And when I listen to her moving about this house, I not only hear her footsteps: I hear the opening and closing of drawers and cupboards, too. She has investigated every nook and cranny, including the basement. She came up from the basement one day and said, "Do you know you've got sixty-three gallons of Sateen Dura-Luxe down there?" She had *counted* them!

It is against the law to dispose of Sateen Dura-Luxe in an ordinary dump because it has been found to degrade over time into a very deadly poison. To get rid of the stuff legally, I would have to ship it to a special disposal area near Pitchfork, Wyoming, and I have never got around to doing that. So there it sits in the basement after all these years.

•   •   •

The one place on the property she hasn't explored is my studio, the potato barn. It is a very long and narrow structure without windows, with sliding doors and a potbellied stove at either end, built for the storage of potatoes and nothing else. The idea was this: a farmer might maintain an even temperature in there, no matter what the weather, with the stoves and the doors, so that his potatoes would neither freeze nor sprout until he was ready to market them.

It was structures with such unusual dimensions, in fact, along with what used to be very cheap property, which caused many painters to move out here when I was young, and especially painters who were working on exceptionally large canvases. I would never have been able to work on the eight panels comprising "Windsor Blue Number Seventeen" as a single piece, if I hadn't rented that potato barn.

• • •

The nosy widow Berman, a.k.a. "Polly Madison," can't get into the studio or even take a peek inside because it has no windows and because two years ago, right after my wife died, I personally nailed the doors at one end shut from the inside with six-inch spikes, and immobilized the doors at the other end on the outside, from top to bottom, with six big padlocks and massive hasps.

I myself haven't been in there since. And, yes, there is something in there. This is no shaggy dog story. After I die and am buried next to my darling Edith, and the executors of my estate open those doors at last, they will find more than just thin air in there. And it won't be some pathetic symbol, such as a paintbrush broken in two or my Purple Heart on an otherwise vacant and clean-swept floor.

And there is no lame joke in there, like a painting of potatoes, as though I were returning the barn to potatoes, or a painting of the Virgin Mary wearing a derby and holding a watermelon, or some such thing.

And no self-portrait.

And nothing with a religious message.

Tantalizing? Here's a hint: it's bigger than a bread box and smaller than the planet Jupiter.

• • • .

Not even Paul Slazinger has come close to guessing what is in there, and he has said more than once that he doesn't see how our friendship can continue, if I feel my secret would not be safe with him.

The barn has become quite famous in the art world. After I show visitors the collection in the house, most of them ask if they can see what is in the barn as well. I tell them that they can see the outside of the barn, if they like, and that the outside is in fact a significant landmark in art history. The first time Terry

Kitchen used a paint-spraying rig, his target was an old piece of beaverboard he had leaned against the barn.

"As for what's *inside* the barn," I tell them, "it's the worthless secret of a silly old man, as the world will discover when I have gone to the big art auction in the sky."

5

O NE ART PUBLICATION claimed to know *exactly* what was in there: the very greatest of the Abstract Expressionist paintings, which I was keeping off the market in order to raise the value of relatively unimportant paintings in the house here.

Not true.

•   •   •

After that article was printed, my fellow Armenian in Southampton, Kevork Hovanessian, made a serious offer of three million dollars for everything in the barn, sight unseen.

"I wouldn't want to cheat you that way," I told him. "That would be un-Armenian."

If I had taken his money, it would have been like selling him Brooklyn Bridge.

•   •   •

One response to that same article wasn't that amusing. A man whose name I did not recognize, said in a letter to the editor that he had known me during the war, which he evidently did. He was at least familiar with my platoon of artists, which he described accurately. He knew the mission we were given after the German Air Force had been knocked out of the sky and there was no longer any need for the big-time camouflage jokes we played. This was the mission, which was like turning children loose in the workshop of Father Christmas: we were to evaluate and catalogue all captured works of art.

This man said he had served in SHAEF, and I must have dealt with him from time to time. It was his belief, as stated in his letter, that I had stolen masterpieces which should have been returned to their rightful owners in Europe. Fearing lawsuits brought by those rightful owners, he said, I had locked them up in the barn.

Wrong.

•   •   •

He is wrong about the contents of the barn. I have to say he is just a little bit right about my having taken advantage of my unusual wartime opportunities. I couldn't have stolen anything which was handed over by the military units which had captured it. I had to give them receipts, and we were visited regularly by auditors from the Finance Corps.

But our travels behind the lines *did* bring us into contact with persons in desperate circumstances who had art to sell. We got some remarkable *bargains*.

Nobody in the platoon got an Old Master, or anything which obviously came from a church or a museum or a great private collection. At least I don't *think* anybody did. I can't be absolutely sure about that. In the Art World, as elsewhere, opportunists are opportunists and thieves are thieves.

But I myself *did* buy from a civilian an unsigned charcoal sketch which looked like a Cézanne to me, and which has since been authenticated as such. It is now a part of the permanent collection of the Rhode Island School of Design. And I bought a Matisse, my favorite painter, from a widow who said her husband had been given it by the artist himself. For that matter, I got stuck with a fake Gauguin, which served me right.

And I sent my purchases for safekeeping to just about the only person I knew and could trust in the whole United States of America anymore, Sam Wu, a Chinese laundryman in New York City who was a cook for a little while for my former master, the illustrator Dan Gregory.

Imagine fighting for a country where the only civilian you know is a Chinese laundryman!

And then one day I and my platoon of artists were ordered into combat, to contain, if we could, the last big German breakthrough of World War Two.

• • •

But none of that stuff is in the barn, or even in my possession. I sold it all when I got home from the war, which gave me a nice little bankroll to invest in the stock market. I had given up my boyhood dream of being an artist. I enrolled in courses in accounting and economics and business law and marketing and so on at New York University. I was going to be a *businessman*.

I thought this about myself and art: that I could catch the likeness of anything I could see—with patience and the best instruments and materials. I had, after all, been an able apprentice under the most meticulous illustrator of this century, Dan Gregory. But cameras could do what he had done and what I could do. And I knew that it was this same thought which had sent the Impressionists and the Cubists and the Dadaists and the Surrealists and so on in their quite successful efforts to make good pictures which cameras and people like Dan Gregory could not duplicate.

I concluded that my mind was so ordinary, which is to say empty, that I could never be anything but a reasonably good camera. So I would content myself with a more common and general sort of achievement than serious art, which was money. I was not saddened about this. I was in fact much *relieved*!

But I still enjoyed engaging in the blather of art, since I could talk if not paint pictures as well as anyone. So I would go to bars around NYU at night, and easily made friends with several painters who thought they were right about almost everything, but who never expected to receive much recognition. I could talk as well as the best of them, and drink as much as they could. Best of all, I could pick up the check at the end of the evening, thanks to the money I was making in the stock market, subsistence payments I was receiving from the government while going to the university, and a lifetime pension from a grateful nation for my having given one eye in defense of Liberty.

To the real painters I seemed a bottomless pit of money. I was good not only for the cost of drinks, but for rent, for a down payment on a car, for a girlfriend's abortion, for a wife's abortion. You name it. However much money they needed for no matter what, they could get it from Diamond Rabo Karabekian.

•   •   •

So I bought those friends. My pit of money wasn't really bottomless. By the end of every month they had taken me for everything I had. But then the pit, a small one, would fill up again.

Fair was fair. I certainly enjoyed their company, especially since they treated me as though I were a painter, too. I was one of them. Here was another big family to replace my lost platoon.

And they paid me back with more than companionship. They settled their debts as best they could with pictures nobody wanted, too.

• • •

I almost forgot to say: I was married and my wife was pregnant at the time. She would be *twice* impregnated by that incomparable lover, Rabo Karabekian.

• • •

I have now returned to this typewriter from the vicinity of the swimming pool, where I asked Celeste and her friends in and around that public teenage athletic facility, if they knew who Bluebeard was. I meant to mention Bluebeard in this book. I wanted to know if I had to explain, for the sake of young readers, who Bluebeard was.

Nobody knew. While I was at it, I asked them if they recognized the names of Jackson Pollock, Mark Rothko, or Terry Kitchen, or Truman Capote, or Nelson Algren, or Irwin Shaw, or James Jones, all of whom had figured not only in the history of arts and letters but in the history of the Hamptons. They did not. So much for achieving immortality via the arts and letters.

So: Bluebeard is a fictitious character in a very old children's tale, possibly based loosely on a murderous nobleman of long ago. In the story, he has married many times. He marries for the umpteenth time, and brings his latest child bride back to his castle. He tells her that she can go into any room but one, whose door he shows her.

Bluebeard is either a poor psychologist or a great one, since all his new wife can think about is what might be behind the door. So she takes a look when she thinks he isn't home, but he really *is* home.

He catches her just at the point she is gazing aghast at the bodies of all his former wives in there, all of whom he has murdered, save for the first one, for looking behind the door. The first one got murdered for something else.

• • •

So—of all the people who know about my locked potato barn, the one who finds the mystery most intolerable is surely

Circe Berman. She is after me all the time to tell her where the six keys are, and I tell her again that they are buried in a golden casket at the foot of Mount Ararat.

I said to her the last time she asked, which was about five minutes ago: "Look: think about something else, anything else. I am Bluebeard, and my studio is my *forbidden chamber* as far as *you're* concerned."

6

THE BLUEBEARD STORY notwithstanding, there are no bodies in my barn. The first of my two wives, who was and is Dorothy, remarried soon after our divorce, remarried *happily,* from all accounts. Dorothy is now a widow in a beachfront condominium in Sarasota, Florida. Her second husband was what we both thought I might become right after the war: a capable and personable insurance man. We each have a beach.

My second wife, dear Edith, is buried in Green River Cemetery out here, where I expect to be buried, too—only a few yards, in fact, from the graves of Jackson Pollock and Terry Kitchen.

If I killed anybody in the war, and I just might have, it would have been during the few seconds before a shell from somewhere knocked me unconscious and took out one eye.

• • •

When I was a two-eyed boy, I was the best draughtsman they had ever seen in the rinky-dink public school system of San Ignacio, which wasn't saying much. Several of my teachers were so impressed that they suggested to my parents that perhaps I should pursue a career as an artist.

But this advice seemed so impractical to my parents that they asked the teachers to stop putting such ideas in my head. They thought that artists lived in poverty, and that they had to die before their works were appreciated. They were generally right about that, of course. The paintings by dead men who were poor most of their lives are the most valuable pieces in my collection.

And if an artist wants to really jack up the prices of his creations, may I suggest this: suicide.

• • •

But in 1927, when I was eleven years old, and was incidentally well on my way to becoming as good a cobbler as my father, my mother read about an American artist who made as much money as many movie stars and tycoons, and was in fact the

friend and equal of movie stars and tycoons, and had a yacht—
and a horse farm in Virginia, and a beach house in Montauk,
not far from here.

Mother would say later, and not all that much later, since she
had only one more year to live, that she never would have read
the article if it hadn't been for a photograph of this rich artist on
his yacht. The name of the yacht was the name of the mountain
as sacred to Armenians as Fujiyama is to the Japanese: *Ararat*.

This man had to be an Armenian, she thought, and so he
was. The magazine said he had been born Dan Gregorian in
Moscow, where his father was a horse trainer, and that he had
been apprenticed to the chief engraver of the Russian Imperial
Mint.

He had come to this country in 1907 as an ordinary immigrant, not a refugee from any massacre, and had changed his
name to Dan Gregory, and had become an illustrator of magazine stories and advertisements, and of books for young people.
The author of the article said he was probably the highest paid
artist in American history.

That could still be true of Dan Gregory, or "Gregorian," as
my parents always called him, if his income in the 1920s, or
especially during the Great Depression, were translated into the
depreciated dollars of today. He could still be the champ, living
or dead.

• • •

My mother was shrewd about the United States, as my father
was not. She had figured out that the most pervasive American
disease was loneliness, and that even people at the top often
suffered from it, and that they could be surprisingly responsive
to attractive strangers who were friendly.

So my mother said to me, and I hardly recognized her, so
sly and witchlike had her face become: "You must *write* to this
Gregorian. You must tell him that you are also Armenian. You
must tell him that you want to be an artist half as good as he
is, and that you think he is the greatest artist who ever lived."

• • •

So I wrote such a letter, or about twenty such letters, in my
childish longhand, until Mother was satisfied that the bait was

irresistible. I did this hard work in an acrid cloud of my father's raillery.

He said things like "He stopped being an Armenian when he changed his name," and "If he grew up in Moscow, he's a Russian not an Armenian," and "You know what a letter like that would mean to me? 'The next one asks for money.' "

And Mother said to him in Armenian: "Can't you see we're fishing? If you make so much noise talking, you'll scare the fish away."

In Turkish Armenia, incidentally, or so I've been told, it was the women and not the men who were the fisherfolk.

And what a terrific bite my letter got!

We hooked Dan Gregory's mistress, a former Ziegfeld Follies showgirl named Marilee Kemp!

This woman would become the very first woman I ever made love to—at the age of *nineteen*! And, oh, my God, what a fuddy-duddy old poop I am, thinking about that sexual initiation as though it were as marvelous as the Chrysler Building—while the fifteen-year-old daughter of my cook is taking birth-control pills!

•   •   •

Marilee Kemp said that she was Mr. Gregory's assistant, and that she and he had been deeply moved by my letter. Mr. Gregory, as I might imagine, was a very busy man, and had asked her to reply for him. This was a four-page letter, written in a scrawl almost as childish as my own. She was then only twenty-one years old—the daughter of an illiterate coal miner in West Virginia.

When she was thirty-seven, she would be the Countess Portomaggiori, with a pink palace in Florence, Italy. When she was fifty, she would be the biggest Sony distributor in Europe, and that old continent's greatest collector of American postwar modern art.

•   •   •

My father said she had to be crazy to write such a long letter to a stranger, and nothing but a boy at that, so far away.

Mother said she must be very lonely, which was true. Gregory kept her as a pet around the house, because she was so beautiful, and he used her as a model sometimes. But she was certainly no assistant in his business. He had no interest in her opinions about anything.

He never included her in his dinner parties, either, never took her on trips or to a show or out to restaurants or to other people's parties, or introduced her to his famous friends.

•   • • •

Marilee Kemp wrote me seventy-eight letters between 1927 and 1933. I can count them because I still have them, now bound in a hand-tooled leather volume in a slipcase in the library. The binding and slipcase were a gift from dear Edith on our tenth wedding anniversary. Mrs. Berman has found it, as she has found everything of any emotional significance here but the keys to the barn.

She has read all the letters without first asking me if I considered them private, which I surely do. And she has said to me, and this is the first time she has ever sounded awed: "Just one of this woman's letters says more wonderful things about life than every picture in this house. They're the story of a scorned and abused woman discovering that she was a great writer, because that is what she became. I hope you know that."

"I know that," I said. It was certainly true: each letter is deeper, more expressive, more confident and self-respecting than the one before.

"How much education did she have?" she asked.

"One year of high school," I said.

Mrs. Berman shook her head in wonder. "What a year that must have been," she said.

• • •

As for my side of the correspondence: my main messages were pictures I had made, which I thought she would show to Dan Gregory, with brief notes attached. •

After I told Marilee that Mother had died of tetanus from the cannery, her letters became very motherly, although she was only nine years older than me. And the first of these motherly letters came not from New York City but from Switzerland, where, she said in the letter, she had gone to ski.

Only after I visited her in her palace in Florence after the war did she tell me the truth: Dan Gregory had sent her alone to a clinic there to get rid of the fetus she was carrying.

"I should have thanked Dan for that," she said to me in Florence. "That's when I got interested in foreign languages." She laughed.

• • •

Mrs. Berman has just told me that my cook has had not just one abortion, like Marilee Kemp, but three—and not in Switzerland but in a doctor's office in Southampton. This wearied me, but then, almost everything about the modern world wearies me.

I didn't ask where the cook's carrying Celeste for a full nine months fit in with the abortions. I didn't want to know, but Mrs. Berman gave me the information anyway. "Two abortions before Celeste, and one after," she said.

"The cook told you that?" I said.

"Celeste told me," she said. "She also told me that her mother was thinking of having her tubes tied."

"I'm certainly glad to know all this," I said, "in case of an emergency."

• • •

Back to the past I go again, with the present nipping at my ankles like a rabid fox terrier:

My mother died believing that I had become a protégé of Dan Gregory, from whom I had never heard directly. Before she got sick, she predicted that "Gregorian" would send me to art school, that "Gregorian" would persuade magazines to hire me as an illustrator when I was old enough, that "Gregorian" would introduce me to all his rich friends, who would tell me how I could get rich, too, investing the money I made as an artist in the stock market. In 1928, the stock market never seemed to do anything but go up and up, just like the one we have today! Whoopee!

So she not only missed the stock market crash a year later, but the realization a couple of years after the crash that I wasn't even indirectly in touch with Dan Gregory, that he probably didn't even know I was alive, that the effusive praise for the artwork I was sending to New York for criticism wasn't coming from the highest paid artist in American history, but from what my father called in Armenian: ". . . maybe his cleaning woman, maybe his cook, maybe his whore."

7

I REMEMBER the afternoon I came home from school when I was about fifteen or so, and Father was sitting at the oil-cloth-covered table in our little kitchen, with Marilee's letters in a stack before him. He had reread them all.

This was not a violation of my privacy. The letters were family property—if you can call only two people a family. They were like bonds we had accumulated, gilt-edged securities of which I would be the beneficiary when they and I reached maturity. Once they paid off, I would be able to take care of Father, too, and he sure needed help. His savings had been wiped out by the failure of the Luma County Savings and Loan Association, which we and everybody in town had taken to calling "El Banco Busto." There was no federal insurance scheme for bank deposits back then.

El Banco Busto, moreover, had held the mortgage on the little building whose first floor was Father's shop and whose second story was our home. Father used to own the building, thanks to a loan from the bank. After the bank failed, though, its receivers liquidated all its assets, foreclosing all the mortgages which were in arrears, which was most of them. Guess why they were in arrears? Practically everybody had been dumb enough to entrust their savings to El Banco Busto.

So the father I found reading Marilee's letters in the afternoon was a man who had become a mere tenant in a building he used to own. As for the shop downstairs: it was vacant, since he couldn't afford to rent that, too. All his machinery had been sold at auction anyway in order to get a few pennies for what we were: people who had been dumb enough to entrust his or her savings to El Banco Busto.

What a comedy!

•   •   •

Father looked up from Marilee's letters when I came in with my schoolbooks, and he said, "You know what this woman is? She has promised you everything, but she has nothing to give."

He named the Armenian sociopath who had swindled him and
Mother in Cairo. "She is the new Vartan Mamigonian," he said.
   "What do you mean?" I said.
   And he said exactly as though the handwritten letters were
bonds or insurance policies or whatever: "I have just read the
fine print." He went on to say that Marilee's first letters had
been rich in phrases like "Mr. Gregory says," and "Mr. Gregory
feels," and "Mr. Gregory wants you to know," but that, since the
third letter, such locutions had entirely disappeared. "This is a
nobody," he said, "who will never be anybody, who is trying to
get somebody anyway, by stealing the reputation of Gregorian!"
   I felt no shock. Some part of me had noticed the same thing
about the letters. Some other part of me had managed to bury
the bad, bad implications.

•   •   •

   I asked Father what had triggered this investigation at this
time. He indicated ten books which had arrived for me from
Marilee soon after I left for school. He had stacked them on the
drainboard of our sink, a sink full of dirty dishes and pans. I
examined them. They were young people's story classics of the
day, *Treasure Island, Robinson Crusoe, The Swiss Family Robinson,
The Adventures of Robin Hood and his Merry Men, Tanglewood
Tales, Gulliver's Travels, Tales from Shakespeare* and so on. Reading matter for young people before the Second World War was
a dozen universes removed from the unwanted pregnancies and
incest and minimum-wage slavery and treacherous high school
friendships and so on in the novels of Polly Madison.
   Marilee had sent me these books because they were vibrantly
illustrated by Dan Gregory. They were not only the most
beautiful artifacts in our apartment: they were about the most
beautiful artifacts in all of Luma County, and I responded to
them as such. "How nice of her!" I exclaimed. "Would you look
at these! Would you *look* at these?"
   "I have," he said.
   "Aren't they beautiful?" I said.
   "Yes," he said, "they are beautiful. But maybe you can explain
to me why Mr. Gregorian, who thinks so highly of you, hasn't
signed at least one of them, and perhaps scribbled a little note
of encouragement to my gifted son?"

All this was said in Armenian. He never talked anything but Armenian at home after the failure of El Banco Busto.

• • •

Whether the advice and encouragement had come from Gregory or Marilee didn't matter much to me at that point. If I do say so myself, I had become one hell of a good artist for a kid in any case. I was so conceited about my prospects, with or without help from New York City, that I defended Marilee mainly to cheer up Father.

"If this Marilee, whoever she is, whatever she is, thinks so much of your pictures," he said, "why doesn't she sell some of them and send you the money?"

"She's been extremely generous," I replied—and so she had been: generous with her time, but also with the finest artist's materials then available anywhere. I had no idea of their value, and neither did she. She had taken them without permission from the supply room in the basement of Gregory's mansion. I myself would see that room in a couple of years, and there was enough stuff in there to take care of Gregory's needs, as prolific as he was, for a dozen lifetimes. She didn't think he would miss what she sent me, and she didn't ask permission because she was scared to death of him.

He used to hit and kick her a lot.

But about the actual value of the stuff: the paints I was using sure weren't Sateen Dura-Luxe. They were Mussini oils and Horadam watercolors from Germany. My brushes came from Winsor and Newton in England. My pastels and colored pencils and inks came from Lefèbvre-Foinet in Paris. My canvas came from Claessen's in Belgium. No other artist west of the Rockies had such priceless art supplies!

For that matter, Dan Gregory was the only illustrator I ever knew who expected his pictures to take their places among the great art treasures of the world, who used materials which might really do what Sateen Dura-Luxe was supposed to do: outlast the smile on the "Mona Lisa." The rest of them were satisfied if their work survived the trip to the print shop. They commonly sneered that they did such hack work only for money, that it was art for people who didn't know anything about art—but not Dan Gregory.

•   •   •

"She is *using* you," said my father.

"For what?" I said.

"So she can feel like a big shot," he said.

•   •   •

The widow Berman agrees that Marilee *was* using me, but not in the way my father thought. "You were her *audience*," she said. "Writers will *kill* for an audience."

"An audience of *one?*" I said.

"That's all she needed," she said. "That's all anybody needs. Just look at how her handwriting improved and her vocabulary grew. Look at all the things she found to talk about, as soon as she realized you were hanging on every word. She certainly couldn't write for that bastard Gregory. There was no point in writing to the folks back home, either. They couldn't even read! Did you really believe her when she said she was describing things she saw around the city because you might want to paint pictures of them?"

"Yes—" I said, "I guess I did." Marilee wrote long descriptions of breadlines for all the people who had been put out of work by the Depression, and of men in nice suits who obviously used to have money, but who were now selling apples on street corners, and of a legless man on a sort of skateboard, who was a World War One veteran or was pretending to be one, selling pencils in Grand Central Station, and of high-society people thrilled to be hobnobbing with gangsters in speakeasies—that sort of thing.

"That's the secret of how to enjoy writing and how to make yourself meet high standards," said Mrs. Berman. "You don't write for the whole world, and you don't write for ten people, or two. You write for just one person."

•   •   •

"Who's the one person *you* write for?" I asked.

And she said, "This is going to sound very strange, because you'd think it would be somebody the same age as my readers, but it isn't. That's the secret ingredient of my books, I think.

That's why they seem so strong and trustworthy to young people, why I don't sound like one dumb teenager talking to another one. I don't put anything down on paper which Abe Berman wouldn't find interesting and truthful."

Abe Berman, of course, was her brain surgeon husband who died of a stroke seven months ago.

• • •

She has asked me for the keys to the barn again. I told her if she ever even *mentioned* the barn again, I was going to tell everybody that she was really Polly Madison—invite the local papers to come on over and interview her, and so on. If I actually did that, it would not only wreck Paul Slazinger: it would also attract a lynch mob of religious fundamentalists to our doorstep.

I happened to watch the sermon of a television evangelist the other night, and he said Satan was making a four-pronged attack on the American family with communism, drugs, rock and roll, and books by Satan's sister, who was Polly Madison.

• • •

To return to my correspondence with Marilee Kemp: My notes to her cooled after Father denounced her as the new Vartan Mamigonian. I was no longer counting on her for anything. Simply as part of the growing-up process, I didn't want her to go on trying to be my substitute mother. I was becoming a man, and didn't need a mother anymore, or so I thought.

Without any help from her, in fact, I had started to make money as an artist, as young as I was, and right there in bankrupt little San Ignacio. I had gone to the local paper, the *Luma County Clarion*, looking for work of any kind after school, and had mentioned that I could draw pretty well. The editor asked me if I could draw a picture of the Italian dictator Benito Mussolini, Dan Gregory's hero of heroes, incidentally, and I did so in two or three minutes maybe, without having to refer to a photograph.

Then he had me draw a beautiful female angel, and I did that.

Then he had me draw a picture of Mussolini pouring a quart of something into the mouth of the angel. He had me label the bottle CASTOR OIL and the angel WORLD PEACE. Mussolini liked to punish people by making them drink a quart of castor oil. That sounded like a comical way to teach somebody a lesson, but it wasn't. The victims often vomited and shit themselves to death. Those who survived were all torn up inside.

That is how I became a paid political cartoonist at a tender age. I did one cartoon a week, with the editor telling me exactly what to draw.

•   •   •

Much to my surprise, Father began to blossom as an artist, too. In all the guessing about where my artistic talent might have come from, one thing seemed certain: it hadn't come from him or from anybody on his side of the family. When he still had his shoe repair shop, I never saw him do anything imaginative with all the scraps lying around, maybe make a fancy belt for me or a purse for Mother. He was a no-nonsense repairman, and that was all.

But then, as though he were in a trance, and using the simplest hand-tools, he began to make perfectly beautiful cowboy boots, which he sold from door to door. They weren't only tough and comfortable: they were dazzling jewelry for manly feet and calves, scintillating with gold and silver stars and eagles and flowers and bucking broncos cut from flattened tin cans and bottle caps.

But this new development in his life wasn't as nice for me to see as you might think.

It gave me the creeps, actually, because I would look into his eyes, and there wasn't anybody home anymore.

•   •   •

I would see the same thing happen to Terry Kitchen years later. He used to be my closest friend. And suddenly he began to paint the pictures which make many people say today that he was the greatest of all the Abstract Expressionists—superior to Pollock, to Rothko.

That was fine, I guess, except that when I looked into my best friend's eyes, there wasn't anybody home anymore.

•   •   •

Ah, me.

Anyway: back around Christmas in 1932, Marilee's most recent letters were lying around somewhere, mostly unread. I had become bored with being her audience.

And then this telegram arrived, addressed to me.

Father would comment before we opened it that it was the first telegram our family had ever received.

The message was this:

> BE MY APPRENTICE. WILL PAY
> TRANSPORTATION HERE PLUS FREE ROOM,
> BOARD, MODEST ALLOWANCE, ART LESSONS.
> DAN GREGORY.

8

THE FIRST PERSON I told about this magnificent opportunity was the old newspaper editor for whom I had been
drawing cartoons. His name was Arnold Coates, and he said
this to me:

"You really are an artist, and you have to get out of here or
you'll shrivel up like a raisin. Don't worry about your father.
He's a perfectly contented, self-sufficient zombie, if you'll
pardon my saying so.

"New York is just going to be a stopover for you," he went
on. "Europe is where the real painters are, and always will be."

He was wrong about that.

"I never prayed before, but I'll pray tonight that you never go
to Europe as a soldier. We should never get suckered again into
providing meat for the cannons and machine guns they love so
much. They could go to war at any time. Look how big their
armies are in the midst of a Great Depression!

"If the cities are still standing when you get to Europe," he
said, "and you sit in a café for hours, sipping coffee or wine
or beer, and discussing painting and music and literature, just
remember that the Europeans around you, who you think are
so much more civilized than Americans, are looking forward to
just one thing: the time when it will become legal to kill each
other and knock everything down again.

"If I had my way," he said, "American geography books
would call those European countries by their right names: 'The
Syphilis Empire,' 'The Republic of Suicide,' 'Dementia Praecox,'
which of course borders on beautiful 'Paranoia.'

"There!" he said. "I've spoiled Europe for you, and you
haven't even seen it yet. And maybe I've spoiled art for you,
too, but I hope not. I don't see how artists can be blamed if
their beautiful and usually innocent creations for some reason
just make Europeans unhappier and more bloodthirsty all the
time."

• • •

That was an ordinary way for a patriotic American to talk back then. It's hard to believe how sick of war we used to be. We used to boast of how small our Army and Navy were, and how little influence generals and admirals had in Washington. We used to call armaments manufacturers "Merchants of Death."

Can you imagine that?

• • •

Nowadays, of course, just about our only solvent industry is the merchandising of death, bankrolled by our grandchildren, so that the message of our principal art forms, movies and television and political speeches and newspaper columns, for the sake of the economy, simply *has* to be this: War is hell, all right, but the only way a boy can become a man is in a shoot-out of some kind, preferably, but by no means necessarily, on a battlefield.

• • •

So I went to New York City to be born again.

It was and remains easy for most Americans to go somewhere else to start anew. I wasn't like my parents. I didn't have any supposedly sacred piece of land or shoals of friends and relatives to leave behind. Nowhere has the number *zero* been more of philosophical value than in the United States.

"Here goes nothing," says the American as he goes off the high diving board.

Yes, and my mind really was as blank as an embryo's as I crossed this great continent on womblike Pullman cars. It was as though there had never been a San Ignacio. Yes, and when the Twentieth Century Limited from Chicago plunged into a tunnel under New York City, with its lining of pipes and wires, I was out of the womb and into the birth canal.

Ten minutes later I was born in Grand Central Station, wearing the first suit I had ever owned, and carrying a cardboard valise and a portfolio of my very best drawings.

Who was there to welcome this beguiling Armenian infant? Not a soul, not a soul.

• • •

I would have made a great Dan Gregory illustration for a
story about a yokel finding himself all alone in a big city he
has never seen before. I had got my suit through the mail from
Sears, Roebuck, and nobody could draw cheap, mail-order
clothes like Dan Gregory. My shoes were old and cracked, but
I had shined them and put new rubber heels on them myself.
I had also threaded in new laces, but one of those had broken
somewhere around Kansas City. A truly observant person
would have noticed the clumsy splice in the broken shoelaces.
Nobody could describe the economic and spiritual condition of
a character in terms of his shoes like Dan Gregory.

My face, however, was wrong for a yokel in a magazine story
back then. Gregory would have had to make me an Anglo-Saxon.

• • •

He could have used my head in a story about Indians. I would
have made a passable Hiawatha. He illustrated an expensive edition of *Hiawatha* one time, and the model he used for the title
character was the son of a Greek fry cook.

In the movies back then, just about any big-nosed person
whose ancestors came from the shores of the Mediterranean or
the Near East, if he could act a little, could play a rampaging
Sioux or whatever. The audiences were more than satisfied.

• • •

Now I yearned to get back on the railroad train! I had been
so *happy* there! How I adored that train! God Almighty Himself
must have been hilarious when human beings so mingled iron
and water and fire as to make a railroad train!

Nowadays, of course, everything must be done with plutonium and laser beams.

• • •

And could Dan Gregory ever paint pictures of railroad trains!
He used to work from blueprints he got from the manufacturers, so that a misplaced rivet or whatever wouldn't spoil his
picture for a railroad man. And if he had done a picture of the
Twentieth Century Limited the day I arrived, the stains and dirt
on the outside would be native to the run between Chicago and
New York. Nobody could paint grime like Dan Gregory.

And where was he now? Where was Marilee? Why hadn't they sent someone to meet me with his great Marmon touring car?

•   •   •

He knew exactly when I was coming. He was the one who had picked the date, an easy one to remember. It was Saint Valentine's Day. And he had done me so many kindnesses through the mail, and not through Marilee or any flunky. All the messages were in his own handwriting. They were brief, but they were incredibly generous, too. I was not only to buy a warm suit for myself at his expense, but one for Father, too.

His notes were so compassionate! He didn't want me to get scared or make a fool of myself on the trains, so he told me how to act in a Pullman berth and on the dining car, and how much and when to tip the waiters and porters, and how to change trains in Chicago. He couldn't have been nicer to his own son, if he had had a son.

He even went to the trouble of sending me expense money as postal money orders rather than personal checks, which indicated that he knew about the failure of the only bank in San Ignacio.

What I didn't know was that, back in December, when he sent me the telegram, Marilee was in the hospital with both legs and one arm broken. He had given her a shove in his studio which sent her backwards and down the staircase. She looked dead when she hit the bottom, and two servants happened to be standing there—at the bottom of the stairs.

So Gregory was scared and remorseful. When he visited Marilee in the hospital the first time, all shamefaced, he told her he was sorry and loved her so much that he would give her anything she could think to ask for—*anything*.

He probably thought it was going to be diamonds or something like that, but she asked for a human being. She asked for me.

•   •   •

Circe Berman has just suggested that I was a replacement for the Armenian baby which had been taken from her womb in Switzerland.

Maybe so.

• • •

And then Marilee told Gregory what to say to me in the telegram and then his letters, and how much money to send me
for what, and on and on. She was still in the hospital when I
reached New York, but she certainly didn't expect him to stand
me up at the station.

But that's what he did.

He was turning mean again.

• • •

That wasn't the whole story, either. I wouldn't get the *whole*
story until I visited Marilee in Florence after the war. Gregory,
incidentally, had been dead and buried in Egypt for about ten
years by then.

Only after the war did Marilee, reborn as the Contessa Portomaggiore, tell me that I was the reason she had been pushed
down the stairs back in 1932. She had sheltered me from that
abashing information, and so, from very different motives, certainly, had Dan Gregory.

But she came up to his studio the night he nearly killed her,
to get him to give his serious attention to pictures of mine for
the very first time. In all the years I had been sending pictures
to New York, he had never looked at one. Marilee thought that
this time might be different, since Gregory was happier than she
had ever seen him. Why? He had that afternoon received a letter
of thanks from the man he believed to be the most brilliant
leader on earth, the Italian dictator Mussolini, the man who
made his enemies drink castor oil.

Mussolini had thanked him for a portrait of himself which
Gregory had painted as a gift. Mussolini was depicted as a general of Alpine troops on a mountaintop at sunrise, and you can
bet that every bit of leather and piping and braid and brass and
pleating, and all the decorations, were exactly as they should be.
Nobody could paint uniforms like Dan Gregory.

Gregory would be shot dead in Egypt eight years later, incidentally, by the British, while wearing an Italian uniform.

• • •

But the point is this: Marilee spread out my pictures on a refectory table in his studio, and he knew what they were. As she had hoped, he ambled over to them with all possible amiability. The moment he looked at them closely, though, he flew into a rage.

But it wasn't the nature of my pictures which infuriated him. It was the quality of the art materials I had used. No boy artist in California could afford such expensive imported colors and paper and canvas. Marilee, obviously, had taken them from his supply room.

So he gave her a shove, and she fell backwards down the stairs.

•   •   •

Somewhere in here I want to tell about the suit I ordered from Sears, Roebuck along with my own. Father and I measured each other up for the suits, which was strange even in itself, since I can't recall our ever having touched before.

But when the suits arrived, it was obvious that somebody somewhere had misplaced a decimal point where Father's pants were concerned. As short as his legs were, his pants were much shorter. As scrawny as he was around the middle, he couldn't button the pants at the waist. The coat was just perfect, though.

So I said to him, "I'm really sorry about the pants. You'll have to send them back."

And he said, "No. I like it very much. It's a very good funeral suit."

And I said, "What do you mean, 'funeral suit'?" I had this vision of his going to other people's funerals without any pants on—not that he had ever gone to anybody's funeral but my mother's, as far as I know.

And he said, "You don't have to wear pants to your own funeral," he said.

•   •   •

When I went back to San Ignacio for his funeral five years later, he was laid out in the *coat* of that suit at least, but the bottom half of the casket was closed, so I had to ask the mortician if Father had pants on.

It turned out that he did, and that the pants fit nicely. So Father had gone to the trouble of getting pants that fit from Sears, Roebuck.

But there were two unexpected fillips to the mortician's answer. He wasn't the one who had buried my mother, incidentally. The one who had buried my mother had gone bankrupt and left town to seek his fortune elsewhere. The one who was burying my father had come to seek his fortune in San Ignacio, where the streets were paved with gold.

One surprising piece of news from him was that my father was going to be buried wearing a pair of his own cowboy boots, which he had been wearing when he died at the movies.

The other fillip was the undertaker's assumption that Father was a Mohammedan. This was exciting to him. It was his biggest adventure in being uncritically pious in a madly pluralistic democracy.

"Your father is the first Mohammedan I've taken care of," he said. "I hope I haven't done anything wrong so far. There weren't any other Mohammedans to advise me. I would have had to go all the way to Los Angeles."

I didn't want to spoil his good time, so I told him that everything looked perfect to me. "Just don't eat pork too near the casket," I said.

"That's all?" he said.

"That—" I said, "and of course you say 'Praise Allah' when you close the lid."

Which he did.

9

How GOOD were those pictures of mine which Dan Gregory looked at so briefly before he shoved Marilee down the stairs? Technically, if not spiritually, they were pretty darn good for a kid my age—a kid whose self-imposed lessons had consisted of copying, stroke by stroke, illustrations by Dan Gregory.

I was obviously born to draw better than most people, just as the widow Berman and Paul Slazinger were obviously born to tell stories better than most people can. Other people are obviously born to sing and dance or explain the stars in the sky or do magic tricks or be great leaders or athletes, and so on.

I think that could go back to the time when people had to live in small groups of relatives—maybe fifty or a hundred people at the most. And evolution or God or whatever arranged things genetically, to keep the little families going, to cheer them up, so that they could all have somebody to tell stories around the campfire at night, and somebody else to paint pictures on the walls of the caves, and somebody else who wasn't afraid of anything and so on.

That's what I think. And of course a scheme like that doesn't make sense anymore, because simply moderate giftedness has been made worthless by the printing press and radio and television and satellites and all that. A moderately gifted person who would have been a community treasure a thousand years ago has to give up, has to go into some other line of work, since modern communications put him or her into daily competition with nothing but world's champions.

The entire planet can get along nicely now with maybe a dozen champion performers in each area of human giftedness. A moderately gifted person has to keep his or her gifts all bottled up until, in a manner of speaking, he or she gets drunk at a wedding and tap-dances on the coffee table like Fred Astaire or Ginger Rogers. We have a name for him or her. We call him or her an "exhibitionist."

How do we reward such an exhibitionist? We say to him or her the next morning, "Wow! Were you ever *drunk* last night!"

• • •

So when I became an apprentice to Dan Gregory, I was going into the ring with the world's champion of commercial art. His illustrations must have made any number of gifted young artists give up on art, thinking, "My God, I could never do anything *that* wonderful."

I was a really cocky kid, I now realize. From the very first, when I began copying Gregory, I was saying to myself, in effect, "If I work hard enough, by golly, *I* can do that, too!"

• • •

So there I was in Grand Central Station, with everybody but me being hugged and kissed by everybody, seemingly. I had doubted that Dan Gregory would come to greet me, but where was Marilee?

Did she know what I looked like? Of course. I had sent her many self-portraits, and snapshots taken by my mother, too.

Father, by the way, refused to touch a camera, saying that all it caught was dead skin and toenails and hair which people long gone had left behind. I guess he thought photographs were a poor substitute for all the people killed in the massacre.

Even if Marilee hadn't seen those pictures of me, I would have been easy to spot, since I was the darkest passenger by far on any of the Pullman cars. Any passenger much darker than me in those days would have been excluded by custom from Pullman cars—and almost all hotels and theaters and restaurants.

• • •

Was I sure I could spot Marilee at the station? Funnily enough: no. She had sent me nine photographs over the years, which are now bound together with her letters. They were made with the finest equipment by Dan Gregory himself, who could easily have become a successful photographer. But Gregory had also costumed and posed her each time as a character in some story he was illustrating—the Empress Josephine, an F. Scott Fitzgerald flapper, a cave woman, a pioneer wife, a mermaid, tail and all, and so on. It was and remains hard to believe that these weren't pictures of nine different women.

There were many beauties on the platform, since the Twentieth Century Limited was the most glamorous train of its time. So I locked eyes with woman after woman, hoping to fire the flashbulb of recognition inside her skull. But all I succeeded in doing, I am afraid, was to confirm for each woman that the darker races were indeed leeringly lecherous, being closer than the whiter ones to the gorillas, the chimpanzees.

• • •

Polly Madison, a.k.a. Circe Berman, has just come and gone, having read what is in my typewriter without asking if I minded. I mind a lot!

"I'm in the middle of a sentence," I said.

"Who isn't?" she said. "I just wondered if it wasn't making you feel creepy, writing about people so long ago."

"Not that I've noticed," I said. "I've gotten upset by a lot of things I hadn't thought about for years, but that's about the size of it. Creepy? No."

"Just think about it," she said. "You know about all sorts of terrible things that are going to happen to these people, yourself included. Wouldn't you like to hop into a time machine and go back and warn them, if you could?" She described an eerie scene in the Los Angeles railroad station back in 1933. "An Armenian boy with a cardboard suitcase and a portfolio is saying good-bye to his immigrant father. He is about to seek his fortune in a great city twenty-five hundred miles away. An old man wearing an eye patch, who has just arrived in a time machine from 1987, sidles up. What does the old man say to him?"

"I'd have to think about it," I said. I shook my head. "Nothing. Cancel the time machine."

"Nothing?" she said.

I told her this: "I want him to believe for as long as possible that he is going to become a great painter and a good father."

• • •

Only half an hour later: she has popped in and out again. "I just thought of something maybe you could use somewhere," she said. "What made me think of it was what you wrote earlier about how, after your father started making beautiful cowboy boots, you looked into his eyes and there wasn't anybody home anymore—or when your friend Terry Kitchen started painting his best pictures with his spray gun, and you looked into his eyes and there wasn't anybody home anymore."

I gave up. I switched off this electric typewriter. Where did I learn to touch-type? I had taken a course in typing after the war, when I thought I was going to become a businessman.

I sat back in this chair and I closed my eyes. Ironies go right over her head, and especially those relating to privacy, but I tried one anyway. "I'm all *ears*," I said.

"I never told you the very last thing Abe said before he died, did I?" she said.

"Never did," I agreed.

"That was what I was thinking about that first day—when you came down on the beach," she said.

"O.K.," I said.

At the very end, her brain-surgeon husband couldn't talk anymore, but he could still scrawl short messages with his left hand, although he was normally right handed. His left hand was all he had left that still worked a little bit.

According to Circe, this was his ultimate communiqué: "I was a radio repairman."

"Either his damaged brain believed that this was a literal truth," she said, "or he had come to the conclusion that all the brains he had operated on were basically just receivers of signals from someplace else. Do you get the concept?"

"I think I do," I said.

"Just because music comes from a little box we call a radio," she said, and here she came over and rapped me on my pate with her knuckles as though it were a radio, "that doesn't mean there's a symphony orchestra inside."

"What's that got to do with Father and Terry Kitchen?" I said.

"Maybe, when they suddenly started doing something they'd never done before, and their personalities changed, too—" she said, "maybe they had started picking up signals from another station, which had very different ideas about what they should say and do."

• • •

I have since tried out this human-beings-as-nothing-but-radio-receivers theory on Paul Slazinger, and he toyed with it some. "So Green River Cemetery is full of busted radios," he mused, "and the transmitters they were tuned to still go on and on."

"That's the theory," I said.

He said that all he'd been able to receive in his own head for the past twenty years was static and what sounded like weather reports in some foreign language he'd never heard before. He said, too, that toward the end of his marriage to Barbira Mencken, the actress, she acted "as though she was wearing headphones and listening to the *1812 Overture* in stereo. That's when she was becoming a real actress, and not just another pretty girl onstage that everybody liked a lot. She wasn't even 'Barbara' anymore. All of a sudden she was 'Bar-*beer*-ah!' "

He said that the first he heard of the name change was during the divorce proceedings, when her lawyer referred to her as "Barbira," and spelled it for the court stenographer.

Out in the courthouse corridor afterwards, Slazinger asked her: "Whatever happened to Barbara?"

She said Barbara was dead!

So Slazinger said to her: "Then what on Earth did we waste all this money on lawyers for?"

•   •   •

I said that I had seen the same sort of thing happen to Terry Kitchen the first time he played with a spray rig, shooting bursts of red automobile paint at an old piece of beaverboard he'd leaned against the potato barn. All of a sudden, he, too, was like somebody listening through headphones to a perfectly wonderful radio station I couldn't hear.

Red was the only color he had to play with. We'd gotten two cans of the red paint along with the spray rig, which we'd bought from an automobile repair shop in Montauk a couple of hours before. "Just *look* at it! Just *look* at it!" he'd say, after every burst.

"He'd just about given up on being a painter, and was going into law practice with his father before we got that spray rig," I said.

"Barbira was just about to give up being an actress and have a baby instead," said Slazinger. "And then she got the part of Tennessee Williams's sister in *The Glass Menagerie*."

•   •   •

Actually, now that I think back: Terry Kitchen went through a radical personality change the moment he saw the spray rig for sale, and not when he fired those first bursts of red at the beaverboard. I happened to spot the rig, and said that it was probably war surplus, since it was identical with rigs I had used in the Army for camouflage.

"Buy it for me," he said.

"What for?" I said.

"Buy it for me," he said again. He had to have it, and he wouldn't even have known what it was if I hadn't told him.

He never had any money, although he was from a very rich old family, and the only money I had was supposed to go for a crib and a youth bed for the house I'd bought in Springs. I was in the process of moving my family, much against their will, from the city to the country.

"Buy it for me," he said again.

And I said, "O.K., take it easy. O.K., O.K."

•   •   •

And now, let us hop into our trusty old time machine, and go back to 1932 again:

Was I angry to be stood up at Grand Central Station? Not a bit. As long as I believed Dan Gregory to be the greatest artist alive, he could do no wrong. And before I was done with him and he with me, I would have to forgive him for a lot worse things than not meeting my train.

•   •   •

What kept him from coming anywhere near to greatness, although no more marvelous technician ever lived? I have thought hard about this, and any answer I give refers to me, too. I was the best technician by far among the Abstract Expressionists, but I never amounted to a hill of beans, either, and couldn't have—and I am not talking about my fiascoes with Sateen Dura-Luxe. I had painted plenty of pictures before

Sateen Dura-Luxe, and quite a few afterwards, but they were no damned good.

But let's forget me for the moment, and focus on the works of Gregory. They were truthful about material things, but they lied about time. He celebrated moments, anything from a child's first meeting with a department store Santa Claus to the victory of a gladiator at the Circus Maximus, from the driving of the golden spike which completed a transcontinental railroad to a man's going on his knees to ask a woman to marry him. But he lacked the guts or the wisdom, or maybe just the talent, to indicate somehow that time was liquid, that one moment was no more important than any other, and that all moments quickly run away.

Let me put it another way: Dan Gregory was a taxidermist. He stuffed and mounted and varnished and mothproofed supposedly great moments, all of which turn out to be depressing dust-catchers, like a moosehead bought at a country auction or a sailfish on the wall of a dentist's waiting room.

Clear?

Let me put it yet another way: life, by definition, is never still. Where is it going? From birth to death, with no stops on the way. Even a picture of a bowl of pears on a checkered tablecloth is liquid, if laid on canvas by the brush of a master. Yes, and by some miracle I was surely never able to achieve as a painter, nor was Dan Gregory, but which was achieved by the best of the Abstract Expressionists, in the paintings which have greatness birth and death are always there.

Birth and death were even on that old piece of beaverboard Terry Kitchen sprayed at seeming random so long ago. I don't know how he got them in there, and neither did he.

I sigh. "Ah, me," says old Rabo Karabekian.

10

B ACK IN 1933:
    I told a policeman in Grand Central Station Dan Gregory's address. He said it was only eight blocks away, and that I couldn't get lost, since that part of the city was as simple as a checkerboard. The Great Depression was going on, so that the station and the streets teemed with homeless people, just as they do today. The newspapers were full of stories of worker layoffs and farm foreclosures and bank failures, just as they are today. All that has changed, in my opinion, is that, thanks to television, we can *hide* a Great Depression. We may even be hiding a Third World War.

So it was an easy walk, and I soon found myself standing in front of a noble oak door which my new master had used on the cover of the Christmas issue of *Liberty* magazine. The massive iron hinges were rusty. Nobody could counterfeit rust and rust-stained oak like Dan Gregory. The knocker was in the shape of a Gorgon's head, with intertwined asps forming her necklace and hair.

If you looked directly at a Gorgon, supposedly, you were turned to stone. I told that today to the kids around my swimming pool. They had never heard of a Gorgon. I don't think they've heard of anything that wasn't on TV less than a week ago.

• • •

On the *Liberty* cover, as in real life, the lines in the Gorgon's malevolent face and the creases between the writhing asps were infected with verdigris. Nobody could counterfeit verdigris like Dan Gregory. There was a holly wreath around the knocker on the cover, which had been taken down by the time I got there. Some of the leaves had been brown around the edges or spotted. Nobody could counterfeit plant diseases like Dan Gregory.

So I lifted the Gorgon's heavy necklace and let it fall. The *boom* reverberated in an entrance hall whose chandelier and

68

spiral staircase would also be old stuff to me. I had seen them in an illustration of a story about a fabulously rich girl who fell in love with her family's chauffeur: in *Collier's*, I believe.

The face of the man who answered my *boom* was also well known to me, if not his name, since he had been a model for many of Gregory's pictures—including one about a rich girl and her chauffeur. He had been the chauffeur, who in the story would save the girl's father's business after everybody but the girl scorned him as being nothing but a chauffeur. That story, incidentally, was made into the movie *You're Fired*, the second movie to star sound as well as images. The first one was *The Jazz Singer*, starring Al Jolson, who was a friend of Dan Gregory until they had a falling out about Mussolini during my first night there.

The man who opened the door to me had a very good face for an American-style hero, and had in fact been an aviator during the First World War. He was truly Gregory's assistant, what Marilee Kemp had only claimed to be, and would become the only friend who stuck with Gregory to the bitter end. He, too, would be shot while wearing an Italian uniform in Egypt during not his First but his Second World War.

So says this one-eyed Armenian fortune-teller as he peers into his crystal ball.

•   •   •

"Can I help you?" he said. There wasn't a flicker of recognition in his eyes, although he knew who I was and that I would be coming to the house at any time. He and Gregory had resolved to give me a chilly welcome. I can only guess at their deliberations prior to my arrival, but they must have been along the lines of my being a parasite which Marilee had brought into the house, a thief who had already stolen hundreds of dollars' worth of art materials.

They must have persuaded themselves, too, that Marilee was wholly to blame for her backward somersaults down the studio staircase, and that she had unjustly blamed Gregory. As I say, I myself would believe that until she told me the truth of the matter after the war.

So, just to start somewhere in proving that I was right to be on the doorstep, I asked for Marilee.

"She's in the hospital," he said, still barring the way.

"Oh," I said. "I'm sorry." And I told him my name.

"That's what I figured," he said. But still he wasn't going to ask me in.

So then Gregory, who was about halfway down the spiral staircase, asked him who was at the door, and the man, whose name was Fred Jones, said, as though "apprentice" were another name for tapeworm, "It's your apprentice."

"My what?" said Gregory.

"Your apprentice," said Jones.

And Gregory now addressed a problem I myself had pondered: what was a painter's apprentice supposed to do in modern times, when paints and brushes and so on no longer had to be made right in the painter's workplace?

He said this: "I need an apprentice about as much as I need a squire or a troubadour."

• • •

His accent wasn't Armenian or Russian—or American. It was British upper class. If he had so chosen, up there on the spiral staircase, looking at Fred Jones, not at me, he might have sounded like a movie gangster or cowboy, or a German or Irish or Italian or Swedish immigrant, and who knows what else? Nobody could counterfeit more accents from stage, screen and radio than Dan Gregory.

• • •

That was only the *beginning* of the hazing they had planned so lovingly. This was in the late afternoon, and Gregory went back upstairs without greeting me, and Fred Jones took me down into the basement, where I was served a supper of cold leftovers in the servants' dining room off the kitchen.

That room was actually a pleasant one, furnished with early American antiques which Gregory had used in illustrations. I remembered the long table and the corner cupboard full of pewter and the rustic fireplace with a blunderbuss resting on pegs driven into its chimney breast, from a painting he had done of Thanksgiving at Plymouth Colony.

I was put at one end of the table, with my silverware thrown down any which way, and no napkin. I still remember no napkin. While at the other end five places were very nicely set, with linen napkins and crystal and fine china and neatly deployed silverware, and with a candelabrum at their center. The servants were going to have a fine dinner party to which the apprentice was not invited. I was not to consider myself one of them.

Nor did any of the servants speak to me. I might as well have been a bum off the street. Fred Jones moreover stood over me while I ate—like a sullen prison guard.

While I was eating, and more lonesome than I had ever been in my life, a Chinese laundryman, Sam Wu, came in with clean shirts for Gregory. *Pow!* A flash of recognition went off in my skull. I *knew* him! And he must know me! Only days later would I realize why I thought I knew Sam Wu, although he certainly didn't know me. All dressed up in silk robes and wearing a skullcap, this simperingly polite laundryman had been the model for Dan Gregory's pictures of one of the most sinister characters in all of fiction, the Yellow Menace personified, the master criminal Fu Manchu!

• • •

Sam Wu would eventually become Dan Gregory's cook, and then go back to being a laundryman again. And he would be the person to whom I sent the paintings I bought in France during the war.

It was a curious and touching relationship we had during the war. I happened to run into Sam in New York City just before I went overseas, and he asked for my address. He had heard on the radio, he said, about how lonesome soldiers could be overseas, and that people should write to them often. He said I was the only soldier he knew well, so he would write to me.

It became a joke in our platoon at mail call. People would say to me things like: "What's the latest news from Chinatown?" or "No letter from Sam Wu this week? Maybe somebody poisoned his chow mein," and so on.

After I got my pictures from him after the war, I never heard from him again. He may not even have liked me much. For him, I was strictly a wartime activity.

• • •

Back to 1933:

Since supper was so nasty, I would not have been surprised to be escorted next to a windowless room by the furnace, and told that that was to be my bedroom. But I was led up three flights of stairs to the most sumptuous chamber any Karabekian had ever occupied, and told to wait there until Gregory had time to see me, which would be in about six hours, at about midnight, Fred Jones estimated. Gregory was giving a dinner party in the dining room right below me for, among others, Al Jolson and the comedian W. C. Fields, and the author whose stories Gregory had illustrated countless times, Booth Tarkington. I would never meet any of them because they would never come back to the house again—after a bitter argument with Gregory about Benito Mussolini.

About this room Jones put me in: It was Dan Gregory's counterfeit, with genuine French antiques, of the bedroom of Napoleon's Empress Josephine. The chamber was a guest room and not Gregory's and Marilee's bedroom. Imprisoning me there for six hours was subtle sadism of a high order indeed. For one thing, Jones, with a perfectly straight face, indicated that this was to be my bedroom during my apprenticeship, as though anybody but a person as lowborn as myself would find it a perfectly ordinary place to sleep. For another: I didn't dare touch anything. Just to be sure I didn't, Jones said to me, "Please be as quiet as possible, and don't touch anything."

One might have thought they were trying to get rid of me.

• • •

I have just given this snap quiz to Celeste and her friends out by the tennis courts: "Identify the following persons in history: 'W. C. Fields, the Empress Josephine, Booth Tarkington, and Al Jolson.'"

The only one they got was W. C. Fields, whose old movies are shown on TV.

And I say I never met Fields, but that first night I tiptoed out of my gilded cage and to the top of the spiral staircase to listen to the arrival of the famous guests. I heard the unmistakable bandsaw twang of Fields as he introduced the woman with him to Gregory with these words: "This, my child, is Dan Gregory, the love child of Leonardo da Vinci's sister and a sawed-off Arapahoe."

• • •

I complained to Slazinger and Mrs. Berman at supper last night that the young people of today seemed to be trying to get through life with as little information as possible. "They don't even know anything about the Vietnam War or the Empress Josephine, or what a Gorgon is," I said.

Mrs. Berman defended them. She said that it was a little late for them to do anything about the Vietnam War, and that they had more interesting ways of learning about vanity and the power of sex than studying a woman who had lived in another country one hundred and seventy-five years ago. "All that anybody needs to know about a Gorgon," she said, "is that there *is* no such thing."

Slazinger, who still believes her to be only semiliterate, patronized her most daintily with these words: "As the philosopher George Santayana said, 'Those who cannot remember the past are condemned to repeat it.' "

"Is that a fact?" she said. "Well—I've got news for Mr. Santayana: we're doomed to repeat the past no matter what. That's what it is to be alive. It's pretty dense kids who haven't figured that out by the time they're ten."

"Santayana was a famous philosopher at Harvard," said Slazinger, a Harvard man.

And Mrs. Berman said, "Most kids can't afford to go to Harvard to be misinformed."

• • •

I happened to see in *The New York Times* the other day a picture of a French Empire escritoire which was auctioned off to a Kuwaiti for three quarters of a million dollars, and I am almost certain it was in Gregory's guest room back in 1933.

There were two anachronisms in that room, both pictures by Gregory. Over the fireplace was his illustration of the moment in *Robinson Crusoe* when the castaway narrator sees a human footprint on the beach of the island of which he had believed himself to be the sole resident. Over the escritoire was his illustration of the moment when Robin Hood and Little John, strangers who are about to become the best of friends, meet in the middle of a log crossing a stream, each armed with a quarterstaff, and neither one of them willing to back up so that the other one can get to where he would very much like to be.

Robin Hood winds up in the drink, of course.

11

I FELL ASLEEP on the floor of that room. I certainly wasn't going to muss the bed or disturb anything. I dreamed I was back on the train, with its *clickety-clack, clickety-clack, ding-ding-ding* and *whoo-ah*. The *ding-ding-ding* wasn't coming from the train, of course, but from signals at crossings, where anybody who didn't give us the right-of-way would be ripped to smithereens. Serve 'em right! They were nothing. We were everything.

A lot of the people who had to stop for us or be killed were farmers and their families, with all their possessions tied every which way on broken-down trucks. Windstorms or banks had taken away their farms, just as surely as the United States Cavalry had taken the same land from the Indians in their grandfathers' time. The farms that were whisked away by the winds: where are they now? Growing fish food on the floor of the Gulf of Mexico.

These defeated white Indians at the crossings were nothing new to me. I had seen plenty of them passing through San Ignacio, asking the likes of me or my father, or even an emotionally opaque Luma Indian, if we knew of somebody who needed anybody to do work of any kind.

And I was awakened from my railroad dream at midnight by Fred Jones. He said that Mr. Gregory would see me now. He found it unremarkable that I was sleeping on the floor. When I opened my eyes, the tips of his shoes were inches from my nose.

Shoes have played a very important part in the history of the noble Karabekians.

•   •   •

Fred led me to the foot of the staircase down which Marilee had tumbled, which would deliver me up to one end of the holy of holies, the studio. It looked dark up there. I was to climb the stairs alone. It was easy to believe that there was a gallows tree dangling a noose over a trap door up there.

So up I went. I stopped at the head of the stairs, and perceived an impossibility: six free-standing chimneys and fireplaces, with a coal fire glowing in the hearth of every one.

Let me explain architecturally what was really going on. Gregory, you see, had bought three typical New York brownstones, each one three windows wide, four floors high, and fifty feet deep, with two fireplaces on each floor. I had supposed that he owned only the townhouse with the oak door and the Gorgon knocker infected with verdigris. So I was unprepared for the vista on the top floor, which seemed to violate all laws of time and space by going on and on and on. Down on the lower floors, including the basement, he had joined up to three houses with doors and archways. On the top floor, though, he had ripped out the dividing walls entirely, from end to end and side to side, leaving only those six free-standing fireplaces.

• • •

The only illumination that first night came from the six coal fires, and from pale zebra stripes on the ceiling. The stripes were light from a streetlamp below—cut to ribbons by nine windows overlooking East Forty-eighth Street.

Where was Dan Gregory? I could not see him at first. He was motionless and silent—and shapeless in a voluminous black caftan, displaying his back to me, and low, hunched over on a camel saddle before a fireplace in the middle, about twenty feet from me. I identified the objects on the mantelpiece above him before I understood where he was. They were the whitest things in the grotto. They were eight human skulls, an octave arranged in order of size, with a child's at one end and a great-grandfather's at the other—a marimba for cannibals.

There was a kind of music up there, a tedious fugue for pots and pans deployed under a leaking skylight to the right of Gregory. The skylight was under a blanket of melting snow.

• • •

"*Ker-plunk.*" Silence. "*Plink-pank.*" Silence. "*Ploop.*" Silence. That was how the song of the skylight went as my gaze probed Dan Gregory's one indubitable masterpiece, that studio—his one work of breathtaking originality.

A simple inventory of the weapons and tools and idols and icons and hats and helmets and ship models and airplane models and stuffed animals, including a crocodile and an upright polar bear, in the masterpiece would be amazing enough. But think of this: there were fifty-two mirrors of every conceivable period and shape, many of them hung in unexpected places at crazy angles, to multiply even the bewildered observer to infinity. There at the top of the stairs, with Dan Gregory invisible to me, I myself was everywhere!

I know there were fifty-two mirrors because I counted them the next day. Some I was supposed to polish every week. Others I was not to dust on penalty of *death*, according to my master. Nobody could counterfeit images in dusty mirrors like Dan Gregory.

Now he spoke, and rolled his shoulders some, so I could see where he was. And he said this: "I was never welcome anywhere either." He was using his British accent again, which was the only one he ever used, except in fun. He went on: "It was very good for me to be so unwelcome, so unappreciated by my own master, because look what I have become."

• • •

He said that his father, the horse trainer, had come close to killing him when he was an infant because his father couldn't stand to hear him cry. "If I started to cry, he did everything he could to make me stop right away," he said. "He was only a child himself, which is easy to forget about a father. How old are you?"

I spoke my first word to him: "Seventeen."

• • •

"My father was only one year older than you are when I was born," said Dan Gregory. "If you start copulating right now, you, too, can have a squalling baby by the time you're eighteen, in a big city like this one—and far from home. You think you're going to set this city on its ear as an artist, do you? Well—my father thought he was going to set Moscow on its ear as a horse trainer, and he found out quickly enough that the horse world there was run by Polacks, and that the highest he was ever going to rise, no matter how good he was, was to the rank of lowest stableboy. He had stolen my mother away from her people and all she knew when she was only sixteen, promising her that they would soon be rich and famous in Moscow."

He stood and faced me. I had not budged from the top of the stairs. The new rubber heels I had put on my old broken shoes were cantilevered in air past the lip of the top step, so reluctant was I to come any farther into this dumbfoundingly complex and mirrored environment.

Gregory himself was only a head and hands now, since his caftan was black. The head said to me, "I was born in a stable like Jesus Christ, and I cried like this:"

From his throat came a harrowing counterfeit of the cries of an unwanted baby who could do nothing but cry and cry.

My hair stood on end.

12

D AN GREGORY, or *Gregorian*, as he was known in the
Old World, was rescued from his parents when he was
about five years old by the wife of an artist named Beskudnikov,
who was the engraver of plates for Imperial bonds and paper
currency. She did not love him. He was simply a stray, mangy
animal in the city she could not stand to see abused. So she did
with him what she had done with several stray cats and dogs she
had brought home—handed him over to the servants to clean
and raise.

"Her servants felt about me the way my servants feel about
you," Gregory said to me. "I was just one more job to do, like
shoveling ashes from the stoves or cleaning the lamp chimneys
or beating the rugs."

He said he studied what the dogs and cats did to get along,
and then he did that, too. "The animals spent a lot of time in
Beskudnikov's workshop, which was behind his house," he
said. "The apprentices and journeymen would pet them and
give them food, so I did that, too. I did some things the other
animals *couldn't* do. I learned all the languages spoken there.
Beskudnikov himself had studied in England and France, and
he liked to give his helpers orders in one or the other of those
languages, which he expected all of them to understand. Very
soon I made myself useful as a translator, telling them exactly
what their master had said to them. I already knew Polish and
Russian, which the servants had taught me."

"And Armenian," I suggested.

"No," he said. "All I ever learned from my drunken parents
was how to bray like a jackass or gibber like a monkey—or snarl
like a wolf."

He said that he also mastered every craft practiced in the
shop, and, like me, had a knack for catching in a quick sketch a
passable likeness of almost anybody or anything. "At the age of
ten I myself was made an apprentice," he said.

"By the age of fifteen," he went on, "it was obvious to everyone that I was a genius. Beskudnikov himself felt threatened,
so he assigned me a task which everyone agreed was impossible.

He would promote me to journeyman only after I had drawn by hand a one-ruble note, front and back, good enough to fool the sharp-eyed merchants in the marketplace."

He grinned at me. "The penalty for counterfeiting in those days," he said, "was a public hanging in that same marketplace."

• • •

Young Dan Gregorian spent six months making what he and all his co-workers agreed was a perfect note. Beskudnikov called the effort childish, and tore it into little pieces.

Gregorian made an even better one, again taking six months to do so. Beskudnikov declared it to be worse than the first, and threw it into the fire.

Gregorian made still a better one, spending a full year on it this time. All the while, of course, he was also carrying out his regular chores around the shop and house. When he completed his third counterfeit, however, he put it in his pocket. He showed Beskudnikov the genuine ruble he had been copying instead.

As he had expected, the old man laughed at that one, too. But before Beskudnikov could destroy it, young Gregorian snatched it away and ran out into the marketplace. He bought a box of cigars with the genuine ruble, telling the tobacconist that the note was *surely* genuine, since it had come from Beskudnikov, engraver of the plates for the Imperial paper currency.

Beskudnikov was horrified when the boy returned with the cigars. He had never meant for him to actually spend his counterfeit in the marketplace. He had named negotiability simply as his standard for excellence. His bugging eyes and sweaty brow and gasping proved that he was an honest man whose judgment was clouded by jealousy. Because his brilliant apprentice had handed him the ruble, his own work, incidentally, it really did look like a fake to him.

What could the old man do, now? The tobacconist would surely recognize the note as a fake, too, and know where it had come from. After that? The law was the law. The Imperial engraver and his apprentice would be hanged side by side in the marketplace.

"To his eternal credit," Dan Gregory said to me, "he himself resolved to retrieve what he thought was a fatal piece of paper.

He asked me for the ruble I had copied. I of course handed him my perfect counterfeit."

•   •   •

Beskudnikov told the tobacconist a preposterous story about how the ruble his apprentice had spent on cigars had great sentimental value. It was a matter of indifference to the tobacconist, who traded him the real one for the fake.

The old man returned to the workshop beaming. The moment he was inside, however, he promised Gregorian the beating of his life. Until that time, Gregorian had always stood still for his beatings, as a good apprentice should.

This time the boy ran a short distance away and turned to laugh at his master.

"How dare you laugh at a time like this?" cried Beskudnikov.

"I dare to laugh at you now and for the rest of my life," the apprentice replied. He told what he had done with his counterfeit ruble and the real one. "You can teach me no more. I have surpassed you by far," he said. "I am such a genius that I have tricked the engraver of the Imperial currency into passing a counterfeit ruble in the marketplace. My last words on Earth will be a confession to you, should we find ourselves side by side with nooses around our necks in the marketplace. I will say, 'You were right after all. I wasn't as talented as I thought I was. Good-bye, cruel world, good-bye.'"

13

COCKY DAN GREGORIAN left Beskudnikov's employ that day, and easily became a journeyman under another master engraver and silk screen artist, who made theatrical posters and illustrations for children's books. His counterfeit was never detected, or at any rate was not traced to him or Beskudnikov.

"And Beskudnikov surely never told anyone the true story," he said to me, "of how he and his most promising apprentice came to a parting of the ways."

• • •

He said he had so far done me the favor of making me feel unwelcome. "Since you are so much older than I was when I surpassed Beskudnikov," he went on, "we should waste no time in assigning you work roughly equivalent to copying a ruble by hand." He appeared to consider many possible projects, but I am sure he had settled on the most diabolical one imaginable well before my arrival.

"Aha!" he said. "I've got it! I want you to set up an easel about where you're standing now. You should then paint a picture of this room—*indistinguishable* from a photograph. Does that sound fair? I hope not."

I swallowed hard. "No, sir," I said, "it sure isn't fair."

And he said, "Excellent!"

• • •

I have just been to New York City for the first time in two years. It was Circe Berman's idea that I do this, and that I do it alone—so as to prove to myself that I was still a perfectly healthy man, in no way in need of assistance, in no way an invalid. It is now the middle of August. She has been here for two months and a little more, which means that I have been writing this book for two months!

She swore that the city of New York could be a Fountain of Youth for me, if only I would retrace some of the steps I had taken when I first got there from California so long ago. "Your muscles will tell you that they are nearly as springy as they were back then," she said. "If you will only let it," she said, "your brain will show you that it can be exactly as cocky and *excited* as it was back then."

It sounded good. But guess what? She was assembling a booby trap.

• • •

Her promise came true for a little while, not that she gave a damn whether it was hollow or not. All she wanted was to get me out of here for a little while, so she could do what she pleased with this property.

At least she didn't break into the potato barn, which she could have done herself, given enough time—and a crowbar and an axe. She had only to go into the carriage house to find a crowbar and an axe.

• • •

I really did feel spry and cocky again when I retraced my first steps from Grand Central Station to the three brownstones which had been the mansion of Dan Gregory. They were three separate houses again, as I already knew. They had been made separate again about the time my father died, three years before the United States got into the war. Which war? The Peloponnesian War, of course. Doesn't anybody but me remember the Peloponnesian War?

• • •

I begin again:

Dan Gregory's mansion became three separate brownstones again soon after he and Marilee and Fred Jones left for Italy to take part in Mussolini's great social experiment. Although he and Fred were well into their fifties by then, they would ask for and receive permission from Mussolini himself to don Italian infantry officers' uniforms, but without any badges of rank or unit, and to make paintings of the Italian Army in action.

They would be killed almost exactly one year before the United States joined the war—against Italy, by the way, and against Germany and Japan and some others. They were killed around December seventh of 1940 at Sidi Barrani, Egypt, where only thirty thousand British overwhelmed eighty thousand

Italians, I learn from the *Encyclopaedia Britannica*, capturing forty thousand Italians and four hundred guns.

When the *Britannica* talks about captured guns, it doesn't mean rifles and pistols. It means great big guns.

Yes, and since Gregory and his sidekick Jones were such weapons nuts, let it be said that it was Matilda tanks, and Stens and Brens and Enfield rifles with fixed bayonets which did them in.

•   •   •

Why did Marilee go to Italy with Gregory and Jones? She was in love with Gregory, and he was in love with her.

How is that for simplicity?

•   •   •

The easternmost house of the three which used to belong to Gregory, I only discovered on this most recent trip to New York, is now the office and dwelling of the Delegation to the United Nations of the Emirate of Salibaar. That was the first I had ever heard of the Emirate of Salibaar, which I can't find anywhere in my *Encyclopaedia Britannica*. I can only find a desert town by that name, population eleven thousand, about the population of San Ignacio. Circe Berman says it is time I got a new encyclopedia, and some new neckties, too.

The big oak door and its massive hinges are unchanged, except that the Gorgon knocker is gone. Gregory took it with him to Italy, and I saw it again on the front door of Marilee's palace in Florence after the war.

Maybe it has now migrated elsewhere, since Italy's and my beloved Contessa Portomaggiore died of natural causes in her sleep in the same week my beloved Edith passed away.

Some *week* for old Rabo Karabekian!

•   •   •

The middle brownstone has been divided into five apartments, one on each floor, including the basement, as I learned by the mailboxes and doorbells in the foyer.

But don't mention foyers to me! More about that in a little bit! All things in good time.

•   •   •

That middle house used to contain the guest room where I was first incarcerated, and Gregory's grand dining room right below that, and his research library below that, and the storage room for his art materials in the basement. I was mostly curious, though, about the top floor, which used to be the part of Gregory's studio with the big, leaky skylight. I wanted to know whether there was still a skylight up there, and, if so, if anybody had ever found a way to stop its leaks, or whether there were still pots and pans making John Cage music underneath it when it rained or snowed.

But there was nobody to ask, so I never found out. So there is one storytelling fizzle for you, dear Reader. I never found out.

And here is another one. The house to the west of that one is, judging from the mailboxes and bells, evidentally a triplex at the bottom, with a duplex on top of that. It was this third of Gregory's establishment which the live-in servants had inhabited, and where I, too, was given a small but cheerful bedroom. Fred Jones's bedroom, by the way, was right in back of Gregory's and Marilee's room in the Emirate of Salibaar.

• • •

This woman came out of the brownstone with the duplex and triplex. She was old and trembly, but her posture was good, and it was easy to see that she had been very beautiful at one time. I locked my gaze to hers, and a flash of recognition went off in my skull. I knew *her*, but she didn't know *me*. We had never met. I realized that I had seen her in motion pictures when she was much younger. A second later, I came up with her name. She was Barbira Mencken, the ex-wife of Paul Slazinger. He had lost touch with her years ago, had no idea where she lived. She hadn't done a movie or a play for a long, long time, but there she was. Greta Garbo and Katharine Hepburn also live in that same general neighborhood.

I didn't speak to her. Should I have spoken to her? What would I have had to say to her? "Paul is fine and sends his best"? Or how about this one: "Tell me how your parents died"?

• • •

I had supper at the Century Club, to which I have belonged for many years. There was a new maître d', and I asked him what had happened to the old one, Roberto. He said that Roberto had been killed by a bicycle messenger going the wrong way on a one-way street right in front of the club.

I said that was too bad, and he heartily agreed with me.

I didn't see anybody I knew, which was hardly surprising, since everybody I know is dead. But I made friends in the bar with a man considerably my junior, who was a writer of young adult novels, like Circe Berman. I asked him if he had ever heard of the Polly Madison books and he asked me if I had ever heard of the Atlantic Ocean.

So we had supper together. His wife was out of town lecturing, he said. She was a prominent sexologist.

I asked him as delicately as I could if making love to a woman so sophisticated in sexual techniques was in any way unusually burdensome. He replied, rolling his eyes at the ceiling, that I had certainly hit the nail on the head. "I have to reassure her that I really love her practically *incessantly*," he said.

• • •

I spent an uneventful late evening watching pornographic TV programs in my room at the Algonquin Hotel. I watched and didn't watch at the very same time.

I planned to catch a train back the next afternoon, but met a fellow East Hamptonite, Floyd Pomerantz, at breakfast. He, too, was headed home later in the day, and offered me a ride in his Cadillac stretch limousine. I accepted with alacrity.

What a satisfactory form of transportation that proved to be! That Cadillac was better than womblike. The Twentieth Century Limited, as I have said, really was womblike, in constant motion, with all sorts of unexplained thumps and bangs outside. But the Cadillac was *coffin*like. Pomerantz and I got to be *dead* in there. The hell with this baby stuff. It was so cozy, two of us in a single, roomy, gangster-style casket. Everybody should be buried with somebody else, just about anybody else, whenever feasible.

• • •

Pomerantz talked some about picking up the pieces of his life and trying to put them back together again. He is Circe Berman's age, which is forty-three. Three months before, he had been given eleven million dollars to resign as president of a big TV network. "Most of my life still lies ahead of me," he said.

"Yes," I said. "I guess it does."

"Do you think there is still time for me to be a painter?" he said.

"Never too late," I said.

•   •   •

Earlier, I knew, he had asked Paul Slazinger if there was still time for him to become a writer. He thought people might be interested in his side of the story about what happened to him at the network.

Slazinger said afterwards that there ought to be some way to persuade people like Pomerantz, and the Hamptons teem with people like Pomerantz, that they had already extorted more than enough from the economy. He suggested that we build a Money Hall of Fame out here, with busts of the arbitrageurs and hostile-takeover specialists and venture capitalists and investment bankers and golden handshakers and platinum parachutists in niches, with their statistics cut into stone—how many millions they had stolen legally in how short a time.

I asked Slazinger if *I* deserved to be in the Money Hall of Fame. He thought that over, and concluded that I belonged in some sort of Hall of Fame, but that all my money had come as a result of accidents rather than greed.

"You belong in the Dumb *Luck* Hall of Fame," he said. He thought it should be built in Las Vegas or Atlantic City, maybe, but then changed his mind. "The Klondike, I think," he said. "People should have to come by dogsled or on snowshoes if they want to see Rabo Karabekian's bust in the Dumb Luck Hall of Fame."

He can't *stand* it that I inherited a piece of the Cincinnati Bengals, and don't give a damn. He is an avid football fan.

14

S o Floyd Pomerantz's chauffeur delivered me to the first flagstone of my doorpath. I clambered out of our fancy casket like Count Dracula, blinded by the setting sun. I groped my way to my front door and entered.

Let me tell you about the foyer I had every right to expect to see. Its walls should have been oyster white, like every square foot of wall space in the entire house, except for the basement and servants' quarters. Terry Kitchen's painting "Secret Window" should have loomed before me like the City of God. To my left should have been a Matisse of a woman holding a black cat in her arms and standing before a brick wall covered with yellow roses, which dear Edith had bought fair and square from a gallery as a present to me on our fifth wedding anniversary. On my right should have been a Hans Hofmann which Terry Kitchen got from Philip Guston in trade for one of his own pictures, and which he gave to me after I paid for a new transmission for his babyshit-brown convertible Buick Roadmaster.

• • •

Those who wish to know more about the foyer need only dig out a copy of the February 1981 issue of *Architect & Decorator*. The foyer is on the cover, is viewed through the open front door from the flagstone walk, which was lined on both sides with hollyhocks back then. The lead article is about the whole house as a masterpiece of redecorating a Victorian house to accommodate modern art. Of the foyer itself it says, "The Karabekians' entrance hall alone contains what might serve as the core of a small museum's permanent collection of modern art, marvelous enough in itself, but in fact a mere *hors d'oeuvre* before the incredible feast of art treasures awaiting in the high-ceilinged, stark-white rooms beyond."

And was I, the great Rabo Karabekian, the mastermind behind this happy marriage of the old and the new? No. Dear Edith was. It was all her idea that I bring my collection out of storage. This house, after all, was an heirloom of the Taft family, full not only of memories of Edith's happy childhood in summertimes here, but of her very good first marriage, too. When I moved in here from the potato barn, she asked me if I was comfortable in such old-fashioned surroundings. I said truthfully and from the bottom of my heart that I loved it for what it was, and that she shouldn't change a thing for me.

So by God if it wasn't *Edith* who called in the contractors, and had them strip off all the wallpaper right down to bare plaster, and take down the chandeliers and put up track lights—and paint the oak baseboards and trim and doors and window sashes and walls a solid oyster-white!

When the work was done, she looked about twenty years younger. She said she had almost gone to her grave without ever realizing what a gift she had for remodeling and decorating. And then she said, "Call Home Sweet Home Moving and Storage," in whose warehouse I had stored my collection for years and years. "Let them tell your glorious paintings as they bring them out into the daylight, 'You are going *home!*' "

• • •

When I walked into my foyer after my trip to New York City, though, a scene so shocking enveloped me that, word of honor, I thought an axe murder had happened there. I am not joking! I thought I was looking at blood and gore! It may have taken me as long as a minute to realize what I was really seeing: wallpaper featuring red roses as big as cabbages against a field of black, babyshit-brown baseboards, trim and doors, and six chromos of little girls on swings, with mats of purple velvet, and with gilded frames which must have weighed as much as the limousine which had delivered me to this catastrophe.

Did I yell? They tell me I did. What did I yell? They had to tell me afterwards what I yelled. They heard it, and I did not. When the cook and her daughter, the first to arrive, came running, I was yelling this, they say, over and over: "I am in the wrong house! I am in the wrong house!"

Think of this: my homecoming was a surprise party they had been looking forward to all day long. Now it was all they could do, despite how generous I had always been with them, not to laugh out loud at my maximum agony!

What a world!

• • •

I said to the cook, and I could hear myself now: "Who *did* this?"

"Mrs. Berman," she said. She behaved as though she couldn't imagine what the trouble was.

"How could you allow this to happen?" I said.

"I'm just the cook," she said.

"I also hope you're my *friend*," I said.

"Think what you want," she said. The truth be told, we had never been close. "I like how it looks," she said.

"*Do* you!" I said.

"Looks better than it did," she said.

So I turned to her daughter. "You think it looks better than it did?"

"Yes," she said.

"Well—" I said, "isn't this just wonderful! The minute I was out of the house, Mrs. Berman called in the painters and paperhangers, did she?"

They shook their heads. They said that Mrs. Berman had done the whole job herself, and that she had met her husband the doctor while papering his office. She used to be a professional paperhanger! Can you beat it?

"After his office," said Celeste, "he had her paper his home."

"He was lucky she didn't paper *him*!" I said.

And Celeste said, "You know you dropped your patch?"

"My what?" I said.

"Your eye patch," she said. "It's on the floor and you're stepping on it."

It was true! I was so upset that at some point, maybe while tearing my hair, I had stripped the patch from my head. So now they were seeing the scar tissue which I had never even shown Edith. My first wife had certainly seen a lot of it, but she was my nurse in the Army hospital at Fort Benjamin Harrison, where a plastic surgeon tried to clean up the mess a little bit after the war. He would have had to do a lot more surgery to get it to the point where it would hold a glass eye, so I chose an eye patch instead.

The patch was on the floor!

• • •

My most secret disfigurement was in plain view of the cook and her daughter! And now Paul Slazinger came into the foyer in time to see it, too.

They were all very cool about what they saw. They didn't recoil in horror or cry out in disgust. It was almost as though I looked just about the same, with or without the eye patch on.

After I got the eye patch back in place, I said to Slazinger: "Were you here while this was going on?"

"Sure," he said. "I wouldn't have missed it for anything."

"Didn't you know how it would make me feel?" I said.

"That's why I wouldn't have missed it for anything," he said.

"I just don't understand this," I said. "Suddenly it sounds as though you're all my enemies."

"I don't know about these two," said Slazinger, "but I'm sure as hell your enemy. Why didn't you tell me she was Polly Madison?"

"How did you find out?" I said.

"She told me," he said. "I saw what she was doing here, and I begged her not to—because I thought it might kill you. She said it would make you ten years younger.

"I thought it might really be a life-and-death situation," he went on, "and that I had better take some direct physical action." This was a man, incidentally, who had won a Silver Star for protecting his comrades on Okinawa by lying down on a fizzing Japanese hand grenade.

"So I gathered up as many rolls of wallpaper as I could," he said, "and ran out into the kitchen and hid them in the deep freeze. How's that for friendship?"

"God *bless* you!" I exclaimed.

"Yes, and God fuck you," he said. "She came right after me, and wanted to know what I'd done with the wallpaper. I called her a crazy witch, and she called me a freeloader and 'the spit-filled penny whistle of American literature.' 'Who are you to talk about literature?' I asked her. So she told me."

What she said to him was this: "My novels sold seven million copies in the United States alone last year. Two are being made into major motion pictures as we stand here, and one of them made into a movie last year won Academy Awards for Best Cinematography, Best Supporting Actress and Best Score. Shake hands, Buster, with Polly Madison, Literary Middleweight

Champion of the World! And then give me back my wallpaper, or I'll break your arms!"

•   •   •

"How could you have let me make such a fool of myself for so long, Rabo—" he said, "giving her tips on the ins and outs of the writing game?"

"I was waiting for the opportune time," I said.

"You missed it by a mile, you son of a bitch," he said.

"She's in a different league from you anyway," I said.

"That's right," he said. "She's richer and she's better."

"Not better, surely," I said.

"This woman is a monster," he said, "but her books are marvelous! She's the new Richard Wagner, one of the most awful people who ever lived."

"How would you know about her books?" I said.

"Celeste has them all, so I read them," he said. "How's that for an irony? There I was all summer, reading her books and admiring the hell out of them, and meanwhile treating her like a half-wit, not knowing who she was."

So that's what *he* did with this summer, anyway: he read all the Polly Madison books!

•   •   •

"After I found out who she was," he said, "and the way you'd kept it from me, I became more enthusiastic than she was about redoing the foyer. I said that if she really wanted to make you happy, she would paint the woodwork babyshit brown."

He knew that I had had at least two unhappy experiences with the color practically everybody calls "babyshit brown." Even in San Ignacio when I was a boy, people called it "babyshit brown."

One experience took place outside Brooks Brothers years ago, where I had bought a summer suit which I thought looked pretty nice, which had been altered for me, and which I decided to wear home. I was then married to Dorothy, and we were still living in the city, and both still planning on my being a businessman. The minute I stepped outside, two policemen grabbed me for hard questioning. Then they let me go with an apology, explaining that a man had just robbed a bank down the street, with a lady's nylon stocking over his head. "All that anybody could tell us about him," one of them said to me, "was that his suit was babyshit brown."

My other unhappy association with that color had to do with Terry Kitchen. After Terry and I and several others in our gang moved out here for the cheap real estate and potato barns, Terry did his afternoon drinking at bars which were, in effect, private clubs for native working men. This was a man, incidentally, who was a graduate of Yale Law School, who had been a clerk to Supreme Court Justice John Harlan, and a major in the 82nd Airborne. I was not only supporting him in large measure: I was the one he called or had somebody else call from some bar when he was too drunk to drive home.

And here is what Kitchen, arguably the most important artist ever to paint in the Hamptons, with the possible exception of Winslow Homer, is called in the local bars by the few who still remember him: "The guy in the babyshit-brown convertible."

15

"WHERE IS Mrs. Berman at this moment?" I wished to
know.

"Upstairs—getting dressed for a big date," said Celeste. "She
looks terrific. Wait till you see."

"Date?" I said. She had never gone on a date as long as she had
been living here. "Who would she have a date with?"

"She met a psychiatrist on the beach," said the cook.

"He drives a Ferrari," said her daughter. "He held the ladder
for her while she hung the paper. He's taking her to a big dinner
party for Jackie Kennedy over in Southampton, and then they're
going dancing in Sag Harbor afterwards."

At that moment, Mrs. Berman arrived in the foyer, as serene
and majestic as the most beautiful motor ship ever built, the
French liner *Normandie*.

• • •

When I was a hack artist in an advertising agency before the
war, I had painted a picture of the *Normandie* for a travel poster.
And when I was about to sail as a soldier for North Africa on
February 9, 1942, and was giving Sam Wu the address where
he could write to me, the sky over New York Harbor was thick
with smoke.

Why?

Workmen converting an ocean liner into a troopship had
started an uncontrollable fire in the belly of the most beautiful
motor ship ever built. Her name again, and may her soul rest in
peace: the *Normandie*.

• • •

"This is an absolute outrage," I said to Mrs. Berman.

She smiled. "How do I look?" she said. She was overwhelm-
ingly erotic—her voluptuous figure exaggerated and cocked
this way and that way as she teetered on high-heeled, golden
dancing shoes. Her skintight cocktail dress was cut low in front,
shamelessly displaying her luscious orbs. What a sexual bully
she could be!

"Who gives a damn what *you* look like?" I said.

"Somebody will," she said.

"What have you *done* to this foyer?" I said. "That's what I'd like to discuss with you, and the *hell* with your clothes!"

"Make it fast," she said. "My date will be here at any time."

"O.K.," I said. "What you have done here is not only an unforgivable insult to the history of art, but you have spit on the grave of my *wife*! You knew perfectly well that she created this foyer, not I. I could go on to speak of sanity as compared with *in*sanity, decency as compared with vandalism, friendship as compared with rabies. But since you, Mrs. Berman, have called for speed and clarity in my mode of self-expression, because your concupiscent shrink will be arriving in his Ferrari at any moment, try this: Get the hell out of here, and never come back again!"

"Bushwa," she said.

" 'Bushwa'?" I echoed scornfully. "I suppose that's the high level of intellectual discourse one might expect from the author of the Polly Madison books."

"It wouldn't hurt *you* to read one," she said. "They're about life right now." She indicated Slazinger. "You and your ex-pal here never got past the Great Depression and World War Two."

She was wearing a gold wristwatch encrusted with diamonds and rubies which I had never seen before, and it fell to the floor.

The cook's daughter laughed, and I asked her loftily what she thought was funny.

She said, "Everybody's got the dropsies today."

So Circe, picking up the watch, asked who else had dropped something, and Celeste told her about my eye patch.

Slazinger took the opportunity to mock what was under the eye patch. "Oh, you should *see* that scar," he said. "It is the most *horrible* scar! I have never seen such disgusting disfigurement."

I wouldn't have taken that from anybody else, but I had to take it from him. He had a wide scar that looked like a map of the Mississippi Valley running from his sternum to his crotch, where he had been laid open by the hand grenade.

• • •

He has only one nipple left, and he asked me a riddle one time: "What has three eyes, three nipples and two assholes?"

"I give up," I said.

And he said, "Paul Slazinger and Rabo Karabekian."

•   •   •

There in the foyer, he said to me, "Until you dropped your eye patch, I had no idea how *vain* you were. That's a perfectly acceptable wink under there."

"Now that you know," I said, "I hope that *both* you and Polly Madison clear the hell out of here and never come back again. How you two took advantage of my hospitality!"

"I paid my share," said Mrs. Berman. This was true. From the very first, she had insisted on paying for the cook and the food and liquor.

"You are so deep in my debt for so many things besides money," she went on, "you could never pay me back in a million years. After I'm gone, you're going to realize what a favor I did you with this foyer alone."

"Favor? Did you say *favor*?" I jeered. "You know what these pictures are to anybody with half a grain of sense about art? They are a *negation* of art! They aren't just neutral. They are black holes from which no intelligence or skill can ever escape. Worse than that, they suck up the dignity, the self-respect, of anybody unfortunate enough to have to look at them."

"Seems like a lot for just a few little pictures to do," she said, meanwhile trying without any luck to clip her watch around her wrist again.

"Is it still running?" I said.

"It hasn't run for years," she said.

"Then why do you wear it?" I said.

"To look as nice as possible," she said, "but now the clasp is broken." She offered the watch to me, and made an allusion to my tale of how my mother had become rich in jewels during the massacre. "Here! Take it, and buy yourself a ticket to someplace where you'll be happier—like the Great Depression or World War Two."

I waved the gift away.

"Why not a ticket back to what you were before I got here?" she said. "Except you don't *need* a ticket. You'll be back there quick enough, as soon as I move out."

"I was quite content in June," I said, "and then you appeared."

"Yes," she said, "and you were also fifteen pounds lighter and ten shades paler, and a thousand times more listless, and your personal hygiene was so careless that I almost didn't come to supper. I was afraid I might get leprosy."

"You're *too* kind," I said.

"I brought you back to life," she said. "You're my Lazarus. All Jesus did for Lazarus was bring him back to life. I not only brought you back to life—I got you writing your autobiography."

"That was a big joke, too, I guess," I said.

"Big joke like what?" she said.

"Like this foyer," I said.

"These pictures are twice as serious as yours, if you give them half a chance," she said.

• • •

"You had them sent up from Baltimore?" I said.

"No," she said. "I ran into another collector at an antique show in Bridgehampton last week, and she sold them to me. I didn't know what to do with them at first, so I hid them in the basement—behind all the Sateen Dura-Luxe."

"I hope this babyshit brown isn't Sateen Dura-Luxe," I said.

"No," she said. "Only an idiot would use Sateen Dura-Luxe. And you want me to tell you what's great about these pictures?"

"No," I said.

"I've done my best to understand and respect *your* pictures," she said. "Why won't you do the same for *mine?*"

"Do you know the meaning of the word 'kitsch'?" I said.

"I wrote a book called *Kitsch*," she said.

"I read it," said Celeste. "It's about a girl whose boyfriend tried to make her think she has bad taste, which she does—but it doesn't matter much."

"You don't call these pictures of little girls on swings serious art?" jeered Mrs. Berman. "Try thinking what the Victorians thought when they looked at them, which was how sick or unhappy so many of these happy, innocent little girls would be in just a little while—diphtheria, pneumonia, smallpox, miscarriages, violent husbands, poverty, widowhood, prostitution—death and burial in potter's field."

There was the swish of tires in the gravel driveway. "Time to go," she said. "Maybe you can't stand truly serious art. Maybe you'd better use the back door from now on."

And she was gone!

16

N O SOONER had the snarl and burble of the psychiatrist's
Ferrari died away in the sunset than the cook said she and
her daughter would be leaving too. "This is your two weeks'
notice," she said.

What a blow! "What made you decide so suddenly?" I asked.

"Nothing sudden about it," she said. "Celeste and I were
about to leave right before Mrs. Berman came. It was so *dead*
here. She made things exciting, so we stayed. But we've always
said to each other: 'When she goes, we go, too.' "

"I really *need* you," I said. "What could I do to persuade you
to stay?" I mean: my God—they already had rooms with ocean
views, and Celeste's young friends had the run of the property,
and no end of free snacks and refreshments. The cook could
take any of the cars anytime she wanted to, and I was paying
her like a movie star.

"You could learn my name," she said.

What was going on? "Do what?" I said.

"Whenever I hear you talk about me, all you ever call me is
'the cook.' I have a name. It's 'Allison White,' " she said.

"Goodness!" I protested with terrified joviality, "I know that
perfectly well. That's who I make out your check to every week.
Did I misspell it or something—or get your Social Security
wrong?"

"That's the only time you ever think of me," she said, "when
you make out my check—and I don't think you think about
me then. Before Mrs. Berman came, and Celeste was in school,
and there were just the two of us in the house alone, and we'd
slept under the same roof night after night, and you ate my
food—"

Here she stopped. She hoped she'd said enough, I guess. I
now realize that this was very hard for her.

"Yes—?" I said.

"This is so *stupid*," she said.

"I can't tell if it is or not," I said.

And then she blurted: "I don't want to marry you!"

My God! "Who *would*?" I said.

"I just want to be a human being and not a nobody and a nothing, if I have to live under the same roof with a man—*any* man," she said. She revised that instantly: "Any *person*," she said.

This was dismayingly close to what my first wife Dorothy had said to me: that I often treated her as though I didn't even care what her name was, as though she really weren't there. The next thing the cook said I had also heard from Dorothy:

"I think you're scared to death of women," she said.

"Me, too," said Celeste.

•   •   •

"Celeste—" I said, "you and I have been close, haven't we?"

"That's because you think I'm stupid," said Celeste.

"And she's still too young to be threatening," her mother said.

"So *everybody's* leaving now," I said. "Where's Paul Slazinger?"

"Out the door," said Celeste.

•   •   •

What had I done to deserve this? All I had done was go to New York City for one night, giving the widow Berman time to redecorate the foyer! And now, as I stood in the midst of a life she had ruined, she was off hobnobbing in Southampton with Jackie Kennedy!

"Oh, my," I said at last. "And I know you hate my famous art collection, too."

They brightened some, because, I suppose, I had broached a subject which was a lot easier to discuss than the relationship between women and men.

"I don't hate them," said the cook—said *Allison White, Allison White, Allison White*! This is a perfectly presentable woman, with even features and a trim figure and nice brown hair. I'm the problem. I am not a presentable man.

"They just don't *mean* anything to me," she went on. "I'm sure that's because I'm uneducated. Maybe if I went to college, I would finally realize how wonderful they are. The only one I really liked, you sold."

"Which one was that?" I said. I myself perked up some, hoping to salvage something, at least, from this nightmare: a statement from these unsophisticated people as to which of my paintings, one I had sold, evidently, had had such power that even *they* had liked it.

"The one with the two little black boys and the two little white boys," she said.

I ransacked my mind for any painting in the house which might have been misread in that way by an imaginative and simple person. Which one had two black blobs and two white ones? Again: it sounded a lot like a Rothko.

But then I caught on that she was talking about a painting I had never considered a part of my collection, but simply a souvenir. It was by none other than Dan Gregory! It was a magazine illustration for a Booth Tarkington story about an encounter in the back alley of a middle-western town, not in this century but in the one before, between two white boys and two black—about ten years old.

In the picture, they were obviously wondering if they could be playmates, or whether they had better go their separate ways.

In the story, the two black boys had very comical names: "Herman" and "Verman." I often heard it said that nobody could paint black people like Dan Gregory, but he did it entirely from photographs. One of the first things he ever said to me was that he would never have a black person in his house.

I thought that was great. I thought everything he said was great for a little while. I was going to become what *he* was, and regrettably *did* in many ways.

• • •

I sold that painting of the two black boys and the two white boys to a real-estate and insurance millionaire in Lubbock, Texas, who has the most complete collection of Dan Gregory paintings in the world, he told me. As far as I know, he has the *only* such collection, for which he has built a large private museum.

He discovered somehow that I used to be Gregory's apprentice, and he called me up to ask if I had any of my master's works I was willing to part with. I had only that one, which I hadn't looked at for years, since it hung in the bathroom of one of the many guest rooms here which I had had no reason to enter.

"You sold the only picture that was really about something," said Allison White. "I used to look at it and try and guess what would happen next."

• • •

Oh: one last thing Allison White said to me before she and Celeste went upstairs to their quarters which had priceless ocean views: "We'll get out of your way now," she said, "and we don't care if we never find out what's in the potato barn."

• • •

So there I was all alone downstairs. I was afraid to go upstairs. I didn't want to be in the house at all, and seriously considered taking up residence again as what I had been to dear Edith after her first husband died: a half-tamed old raccoon in the potato barn.

So I went walking for hours on the beach—all the way to Sagaponack and back again, reliving my blank-brained, deep-breathing hermit days.

There was a note on the kitchen table from the cook, from *Allison White*, saying my supper was in the oven. So I ate it. My appetite is always good. I had a few drinks, and listened to some music. There was one thing I learned during my eight years as a professional soldier which proved to be very useful in civilian life: how to fall asleep almost anywhere, no matter how bad the news may be.

I was awakened at two in the morning by someone's rubbing the back of my neck *so* gently. It was Circe Berman.

"Everybody's leaving," I said. "The cook gave notice. In two weeks, she and Celeste will be gone."

"No, no," she said. "I've talked to them, and they're staying."

"Thank God!" I said. "What did you *say* to them? They hate it here."

"I promised them I wasn't leaving," she said, "so they'll stay, too. Why don't you go up to bed now? You'll be very stiff in the morning if you spend all night down here."

"O.K.," I said groggily.

"Mama's been out dancing, but she's home again," she said. "Go to bed, Mr. Karabekian. All's well with the world."

"I'll never see Slazinger again," I said.

"What do you care?" she said. "He never liked you and you never liked him. Don't you know *that*?"

17

WE MADE some sort of contract that night. It was as though we had been negotiating its terms for quite some time: she wanted this, I wanted that.

For reasons best known to herself, the widow Berman wants to go on living and writing here rather than return to Baltimore. For reasons all too clear to myself, I am afraid, I want someone as vivid as she is to keep me alive.

What is the biggest concession she has made? She no longer mentions the potato barn.

• • •

To return to the past:

After Dan Gregory at our first meeting ordered me to make a super-realistic painting of his studio, he said that there was a very important sentence he wanted me to learn by heart. This was it: "The Emperor has no clothes."

"Let me hear you say it," he said. "Say it several times."

So I did. "The Emperor has no clothes, the Emperor has no clothes, the Emperor has no clothes."

"That was a really fine performance," he said, "really topping, really first rate." He clapped his hands appreciatively.

How was I supposed to respond to that? I felt like Alice in Wonderland.

"I want you to say that out loud and with just that degree of conviction," he said, "anytime anyone has anything good to say about so-called modern art."

"O.K.," I said.

"It's the work of swindlers and lunatics and degenerates," he said, "and the fact that many people are now taking it seriously proves to me that the world has gone mad. I hope you agree."

"I do, I do," I said. It sounded right to me.

"Mussolini thinks so, too," he said. "Do you admire Mussolini as much as I do?"

"Yes, sir," I said.

"You know the first two things Mussolini would do if he took over this country?" he said.

"No, sir," I said.

"He would burn down the Museum of Modern Art and outlaw the word *democracy*. After that he would make up a word for what we really are, make us face up to what we really are and always have been, and then strive for efficiency. Do your job right or drink castor oil!"

About a year later, I got around to asking him what he thought the people of the United States really were, and he said, "Spoiled children, who are begging for a frightening but just Daddy to tell them exactly what to do."

• • •

"Draw everything the way it really is," he said.

"Yes, sir," I said.

He pointed to a clipper ship model on a mantelpiece in the murky distance. "That, my boy, is the *Sovereign of the Seas*," he said, "which, using nothing but wind power, was faster than most freighters are today! Think of that!"

"Yes, sir," I said.

"And when you put it into the wonderful picture you are going to paint of this studio, you and I are going to go over your rendering of it with a magnifying glass. Any line in the rigging I care to point to: I expect you to tell me its name and what its function is."

"Yes, sir," I said.

"Pablo Picasso could never do that," he said.

"No, sir," I said.

He removed from a gun rack a Springfield 1906 rifle, then the basic weapon for the United States Infantry. There was an Enfield rifle in there, too, the basic weapon of the British Infantry, a sort of gun which may have killed him. "When you include this perfect killing machine in your picture," he said of the Springfield, "I want it so real that I can load it and shoot a burglar." He pointed to a nubbin near the muzzle and asked me what it was.

"I don't know, sir," I said.

"The bayonet stud," he said. He promised me that he was going to triple or quadruple my vocabulary, starting with the parts of the rifle, each of which had a specific name. We would go from that simple exercise, he said, required of every Army recruit, to the nomenclature of all the bones, sinews, organs, tubes and wires in the human body, required of every student in medical school. This had been required of him as well, he said, during his Moscow apprenticeship.

He asserted that there would be a spiritual lesson for me in my study of the simple rifle and then the bewilderingly complex human body, since it was the human body the rifle was meant to destroy.

"Which represents good and which represents evil—" he asked me, "the rifle or the rubbery, jiggling, giggling bag of bones we call the body?"

I said that the rifle was evil and the body was good.

"But don't you know that this rifle was designed to be used by Americans defending their homes and honor against wicked enemies?" he said.

So I said a lot depended on whose body and whose rifle we were talking about, that either one of them could be good or evil.

"And who renders the final decision on that?" he said.

"God?" I said.

"I mean here on *Earth*," he said.

"I don't know," I said.

"Painters—and storytellers, including poets and playwrights and historians," he said. "They are the justices of the Supreme Court of Good and Evil, of which I am now a member, and to which you may belong someday!"

How was *that* for delusions of moral grandeur!

Yes, and now that I think about it: maybe the most admirable thing about the Abstract Expressionist painters, since so much senseless bloodshed had been caused by cockeyed history lessons, was their refusal to serve on such a court.

• • •

Dan Gregory kept me around as long as he did, about three years, because I was servile and because he needed company, since he had alienated most of his famous friends with his humorlessness and rage during political arguments. When I said to Gregory that first night that I had heard the famous voice of W. C. Fields from the top of the spiral staircase, he replied that Fields would never be welcome in his house again, and neither would Al Jolson or any of the others who had drunk his liquor and eaten his food that night.

"They simply do not, will not understand!" he said.

"No, sir," I said.

And he changed the subject to Marilee Kemp. He said she was clumsy to begin with, but had gotten drunk on top of that, and had fallen downstairs. I think he honestly believed that by then. He could easily have indicated which stairs she had fallen down, since I was standing right at the top of them. But he didn't. He felt it sufficed to let me know that she had fallen downstairs *somewhere*. What did it matter where?

While he went on talking about Marilee, he never mentioned her name again. She simply became "women." "Women will never take the blame for anything," he said. "No matter what troubles they bring on themselves, they won't rest until they've found some man to blame for it. Right?"

"Right," I said.

"There's only one way they can take anything, and that's *personally*," he said. "You're not even talking about them, don't even know they're in the room, but they will still take anything you say as though it were aimed right at them. Ever notice that?"

"Yes, sir," I said. It seemed that I *had* noticed that, now that he mentioned it.

"Every so often they will get it into their heads that they understand what you're doing better than you do yourself," he said. "You've just got to throw them out, or they will screw up everything! They've got their jobs and we've got ours. We never try to horn in on them, but they'll horn in us every chance they get. You want some good advice?"

"Yes, sir," I said.

"Never have anything to do with a woman who would rather be a man," he said. "That means she's never going to do what a woman is supposed to do—which leaves you stuck with both what a man's supposed to do and what a woman's supposed to do. You understand what I am saying?"

"Yes, sir, I do," I said.

He said that no woman could succeed in the arts or sciences or politics or industry, since her basic job was to have children and encourage men and take care of the housework. He invited me to test this statement by naming, if I could, ten women who had amounted to anything in any field but domesticity.

I think I could name ten now, but back then all I could come up with was Saint Joan of Arc.

"Jeanne d'Arc," he said, "was a hermaphrodite!"

18

I DON'T KNOW where this fits into my story, and probably it doesn't fit in at all. It is certainly the most trivial footnote imaginable in a history of Abstract Expressionism, but here it is:

The cook who had begrudgingly fed me my first supper in New York City, and who kept asking, "What next, what next?" died two weeks after I got there. That finally became what was going to happen next: she would drop dead in Turtle Bay Chemists, a drugstore two blocks away.

But here was the thing: the undertaker discovered that she wasn't just a woman, and she wasn't just a man, either. She was somewhat both. She was a hermaphrodite.

An even more trivial footnote: she would be promptly replaced as Dan Gregory's cook by Sam Wu, the laundryman.

• • •

Marilee arrived home from the hospital in a wheelchair two days after my arrival. Dan Gregory did not come down to greet her. I don't think he would have stopped working if the house were on fire. He was like my father making cowboy boots or Terry Kitchen with his spray gun or Jackson Pollock dribbling paint on a canvas on the floor: when he was doing art, the whole rest of the world dropped away.

And I would be like that, too, after the war, and it would wreck my first marriage and my determination to be a good father. I had a very hard time getting the hang of civilian life after the war, and then I discovered something as powerful and irresponsible as shooting up with heroin: if I started laying on just one color of paint to a huge canvas, I could make the whole world drop away.

• • •

And Gregory's total concentration on his work for twelve or more hours a day meant that I, as his apprentice, had a very easy job indeed. He had nothing for me to do, and did not want to waste time inventing tasks. He had told me to make a painting of his studio, but, once he himself got back to work, I think he forgot all about it.

•   •   •

Did I make a painting of his studio which was virtually indistinguishable from a photograph? Yes, I did, yes I did.

But I was the only person who gave a damn if I even *tried* to work such a miracle, or not. I was so unworthy of his attention, so far from being a genius, a Gregorian to his Beskudnikov, a threat or a son or whatever, that I might as well have been his cook, who had to be told what to prepare for dinner.

Anything! Anything! Roast beef! Paint a picture of this studio! Who cares? Broccoli!

O.K. I would show *him*.

And I did.

•   •   •

It was up to his real assistant, Fred Jones, the World War One aviator, to think up work for me to do. Fred made me a messenger, which must have been a terrible blow for the messenger service he had been using. Somebody who desperately needed a job, any kind of job, must have been thrown out of work when Fred gave me a handful of subway tokens and a map of New York City.

He also set me the task of cataloguing all the valuable objects in Gregory's studio.

"Won't that bother Mr. Gregory while he's working?" I said.

And he said: "You could saw him off at the waist while singing 'The Star-Spangled Banner,' and he wouldn't notice. Just keep away from his eyes and hands."

•   •   •

So I was up in the studio, just a few feet from Dan Gregory, itemizing in a ledger his extensive collection of bayonets, when Marilee came home. I remember still how full of bad magic all those spearpoints to be put on the ends of rifles seemed to be. One was like a sharpened curtain rod. Another was triangular in cross-section, so that the wound it made wouldn't close up again and keep the blood and guts from falling out. Another

one had sawteeth—so it could work its way through bone,
I guess. I can remember thinking that war was so horrible
that, at last, thank goodness, nobody could ever be fooled by
romantic pictures and fiction and history into marching to war
again.

Nowadays, of course, you can buy a machine gun with a
plastic bayonet for your little kid at the nearest toy boutique.

•   •   •

The sounds of Marilee's homecoming floated up from down
below. I myself, so much in her debt, didn't hurry down to
greet her. I think the cook and my first wife were right: I have
always been leery of women—possibly because, as Circe Berman
suggested at breakfast this morning, I considered my mother
faithless, since she had up and died on me.

Maybe so.

Anyway: she had to send for me, and I behaved with formality. I did not know that Gregory had almost killed her because
of the art materials she had sent to me. If I had known that, I
might still have been very formal. One thing, surely, which prevented my being effusive, was my sense of my own homeliness
and powerlessness and virginity. I was unworthy of her, since
she was as beautiful as Madeleine Carroll, the most beautiful of
all movie stars.

She was cool and stiff with me, too, I have to say, possibly
answering formality with formality. There was probably this
factor, too: she wanted to make it clear to me, to Fred, to Gregory, to the hermaphrodite cook, to everybody, that she had not
caused me to be brought all the way from the West Coast for
purposes of hanky-panky.

And if only I could get back there in a time machine, what
incredible fortune I could tell for her:

"You will be as beautiful as you are now, but much, much
wiser, when you and I are reunited in Florence, Italy, after
World War Two. What a war you will have had!

"You and Fred and Gregory will have moved to Italy, and
Fred and Gregory will have been killed in the Battle of Sidi
Barrani—in Egypt. You will have then won the heart of Mus-
solini's minister of culture, Bruno, the Oxford-educated Count
Portomaggiore, one of Italy's largest landowners. He will also

have been head of the British spy apparatus in Italy all through
the war."

• • •

When I visited her in her palace after the war, incidentally,
she showed me a painting given to her by the mayor of Florence.
It depicted the death of her late husband before a Fascist firing
squad near the end of the war.

The painting was the sort of commercial kitsch Dan Gregory
used to do, and of which I myself was and remain capable.

• • •

Her sense of her place in the world back in 1933, with the
Great Depression going on, revealed itself, I think, in a conversation we had about *A Doll's House*, the play by Henrik Ibsen. A
new reader's edition of that play had just come out, with illustrations by Dan Gregory, so we both read it and then discussed it
afterwards.

Gregory's most compelling illustration showed the very end
of the play, with the leading character, Nora, going out the
front door of her comfortable house, leaving her middle-class
husband and children and servants behind, declaring that she
had to discover her own identity out in the real world before she
could be a strong mother and wife.

• • •

That is how the play *ends*. Nora isn't going to allow herself to
be patronized for being as uninformed and helpless as a child
anymore.

And Marilee said to me, "That's where the play *begins* as far
as I'm concerned. We never find out how she survived. What
kind of job could a woman get back then? Nora didn't have any
skills or education. She didn't even have money for food and a
place to stay."

• • •

That was precisely Marilee's situation, too, of course. There
was nothing waiting for her outside the door of Gregory's very
comfortable dwelling except hunger and humiliation, no matter
how meanly he might treat her.

A few days later, she told me that she had solved the problem. "That ending is a *fake!*" she said, delighted with herself. "Ibsen just tacked it on so the audience could go home *happy.* He didn't have the nerve to tell what really happened, what the whole rest of the play says *has* to happen."

"What *has* to happen?" I said.

"She has to commit *suicide,*" said Marilee. "And I mean *right* away—in front of a streetcar or something before the curtain comes down. *That's* the play. Nobody's ever seen it, but *that's* the play!"

•   •   •

I have had quite a few friends commit suicide, but was never able to see the dramatic necessity for it that Marilee saw in Ibsen's play. That I can't see that necessity is probably yet another mark of my shallowness as a participant in a life of serious art.

These are just my *painter* friends who killed themselves, all with considerable artistic successes behind them or soon to come:

Arshile Gorky hanged himself in 1948. Jackson Pollock, while drunk, drove his car into a tree along a deserted road in 1956. That was right before my first wife and kids walked out on me. Three weeks later, Terry Kitchen shot himself through the roof of his mouth with a pistol.

Back when we all lived in New York City, Pollock and Kitchen and I, heavy drinkers all, were known in the Cedar Tavern as the "Three Musketeers."

Trivia question: How many of the Three Musketeers are alive today? Answer: me.

Yes, and Mark Rothko, with enough sleeping pills in his medicine cabinet to kill an elephant, slashed himself to death with a knife in 1970.

What conclusion can I draw from such grisly demonstrations of terminal discontent? Only this: some people are a lot harder than others, with Marilee and me typifying those others, to satisfy.

Marilee said this about Nora in *A Doll's House*: "She should have stayed home and made the best of things."

19

B ELIEF IS NEARLY the whole of the Universe, whether based on truth or not, and I believed back then that sperm, if not ejaculated, was reprocessed by healthy males into substances which made them athletic, merry, brave and creative. Dan Gregory believed this, too, and so did my father, and so did the United States Army and the Boy Scouts of America and Ernest Hemingway. So I cultivated erotic fantasies about making love to Marilee, and behaved as though we were courting sometimes, but only in order to generate more sperm which could be converted into the beneficial chemicals.

I used to shuffle my feet for a long time on a carpet, and then give Marilee an electric shock with my fingertips when she wasn't expecting it—on the back of her neck or her cheek or a hand. How is that for pornography?

I also got her to sneak off with me and do something which would have made Gregory furious, if he had found out about it, which was to go to the Museum of Modern Art.

But she certainly wasn't about to promote me erotically above the rank of pest and playmate. Not only did she love Gregory, but he was also making it very easy for both of us to get through the Great Depression. First things first.

Meanwhile, though, we were innocently exposing ourselves to a master seducer against whose blandishments we were defenseless. It was too late for either of us to turn back by the time we realized how deeply embroiled we had let ourselves become.

Want to guess who or what it was?

It was the Museum of Modern Art.

• • •

The theory that sperm, if unspent, was converted into cosmic vitamins seemed validated by my own performances. Running errands for Gregory, I became as cunning as a sewer rat about the fastest ways to get from anywhere to anywhere on the island of Manhattan. I quintupled my vocabulary, learning the names and functions of every important part of every sort of organism and artifact. My most thrilling accomplishment, however, was this: I finished a meticulously accurate painting of Gregory's studio in only six months! The bone was bone, the fur was fur, the hair was hair, the dust was dust, the soot was soot, the wool was wool, the cotton was cotton, the walnut was walnut, the oak was oak, the horsehide was horsehide, the cowhide was cowhide, the iron was iron, the steel was steel, the old was old and the new was new.

Yes, and the water dripping from the skylight in my painting was not only the wettest water you ever saw: in each droplet, if you looked at it through a magnifying glass, there was the whole damned studio! Not bad! Not bad!

•   •   •

An idea has just come to me from nowhere, to wit: Might not the ancient and nearly universal belief that sperm could be metabolized into noble actions have been the inspiration for Einstein's very similar formula: "E equals MC squared"?

•   •   •

"Not bad, not bad," said Dan Gregory of my painting, and I imagined his feeling like Robinson Crusoe on the occasion of Crusoe's understanding that he no longer had his little island all to himself. There was now *me* to reckon with.

But then he said, "However, *not bad* is another term for *disappointing* or worse, wouldn't you say?"

Before I could frame a reply, he had put the picture atop the glowing coals in the fireplace with the skulls on its mantelpiece. Six months' painstaking work went up the flue in a moment.

I managed to ask chokingly, perfectly aghast, "What was the *matter* with it?"

"No *soul*," he said complacently.

So there I was in the thrall of the new Imperial engraver Beskudnikov!

•   •   •

I knew what he was complaining about, and the complaint wasn't laughable, coming from him. His own pictures were vibrant with the full spectrum of his own loves, hates and neutralities, as dated as that spectrum might seem today. If I were to visit that private museum in Lubbock, Texas, where so many of his works are on permanent display, the pictures would create for me a sort of hologram of Dan Gregory. I could pass my hand through it, but it would be Dan Gregory in three dimensions all the same. He lives!

If I, on the other hand, were to die, God forbid, and if some magician were to recover every painting of mine, from the one Gregory incinerated to the last one I will ever do, and if these were to be hung in a great domed rotunda so as to concentrate the soul in each one at the same focal point, and if my own mother and the women who swore they loved me, which would be Marilee and Dorothy and Edith, were to stand for hours at that focal point, along with the best friend I ever had, who was Terry Kitchen, not one of them would find any reason to think about me except randomly. There would not be a trace of their dear departed Rabo Karabekian, or of spiritual energy of any sort, at the focal point!

What an experiment!

• • •

Oh, I know: I bad-mouthed Gregory's works a while back, saying he was a taxidermist, and that his pictures were always about a single moment rather than the flow of life, and so on. But he was sure a better painter than I could ever hope to be. Nobody could put more of the excitement of a single moment into the eyes of stuffed animals, so to speak, than Dan Gregory.

• • •

Circe Berman has just asked me how to tell a good picture from a bad one.

I said that the best answer I had ever heard to that question, although imperfect, came from a painter named Syd Solomon, a man about my age who summers not far from here. I overheard him say it to a very pretty girl at a cocktail party maybe fifteen years ago. She was so wide-eyed and on tippy-toe! She sure wanted to learn all about art from him.

"How can you tell a good painting from a bad one?" he said. This is the son of a Hungarian horse trainer. He has a magnificent handlebar mustache.

"All you have to do, my dear," he said, "is look at a million paintings, and then you can never be mistaken."

It's true! It's true!

•   •   •

The present again:

I must tell what happened here yesterday afternoon, when I received the first visitors to my collection since the foyer was, to use the decorator's term, "redone." A young man from the State Department escorted three writers from the Soviet Union, one from Tallin, Estonia, where Mrs. Berman's ancestors came from, after the Garden of Eden, of course, and two from Moscow, Dan Gregory's old hometown. Small world. They spoke no English, but their guide was an able interpreter.

They made no comment on the foyer when they came in, and proved to be sophisticated and appreciative with respect to Abstract Expressionism, quite a contrast with many other guests from the USSR. As they were leaving, though, they had to ask me why I had such trashy pictures in the foyer.

So I gave them Mrs. Berman's lecture on the horrors which awaited these children, bringing them close to tears. They were terribly embarrassed. They apologized effusively for not understanding the true import of the chromos, and said that, now that I had explained them, they were unanimous in agreeing that these were the most important pictures in the house. And then they went from picture to picture, bewailing all the pain each girl would go through. Most of this wasn't translated, but I gathered that they were predicting cancer and war and so on.

I was quite a hit, and was hugged and hugged.

Never before had visitors bid me farewell so ardently! Usually they can hardly think of anything to say.

And they called something to me from the driveway, grinning affectionately and shaking their heads. So I asked the man from the State Department what they had said, and he translated: "No more war, no more war."

20

B ACK TO THE PAST:
   When Dan Gregory burned up my painting, why didn't
I do to him what he had done to Beskudnikov? Why didn't I
mock him and walk out and find a better job? For one thing, I
had learned a lot about the commercial art world by then, and
knew that artists like me were a dime a dozen and all starving
to death.

Consider all I had to lose: a room of my own, three square
meals a day, entertaining errands to run all over town, and lots
of playtime with the beautiful Marilee.

What a fool I would have been to let self-respect interfere
with my happiness!

•   •   •

After the hermaphroditic cook died, incidentally, Sam Wu,
the laundryman, asked for the job and got it. He was a wonderful cook of good, honest American food as well as Chinese
delicacies, and Gregory continued to use him as a model for the
sinister master criminal Fu Manchu.

•   •   •

Back to the present:

Circe Berman said to me at lunch today that I ought to try
painting again, since it used to give me such pleasure.

My dear wife Edith made the same suggestion one time, and
I told Mrs. Berman what I told her: "I have had all I can stand
of not taking myself seriously."

She asked me what had been the most pleasing thing about
my professional life when I was a full-time painter—having my
first one-man show, getting a lot of money for a picture, the
comradeship with fellow painters, being praised by a critic, or
what?

"We used to talk a lot about that in the old days," I said.
"There was general agreement that if we were put into individual capsules with our art materials, and fired out into different

parts of outer space, we would still have everything we loved about painting, which was the opportunity to lay on paint."

I asked her in turn what the high point was for writers—getting great reviews, or a terrific advance, or selling a book to the movies, or seeing somebody reading your book, or what?

She said that she, too, could find happiness in a capsule in outer space, provided that she had a finished, proofread manuscript by her in there, along with somebody from her publishing house.

"I don't understand," I said.

"The orgastic moment for me is when I hand a manuscript to my publisher and say, 'Here! I'm all through with it. I never want to see it again,'" she said.

•   •   •

Back to the past again:

Marilee Kemp wasn't the only one who was trapped like Nora in *A Doll's House* before Nora blew her cork. I was another one. And then I caught on: Fred Jones was still another one. He was so handsome and dignified and honored, seemingly, to be of assistance to the great artist Dan Gregory in any way possible—but he was a Nora, too.

His life had been all downhill since World War One, when he had discovered a gift for flying rattletrap kites which were machine-gun platforms. The first time he got his hands on the joystick of an airplane, he must have felt what Terry Kitchen felt when he gripped a spray gun. He must have felt like Kitchen again when he fired his machine guns up in the wild blue yonder, and saw a plane in front of him draw a helix of smoke and flame—ending in a sunburst far below.

What beauty! So unexpected and pure! So easy to achieve!

Fred Jones told me one time that the smoke trails of falling airplanes and observation balloons were the most beautiful things he ever expected to see. And I now compare his elation over arcs and spirals and splotches in the atmosphere with what Jackson Pollock used to feel as he watched what dribbled paint chose to do when it struck a canvas on his studio floor.

Same sort of happiness!

Except that what Pollock did lacked that greatest of all crowd pleasers, which was human sacrifice.

● ● ●

But my point about Fred Jones is this: he had found a home in the Air Corps, just as I would find a home in the Corps of Engineers.

And then he was kicked out for the same reason that I was: he had lost an eye somewhere.

So there is something startling I might tell myself as a youth, if I could get back to the Great Depression in a time machine: "Pst—you, the cocky little Armenian kid. Yes, you. You think Fred Jones is funny and sad at the same time? That's what you'll be someday, too: a one-eyed old soldier, afraid of women and with no talent for civilian life."

I used to wonder back then what it was like to have one eye instead of two, and experiment by covering one eye with a hand. The world didn't seem all that diminished when I looked at it with only one eye. Nor do I feel today that having only one eye is a particularly serious handicap.

Circe Berman asked me about being one eyed after we had known each other less than an hour. She will ask anybody anything at any time.

"It's a piece of cake," I said.

● ● ●

I remember Dan Gregory now, and he really did resemble, as W. C. Fields had said, "a sawed-off Arapahoe," and of Marilee and Fred Jones at his beck and call. I think what great models they would make for a Gregory illustration of a story about a Roman emperor with a couple of blond, blue-eyed Germanic captives in tow.

It is curious that Fred and not Marilee was the captive Gregory liked to parade in public all the time. It was Fred he took to parties and on fox hunts in Virginia and cruises on his yacht, the *Ararat.*

I do not propose to explain this, beyond declaring for a certainty that Gregory and Fred were men's men. They were not homosexuals.

Whatever the explanation, Gregory did not mind at all that Marilee and I took long walks all over Manhattan, with heads snapping around to take second, third, and fourth looks at her.

People must have wondered, too, how somebody like me, obviously not a relative, could have won the companionship of a woman that beautiful.

"People think we're in love," I said to her on a walk one day. And she said, "They're right."

"You know what I mean," I said.

"What do you think love is anyway?" she said.

"I guess I don't know," I said.

"You know the best part—" she said, "walking around like this and feeling good about everything. If you missed the rest of it, I certainly wouldn't cry for you."

So we went to the Museum of Modern Art for maybe the fiftieth time. I had been with Gregory for almost three years then, and was just a shade under twenty years old. I wasn't a budding artist anymore. I was an *employee* of an artist, and lucky to have a job of any kind. An awful lot of people were putting up with any sort of job, and waiting for the Great Depression to end, so that real life could get going again. But we would also have to get through another World War before *real* life could get going again.

Don't you *love* it? This is real life we are now experiencing.

• • •

But let me tell you that life seemed as real as Hell back in 1936, when Dan Gregory caught Marilee and me coming out of the Museum of Modern Art.

21

D AN GREGORY caught Marilee and me coming out of the Museum of Modern Art while a Saint Patrick's Day parade was blatting and booming northward on Fifth Avenue, a half a block away. The parade caused Gregory's automobile, a convertible Cord, the most beautiful American means of transportation ever manufactured, to be stuck in traffic right in front of the Museum of Modern Art. This was a two-seater with the top down, and with Fred Jones, the old World War One aviator, at the wheel.

What Fred may have been doing with his sperm I never found out. If I had to guess, I would say that he was saving it up like me. He had that *look* as he sat at the wheel of that sublime motorcar, but the hell with Fred. He was going to be O.K. for quite a while longer, until he was shot dead in Egypt—whereas I was about to go into the real world, ready or not, and try to stand on my own two feet!

Everybody was wearing something green! Then as now, even black people and Orientals and Hasidic Jews were wearing something green in order not to provoke arguments with Roman Catholic Irishmen. Marilee and Dan Gregory and I and Fred Jones were all wearing green. Back in Gregory's kitchen, Sam Wu was wearing green.

Gregory pointed a finger at us. He was trembling with rage. "Caught you!" he shouted. "Stay right there! I want to *talk* to you!"

He clambered over the car door, pushed his way through the crowd and planted himself in front of us, his feet far apart, his hands balled into fists. He had often hit Marilee, but he had certainly never hit me. Oddly enough, nobody had ever hit me. Nobody has *ever* hit me.

Sex was the cause of our excitement: youth versus age, wealth and power versus physical attractiveness, stolen moments of forbidden fun and so on—but Gregory spoke only of gratitude, loyalty and modern art.

As for the pictures in the museum's being genuinely modern: most of them had been painted before the First World War, before Marilee and I had been born! The world back then was very slow to accept changes in painting styles. Nowadays, of course, *every* novelty is celebrated immediately as a masterpiece!

•   •   •

"You parasites! You ingrates! You rotten-spoiled little kids!" seethed Dan Gregory. "Your loving Papa asked just one thing of you as an expression of your loyalty: 'Never go into the Museum of Modern Art.' "

I doubt that many people who heard him even knew that we were in front of a museum. They probably thought he had caught us coming out of a hotel or an apartment house—some-place with beds for lovers. If they took him literally when he called himself a "Papa," they would have had to conclude that he was *my* Papa and not hers, since we looked so much alike.

"It was *symbolic*!" he said. "Don't you understand that? It was a way of proving you were on my side and not theirs. I'm not afraid to have you look at the junk in there. You were part of *my* gang, and proud of it." He was all choked up now, and he shook his head. "That's why I made that very simple, very modest, very easily complied-with request: 'Stay out of the Museum of Modern Art.' "

•   •   •

Marilee and I were so startled by this confrontation, we may even have gone on holding hands. We had come skipping out and holding hands like Jack and Jill. We probably did go on holding hands—like Jack and Jill.

Only now do I realize that Dan Gregory caught us at a moment when we had somehow agreed that we were going to make love that afternoon. I now think we were out of control, and would have made love whether we had run into him or not. Every time I have told this story before, I have indicated that there would have been no lovemaking if it hadn't been for the confrontation.

Not so.

•   •   •

"I don't give a *hoot* what pictures you look at," he said. "All I asked was that you not pay your respects to an institution which thinks that the smears and spatters and splotches and daubs and dribbles and vomit of lunatics and degenerates and charlatans are great treasures we should all admire."

Reconstructing what he said to us long ago, I am touched by how careful he and almost all angry males used to be, when in mixed company, not to use words which might offend women and children, such as *shit* and *fuck*.

Circe Berman argues that the inclusion of once-taboo words into ordinary conversations is a good thing, since women and children are now free to discuss their bodies without shame, and so to take care of themselves more intelligently.

I said to her, "Maybe so. But don't you think all this frankness has also caused a collapse of eloquence?" I reminded her of the cook's daughter's habit of referring to anybody she didn't like for whatever reason as "an asshole." I said: "Never did I hear Celeste give a thoughtful explanation of what it was that such a person might have done to earn that proctological sobriquet."

• • •

"Of all the ways to hurt me," Gregory went on in that British accent of his, "you could not have picked a crueler one. I have treated you as a son," he said to me, "and you like a daughter," he said to Marilee, "and this is the thanks I get. And it's not your going in there which is the most insulting. No, it isn't that. It's how *happy* you were when you were coming out! What could that happiness be but a mockery of me and of every person who ever tried to keep control of a paintbrush?"

He said that he was going to have Fred drive him to City Island, where his yacht the *Ararat* was in dry dock, and he was going to live aboard her until Fred could assure him that we were out of his house on Forty-eighth Street, and that every trace of our ever having been there had been removed.

"Out you go!" he said. "Good riddance of bad rubbish!" What a surreal thing this master realist was about to do! He was going to take up residence on an eighty-foot sailing yacht in dry dock! He would have to come and go by ladder, would have to use a boatyard toilet and telephone!

And think of what a bizarre creation his studio was, an hallucination created at tremendous expense and effort!

And he would eventually arrange to have himself and his only friend killed while wearing Italian uniforms!

Everything about Dan Gregory, except for his paintings, had fewer connections with reality and common sense than the most radical modern art!

• • •

Bulletin from the present: Circe Berman has just discovered, after questioning me closely, that I have never actually read a whole book by Paul Slazinger, my former best friend.

She, it turns out, has read them all since moving in. I *own* them all. They have a little shelf of honor in the library, and are autographed beneath testimonials as to how close Paul and I have been for so many years. I have read reviews of most of them, and have a pretty good idea of how they go.

I think Paul knew this about me, although we have certainly never discussed it openly. It is impossible for me to take his writings seriously, knowing how reckless he has been in real life. How can I study his published opinions on love and hate and God and man and whether the ends ever justify the means and all that with solemnity? As for a quid pro quo: I don't owe him one. He has never honored me as a painter or collector, nor should he have.

So what was our bond?

Loneliness and wounds from World War Two which were quite grave.

• • •

Circe Berman has broken her silence about the mystery of the locked potato barn. She found a big picture book in the library whose spine is split and whose pages are not only dog eared but splotched with painty fingerprints, although it was published only three years ago. It depicts virtually all the uniforms worn by every sort of regular soldier or sailor or airman during World War Two. She asked me point blank if it had anything to do with what was in the barn.

"Maybe it does and maybe it doesn't," I said.

But I will tell you a secret: it does, it does.

• • •

So Marilee and I slouched home from the Museum of Modern Art like whipped children. We laughed sometimes, too, just fell into each other's arms and laughed and laughed. So we were feeling each other up and liking each other terrifically all the way home.

We stopped to watch a fight between two white men in front of a bar on Third Avenue. Neither one was wearing green. They snarled in some language we did not understand. They may have been Macedonians or Basques or Frisian Islanders, or something like that.

Marilee had a slight limp and a list to the left, as permanent consequences of her having been pushed down the stairs by an Armenian. But another Armenian was groping her and nuzzling her hair and so on, and had an erection with which you might have smashed coconuts. I like to think we were man and wife. Life itself can be sacramental. The supposition was that we would be leaving the Garden of Eden together, and would cleave to one another in the wilderness through thick and thin.

I don't know why we laughed so much.

Our ages again: I was almost twenty, and she was twenty-nine. The man we were about to cuckold or whatever was fifty-three, with only seven more years to go, a mere stripling in retrospect. Imagine having all of seven more years to go!

• • •

Maybe Marilee and I laughed so much because we were about to do the one thing other than eat and drink and sleep which our bodies said we were on Earth to do. There was no vengeance or defiance or defilement in it. We did not do it in the bed she and Gregory shared, or in Fred Jones's bed next door, or in the immaculate French Empire guest-room, or in the studio—and not even on my own bed, although we could have done it almost anywhere except in the basement, since Fu Manchu was the only other person in the house just then. Our brainless lovemaking anticipated Abstract Expressionism in a way, since it was about absolutely nothing but itself.

Yes, and I am reminded now of what the painter Jim Brooks said to me about how he operated, about how all the Abstract Expressionists operated: "I lay on the first stroke of color. After that, the canvas has to do at least half the work." The canvas, if things were going well, would, after that first stroke, begin suggesting or even demanding that he do this or that. In Marilee's and my case, the first stroke was a kiss just inside the front door, a big, wet, hot, hilariously smeary thing.

Talk about paint!

•   •   •

Marilee's and my canvas, so to speak, called for more and wetter kisses, and then a groping, goosey, swooning tango up the spiral staircase and through the grand dining room. We knocked over a chair, which we set upright again. The canvas, doing *all* the work and not just half of it, sent us through the butler's pantry and into an unused storage room about eight feet square. The only thing in there was a broken-down sofa which must have been left by the previous owners. There was one tiny window, looking northward, into the leafless treetops of the back garden.

We needed no further instructions from the canvas as to what to do, should we wish to complete a masterpiece. This we did.

•   •   •

Nor did I need instructions from the experienced older woman as to what to do.

Bull's-eye and bull's-eye and bull's-eye again!

And it was so *retroactive*! This was something I had been doing all my life! It was so *prospective*, too! I would be doing one hell of a lot of this for the rest of my life.

And so I did. Except that it would never be that good again.

Never again would the canvas of life, so to speak, help me and a partner create a sexual masterpiece.

Rabo Karabekian, then, created at least one masterpiece as a lover, which was necessarily created in private and vanished from the Earth even more quickly than the paintings which made me a footnote in Art History. Is there nothing I have done which will outlive me, other than the opprobrium of my first wife and sons and grandchildren?

Do I care?

Doesn't everybody?

Poor me. Poor practically everybody, with so little durable good to leave behind!

• • •

After the war, when I told Terry Kitchen something about my three hours of ideal lovemaking with Marilee, and how contentedly adrift in the cosmos they made me feel, he said this: "You were experiencing a *non-epiphany*."

"A what?" I said.

"A concept of my own invention," he said. This was back when he was still a talker instead of a painter, long before I bought him the spray rig. As far as that goes, I was nothing but a talker and a painters' groupie. I was still going to become a businessman.

"The trouble with God isn't that He so seldom makes Himself known to us," he went on. "The trouble with God is exactly the opposite: He's holding you and me and everybody else by the scruff of the neck practically *constantly*."

He said he had just come from an afternoon at the Metropolitan Museum of Art, where so many of the paintings were about God's giving instructions, to Adam and Eve and the Virgin Mary, and various saints in agony and so on. "These moments are very rare, if you can believe the painters—but who was ever nitwit enough to believe a painter?" he said, and he ordered another double Scotch, I'm sure, for which I would pay. "Such moments are often called 'epiphanies' and I'm here to tell you they are as common as houseflies," he said.

"I see," I said. I think Pollock was there listening to all this, although he and Kitchen and I were not yet known as the "Three Musketeers." He was a real painter, so he hardly talked at all. After Terry Kitchen became a real painter, he, too, hardly talked at all.

" 'Contentedly adrift in the cosmos,' were you?" Kitchen said to me. "That is a perfect description of a non-epiphany, that rarest of moments, when God Almighty lets go of the scruff of your neck and lets you be human for a little while. How long did the feeling last?"

"Oh—maybe half an hour," I said.

And he leaned back in his chair and he said with deep satisfaction: "And there you are."

• • •

That could have been the same afternoon I rented studio space for the two of us in a loft owned by a photographer at the top of a building on Union Square. Studio space in Manhattan was dirt cheap back then. An artist could actually afford to live in New York City! Can you imagine that?

After we had rented the studio space, I said to him: "My wife will kill me, if she hears about this."

"Just give her seven epiphanies a week," he said, "and she'll be so grateful that she'll let you get away with anything."

"Easier said than done," I said.

• • •

The same people who believe that Circe Berman's Polly Madison books are destroying the fabric of American society, telling teenage girls that they can get pregnant if they're not careful and so on, would surely consider Terry Kitchen's concept of non-epiphanies blasphemous. But I can't think of anybody who tried harder than he did to find worthwhile errands to run for God. He could have had brilliant careers in law or business or finance or politics. He was a magnificent pianist, and a great athlete, too. He might have stayed in the Army and soon become a general and maybe Chairman of the Joint Chiefs of Staff.

When I met him, though, he had given all that up in order to be a painter, even though he couldn't draw for sour apples, and had never had an art lesson in his life! "Something's just got to be worth doing!" he said. "And painting is one of the few things I haven't tried."

• • •

A lot of people, I know, think that Terry could draw realistically, if he wanted to do so. But their only proof of that is a small patch in a painting that used to hang in my foyer here. He never gave the picture a title, but it is now generally known as *Magic Window*.

Except for one little patch, that picture is a typical Kitchen airbrush view of a brightly colored storm system as viewed from an orbiting satellite, or whatever you want to call it. But the little patch, if examined carefully, turns out to be an upside-down copy of John Singer Sargent's full-length "Portrait of Madame

X," with her famous milk-white shoulders and ski-jump nose and so on.

I'm sorry, folks: that whimsical insert, that magic window, wasn't Terry's work, and *couldn't* have been Terry's work. It was done at Terry's insistence by a hack illustrator with the unlikely name of Rabo Karabekian.

• • •

Terry Kitchen said that the only moments he ever experienced as non-epiphanies, when God left him alone, were those following sex and the two times he took heroin.

22

B ULLETIN FROM THE PRESENT: Paul Slazinger has gone to Poland, of all places. According to *The New York Times* this morning, he was sent there for a week by the international writers' organization called "PEN"—as a part of a delegation to investigate the plight of his suffocated colleagues there.

Perhaps the Poles will reciprocate, and investigate his plight in turn. Who is more to be pitied, a writer bound and gagged by policemen or one living in perfect freedom who has nothing more to say?

•   •   •

Bulletin from the present: the widow Berman has installed an old-fashioned pool table dead center in my living room, having sent the furniture it displaced to Home Sweet Home Moving and Storage. This is a real elephant, so heavy that jack posts had to be put in the basement to keep it from winding up down there amid the cans of Sateen Dura-Luxe.

I haven't played this game since my Army days, and never played it very well. But you should see Mrs. Berman clear the table of balls no matter where they are!

"Where did you ever learn to shoot pool like that?" I asked her.

She said that after her father committed suicide she dropped out of high school and, rather than be sexually promiscuous or become an alcoholic in Lackawanna, she spent ten hours a day shooting pool instead.

I don't have to play with her. Nobody has to play with her, and I don't suppose anybody had to play with her in Lackawanna. But a funny thing will happen. She will suddenly lose her deadly accuracy, and have a fit of yawns and will scratch herself as though she had a fit of itching, too. Then she will go up to bed, and sometimes sleep until noon the next day.

She is the moodiest woman I ever knew.

•   •   •

And what of the broad hints I have given as to the secret of the potato barn? Won't she read them in this manuscript, and easily guess the rest? No.

She keeps her promises, and she promised me when I began to write that, once I reached one hundred and fifty pages, if I ever reached one hundred and fifty pages, she would reward me with perfect privacy in this writing room.

She said further that when I got this far, if I got that far, this book and I would have become so intimate that it would be indecent for her to intrude. And that is nice, I guess, to have earned through hard work certain privileges and marks of respect, except that I have to ask myself: "Who is she to reward or punish me, and what the hell is this: a nursery school or a prison camp?" I don't ask her that, because then she might take away all my privileges.

• • •

Two dandified young German businessmen from Frankfurt came to see my wonderful collection yesterday afternoon. They were typical successful post-Nazi entrepreneurs, to whom history was a clean slate. They were so new, new, new. Like Dan Gregory, they spoke English with upper-class British accents, but asked early on if Circe and I understood any German. They wanted to know, it became evident, whether or not they could communicate frankly to each other in that language without being understood. Circe and I said that we did not, although she was fluent in Yiddish, and so understood quite a lot, and so did I, having heard so much of it as a prisoner of war.

We were able to crack their code to this extent: they were only pretending interest in my pictures. They were really after my real estate. They had come seeking signs in me of failing health or intelligence, or domestic or financial distress, which might make it easy for them to diddle me out of my priceless beachfront, where they would be pleased to erect condominiums.

They got precious little satisfaction. After they had departed in their Mercedes coupe, Circe, the child of a Jewish pants manufacturer, said to me, the child of an Armenian shoemaker, "*We* are the Indians now."

• • •

They were West Germans, as I say, but they could just as easily have been fellow citizens of mine from right down the beach. And I wonder now if that isn't a secret ingredient in the attitudes of so many people here, citizens or not: that this is still a virgin continent, and that everybody else is an Indian who does not appreciate its value, or is at least too weak and ignorant to defend himself?

• • •

The darkest secret of this country, I am afraid, is that too many of its citizens imagine that they belong to a much higher civilization somewhere else. That higher civilization doesn't have to be another country. It can be the past instead—the United States as it was before it was spoiled by immigrants and the enfranchisement of the blacks.

This state of mind allows too many of us to lie and cheat and steal from the rest of us, to sell us junk and addictive poisons and corrupting entertainments. What are the rest of us, after all, but sub-human aborigines?

• • •

This state of mind explains a lot of American funeral customs, too. The message of so many obsequies here, if you think about it, is this: that the dead person has looted this alien continent, and is now returning to his or her real home with the gold of El Dorado.

• • •

But back to 1936 again! Listen:

Marilee's and my non-epiphany was soon over. We used it well. Each of us gripped the other's upper arms, and palpated what there was to palpate there, initiating, I suppose, an exploration from the very beginning of what sorts of devices we might be. There was warm, rubbery stuff over rods of some kind.

But then we heard the big front door open and close downstairs. As Terry Kitchen once said of a postcoital experience of his own: "The epiphany came back, and everybody had to put on their clothes and run around again like chickens with their heads cut off."

• • •

As Marilee and I were dressing, I whispered to her that I loved her with all my heart. What else was there to say?

"You don't. You can't," she said. She was treating me like a stranger.

"I will be as great an illustrator as he is," I said.

"With some other woman," she said. "Not with me." Here we had made all this love, but she was acting as though I were a nobody trying to pick her up in a public place.

"Did I do something wrong?" I said.

"You didn't do anything right or wrong," she said, "and neither did I." She stopped dressing to look me straight in the eyes. I still had two. "This never happened." She resumed the making of her toilette.

"Feel better?" she said.

I told her that I certainly did.

"So do I," she said, "but it won't last long."

Talk about *realism*!

I thought we had made a contract to pair off permanently. Many people used to think that about sexual intercourse. I thought, too, that Marilee might now bear my child. I did not know that she had been rendered sterile by an infection she picked up during an abortion in supposedly germ-free Switzerland. There was so much I didn't know about her, and which I wouldn't find out for fourteen years!

"Where do you think we should go next?" I said.

"Where do I think *who* should go next?" she said.

"Us," I said.

"You mean after we go leave this warm house forever, smiling bravely and holding hands?" she said. "There's an opera for you that'll break your heart."

"Opera?" I said.

"The beautiful, worldly mistress of a great painter twice her age seduces his apprentice, almost young enough to be her son," she said. "They are discovered. They are cast out into the world. She believes that her love and advice will make the boy a great painter, too, and they freeze to death."

That is just about what would have happened, too.

• • •

"You have to go, but I have to stay," she said. "I've got a little money saved up—enough to take care of you for a week or two. It's time you got out of here anyway. You were getting much too comfortable."

"How could we ever part after what we just did?" I said.

"The clocks stopped while we did it," she said, "and now they've started up again. It didn't count, so forget it."

"How *could* I?" I said.

"*I* already have," she said. "You're still a little boy, and I need a man to take care of me. Dan is a man."

So I slunk to my room, confused and humiliated. I packed up my belongings. She did not see me out. I had no idea what room she had gone to, or what she might be doing there. Nobody saw me out.

And I left that house forever as the sun went down on Saint Patrick's Day, 1936, without a backward glance at the Gorgon on the front door of Dan Gregory.

• • •

I spent my first night on my own only a block away, at the Vanderbilt YMCA, but would not see or hear from her again for fourteen years. It seemed to me that she had dared me to become a great financial success, and then to come back and take her away from Dan Gregory. I fantasized about that as a real possibility for perhaps a month or two. Such things happened all the time in stories Dan Gregory was given to illustrate.

She would not see me again until I was worthy of her. Dan Gregory was working on a new edition of *Tales of King Arthur and His Knights* when he got rid of me. Marilee had posed as Guinevere. I would bring her the Holy Grail.

• • •

But the Great Depression soon made clear to me that I would never amount to anything. I couldn't even provide decent food and a bed for my worthless self, and was frequently a bum among bums in soup kitchens and shelters for the homeless. I improved myself in libraries while keeping warm, reading histories and novels and poems said to be great—and encyclopedias and dictionaries, and the latest self-help books about how to get ahead in the United States of America, how to learn from failures, how to make strangers like and trust you immediately, how to start your own business, how to sell anybody anything, how to put yourself into the hands of God and stop wasting so much time and precious energy worrying. How to eat right.

I was certainly a child of Dan Gregory, and of the times, too, when I tried to make my vocabulary and familiarity with great issues and events and personalities throughout recorded time equal to those of graduates of great universities. My accent, moreover, was as synthetic as Gregory's, and so, by the way, was Marilee's. Marilee and I, a coal miner's daughter and an Armenian shoemaker's son, remember, had sense enough not to pretend to be upper-class British. We obscured our humble origins in vocal tones and inflections which had no name back then, as nearly as I can remember, but which are now known as "trans-Atlantic"—cultivated, pleasant to the ear, and neither British nor American. Marilee and I were brother and sister in that regard: we sounded the same.

• • •

But when I roamed New York City, knowing so much and capable of speaking so nicely, and yet so lonely, and often hungry and cold, I learned the joke at the core of American self-improvement: knowledge was so much junk to be processed one way or another at great universities. The real treasure the great universities offered was a lifelong membership in a respected artificial extended family.

• • •

My parents were born into biological families, and big ones, too, which were respected by Armenians in Turkey. I, born in America far from any other Armenians, save for my parents, eventually became a member of two artificial extended families which were reasonably respectable, although surely not the social equals of Harvard or Yale:

1. The Officer Corps of the United States Army in time of war,
2. the Abstract Expressionist school of painting after the war.

23

I COULD NOT get work with any of the companies which had come to know me as Dan Gregory's messenger boy. He had told them, I imagine, although I have no proof of this, that I was self-serving, disloyal, untalented, and so on. True enough. Jobs were so scarce anyway, so why should they give one to anyone as unlike themselves as an Armenian? Let the Armenians take care of their own unemployed.

And it was, in fact, an Armenian who came to my rescue while I was caricaturing willing sitters in Central Park—for the price of a cup of coffee and little more. He was neither a Turkish nor a Russian Armenian, but a Bulgarian Armenian, whose parents had taken him to Paris, France, in his infancy. He and they had become members of the lively and prosperous Armenian community in that city, then the Art Capital of the World. As I have said, my own parents and I would have become Parisians, too, had we not been diverted to San Ignacio, California, by the criminal Vartan Mamigonian. My savior's original name had been Marktich Kouyoumdjian, subsequently Frenchified to Marc Coulomb.

The Coulombs, then as now, were giants in the tourist industry, with travel agencies all over the world, and orchestrators of tours to almost anywhere. When he struck up a conversation with me in Central Park, Marc Coulomb was only twenty-five, and had been sent from Paris to find an advertising agency to make his family's services better known in the U.S.A. He admired my facility with drawing materials, and said that, if I really wished to become an artist, I would have to come to Paris.

There was an irony lying in wait in the distant future, of course: I would eventually become a member of that small group of painters which would make New York City and not Paris the Art Capital of the World.

Purely on the basis of race prejudice, I think, one Armenian taking care of another, he bought me a suit, a shirt, a necktie, and a new pair of shoes, and took me to the advertising agency he liked best, which was Leidveld and Moore. He told them they could have the Coulomb account if they would hire me as an artist. Which they did.

I never saw or heard from him again. But guess what? On this very morning, as I am thinking about Marc Coulomb hard for the first time in half a century, *The New York Times* carries his obituary. He was a hero of the French Resistance, they say, and was, at the time of his death, chairman of the board of Coulomb Frères et Cie, the most extensive travel organization in the world.

What a coincidence! But that is all it is. One mustn't take such things too seriously.

•   •   •

Bulletin from the present: Circe Berman has gone mad for dancing. She gets somebody, simply anybody of any age or station, to squire her to every public dance she hears about within thirty miles of here, many of them fund-raisers for volunteer fire departments. The other morning she came home at three in the morning wearing a fire hat.

She is after me to take ballroom dancing lessons being offered at the Elks Lodge in East Quogue.

I said to her: "I am not going to sacrifice my one remaining shred of dignity on the altar of Terpsichore."

•   •   •

I experienced modest prosperity at Leidveld and Moore. It was there that I did my painting of the most beautiful ocean liner in the world, the *Normandie*. In the foreground was the most beautiful automobile in the world, the Cord. In the background was the most beautiful skyscraper in the world, the Chrysler Building. Getting out of the Cord was the most beautiful actress in the world, who was Madeleine Carroll. What a time to be alive!

Improved diet and sleeping conditions did me the disservice of sending me one evening to the Art Students League with a portfolio under my arm. I wished to take lessons in how to be a serious painter, and presented myself and my work to a teacher named Nelson Bauerbeck, a representational painter, as were almost all of the painting teachers then. He was principally known as a portraitist, and his work can still be viewed in at least one place I know of—at New York University, my old alma mater. He did portraits of two of that institution's presidents before my time. He made them immortal, as only paintings can.

• • •

There were about twelve students in the room and busy at their easels, all making pictures of the same nude model. I looked forward to joining them. They seemed to be a happy family, and I needed one. I was not a member of the family at Leidveld and Moore. There was resentment there about how I'd got my job.

Bauerbeck was old to be teaching—about sixty-five, I'd guess. I knew from the head of the art department at the ad agency, who had studied under him, that he was a native of Cincinnati, Ohio, but had spent most of his adult life in Europe, as so many American painters used to do. He was so old that he had conversed, however briefly, with James Whistler and Henry James and Émile Zola and Paul Cézanne! He also claimed to have been a friend of Hitler in Vienna, when Hitler was a starving artist before the First World War.

Old Bauerbeck must have himself been a starving artist when I met him. Otherwise, he would not have been teaching at the Art Students League at that advanced age. I have never been able to find out what finally became of him. Now you see him, now you don't.

We did not become friends. He leafed through my portfolio while saying things like this, very quietly, thank God, so his students could not hear: "Oh, dear, dear, dear," and "My poor boy," and "Who did this to you—or did you do it to yourself?"

I asked him what on Earth was wrong, and he said, "I'm not sure I can put it into words." He really did have to think hard about it. "This is going to sound very odd—" he said at last, "but, technically speaking, there's nothing you can't do. Do you understand what I'm saying?"

"No," I said.

"I'm not sure I do, either," he said. He screwed up his face, "I think—I think—it is somehow very useful, and maybe even essential, for a fine artist to have to somehow make his peace on the canvas with all the things he *cannot* do. That is what attracts us to serious paintings, I think: that shortfall, which we might call 'personality,' or maybe even 'pain.' "

"I see," I said.

He relaxed. "I think *I* do, too," he said. "It's something I've never had to articulate before. How *interesting!*"

"I can't tell if you've accepted me as a student or not," I said.

"No, I've rejected you," he said. "It wouldn't be fair to either one of us if I were to take you on."

I was angry. "You've rejected me on the basis of some high-flown theory you just made up," I protested.

"Oh, no, no, no," he said. "I rejected you before I thought of the theory."

"On the basis of what?" I demanded.

"On the basis of the very first picture in your portfolio," he said. "It told me, 'Here is a man without passion.' And I asked myself what I now ask you: 'Why should I teach him the language of painting, since there seems to be absolutely nothing which he is desperate to talk about?' "

• • •

Hard times!

So I signed up for a course in creative writing instead—taught three nights a week at City College by a fairly famous short-story writer named Martin Shoup. His stories were about black people, although he himself was white. Dan Gregory had illustrated at least a couple of them—with the customary delight and sympathy he felt for people he believed to be orangutans.

Shoup said about my writing that I wasn't going to get very far until I became more enthusiastic about describing the looks of things—and particularly people's faces. He knew I could draw, so he found it odd that I wouldn't want to go on and on about the looks of things.

"To anybody who can draw," I said, "the idea of putting the appearance of anything into words is like trying to make a Thanksgiving dinner out of ball bearings and broken glass."

"Then perhaps you had better resign from this course," he said. Which I did.

I have no idea what finally became of Martin Shoup, either. Maybe he got killed in the war. Circe Berman never heard of him. Now you see him, now you don't.

• • •

Bulletin from the present: Paul Slazinger, who himself teaches creative writing from time to time, has come back into our lives in a great big way! All is forgiven, apparently. He is sound asleep here now in an upstairs bedroom. When he wakes up, we shall see what we shall see.

The Rescue Squad of the Springs Volunteer Fire Department brought him here at about midnight last night. He had awakened his neighbors in Springs by yelling for help out different windows of his house—maybe every window he owned before he was through. The Rescue Squad wanted to take him to the Veterans Administration hospital at Riverhead. It was well known that he was a veteran. It is well known that *I* am a veteran.

But he calmed down, and he promised the rescuers that he would be all right if they brought him over here. So they rang my doorbell, and I received them in the foyer with its pictures of little girls on swings. Supported and restrained in the midst of the compassionate volunteers was a straitjacket containing the frantic meat of Slazinger. If I gave them permission, they were going to turn him loose as an experiment.

Circe Berman had come down by then. We were both in our nightclothes. People do strange things when suddenly confronted by a person out of his or her mind. After taking one long, hard look at Slazinger, Circe turned her back on all of us and started straightening the pictures of the little girls on swings. So there was something this seemingly fearless woman was afraid of. She was petrified by insanity.

Insane people are evidently Gorgons to her. If she looks at one, she turns to stone. There must be a story there.

24

S LAZINGER WAS A LAMB when they unswaddled him. "Just put me to bed," he said. He named the room he wanted to be put in, the one on the second floor with Adolph Gottlieb's "Frozen Sounds Number Seven" over the fireplace and a bay window looking across the dunes to the ocean. He wanted that room and no other, and seemed to feel entitled to sleep there. So he must have been dreaming in detail of moving in with me for hours at least, and maybe even for decades. I was his insurance plan. Sooner or later, he would simply give up, go limp, and have himself delivered to the beach house of a fabulously well-to-do Armenian.

He, incidentally, was from a very old American family. The first Slazinger on this continent was a Hessian grenadier serving as a mercenary with General John Burgoyne, the British general who was defeated by forces commanded in part by the rebel General Benedict Arnold, who would later desert to the British, at the second Battle of Freeman's Farm, north of Albany, two hundred years ago. Slazinger's ancestor was taken prisoner during the battle, and never went home, which was in Wiesbaden, Germany, where he had been the son of—guess what?

A cobbler.

•   •   •

"All God's chilluns got shoes."
—Old Negro spiritual.

•   •   •

I would have to say that the widow Berman was a lot scarier than Slazinger the night Slazinger arrived in a straitjacket. He was pretty much the same old Slazinger when the Rescue Squad turned him loose in the foyer. But Circe, almost catatonic, was a Circe I had never seen before.

So I put Slazinger to bed unassisted. I didn't undress him. He didn't have that many clothes on anyway—just Jockey shorts and a T-shirt that said, STOP SHOREHAM. Shoreham is a nuclear generating plant not far away. If it didn't work the way it was supposed to, it might kill hundreds of thousands of people and render Long Island uninhabitable for centuries. A lot of people were opposed to it. A lot of people were for it. I myself think about it as little as possible.

I will say this about it, although I have only seen it in photographs. Never have I contemplated architecture which said more pointedly to one and all: "I am from another planet. I have no way of caring what you are or what you want or what you do. Buster, you have been *colonized*."

• • •

A good subtitle for this book might be this: *Confessions of an Armenian Late Bloomer or Always the Last to Learn*. Listen to this: I never even *suspected* that the widow Berman was a pill freak until the night Slazinger moved in.

After I had put him to bed, with the Belgian linen sheets pulled right up to the nostrils of his big Hessian nose, I thought it might be a good idea to give him a sleeping pill. I didn't have any, but I hoped Mrs. Berman might have some. I had heard her come up the stairs very slowly and go into her bedroom.

Her door was wide open, so I paid her a call. She was sitting on the edge of her bed, staring straight ahead. I asked her for a sleeping pill, and she told me to help myself in the bathroom. I hadn't entered that bathroom since she took up residence. In fact, I don't think I had been in it for years and years. There is a good chance that I had *never* been in that bathroom before.

And, my God—I wish you could see the pills she had! They were apparently samples from drug salesmen which her late doctor husband had accumulated over decades! The medicine cabinet couldn't begin to hold them all! The marble counter-top around the washbasin was about five feet long and two feet wide, I would estimate, and an entire *regiment* of little bottles was deployed there. The scales dropped from my eyes! So much was suddenly *explicable*—the strange salutation when we first met on the beach, the impulsive redecoration of the foyer, the unbeatable pool game, the dancing madness, and on and on.

And which patient needed me most now in the dead of night?

Well—what could I do for a pill freak that she couldn't do better or worse for herself? So I went back to Slazinger empty handed, and we talked about his trip to Poland for a while. Why not? Any port in a storm.

• • •

Here is the solution to the American drug problem suggested a couple of years back by the wife of our President: "Just say no."

• • •

Maybe Mrs. Berman could say no to her pills, but poor Paul Slazinger had no control over the dangerous substances his own body was manufacturing and dumping in his bloodstream. He had no choice but to think all kinds of crazy things. And I listened to him rave on a while about how well he could write, if only he were in hiding or in prison in Poland, and how the Polly Madison books were the greatest works of literature since *Don Quixote*.

He did get off one pretty good crack about her, but I don't think it was meant to be a crack, since he was so rapt when he said it. He called her "the Homer of the bubblegum crowd."

And let's just get it out of the way right here and now about the merits of the Polly Madison books. To settle this question in my own mind, without having to actually read them, I have just solicited by telephone the opinions of a bookseller and a librarian in East Hampton, and also the widows of a couple of the old Abstract Expressionist gang who have teenage grandchildren now.

They all said about the same thing, boiling down to this: "Useful, frank, and intelligent, but as literature hardly more than workmanlike."

So there it is. If Paul Slazinger wants to keep out of the nuthouse, it certainly isn't going to help his case if he says he spent this past summer reading all the Polly Madison books.

• • •

It won't help his case much, either, that when he was a mere stripling he lay face down on a Japanese hand grenade, and has been in and out of laughing academies ever since. He was seemingly born not only with a gift for language, but with a particularly nasty clock which makes him go crazy every three years or so. Beware of gods bearing gifts!

Before he went to sleep the other night, he said that he could not help being what he was, for good or ill, that he was "that sort of molecule."

"Until the Great Atom Smasher comes to get me, Rabo," he said, "this is the kind of molecule I have to be."

• • •

"And what is literature, Rabo," he said, "but an insider's newsletter about affairs relating to molecules, of no importance to anything in the Universe but a few molecules who have the disease called 'thought.'"

• • •

"It's all so clear to me now," he said. "I understand everything."

"That's what you said the last time," I reminded him.

"Well—it's clear to me again," he said. "I was put on Earth with only two missions: to get the Polly Madison books the recognition they deserve as great literature, and to publish my Theory of Revolution."

"O.K.," I said.

"Does that sound crazy?" he said.

"Yes," I said.

"Good," he said. "Two monuments I must build! One to her and one to me. A thousand years from now her books will still be read and people will still be discussing Slazinger's Theory of Revolution."

"That's nice to think about," I said.

He became foxy. "I never *told* you my theory, did I?" he said.

"No," I said.

He tapped his temple with his fingertips. "That's because I've kept it locked up here all these years in this potato barn," he said. "You're not the only old man, Rabo, who has saved the best for last."

"What do you know about the potato barn?" I said.

"Nothing—word of honor: nothing. But why does an old man lock up anything so tight, so tight, unless he's saving the best for last?" he said. "It takes a molecule to know a molecule."

"What's in *my* barn is not the best and is not the worst, although it wouldn't have to be very good to be the best I ever did, and it would have to be pretty awful to be the worst," I said. "You want to know what's in there?"

"Sure, if you want to tell me," he said.

"It's the emptiest and yet the fullest of all human messages," I said.

"Which *is*?" he said.

" 'Good-bye,' " I said.

•   •   •

House party!

And who prepares the meals and makes the beds for these increasingly fascinating guests of mine?

The indispensable Allison White! Thank goodness Mrs. Berman talked her into staying!

And while Mrs. Berman, who says she is nine tenths of the way through her latest epic, can be expected to return to Baltimore in the near future, Allison White will not leave me high and dry. For one thing, the stock market crash two weeks ago has reduced the demand for domestic help out this way. For another, she is pregnant again, and determined to carry the fetus to term. So she has *begged* permission to stay on with Celeste for the winter at least, and I have told her: "The more the merrier."

•   •   •

Perhaps I should have scattered milestones along the route this book has taken, saying, "It is now the Fourth of July," and "They say this is the coolest August on record, and may have something to do with the disappearance of ozone over the North Pole," and so on. But I had no idea that this was going to be a diary as well as an autobiography.

Let me say now that Labor Day was two weeks ago, just like the stock-market crash. So *zingo!* There goes prosperity! And *zingo!* There goes another summertime!

•   •   •

Celeste and her friends are back in school, and she asked me this morning what I knew about the Universe. She has to write a theme about it.

"Why ask me?" I said.

"You read *The New York Times* every day," she said.

So I told her that the Universe began as an eleven-pound strawberry which exploded at seven minutes past midnight three trillion years ago.

"I'm *serious!*" she said.

"All I can tell you is what I read in *The New York Times*," I said.

• • •

Paul Slazinger has had all his clothes and writing materials brought here. He is working on his first volume of nonfiction, to which he has given this title: *The Only Way to Have a Successful Revolution in Any Field of Human Activity.*

For what it is worth: Slazinger claims to have learned from history that most people cannot open their minds to new ideas unless a mind-opening team with a peculiar membership goes to work on them. Otherwise, life will go on exactly as before, no matter how painful, unrealistic, unjust, ludicrous, or downright dumb that life may be.

The team must consist of three sorts of specialists, he says. Otherwise, the revolution, whether in politics or the arts or the sciences or whatever, is sure to fail.

The rarest of these specialists, he says, is an authentic genius— a person capable of having seemingly good ideas not in general circulation. "A genius working alone," he says, "is invariably ignored as a lunatic."

The second sort of specialist is a lot easier to find: a highly intelligent citizen in good standing in his or her community, who understands and admires the fresh ideas of the genius, and who testifies that the genius is far from mad. "A person like that working alone," says Slazinger, "can only yearn out loud for changes, but fail to say what their shapes should be."

The third sort of specialist is a person who can explain anything, no matter how complicated, to the satisfaction of most people, no matter how stupid or pigheaded they may be. "He

will say almost anything in order to be interesting and exciting,"
says Slazinger. "Working alone, depending solely on his own
shallow ideas, he would be regarded as being as full of shit as a
Christmas turkey."

•   •   •

Slazinger, high as a kite, says that every successful revolution,
including Abstract Expressionism, the one I took part in, had
that cast of characters at the top—Pollock being the genius in
our case, Lenin being the one in Russia's, Christ being the one
in Christianity's.

He says that if you can't get a cast like that together, you can
forget changing *anything* in a great big way.

•   •   •

Just think! This one house by the seaside, so empty and dead
only a few months ago, is now giving birth to a book about how
to revolt successfully, a book about how poor girls feel about
rich boys, and the memoirs of a painter whose pictures all came
unstuck from canvas.

And we are expecting a baby, too!

•   •   •

I look out my window and see a simple man astride a tractor
which drags a madly chattering gang of mowers across my lawns.
I know little more about him than his name is Franklin Cooley,
and that he drives an old, babyshit-brown Cadillac Coupe de
Ville, and has six kids. I don't even know if Mr. Cooley can
read and write. At least forty million Americans can't read and
write, according to this morning's *New York Times*. That is six
times as many illiterates as there are people of Armenian descent
anywhere! So many of them and so few of us!

Does Franklin Cooley, that poor, dumb bastard with six kids,
his ears filled with the clashing gibberish of the mowers, have
the least suspicion that earthshaking work is going on in here?

•   •   •

Yes, and guess what *else The New York Times* said this morning? Geneticists have *incontrovertible* evidence that men and

women were once separate races, men evolving in Asia and women evolving in Africa. It was simply a coincidence that they were interfertile when they met.

The clitoris, so goes the speculation in the paper, is the last vestige of the inseminating organ of a conquered, enslaved, trivialized and finally emasculated race of weaker, but not necessarily dumber, anthropoids!

Cancel my subscription!

25

BACK TO THE GREAT DEPRESSION!
To make a long story short: Germany invaded Austria
and then Czechoslovakia and then Poland and then France, and
I was a pipsqueak casualty in faraway New York City. Coulomb
Frères et Cie was out of business, so I lost my job at the agency—
not that long after my father's Moslem obsequies. So I joined
what was still a peacetime United States Army, and scored high
on their classification test. The Great Depression was as discouraging as ever, and the Army was still a very little family in this
country, so I was lucky to be accepted. The recruiting sergeant
on Times Square, I remember, had indicated that I might be a
more attractive relative in prospect if I were to have my name
legally changed to something more American.

I even remember his helpful suggestion: that I become
"Robert King." Just think: somebody might now be trespassing on my private beach and gazing in awe at this mansion, and
wondering who could be rich enough to live this well, and the
answer could so easily have been this: "Robert King."

•   •   •

But the Army adopted me as Rabo Karabekian—as I was soon
to discover, for this reason: Major General Daniel Whitehall,
then the commander of the combat troops of the Corps of Engineers, wanted an oil painting of himself in full uniform, and
believed that somebody with a foreign-sounding name could
do the best job. As an Army regular, of course, I would have
to paint him for free. And this was a man ravenous for immortality. He was going to be retired in six months, by reason of
failing kidneys, having barely missed service in two world wars.

God only knows what became of the portrait I did of him—
after hours during basic training. I used the most expensive
materials, which he was more than glad to buy for me. There is
one painting of mine which might actually outlive the "Mona
Lisa"! If I had realized that at the time I might have given him
a puzzling half-smile, whose meaning only I knew for certain:

he had become a general, but had missed the two big wars of
his lifetime.

•   •   •

Another painting of mine which just might outlive the
"Mona Lisa," for better or for worse, is the gigantic son of a
bitch out in the potato barn.

•   •   •

So much I only *now* realize! When I did the portrait of General Whitehall in a mansion nearly as grand as this one, which
was the property of the Army, I was stereotypically Armenian!
Welcome home to my true nature! I was a scrawny recruit and
he was a Pasha weighing more than two hundred pounds, who
could squash me like an insect anytime he pleased.

But what sly and self-serving advice, but actually very good
advice, too, I was able to give him along with flattery on this
order: "You have a very strong chin. Did you know that?"

In what must surely have been the manner of powerless
Armenian advisors in Turkish courts, I congratulated him on
having ideas he might never have had before. An example: "You
must be thinking very hard how important aerial photography
is going to be, if war should come." War, of course, had come to
practically everybody but the United States by then.

"Yes," he said.

"Would you turn your head the least little bit to the left?" I
said. "Wonderful! That way there aren't such deep shadows in
your eye sockets. I certainly don't want to lose those eyes. And
could you imagine now that you are looking from a hilltop at
sunset—over a valley where a battle is going to take place the
next day?"

So he did that as best he could, and he couldn't talk without ruining everything. But, like a dentist, I was perfectly free
to go on jabbering. "Good! Wonderful! Perfect! Don't move
anything!" I said. And then I added almost absentmindedly
as I laid the paint on: "Every branch of the service is claiming
camouflage from the air as their specialty, even though it's obviously the business of the Engineers."

And I said a little later: "Artists are so naturally good at camouflage, I guess I'm just the first of many to be recruited by the
Corps of Engineers."

• • •

Did such a sly and smarmy and Levantine seduction work?
You be the judge:

The painting was unveiled at the General's retirement ceremonies. I had completed my basic training and been promoted
to private first class. I was simply another soldier with an obsolescent Springfield rifle, standing in ranks before the bunting-
draped scaffold which supported the painting on an easel, and
from which the General spoke.

He lectured on aerial photography, and the clear mission of
the Engineers to teach the other branches of the service about
camouflage. He said that among the last orders he would ever
give was one which called for all enlisted men with what he
called "artistic experiences" to be assigned to a new camouflage
unit under the command of, now get this: "Master Sergeant
Rabo Karabekian. I hope I pronounced his name right."

He had, he *had*!

• • •

I was a master sergeant at Fort Belvoir when I read of the
deaths of Dan Gregory and Fred Jones in Egypt. There was
no mention of Marilee. They had died as civilians, although
in uniforms, and they both got respectful obituaries, since the
United States was still a neutral nation in the war. The Italians
weren't our enemies yet, and the British who killed Gregory and
Fred weren't yet our allies. Gregory, I remember, was bid farewell in the papers as possibly the best-known American artist in
history. Fred was sent on to Judgment Day as a World War One
ace, which he wasn't, and an aviation pioneer.

I, of course, wondered what had become of Marilee. She was
still young and I presumed beautiful, and had a good chance of
finding some man a lot richer than I was to look after her. I was
certainly in no position to make her my own. Military pay was
still very low even for a master sergeant. There were no Holy
Grails for sale at the Post Exchange.

• • •

When my country finally went to war like everybody else, I was commissioned a lieutenant and served, if not fought, in North Africa and Sicily and England and France. I was forced to fight at last on the border of Germany, and was wounded and captured without having fired a shot. There was this white flash.

The war in Europe ended on May 8, 1945. My prison camp had not yet been captured by the Russians. I, with hundreds of other captured officers from Great Britain, from France, from Belgium, from Yugoslavia, from Russia, from Italy, which country had switched sides, from Canada and New Zealand and South Africa and Australia, from everywhere, was marched at route step out of our prison and into the still-to-be-conquered countryside. Our guards vanished one night, and we awoke the next morning on the rim of a great green valley on what is now the border between East Germany and Czechoslovakia. There may have been as many as ten thousand people below us— concentration camp survivors, slave laborers, lunatics released from asylums and ordinary criminals released from jails and prisons, captured officers and enlisted men from every Army which had fought the Germans.

What a *sight*! And, if that weren't enough for a person to see and then marvel about for a lifetime, listen to this: the very last remains of Hitler's armies, their uniforms in tatters but their killing machines still in working order, were also there.

Unforgettable!

26

A T THE END of my war, my country, where the only person
I knew was a Chinese laundryman, paid in full for cos-
metic surgery performed on the place where my eye used to be.
Was I bitter? No, I was simply blank, which I came to realize
was what Fred Jones used to be. Neither one of us had anything
to come home to.

Who paid for my eye operation at Fort Benjamin Harrison
outside Indianapolis? He was a tall, skinny fellow, tough but
fair-minded, plain spoken but shrewd. No, I am not speaking of
Santa Claus, whose image in shopping malls at Christmas time
nowadays is largely based on a painting Dan Gregory made for
Liberty magazine in 1923. No. I am speaking of my Uncle Sam.

• • •

As I've said, I married my nurse at the hospital. As I've
said, we had two sons who no longer speak to me. They aren't
even Karabekians anymore. They had their last names legally
changed to that of their stepfather, whose name was Roy Steel.

Terry Kitchen asked me one time why, since I had so few
gifts as a husband and father, I had gotten married. And I heard
myself say: "That's the way the postwar movie goes."

That conversation must have taken place about five years after
the war.

The two of us must have been lying on cots I had bought for
the studio space we had rented above Union Square. That loft
had become not only Kitchen's workplace but his home. I myself
had taken to spending two or three nights a week there, as I
found myself less and less beloved in the basement apartment
three blocks away, where my wife and children lived.

• • •

What did my wife have to complain about? I had quit my
job as a salesman of life insurance for Connecticut General. I
was intoxicated most of the time not only by alcohol but by the
creation of huge fields of a single color of Sateen Dura-Luxe. I

had rented a potato barn and made a down payment on a house out here, which was then a wilderness.

And in the midst of that domestic nightmare there arrived a registered letter from Italy, a country I had never seen. It asked me to come to Florence, all expenses paid for one, to testify in a lawsuit there about two paintings, a Giotto and a Masaccio, which had been taken by American soldiers from a German general in Paris. They had been turned over to my platoon of art experts to be catalogued and shipped to a warehouse in Le Havre, where they were to be crated and stored. The general had evidently stolen them from a private house while retreating north through Florence.

The crating in Le Havre was done by Italian prisoners of war, who had done that sort of work in civilian life. One of them evidently found a way to ship both paintings to his wife in Rome, where he kept them hidden, except to show to close friends after the war. The rightful owners were suing to recover them.

So I went over there alone, and I got my name in the papers for accounting for the trip the paintings made from Paris to Le Havre.

• • •

But I had a secret, which I have never told anybody before: "Once an illustrator, always an illustrator!" I couldn't help seeing stories in my own compositions of strips of colored tape applied to vast, featureless fields of Sateen Dura-Luxe. This idea came into my head uninvited, like a nitwit tune for a singing commercial, and would not get out again; each strip of tape was the soul at the core of some sort of person or lower animal.

So whenever I stuck on a piece of tape, the voice of the illustrator in me who would not die would say, for example, "The orange tape is the soul of an Arctic explorer, separated from his companions, and the white one is the soul of a charging polar bear."

This secret fantasy, moreover, infected and continues to infect my way of seeing scenes in real life. If I watch two people talking on a street corner, I see not only their flesh and clothes, but narrow, vertical bands of color inside them—not so much like tape, actually, but more like low-intensity neon tubes.

• • •

When I got back to my hotel at about noon on my last day in Florence, there was a note for me in my pigeonhole. As far as I knew, I had no friends in all of Italy. The note on expensive paper with a noble crest at the top said this:

There can't be all that many Rabo Karabekians in the world. If you're the wrong one, come on over anyway. I'm mad for Armenians. Isn't everybody? You can rub your feet on my carpets and make sparks. Sound like fun? Down with modern art! Wear something green.

And it was signed, *Marilee, Countess Portomaggiore (the coal miner's daughter).*
Wow!

27

I TELEPHONED HER at once from the hotel. She asked if I could come to tea in an hour! I said I sure *could*! My heart was beating like mad!

She was only four blocks away—in a palazzo designed for Innocenzo "the Invisible" de Medici by Leon Battista Alberti in the middle of the fifteenth century. It was a cruciform structure whose four wings abutted on a domed rotunda twelve meters in diameter and in whose walls were half embedded eighteen Corinthian columns four and a half meters high. Above the capitals of the columns was a clerestory, a wall pierced with thirty-six windows. Above this was the dome—on whose underside was an epiphany, God Almighty and Jesus and the Virgin Mary and angels looking down through clouds, painted by Paolo Uccello. The terrazzo floor, its designer unknown, but almost surely a Venetian, was decorated with the backs of peasants planting and harvesting and cooking and baking and making wine and so on.

• • •

The incomparable Rabo Karabekian is not here demonstrating his connoisseurship nor his Armenian gift for total recall—nor his fluency with the metric system, for that matter. All the information above comes from a brand new book published by Alfred A. Knopf, Incorporated, called *Private Art Treasures of Tuscany*, with text and photographs by a South Korean political exile named Kim Bum Suk. According to the preface, it was originally Kim Bum Suk's doctoral thesis for a degree in the history of architecture from Massachusetts Institute of Technology. He managed to examine and photograph the interiors of many opulent private homes in and around Florence which few scholars had ever seen, and whose art treasures had never before been photographed by an outsider or noted in any public catalogue.

Among these hitherto impenetrable private spaces was, hey presto, the palazzo of Innocenzo "the Invisible" de Medici, which I myself penetrated thirty-seven years ago.

• • •

The palazzo and its contents, uninterruptedly private property for five and a half centuries now, remains private property, following the death of my friend, Marilee, Contessa Portomaggiore, who was the person who, according to the book, gave Kim Bum Suk and his camera and his metric measuring instruments the run of the place. Ownership, upon Marilee's death two years ago, passed on to her late husband's nearest male blood relative, a second cousin, an automobile dealer in Milan, who sold it at once to an Egyptian man of mystery, believed to be an arms dealer. His name? Hold on to your hats: his name is Leo *Mamigonian!*

Small World!

He is the son of Vartan Mamigonian, the man who diverted my parents from Paris to San Ignacio, and who cost me an eye, among other things. How could I ever forgive Vartan Mamigonian?

• • •

Leo Mamigonian bought all the contents of the palazzo, too, and so must own Marilee's collection of Abstract Expressionist paintings, which was the best in Europe, and second in the world only to mine.

What is it about Armenians that they always *do* so well? There should be an investigation.

• • •

How did I come to possess Kim Bum Suk's invaluable doctoral thesis at precisely the moment I must write about my reunion with Marilee in 1950? We have here another coincidence, which superstitious persons would no doubt take seriously.

Two days ago, the widow Berman, made vivacious and supranaturally alert by God only knows what postwar pharmaceutical miracles, entered the bookstore in East Hampton, and heard, by her own account, one book out of hundreds calling out to her. It said that I would like it. So she bought it for me.

She had no way of knowing that I was on the brink of writing about Florence. Nobody did. She gave me the book without herself examining the contents, and so did not know that my old girlfriend's palazzo was therein described.

One would soon go mad if one took such coincidences too seriously. One might be led to suspect that there were all sorts of things going on in the Universe which he or she did not thoroughly understand.

•   •   •

Dr. Kim or Dr. Bum or Dr. Suk, whichever is the family name, if any, has cleared up two questions I had about the rotunda when I myself was privileged to see it. The first puzzle was how the dome was filled with natural light in the daytime. It turns out that there were mirrors on the sills of the clerestory windows—and there were still more mirrors on the roofs outside to capture sunbeams and deflect them upward into the dome.

The second puzzle was this: why were the vast rectangles between the encircling columns at ground level blank? How could any art patron have left them bare? When I saw them, they were painted the palest rose-orange, not unlike the Sateen Dura-Luxe shade yclept "Maui Eventide."

Dr. Kim or Dr. Bum or Dr. Suk explains that lightly clad pagan gods and goddesses used to cavort in these spaces, and that they were lost forever. They had not been merely concealed under coats of paint. They had been *scraped* off the walls during the exile of the Medicis from Florence from 1494, two years after the discovery of this hemisphere by white people, until 1531. The murals were destroyed by the insistence of the Dominican monk Girolamo Savonarola, who wished to dispel every trace of paganism, which he felt had poisoned the city during the reign of the Medicis.

The murals were the work of Giovanni Vitelli, about whom almost nothing else is known, except that he was said to have been born in Pisa. One may assume that he was the Rabo Karabekian of his time, and that Christian fundamentalism was his Sateen Dura-Luxe.

•   •   •

Kim Bum Suk, incidentally, was thrown out of his native South Korea for forming a union of university students which demanded improvements in the curricula.

Girolamo Savonarola, incidentally, was hanged and burned in the piazza in front of what had been the Palazzo of Innocenzo "the Invisible" de Medici in 1494.

I sure love history. I don't know why Celeste and her friends aren't more interested.

• • •

I now think of the rotunda of that palazzo, when it still had its pagan as well as its Christian images, as a Renaissance effort to make an atom bomb. It cost a great deal of money and employed many of the best minds of the time, and it compressed into a small space and in bizarre combinations the most powerful forces of the Universe as the Universe was understood in the fifteenth century.

The Universe has certainly come a long, long way since then.

• • •

As for Innocenzo "the Invisible" de Medici, according to Kim Bum Suk: he was a banker, which I choose to translate as "loan shark and extortionist" or "gangster," in the parlance of the present day. He was simultaneously the richest and least public member of his family. No portrait of him was ever made, save for a bust done of him when a child by the sculptor Lorenzo Ghiberti. He himself smashed that bust when he was fifteen years old, and threw the pieces into the Arno. He attended no parties and gave none when an adult, and never traveled in the city save in a conveyance which hid him from view.

After his palazzo was completed, his most trusted henchmen and even the highest dignitaries, including two of his own cousins who were Popes, never saw him save in the rotunda. They were obliged to stand at the edge of it, while he alone occupied the middle—wearing a shapeless monk's robe and a death's-head mask.

• • •

He drowned while in exile in Venice. This was long before the invention of water wings.

• • •

When Marilee told me on the telephone to come over to her palazzo right away, the tone of her voice, coupled with her confession that there were no men in her life just then, seemed guarantees to me that in no more than two hours, probably, I would be getting more of the greatest loving I had ever had— and not as a callow youth this time, but as a war hero, roué, and seasoned cosmopolite!

I in turn warned her that I had lost an eye in battle, and so would be wearing an eye patch, and that I was married, yes, but that the marriage was on the rocks.

I am afraid that I said, too, in making light of my years as a warrior, that I had spent most of my time ". . . combing pussy out of my hair." This meant that women had made themselves available to me in great numbers. This odd locution was a variant of a metaphor which made a lot more sense: a person who had been shelled a great deal might say that he had been combing tree bursts out of his hair.

So I arrived at the appointed hour in a twanging state of vanity and concupiscence. I was led by a female servant down a long, straight corridor to the edge of the rotunda. All the Contessa Portomaggiore's servants were females—even the porters and gardeners. The one who let me in, I remember, struck me as mannish and unfriendly—and then downright military when she told me to stop just inside the rotunda.

• • •

At the center, clad from neck to floor in the deepest black mourning for her husband, Count Bruno—there stood Marilee.

She wasn't wearing a death's-head mask, but her face was so pale and in the dim light so close to the color of her flaxen hair that her head might have been carved from a single piece of old ivory.

I was aghast.

Her voice was imperious and scornful. "So, my faithless little Armenian protégé," she said, "we meet again."

28

"THOUGHT YOU were going to get laid again, I'll bet," she said. Her words echoed whisperingly in the dome—as though they were being discussed up there by the Divinities.

"Surprise, surprise," she said, "we're not even going to shake hands today."

I wagged my head in unhappy wonderment. "Why are you so mad at me?" I asked.

"During the Great Depression," she said, "I thought you were the one real friend I had in the world. And then we made love, and I never heard from you again."

"I can't believe this," I said. "You told me to go away—for the good of *both* of us. Have you forgotten that?"

"You must have been awfully glad to hear me say that," she said. "You sure went away."

"What did you *expect* me to do?" I said.

"To give some sign, any sign, that you cared how I was," she said. "You've had fourteen years to do it, but you never did it—not one telephone call, not one postcard. Now here you are back like a bad penny: expecting what? Expecting to get laid again."

• • •

"You mean we could have gone on being lovers?" I asked incredulously.

"Lovers? Lovers? Lovers?" she mocked me raucously. The echoes of her scorn for lovers sounded like warring blackbirds overhead.

"There's never been any shortage of lovers for Marilee Kemp," she said. "My father loved me so much he beat me every day. The football team at the high school loved me so much they raped me all night after the Junior Prom. The stage manager at the Ziegfeld Follies loved me so much he told me that I had to be part of his stable of whores or he'd fire me and have somebody throw acid in my face. Dan Gregory loved me so much he threw me down the stairs because I'd sent you some expensive art materials."

"He did *what*?" I said.

So she told me the true story of how I had become the apprentice of Dan Gregory.

I was flabbergasted. "But—but he must have liked my pictures, didn't he?" I stammered.

"No," she said.

•   •   •

"That's one beating I took on account of you," she said. "I took another one after we made love and I never heard from you again. Now let's talk about all the wonderful things you did for me."

"I never felt so ashamed in my life," I said.

"All right—I'll tell you what you did for me: you went for happy, silly, beautiful walks with me."

"Yes—" I said, "I remember those."

"You used to rub your feet on the carpets and then give me shocks on my neck when I least expected it," she said.

"Yes," I said.

"And we were so naughty sometimes," she said.

"When we made love," I said.

She blew up again. "No! No! No! You jerk! You jerk! You incomparable jerk!" she exclaimed. "The Museum of Modern Art!"

•   •   •

"So you lost an eye in the war," she said.

"So did Fred Jones," I said.

"So did Lucrezia and Maria," she said.

"Who are they?" I said.

"My cook," she said, "and the woman who let you in."

•   •   •

"Did you win a lot of medals in the war?" she said.

Actually, I hadn't done too badly. I had a *Bronze Star* with a *Cluster*, and a *Purple Heart* for my wound, and a *Presidential Unit Citation*, a *Soldier's Medal*, a *Good Conduct Badge*, and a *European–African–Middle Eastern Campaign Ribbon* with seven *Battle Stars*.

I was proudest of my *Soldier's Medal*, which is usually awarded to a soldier who has saved the life of another soldier in situations not necessarily related to combat. In 1941, I was giving a course in camouflage techniques to officer candidates at Fort Benning, Georgia. I saw a barracks on fire, and I gave the alarm, and then went in twice, without regard for my own safety, and carried out two unconscious enlisted men.

They were the only two people in there, and nobody was supposed to be in there. They had been drinking, and had accidentally started the fire themselves, for which they were given two years at hard labor—plus loss of all pay and dishonorable discharges.

About my medals: all I said to Marilee was that I guessed I had received my share.

How Terry Kitchen used to envy me for my Soldier's Medal, incidentally. He had a Silver Star, and he said a Soldier's Medal was worth ten of those.

•   •   •

"Whenever I see a man wearing a medal," said Marilee, "I want to cry and hug him, and say, 'Oh, you poor baby—all the terrible things you've *been* through, just so the woman and the children could be safe at home.' "

She said she used to want to go up to Mussolini, who had so many medals that they covered both sides of his tunic right down to his belt, and say to him, "After all you've been through, how can there be anything *left* of you?"

And then she brought up the unfortunate expression I had used when talking to her on the telephone: "Did you say that in the war you were 'combing pussy out of your hair'?"

I said I was sorry I'd said it, and I was.

"I never heard that expression before," she said. "I had to guess what it meant."

"Just forget I said it," I said.

"You want to know what my guess was? I guessed that wherever you went there were women who would do anything for food or protection for themselves and the children and the old people, since the young men were dead or gone away," she said. "How close was I?"

"Oh my, oh my, oh my," I said.

"What's the matter, Rabo?" she said.

"You hit the nail on the head," I said.

•   •   •

"Wasn't very hard to guess," she said. "The whole point of war is to put women everywhere in that condition. It's always men against women, with the men only pretending to fight among themselves."

"They can pretend pretty hard sometimes," I said.

"They know that the ones who pretend the hardest," she said, "get their pictures in the paper and medals afterwards."

•   •   •

"Do you have an artificial leg?" she said.

"No," I said.

"Lucrezia, the woman who let you in, lost a leg along with her eye. I thought maybe you'd lost one, too."

"No such luck," I said.

"Well—" she said, "early one morning she crossed a meadow, carrying two precious eggs to a neighbor who had given birth to a baby the night before. She stepped on a mine. We don't know what army was responsible. We do know the sex. Only a male would design and bury a device that ingenious. Before you leave, maybe you can persuade Lucrezia to show you all the medals she won."

And then she added: "Women are so useless and unimaginative, aren't they? All they ever think of planting in the dirt is the seed of something beautiful or edible. The only missile they can ever think of throwing at anybody is a ball or a bridal bouquet."

I said with utmost fatigue, "O.K., Marilee—you've certainly made your point. I have never felt worse in my life. I only wish the Arno were deep enough to drown myself in. Can I please return to my hotel?"

"No," she said. "I think I've reduced you to the level of self-esteem which men try to force on women. If I have, I would very much like to have you stay for the tea I promised you. Who knows? We might even become friends again."

29

MARILEE LED ME to a small and cozy library which used to house, she said, her late husband's great collection of male homosexual pornography. I asked her what had become of the books, and she said she had sold them for a great deal of money, which she had divided among her servants—all women who had been badly hurt one way or another by war.

We settled into overstuffed chairs, facing each other across a coffee table. She beamed at me fondly and then said this: "Well, well, well, my young protégé—how goes it? Long time no see. Marriage on the rocks, you say?"

"I'm sorry I said that," I said. "I'm sorry I said anything. I feel like something the cat drug in."

We were served tea and little cakes at that point by a woman who had two steel clamps where her hands should have been. Marilee said something to her in Italian, and she laughed.

"What did you say to her?" I asked.

"I said your marriage was on the rocks," she said.

The woman with the clamps said something to her in Italian, and I requested a translation.

"She said you should marry a man next time," said Marilee.

"Her husband plunged her hands into boiling water," she said, "in order to make her tell him who her lovers had been while he was away at war. They were Germans and then Americans, by the way, and gangrene set in."

• • •

Over the fireplace of Marilee's cozy library was the Dan Gregory–style painting I mentioned earlier, a gift to her from the people of Florence: showing her late husband, Count Bruno, refusing a blindfold while facing a firing squad. She said that it hadn't happened exactly that way, but that nothing ever did. So I asked her how it happened that she became the Contessa Portomaggiore, with the beautiful palazzo and rich farms to the north and so on.

When she and Gregory and Fred Jones arrived in Italy, she said, before the United States got into the war, and against Italy and Germany and Japan, they were received as great celebrities. They represented a propaganda victory for Mussolini: " 'America's greatest living artist and one of its greatest aviators and the incomparably beautiful and gifted American actress, Marilee Kemp,' he called us," said Marilee. "He said the three of us had come to take part in the spiritual and physical and economic miracle in Italy, which would become the model for the world for thousands of years to come."

The propaganda value of the three of them was so great that she was accorded in the press and at social events the respect a real and famous actress deserved. "So suddenly I wasn't a dim-witted floozy anymore," she said. "I was a jewel in the crown of the new Roman emperor. Dan and Fred, I must say, found this confusing. They had no choice in public but to treat me more respectfully, and I had fun with that. This country is absolutely crazy about blondes, of course, so that, whenever we had to make an entrance, I came first—and they came along behind me, as part of my entourage.

"And it was somehow very easy for me to learn Italian," she said. "I was soon better at it than Dan, who'd taken lessons in it back in New York. Fred, of course, never learned Italian at all."

•   •   •

Fred and Dan became heroes in Italy after they died fighting more or less for the Italian cause. Marilee's celebrity survived them—as a very beautiful and charming reminder of their supreme sacrifice, and of the admiration many Americans had, supposedly, for Mussolini.

She was still certainly beautiful, by the way, at the time of our reunion, even without makeup and in widow's weeds. She should have been an old lady after all she had been through, but she was only forty-three. She had a third of a century still to go!

And, as I say, she would become Europe's largest Sony distributor, among other things. There was life in the old girl yet!

The Contessa was surely way ahead of her time, too, in believing that men were not only useless and idiotic, but downright dangerous. That idea wouldn't catch on big in her native country until the last three years of the Vietnam War.

• • •

After Dan Gregory's death, her regular escort in Rome was Mussolini's Oxford-educated and unmarried Minister of Culture, the handsome Bruno, Count Portomaggiore. He explained to Marilee at once that they could have no physical relationship, since he was interested sexually only in men and boys. Such a preference, if acted upon, was a capital offense at the time, but Count Bruno felt perfectly safe, no matter how outrageously he might behave. He was confident that Mussolini would protect him, since he was the only member of the old aristocracy who had accepted a high position in his government, and who virtually wallowed in admiration at the upstart dictator's booted feet.

"He was a perfect ass," said Marilee. She said that people laughed at his cowardice and vanity and effeminacy.

"He was also," she added, "the perfect head of British Intelligence in Italy."

• • •

After Dan and Fred were killed, and before the United States got into the war, Marilee was the toast of Rome. She had a wonderful time shopping and dancing, dancing, dancing, with the count, who enjoyed hearing her talk, and was always the perfect gentleman. Her wish was his command, and he never threatened her physically, and never demanded that she do this or that until one night, when he told her that Mussolini himself had ordered him to marry her!

"He had many enemies," said Marilee, "and they had been telling Mussolini that he was a homosexual and a British spy. Mussolini certainly knew he loved men and boys, but didn't even suspect that a man that silly could have the nerve or wit to be a spy."

When Mussolini ordered his Minister of Culture to prove that he wasn't a homosexual by wedding Marilee, he also handed him a document for Marilee to sign. It was designed to placate old aristocrats to whom the idea of an American floozy's inheriting ancient estates would have been intolerable. It set forth that, in the case of the count's death, Marilee would have his property for life, but without the right to sell it or leave it to anyone else. Upon her death, it was to go to the count's nearest male relative, who, as I have said, turned out to be an automobile dealer in Milan.

The next day, the Japanese in a surprise attack sank a major fraction of the United States warships at Pearl Harbor, leaving this still pacifistic, antimilitaristic country no choice but to declare war on not only Japan, but on Japan's allies, Germany and Italy, as well.

• • •

But even before Pearl Harbor, Marilee told the only man ever to propose marriage to her, and a rich nobleman at that, that no, she would not marry him. She thanked him for happiness such as she had never known before. She said that his proposal and the accompanying document had awakened her from what could only be a dream, and that it was time for her to return to the United States, where she could try to deal with who and what she really was, even though she didn't have a home there.

But then, all excited the next morning about going home, Marilee found the spiritual climate of Rome, although the real Sun was shining brightly and the real clouds were somewhere else, to be as dark and chilling as, and this is how she described it to me in Florence, "rain and sleet at midnight."

• • •

Marilee listened to the news about Pearl Harbor on the radio that morning. One item was about the approximately seven thousand American citizens living in Italy. The American Embassy, which was still operating, still technically at peace with Italy, announced that it was making plans to provide transportation back to the United States for as many as possible, as soon as possible. The Italian government responded that it would do all within its power to facilitate their departure, but that there was surely no reason for a mass exodus, since Italy and the United States had close bonds of both blood and history which should not be broken in order to satisfy the demands of Jews and Communists and the decaying British Empire.

Marilee's personal maid came in with the quotidian announcement that some sort of workman wanted to talk to her about the possibility of old, leaking gas pipes in her bedroom, and he wore coveralls and had a toolbox. He tapped the walls and sniffed, and murmured to himself in Italian. And then, when the two of them were surely alone, he began, still facing the wall, to speak softly in middle-western American English.

He said that he was from the War Department of the United States, which is what the Department of Defense used to be called. We had no separate spy organization back then. He said that he had no idea how she felt down deep about democracy or fascism, but that it was his duty to ask her, for the good of their country, to remain in Italy and to continue to curry the favor of Mussolini's government.

By her own account, Marilee then thought about democracy and fascism for the first time in her life. She decided that democracy sounded better.

"Why should I stay here and do that?" she asked.

"Sooner or later, you might hear something we would be very interested in knowing," he said. "Sooner or later, or even possibly never, your country might have some use to make of you."

She said to him that the whole world suddenly seemed to be going crazy.

He commented that there was nothing sudden about it, that it had belonged in a prison or a lunatic asylum for quite some time.

As an example of what she saw as sudden craziness, she told him about Mussolini's ordering his minister of culture to marry her.

He replied, according to Marilee: "If you have one atom of love for America in your heart, you will marry him."

Thus did a coal miner's daughter become the Contessa Portomaggiore.

30

MARILEE DID NOT LEARN until the war was nearly over that her husband was a British agent. She, too, thought him a weakling and a fool, but forgave him that since they lived so well and he was so nice to her. "He had the most amusing and kind and flattering things to say to me. He really enjoyed my company. We both loved to dance and dance."

So there was another woman in my life with a mania for dancing, who would do it with anybody as long as they did it well.

"You never danced with Dan Gregory," I said.

"He wouldn't," she said, "and you wouldn't either."

"I couldn't," I said. "I never had."

"Anybody who wants to can," she said.

• • •

She said that the news that her husband was a British spy made almost no impression on her. "He had all these uniforms for different occasions, and I never cared what any of them were supposed to mean. They were covered with emblems which I never bothered to decode. I never asked him: 'Bruno, what did you get this medal for? What does the eagle on your sleeve mean? What are those two crosses on your collar points?' So when he told me that he was a British spy, that was just more of the junk jewelry of warfare. It had almost nothing to do with me or him."

She said that after he was shot she expected to feel a terrible emptiness, but did not. And then she understood that her real companion and mate for life was the Italian people. "They spoke to me so lovingly wherever I went, Rabo, and I loved them in return, and did not give a damn about what junk jewelry they wore!"

"I'm *home*, Rabo," she said. "I never would have got here if it hadn't been for the craziness of Dan Gregory. Thanks to loose screws in the head of an Armenian from Moscow, I'm home, I'm home."

• • •

"Now tell me what *you've* been doing with all these years," she said.

"For some reason I find myself dismayingly uninteresting," I said.

"Oh, come, come, come," she said. "You lost an eye, you married, you reproduced twice, and you say you've taken up painting again. How could a life be more eventful?"

I thought to myself that there had been events, but very few, certainly, since our Saint Patrick's Day lovemaking so long ago, which had made me proud and happy. I had old soldier's anecdotes I had told my drinking buddies in the Cedar Tavern, so I told her those. She had had a life. I had accumulated anecdotes. She was home. Home was somewhere I never thought I'd be.

• • •

Old Soldier's Anecdote Number One: "While Paris was being liberated," I said, "I went to find Pablo Picasso, Dan Gregory's idea of Satan—to make sure he was O.K.," I said.

"He opened his door a crack, with a chain across it inside, and said he was busy and did not wish to be disturbed. You could still hear guns going off only a couple of blocks away. Then he shut and locked the door again."

Marilee laughed and said, "Maybe he knew all the terrible things our lord and master used to say about him." She said that if she had known I was still alive, she would have saved a picture in an Italian magazine which only she and I could fully appreciate. It showed a collage Picasso had made by cutting up a poster advertising American cigarettes. He had reassembled pieces of the poster, which originally showed three cowboys smoking around a campfire at night, to form a cat.

Of all the art experts on Earth, only Marilee and I, most likely, could identify the painter of the mutilated poster as Dan Gregory.

How is that for trivia?

• • •

"So that is probably the only point at which Picasso paid the least bit of attention to one of the most popular American artists in history," I speculated.

"Probably," she said.

• • •

Old Soldier's Anecdote Number Two: "I was captured when the war had only a few more months to go," I said. "I was patched up in a hospital and then sent to a camp south of Dresden, where they were practically out of food. Everything in what was left of Germany had been eaten up. So we were all getting skinnier and skinnier except for the man we'd elected to divide what food there was into equal shares.

"There was never a time when he had the food to himself. We saw it delivered, and then he divided it up with all of us watching. Still, he somehow remained sleek and contented-looking while the rest of us became skeletons.

"He was feasting absentmindedly on crumbs and dribblings that fell on the tabletop and clung to his knife and ladle."

This same innocent phenomenon, by the way, explains the great prosperity of many of my neighbors up and down the beach here. They are in charge of such wealth as remains in this generally bankrupt country, since they are so *trustworthy*. A little bit of it is bound to try to find its way to their mouths from their busy fingers and implements.

• • •

Old Soldier's Anecdote Number Three: "One evening in May," I said, "we were marched out of our camp and into the countryside. We were halted at about three in the morning, and told to sleep under the stars as best we could.

"When we awoke at sunrise, the guards were gone, and we found that we were on the rim of a valley near the ruins of an ancient stone watchtower. Below us, in that innocent farmland, were thousands upon thousands of people like us, who had been brought there by their guards, had been *dumped*. These weren't only prisoners of war. They were people who had been marched out of concentration camps and factories where they had been slaves, and out of regular prisons for criminals, and out of lunatic asylums. The idea was to turn us loose as far as possible from the cities, where we might raise hell.

"And there were civilians there, too, who had run and run from the Russian front or the American and British front. The fronts had actually met to the north and south of us.

"And there were hundreds in German uniforms, with their weapons still in working order, but docile now, waiting for whomever they were expected to surrender to."

"The Peaceable Kingdom," said Marilee.

• • •

I changed the subject from war to peace. I told Marilee that I had returned to the arts after a long hiatus, and had, to my own astonishment, become a creator of serious paintings which would make Dan Gregory turn over in his hero's grave in Egypt, paintings such as the world had never seen before.

She protested in mock horror. "Oh, please—not the arts again," she said. "They're a swamp I'll never get out of as long as I live."

But she listened thoughtfully when I told her about our little gang in New York City, whose paintings were nothing alike except for one thing: they were about nothing but themselves.

When I was all talked out, she sighed, and she shook her head. "It was the last conceivable thing a painter could do to a canvas, so you *did* it," she said. "Leave it to Americans to write, 'The End.'"

"I hope that's not what we're doing," I said.

"I hope very much that it *is* what you're doing," she said. "After all that men have done to the women and children and every other defenseless thing on this planet, it is time that not just every painting, but every piece of music, every statue, every play, every poem and book a man creates, should say only this: 'We are much too horrible for this nice place. We give up. We quit. The end!'"

• • •

She said that our unexpected reunion was a stroke of luck for her, since she thought I might have brought the solution to an interior decorating problem which had been nagging at her for years, namely: what sort of pictures, if any, should she put on the inane blanks between the columns of her rotunda? "I want to leave some sort of mark on this place while I have it," she said, "and the rotunda seems the place to do it.

"I considered hiring women and children to paint murals of the death camps and the bombing of Hiroshima and the planting of land mines, and maybe the burning of witches and the feeding of Christians to wild animals in olden times," she said. "But I think that sort of thing, on some level, just eggs men on to be even more destructive and cruel, makes them think: 'Ha! We are as powerful as gods! There has never been anything to stop us from doing even the most frightful things, if even the most frightful things are what we *choose* to do.'

"So your idea is a much better one, Rabo. Let men come into my rotunda, and wherever they look at eye level let them receive no encouragement. Let the walls cry out: 'The end! The end!' "

• • •

Thus began the second great collection of American Abstract Expressionist art—the first being my own, the storage bills for which were making paupers of me and my wife and children. Nobody else wanted those pictures at any price!

Marilee ordered ten of them sight unseen—to be selected by me and at one thousand dollars each!

"You're joking!" I said.

"The Countess Portomaggiore never jokes," she said. "And I'm as noble and rich as anybody who ever lived here, so you do what I say."

So I did.

• • •

She asked if our gang had come up with a name for ourselves, and we hadn't. It was critics who would finally name us. She said that we should call ourselves the "Genesis Gang," since we were going right back to the beginning, when subject matter had yet to be created.

I found that a good idea, and would try to sell it to the others when I got home. But it never caught on somehow.

• • •

Marilee and I talked for hours, until it was dark outside. She said at last, "I think you had better go now."

"Sounds like what you said to me on Saint Patrick's Day four- teen years ago," I said.

"I hope you won't be so quick to forget me this time," she said.

"I never did that," I said.

"You forgot to *worry* about me," she said.

"I give you my word of honor, Contessa," I said, standing. "I can never do that again."

That was the last time we met. We exchanged several letters, though. I have dug one of hers from the archives here. It is dated three years after our reunion, June 7, 1953, and says that we have failed to paint pictures of nothing after all, that she easily identifies chaos in every canvas. This is a pleasant joke, of course. "Tell that to the rest of the Genesis Gang," she says.

I answered that letter with a cable, of which I have a copy. "NOT EVEN CHAOS IS SUPPOSED TO BE THERE," it reads. "WE'LL COME OVER AND PAINT IT OUT. ARE OUR FACES RED. SAINT PATRICK."

• • •

Bulletin from the present: Paul Slazinger has voluntarily committed himself to the psychiatric ward at the Veterans Administration hospital over at Riverhead. I certainly didn't know what to do about the bad chemicals his body was dumping into his bloodstream, and he was becoming a maniac even to himself. Mrs. Berman was glad to see him *out* of here.

Better he should be looked after by his Uncle Sam.

31

O F ALL THE THINGS I have to be ashamed of, the most troublesome of this old heart of mine is my failure as a husband of the good and brave Dorothy, and the consequent alienation of my own flesh and blood, Henri and Terry, from me, their Dad.

What will be found written after the name of Rabo Karabekian in the Big Book on Judgment Day?

"Soldier: Excellent.

"Husband and Father: Floparroo.

"Serious artist: Floparroo."

• • •

There was Hell to pay when I got home from Florence. The good and brave Dorothy and both boys had a brand new kind of influenza, yet another postwar miracle. A doctor had been to see them and would come again, and a woman upstairs was feeding them. It was agreed that I could only be in the way until Dorothy got back to her feet, and that I should spend the next few nights at the studio Terry Kitchen and I had rented above Union Square.

How smart we would have been to have me stay away for a hundred years instead!

"Before I go, I want to tell you I've got some really good news," I said.

"We're not going to move out to that godforsaken house in the middle of nowhere?" she said.

"That isn't it," I said. "You and the kids will get to love it out there, with the ocean and lots of fresh air."

"Somebody's offered you a steady job out there?" she said.

"No," I said.

"But you're going to look for one," she said. "You're going to take your degree in business administration that we all sacrificed so much for, and knock on doors out there till somebody in some decent business hires you, so we'll have steady money coming in."

"Honeybunch, listen to me," I said. "When I was in Florence I sold ten thousand dollars' worth of paintings."

Our basement apartment resembled a storage room for scenery in a theater, there were so many huge canvases in there—which I had accepted in lieu of repayments of debts. So she got off this joke: "Then you're going to end up in prison," she said, "because we don't even have three dollars' worth of paintings here."

I had made her so unhappy that she had developed a sense of humor, which she certainly didn't have when I married her.

• • •

"You're supposed to be thirty-four years old," she said. She herself was twenty-three!

"I *am* thirty-four," I said.

"Then *act* thirty-four," she said. "Act like a man with a wife and family who'll be forty before he knows it, and nobody will give him a job doing anything but sacking groceries or pumping gas."

"That's really laying it on the line, isn't it?" I said.

"I don't lay it on the line like that," she said. "Life lays it on the line like that. Rabo! What's happened to the man I married? We had such sensible plans for such a sensible life. And then you met these people—these bums."

"I always wanted to be an artist," I said.

"You never told me that," she said.

"I didn't think it was possible," I said. "Now I do."

"Too late—and much too risky for a family man. Wake up!" she said. "Why can't you just be happy with a nice family? Everybody else is."

"I'll tell you again: I sold ten thousand dollars' worth of paintings in Florence," I said.

"That'll fall through like everything else," she said.

"If you loved me, you'd have more faith in me as a painter," I said.

"I love you, but I hate your friends and your paintings," she said, "and I'm scared for me and my babies, the way things are going. The war is *over*, Rabo!"

"What is *that* supposed to mean?" I said.

"You don't have to do wild things, great big things, dangerous things that don't have a chance," she said. "You've already
got all the medals anybody could want. You don't have to conquer France." This last was a reference to our grandiose talk
about making New York City rather than Paris the Art Capital
of the World.

"They were on our side anyway, weren't they?" she said.
"Why do you have to go conquer them? What did they ever
do to you?"

I was already outside the apartment when she asked me that,
so all she had to do to end the conversation was what Picasso
had done to me, which was to close the door and lock it.

I could hear her crying inside. Poor soul! Poor soul!

•   •   •

It was late afternoon. I took my suitcase over to Kitchen's and
my studio. Kitchen was asleep on his cot. Before I woke him up,
I had a look at what he had been doing in my absence. He had
slashed all his paintings with an ivory-handled straight razor
inherited from his paternal grandfather, who had been president
of the New York Central Railroad. The Art World certainly
wasn't any the poorer for what he had done. I had the obvious
thought: "It's a miracle he didn't slash his wrists as well."

This was a great big beautiful Anglo-Saxon sleeping there,
like Fred Jones a model for a Dan Gregory illustration of a story
about an ideal American hero. And when he and I went places
together, we really *did* look like Jones and Gregory. Not only
that, but Kitchen treated me as respectfully as Fred had treated
Gregory, which was preposterous! Fred had been a genuine,
dumb, sweet lunk, whereas my own buddy, sleeping there, was
a graduate of Yale Law School, could have been a professional
pianist or tennis player or golfer.

He had inherited a world of talent along with that straight
razor. His father was a first-rate cellist and chess player and hor-
ticulturalist, as well as a corporation lawyer and a pioneer in
winning civil rights for the black people.

My sleeping buddy had also outranked me in the Army, as a
lieutenant colonel in the Paratroops, and in deeds of derring-
do! But he chose to stand in awe of me because I could do one

thing he could never do, which was to draw or paint a likeness of anything my eye could see.

As for my own work there in the studio, the big fields of color before which I could stand intoxicated for hour after hour: they were meant to be *beginnings*. I expected them to become more and more complicated as I slowly but surely closed in on what had so long eluded me: soul, soul, soul.

• • •

I woke him up, and said I would buy him an early supper at the Cedar Tavern. I didn't tell him about the big deal I had pulled off in Florence, since he couldn't be a part of it. He wouldn't get his hands on the spray rig for two more days.

When the Contessa Portomaggiore died, incidentally, her collection would include *sixteen* Terry Kitchens.

• • •

"Early supper" meant early drinking too. There were already three painters at what had become our regular table in the back. I will call them "Painters X, Y and Z." And, lest I give aid and comfort to Philistines eager to hear that the first Abstract Expressionists were a bunch of drunks and wild men, let me say who these three *weren't*.

They were *not*, repeat, were *not*: William Baziotes, James Brooks, Willem de Kooning, Arshile Gorky, who was already dead by then anyway, Adolph Gottlieb, Philip Guston, Hans Hofmann, Barnett Newman, Jackson Pollock, Ad Reinhardt, Mark Rothko, Clyfford Still, Syd Solomon or Bradley Walker Tomlin.

Pollock would show up that evening, all right, but he was on the wagon. He would not say a word, and would soon go home again. And one person there wasn't a painter at all, as far as we knew. He was a tailor. His name was Isadore Finkelstein, and his shop was right above the tavern. After a couple of drinks, he could talk painting as well as anyone. His grandfather, he said, had been a tailor in Vienna, and had made several suits for the painter Gustav Klimt before the First World War.

And we got on the subject of why, even though we had been given shows which had excited some critics, and which had inspired a big story in *Life* magazine about Pollock, we still weren't making anywhere near enough to live on.

We concluded that it was our clothing and grooming which were holding us back. This was a kind of joke. Everything we said was a kind of joke. I still don't understand how things got so gruesomely serious for Pollock and Kitchen after only six more years went by.

•   •   •

Slazinger was there, too. That was where I met him. He was gathering material for a novel about painters—one of dozens of novels he never wrote.

At the end of that evening, I remember, he said to me: "I can't get over how passionate you guys are, and yet so absolutely *unserious*."

"Everything about life is a joke," I said. "Don't you know that?"

"No," he said.

•   •   •

Finkelstein declared himself eager to solve the clothing problem of anybody who thought he had one. He would do it for a small down payment and a manageable installment plan. So the next thing I knew, Painters X, Y and Z and I and Kitchen were all upstairs in Finkelstein's shop, getting measured for suits. Pollock and Slazinger came along, but only as spectators. Nobody else had any money, so, in character, I made everybody's down payment with the traveler's checks I had left over from my trip to Florence.

Painters X, Y and Z, incidentally, would pay me back with pictures the very next afternoon. Painter X had a key to our apartment, which I had given him after he was thrown out of his fleabag hotel for setting his bed on fire. So he and the other two delivered their paintings and got out again before poor Dorothy could defend herself.

•   •   •

Finkelstein the tailor had been a real killer in the war, and so had Kitchen been. I never was.

Finkelstein was a tank gunner in Patton's Third Army. When he measured me for my suit, a suit I still own, he told me, his mouth full of pins, about how a track was blown off his tank by a boy with a rocket launcher two days before the war in Europe ended.

So they shot him before they realized that he was just a boy.

• • •

And here is a surprise: when Finkelstein died of a stroke three years later, when we were all starting to do quite well financially, it turned out that he had been a secret painter all along!

His young widow Rachel, who looked a lot like Circe Berman, now that I think about it, gave him a one-man show in his shop before she closed it up forever. His stuff was unambitious but strong: as representational as he could make it, much like what his fellow war heroes Winston Churchill and Dwight David Eisenhower used to do.

Like them, he enjoyed paint. Like them, he appreciated reality. That was the late painter Isadore Finkelstein.

• • •

After we had been measured for suits we went back down to the tavern for more food and drink and talk, talk, talk, we were joined by a seemingly rich and distinguished gentleman, about sixty years old. I had never seen him before, and neither had any of the others, as nearly as I could tell.

"I hear you are painters," he said. "Do you mind if I just sit here and listen in?" He was between me and Pollock, and across the table from Kitchen.

"Most of us are painters," I said. We weren't about to be rude to him. It was possible that he was an art collector, or maybe on the board of directors of an important museum. We knew what all the critics and dealers looked like. He was much too honest, obviously, to take part in either of those scruffy trades.

"Most of you are painters," he echoed. "Aha! So the simplest thing would be for you to tell me who *isn't* one."

Finkelstein and Slazinger so identified themselves.

"Oh—guessed wrong," he said. He indicated Kitchen. "I wouldn't have thought he was a painter, either," he said, "despite his rough clothes. A musician maybe, or a lawyer or a professional athlete, maybe. A painter? He sure fooled me."

He had to be a clairvoyant, I thought, to home in on the truth about Kitchen with such accuracy! Yes, and he kept his attention locked on Kitchen, as though he were reading his mind. Why would he be more fascinated by somebody who had yet to paint a single interesting picture, than by Pollock, whose work was causing such controversy, and who was sitting right next to him?

He asked Kitchen if he had by any chance seen service in the war.

Kitchen said that he had. He did not elaborate.

"Did that have something to do with your decision to be a painter?" asked the old gentleman.

"No," said Kitchen.

Slazinger would say to me later that he thought that the war had embarrassed Kitchen about how privileged he had always been, easily mastering the piano, easily getting through the best schools, easily beating most people at almost any game, easily getting to be a lieutenant colonel in no time at all, and so on. "To teach himself something about real life," said Slazinger, "he picked one of the few fields where he could not help being a hopeless bungler."

Kitchen said as much to his questioner. "Painting is my Mount Everest," he said. Mount Everest hadn't been climbed yet. That wouldn't happen until 1953, the same year Finkelstein would be buried and have his one-man show.

The old gentleman sat back, seemingly much pleased by this answer.

But then he got much too personal, in my opinion, asking Kitchen if he was independently wealthy, or if his family was supporting him while he made such an arduous climb. I knew that Kitchen would become a very rich man if he outlived his mother and father, and that his parents had refused to give him any money, in the hopes of forcing him to start practicing law or enter politics or take a job on Wall Street, where success was assured.

I didn't think that was any of the old gentleman's business, and I wanted Kitchen to tell him so. But Kitchen told him all—and when he was done answering, his expression indicated that he was ready for another question, no matter what it might be.

This was the next one: "You are married, of course?"

"No," said Kitchen.

"But you *like* women?" said the old gentleman.

He was putting that question to a man who before the end of the war was one of the planet's greatest cocksmen.

"At this point in my life, sir," said Kitchen, "I am a waste of time for women, and women are a waste of time for me."

The old man stood. "I thank you for being so frank and polite with me," he said.

"I try," said Kitchen.

The old gentleman departed. We made guesses as to who and what he might have been. Finkelstein said, I remember, that whoever he was, his clothes had come from England.

•   •   •

I said I was going to have to borrow or rent a car the next day—to get the house out here ready for my family. I also wanted to have another look at the potato barn I'd rented.

Kitchen asked if he could come along, and I said, "Sure."

And there was this spray rig waiting for him in Montauk. Talk about fate!

•   •   •

Before we dropped off to sleep on our cots that night, I asked him if he had the least idea who the old gentleman who had questioned him so closely could have been.

"I'll make a really wild guess," he said.

"What is it?" I said.

"I could be wrong, but I think that was my father," he said. "Looked like Dad, sounded like Dad, dressed like Dad, made wry jokes like Dad. I watched him like a hawk, Rabo, and I said to myself, 'Either this is a very clever imitator, or this is the man who fathered me.' You're smart, and you're my best and only friend. Tell me: if he was simply a good imitator of my father, what could his game have been?"

32

I WOUND UP renting a truck instead of a car for Kitchen's and my fateful foray out here. Talk about Fate: if I hadn't rented a truck, Kitchen might be practicing law now, since there is no way we could have fit the spray rig into a closed sedan, which is the kind of car I would have rented.

Every so often, but not often enough, God knows, I would think of something which would make my wife and family a little less unhappy, and the truck was a case in point. The least I could do was get all the canvases out of our apartment, since they made poor Dorothy feel sick as a dog, even when she was well.

"You're not going to put them in the new house, are you?" she said.

That is what I *had* intended to do. I have never been famous for thinking far ahead. But I said, "No." I formulated a new scheme, which was to put them into the potato barn, but I didn't say so. I hadn't had the nerve to tell her I had rented a potato barn. But she'd found out about it someway. She would find out someway, too, that I had bought myself and Painters X, Y and Z and Kitchen tailor-made suits of the finest materials and workmanship the night before.

"Put them in the potato barn," she said, "and bury them under potatoes. Potatoes we can always use."

• • •

That truck should have been an armored car in a convoy of state police, considering what some of the paintings in there are worth today. I myself considered them valuable, but certainly not *that* valuable. So I could not bring myself to put them in the barn, which was then a musty place, having been home for so long for nothing but potatoes and the earth and bacteria and fungi which so loved to cling to them.

So I rented a dry, clean space under lock and key at Home Sweet Home Moving and Storage out here instead. The rental over the years would absorb a major part of my income. Nor did I overcome my habit of helping painter pals in trouble with whatever cash I had or could lay my hands on, and accepting pictures in return. At least Dorothy did not have to look at the detritus of this habit. Every painting which settled a debt in full went straight from the needy painter's studio to Home Sweet Home.

Her parting words to Kitchen and me when we at last got the pictures out of the apartment were these: "One thing I like about the Hamptons: every so often you see a sign that says 'Town Dump.'"

•   •   •

If Kitchen had been a perfect Fred Jones to my Dan Gregory, he would have driven the truck. But he was very much the passenger, and I was the chauffeur. He had grown up with chauffeurs, so he didn't think twice when he got in on the passenger side.

I talked about my marriage and the war and the Great Depression, and about how much older Kitchen and I both were, compared with the typical returning veteran. "I should have started a family and settled down years ago," I said. "But how could I have done that when I was the right age to do it? What women did I know anyway?"

"All the returning veterans in the movies are our age or older," he said. That was true. In the movies you seldom saw the babies who had done most of the heavy fighting on the ground in the war.

"Yes—" I said, "and most of the actors in the movies never even went to war. They came home to the wife and kids and swimming pool after every grueling day in front of the cameras, after firing off blank cartridges while men all around them were spitting catsup."

"That's what the young people will think our war was fifty years from now," said Kitchen, "old men and blanks and catsup." So they would. So they do.

"Because of the movies," he predicted, "nobody will believe that it was babies who fought the war."

•   •   •

"Three years out of our lives," he said about the war.

"You keep forgetting I was a regular," I said. "It was eight years out of mine. And there went my youth, and God, I still want it." Poor Dorothy thought she was marrying a mature, fatherly retired military gentleman. What she got instead was an impossibly self-centered and undisciplined jerk of nineteen or so!

"I can't help it," I said. "My soul knows my meat is doing bad things, and is embarrassed. But my meat just keeps right on doing bad, dumb things."

"Your what and your what?" he said.

"My soul and my meat," I said.

"They're separate?" he said.

"I sure hope they are," I said. I laughed. "I would hate to be responsible for what my meat does."

I told him, only half joking, about how I imagined the soul of each person, myself included, as being a sort of flexible neon tube inside. All the tube could do was receive news about what was happening with the meat, over which it had no control.

"So when people I like do something terrible," I said, "I just flense them and forgive them."

"*Flense?*" he said. "What's flense?"

"It's what whalers used to do to whale carcasses when they got them on board," I said. "They would strip off the skin and blubber and meat right down to the skeleton. I do that in my head to people—get rid of all the meat so I can see nothing but their souls. Then I forgive them."

"Where would you ever come across a word like *flense?*" he said.

And I said: "In an edition of *Moby-Dick* illustrated by Dan Gregory."

• • •

He talked about his father, who is still alive, by the way, and who has just celebrated his hundredth birthday! Think of that.

He adored his father. He also said that he would never want to compete with him, to try to beat him at anything. "I would hate that," he said.

"Hate what?" I said.

"To beat him," he said.

He said that the poet Conrad Aiken had lectured at Yale when Kitchen was in law school there, and had said that sons of gifted men went into fields occupied by their fathers, but where their fathers were weak. Aiken's own father had been a great physician and politician and ladies' man, but had also fancied himself a poet. "His poetry was no damn good, so Aiken became a poet," said Kitchen. "I could never do such a thing to my old man."

•   •   •

What he *would* do to his father six years later, in the front yard of Kitchen's shack about six miles from here, was take a shot at him with a pistol. Kitchen was drunk then, as he often was, and his father had come for the umpteenth time to beg him to get treatment for his alcoholism. It can never be proved, but that shot had to have been intended as a gesture.

When Kitchen saw that he had actually gunned down his father, with a bullet in the shoulder, it turned out, nothing would do but that Kitchen put the pistol barrel in his own mouth and kill himself.

It was an accident.

•   •   •

It was on that fateful truck trip, too, that I got my first look at Edith Taft Fairbanks, who would be my second wife. I had negotiated the rental of the barn from her husband, who was an affable idler, who seemed a useless, harmless waster of life to me back then, but who would become the role model I kept in mind when he died and I became her husband.

Prophetically, she was carrying a tamed raccoon in her arms. She was a magical tamer of almost any sort of animal, an over-whelmingly loving and uncritical nurturer of anything and everything that looked half alive. That's what she would do to me when I was living as a hermit in the barn and she needed a new husband: she tamed me with nature poems and good things to eat which she left outside my sliding doors. I'm sure she tamed her first husband, too, and thought of him lovingly and patronizingly as some kind of dumb animal.

She never said what kind of animal she thought he was. I know what kind of animal she thought *I* was, because she came right out and said it to a female relative from Cincinnati at our wedding reception, when I was all dressed up in my Izzy Fin-kelstein suit: "I want you to meet my tamed raccoon."

•   •   •

I will be *buried* in that suit, too. It says so in my will: "I am
to be buried next to my wife Edith in Green River Cemetery
in the dark blue suit whose label says: 'Made to order for Rabo
Karabekian by Isadore Finkelstein.' " It wears and wears.

•   •   •

Well—the execution of that will still lies in the future, but
just about everything else has vanished into the past, including Circe Berman. She finished up her book and returned to
Baltimore two weeks ago.

On her last night here, she wanted me to take her dancing,
and I again refused. I took her to supper at the American Hotel
in Sag Harbor instead. Just another tourist trap nowadays, Sag
Harbor used to be a whaling port. You can still see the man-
sions of the brave captains who sailed from there to the Pacific
Ocean, around the tip of South America, and then came home
millionaires.

In the lobby of the hotel is a guest register opened to a date
at the peak of the whale-killing industry, so disreputable nowadays: March 1, 1849. Back then, Circe's ancestors were in the
Russian Empire and mine in the Turkish Empire, which would
have made them enemies.

We feasted on lobsters, and drank in moderation in order to
become voluble. It is a bad thing to need a drink, everybody is
saying now, and I in fact went without alcohol the whole time
I was a hermit. But my feelings about Mrs. Berman on the eve
of her departure were so contradictory that, without a drink,
I might have eaten in wooden silence. But I certainly wasn't
going to drive with a couple of drinks in me, and neither was
she. It used to be almost fashionable to drive when drunk, but
no more, no more.

So I hired a boyfriend of Celeste's to drive us over there in his
father's car, and then pick us up again.

•   •   •

In the simplest terms: I was sorry that she was leaving,
because she was exciting to have around. But she could also be
too exciting, telling everybody exactly what to do. So I was also

glad that she was going, since what I wanted most, with my own book so nearly finished, was peace and quiet for a change. To put it another way: we were acquaintances, despite our months together. We had not become great friends.

That would change, however, once I had shown her what was in the potato barn.

Yes, that's right: this determined widow from Baltimore, before she left, persuaded this old Armenian geezer to unlock the locks and turn on the floodlights in the potato barn.

What did I get in exchange? I think we're really friends now.

33

W HEN WE GOT HOME from the American Hotel, the first thing she said was: "One thing you don't have to worry about: I'm not going to badger you about the keys to the potato barn."

"Thank God!" I said.

I think she was certain right then that, before the night was over, one way or another, she was damn well going to see what was in the potato barn.

"I only want you to draw me a picture," she said.

"Do what?" I said.

"You're a very modest man—" she said, "to the point where anybody who believed you would think you were no good at anything."

"Except camouflage," I said. "You're forgetting camouflage. I was awarded a Presidential Unit Citation, my platoon was so good at camouflage."

"O.K.—camouflage," she said.

"We were so good at camouflage," I said, "that half the things we hid from the enemy have to this very day never been seen again!"

"And that's not true," she said.

"We're having a celebration, so all sorts of things have been said which are not true," I said. "That's how to act at a party."

• • •

"You want me to go home to Baltimore knowing a whole lot of things about you which are not true?" she said.

"Everything that's true about me you should have learned before now, given your profound powers of investigation," I said. "This is just a party."

"I still don't know whether you can really draw or not," she said.

"Don't worry about it," I said.

"That's the bedrock of your life, to hear you tell it," she said. "That and camouflage. You were no good as a commercial artist, and you were no good as a serious artist, and you were no good as a husband or a father, and your great collection of paintings is an accident. But you keep coming back to one thing you're proud of: you could really draw."

"It's true," I said. "I didn't realize that, but now that you mention it, it's true."

"So prove it," she said.

"It's a very small boast," I said. "I wasn't an Albrecht Dürer. I could draw better than you or Slazinger or the cook—or Pollock or Terry Kitchen. I was born with this gift which certainly doesn't look like much when you compare me with all the far superior draughtsmen who've lived and died. I wowed the grade school and then the high school in San Ignacio, California. If I'd lived ten thousand years ago, I might have wowed the cave dwellers of Lascaux, France—whose standards for draughtsmanship must have been on about the same level as those of San Ignacio."

• • •

"If your book is actually published," she said, "you're going to have to include at least one picture that proves you can draw. Readers will insist on that."

"Poor souls," I said. "And the worst thing about getting as old as I am—"

"You're not that old," she said.

"Old enough!" I said. "And the worst thing is that you keep finding yourself in the middle of the same old conversations, no matter who you're talking to. Slazinger didn't think I could draw. My first wife didn't think I could draw. My second wife didn't care whether I could or not. I was just an old raccoon she brought in from the barn and turned into a house pet. She loved animals whether they could draw or not."

• • •

"What did you say to your first wife when she bet you couldn't draw?" she said.

"We had just moved out in the country where she didn't know a soul," I said. "There still wasn't heat in the house, and I was trying to keep us warm with fires in the three fireplaces—like my pioneer ancestors. And Dorothy was finally trying to catch up on art, reading up on it, since she had resigned herself to being stuck with an artist. She had never seen me draw—because not drawing and forgetting everything I knew about art, I thought, was the magic key to my becoming a serious painter.

"So, sitting in front of a fire in the kitchen fireplace, with all the heat going up the flue instead of coming out in the room," I said, "Dorothy read in an art magazine what an Italian sculptor had said about the first Abstract Expressionist paintings ever to be shown in a major show in Europe—at the Venice Biennale in 1950, the same year I had my reunion with Marilee."

"You had a painting there?" said Circe.

"No," I said. "It was just Gorky and Pollock and de Kooning. And this Italian sculptor, who was supposedly very important back then, but who is all but forgotten now, said this about what we thought we were up to: 'These Americans are very interesting. They dive into the water before they learn to swim.' He meant we couldn't draw.

"Dorothy picked up on that right away. She wanted to hurt me as much as I had hurt her, so she said, 'So that's it! You guys all paint the way you do because you couldn't paint something real if you *had* to.'

"I didn't rebut her with words. I snatched a green crayon Dorothy had been using to make a list of all the things inside and outside the house that had to be repaired, and I drew portraits on the kitchen wall of our two boys, who were asleep in front of the fireplace in the living room. I just did their heads—life size. I didn't even go into the living room to look at them first. The wall was new Sheetrock which I had nailed over the cracked plaster. I hadn't got around to filling and taping the joints between the sheets yet, and covering the nailheads. I never would.

"Dorothy was flabbergasted," I said to Circe. "She said to me: 'Why don't you do that all the time?' And I said to her, and this was the first time I ever said 'fuck' to her, no matter how angry we might have been with each other: 'It's just too fucking *easy*.' "

•   •   •

"You never did fill in the joints between the Sheetrock?" said Mrs. Berman.

"That is certainly a woman's question," I said. "And my manly answer is this one: 'No, I did not.' "

"So what happened to the portraits?" she said. "Were they painted over?"

"No," I said. "They stayed there on the Sheetrock for six years. But then I came home half drunk one afternoon, and found my wife and children and the pictures gone, and a note from Dorothy saying they were gone forever. She had cut the pictures out of the Sheetrock and taken them with her. There were two big square holes where the pictures used to be."

"You must have felt awful," said Mrs. Berman.

"Yes," I said. "Pollock and Kitchen had killed themselves only a few weeks before that, and my own paintings were falling apart. So when I saw those two squares cut out of the Sheetrock in that empty house—" I stopped. "Never mind," I said.

"Finish the sentence, Rabo," she begged.

"That was as close as I'll ever be," I said, "to feeling what my father must have felt when he was a young teacher—and found himself all alone in his village after the massacre."

•   •   •

Slazinger was another one who had never seen me draw, who wondered if I could really draw. I had been living out here for a couple of years by then, and he came by to watch me paint in the potato barn. I had set up a stretched and primed canvas eight by eight feet, and was about to lay on a coat of Sateen Dura-Luxe with a roller. It was a shade of greenish burnt orange called "Hungarian Rhapsody." Little did I know that Dorothy, back at the house, was slathering our whole bedroom with "Hungarian Rhapsody." But that is another story.

"Tell me, Rabo—" said Slazinger, "if I put on that same paint with that same roller, would the picture still be a Karabekian?"

"Absolutely," I said, "provided you have in reserve what Karabekian has in reserve."

"Like what?" he said.

"Like this," I said. There was dust in a pothole in the floor, and I picked up some of it on the balls of both my thumbs. Working both thumbs simultaneously, I sketched a caricature of Slazinger's face on the canvas in thirty seconds.

"Jesus!" he said. "I had no idea you could draw like that!"

"You're looking at a man who has *options*," I said.

And he said: "I guess you do, I guess you *do*."

• • •

I covered up that caricature with a couple of coats of "Hungarian Rhapsody," and laid on tapes which were supposed to be pure abstraction, but which to me were secretly six deer in a forest glade. The deer were near the left edge. On the right was a red vertical band, which to me, again secretly, was the soul of a hunter drawing a bead on one of them. I called it "Hungarian Rhapsody Number Six," which was bought by the Guggenheim Museum.

That picture was in storage when it started to fall apart like all the rest of them. A woman curator just happened to walk by and see all this tape and flakes of Sateen Dura-Luxe on the floor, so she called me up to ask what could be done to restore the picture, and whether they might be at fault someway. I didn't know where she had been the past year, when my pictures had become notorious for falling apart everywhere. She honestly thought maybe the Guggenheim hadn't provided proper humidity controls or whatever. I was at that time living like an animal in the potato barn, friendless and unloved. But I did have a telephone.

"One very strange thing—" she went on, "this big face has emerged from the canvas." It was the caricature, of course, which I had drawn with filthy thumbs.

"You should notify the Pope," I said.

"The Pope?" she said.

"Yes," I said. "You may have the next best thing to the *Shroud of Turin.*"

I had better explain to young readers that the *Shroud of Turin* is a linen sheet in which a dead person has been wrapped, which bears the imprint of an adult male who has been crucified, which the best scientists of today agree may indeed be two thousand years old. It is widely believed to have swaddled none other than Jesus Christ, and is the chief treasure of the Cathedral of San Giovanni Battista in Turin, Italy.

My joke with the lady at the Guggenheim suggested that it might be the face of Jesus emerging from the canvas—possibly just in time to prevent World War Three.

But she topped my joke. She said, "Well—I would call the Pope right away, except for one thing."

"What's that?" I said.

And she said: "You happen to be talking to somebody who used to date Paul Slazinger."

• • •

I made her the same offer I had made everybody else: that I would duplicate the painting exactly in more durable materials, paints and tapes which really *would* outlive the smile on the "Mona Lisa."

But the Guggenheim, like everybody else, turned me down. Nobody wanted to spoil the hilarious footnote I had become in art history. With a little luck, my last name might actually find its way into dictionaries:

kar • a • bek • i • an (ˌkar-a-'bek-ē-an), n. (from Rabo Kara-bekian, U.S. 20th cent. painter). Fiasco in which a person causes total destruction of own work and reputation through stupidity, carelessness or both.

34

W HEN I REFUSED to draw a picture for Mrs. Berman, she said, "Oh—you are such a *stubborn* little boy!"

"I am a stubborn little old *gentleman*," I said, "clinging to his dignity and self-respect as best he can."

"Just tell me what *kind* of thing it is in the barn—" she wheedled, "animal, vegetable or mineral?"

"All three," I said.

"How big?" she said.

I told her the truth: "Eight feet high and sixty-four feet long."

"You're kidding me again," she surmised.

"Of course," I said.

Out in the barn were eight panels of primed and stretched canvas placed side by side, each one eight feet by eight feet. They formed, as I had told her, a continuous surface sixty-four feet long. They were held upright in back by two-by-fours, and ran like a fence down the middle of the potato barn. These were the same panels which had shed the paint and tape of what had been my most famous and then most infamous creation, the picture which had graced and then disgraced the lobby of the GEFFCo headquarters on Park Avenue: "Windsor Blue Number Seventeen."

• • •

Here is how they came back into my possession, three months before dear Edith died:

They were found entombed in a locked chamber in the bottommost of the three basement floors under the Matsumoto Building, formerly the GEFFCo Building. They were recognized for what they were, with shreds of Sateen Dura-Luxe clinging to them here and there, by an inspector from Matsumoto's insurance company, who was looking for fire hazards deep underground. There was a locked steel door, and nobody had any idea what was on the other side.

The inspector got permission to break in. This was a woman and, as she told me on the telephone: she was the first female safety inspector for her company, and also the first black. "I

am two birds with one stone," she said, and she laughed. She
had a very nice laugh. There was no malice or mockery in it.
In offering to return my canvases to me after all those years,
with the absentminded approval of Matsumoto, she was simply
expressing her reluctance to see anything go to waste.

"I'm the only one who cares one way or another," she said,
"so *you* tell me what to do. You'd have to pick them up yourself,"
she said.

"How did you know what they *were*?" I said.

She had been a prenursing student at Skidmore College, she
said, and had taken, as one of her precious few electives, a course
in art appreciation. She was a registered nurse like my first wife
Dorothy, but had given up that profession because doctors, she
said, treated her like an idiot and a slave. Also: the hours were
long and the pay was low, and she had an orphaned niece to
support and keep company.

Her art appreciation teacher showed slides of famous pictures,
and two of these were of "Windsor Blue Number Seventeen,"
before and after it fell apart.

"How can I thank him?" I said.

"I think he was trying to lighten up the course," she said.
"The rest of it was so *serious*."

• • •

"Do you want the canvases or not?" she said. There was a long
silence, so she finally said, "Hello? Hello?"

"Sorry," I said. "That may seem like a simple question to you,
but it's a biggie to me. To me it's as though you called me up
out of the blue on a day like any other day, and asked me if I
was grown up yet."

If harmless objects like those rectangles of stretched canvas
were hobgoblins to me, could fill me with shame, yes, with rage
at a world which had entrapped me into being a failure and a
laughingstock and so on, then I *wasn't* a grown-up yet, although
I was then sixty-eight years old.

"So what is your answer?" she said on the telephone.

"I'm waiting myself to hear it," I said. I had no use for the
canvases—or so I thought back then. I honestly never expected
to paint again. Storing them would be no problem, since there
was plenty of space in the potato barn. Could I sleep well here

with the worst of the embarrassments from my past right here on the property? I hoped so.

I heard myself say this at last: "Please—don't throw them away. I will call Home Sweet Home Moving and Storage out here, and have them picked up as soon as possible. Please tell me your name again—so they can ask for you."

And she said this: "Mona Lisa Trippingham."

• • •

When GEFFCo hung "Windsor Blue Number Seventeen" in its lobby, with fanfare about such an old company's keeping on top of the latest developments not only in technology but in the arts, the company's publicity people hoped to say that "Windsor Blue Number Seventeen" was superlative in terms of size—if not the largest painting in the world, then at least the largest painting in New York City, or whatever. But there were several murals right in the city, and God knows in the world, which easily exceeded my painting's 512 square feet.

The publicity people wondered if it might not be a record holder for a painting *hung on a wall*—ignoring the fact that it was in fact eight separate panels, mated in back with C-clamps. But that wouldn't do, either, since it turned out that the Museum of the City of New York had three *continuous* paintings on canvas, *stitched* together to be sure, as high as mine and a third again as long! They were curious artifacts—an early effort at making movies, you might say, since they had rollers at either end. They could be unwound from one and rewound on the other. An audience could see only a small part of the whole at any time. These Brobdingnagian ribbons were decorated with mountains and rivers and virgin forests and limitless grasslands on which buffalo grazed, and deserts where diamonds or rubies or gold nuggets might be had for the stooping. These were the United States of America.

Lecturers traveled all over Northern Europe with such pictures in olden times. With assistants to unroll one end and roll up the other, they urged all ambitious and able persons to abandon tired old Europe and lay claim to rich and beautiful properties in the Promised Land, which were practically theirs for the asking.

Why should a real man stay home when he could be raping a virgin continent?

•   •   •

I had the eight panels purged of every trace of faithless Sateen Dura-Luxes, and restretched and reprimed. I had them set up in the barn, dazzling white in their restored virginity, just as they had been before I transmuted them into "Windsor Blue Number Seventeen."

I explained to my wife that this eccentric project was an exorcism of an unhappy past, a symbolic repairing of all the damage I had done to myself and others during my brief career as a painter. That was yet another instance, though, of putting into words what could not be put into words: why and how a painting had come to be.

The long and narrow barn, a century old, was as much a part of it as all that white, white, white.

The powerful floodlights dangling from tracks on the ceiling were part of it, pouring megawatts of energy into all that white sizing, making it far whiter than I would have believed white could ever be. I had caused those artificial suns to be installed when I received the commission to create "Windsor Blue Number Seventeen."

"What are you going to do with it next?" dear Edith asked.

"It's done," I said.

"Are you going to sign it?" she said.

"That would spoil it," I replied. "A flyspeck would spoil it."

"Does it have a title?" she said.

"Yes," I said, and I gave it a title on the spot, one as long as the title Paul Slazinger had given his book on successful revolutions: "I Tried and Failed and Cleaned Up Afterwards, so It's *Your* Turn Now."

•   •   •

I had my own death in mind—and what people would say about me afterwards. That was when I first locked up the barn, but with only a single padlock and hasp. I assumed, as my father had and as most husbands do, that I would of course be the first of our pair to die. So I had whimsically self-pitying instructions for Edith as to what she was to do immediately following my burial.

"Hold my wake in the barn, Edith," I said, "and when people ask you about all the white, white, white, you tell them that it was your husband's last painting, even though he didn't paint it. And then you tell them what the title is."

• • •

But she died first, and only two months after that. Her heart stopped, and down she fell into a flower bed.

"No pain," the doctor said.

At her burial at noon in Green River Cemetery, in a grave only a few yards from those of the other two Musketeers, Jackson Pollock and Terry Kitchen, I had my strongest vision yet of human souls unencumbered, unembarrassed by their unruly meat. There was this rectangular hole in the ground, and standing around it were all these pure and innocent neon tubes.

Was I crazy? You bet.

Her wake was in the home of a friend of hers, not mine, a mile up the beach from here. The husband did not attend!

Nor did he reenter this house, where he had been so useless and contented and loved without reason for one third of his life and one quarter of the twentieth century.

He went out to the barn, unlocked the sliding doors and turned on the lights. He stared at all that white.

Then he got into his Mercedes and drove to a hardware store in East Hampton, which carried art supplies. I bought everything a painter could ever wish for, save for the ingredient he himself would have to supply: soul, soul, soul.

The clerk was new to the area, and so did not know who I was. He saw a nameless old man in a shirt and tie and a suit made to order by Izzy Finkelstein—and a patch over one eye. The cyclops was in a high state of agitation.

"You're a painter, are you, sir?" said the clerk. He was perhaps twenty years old. He hadn't even been born when I stopped painting, stopped making pictures of any kind.

I spoke one word to him before leaving. This was it: "Renaissance."

• • •

The servants quit. I had become an untamed old raccoon again, who spent all his life in and around the potato barn. I kept the sliding doors closed, so that nobody could see what it was that I did in there. I did it for six months!

When I was done, I bought five more locks and hasps for the sliding doors, and snapped them shut. I hired new servants, and had a lawyer draw up a new will, which stipulated, as I have said, that I be buried in my Izzy Finkelstein suit, that all I owned was to go to my two sons, provided that they did a certain thing in memory of their Armenian ancestors, and that the barn was not to be unlocked until after my burial.

My sons have done quite well in the world, despite the horrors of their childhood. As I've said, their last name now is that of their good stepfather. Henri Steel is a civilian contract compliance officer at the Pentagon. Terry Steel is a publicity man for the Chicago Bears, which, since I own a piece of the Cincinnati Bengals, makes us sort of a football family.

•   •   •

Having done all that, I found I was able to take up residence in this house again, to hire new servants, and to become the empty and peaceful old man to whom Circe Berman addressed this question on the beach four months ago: "Tell me how your parents died."

On her last night in the Hamptons, she now said to me: "Animal, vegetable *and* mineral? All three?"

"Word of honor," I said. "All three, all three." With colors and binders taken from creatures and plants and the ground beneath us, every painting was surely all three, all three.

"Why won't you show it to me?" she said.

"Because it is the last thing I have to give to the world," I said. "I don't want to be around when people say whether it is any good or not."

"Then you are a coward," she said, "and that is how I will remember you."

I thought that over, and then I heard myself say: "All right, I will go get the keys. And then, Mrs. Berman, I would be most grateful if you would come with me."

•   •   •

Out into the dark we went, a flashlight beam dancing before us. She was subdued, humble, awed and virginal. I was elated, high as a kite and absolutely petrified.

We walked on flagstones at first, but then they veered off in the direction of the carriage house. After that we trod the stubble path cut through the wilderness by Franklin Cooley and his mowing machine.

I unlocked the barn doors and reached inside, my fingers on the light switch. "Scared?" I said.

"Yes," she said.

"So am I," I said.

Remember now: we were standing at the extreme right end of a painting eight feet high and sixty-four feet long. When I turned on the floodlights, we would be seeing the picture compressed by foreshortening to a seeming triangle eight feet high, all right, but only five feet wide. There was no telling from that vantage point what the painting really was—what the painting was all *about*.

I flicked on the switch.

There was a moment of silence, and then Mrs. Berman gasped in wonderment.

"Stay right where you are," I told her, "and tell me what you think of it."

"I can't come any farther?" she said.

"In a minute," I said, "but first I want to hear you say what it looks like from here."

"A big fence," she said.

"Go on," I said.

"A very big fence, an incredibly high and long fence," she said, "every square inch of it encrusted with the most gorgeous jewelry."

"Thank you very much," I said. "And now take my hand and close your eyes. I am going to lead you to the middle, and you can look again."

She closed her eyes, and she followed me as unresistingly as a toy balloon.

When we were in the middle, with thirty-two feet of the painting extending to either side, I told her to open her eyes again.

We were standing on the rim of a beautiful green valley in the springtime. By actual count, there were five thousand, two hundred and nineteen people on the rim with us or down below. The largest person was the size of a cigarette, and the smallest a flyspeck. There were farmhouses here and there, and the ruins of a medieval watchtower on the rim where we stood. The picture was so realistic that it might have been a photograph.

"Where are we?" said Circe Berman.

"Where I was," I said, "when the sun came up the day the Second World War ended in Europe."

35

I T IS ALL PART of the regular tour of my museum now. First come the doomed little girls on swings in the foyer, and then the earliest works of the first Abstract Expressionists, and then the perfectly tremendous whatchamacallit in the potato barn. I have unspiked the sliding doors at the far end of the barn, so that the greatly increased flow of visitors can move past the whatchamacallit without eddies and backwash. In one end they go, and out the other. Many of them will go through two times or more: not the whole show, just through the potato barn.

Ha!

No solemn critic has yet appeared. Several laymen and laywomen have asked me, however, to say what sort of a painting I would call it. I told them what I will tell the first critic to show up, if one ever comes, and one may never come, since the whatchamacallit is so exciting to the common people:

"It isn't a painting at all! It's a tourist attraction! It's a World's Fair! It's a Disneyland!"

•   •   •

It is a gruesome Disneyland. Nobody is cute there.

On an average, there are ten clearly drawn World War Two survivors to each square foot of the painting. Even the figures in the distance, no bigger than flyspecks, when examined through one of several magnifying glasses I keep in the barn, prove to be concentration-camp victims or slave laborers or prisoners of war from this or that country, or soldiers from this or that military unit on the German side, or local farmers and their families, or lunatics set free from asylums, and on and on.

There is a war story to go with every figure in the picture, no matter how small. I made up a story, and then painted the person it had happened to. I at first made myself available in the barn to tell anyone who asked what the story was of this person or that one, but soon gave up in exhaustion. "Make up your own war stories as you look at the whatchamacallit," I tell people. I stay in the house here, and simply point the way out to the potato barn.

• • •

That night with Circe Berman, though, I was glad to tell her any of the stories she wished to hear.

"Are you in there?" she said.

I pointed out myself at the bottom and right above the floor. I pointed with the toe of my shoe. I was the largest figure—the one as big as a cigarette. I was also the only one of the thousands with his back to the camera, so to speak. The crack between the fourth and fifth panels ran up my spine and parted my hair, and might be taken for the soul of Rabo Karabekian.

"This man clinging to your leg is looking up at you as though you were God," she said.

"He is dying of pneumonia, and will be dead in two hours," I said. "He is a Canadian bombardier who was shot down over an oil field in Hungary. He doesn't know who I am. He can't even see my face. All he can see is a thick fog which isn't there, and he's asking me if we are home yet."

"And what are you telling him?" she said.

"What would *you* tell him?" I said. "I'm telling him, 'Yes! We're home! We're home!' "

"Who is this man in the funny-looking suit?" she said.

"That is a concentration-camp guard who threw away his SS uniform and stole the suit from a scarecrow," I said. I pointed out a group of concentration camp victims far away from the masquerading guard. Several of them were on the ground and dying, like the Canadian bombardier. "He brought these people to the valley and dumped them, but doesn't know where to go next. Anybody who catches him will know he is an SS man—because he has his serial number tattooed on his upper left arm."

"And these two?" she said.

"Yugoslavian partisans," I said.

"This one?" she said.

"A sergeant major in the Moroccan Spahis, captured in North Africa," I said.

"And this one with a pipe in his mouth?" she said.

"A Scottish glider pilot captured on D-Day," I said.

"They're just from everywhere, aren't they?" she said.

"This is a Gurkha here," I said, "all the way from Nepal. And this machine-gun squad in German uniforms: they're

Ukrainians who changed sides early in the war. When the Russians finally reach the valley, they'll be hanged or shot."

"There don't seem to be any women," she said.

"Look closer," I said. "Half the concentration camp people and half the people from the lunatic asylums are women. They just don't look much like women anymore. They aren't what you might call 'movie stars.' "

"There don't seem to be any *healthy* women," she said.

"Wrong again," I said. "You'll find healthy ones at either end—in the corners at the bottom."

We went to the extreme right end for a look. "My goodness," she said, "it's like a display in a museum of natural history." So it was. There was a farmhouse down at the bottom of both ends: each one buttoned up tight like a little fort, its high gates closed, and all the animals in the courtyard. And I had made a schematic cut through the earth below them, so as to show their cellars, too, just as a museum display might give away the secrets of animals' burrows underground.

"The healthy women are in the cellar with the beets and potatoes and turnips," I said. "They are putting off being raped as long as possible, but they have heard the history of other wars in the area, so they know that rape will surely come."

"Does the picture have a title?" she said, rejoining me at the middle.

"Yes it does," I said.

"What is it?" she said.

And I said: " 'Now It's the Women's Turn.' "

•   •   •

"Am I crazy," she said, indicating a figure lurking near the ruined watchtower, "or is this a Japanese soldier?"

"That's what he is," I said. "He is a major in the army. You can tell that from the gold star and two brown stripes on the cuff of his left sleeve. And he still has his sword. He would rather die than give up his sword."

"I'm surprised that there were any Japanese there," she said.

"There weren't," I said, "but I thought there should be one there so I put one there."

"Why?" she said.

"Because," I said, "the Japanese were as responsible as the Germans for turning Americans into a bunch of bankrupt militaristic fuckups—after we'd done such a good job of being sincere war-haters after the First World War."

"And this woman lying here—" she said, "she's dead?"

"She's dead," I said. "She's an old queen of the Gypsies."

"She's so fat," she said. "Is she the only fat person? Everybody else is so skinny."

"Dying is the only way to get fat in Happy Valley," I said. "She's as fat as a circus freak because she's been dead three days."

" 'Happy Valley,' " echoed Circe.

"Or 'Peacetime' or 'Heaven' or 'the Garden of Eden' or 'Springtime' or whatever you want to call it," I said.

"She's the only one who's all alone," said Circe. "Or is she?"

"Just about," I said. "People don't smell too nice after they've been dead three days. She was the first stranger to arrive in Happy Valley, and she came all alone, and she died almost right away."

"Where are the other Gypsies?" she said.

"With their fiddles and tambourines and brightly painted caravans?" I said. "And their reputation for thieving, which was much deserved?"

• • •

Mrs. Berman told me a legend about Gypsies I had never heard before: "They stole the nails from the Roman soldiers who were about to crucify Jesus," she said. "When the soldiers looked for the nails, they had disappeared mysteriously. Gypsies had stolen them, and Jesus and the crowd had to wait until the soldiers sent for new nails. After that, God Almighty gave permission to all Gypsies to steal all they could." She pointed to the bloated Gypsy queen. "She believed that story. All Gypsies do."

"Too bad for her that she believed it," I said. "Or maybe it didn't matter whether she believed it or not, since she was starving to death when she arrived all alone in Happy Valley.

"She tried to steal a chicken from the farmhouse," I said. "The farmer saw her from this bedroom window, and took a shot at her with a small-caliber rifle he kept under his feather mattress. She ran away. He thought he had missed her, but he hadn't. She had a little bullet in her abdomen, and she lay down there and died. Three days later, the rest of us came along."

• • •

"If she's a queen of the Gypsies, where are her subjects?" Circe asked again.

I explained that she had been queen of only about forty people at the peak of her power, including babes in arms. While there were notorious disputes in Europe as to which races and sub-races were vermin, all Europeans could agree that the thieving, fortune-telling, child-stealing Gypsies were the enemies of all decent humankind. So they were hunted down everywhere. The queen and her people gave up their caravans, and their traditional costumes, too—gave up everything which might identify them as Gypsies. They hid in forests in the daytime, and foraged for food at night.

One night, when the queen went out alone to look for food, one of her subjects, a fourteen-year-old boy, was caught stealing a ham from a Slovak mortar squad which had deserted the German lines on the Russian front. They were headed home, which wasn't far from Happy Valley. They made the boy lead them to the Gypsy camp, where they killed everybody. So when the queen came back, she didn't have any subjects.

Such was the story I made up for Circe Berman.

• • •

Circe provided the missing link in the narrative. "So she wandered into Happy Valley, looking for other Gypsies," she said.

"Right!" I said. "But there weren't many Gypsies to be found anywhere in Europe. Most of them had been rounded up and gassed in extermination camps, which was fine with everybody. Who likes thieves?"

She took a closer look at the dead woman and turned away in disgust. "Ugh!" she said. "What's coming from her mouth? Blood and maggots?"

"Rubies and diamonds," I said. "She smells so awful, and looks like such bad luck, that nobody has come close enough to notice yet."

"And of all these people here," she said wonderingly, "who will be the first to notice?"

I indicated the former concentration camp guard in the rags of a scarecrow. "This man," I said.

36

"SOLDIERS, SOLDIERS, SOLDIERS," she marveled. "Uniforms, uniforms, uniforms."

The uniforms, what was left of them, were as authentic as I could make them. That was my homage to my master, Dan Gregory.

"Fathers are always so proud, the first time they see their sons in uniform," she said.

"I know Big John Karpinski was," I said. He is my neighbor to the north, of course. Big John's son Little John did badly in high school, and the police caught him selling dope. So he joined the Army while the Vietnam War was going on. And the first time he came home in uniform, I never saw Big John so happy, because it looked to him as though Little John was all straightened out and would finally amount to something.

But then Little John came home in a body bag.

•   •   •

Big John and his wife Dorene, incidentally, are dividing their farm, where three generations of Karpinskis grew up, into six-acre lots. It was in the local paper yesterday. Those lots will sell like hotcakes, since so many of the second-story windows of houses built on them, overlooking my property, will have a water view.

Big John and Dorene will become cash millionaires in a condominium in Florida, where winter never comes. So they are losing their own sacred plot of earth at the foot of their own Mount Ararat, so to speak—without experiencing that ultimate disgrace: a massacre.

"Was *your* father proud of you when he saw *you* for the first time in a uniform?" Circe asked me.

"He didn't live to see it," I said, "and I'm glad he didn't. If he had, he would have thrown an awl or a boot at me."

"Why?" she said.

"Don't forget that it was young soldiers whose parents thought they were finally going to amount to something who killed everybody he'd ever known and loved. If he'd seen me in a uniform, he would have bared his teeth like a dog with rabies. He would have said, 'Swine!' He would have said, 'Pig!' He would have said, 'Murderer! Get out of here!' "

•   •   •

"What do you think will eventually become of this painting?" she said.

"It's too big to throw away," I said. "Maybe it'll go to that private museum in Lubbock, Texas, where they have most of the paintings of Dan Gregory. I thought it might wind up behind the longest bar in the world, wherever that is—probably in Texas, too. But the customers would be climbing up on the bar all the time, trying to see what was really going on—kicking over glasses, stepping on the complimentary hors d'oeuvres."

I said that it would eventually be up to my two sons, Terry and Henri, to decide what was to become of "Now It's the Women's Turn."

"You're leaving it to *them*?" she said. She knew that they hated me, and had had their last name legally changed to that of Dorothy's second husband, Roy—the only *real* father they'd ever had.

"You think it's kind of a *joke* to leave them this?" said Circe. "You think it's worthless? I'm here to tell you this is a *terribly* important painting *some*way."

"I think maybe it's terribly important the same way a head-on collision is important," I said. "There's undeniable impact. Something has sure as hell happened."

"You leave those ingrates this," she said, "and you'll make them multimillionaires."

"They'll be that in any case," I said. "I'm leaving them everything I own, including your pictures of the little girls in swings and the pool table, unless you want those back. After I die, they'll have to do only one little thing to get it all."

"What's that?" she said.

"Merely have their names and those of my grandchildren legally changed back to 'Karabekian,' " I said.

"You care that much?" she said.

"I'm doing it for my mother," I said. "She wasn't even a Karabekian by birth, but she was the one who wanted, no matter where, no matter what, the name Karabekian to live on and on."

•   •   •

"How many of these are portraits of actual people?" she said.

"The bombardier clinging to my leg: that's his face, as I remember it. These two Estonians in German uniforms are Laurel and Hardy. This French collaborator here is Charlie Chaplin. These two Polish slave laborers on the other side of the tower from me are Jackson Pollock and Terry Kitchen."

"So there you are across the bottom: the Three Musketeers," she said.

"There we are," I agreed.

"The death of the other two so close together must have been a terrible blow to you," she said.

"We'd stopped being friends long before then," I said. "It was all the boozing we did together that made people call us that. It didn't have anything to do with painting. We could have been plumbers. One or the other of us would stop drinking for a little while, and sometimes all three of us—and that was that for the Three Musketeers, long before the other two killed themselves. 'Quite a blow,' you say, Mrs. Berman? Not at all. The only thing I did after I heard about it was become a hermit for eight years or so."

•   •   •

"And then Rothko killed himself after that," she said.

"Yup," I said. We were extricating ourselves from Happy Valley, and returning to real life. The melancholy roll-call of real-life suicides among the Abstract Expressionists again: Gorky by hanging in 1948, Pollock and then almost immediately Kitchen, by drunken driving and then pistol in 1956—and then Rothko with all possible messiness by knife in 1970.

I told her with sharpness which surprised me, and surprised her, too, that those violent deaths were like our drinking, and had nothing to do with our painting.

"I certainly won't argue with you," she said.

"Really!" I said. "Word of honor!" I said, my vehemence unspent. "The whole magical thing about our painting, Mrs. Berman, and this was old stuff in music, but it was brand new in painting: it was pure *essence of human wonder*, and wholly apart from food, from sex, from clothes, from houses, from drugs, from cars, from news, from money, from crime, from punishment, from games, from war, from peace—and surely apart from the universal human impulse among painters and plumbers alike toward inexplicable despair and self-destruction!"

• • •

"You know how old I was when you were standing on the rim of this valley?" she said.

"No," I said.

"One year old," she said. "And I don't mean to be rude, Rabo, but this picture is so rich, I don't think I can look at it any more tonight."

"I understand," I said. We had been out there for two hours. I myself was all worn out, but also twangingly proud and satisfied.

• • •

So there we were back in the doorway again, and I had my hand on the light switch. Since there were no stars that night, and no moon, a flick of that switch would plunge us into total darkness.

She asked me this: "Is there anything anywhere in the picture which says when and where this happened?"

"Nothing to say *where* it was," I said. "There's one place that says *when* it was, but that's at the other end and way up high. If you really want to see it, I'll have to get not only a stepladder but a magnifying glass."

"Some other time," she said.

I described it for her. "There's this Maori, a corporal in the New Zealand Field Artillery who was captured in a battle outside Tobruk, Libya. I'm sure you know who the Maoris are," I said.

"They're Polynesians," she said. "They're the aborigines of New Zealand."

"Exactly!" I said. "They were cannibals and were divided into many warring tribes until the white man came. So this Polynesian is sitting on a discarded German ammunition box. There are three bullets still in the bottom of it, in case anybody needs one. He is trying to read what is an inside page from a newspaper. He has grabbed it as it scuttled across the valley in the breeze that came with sunrise."

I went on, my fingertips touching the light switch: "The page is from an anti-Semitic weekly published in Riga, Latvia, during the German occupation of that little country. It is six months old, and offers tips on gardening and home canning. The Maori is studying it very earnestly, in the hopes of learning what we would all like to know about ourselves: where he is, what is going on, and what is likely to happen next.

"If we had a stepladder and a magnifying glass, Mrs. Berman, you could see for yourself that written in tiny characters on the ammunition box is this date, when you were only one year old: 'May 8, 1945.'"

•   •   •

I took one last look at "Now It's the Women's Turn," which was foreshortened again into a seeming triangle of close-packed jewels. I did not have to wait for the neighbors and Celeste's schoolmates to arrive before knowing that it was going to be the most popular painting in my collection.

"Jesus, Circe!" I said. "It looks like a million bucks!"

"It really does," she said.

Out went the lights.

37

W HEN WE SAUNTERED back to this house through the darkness, she held my hand, and she said I had taken her dancing after all.

"When was that?" I said.

"We're dancing now," she said.

"Oh," I said.

She said again that she couldn't imagine how I or anybody could have made such a big, beautiful painting about something so important.

"I can't believe I did it myself," I said. "Maybe I didn't. Maybe it was done by potato bugs."

She said that she looked at all the Polly Madison books in Celeste's room one time, and couldn't believe she'd written them.

"Maybe you're a plagiarist," I said.

"That's what I feel like sometimes," she said.

When we reached this house, and although we had not and never would make love, our moods were postcoital. May I say, without seeming boastful, that I had never seen her so *languorous*?

•   •   •

She surrendered her body, ordinarily so restless, so twitchy and itchy, to a voluptuously cushioned easy chair in the library. Marilee Kemp was in the room, too, in a ghostly way. The bound volume of letters she had written to an Armenian child in California was on the coffee table between me and Mrs. Berman.

I asked Mrs. Berman what she would have thought if the barn had been empty, or if the eight panels had been blanks, or if I had reconstructed "Windsor Blue Number Seventeen."

"If you had really been that empty, which I thought you were," she said, "I guess I would have had to give you an A-plus for sincerity."

•   •   •

I asked her if she would write. I meant letters to me, but she thought I meant books. "That's all I do—that and dancing," she said. "As long as I keep that up, I keep grief away." All summer long, she had made it easy to forget that she had recently lost a husband who was evidently brilliant and funny and adorable.

"One other thing helps a little bit," she said. "It works for me. It probably wouldn't work for you. That's talking loud and brassy, telling everybody when they're right and wrong, giving orders to everybody: 'Wake up! Cheer up! Get to work!' "

"Twice now I've been a Lazarus," I said. "I died with Terry Kitchen, and Edith brought me back to life again. I died with dear Edith, and Circe Berman brought me back to life again."

"Whoever that is," she said.

• • •

We talked some about Gerald Hildreth, the man who would come at eight in the morning to take her and her luggage to the airport in his taxicab. He was a local character about sixty years old. Everybody out this way knows Gerald Hildreth and his taxicab.

"He used to be on the Rescue Squad," I said, "and I think he and my first wife might have had a little fling. He was the one who found Jackson Pollock's body sixty feet from where his car hit the tree. Then, in a few weeks, he was gathering up the pieces of Terry Kitchen's head in a plastic bag. You'd have to say he's played an important part in Art History."

"The last time I rode with him," she said, "he told me his family had been working hard out here for three hundred years, but that all he had to show for it was his taxicab."

"It's a nice taxicab," I said.

"Yes, he keeps it polished on the outside and vacuumed on the inside," she said. "I guess that's how *he* keeps grief away— whatever it is he's got to grieve about."

"Three hundred years," I said.

• • •

We worried about Paul Slazinger. I speculated as to what his helpless soul must have felt like when it realized that his meat had thrown itself down on a hand grenade which was about to go off.

"Why didn't it kill him?" she said.

"Unforgivably sloppy workmanship at the hand grenade factory," I said.

"His meat did that, and *your* meat made the picture in the potato barn," she said.

"Sounds right," I said. "My soul didn't know what kind of picture to paint, but my meat sure did."

She cleared her throat. "Well, then," she said, "isn't it time for your soul, which has been ashamed of your meat for so long, to thank your meat for finally doing something wonderful?"

I thought that over. "That sounds right, too," I said.

"You have to actually *do* it," she said.

"How?" I said.

"Hold your hands in front of your eyes," she said, "and look at those strange and clever animals with love and gratitude, and tell them out loud: 'Thank you, Meat.' "

So I did.

I held my hands in front of my eyes, and I said out loud and with all my heart: 'Thank you, Meat.' "

Oh, happy Meat. Oh, happy Soul. Oh, happy Rabo Karabekian.

HOCUS POCUS

The author of this book did not have access to writing paper of uniform size and quality. He wrote in a library housing some eight hundred thousand volumes of interest to no one else. Most had never been read and probably never would be read, so there was nothing to stop him from tearing out their blank endpapers for stationery. This he did not do. Why he did not do this is not known. Whatever the reason, he wrote this book in pencil on everything from brown wrapping paper to the backs of business cards. The unconventional lines separating passages within chapters indicate where one scrap ended and the next began. The shorter the passage, the smaller the scrap.

One can speculate that the author, fishing through trash for anything to write on, may have hoped to establish a reputation for humility or insanity, since he was facing trial. It is equally likely, though, that he began this book impulsively, having no idea it would become a book, scribbling words on a scrap which happened to be right at hand. It could be that he found it congenial, then, to continue on from scrap to scrap, as though each were a bottle for him to fill. When he filled one up, possibly, no matter what its size, he could satisfy himself that he had written everything there was to write about this or that.

He numbered all the pages so there could be no doubt about their being sequential, nor about his hope that someone, undaunted by their disreputable appearance, would read them as a book. He in fact says here and there, with increasing confidence as he nears the end, that what he is doing is writing a book.

There are several drawings of a tombstone. The author made only one such drawing. The others are tracings of the original, probably made by superimposing translucent pieces of paper and pressing them against a sunlit library windowpane. He wrote words on the face of each burial marker, and in one case simply a question mark. These did not reproduce well on a printed page. So they have been set in type instead.

The author himself is responsible for the capitalization of certain words whose initial letters a meticulous editor might prefer to see in lowercase. So, too, did Eugene Debs Hartke choose for reasons unexplained to let numbers stand for themselves, except at the heads of sentences, rather than put them into words: for example, "2" instead of "two." He may have felt that numbers lost much of their potency when diluted by an alphabet.

To virtually all of his idiosyncrasies I, after much thought, have applied what another author once told me was the most sacred word in a great editor's vocabulary. That word is "stet."

                                                                    K.V.

This work of pure fiction is dedicated to the memory of

EUGENE VICTOR DEBS
1855–1926

"While there is a lower class
I am in it.
While there is a criminal element
I am of it.
While there is a soul in prison
I am not free."

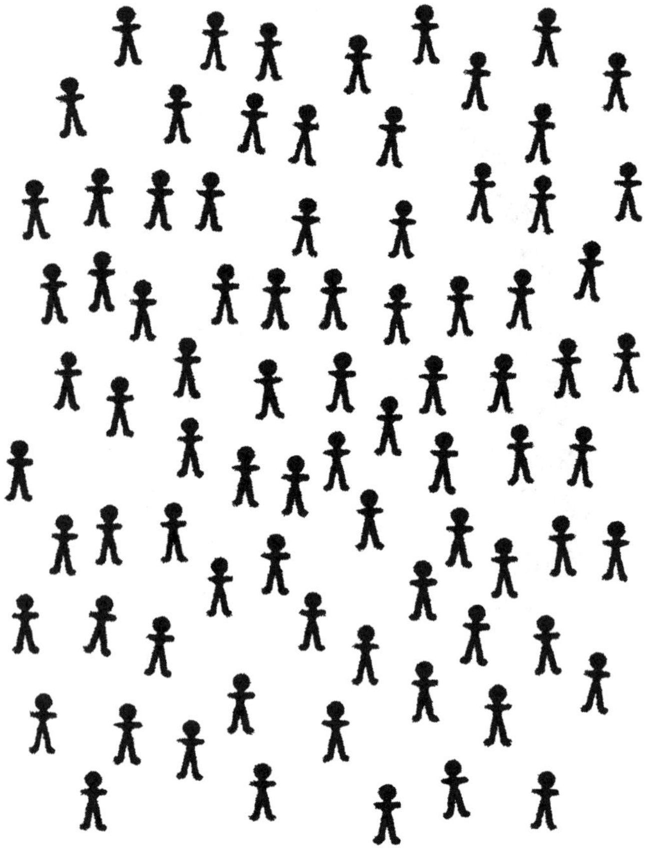

1

M Y NAME is Eugene Debs Hartke, and I was born in 1940. I was named at the behest of my maternal grandfather, Benjamin Wills, who was a Socialist and an Atheist, and nothing but a groundskeeper at Butler University, in Indianapolis, Indiana, in honor of Eugene Debs of Terre Haute, Indiana. Debs was a Socialist and a Pacifist and a Labor Organizer who ran several times for the Presidency of the United States of America, and got more votes than has any other candidate nominated by a third party in the history of this country.

Debs died in 1926, when I was a negative 14 years of age.

The year is 2001 now.

If all had gone the way a lot of people thought it would, Jesus Christ would have been among us again, and the American flag would have been planted on Venus and Mars.

No such luck!

At least the World will end, an event anticipated with great joy by many. It will end very soon, but not in the year 2000, which has come and gone. From that I conclude that God Almighty is not heavily into Numerology.

Grandfather Benjamin Wills died in 1948, when I was a plus 8 years of age, but not before he made sure that I knew by heart the most famous words uttered by Debs, which are:

"While there is a lower class I am in it. While there is a criminal element I am of it. While there is a soul in prison I am not free."

I, Debs' namesake, however, became anything but a bleeding heart. From the time I was 21 until I was 35 I was a professional soldier, a Commissioned Officer in the United States Army. During those 14 years I would have killed Jesus Christ Himself or Herself or Itself or Whatever, if ordered to do so by a superior officer. At the abrupt and humiliating and dishonorable end of the Vietnam War, I was a Lieutenant Colonel, with 1,000s and 1,000s of my own inferiors.

During that war, which was about nothing but the ammunition business, there was a microscopic possibility, I suppose, that I called in a white-phosphorus barrage or a napalm air strike on a returning Jesus Christ.

I never wanted to be a professional soldier, although I turned out to be a good one, if there can be such a thing. The idea that I should go to West Point came up as unexpectedly as the finale of the Vietnam War, near the end of my senior year in high school. I was all set to go to the University of Michigan, and take courses in English and History and Political Science, and work on the student daily paper there in preparation for a career as a journalist.

But all of a sudden my father, who was a chemical engineer involved in making plastics with a half-life of 50,000 years, and as full of excrement as a Christmas turkey, said I should go to West Point instead. He had never been in the military himself. During World War II, he was too valuable as a civilian deep-thinker about chemicals to be put in a soldier suit and turned into a suicidal, homicidal imbecile in 13 weeks.

I had already been accepted by the University of Michigan, when this offer to me of an appointment to the United States Military Academy came out of the blue. The offer arrived at a low point in my father's life, when he needed something to boast about which would impress our simple-minded neighbors. They would think an appointment to West Point was a great prize, like being picked for a professional baseball team.

So he said to me, as I used to say to infantry replacements fresh off the boat or plane in Vietnam, "This is a great opportunity."

What I would really like to have been, given a perfect world, is a jazz pianist. I mean jazz. I don't mean rock and roll. I mean the never-the-same-way-twice music the American black people gave the world. I played piano in my own all-white band in my all-white high school in Midland City, Ohio. We called ourselves "The Soul Merchants."

How good were we? We had to play white people's popular music, or nobody would have hired us. But every so often we would cut loose with jazz anyway. Nobody else seemed to notice the difference, but we sure did. We fell in love with ourselves. We were in ecstasy.

Father should never have made me go to West Point.

Never mind what he did to the environment with his nonbio-degradable plastics. Look what he did to me! What a boob he was! And my mother agreed with every decision he ever made, which makes *her* another blithering nincompoop.

They were both killed 20 years ago in a freak accident in a gift shop on the Canadian side of Niagara Falls, which the Indians in this valley used to call "Thunder Beaver," when the roof fell in.

There are no dirty words in this book, except for "hell" and "God," in case someone is fearing that an innocent child might see 1. The expression I will use here and there for the end of the Vietnam War, for example, will be: "when the excrement hit the air-conditioning."

Perhaps the only precept taught me by Grandfather Wills that I have honored all my adult life is that profanity and obscenity entitle people who don't want unpleasant information to close their ears and eyes to you.

The more alert soldiers who served under me in Vietnam would comment in some amazement that I never used profanity, which made me unlike anybody else they had ever met in the Army. They might ask if this was because I was religious.

I would reply that religion had nothing to do with it. I am in fact pretty much an Atheist like my mother's father, although I kept that to myself. Why argue somebody else out of the expectation of some sort of an Afterlife?

"I don't use profanity," I would say, "because your life and the lives of those around you may depend on your understanding what I tell you. OK? OK?"

I resigned my commission in 1975, after the excrement hit the air-conditioning, not failing, however, to father a son on my way home, unknowingly, during a brief stopover in the Philippines. I thought surely that the subsequent mother, a young female war correspondent for *The Des Moines Register*, was using foolproof birth control.

Wrong again!

Booby traps everywhere.

The biggest booby trap Fate set for me, though, was a pretty and personable young woman named Margaret Patton, who allowed me to woo and marry her soon after my graduation from West Point, and then had 2 children by me without telling me that there was a powerful strain of insanity on her mother's side of her family.

So then her mother, who was living with us, went insane, and then she herself went insane. Our children, moreover, had every reason to suspect that they, too, might go crazy in middle age.

Our children, full-grown now, can never forgive us for reproducing. What a mess.

I realize that my speaking of my first and only wife as something as inhuman as a booby trap risks my seeming to be yet another infernal device. But many other women have had no trouble relating to me as a person, and ardently, too, and my interest in them has gone well beyond the merely mechanical. Almost invariably, I have been as enchanted by their souls, their intellects, and the stories of their lives as by their amorous propensities.

But after I came home from the Vietnam War, and before either Margaret or her mother had shown me and the children and the neighbors great big symptoms of their inherited craziness, that mother-daughter team treated me like some sort of boring but necessary electrical appliance like a vacuum cleaner.

Good things have also happened unexpectedly, "manna from Heaven" you might want to call them, but not in such quantities as to make life a bowl of cherries or anything approaching that. Right after my war, when I had no idea what to do with the rest of my life, I ran into a former commanding officer of mine who had become President of Tarkington College, in Scipio, New York. I was then only 35, and my wife was still sane, and my mother-in-law was only slightly crazy. He offered me a teaching job, which I accepted.

I could accept that job with a clear conscience, despite my lack of academic credentials beyond a mere BS Degree from West Point, since all the students at Tarkington were learning-disabled in some way, or plain stupid or comatose or whatever. No matter what the subject, my old CO assured me, I would have little trouble keeping ahead of them.

The particular subject he wanted me to teach, what's more, was 1 in which I had excelled at the Academy, which was Physics.

The greatest stroke of luck for me, the biggest chunk of manna from Heaven, was that Tarkington had need of somebody to play the Lutz Carillon, the great family of bells at the top of the tower of the college library, where I am writing now.

I asked my old CO if the bells were swung by ropes.

He said they used to be, but that they had been electrified and were played by means of a keyboard now.

"What does the keyboard look like?" I said.

"Like a piano," he said.

I had never played bells. Very few people have that clanging opportunity. But I could play a piano. So I said, "Shake hands with your new carillonneur."

The happiest moments in my life, without question, were when I played the Lutz Carillon at the start and end of every day.

I went to work at Tarkington 25 years ago, and have lived in this beautiful valley ever since. This is home.

I have been a teacher here. I was a Warden for a little while, after Tarkington College officially became Tarkington State Reformatory in June of 1999, 20 months ago.

Now I myself am a prisoner here, but with pretty much the run of the place. I haven't been convicted of anything yet. I am awaiting trial, which I guess will take place in Rochester, for supposedly having masterminded the mass prison break at the New York State Maximum Security Adult Correctional Institution at Athena, across the lake from here.

It turns out that I also have tuberculosis, and my poor, addled wife Margaret and her mother have been put by court order into a lunatic asylum in Batavia, New York, something I had never had the guts to do.

I am so powerless and despised now that the man I am named after, Eugene Debs, if he were still alive, might at last be somewhat fond of me.

2

I N MORE optimistic times, when it was not widely under-stood that human beings were killing the planet with the by-products of their own ingenuity and that a new Ice Age had begun in any case, the generic name for the sort of horse-drawn covered wagon that carried freight and settlers across the prairies of what was to become the United States of America, and eventually across the Rocky Mountains to the Pacific Ocean, was "Conestoga"—since the first of these were built in the Conestoga Valley of Pennsylvania.

They kept the pioneers supplied with cigars, among other things, so that cigars nowadays, in the year 2001, are still called "stogies" sometimes, which is short for "Conestoga."

By 1830, the sturdiest and most popular of these wagons were in fact made by the Mohiga Wagon Company right here in Scipio, New York, at the pinched waist of Lake Mohiga, the deepest and coldest and westernmost of the long and narrow Finger Lakes. So sophisticated cigar-smokers might want to stop calling their stinkbombs "stogies" and call them "mogies" or "higgies" instead.

The founder of the Mohiga Wagon Company was Aaron Tarkington, a brilliant inventor and manufacturer who never-theless could not read or write. He now would be identified as a blameless inheritor of the genetic defect known as dyslexia. He said of himself that he was like the Emperor Charlemagne, "too busy to learn to read and write." He was not too busy, however, to have his wife read to him for 2 hours every evening. He had an excellent memory, for he delivered weekly lectures to the workmen at the factory that were laced with lengthy quotations from Shakespeare and Homer and the Bible, and on and on.

He sired 4 children, a son and 3 daughters, all of whom could read and write. But they still carried the gene of dyslexia, which would disqualify several of their own descendants from getting very far in conventional schemes of education. Two of Aaron Tarkington's children were so far from being dyslexic,

in fact, as to themselves write books, which I have read only
now, and which nobody, probably, will ever read again. Aaron's
only son, Elias, wrote a technical account of the construction
of the Onondaga Canal, which connected the northern end of
Lake Mohiga to the Erie Canal just south of Rochester. And
the youngest daughter, Felicia, wrote a novel called *Carpathia*,
about a headstrong, high-born young woman in the Mohiga
Valley who fell in love with a half-Indian lock-tender on that
same canal.

That canal is all filled in and paved over now, and is Route
53, which forks at the head of the lake, where the locks used to
be. One fork leads southwest through farm country to Scipio.
The other leads southeast through the perpetual gloom of the
Iroquois National Forest to the bald hilltop crowned by the
battlements of the New York State Maximum Security Adult
Correctional Institution at Athena, a hamlet directly across the
lake from Scipio.

Bear with me. This is history. I am trying to explain how this
valley, this verdant cul-de-sac, got to be what it is today.

All 3 of Aaron Tarkington's daughters married into prosperous and enterprising families in Cleveland, New York,
and Wilmington, Delaware—innocently making the threat of
dyslexia pandemic in an emerging ruling class of bankers and
industrialists, largely displaced in my time by Germans, Koreans, Italians, English, and, of course, Japanese.

The son of Aaron, Elias, remained in Scipio and took over
his father's properties, adding to them a brewery and a steam-
driven carpet factory, the first such in the state. There was no
water power in Scipio, whose industrial prosperity until the
introduction of steam was based not on cheap energy and
locally available raw materials but on inventiveness and high
standards of workmanship.

Elias Tarkington never married. He was severely wounded
at the age of 54 while a civilian observer at the Battle of Gettysburg, top hat and all. He was there to see the debuts of 2 of
his inventions, a mobile field kitchen and a pneumatic recoil

mechanism for heavy artillery. The field kitchen, incidentally, with slight modifications, would later be adopted by the Barnum & Bailey Circus, and then by the German Army during World War I.

Elias Tarkington was a tall and skinny man with chin whiskers and a stovepipe hat. He was shot through the right chest at Gettysburg, but not fatally.

The man who shot him was 1 of the few Confederate soldiers to reach the Union lines during Pickett's Charge. That Johnny Reb died in ecstasy among his enemies, believing that he had shot Abraham Lincoln. A crumbling newspaper account I have found here in what used to be the college library, which is now the prison library, gives his last words as follows: "Go home, Bluebellies. Old Satan's daid."

During my 3 years in Vietnam, I certainly heard plenty of last words by dying American footsoldiers. Not 1 of them, however, had illusions that he had somehow accomplished something worthwhile in the process of making the Supreme Sacrifice.

One boy of only 18 said to me while he was dying and I was holding him in my arms, "Dirty joke, dirty joke."

3

E LIAS TARKINGTON, the severely wounded Abraham Lincoln look-alike, was brought home in 1 of his own wagons to Scipio to his estate overlooking the town and lake.

He was not well educated, and was more a mechanic than a scientist, and so spent his last 3 years trying to invent what anyone familiar with Newton's Laws would have known was an impossibility, a perpetual-motion machine. He had no fewer than 27 contraptions built, which he foolishly expected to go on running, after he had given them an initial spin or whack, until Judgment Day.

I found 19 of those stubborn, mocking machines in the attic of what used to be their inventor's mansion, which in my time was the home of the College President, about a year after I came to work at Tarkington. I brought them back downstairs and into the 20th Century. Some of my students and I cleaned them up and restored any parts that had deteriorated during the intervening 100 years. At the least they were exquisite jewelry, with garnets and amethysts for bearings, with arms and legs of exotic woods, with tumbling balls of ivory, with chutes and counterweights of silver. It was as though dying Elias hoped to overwhelm science with the magic of precious materials.

The longest my students and I could get the best of them to run was 51 seconds. Some eternity!

To me, and I passed this on to my students, the restored devices demonstrated not only how quickly anything on Earth runs down without steady infusions of energy. They reminded us, too, of the craftsmanship no longer practiced in the town below. Nobody down there in our time could make things that cunning and beautiful.

Yes, and we took the 10 machines we agreed were the most beguiling, and we put them on permanent exhibit in the foyer of this library underneath a sign whose words can surely be applied to this whole ruined planet nowadays:

THE COMPLICATED FUTILITY OF IGNORANCE

I have discovered from reading old newspapers and letters and diaries from back then that the men who built the
machines for Elias Tarkington knew from the first that they
would never work, whatever the reason. Yet what love they
lavished on the materials that comprised them! How is this for
a definition of high art: "Making the most of the raw materials
of futility"?

Still another perpetual-motion machine envisioned by Elias
Tarkington was what his Last Will and Testament called "The
Mohiga Valley Free Institute." Upon his death, this new school
would take possession of his 3,000-hectare estate above Scipio,
plus half the shares in the wagon company, the carpet company,
and the brewery. The other half was already owned by his sisters
far away. On his deathbed he predicted that Scipio would 1 day
be a great metropolis and that its wealth would transform his
little college into a university to rival Harvard and Oxford and
Heidelberg.

It was to offer a free college education to persons of either
sex, and of any age or race or religion, living within 40 miles
of Scipio. Those from farther away would pay a modest fee. In
the beginning, it would have only 1 full-time employee, the
President. The teachers would be recruited right here in Scipio.
They would take a few hours off from work each week, to teach
what they knew. The chief engineer at the wagon company, for
example, whose name was André Lutz, was a native of Liège,
Belgium, and had served as an apprentice to a bell founder
there. He would teach Chemistry. His French wife would teach
French and Watercolor Painting. The brewmaster at the brewery, Hermann Shultz, a native of Leipzig, would teach Botany
and German and the flute. The Episcopalian priest, Dr. Alan
Clewes, a graduate of Harvard, would teach Latin, Greek,
Hebrew, and the Bible. The dying man's physician, Dalton Polk,
would teach Biology and Shakespeare, and so on.

And it came to pass.

In 1869 the new college enrolled its first class, 9 students in all, and all from right here in Scipio. Four were of ordinary college age. One was a Union veteran who had lost his legs at Shiloh. One was a former black slave 40 years old. One was a spinster 82 years old.

The first President was only 26 years old, a schoolteacher from Athena, 2 kilometers by water from Scipio. There was no prison over there back then, but only a slate quarry and a sawmill and a few subsistence farms. His name was John Peck. He was a cousin of the Tarkingtons. His branch of the family, however, was and remains unhampered by dyslexia. He has numerous descendants in the present day, 1 of whom, in fact, is a speech writer for the Vice-President of the United States.

Young John Peck and his wife and 2 children and his mother-in-law arrived at Scipio by rowboat, with Peck and his wife at the oars, their children seated in the stern, and their luggage and the mother-in-law in another boat they towed behind.

They took up residence on the third floor of what had been Elias Tarkington's mansion. The rooms on the first 2 floors would be classrooms, a library, which was already a library with 280 volumes collected by the Tarkingtons, study halls, and a dining room. Many treasures from the past were taken up to the attic to make room for the new activities. Among these were the failed perpetual-motion machines. They would gather dust and cobwebs until 1978, when I found them up there, and realized what they were, and brought them down the stairs again.

One week before the first class was held, which was in Latin, taught by the Episcopalian priest Alan Clewes, André Lutz the Belgian arrived at the mansion with 3 wagons carrying a very heavy cargo, a carillon consisting of 32 bells. He had cast them on his own time and at his own expense in the wagon factory's foundry. They were made from mingled Union and Confederate rifle barrels and cannonballs and bayonets gathered up after the Battle of Gettysburg. They were the first bells and surely the last bells ever to be cast in Scipio.

Nothing, in my opinion, will ever again be cast in Scipio. No industrial arts of any sort will ever again be practiced here.

André Lutz gave the new college all those bells, even though there was no place to hang them. He said he did it because he was so sure that it would 1 day be a great university with a bell tower and everything. He was dying of emphysema as a result of the fumes from molten metals that he had been breathing since he was 10 years old. He had no time to wait for a place to hang the most wonderful consequence of his having been alive for a little while, which was all those bells, bells, bells.

They were no surprise. They had been 18 months in the making. The founders whose work he supervised had shared his dreams of immortality as they made things as impractical and beautiful as bells, bells, bells.

So all the bells but 1 from a middle octave were slathered with grease to prevent their rusting and stored in 4 ranks in the estate's great barn, 200 meters from the mansion. The 1 bell that was going to get to sing at once was installed in the cupola of the mansion, with its rope running all the way down to the first floor. It would call people to classes and, if need be, also serve as a fire alarm.

The rest of the bells, it turned out, would slumber in the loft for 30 years, until 1899, when they were hanged as a family, the 1 from the cupola included, on axles in the belfry of the tower of a splendid library given to the school by the Moellenkamp family of Cleveland.

The Moellenkamps were also Tarkingtons, since the founder of their fortune had married a daughter of the illiterate Aaron Tarkington. Eleven of them so far had been dyslexic, and they had all gone to college in Scipio, since no other institution of higher learning would take them in.

The first Moellenkamp to graduate from here was Henry, who enrolled in 1875, when he was 19, and when the school was only 6 years old. It was at that time that its name was changed to Tarkington College. I have found the crumbling minutes

of the Board of Trustees meeting at which that name change
was made. Three of the 6 trustees were men who had married
daughters of Aaron Tarkington, 1 of them the grandfather of
Henry Moellenkamp. The other 3 trustees were the Mayor of
Scipio, and a lawyer who looked after the Tarkington daughters' interests in the valley, and the area Congressman, who was
surely the sisters' faithful servant, too, since they were partners
with the college in his district's most important industries.

And according to the minutes, which fell apart in my hands
as I read them, it was the grandfather of young Henry Moellenkamp who proposed the name change, saying that "The
Mohiga Valley Free Institute" sounded too much like a poor-
house or a hospital. It is my guess that he would not have
minded having the place sound like a catchment for the poor,
if only he had not suffered the misfortune of having his own
grandson go there.

It was in that same year, 1875, that work began across the
lake from Scipio, on a hilltop above Athena, on a prison camp
for young criminals from big-city slums. It was believed that
fresh air and the wonders of Nature would improve their souls
and bodies to the point that they would find it natural to be
good citizens.

When I came to work at Tarkington, there were only 300
students, a number that hadn't changed for 50 years. But the
rustic work-camp across the lake had become a brutal fortress
of iron and masonry on a naked hilltop, the New York State
Maximum Security Adult Correctional Institution at Athena,
keeping 5,000 of the state's worst criminals under lock and key.

Two years ago, Tarkington still had only 300 students, but
the population of the prison, under hideously overcrowded conditions, had grown to 10,000. And then, 1 cold winter's night,
it became the scene of the biggest prison break in American
history. Until then, nobody had ever escaped from Athena.

Suddenly, everybody was free to leave, and to take a weapon
from the prison armory, too, if he had use for 1. The lake

between the prison and the little college was frozen solid, as easily traversed as the parking lot of a great shopping mall.

What next?

Yes, and by the time André Lutz's bells were at last made to sing as a carillon, Tarkington College had not only a new library but luxurious dormitories, a science building, an art building, a chapel, a theater, a dining hall, an administration building, 2 new buildings of classrooms, and athletic facilities that were the envy of the institutions with which it had begun to compete in track and fencing and swimming and baseball, which were Hobart, the University of Rochester, Cornell, Union, Amherst, and Bucknell.

These structures bore the names of wealthy families as grateful as the Moellenkamps for all the college had managed to do for offspring of theirs whom conventional colleges had deemed ineducable. Most were unrelated to the Moellenkamps or to anyone who carried the Tarkington gene of dyslexia. Nor were the young they sent to Tarkington necessarily troubled by dyslexia. All sorts of different things were wrong with them, including an inability to write legibly with pen and ink, although what they tried to write down made perfect sense, and stammering so severe as to prevent their saying a word in class, and petit mal, which caused their minds to go perfectly blank for seconds or minutes anywhere, anytime, and so on.

It was simply the Moellenkamps who first challenged the new little college to do what it could for a seemingly hopeless case of plutocratic juvenile incapacity, namely Henry. Not only would Henry graduate with honors from Tarkington. He would go on to Oxford, taking with him a male companion who read aloud to him and wrote down thoughts Henry could only express orally. Henry would become 1 of the most brilliant speakers in a golden age of American purple, bow-wow oratory, and serve as a Congressman and then a United States Senator from Ohio for 36 years.

That same Henry Moellenkamp was author of the lyrics to one of the most popular turn-of-the-century ballads, "Mary, Mary, Where Have You Gone?"

The melody of that ballad was composed by Henry's friend Paul Dresser, brother of the novelist Theodore Dreiser. This was 1 of the rare instances in which Dresser set another man's words to music instead of his own. And then Henry appropriated that tune and wrote, or rather dictated, new words which sentimentalized student life in this valley.

Thus was "Mary, Mary, Where Have You Gone?" transmogrified into the alma mater of this campus until it became a penitentiary 2 years ago.

History.

Accident after accident has made Tarkington what it is today. Who would dare to predict what it will be in 2021, only 20 years from now? The 2 prime movers in the Universe are Time and Luck.

As the tag line of my favorite dirty joke would have it: "Keep your hat on. We could wind up miles from here."

If Henry Moellenkamp had not come out of his mother's womb dyslexic, Tarkington College wouldn't even have been called Tarkington College. It would have gone on being The Mohiga Valley Free Institute, which would have died right along with the wagon factory and the carpet factory and the brewery when the railroads and highways connecting the East and West were built far to the north and south of Scipio—so as not to bridge the lake, so as not to have to penetrate the deep and dark virgin hardwood forest, now the Iroquois National Forest, to the east and south of here.

If Henry Moellenkamp hadn't come out of his mother's womb dyslexic, and if that mother hadn't been a Tarkington and so known about the little college on Lake Mohiga, this library would never have been built and filled with 800,000 bound volumes. When I was a professor here, that was 70,000 more bound volumes than Swarthmore College had! Among small colleges, this library used to be second only to the 1 at Oberlin, which had 1,000,000 bound volumes.

So what is this structure in which I sit now, thanks to Time and Luck? It is nothing less, friends and neighbors, than the greatest prison library in the history of crime and punishment!

It is very lonely in here. Hello? Hello?

———————————

I might have said the same sort of thing back when this was an 800,000-bound-volume college library: "It is very lonely in here. Hello? Hello?"

———————————

I have just looked up Harvard University. It has 13,000,000 bound volumes now. What a read!

And almost every book written for or about the ruling class.

———————————

If Henry Moellenkamp hadn't come out of his mother's womb dyslexic, there would never have been a tower in which to hang the Lutz Carillon.

Those bells might never have gotten to reverberate in the valley or anywhere. They probably would have been melted up and made back into weapons during World War I.

———————————

If Henry Moellenkamp had not come out of his mother's womb dyslexic, these heights above Scipio might have been all darkness on the cold winter night 2 years ago, with Lake Mohiga frozen hard as a parking lot, when 10,000 prisoners at Athena were suddenly set free.

Instead, there was a little galaxy of beckoning lights up here.

4

REGARDLESS of whether Henry Moellenkamp came out of his mother's womb dyslexic or not, I was born in Wilmington, Delaware, 18 months before this country joined the fighting in World War II. I have not seen Wilmington since. That is where they keep my birth certificate. I was the only child of a housewife and, as I've said, a chemical engineer. My father was then employed by E. I. Du Pont de Nemours & Company, a manufacturer of high explosives, among other things.

When I was 2 years old, we moved to Midland City, Ohio, where a washing-machine company named Robo-Magic Corporation was beginning to make bomb-release mechanisms and swivel mounts for machine guns on B-17 bombers. The plastics industry was then in its infancy, and Father was sent to Robo-Magic to determine what synthetic materials from Du Pont could be used in the weapons systems in place of metal, in order to make them lighter.

By the time the war was over, the company had gotten out of the washing-machine business entirely, had changed its name to Barrytron, Limited, and was making weapon, airplane, and motor vehicle parts composed of plastics it had developed on its own. My father had become the company's Vice-President in Charge of Research and Development.

When I was about 17, Du Pont bought Barrytron in order to capture several of its patents. One of the plastics Father had helped to develop, I remember, had the ability to scatter radar signals, so that an airplane clad in it would look like a flock of geese to our enemies.

This material, which has since been used to make virtually indestructible skateboards and crash helmets and skis and motorcycle fenders and so on, was an excuse, when I was a boy, for increasing security precautions at Barrytron. To keep Communists from finding out how it was made, a single fence topped with barbed wire was no longer adequate. A second fence was put outside that one, and the space between them was patrolled around the clock by humorless, jackbooted armed guards with lean and hungry Dobermans.

When Du Pont took over Barrytron, the double fence, the Dobermans, my father and all, I was a high school senior, all set to go to the University of Michigan to learn how to be a journalist, to serve John Q. Public's right to know. Two members of my 6-piece band, The Soul Merchants, the clarinet and the string bass, were also going to Michigan.

We were going to stick together and go on making music at Ann Arbor. Who knows? We might have become so popular that we went on world tours and made great fortunes, and been superstars at peace rallies and love-ins when the Vietnam War came along.

Cadets at West Point did not make music. The musicians in the dance band and the marching band were Regular Army enlisted men, members of the servant class.

They were under orders to play music as written, note for note, and never mind how they felt about the music or about anything.

For that matter, there wasn't any student publication at West Point. So never mind how the cadets felt about anything. Not interesting.

I was fine, but all kinds of things were going wrong with my father's life. Du Pont was looking him over, as they were looking over everybody at Barrytron, deciding whether to keep him on or not. He was also having a love affair with a married woman whose husband caught him in the act and beat him up.

This was a sensitive subject with my parents, naturally, so I never discussed it with them. But the story was all over town, and Father had a black eye. He didn't play any sports, so he had to make up a story about falling down the basement stairs. Mother weighed about 90 kilograms by then, and berated him all the time about his having sold all his Barrytron stock 2 years too soon. If he had hung on to it until the Du Pont takeover, he would have had $1,000,000, back when it meant something to be a millionaire. If I had been learning-disabled, he could easily have afforded to send me to Tarkington.

Unlike me, he was the sort of man who had to be in extremis in order to commit adultery. According to a story I heard from enemies at high school, Father had done the jumping-out-the-window thing, hippity-hopping like Peter Cottontail across backyards with his pants around his ankles, and getting bitten by a dog, and getting tangled up in a clothesline, and all the rest of it. That could have been an exaggeration. I never asked.

I myself was deeply troubled by our little family's image problem, which was complicated when Mother broke her nose 2 days after Father got the black eye. To the outside world it looked as though she had said something to Father about the reason he had a black eye, and his reply had been to slug her. I didn't think he would ever slug her, no matter what.

There is a not quite remote possibility that he really did slug her, of course. Lesser men would have slugged her under similar circumstances. The real truth of the matter became unavailable to historians forever when the falling ceiling of a gift shop on the Canadian side of Niagara Falls killed both participants, as I've said, some 20 years ago. They were said to have died instantly. They never knew what hit them, which is the best way to go.

There was no argument about that in Vietnam or, I suppose, on any battlefield. One kid I remember stepped on an antipersonnel mine. The mine could have been one of our own. His best friend from Basic Training asked him what he could do for him, and the kid replied: "Turn me off like a light bulb, Sam."

The dying kid was white. The kid who wanted to help him was black, or a light tan, actually. His features were practically white, you would have to say.

A woman I was making love to a few years ago asked me if my parents were still alive. She wanted to know more about me, now that we had our clothes off.

I told her that they had suffered violent deaths in a foreign country, which was true. Canada is a foreign country.

But then I heard myself spinning this fantastic tale of their being on a safari in Tanganyika, a place about which I know almost nothing. I told that woman, and she believed me, that my parents and their guide were shot by poachers who were killing elephants for their ivory and mistook them for game wardens. I said that the poachers put their bodies on top of anthills, so that their skeletons were soon picked clean. They could be positively identified only by their dental work.

I used to find it easy and even exhilarating to lie that elaborately. I don't anymore. And I wonder now if I didn't develop that unwholesome habit very young, and because my parents were such an embarrassment, and especially my mother, who was fat enough to be a circus freak. I described much more attractive parents than I really had, in order to make people who knew nothing about them think well of me.

And during my final year in Vietnam, when I was in Public Information, I found it as natural as breathing to tell the press and replacements fresh off the boats or planes that we were clearly winning, and that the folks back home should be proud and happy about all the good things we were doing there.

I learned to lie like that in high school.

Another thing I learned in high school that was helpful in Vietnam: Alcohol and marijuana, if used in moderation, plus loud, usually low-class music, make stress and boredom infinitely more bearable. It was manna from Heaven that I came into this world with a gift for moderation in my intake of mood-modifying substances. During my last 2 years in high school, I don't think my parents even suspected that I was half in the bag a lot of the time. All they ever complained about was the music, when I played the radio or the phonograph or when The Soul Merchants rehearsed in our basement, which Mom and Dad said was jungle music, and much too loud.

In Vietnam, the music was always much too loud. Practically everybody was half in the bag, including Chaplains. Several of the most gruesome accidents I had to explain to the press during my last year over there were caused by people who had rendered themselves imbecilic or maniacal by ingesting too much of what, if taken in moderation, could be a helpful chemical. I ascribed all such accidents, of course, to human error. The press understood. Who on this Earth hasn't made a mistake or 2?

The assassination of an Austrian archduke led to World War I, and probably to World War II as well. Just as surely, my father's black eye brought me to the sorry state in which I find myself today. He was looking for some way, almost any way, to recapture the respect of the community, and to attract favorable attention from Barrytron's new owner, Du Pont. Du Pont, of course, has now been taken over by I. G. Farben of Germany, the same company that manufactured and packaged and labeled and addressed the cyanide gas used to kill civilians of all ages, including babes in arms, during the Holocaust.

What a planet.

So Father, his injured eye looking like a slit in a purple and yellow omelet, asked me if I was likely to receive any sort of honors at high school graduation. He didn't say so, but he was frantic for something to brag about at work. He was so desperate that he was trying to get blood out of the turnip of my nonparticipation in high school sports, student government, or school-sponsored extracurricular activities. My grade average was high enough to get me into the University of Michigan, and on the honor roll now and then, but not into the National Honor Society.

It was so pitiful! It made me mad, too, because he was trying to make me partly responsible for the family's image problem, which was all his fault. "I was always sorry you didn't go out for football," he said, as though a touchdown would have made everything all right again.

"Too late now," I said.

"You let those 4 years slip by without doing anything but making jungle music," he said.

It occurs to me now, a mere 43 years later, that I might have said to him that at least I managed my sex life better than he had managed his. I was getting laid all the time, thanks to jungle music, and so were the other Soul Merchants. Certain sorts of not just girls but full-grown women, too, found us glamorous free spirits up on the bandstand, imitating black people and smoking marijuana, and loving ourselves when we made music, and laughing about God knows what just about anytime.

———————

I guess my love life is over now. Even if I could get out of prison, I wouldn't want to give some trusting woman tuberculosis. She would be scared to death of getting AIDS, and I would give her TB instead. Wouldn't that be nice?

So now I will have to make do with memories. As a prosthesis for my memory, I have begun to list all the women, excluding my wife and prostitutes, with whom I have "gone all the way," as we used to say in high school. I find it impossible to remember any conquest I made as a teenager with clarity, to separate fact from fantasy. It was all a dream. So I begin my list with Shirley Kern, to whom I made love when I was 20. Shirley is my datum.

How many names will there be on the list? Too early to tell, but wouldn't that number, whatever it turns out to be, be as good a thing as any to put on my tombstone as an enigmatic epitaph?

———————

I am certainly sorry if I ruined the lives of any of those women who believed me when I said I loved them. I can only hope against hope that Shirley Kern and all the rest of them are still OK.

If it is any consolation to those who may not be OK, my own life was ruined by a Science Fair.

Father asked me if there wasn't some school-sponsored extracurricular activity I could still try out for. This was only 8 weeks before my graduation! So I said, in a spirit of irony, since he knew science did not delight me as it delighted him, that my last opportunity to amount to anything was the County Science Fair. I got Bs in Physics and Chemistry, but you could stuff both those subjects up your fundament as far as I was concerned.

But Father rose from his chair in a state of sick excitement. "Let's go down in the basement," he said. "There's work to do."

"What kind of work?" I said. This was about midnight.

And he said, "You are going to enter and win the Science Fair."

───────────────

Which I did. Or, rather, Father entered and won the Science Fair, requiring only that I sign an affidavit swearing that the exhibit was all my own work, and that I memorize his explanation of what it proved. It was about crystals and how they grew and why they grew.

His competition was weak. He was, after all, a 43-year-old chemical engineer with 20 years in industry, taking on teenagers in a community where few parents had higher educations. The main business in the county back then was still agriculture, corn and pigs and beef cattle. Barrytron was the sole sophisticated industry, and only a handful of people such as Father understood its processes and apparatus. Most of the company's employees were content to do what they were told and incurious as to how it was, exactly, that they had worked the miracles that somehow arrived all packaged and labeled and addressed on the loading docks.

I am reminded now of dead American soldiers, teenagers mostly, all packaged and labeled and addressed on loading docks in Vietnam. How many people knew or cared how these curious artifacts were actually manufactured?

A few.

───────────────

Why Father and I were not branded as swindlers, why my exhibit was not thrown out of the Science Fair, why I am a prisoner awaiting trial now instead of a star reporter for the Korean owners of *The New York Times* has to do with compassion, I now believe. The feeling was general in the community,

I think, that our little family had suffered enough. Nobody in the county gave much of a darn about science anyway.

The other exhibits were so dumb and pitiful, too, that the best of them would make the county look stupid if it and its honest creator went on to the statewide competition in Cleveland. Our exhibit sure looked slick and tidy. Another big plus from the judges' point of view, maybe, when they thought about what the county's best was going to be up against in Cleveland: our exhibit was extremely hard for an ordinary person to understand or find at all interesting.

I remained philosophical, thanks to marijuana and alcohol, while the community decided whether to crucify me as a fraud or to crown me as a genius. Father may have had a buzz on, too. Sometimes it's hard to tell. I served under 2 Generals in Vietnam who drank a quart of whiskey a day, but it was hard to detect. They always looked serious and dignified.

So off Father and I went to Cleveland. His spirits were high. I knew we would go smash up there. I don't know why he didn't know we would go smash up there. The only advice he gave me was to keep my shoulders back when I was explaining my exhibit and not to smoke where the judges might see me doing it. He was talking about ordinary cigarettes. He didn't know I smoked the other kind.

I make no apologies for having been zapped during my darkest days in high school. Winston Churchill was bombed out of his skull on brandy and Cuban cigars during the darkest days of World War II.

Hitler, of course, thanks to the advanced technology of Germany, was among the first human beings to turn their brains to cobwebs with amphetamine. He actually chewed on carpets, they say. Yum yum.

Mother did not come to Cleveland with Father and me. She was ashamed to leave the house, she was so big and fat. So I had to do most of the marketing after school. I also had to do most of the housework, she had so much trouble getting around. My familiarity with housework was useful at West Point, and then again when my mother-in-law and then my wife went nuts. It was actually sort of relaxing, because I could see that I had accomplished something undeniably good, and I didn't have to think about my troubles while I was doing it. How my mother's eyes used to shine when she saw what I had cooked for her!

My mother's story is 1 of the few real success stories in this book. She joined Weight Watchers when she was 60, which is my age now. When the ceiling fell on her at Niagara Falls she weighed only 52 kilograms!

This library is full of stories of supposed triumphs, which makes me very suspicious of it. It's misleading for people to read about great successes, since even for middle-class and upper-class white people, in my experience, failure is the norm. It is unfair to youngsters particularly to leave them wholly unprepared for monster screw-ups and starring roles in Keystone Kops comedies and much, much worse.

The Ohio Science Fair took place in Cleveland's beautiful Moellenkamp Auditorium. The theater seats had been removed and replaced with tables for all the exhibits. There was a hint of my then distant future in the auditorium's having been given to the city by the Moellenkamps, the same coal and shipping family that gave Tarkington College this library. This was long before they sold the boats and mines to a British and Omani consortium based in Luxembourg.

But the present was bad enough. Even as Father and I were setting up our exhibit, we were spotted by other contestants as a couple of comedians, as Laurel and Hardy, maybe, with Father as the fat and officious one and me as the dumb and skinny one. The thing was, Father was doing all the setting up, and I was standing around looking bored. All I wanted to do was go outside and hide behind a tree or something and smoke a cigarette. We were violating the most basic rule of the Fair, which was that the young exhibitors were supposed to do all the work, from start to finish. Parents or teachers or whatever were forbidden in writing to help at all.

It was as though I had entered the Soapbox Derby over in Akron, Ohio, in a car for coasting down hills that I had supposedly built myself but was actually my dad's Ferrari Gran Turismo.

———————————

We hadn't made any of the exhibit in the basement. When, at the very beginning, Father said that we should go down in the basement and get to work, we had actually gone down in the basement. But we stayed down there for only about 10 minutes while he thought and thought, growing ever more excited. I didn't say anything.

Actually, I *did* say one thing. "Mind if I smoke?" I said.

"Go right ahead," he said.

That was a breakthrough for me. It meant I could smoke in the house whenever I pleased, and he wouldn't say anything.

Then he led the way back up to the living room. He sat down at Mother's desk and made a list of things that should go into the exhibit.

"What are you doing, Dad?" I said.

"Shh," he said. "I'm busy. Don't bother me."

———————————

So I didn't bother him. I had more than enough to think about as it was. I was pretty sure I had gonorrhea. It was some sort of urethral infection, which was making me very uncomfortable. But I hadn't seen a doctor about it, because the doctor, by law, would have had to report me to the Department of Health, and my parents would have been told about it, as though they hadn't had enough heartaches already.

Whatever the infection was, it cleared itself up without my doing anything about it. It couldn't have been gonorrhea, which never stops eating you up of its own accord. Why should it ever stop of its own accord? It's having such a nice time. Why call off the party? Look how healthy and happy the kids are.

Twice in later life I would contract what was unambiguously gonorrhea, once in Tegucigalpa, Honduras, and then again in Saigon, now Ho Chi Minh City, in Vietnam. In both instances I told the doctors about the self-healing infection I had had in high school.

It might have been yeast, they said. I should have opened a bakery.

So Father started coming home from work with pieces of the exhibit, which had been made to his order at Barrytron: pedestals and display cases, and explanatory signs and labels made by the print shop that did a lot of work for Barrytron. The crystals themselves came from a Pittsburgh chemical supply house that did a lot of business with Barrytron. One crystal, I remember, came all the way from Burma.

The chemical supply house must have gone to some trouble to get together a remarkable collection of crystals for us, since what they sent us couldn't have come from their regular stock. In order to please a big customer like Barrytron, they may have gone to somebody who collected and sold crystals for their beauty and rarity, not as chemicals but as jewelry.

At any rate, the crystals, which were of museum quality, caused Father to utter these famous last words after he spread them out on the coffee table in our living room, gloatingly: "Son, there is no way we can lose."

Well, as Jean-Paul Sartre says in Bartlett's *Familiar Quotations*, "Hell is other people." Other people made short work of Father's and my invincible contest entry in Cleveland 43 years ago.

Generals George Armstrong Custer at the Little Bighorn, and Robert E. Lee at Gettysburg, and William Westmoreland in Vietnam all come to mind.

Somebody said 1 time, I remember, that General Custer's famous last words were, "Where are all these blankety-blank Injuns comin' from?"

Father and I, and not our pretty crystals, were for a little while the most fascinating exhibit in Moellenkamp Auditorium. We were a demonstration of abnormal psychology. Other contestants and their mentors gathered around us and put us through our paces. They certainly knew which buttons to push, so to speak, to make us change color or twist and turn or grin horribly or whatever.

One contestant asked Father how old he was and what high school he was attending.

That was when we should have packed up our things and gotten out of there. The judges hadn't had a look at us yet, and neither had any reporters. We hadn't yet put up the sign that said what my name was and what school system I represented. We hadn't yet said anything worth remembering.

If we had folded up and vanished quietly right then and there, leaving nothing but an empty table, we might have entered the history of American science as no-shows who got sick or something. There was already an empty table, which would stay empty, only 5 meters away from ours. Father and I had heard that it was going to stay empty and why. The would-be exhibitor and his mother and father were all in the hospital in Lima, Ohio, not Lima, Peru. That was their hometown. They had scarcely backed out of their driveway the day before, headed for Cleveland, they thought, with the exhibit in the trunk, when they were rear-ended by a drunk driver.

The accident wouldn't have been half as serious as it turned out to be if the exhibit hadn't included several bottles of different acids which broke and touched off the gasoline. Both vehicles were immediately engulfed in flames.

The exhibit was, I think, meant to show several important services that acids, which most people were afraid of and didn't like to think much about, were performing every day for Humanity.

The people who looked us over and asked us questions, and did not like what they saw and heard, sent for a judge. They wanted us disqualified. We were worse than dishonest. We were ridiculous!

I wanted to throw up. I said to Father, "Dad, honest to God, I think we better get out of here. We made a mistake."

But he said we had nothing to be ashamed of, and that we certainly weren't going to go home with our tails between our legs.

Vietnam!

So a judge did come over, and easily determined that I had no understanding whatsoever of the exhibit. He then took Father aside and negotiated a political settlement, man to man. He did not want to stir up bad feelings in our home county, which had sent me to Cleveland as its champion. Nor did he want to humiliate Father, who was an upstanding member of his community who obviously had not read the rules carefully. He would not humiliate us with a formal disqualification, which might attract unfavorable publicity, if Father in turn would not insist on having my entry put in serious competition with the rest as though it were legitimate.

When the time came, he said, he and the other judges would simply pass us by without comment. It would be their secret that we couldn't possibly win anything.

That was the deal.

History.

5

T HE PERSON who won that year was a girl from Cincinnati. As it happened, she too had an exhibit about crystallography. She, however, had either grown her own or gathered specimens herself from creek beds and caves and coal mines within 100 kilometers of her home. Her name was Mary Alice French, I remember, and she would go on to place very close to the bottom in the National Finals in Washington, D.C.

When she set off for the Finals, I heard, Cincinnati was so proud of her and so sure she would win, or at least place very high with her crystals, that the Mayor declared "Mary Alice French Day."

I have to wonder now, with so much time in which to think about people I've hurt, if Father and I didn't indirectly help set up Mary Alice French for her terrible disappointment in Washington. There is a good chance that the judges in Cleveland gave her First Prize because of the moral contrast between her exhibit and ours.

Perhaps, during the judging, science was given a backseat, and because of our ill fame, she represented a golden opportunity to teach a rule superior to any law of science: that honesty was the best policy.

But who knows?

Many, many years after Mary Alice French had her heart broken in Washington, and I had become a teacher at Tarkington, I had a male student from Cincinnati, Mary Alice French's hometown. His mother's side of the family had just sold Cincinnati's sole remaining daily paper and its leading TV station, and a lot of radio stations and weekly papers, too, to the Sultan of Brunei, reputedly the richest individual on Earth.

This student looked about 12 when he came to us. He was actually 21, but his voice had never changed, and he was only 150 centimeters tall. As a result of the sale to the Sultan, he personally was said to be worth $30,000,000, but he was scared to death of his own shadow.

He could read and write and do math all the way up through algebra and trigonometry, which he had taught himself. He was also probably the best chess player in the history of the college. But he had no social graces, and probably never would have any, because he found everything about life so frightening.

I asked him if he had ever heard of a woman about my age in Cincinnati whose name was Mary Alice French.

He replied: "I don't know anybody or anything. Please don't ever talk to me again. Tell everybody to stop talking to me."

I never did find out what he did with all his money, if anything. Somebody said he got married. Hard to believe!

Some fortune hunter must have got him.

Smart girl. She must be on Easy Street.

But to get back to the Science Fair in Cleveland: I headed for the nearest exit after Father and the judge made their deal. I needed fresh air. I needed a whole new planet or death. Anything would be better than what I had.

The exit was blocked by a spectacularly dressed man. He was wholly unlike anyone else in the auditorium. He was, incredibly, what I myself would become: a Lieutenant Colonel in the Regular Army, with many rows of ribbons on his chest. He was in full-dress uniform, with a gold citation cord and paratrooper's wings and boots. We were not then at war anywhere, so the sight of a military man all dolled up like that among civilians, especially so early in the day, was startling. He had been sent there to recruit budding young scientists for his alma mater, the United States Military Academy at West Point.

The Academy had been founded soon after the Revolutionary War because the country had so few military officers with mathematical and engineering skills essential to victories in what was modern warfare way back then, mainly mapmaking and cannonballs. Now, with radar and rockets and airplanes and nuclear weapons and all the rest of it, the same problem had come up again.

And there I was in Cleveland, with a great big round badge pinned over my heart like a target, which said:

EXHIBITOR.

This Lieutenant Colonel, whose name was Sam Wakefield, would not only get me into West Point. In Vietnam, where he was a Major General, he would award me a Silver Star for extraordinary valor and gallantry. He would retire from the Army when the war still had a year to go, and become President of Tarkington College, now Tarkington Prison. And when I myself got out of the Army, he would hire me to teach Physics and play the bells, bells, bells.

Here are the first words Sam Wakefield ever spoke to me, when I was 18 and he was 36:

"What's the hurry, Son?"

6

"W HAT'S THE HURRY, Son?" he said. And then, "If you've got a minute, I'd like to talk to you."

So I stopped. That was the biggest mistake of my life. There were plenty of other exits, and I should have headed for 1 of those. At that moment, every other exit led to the University of Michigan and journalism and music-making, and a lifetime of saying and wearing what I goshdarned pleased. Any other exit, in all probability, would have led me to a wife who wouldn't go insane on me, and kids who gave me love and respect.

Any other exit would have led to a certain amount of misery, I know, life being what it is. But I don't think it would have led me to Vietnam, and then to teaching the unteachable at Tarkington College, and then getting fired by Tarkington, and then teaching the unteachable at the penitentiary across the lake until the biggest prison break in American history. And now I myself am a prisoner.

But I stopped before the 1 exit blocked by Sam Wakefield.

There went the ball game.

Sam Wakefield asked me if I had ever considered the advantages of a career in the military. This was a man who had been wounded in World War II, the 1 war I would have liked to fight in, and then in Korea. He would eventually resign from the Army with the Vietnam War still going on, and then become President of Tarkington College, and then blow his brains out.

I said I had already been accepted by the University of Michigan and had no interest in soldiering. He wasn't having any luck at all. The sort of kid who had reached a state-level Science Fair honestly wanted to go to Cal Tech or MIT, or someplace a lot friendlier to freestyle thinking than West Point. So he was desperate. He was going around the country recruiting the dregs of Science Fairs. He didn't ask me about my exhibit. He didn't ask about my grades. He wanted my body, no matter what it was.

And then Father came along, looking for me. The next thing I knew, Father and Sam Wakefield were laughing and shaking hands.

Father was happier than I had seen him in years. He said to me, "The folks back home will think that's better than any prize at a Science Fair."

"What's better?" I said.

"You have just won an appointment to the United States Military Academy," he said. "I've got a son I can be proud of now."

Seventeen years later, in 1975, I was a Lieutenant Colonel on the roof of the American Embassy in Saigon, keeping everybody but Americans off helicopters that were ferrying badly rattled people out to ships offshore. We had lost a war!

Losers!

I wasn't the worst young scientist Sam Wakefield persuaded to come to West Point. One classmate of mine, from a little high school in Wyoming, had shown early promise by making an electric chair for rats, with little straps and a little black hood and all.

That was Jack Patton. He was no relation to "Old Blood and Guts" Patton, the famous General in World War II. He became my brother-in-law. I married his sister Margaret. She came with her folks from Wyoming to see him graduate, and I fell in love with her. We sure could dance.

Jack Patton was killed by a sniper in Hué—pronounced "whay." He was a Lieutenant Colonel in the Combat Engineers. I wasn't there, but they say he got it right between the eyes. Talk about marksmanship! Whoever shot him was a real winner.

The sniper didn't stay a winner very long, though, I heard. Hardly anybody does. Some of our people figured out where he was. I heard he couldn't have been more than 15 years old. He was a boy, not a man, but if he was going to play men's games he was going to have to pay men's penalties. After they killed him, I heard, they put his little testicles and penis in his mouth as a warning to anybody else who might choose to be a sniper.

Law and order. Justice swift and justice sure.

Let me hasten to say that no unit under my command was encouraged to engage in the mutilation of bodies of enemies, nor would I have winked at it if I had heard about it. One platoon in a battalion I led, on its own initiative, took to leaving aces of spades on the bodies of enemies, as sort of calling cards, I guess. This wasn't mutilation, strictly speaking, but still I put a stop to it.

What a footsoldier can do to a body with his pipsqueak technology is nothing, of course, when compared with the ordinary, unavoidable, perfectly routine effects of aerial bombing and artillery. One time I saw the severed head of a bearded old man resting on the guts of an eviscerated water buffalo, covered with flies in a bomb crater by a paddy in Cambodia. The plane whose bomb made the crater was so high when it dropped it that it couldn't even be seen from the ground. But what its bomb did, I would have to say, sure beat the ace of spades for a calling card.

I don't think Jack Patton would have wanted the sniper who killed him mutilated, but you never know. When he was alive he was like a dead man in 1 respect: everything was pretty much all right with him.

Everything, and I mean everything, was a joke to him, or so he said. His favorite expression right up to the end was, "I had to laugh like hell." If Lieutenant Colonel Patton is in Heaven, and I don't think many truly professional soldiers have ever expected to wind up there, at least not recently, he might at this very moment be telling about how his life suddenly stopped in Hué, and then adding, without even smiling, "I had to laugh like hell." That was the thing: Patton would tell about some supposedly serious or beautiful or dangerous or holy event during which he had had to laugh like hell, but he hadn't really laughed. He kept a straight face, too, when he told about it afterward. In all his life, I don't think anybody ever heard him do what he said he had to do all the time, which was laugh like hell.

He said he had to laugh like hell when he won a science prize in high school for making an electric chair for rats, but he hadn't.

A lot of people wanted him to stage a public demonstration of the chair with a tranquilized rat, wanted him to shave the head of a groggy rat and strap it to the chair, and, according to Jack, ask it if it had any last words to say, maybe wanted to express remorse for the life of crime it had led.

The execution never took place. There was enough common sense in Patton's high school, although not in the Science Department, apparently, to have such an event denounced as cruelty to dumb animals. Again, Jack Patton said without smiling, "I had to laugh like hell."

He said he had to laugh like hell when I married his sister Margaret. He said Margaret and I shouldn't take offense at that. He said he had to laugh like hell when anybody got married.

I am absolutely sure that Jack did not know that there was inheritable insanity on his mother's side of the family, and neither did his sister, who would become my bride. When I married Margaret, their mother seemed perfectly OK still, except for a mania for dancing, which was a little scary sometimes, but harmless. Dancing until she dropped wasn't nearly as loony as wanting to bomb North Vietnam back to the Stone Age, or bombing anyplace back to the Stone Age.

My mother-in-law Mildred grew up in Peru, Indiana, but never talked about Peru, even after she went crazy, except to say that Cole Porter, a composer of ultrasophisticated popular songs during the first half of the last century, was also born in Peru.

My mother-in-law ran away from Peru when she was 18, and never went back again. She worked her way through the University of Wyoming, in Laramie, of all places, which I guess was about as far away from Peru as she could get without leaving the Milky Way. That was where she met her husband, who was then a student in the university's School of Veterinary Science.

Only after the Vietnam War, with Jack long dead, did Margaret and I realize that she wanted nothing more to do with

Peru because so many people there knew she came from a family famous for spawning lunatics. And then she got married, keeping her family's terrifying history to herself, and she reproduced.

My own wife married and reproduced in all innocence of the danger she herself was in, and the risk she would pass on to our children.

Our own children, having grown up with a notoriously insane grandmother in the house, fled this valley as soon as they could, just as she had fled Peru. But they haven't reproduced, and with their knowing what they do about their booby-trapped genes, I doubt that they ever will.

Jack Patton never married. He never said he wanted kids. That could be a clue that he did know about his crazy relatives in Peru, after all. But I don't believe that. He was against everybody's reproducing, since human beings were, in his own words, "about 1,000 times dumber and meaner than they think they are."

I myself, obviously, have finally come around to his point of view.

During our plebe year, I remember, Jack all of a sudden decided that he was going to be a cartoonist, although he had never thought of being that before. He was compulsive. I could imagine him back in high school in Wyoming, all of a sudden deciding to build an electric chair for rats.

The first cartoon he ever drew, and the last one, was of 2 rhinoceroses getting married. A regular human preacher in a church was saying to the congregation that anybody who knew any reason these 2 should not be joined together in holy matrimony should speak now or forever hold his peace.

This was long before I had even met his sister Margaret.

We were roommates, and would be for all 4 years. So he showed me the cartoon and said he bet he could sell it to *Playboy*.

I asked him what was funny about it. He couldn't draw for sour apples. He had to tell me that the bride and groom were rhinoceroses. I thought they were a couple of sofas maybe, or maybe a couple of smashed-up sedans. That would have been fairly funny, come to think of it: 2 smashed-up sedans taking wedding vows. They were going to settle down.

"What's funny about it?" said Jack incredulously. "Where's your sense of humor? If somebody doesn't stop the wedding, those two will mate and have a baby rhinoceros."

"Of course," I said.

"For Pete's sake," he said, "what could be uglier and dumber than a rhinoceros? Just because something can reproduce, that doesn't mean it should reproduce."

I pointed out that to a rhinoceros another rhinoceros was wonderful.

"That's the point," he said. "Every kind of animal thinks its own kind of animal is wonderful. So people getting married think they're wonderful, and that they're going to have a baby that's wonderful, when actually they're as ugly as rhinoceroses. Just because we think we're so wonderful doesn't mean we really are. We could be really terrible animals and just never admit it because it would hurt so much."

During Jack's and my cow year at the Point, I remember, which would have been our junior year at a regular college, we were ordered to walk a tour for 3 hours on the Quadrangle, in a military manner, as though on serious guard duty, in full uniform and carrying rifles. This was punishment for our having failed to report another cadet who had cheated on a final examination in Electrical Engineering. The Honor Code required not only that we never lie or cheat but that we snitch on anybody who had done those things.

We hadn't seen the cadet cheat. We hadn't even been in the same class with him. But we were with him, along with one other cadet, when he got drunk in Philadelphia after the Army–Navy game. He got so drunk he confessed that he had cheated on the exam the previous June. Jack and I told him to shut up, that we didn't want to hear about it, and that we were going to forget about it, since it probably wasn't true anyway.

But the other cadet, who would later be fragged in Vietnam, turned all of us in. We were as corrupt as the cheater, supposedly, for trying to cover up for him. "Fragging," incidentally, was a new word in the English language that came out of the

Vietnam War. It meant pitching a fizzing fragmentation grenade into the sleeping quarters of an unpopular officer. I don't
mean to boast, but the whole time I was in Vietnam nobody
offered to frag me.

The cheater was thrown out, even though he was a firstie,
which meant he would graduate in only 6 more months. And
Jack and I had to walk a 3-hour tour at night and in an ice-cold
rain. We weren't supposed to talk to each other or to anyone.
But the nonsensical posts he and I had to march intersected at 1
point. Jack muttered to me at one such meeting, "What would
you do if you heard somebody had just dropped an atom bomb
on New York City?"

It would be 10 minutes before we passed again. I thought
of a few answers that were obvious, such as that I would be
horrified, I would want to cry, and so on. But I understood
that he didn't want to hear my answer. Jack wanted me to hear
his answer.

So here he came with his answer. He looked me in the eye,
and he said without a flicker of a smile, "I'd laugh like hell."

———————————

The last time I heard him say that he had to laugh like hell
was in Saigon, where I ran into him in a bar. He told me that he
had just been awarded a Silver Star, which made him my equal,
since I already had one. He had been with a platoon from his
company, which was planting mines on paths leading to a village believed to be sympathetic with the enemy when a firefight
broke out. So he called for air support, and the planes dropped
napalm, which is jellied gasoline developed by Harvard University, on the village, killing Vietnamese of both sexes and all
ages. Afterward, he was ordered to count the bodies, and to
assume that they had all been enemies, so that the number of
bodies could be in the news that day. That engagement was
what he got the Silver Star for. "I had to laugh like hell," he said,
but he didn't crack a smile.

———————————

He would have wanted to laugh like hell if he had seen me on
the roof of our embassy in Saigon with my pistol drawn. I had
won my Silver Star for finding and personally killing 5 enemy

soldiers who were hiding in a tunnel underground. Now I was on a rooftop, while regiments of the enemy were right out in the open, with no need to hide from anybody, taking possession without opposition of the streets below. There they were down there, in case I wanted to kill lots more of them. *Pow! Pow! Pow!*

I was up there to keep Vietnamese who had been on our side from getting onto helicopters that were ferrying Americans only, civilian employees at the embassy and their dependents, to our Navy ships offshore. The enemy could have shot down the helicopters and come up and captured or killed us, if they had wanted. But all they had ever wanted from us was that we go home. They certainly captured or killed the Vietnamese I kept off the helicopter after the very last of the Americans, who was Lieutenant Colonel Eugene Debs Hartke, was out of there.

The rest of that day:

The helicopter carrying the last American to leave Vietnam joined a swarm of helicopters over the South China Sea, driven from their roosts on land and running out of gasoline. How was that for Natural History in the 20th Century: the sky filled with chattering, manmade pterodactyls, suddenly homeless, unable to swim a stroke, about to drown or starve to death.

Below us, deployed as far as the eye could see, was the most heavily armed armada in history, in no danger whatsoever from anyone. We could have all the deep blue sea we wanted, as far as the enemy was concerned. Enjoy! Enjoy!

My own helicopter was told by radio to hover with 2 others over a minesweeper, which had a landing platform for 1 pterodactyl, its own, which took off so ours could land. Down we came, and we got out, and sailors pushed our big, dumb, clumsy bird overboard. That process was repeated twice, and then the ship's own improbable creature claimed its roost again. I had a look inside it later on. It was loaded with electronic gear that could detect mines and submarines under the water, and incoming missiles and planes in the sky above.

And then the Sun itself followed the last American helicopter to leave Saigon to the bottom of the deep blue sea.

At the age of 35, Eugene Debs Hartke was again as dissolute with respect to alcohol and marijuana and loose women as he

had been during his last 2 years in high school. And he had lost
all respect for himself and the leadership of his country, just as,
17 years earlier, he had lost all respect for himself and his father
at the Cleveland, Ohio, Science Fair.

———————

His mentor Sam Wakefield, the man who recruited him for
West Point, had quit the Army a year earlier in order to speak
out against the war. He had become President of Tarkington
College through powerful family connections.

Three years after that, Sam Wakefield would commit suicide.
So there is another loser for you, even though he had been a
Major General and then a College President. I think exhaustion
got him. I say that not only because he seemed very tired all the
time to me, but because his suicide note wasn't even original
and didn't seem to have that much to do with him personally. It
was word for word the same suicide note left way back in 1932,
when I was a negative 8 years old, by another loser, George
Eastman, inventor of the Kodak camera and founder of Eastman Kodak, now defunct, only 75 kilometers north of here.

Both notes said this and nothing more: "My work is done."

In Sam Wakefield's case, that completed work, if he didn't
want to count the Vietnam War, consisted of 3 new buildings,
which probably would have been built anyway, no matter who
was Tarkington's President.

———————

I am not writing this book for people below the age of 18,
but I see no harm in telling young people to prepare for failure
rather than success, since failure is the main thing that is going
to happen to them.

In terms of basketball alone, almost everybody has to lose.
A high percentage of the convicts in Athena, and now in this
much smaller institution, devoted their childhood and youth to
nothing but basketball and still got their brains knocked out in
the early rounds of some darn fool tournament.

———————

Let me say further to the chance young reader that I would
probably have wrecked my body and been thrown out of the

University of Michigan and died on Skid Row somewhere if I had not been subjected to the discipline of West Point. I am talking about my body now, and not my mind, and there is no better way for a young person to learn respect for his or now her bones and nerves and muscles than to accept an appointment to any one of the 3 major service academies.

I entered the Point a young punk with bad posture and a sunken chest, and no history of sports participation, save for a few fights after dances where our band had played. When I graduated and received my commission as a Second Lieutenant in the Regular Army, and tossed my hat in the air, and bought a red Corvette with the back pay the Academy had put aside for me, my spine was as straight as a ramrod, my lungs were as capacious as the bellows of the forge of Vulcan, I was captain of the judo and wrestling teams, and I had not smoked any sort of cigarette or swallowed a drop of alcohol for 4 whole years! Nor was I sexually promiscuous anymore. I never felt better in my life.

I can remember saying to my mother and father at graduation, "Can this be me?"

They were so proud of me, and I was so proud of me.

I turned to Jack Patton, who was there with his booby-trapped sister and mother and his normal father, and I asked him, "What do you think of us now, Lieutenant Patton?" He was the goat of our class, meaning he had the lowest grade average. So had General George Patton been, again no relative of Jack's, who had been such a great leader in World War II.

What Jack replied, of course, unsmilingly, was that he had to laugh like hell.

7

I HAVE BEEN READING issues of the Tarkington College alumni magazine, *The Musketeer*, going all the way back to its first issue, which came out in 1910. It was so named in honor of Musket Mountain, a high hill not a mountain, on the western edge of the campus, at whose foot, next to the stable, so many victims of the escaped convicts are buried now.

Every proposed physical improvement of the college plant triggered a storm of protest. When Tarkington graduates came back here, they wanted it to be exactly as they remembered it. And 1 thing at least never did change, which was the size of the student body, stabilized at 300 since 1925. Meanwhile, of course, the growth of the prison population on the other side of the lake, invisible behind walls, was as irresistible as Thunder Beaver, as Niagara Falls.

Judging from letters to *The Musketeer*, I think the change that generated the most passionate resistance was the modernization of the Lutz Carillon soon after World War II, a memorial to Ernest Hubble Hiscock. He was a Tarkington graduate who at the age of 21 was a nose-gunner on a Navy bomber whose pilot crashed his plane with a full load of bombs onto the flight deck of a Japanese aircraft carrier in the Battle of Midway during World War II.

I would have given anything to die in a war that meaningful.

Me? I was in show business, trying to get a big audience for the Government on TV by killing real people with live ammunition, something the other advertisers were not free to do.

The other advertisers had to fake everything.

Oddly enough, the actors always turned out to be a lot more believable on the little screen than we were. Real people in real trouble don't come across, somehow.

There is still so much we have to learn about TV!

Hiscock's parents, who were divorced and remarried but still friends, chipped in to have the bells mechanized, so that one person could play them by means of a keyboard. Before that, many people had to haul away on ropes, and once a bell was set swinging, it stopped swinging in its own sweet time. There was no way of damping it.

In the old days 4 of the bells were famously off-key, but beloved, and were known as "Pickle" and "Lemon" and "Big Cracked John" and "Beelzebub." The Hiscocks had them sent to Belgium, to the same bell foundry where André Lutz had been an apprentice so long ago. There they were machined and weighted to perfect pitch, their condition when I got to play them.

It can't have been music the carillon made in the old days. Those who used to make whatever it was described it in their letters to *The Musketeer* with the same sort of batty love and berserk gratitude I hear from convicts when they tell me what it was like to take heroin laced with amphetamine, and angel dust laced with LSD, and crack alone, and on and on. I think of all those learning-disabled kids in the old days, hauling away on ropes with the bells clanging sweet and sour and as loud as thunder directly overhead, and I am sure they were finding the same undeserved happiness so many of the convicts found in chemicals.

And haven't I myself said that the happiest parts of my life were when I played the bells? With absolutely no basis in reality, I felt like many an addict that I'd won, I'd won, I'd won!

When I was made carillonneur, I taped this sign on the door of the chamber containing the keyboard: "Thor." That's who I felt like when I played, sending thunderbolts down the hillside and through the industrial ruins of Scipio, and out over the lake, and up to the walls of the prison on the other side.

There were echoes when I played—bouncing off the empty factories and the prison walls, and arguing with notes just leaving the bells overhead. When Lake Mohiga was frozen, their argument was so loud that people who had never been in the area before thought the prison had its own set of bells, and that their carillonneur was mocking me.

And I would yell into the mad clashing of bells and echoes, "Laugh, Jack, laugh!"

After the prison break, the College President would shoot convicts down below from the belfry. The acoustics of the valley would cause the escapees to make many wrong guesses as to where the shots were coming from.

8

I N MY DAY, the bells no longer swung. They were welded to rigid shafts. Their clappers had been removed. They were struck instead by bolts thrust by electricity from Niagara Falls. Their singing could be stopped in an instant by brakes lined with neoprene.

The room in which a dozen or more learning-disabled bell-pullers used to be zonked out of their skulls by hellishly loud cacophony contained a 3-octave keyboard against 1 wall. The holes for the ropes in the ceiling had been plugged and plastered over.

Nothing works up there anymore. The room with the keyboard and the belfry above were riddled by bullets and also bazooka shells fired by escaped convicts down below after a sniper up among the bells shot and killed 11 of them, and wounded 15 more. The sniper was the President of Tarkington College. Even though he was dead when the convicts got to him, they were so outraged that they crucified him in the loft of the stable where the students used to keep their horses, at the foot of Musket Mountain.

So a President of Tarkington, my mentor Sam Wakefield, blew his brains out with a Colt .45. And his successor, although he couldn't feel anything, was crucified.

One would have to say that that was extra-heavy history.

As for light history: The no longer useful clappers of the bells were hung in order of size, but unlabeled, on the wall of the foyer of this library, above the perpetual-motion machines. So it became a college tradition for upperclass-persons to tell incoming freshmen that the clappers were the petrified penises of different mammals. The biggest clapper, which had once belonged to Beelzebub, the biggest bell, was said to be the penis of none other than Moby Dick, the Great White Whale.

Many of the freshmen believed it, and were watched to see how long they went on believing it, just as they had been watched when they were little, no doubt, to see how long they would go on believing in the Tooth Fairy, the Easter Bunny, and Santa Claus.

———————

Vietnam.

———————

Most of the letters to *The Musketeer* protesting the modernization of the Lutz Carillon are from people who had somehow hung on to the wealth and power they had been born to. One, though, is from a man who admitted that he was in prison for fraud, and that he had ruined his life and that of his family with his twin addictions to alcohol and gambling. His letter was like this book, a gallows speech.

One thing he had still looked forward to, he said, after he had paid his debt to society, was returning to Scipio to ring the bells with ropes again.

"Now you take that away from me," he said.

———————

One letter is from an old bell-puller, very likely dead by now, a member of the Class of 1924 who had married a man named Marthinus de Wet, the owner of a gold mine in Krugersdorp, South Africa. She knew the history of the bells, that they had been made from weapons gathered up after the Battle of Gettysburg. She did not mind that the bells would soon be played electrically. The bad idea, as far as she was concerned, was that the sour bells, Pickle and Lemon and Big Cracked John and Beelzebub, were going to be turned on lathes in Belgium until they were either in tune or on the scrap heap.

"Are Tarkington students no longer to be humanized and humbled as I was day after day," she asked, "by the cries from the bell tower of the dying on the sacred, blood-soaked grounds of Gettysburg?"

The bells controversy inspired a lot of purple prose like that, much of it dictated to a secretary or a machine, no doubt. It is quite possible that Mrs. de Wet graduated from Tarkington without being able to write any better than most of the ill-educated prisoners across the lake.

If my Socialist grandfather, nothing but a gardener at Butler University, could read the letter from Mrs. de Wet and note its South African return address, he would be grimly gratified. There was a clear-as-crystal demonstration of a woman living high on profits from the labor of black miners, overworked and underpaid.

He would have seen exploitation of the poor and powerless in the growth of the prison across the lake as well. The prison to him would have been a scheme for depriving the lower social orders of leadership in the Class Struggle and for providing them with a horrible alternative to accepting whatever their greedy paymasters would give them in the way of working conditions and subsistence.

By the time I got to Tarkington College, though, he would have been wrong about the meaning of the prison across the lake, since poor and powerless people, no matter how docile, were no longer of use to canny investors. What they used to do was now being done by heroic and uncomplaining machinery.

So an appropriate sign to put over the gate to Athena might have been, instead of "Work Makes Free," for example: "Too bad you were born. Nobody has any use for you," or maybe: "Come in and stay in, all you burdens on Society."

9

A FORMER ROOMMATE of Ernest Hubble Hiscock, the dead war hero, who had also been in the war, who had lost an arm as a Marine on Iwo Jima, wrote that the memorial Hiscock himself would have wanted most was a promise by the Board of Trustees at the start of each academic year to keep the enrollment the same size it had been in his time.

So if Ernest Hubble Hiscock is looking down from Heaven now, or wherever it is that war heroes go after dying, he would be dismayed to see his beloved campus surrounded by barbed wire and watchtowers. The bells are shot to hell. The number of students, if you can call convicts that, is about 2,000 now.

When there were only 300 "students" here, each one had a bedroom and a bathroom and plenty of closets all his or her own. Each bedroom was part of a 2-bedroom, 2-bathroom suite with a common living room for 2. Each living room had couches and easy chairs and a working fireplace, and state-of-the-art sound-reproduction equipment and a big-screen TV.

At the Athena state prison, as I would discover when I went to work over there, there were 6 men to each cell and each cell had been built for 2. Each 50 cells had a recreation room with one Ping-Pong table and one TV. The TV, moreover, showed only tapes of programs, including news, at least 10 years old. The idea was to keep the prisoners from becoming distressed about anything going on in the outside world that hadn't been all taken care of one way or the other, presumably, in the long-ago.

They could feast their eyes on whatever they liked, just so long as it wasn't relevant.

How those letter-writers loved not just the college but the whole Mohiga Valley—the seasons, the lake, the forest primeval on the other side. And there were few differences between student pleasures in their times and my own. In my time, students didn't skate on the lake anymore, but on an indoor rink given in 1971 by the Israel Cohen Family. But they still had sailboat races and canoe races on the lake. They still had picnics by the ruins of the locks at the head of the lake. Many students still brought their own horses to school with them. In my time, several students brought not just 1 horse but 3, since polo was a major sport. In 1976 and again in 1980, Tarkington College had an undefeated polo team.

There are no horses in the stable now, of course. The escaped convicts, surrounded and starving a mere 4 days after the prison break, calling themselves "Freedom Fighters" and flying an American flag from the top of the bell tower of this library, ate the horses and the campus dogs, too, and fed pieces of them to their hostages, who were the Trustees of the college.

The most successful athlete ever to come from Tarkington, arguably, was a horseman from my own time, Lowell Chung. He won a Bronze Medal as a member of the United States Equestrian Team in Seoul, South Korea, back in 1988. His mother owned half of Honolulu, but he couldn't read or write or do math worth a darn. He could sure do Physics, though. He could tell me how levers and lenses and electricity and heat and all sorts of power plants worked, and predict correctly what an experiment would prove before I'd performed it—just as long as I didn't insist that he quantify anything, that he tell me what the numbers were.

He earned his Associate in the Arts and Sciences Degree in 1984. That was the only degree we awarded, fair warning to other institutions and future employers, and to the students themselves, that our graduates' intellectual achievements, while respectable, were unconventional.

Lowell Chung got me on a horse for the first time in my life when I was 43 years old. He dared me. I told him I certainly wasn't going to commit suicide on the back of one of his fire-cracker polo ponies, since I had a wife and a mother-in-law and 2 children to support. So he borrowed a gentle, patient old mare from his girlfriend at the time, who was Claudia Roosevelt.

Comically enough, Lowell's then girlfriend was a whiz at arithmetic, but otherwise a nitwit. You could ask her, "What is 5,111 times 10,022 divided by 97?" Claudia would reply, "That's 528,066.4. So what? So what?"

So what indeed! The lesson I myself learned over and over again when teaching at the college and then the prison was the uselessness of information to most people, except as entertainment. If facts weren't funny or scary, or couldn't make you rich, the heck with them.

When I later went to work at the prison, I encountered a mass murderer named Alton Darwin who also could do arithmetic in his head. He was Black. Unlike Claudia Roosevelt, he was highly intelligent in the verbal area. The people he had murdered were rivals or deadbeats or police informers or cases of mistaken identity or innocent bystanders in the illegal drug industry. His manner of speaking was elegant and thought-provoking.

He hadn't killed nearly as many people as I had. But then again, he hadn't had my advantage, which was the full cooperation of our Government.

Also, he had done all his killing for reasons of money. I had never stooped to that.

When I found out that he could do arithmetic in his head, I said to him, "That's a remarkable gift you have."

"Doesn't seem fair, does it," he said, "that somebody should come into the world with such a great advantage over the common folk? When I get out of here, I'm going to buy me a pretty striped tent and put up a sign saying 'One dollar. Come on in and see the Nigger do arithmetic.'" He wasn't ever going to get out of there. He was serving a life sentence without hope of parole.

Darwin's fantasy about starring in a mental-arithmetic show when he got out, incidentally, was inspired by something 1 of his great-grandfathers did in South Carolina after World War I. All the airplane pilots back then were white, and some of them did stunt flying at country fairs. They were called "barnstormers."

And 1 of these barnstormers with a 2-cockpit plane strapped Darwin's great-grandfather in the front cockpit, even though the great-grandfather couldn't even drive an automobile. The barnstormer crouched down in the rear cockpit, so people couldn't see him but he could still work the controls. And people came from far and wide, according to Darwin, "to see the Nigger fly the airplane."

He was only 25 years old when we first met, the same age as Lowell Chung when Lowell won the Bronze Medal for horseback riding in Seoul, South Korea. When I was 25, I hadn't killed anybody yet, and hadn't had nearly as many women as Darwin had. When he was only 20, he told me, he paid cash for a Ferrari. I didn't have a car of my own, which was a good car, all right, a Chevrolet Corvette, but nowhere near as good as a Ferrari, until I was 21.

At least I, too, had paid cash.

When we talked at the prison, he had a running joke that was the assumption that we came from different planets. The prison was all there was to his planet, and I had come in a flying saucer from one that was much bigger and wiser.

This enabled him to comment ironically on the only sexual activities possible inside the walls. "You have little babies on your planet?" he asked.

"Yes, we have little babies," I said.

"We got people here trying to have babies every which way," he said, "but they never get babies. What do you think they're doing wrong?"

He was the first convict I heard use the expression "the PB." He told me that sometimes he wished he had "the PB." I thought he meant "TB," short for "tuberculosis," another common affliction at the prison—common enough that I have it now.

It turned out that "PB" was short for "Parole Board," which is what the convicts called AIDS.

That was when we first met, back in 1991, when he said that sometimes he wished he had the PB, and long before I myself contracted TB.

Alphabet soup!

He was hungry for descriptions of this valley, to which he had been sentenced for the rest of his life and where he could expect to be buried, but which he had never seen. Not only the convicts but their visitors, too, were kept as ignorant as possible of the precise geographical situation of the prison, so that anybody escaping would have no clear idea of what to watch out for or which way to go.

Visitors were brought into the cul-de-sac of the valley from Rochester in buses with blacked-out windows. Convicts themselves were delivered in windowless steel boxes capable of holding 10 of them wearing leg irons and handcuffs, mounted on the beds of trucks. The buses and the steel boxes were never opened until they were well inside the prison walls.

These were exceedingly dangerous and resourceful criminals, after all. While the Japanese had taken over the operation of Athena by the time I got there, hoping to operate it at a profit, the blacked-out buses and steel boxes had been in use long before they got there. Those morbid forms of transportation became a common sight on the road to and from Rochester in maybe 1977, about 2 years after I and my little family took up residence in Scipio.

The only change the Japanese made in the vehicles, which was under way when I went to work over there in 1991, was to remount the old steel boxes on new Japanese trucks.

So it was in violation of long-standing prison policy that I told Alton Darwin and other lifers all they wanted to know about the valley. I thought they were entitled to know about the great forest, which was their forest now, and the beautiful lake, which was their lake now, and the beautiful little college, which was where the music from the bells was coming from.

And of course, this enriched their dreams of escaping, but what were those but what we could call in any other context the virtue hope? I never thought they would ever really get out of here and make use of the knowledge I had given them of the countryside, and neither did they.

I used to do the same sort of thing in Vietnam, too, helping mortally wounded soldiers dream that they would soon be well and home again.

Why not?

I am as sorry as anybody that Darwin and all the rest really tasted freedom. They were horrible news for themselves and everyone. A lot of them were real homicidal maniacs. Darwin wasn't 1 of those, but even as the convicts were crossing the ice to Scipio, he was giving orders as if he were an Emperor, as if the break were his idea, although he had had nothing to do with it. He hadn't known it was coming.

Those who had actually breached the walls and opened the cells had come down from Rochester to free only 1 convict. They got him, and they were headed out of the valley and had no interest in conquering Scipio and its little army of 6 regular policemen and 3 unarmed campus cops, and an unknown number of firearms in private hands.

Alton Darwin was the first example I had ever seen of leadership in the raw. He was a man without any badges of rank, and with no previously existing organization or widely understood plan of action. He had been a modest, unremarkable man in prison. The moment he got out, though, sudden delusions of grandeur made him the only man who knew what to do next, which was to attack Scipio, where glory and riches awaited all who dared to follow him.

"Follow me!" he cried, and some did. He was a sociopath, I think, in love with himself and no one else, craving action for its own sake, and indifferent to any long-term consequences, a classic Man of Destiny.

Most did not even follow him down the slope and out onto the ice. They returned to the prison, where they had beds of their own, and shelter from the weather, and food and water, although no heat or electricity. They chose to be good boys, concluding correctly that bad boys roaming free in the valley, but completely surrounded by the forces of law and order, would be shot on sight in a day or 2, or maybe even sooner. They were color-coded, after all.

In the Mohiga Valley, their skin alone sufficed as a prison uniform.

About half of those who followed Darwin out onto the ice turned back before they reached Scipio. This was before they were fired upon and suffered their first casualty. One of those who went back to the prison told me that he was sickened when he realized how much murder and rape there would be when they reached the other side in just a few minutes.

"I thought about all the little children fast asleep in their beds," he said. He had handed over the gun he had stolen from the prison armory to the man next to him, there in the middle of beautiful Lake Mohiga. "He didn't have a gun," he said, "until I gave him 1."

"Did you wish each other good luck or anything like that?" I asked him.

"We didn't say anything," he told me. "Nobody was saying anything but the man in front."

"And what was he saying?" I asked.

He replied with terrible emptiness, " 'Follow me, follow me, follow me.' "

"Life's a bad dream," he said. "Do you know that?"

Alton Darwin's charismatic delusions of grandeur went on and on. He declared himself to be President of a new country. He set up his headquarters in the Board of Trustees Room of Samoza Hall, with the big long table for his desk.

I visited him there at high noon on the second day after the great escape. He told me that this new country of his was going to cut down the virgin forest on the other side of the lake and sell the wood to the Japanese. He would use the money to refurbish the abandoned industrial buildings in Scipio down below. He didn't know yet what they would manufacture, but he was thinking hard about that. He would welcome any suggestions I might have.

Nobody would dare attack him, he said, for fear he would harm his hostages. He held the entire Board of Trustees captive, but not the College President, Henry "Tex" Johnson, nor his wife, Zuzu. I had come to ask Darwin if he had any idea what had become of Tex and Zuzu. He didn't know.

Zuzu, it would turn out, had been killed by a person or persons unknown, possibly raped, possibly not. We will never know. It was not an ideal time for Forensic Medicine. Tex, meanwhile, was ascending the tower of the library here with a rifle and ammunition. He was going clear to the top, to turn the belfry itself into a sniper's nest.

Alton Darwin was never worried, no matter how bad things got. He laughed when he heard that paratroops, advancing on foot, had surrounded the prison across the lake and, on our side, were digging in to the west and south of Scipio. State Police and vigilantes had already set up a roadblock at the head of the lake. Alton Darwin laughed as though he had achieved a great victory.

I knew people like that in Vietnam. Jack Patton had that sort of courage. I could be as brave as Jack over there. In fact, I am pretty sure that I was shot at more and killed more people. But I was worried sick most of the time. Jack never worried. He told me so.

I asked him how he could be that way. He said, "I think I must have a screw loose. I can't care about what might happen next to me or anyone."

Alton Darwin had the same untightened screw. He was a convicted mass murderer, but never showed any remorse that I could see.

During my last year in Vietnam, I, too, reacted at press briefings as though our defeats were victories. But I was under orders to do that. That wasn't my natural disposition.

Alton Darwin, and this was true of Jack Patton, too, spoke of trivial and serious matters in the same tone of voice, with the same gestures and facial expressions. Nothing mattered more or less than anything else.

Alton Darwin, I remember, was talking to me with seemingly deep concern about how many of the convicts who had crossed the ice with him to Scipio were deserting, were going back across the ice to the prison, or turning themselves in at the roadblock at the head of the lake in hopes of amnesty. The deserters were worriers. They didn't want to die, and they didn't want to be held responsible, even though many of them were responsible, for the murders and rapes in Scipio.

So I was pondering the desertion problem when Alton Darwin said with exactly the same intensity, "I can skate on ice. Do you believe that?"

"I beg your pardon?" I said.

"I could always roller-skate," he said. "But I never got a chance to ice-skate till this morning."

That morning, with the phones dead and the electricity cut off, with unburied bodies everywhere, and with all the food in Scipio already consumed as though by a locust plague, he had gone up to Cohen Rink and put on ice skates for the first time in his life. After a few tottering steps, he had found himself gliding around and around, and around and around.

"Roller-skating and ice-skating are just about the very same thing!" he told me triumphantly, as though he had made a scientific discovery that was going to throw an entirely new light on what had seemed a hopeless situation. "Same muscles!" he said importantly.

That's what he was doing when he was fatally shot about an hour later. He was out on the rink, gliding around and around, and around and around. I'd left him in his office, and I assumed that he was still up there. But there he was on the rink instead, going around and around, and around and around.

A shot rang out, and he fell down.

Several of his followers went to him, and he said something to them, and then he died.

It was a beautiful shot, if Darwin was really the man the College President was shooting at. He could have been shooting at me, since he knew I used to make love to his wife Zuzu when he was out of the house.

If he was shooting at Darwin instead of me, he solved one of the most difficult problems in marksmanship, the same problem solved by Lee Harvey Oswald when he shot President Kennedy, which is where to aim when you are high above your target.

As I say, "Beautiful shot."

I asked later what Alton Darwin's last words had been, and was told that they made no sense. His last words had been, "See the Nigger fly the airplane."

10

SOMETIMES Alton Darwin would talk to me about the planet he was on before he was transported in a steel box to Athena. "Drugs were food," he said. "I was in the food business. Just because people on one planet eat a certain kind of food they're hungry for, that makes them feel better after they eat it, that doesn't mean people on other planets shouldn't eat something else. On some planets I'm sure there are people who eat stones, and then feel wonderful for a little while afterwards. Then it's time to eat stones again."

I thought very little about the prison during the 15 years I was a teacher at Tarkington, as big and brutal as it was across the lake, and growing all the time. When we went picnicking at the head of the lake, or went up to Rochester on some errand or other, I saw plenty of blacked-out buses and steel boxes on the backs of trucks. Alton Darwin might have been in one of those boxes. Then again, since the steel boxes were also used to carry freight, there might have been nothing but Diet Pepsi and toilet paper in there.

Whatever was in there was none of my business until Tarkington fired me.

Sometimes when I was playing the bells and getting particularly loud echoes from the prison walls, usually in the dead of the wintertime, I would have the feeling that I was shelling the prison. In Vietnam, conversely, if I happened to be back with the artillery, and the guns were lobbing shells at who knows what in some jungle, it seemed very much like music, interesting noises for the sake of interesting noises, and nothing more.

During a summer field exercise when Jack Patton and I were still cadets, I remember, we were asleep in a tent and the artillery opened up nearby.

We awoke. Jack said to me, "They're playing our tune, Gene. They're playing our tune."

Before I went to work at Athena, I had seen only 3 convicts anywhere in the valley. Most people in Scipio hadn't seen even 1. I wouldn't have seen even 1, either, if a truck with a steel box in back hadn't broken down at the head of the lake. I was picnicking there, near the water, with Margaret, my wife, and Mildred, my mother-in-law. Mildred was crazy as a bedbug by then, but Margaret was still sane, and there seemed a good chance that she always would be.

I was only 45, foolishly confident that I would go on teaching here until I reached the mandatory retirement age of 70 in 2010, 9 years from now. What in fact will happen to me in 9 more years? That is like worrying about a cheese spoiling if you don't put it in the refrigerator. What can happen to a pricelessly stinky cheese that hasn't already happened to it?

My mother-in-law, no danger to herself or anyone else, adored fishing. I had put a worm on her hook for her and pitched it out to a spot that looked promising. She gripped the rod with both hands, sure as always that something miraculous was about to happen.

She was right this time.

I looked up at the top of the bank, and there was a prison truck with smoke pouring out of its engine compartment. There were only 2 guards on board, and 1 of them was the driver. They bailed out. They had already radioed the prison for help. They were both white. This was before the Japanese took over Athena as a business proposition, before the road signs all the way from Rochester were in both English and Japanese.

It looked as though the truck might catch fire, so the 2 guards unlocked the little door in the back of the steel box and told the prisoners to come out. And then they backed off and waited with sawed-off automatic shotguns leveled at the little door.

Out the prisoners came. There were only 3 of them, clumsy in leg irons, and their handcuffs were shackled to chains around their waists. Two were black and 1 was white, or possibly a light

Hispanic. This was before the Supreme Court confirmed that it was indeed cruel and inhuman punishment to confine a person in a place where his or her race was greatly outnumbered by another 1.

The races were still mixed in prisons throughout the country. When I later went to work at Athena, though, there was nothing but people who had been classified as Black in there.

My mother-in-law did not turn around to see the smoking van and all. She was obsessed by what might happen at any moment at the other end of her fishline. But Margaret and I gawked. For us back then, prisoners were like pornography, common things nice people shouldn't want to see, even though the biggest industry by far in this valley was punishment.

When Margaret and I talked about it later, she didn't say it was like pornography. She said it was like seeing animals on their way to a slaughterhouse.

We, in turn, must have looked to those convicts like people in Paradise. It was a balmy day in the springtime. A sailboat race was going on to the south of us. The college had just been given 30 little sloops by a grateful parent who had cleaned out the biggest savings and loan bank in California.

Our brand-new Mercedes sedan was parked on the beach nearby. It cost more than my annual salary at Tarkington. The car was a gift from the mother of a student of mine named Pierre LeGrand. His maternal grandfather had been dictator of Haiti, and had taken the treasury of that country with him when he was overthrown. That was why Pierre's mother was so rich. He was very unpopular. He tried to win friends by making expensive gifts to them, but that didn't work, so he tried to hang himself from a girder of the water tower on top of Musket Mountain. I happened to be up there, in the bushes with the wife of the coach of the Tennis Team.

So I cut him down with my Swiss Army knife. That was how I got the Mercedes.

Pierre would have better luck 2 years later, jumping off the Golden Gate Bridge, and a campus joke was that now I had to give the Mercedes back.

So there were plenty of heartaches in what, as I've said, must have looked to those 3 convicts like Paradise. There was no way they could tell that my mother-in-law was as crazy as a bedbug, as long as she kept her back to them. They could not know, and neither could I, of course, that hereditary insanity would hit my pretty wife like a ton of bricks in about 6 months' time and turn her into a hag as scary as her mother.

If we had had our 2 kids with us on the beach, that would have completed the illusion that we lived in Paradise. They could have depicted another generation that found life as comfortable as we did. Both sexes would have been represented. We had a girl named Melanie and a boy named Eugene Debs Hartke, Jr. But they weren't kids anymore. Melanie was 21, and studying mathematics at Cambridge University in England. Eugene Jr. was completing his senior year at Deerfield Academy in Massachusetts, and was 18, and had his own rock-and-roll band, and had composed maybe 100 songs by then.

But Melanie would have spoiled our tableau on the beach. Like my mother until she went to Weight Watchers, she was very heavy. That must be hereditary. If she had kept her back to the convicts, she might at least have concealed the fact that she had a bulbous nose like the late, great, alcoholic comedian W. C. Fields. Melanie, thank goodness, was not also an alcoholic.

But her brother was.

And I could kill myself now for having boasted to him that on my side of the family the men had no fear of alcohol, since they knew how to drink in moderation. We were not weak and foolish where drugs were concerned.

At least Eugene Jr. was beautiful, having inherited the features of his mother. When he was growing up in this valley, people could not resist saying to me, with him right there to hear it, that he was the most beautiful child they'd ever seen.

I have no idea where he is now. He stopped communicating with me or anybody in this valley years ago.

He hates me.

So does Melanie, although she wrote to me as recently as 2 years ago. She was living in Paris with another woman. They were both teaching English and math in an American high school over there.

My kids will never forgive me for not putting my mother-in-law into a mental hospital instead of keeping her at home, where she was a great embarrassment to them. They couldn't bring friends home. If I had put Mildred into a nuthouse, though, I couldn't have afforded to send Melanie and Eugene Jr. to such expensive schools. I got a free house at Tarkington, but my salary was small.

Also, I didn't think Mildred's craziness was as unbearable as they did. In the Army I had grown used to people who talked nonsense all day long. Vietnam was 1 big hallucination. After adjusting to that, I could adjust to anything.

What my children most dislike me for, though, is my reproducing in conjunction with their mother. They live in constant dread of suddenly going as batty as Mildred and Margaret. Unfortunately, there is a good chance of that.

Ironically enough, I happen to have an illegitimate son about whom I learned only recently. Since he had a different mother, he need not expect to go insane someday. Some of his kids, if he ever has any, could inherit my own mother's tendency to fatness, though.

But they could join Weight Watchers as Mother did.

Heredity is obviously much on my mind these days, and should be. So I have been reading up on it some in a book that also deals with embryology. And I tell you: People who are wary of what they might find in a book if they opened 1 are right to be. I have just had my mind blown by an essay on the embryology of the human eye.

No combination of Time and Luck could have produced a camera that excellent, not even if the quantity of time had been 1,000,000,000,000 years! How is that for an unsolved mystery?

When I went to work at Athena, I hoped to find at least 1 of the 3 convicts who had seen Mildred and Margaret and me having a picnic so long ago. As I've said, I took 1 of them to be a White, or possibly Hispanic. So he would have been transferred to a White or Hispanic prison before I ever got there. The other 2 were clearly black, but I never found either of them. I would have liked to hear what we looked like to them, how contented we seemed to be.

They were probably dead. AIDS could have got them, or murder or suicide, or maybe tuberculosis. Every year, 30 inmates at Athena died for every student who was awarded an Associate in the Arts and Sciences Degree by Tarkington.

Parole.

If I had found a convict who had witnessed our picnic, we might have talked about the fish my mother-in-law hooked while he was watching. He saw her rod bend double, heard the reel scream like a little siren. But he never got to see the monster who had taken her bait and was headed south for Scipio. Before he could see it, he was back in darkness in another van.

It was heavy test line I had put on the reel. This was deep-sea stuff made for tuna and shark, although, as far as we knew, there was nothing in Lake Mohiga but eels and perch and little catfish. That was all Mildred had ever caught before.

One time, I remember, she caught a perch too little to keep. So I turned it loose, even though the barb of the hook had come out through one eye. A few minutes later she hooked that same perch again. We could tell by the mangled eye. Think about that. Miraculous eyes, and no brains whatsoever.

I put such heavy test line on Mildred's reel so that nothing could ever get away from her. In Honduras 1 time I did the same thing for a 3-star General, whose aide I was.

Mildred's fish couldn't snap the line, and Mildred wouldn't let go of the rod. She didn't weigh anything, and the fish weighed a lot for a fish. Mildred went down on her knees in the water, laughing and crying.

I'll never forget what she was saying: "It's God! It's God!"

I waded out to help her. She wouldn't let go of the rod, so I grasped the line and began to haul it in, hand over hand.

How the water swirled and boiled out there!

When I got the fish into shallow water, it suddenly quit fighting. I guess it had used up every bit of its energy. That was that.

This fish, which I picked up by the gills and flung up on the bank, was an enormous pickerel. Margaret looked down at it in horror and said, "It's a crocodile!"

I looked at the top of the bank to see what the convicts and guards thought of a fish that big. They were gone. There was nothing but the broken-down van up there. The little door to its steel box was wide open. Anybody was free to climb inside and close the door, in case he or she wondered what it felt like to be a prisoner.

To those fascinated by Forensic Medicine: The pickerel had not bitten on the worm on the hook. It had bitten on a perch which had bitten on the worm on the hook.

I thought that would be interesting to my mother-in-law during our trip back home in the new Mercedes. But she didn't want to talk about the fish at all. It had scared the daylights out of her, and she wanted to forget it.

As the years went by, I would mention the fish from time to time without getting anything back from her but a stony silence. I concluded that she really had purged it from her memory.

But then, on the night of the prison break, when the 3 of us were living in an old house in the hamlet of Athena, down below the prison walls, there was this terrific explosion that woke us up.

If Jack Patton had been there with us, he might have said to me, "Gene! Gene! They're playing our tune again."

The explosion was in fact the demolition of Athena's main gate from the outside, not the inside. The purported head of the Jamaican drug cartel, Jeffrey Turner, had been brought down to Athena in a steel box 6 months before, after a televised trial lasting a year and a half. He was given 25 consecutive life sentences, said to be a new record. Now a well-rehearsed force of his employees, variously estimated as being anything from a platoon to a company, had arrived outside the prison with explosives, a tank, and several half-tracks taken from the National Guard Armory about 10 kilometers south of Rochester, across the highway from the Meadowdale Cinema Complex. One of their number, it has since come out, moved to Rochester and joined the National Guard, swearing to defend the Constitution and all that, with the sole purpose of stealing the keys to the Armory.

The Japanese guards were wholly unprepared and unmotivated to resist such a force, especially since the attackers were all dressed in American Army uniforms and waving American flags. So they hid or put their hands up or ran off into the virgin forest. This wasn't their country, and guarding prisoners wasn't a sacred mission or anything like that. It was just a business.

The telephone and power lines were cut, so they couldn't even call for help or blow the siren.

The assault lasted half an hour. When it was over, Jeffrey Turner was gone, and he hasn't been seen since. The attackers also disappeared. Their uniforms and military vehicles were subsequently found at an abandoned dairy farm owned by German land speculators a kilometer north of the end of the lake. There were tire tracks of many automobiles, which led police to conclude that it was by means of unremarkable civilian vehicles, seemingly unrelated, and no doubt leaving the farm at timed intervals, that the lawless force had made its 100-percent-successful getaway.

Meanwhile, back at the prison, anyone who didn't want to stay inside the walls anymore was free to walk out of there, first taking, if he was so inclined and got there early, a rifle or a shotgun or a pistol or a tear-gas grenade from the wide-open prison armory.

The police said, too, that the attackers of the prison obviously had had first-class military training somewhere, possibly at a private survival school somewhere in this country, or maybe in Bolivia or Colombia or Peru.

Anyway: Margaret and Mildred and I were awakened by the explosion, which demolished the main gate of the prison. There was no way we could have imagined what was really going on.

The 3 of us were sleeping in separate bedrooms. Margaret was on the first floor, Mildred and I were on the second floor. No sooner had I sat up, my ears ringing, than Mildred came into my room stark naked, her eyes open wide.

She spoke first. She used a slang word for hugeness I had never heard her speak before. It wasn't slang of her generation or even mine. It was slang of my children's generation. I guess she had heard it and liked it, and then held it in reserve for some really important occasion.

Here is what she said, as sporadic small-arms fire broke out at the prison: "Do you remember that *humongous* fish I caught?"

11

A T ONE TIME I fully expected to spend the rest of my life in this valley, but not in jail. I envisioned my mandatory retirement from Tarkington College in 2010. I would be modestly well-off with Social Security and a pension from the College. My mother-in-law would surely be dead by then, I thought, so I would have only Margaret to care for. I would rent a little house in the town below. There were plenty of empty ones.

But that dream would have been blasted even if there hadn't been a prison break, even if the Social Security system hadn't gone bust and the College Treasurer hadn't run off with the pension funds and so on. For, as I've said before, in 1991 Tarkington College fired me.

There I was in late middle age, cut loose in a thoroughly looted, bankrupt nation whose assets had been sold off to foreigners, a nation swamped by unchecked plagues and superstition and illiteracy and hypnotic TV, with virtually no health services for the poor. Where to go? What to do?

The man who got me fired was Jason Wilder, the celebrated Conservative newspaper columnist, lecturer, and television talk-show host. He saved my life by doing that. If it weren't for him, I would have been on the Scipio side of the lake instead of the Athena side during the prison break.

I would have been facing all those convicts as they crossed the ice to Scipio in the moonlight, instead of watching them in mute wonderment from the rear, like Robert E. Lee during Pickett's Charge at the Battle of Gettysburg. They wouldn't have known me, and I would still have seen only 3 Athena convicts in all my time.

I would have tried to fight in some way, although, unlike the College President, I would have had no guns. I would have been killed and buried along with the College President and his wife Zuzu, and Alton Darwin and all the rest of them. I would

have been buried next to the stable, in the shadow of Musket
Mountain when the Sun went down.

The first time I saw Jason Wilder in person was at the Board
meeting when they fired me. He was then only an outraged
parent. He would later join the Board and become by far the
most valuable of the convicts' hostages after the prison break.
Their threat to kill him immobilized units of the 82nd Airborne
Division, which had been brought in by school bus from the
South Bronx. The paratroops sealed off the valley at the head
of the lake and occupied the shoreline across from Scipio and to
the south of Scipio, and dug in on the western slope of Musket
Mountain. But they dared not come any closer, for fear of causing the death of Jason Wilder.

There were other hostages, to be sure, including the rest of
the Trustees, but he was the only famous one. I myself was not
strictly a hostage, although I would probably have been killed if
I had tried to leave. I was a sort of floating, noncombatant wise
man, wandering wherever I pleased in Scipio under siege. As at
Athena Prison, I tried to give the most honest answer I could
to any question anyone might care to put to me. Otherwise I
stayed silent. I volunteered no advice at Athena, and none in
Scipio under siege. I simply described the truth of the inquirer's
situation in the context of the world outside as best I could.
What he did next was up to him.

I call that being a teacher. I don't call that being a mastermind
of a treasonous enterprise. All I ever wanted to overthrow was
ignorance and self-serving fantasies.

I was fired without warning on Graduation Day. I was playing the bells at high noon when a girl who had just completed
her freshman year brought the news that the Board of Trustees,
then meeting in Samoza Hall, the administration building,
wanted to talk to me. She was Kimberley Wilder, Jason Wilder's
learning-disabled daughter. She was stupid. I thought it was
odd but not menacing that the Trustees would have used her for

a messenger. I couldn't imagine what business she might have had that would bring her anywhere near their meeting. She had in fact been testifying before them about my supposed lack of patriotism, and had then asked for the honor of fetching me to my liquidation.

She was one of the few underclasspersons still on the campus. The rest had gone home, and relatives of those about to get their Associate in the Arts and Sciences certificates had taken over their suites. No relative of Kimberley's was about to graduate. She had stayed around for the Trustees' meeting. And her famous father had come by helicopter to back her up. The soccer field was being used as a heliport. It looked like a rookery for pterodactyls.

Others had arrived in conventional aircraft at Rochester, where they had been met by rented limousines provided by the college. One senior's stepmother said, I remember, that she thought she had landed in Yokohama instead of Rochester because there were so many Japanese. The thing was that the changing of the guard at Athena had coincided with Graduation Day. New guards, mostly country boys from Hokkaido, who spoke no English and had never seen the United States, were flown directly to Rochester from Tokyo every 6 months, and taken to Athena by bus. And then those who had served 6 months at the gates, and on the walls and catwalks over the mess halls, and in the watchtowers, and so on, were flown straight home.

"How come you haven't gone home, Kimberley?" I said.

She said that she and her father wanted to hear the graduation address, which was to be delivered by her father's close friend and fellow Rhodes Scholar, Dr. Martin Peale Blankenship, the University of Chicago economist who would later become a quadriplegic as a result of a skiing accident in Switzerland.

Dr. Blankenship had a niece in the graduating class. That was what brought him to Scipio. His niece was Hortense Mellon. I have no idea what became of Hortense. She could play the harp. I remember that, and her upper teeth were false. The real teeth were knocked out by a mugger as she left a friend's coming-out party at the Waldorf-Astoria, which has since burned down. There is nothing but a vacant lot there now, which was bought by the Japanese.

I heard that her father, like so many other Tarkington parents, lost an awful lot of money in the biggest swindle in the history of Wall Street, stock in a company called Microsecond Arbitrage.

I had spotted Kimberley as a snoop, all right, but not as a walking recording studio. All through the academic year now ending, our paths had crossed with puzzling frequency. Again and again I would be talking to somebody, almost anywhere on the campus, and realize that Kimberley was lurking close by. I assumed that she was slightly cracked, and was eavesdropping on everyone, avid for gossip. She wasn't even taking a course of mine for credit, although she did audit both Physics for Nonscientists and Music Appreciation for Nonmusicians. So what could I possibly be to her or she to me? We had never had a conversation about anything.

One time, I remember, I was shooting pool in the new recreation center, the Pahlavi Pavilion, and she was so close that I was having trouble working my cuestick, and I said to her, "Do you like my perfume?"

"What?" she said.

"I find you so close to me so often," I said, "I thought maybe you liked my perfume. I'm very flattered, if that's the case, because that's nothing but my natural body odor. I don't use perfume."

I can quote myself exactly, since those words were on one of the tapes the Trustees would play back for me.

She shrugged as though she didn't know what I was talking about. She didn't leave the Pavilion in great embarrassment. On the contrary! She gave me a little more room for my cuestick but was still practically on top of me.

I was playing 8-ball head to head with the novelist Paul Slazinger, that year's Writer in Residence. He was dead broke and out of print, which is the only reason anybody ever became Writer in Residence at Tarkington. He was so old that he had actually been in World War II. He had won a Silver Star like me when I was only 3 years old!

He asked me who Kimberley was, and I said, and she got this on tape, too, "Pay no attention. She's just another member of the Ruling Class."

So the Board of Trustees would want to know what it was, exactly, that I had against the Ruling Class.

I didn't say so back then, but I am perfectly happy to say now that the trouble with the Ruling Class was that too many of its members were nitwits like Kimberley.

One theory I had about her snooping was that she was titillated by my reputation as the campus John F. Kennedy as far as sex outside of marriage was concerned.

If President Kennedy up in Heaven ever made a list of all the women he had made love to, I am sure it would be 2 or 3 times as long as the one I am making down here in jail. Then again, he had the glamour of his office, and the full cooperation of the Secret Service and the White House Staff. None of the names on my list would mean anything to the general public, whereas many on his would belong to movie stars. He made love to Marilyn Monroe. I sure never did. She evidently expected to marry him and become First Lady, which was a joke to everybody but her.

She eventually committed suicide. She finally found life too embarrassing.

I still hardly knew Kimberley when she appeared in the bell tower on Graduation Day. But she was chatty, as though we were old, old pals. She was still recording me, although what she already had on tape was enough to do me in.

She asked me if I thought the speech Paul Slazinger, the Writer in Residence, gave in Chapel had been a good one. This was probably the most anti-American speech I had ever heard. He gave it right before Christmas vacation, and was never again seen in Scipio. He had just won a so-called Genius Grant from the MacArthur Foundation, $50,000 a year for

5 years. On the same night of his speech he bugged out for Key West, Florida.

He predicted, I remember, that human slavery would come back, that it had in fact never gone away. He said that so many people wanted to come here because it was so easy to rob the poor people, who got absolutely no protection from the Government. He talked about bridges falling down and water mains breaking because of no maintenance. He talked about oil spills and radioactive waste and poisoned aquifers and looted banks and liquidated corporations. "And nobody ever gets punished for anything," he said. "Being an American means never having to say you're sorry."

On and on he went. No matter what he said, he was still going to get $50,000 a year for 5 years.

I said to Kimberley that I thought Slazinger had said some things which were worth considering, but that, on the whole, he had made the country sound a lot worse than it really was, and that ours was still far and away the best one on the planet.

She could not have gotten much satisfaction from that reply.

What do I myself make of that reply nowadays? It was an inane reply.

She asked me about my own lecture in Chapel only a month earlier. She hadn't attended and so hadn't taped it. She was seeking confirmation of things other people had said I said. My lecture had been humorous recollections of my maternal grandfather, Benjamin Wills, the old-time Socialist.

She accused me of saying that all rich people were drunks and lunatics. This was a garbling of Grandfather's saying that Capitalism was what the people with all our money, drunk or sober, sane or insane, decided to do today. So I straightened that out, and explained that the opinion was my grandfather's, not my own.

"I heard your speech was worse than Mr. Slazinger's," she said.

"I certainly hope not," I said. "I was trying to show how outdated my grandfather's opinions were. I wanted people to laugh. They did."

"I heard you said Jesus Christ was un-American," she said, her tape recorder running all the time.

So I unscrambled that one for her. The original had been another of Grandfather's sayings. He repeated Karl Marx's prescription for an ideal society, "From each according to his abilities, to each according to his needs." And then he asked me, meaning it to be a wry joke, "What could be more un-American, Gene, than sounding like the Sermon on the Mount?"

———

"What about putting all the Jews in a concentration camp in Idaho?" said Kimberley.

"What about what-what-what?" I asked in bewilderment. At last, at last, and too late, too late, I understood that this stupid girl was as dangerous as a cobra. It would be catastrophic if she spread the word that I was an anti-Semite, especially with so many Jews, having interbred with Gentiles, now sending their children to Tarkington.

"In all my life, I never said anything like that," I promised.

"Maybe it wasn't Idaho," she said.

"Wyoming?" I said.

"OK, Wyoming," she said. "Lock 'em all up, right?"

"I only said 'Wyoming' because I was married in Wyoming," I said. "I've never been to Idaho or even thought about Idaho. I'm just trying to figure out what you've got so all mixed up and upside down. It doesn't sound even a little bit like me."

"Jews," she said.

"That was my grandfather again," I said.

"He hated Jews, right?" she said.

"No, no, no," I said. "He admired a lot of them."

"But he still wanted to put them in concentration camps," she said. "Right?"

The origin of this most poisonous misunderstanding was in my account in Chapel of riding around with Grandfather in his car one Sunday morning in Midland City, Ohio, when I was a little boy. He, not I, was mocking all organized religions.

When we passed a Catholic church, I recalled, he said, "You think your dad's a good chemist? They're turning soda crackers into meat in there. Can your dad do that?"

When we passed a Pentecostal church, he said, "The mental giants in there believe that every word is true in a book put together by a bunch of preachers 300 years after the birth of Christ. I hope you won't be that dumb about words set in type when you grow up."

I would later hear, incidentally, that the woman my father got involved with when I was in high school, when he jumped out a window with his pants down and got bitten by a dog and tangled in a clothesline and so on, was a member of that Pentecostal church.

What he said about Jews that morning was actually another kidding of Christianity. He had to explain to me, as I would have to explain to Kimberley, that the Bible consisted of 2 separate works, the New Testament and the Old Testament. Religious Jews gave credence only to what was supposedly their own history, the Old Testament, whereas Christians took both works seriously.

"I pity the Jews," said Grandfather, "trying to get through life with only half a Bible."

And then he added, "That's like trying to get from here to San Francisco with a road map that stops at Dubuque, Iowa."

I was angry now. "Kimberley," I asked, "did you by any chance tell the Board of Trustees that I said these things? Is that what they want to see me about?"

"Maybe," she said. She was acting cute. I thought this was a dumb answer. It was in fact accurate. The Trustees had a lot more they wanted to discuss than misrepresentations of my Chapel lecture.

I found her both repulsive and pitiful. She thought she was such a heroine and I was such a viper! Now that I had caught on to what she had been up to, she was thrilled to show me that she was proud and unafraid. Little did she know that I had once thrown a man almost as big as she out of a helicopter. What was to prevent me from throwing her out a tower window? The thought of doing that to her crossed my mind. I was so insulted! That would teach her not to insult me!

The man I threw out of the helicopter had spit in my face and bitten my hand. I had taught him not to insult me.

───────────────

She was pitiful because she was a dimwit from a brilliant family and believed that she at last had done something brilliant, too, in getting the goods on a person whose ideas were criminal. I didn't know yet that her Rhodes Scholar father, a Phi Beta Kappa from Princeton, had put her up to this. I thought she had noted her father's conviction, often expressed in his columns and on his TV show, and no doubt at home, that a few teachers who secretly hated their country were making young people lose faith in its future and leadership.

I thought that, just on her own, she had resolved to find such a villain and get him fired, proving that she wasn't so dumb, after all, and that she was really Daddy's little girl.

Wrong.

"Kimberley," I said, as an alternative to throwing her out the window, "this is ridiculous."

Wrong.

───────────────

"All right," I said, "we're going to settle this in a hurry."

Wrong.

I would stride into the Trustees' meeting, I thought, shoulders squared, and radiant with righteous indignation, the most popular teacher on campus, and the only faculty member who had medals from the Vietnam War. When it comes right down to it, that is why they fired me, although I don't believe they themselves realized that that was why they fired me: I had ugly, personal knowledge of the disgrace that was the Vietnam War.

None of the Trustees had been in that war, and neither had Kimberley's father, and not one of them had allowed a son or a daughter to be sent over there. Across the lake in the prison, of course, and down in the town, there were plenty of somebody's sons who had been sent over there.

12

I MET just 2 people when I crossed the Quadrangle to Samoza Hall. One was Professor Marilyn Shaw, head of the Department of Life Sciences. She was the only other faculty member who had served in Vietnam. She had been a nurse. The other was Norman Everett, an old campus gardener like my grandfather. He had a son who had been paralyzed from the waist down by a mine in Vietnam and was a permanent resident in a Veterans Administration hospital over in Schenectady.

The seniors and their families and the rest of the faculty were having lunch in the Pavilion. Everybody got a lobster which had been boiled alive.

I never considered making a pass at Marilyn, although she was reasonably attractive and unattached. I don't know why that is. There may have been some sort of incest taboo operating, as though we were brother and sister, since we had both been in Vietnam.

She is dead now, buried next to the stable, in the shadow of Musket Mountain when the Sun goes down. She was evidently hit by a stray bullet. Who in his right mind would have taken dead aim at her?

Remembering her now, I wonder if I wasn't in love with her, even though we avoided talking to each other as much as possible.

Maybe I should put her on a very short list indeed: all the women I loved. That would be Marilyn, I think, and Margaret during the first 4 years or so of our marriage, before I came home with the clap. I was also very fond of Harriet Gummer, the war correspondent for *The Des Moines Register*, who, it turns out, bore me a son after our love affair in Manila. I think I felt what could be called love for Zuzu Johnson, whose husband was crucified. And I had a deep, thoroughly reciprocated, multidimensioned friendship with Muriel Peck, who was a bartender at the Black Cat Café the day I was fired, who later became a member of the English Department.

End of list.

Muriel, too, is buried next to the stable, in the shadow of Musket Mountain when the Sun goes down.

Harriet Gummer is also dead, but out in Iowa.

Hey, girls, wait for me, wait for me.

I don't expect to break a world's record with the number of women I made love to, whether I loved them or not. As far as I am concerned, the record set by Georges Simenon, the French mystery writer, can stand for all time. According to his obituary in *The New York Times*, he copulated with 3 different women a day for years and years.

Marilyn Shaw and I hadn't known each other in Vietnam, but we had a friend in common there, Sam Wakefield. Afterward, he had hired both of us for Tarkington, and then committed suicide for reasons unclear even to himself, judging from the plagiarized note he left on his bedside table.

He and his wife, who would become Tarkington's Dean of Women, were sleeping in separate rooms by then.

Sam Wakefield, in my opinion, saved Marilyn's and my lives before he gave up on his own. If he hadn't hired both of us for Tarkington, where we both became very good teachers of the learning-disabled, I don't know what would have become of either of us. When we passed yet again like ships in the night on the Quadrangle, with me on my way to get fired, I was, incredibly, a tenured Full Professor of Physics and she was a tenured Full Professor of Life Sciences!

When I was still a teacher here, I asked GRIOT™, the most popular computer game at the Pahlavi Pavilion, what might have become of me after the war instead of what really happened. The way you play GRIOT™, of course, is to tell the computer the age and race and degree of education and present situation and drug use, if any, and so on of a person. The person doesn't have to be real. The computer doesn't ask if the person is real or not. It doesn't care about anything. It especially doesn't care about hurting people's feelings. You load it up with details about a life, real or imagined, and then it spits out a story about what was likely to happen to him or her. This story is based on what has happened to real persons with the same general specifications.

GRIOT™ won't work without certain pieces of information. If you leave out race, for instance, it flashes the words "ethnic origin" on its screen, and stops cold. If it doesn't know that, it can't go on. The same with education.

I didn't tell GRIOT™ that I had landed a job I loved here. I told it only about my life up to the end of the Vietnam War. It knew all about the Vietnam War and the sorts of veterans it had produced. It made me a burned-out case, on the basis of my length of service over there, I think. It had me becoming a wife-beater and an alcoholic, and winding up all alone on Skid Row.

If I had access to GRIOT™ now, I might ask it what might have happened to Marilyn Shaw if Sam Wakefield hadn't rescued her. But the escaped convicts smashed up the one in the Pavilion soon after I showed them how to work it.

They hated it, and I didn't blame them. I was immediately sorry that I had let them know of its existence. One by one they punched in their race and age and what their parents did, if they knew, and how long they'd gone to school and what drugs they'd taken and so on, and GRIOT™ sent them straight to jail to serve long sentences.

I have no idea how much GRIOT™ back then may have known about Vietnam nurses. The manufacturers claimed then as now that no program in stores was more than 3 months old, and so every program was right up-to-date about what had really happened to this or that sort of person at the time you bought it. The programmers, supposedly, were constantly updating GRIOT™ with the news of the day about plumbers, about podiatrists, about Vietnam boat people and Mexican wetbacks, about drug smugglers, about paraplegics, about everyone you could think of within the continental limits of the United States and Canada.

There is some question now, I've heard, about whether GRIOT™ is as deep and up-to-date as it used to be, since Parker Brothers, the company that makes it, has been taken over by Koreans. The new owners are moving the whole operation to Indonesia, where labor costs next to nothing. They say they will keep up with American news by satellite.

One wonders.

I don't need any help from GRIOT™ to know that Marilyn Shaw had a much rougher war than I did. All the soldiers she had to deal with were wounded, and all of them expected of her what was more often than not impossible: that she make them whole again.

I know that she was married, and that her husband back home divorced her and married somebody else while she was still over there, and that she didn't care. She and Sam Wakefield may have been lovers over there. I never asked.

That seems likely. After the war he went looking for her and found her taking a course in Computer Science at New York University. She didn't want to be a nurse anymore. He told her that maybe she should try being a teacher instead. She asked him if there was a chapter of Alcoholics Anonymous in Scipio, and he said there was.

After he shot himself, Marilyn, Professor Shaw, fell off the wagon for about a week. She disappeared, and I was given the job of finding her. I discovered her downtown, drunk and asleep on a pool table in the back room of the Black Cat Café. She was drooling on the felt. One hand was on the cue ball, as though she meant to throw it at something when she regained consciousness.

As far as I know, she never took another drink.

GRIOT™, in the old days anyway, before the Koreans promised to make Parker Brothers lean and mean in Indonesia, didn't come up with the same biography every time you gave it a certain set of facts. Like life itself, it offered a variety of possibilities, spitting out endings according to what the odds for winning or losing or whatever were known to be.

After GRIOT™ put me on Skid Row 15 years ago, I had it try again. I did a little better, but not as well as I was doing here. It had me stay in the Army and become an instructor at West Point, but unhappy and bored. I lost my wife again, and still drank too much, and had a succession of woman friends who soon got sick of me and my depressions. And I died of cirrhosis of the liver a second time.

GRIOT™ didn't have many alternatives to jail for the escaped convicts, though. If it came up with a parole, it soon put the ex-con back in a cage again.

The same thing happened if GRIOT™ was told that the jailbird was Hispanic. It was somewhat more optimistic about Whites, if they could read and write, and had never been in a mental hospital or been given a Dishonorable Discharge from the Armed Forces. Otherwise, they might as well be Black or Hispanic.

The wild cards among jailbirds, as far as GRIOT™ was concerned, were Orientals and American Indians.

When the Supreme Court handed down its decision that prisoners should be segregated according to race, many jurisdictions did not have enough Oriental or American Indian criminals to make separate institutions for them economically feasible. Hawaii, for example, had only 2 American Indian prisoners, and Wyoming, my wife's home state, had only 1 Oriental.

Under such circumstances, said the Court, Indians and/ or Orientals should be made honorary Whites, and treated accordingly.

This state has plenty of both, however, particularly after Indians began to make tax-free fortunes smuggling drugs over unmapped trails across the border from Canada. So the Indians had a prison all their own at what their ancestors used to call "Thunder Beaver," what we call "Niagara Falls." The Orientals have their own prison at Deer Park, Long Island, conveniently located only 50 kilometers from their heroin-processing plants in New York City's Chinatown.

When you dare to think about how huge the illegal drug business is in this country, you have to suspect that practically everybody has a steady buzz on, just as I did during my last 2 years in high school, and just as General Grant did during the Civil War, and just as Winston Churchill did during World War II.

So Marilyn Shaw and I passed yet again like ships in the night on the Quadrangle. It would be our last encounter there. Without either of us knowing that it would be the last time, she said something that in retrospect is quite moving to me. What she said was derived from our exploratory conversation at the cocktail party that had welcomed us to the faculty so long ago.

I had told her about how I met Sam Wakefield at the Cleveland Science Fair, and what the first words were that he ever spoke to me. Now, as I hastened to my doom, she played back those words to me: "What's the hurry, Son?"

13

THE CHAIRMAN of the Board of Trustees that fired me 10 years ago was Robert W. Moellenkamp of West Palm Beach, himself a graduate of Tarkington and the father of 2 Tarkingtonians, 1 of whom had been my student. As it happened, he was on the verge of losing his fortune, which was nothing but paper, in Microsecond Arbitrage, Incorporated. That swindle claimed to be snapping up bargains in food and shelter and clothing and fuel and medicine and raw materials and machinery and so on before people who really needed them could learn of their existence. And then the company's computers, supposedly, would get the people who really needed whatever it was to bid against each other, running profits right through the roof. It was able to do this with its clients' money, supposedly, because its computers were linked by satellites to marketplaces in every corner of the world.

The computers, it would turn out, weren't connected to anything but each other and their credulous clients like Tarkington's Board Chairman. He was high as a kite on printouts describing brilliant trades he had made in places like Tierra del Fuego and Uganda and God knows where else, when he agreed with the Panjandrum of American Conservatism, Jason Wilder, that it was time to fire me. Microsecond Arbitrage was his angel dust, his LSD, his heroin, his jug of Thunderbird wine, his cocaine.

I myself have been addicted to older women and housekeeping, which my court-appointed lawyer tells me might be germs we could make grow into a credible plea of insanity. The most amazing thing to him was that I had never masturbated.

"Why not?" he said.

"My mother's father made me promise never to do it, because it would make me lazy and crazy," I said.

"And you believed him?" he said. He is only 23 years old, fresh out of Syracuse.

And I said, "Counselor, in these fast-moving times, with progress gone hog-wild, grandfathers are bound to be wrong about everything."

Robert W. Moellenkamp hadn't heard yet that he and his wife and kids were as broke as any convict in Athena. So when I came into the Board Room back in 1991, he addressed me in the statesmanlike tones of a prudent conservator of a noble legacy. He nodded in the direction of Jason Wilder, who was then simply a Tarkington parent, not a member of the Board. Wilder sat at the opposite end of the great oval table with a manila folder, a tape recorder and cassettes, and a Polaroid photograph deployed before him.

I knew who he was, of course, and something of how his mind worked, having read his newspaper column and watched his television show from time to time. But we had not met before. The Board members on either side of him had crowded into one another in order to give him plenty of room for some kind of performance.

He was the only celebrity there. He was probably the only true celebrity ever to set foot in that Board Room.

There was 1 other non-Trustee present. That was the College President, Henry "Tex" Johnson, whose wife Zuzu, as I've already said, I used to make love to when he was away from home any length of time. Zuzu and I had broken up for good about a month before, but we were still on speaking terms.

"Please take a seat, Gene," said Moellenkamp. "Mr. Wilder, who I guess you know is Kimberley's father, has a rather disturbing story he wants to tell to you."

"I see," I said, a good soldier doing as he was told. I wanted to keep my job. This was my home. When the time came, I wanted to retire here and then be buried here. That was before it was clear that glaciers were headed south again, and that anybody buried here, including the gang by the stable, along with Musket Mountain itself, would eventually wind up in Pennsylvania or West Virginia. Or Maryland.

Where else could I become a Full Professor or a college teacher of any rank, with nothing but a Bachelor of Science Degree from West Point? I couldn't even teach high school or grade school, since I had never taken any of the required courses in education. At my age, which was then 51, who would hire me for anything, and especially with a demented wife and mother-in-law in tow.

I said to the Trustees and Jason Wilder, "I believe I know most of what the story is, ladies and gentlemen. I've just been with Kimberley, and she gave me a pretty good rehearsal for what I'd better say here.

"When listening to her charges against me, I can only hope you did not lose sight of what you yourselves have learned about me during my 15 years of faithful service to Tarkington. This Board itself, surely, can provide all the character witnesses I could ever need. If not, bring in parents and students. Choose them at random. You know and I know that they will all speak well of me."

I nodded respectfully in Jason Wilder's direction. "I am glad to meet you in person, sir. I read your columns and watch your TV show regularly. I find what you have to say invariably thought-provoking, and so do my wife and her mother, both of them invalids." I wanted to get that in about my 2 sick dependents, in case Wilder and a couple of new Trustees hadn't heard about them.

Actually, I was laying it on pretty thick. Although Margaret and her mother read to each other a lot, taking turns, and usually by flashlight in a tent they'd made inside the house out of bedspreads and chairs or whatever, they never read a newspaper. They didn't like television, either, except for *Sesame Street*, which was supposedly for children. The only time they saw Jason Wilder on the little screen as far as I can remember, my mother-in-law started dancing to him as though he were modern music.

When one of his guests on the show said something, she froze. Only when Wilder spoke did she start to dance again.

I certainly wasn't going to tell him that.

"I want to say first," said Wilder, "that I am in nothing less than awe, Professor Hartke, of your magnificent record in the

Vietnam War. If the American people had not lost their courage and ceased to support you, we would be living in a very different and much better world, and especially in Asia. I know, too, of your kindness and understanding toward your wife and her mother, to which I am glad to apply the same encomium your behavior earned in Vietnam, 'beyond the call of duty.' So I am sorry to have to warn you that the story I am about to tell you may not be nearly as simple or easy to refute as my daughter may have led you to expect."

"Whatever it is, sir," I said, "let's hear it. Shoot."

So he did. He said that several of his friends had attended Tarkington or sent their children here, so that he was favorably impressed with the institution's successes with the learning-disabled long before he entrusted his own daughter to us. An usher and a bridesmaid at his wedding, he said, had earned Associate in the Arts and Sciences Degrees in Scipio. The usher had gone on to be Ambassador to Iceland. The bridesmaid was on the Board of Directors of the Chicago Symphony Orchestra.

He felt that Tarkington's highly unconventional techniques would be useful if applied to the country's notoriously beleaguered inner-city schools, and he planned to say so after he had learned more about them. The ratio of teachers to students at Tarkington, incidentally, was then 1 to 6. In inner-city schools, that ratio was then 1 to 65.

There was a big campaign back then, I remember, to get the Japanese to buy up inner-city public schools the way they were buying up prisons and hospitals. But they were too smart. They wouldn't touch schools for unwelcome children of unwelcome parents with a 10-foot pole.

He said he hoped to write a book about Tarkington called "Little Miracle on Lake Mohiga" or "Teaching the Unteachable." So he wired his daughter for sound and told her to follow the best teachers in order to record what they said and how they said it. "I wanted to learn what it was that made them good, Professor Hartke, without their knowing they were being studied," he said. "I wanted them to go on being whatever they were, warts and all, without any self-consciousness."

This was the first I heard of the tapes. That chilling news explained Kimberley's lurking, lurking, lurking all the time. Wilder spared me the suspense, at least, of wondering what all of Kimberley's apparatus might have overheard. He punched the playback button on the recorder before him, and I heard myself telling Paul Slazinger, privately, I'd thought, that the two principal currencies of the planet were the Yen and fellatio. This was so early in the academic year that classes hadn't begun yet! This was during Freshman Orientation Week, and I had just told the incoming Class of 1994 that merchants and tradespeople in the town below preferred to be paid in Japanese Yen rather than dollars, so that the freshmen might want their parents to give them their allowances in Yen.

I had told them, too, that they were never to go into the Black Cat Café, which the townspeople considered their private club. It was one place they could go and not be reminded of how dependent they were on the rich kids on the hill, but I didn't say that. Neither did I say that free-lance prostitutes were sometimes found there, and in the past had been the cause of outbreaks of venereal disease on campus.

I had kept it simple for the freshmen: "Tarkingtonians are more than welcome anywhere in town but the Black Cat Café."

If Kimberley recorded that good advice, her father did not play it back for me. He didn't even play back what Slazinger had said to me, and it was during a coffee break, that stimulated me to name the planet's two most acceptable currencies. He was the agent provocateur.

What he said, as I recall, was, "They want to get paid in Yen?" He was as new to Scipio as any freshman, and we had just met. I hadn't read any of his books, and so far as I knew neither had anybody else on the faculty. He was a last-minute choice for Writer in Residence, and had come to orientation because he was lonesome and had nothing else to do. He wasn't supposed to be there, and he was so old, so old! He had been sitting among all those teenagers as though he were just another rich kid who had bottomed out on his Scholastic Aptitude Test, and he was old enough to be their grandfather!

He had fought in World War II! That's how old he was.

So I said to him, "They'll take dollars if they have to, but you'd better have a wheelbarrow."

And he wanted to know if the merchants and tradespeople would also accept fellatio. He used a vernacular word for fellatio in the plural.

But the tape began right after that, with my saying, as though out of the blue, and as a joke, of course, only it didn't sound like a joke during the playback, that, in effect, the whole World was for sale to anyone who had Yen or was willing to perform fellatio.

14

S O THAT WAS TWICE within an hour that I was accused of cynicism that was Paul Slazinger's, not mine. And he was in Key West, well out of reach of punishment, having been unemployment-proofed for 5 years with a Genius Grant from the MacArthur Foundation. In saying what I had about Yen and fellatio, I was being sociable with a stranger. I was echoing him to make him feel at home in new surroundings.

As far as that goes, Professor Damon Stern, head of the History Department and my closest male friend here, spoke as badly of his own country as Slazinger and I did, and right into the faces of students in the classroom day after day. I used to sit in on his course and laugh and clap. The truth can be very funny in an awful way, especially as it relates to greed and hypocrisy. Kimberley must have made recordings of his words, too, and played them back for her father. Why wasn't Damon fired right along with me?

My guess is that he was a comedian, and I was not. He wanted students to leave his presence feeling good, not bad, so the atrocities and stupidities he described were in the distant past. There was nothing a student could do about them but laugh, laugh, laugh.

Whereas Slazinger and I talked about the last half of the 20th Century, in which we had both been seriously wounded physically and psychologically, which was nothing anybody but a sociopath could laugh about.

I, too, might have been acceptable as a comedian if all Kimberley had taped was what I said about Yen and fellatio. That was good, topical Mohiga Valley humor, what with the Japanese taking over the prison across the lake and arousing curiosity among the natives about the relative values of different national currencies. The Japanese were willing to pay their local bills in either dollars or Yen. These bills were for small-ticket items, hardware or toiletries or whatever, which the prison needed in a hurry, usually ordered by telephone. Big-ticket items in quantity came from Japanese-owned suppliers in Rochester or beyond.

So Japanese currency had started to circulate in Scipio. The prison administrators and guards were rarely seen in town, however. They lived in barracks to the east of the prison, and lived lives as invisible to this side of the lake as those of the prisoners.

To the limited extent that anybody on this side of the lake thought about the prison at all until the mass escape, people were generally glad to have the Japanese in charge. The new proprietor had cut waste and corruption to almost nothing. What they charged the State for punishing its prisoners was only 75 percent of what the State used to pay itself for identical services.

The local paper, *The Valley Sentinel*, sent a reporter over there to see what the Japanese were doing differently. They were still using the steel boxes on the back of trucks and showing old TV shows, including news, in no particular order and around the clock. The biggest change was that Athena was drug-free for the first time in its history, and rich prisoners weren't able to buy privileges. The guards weren't easily fooled or corrupted, either, since they understood so little English, and wanted nothing more than to finish up their 6 months overseas and go home again.

A normal tour of duty in Vietnam was twice that long and 1,000 times more dangerous. Who could blame the educated classes with political connections for staying home?

One new wrinkle by the Japanese the reporter didn't mention was that the guards wore surgical masks and rubber gloves when they were on duty, even up in the towers and atop the walls. That wasn't to keep them from spreading infections, of course. It was to ensure that they didn't take any of their loathsome charges' loathsome diseases back home with them.

When I went to work over there, I refused to wear gloves and a mask. Who could teach anybody anything while wearing such a costume?

So now I have tuberculosis.

Cough, cough, cough.

Before I could protest to the Trustees that I certainly wouldn't have said what I'd said about Yen and fellatio if I'd thought there was the slightest chance that a student could hear me, the background noises on the tape changed. I realized that I was about to hear something I had said in a different location. There was the pop-pop-pop of Ping-Pong balls, and a card player asked, "Who dealt this mess?" Somebody else asked somebody else to bring her a hot fudge sundae without nuts on top. She was on a diet, she said. There were rumblings like distant artillery, which were really the sound of bowling balls in the basement of the Pahlavi Pavilion.

Oh Lordy, was I ever drunk that night at the Pavilion. I was out of control. And it was a disgrace that I should have appeared before students in such a condition. I will regret it to my dying day. Cough.

It was on a cold night near the end of November of 1990, 6 months before the Trustees fired me. I know it wasn't December, because Slazinger was still on campus, talking openly of suicide. He hadn't yet received his Genius Grant.

When I came home from work that afternoon, to tidy up the house and make supper, I found an awful mess. Margaret and Mildred, both hags by then, had torn bedsheets into strips. I had laundered the sheets that morning, and was going to put them on our beds that night. What did they care?

They had constructed what they said was a spider web. At least it wasn't a hydrogen bomb.

White cotton strips spliced end to end crisscrossed every which way in the front hall and living room. The newel post of the stairway was connected to the inside doorknob of the front door, and the doorknob was connected to the living room chandelier, and so on ad infinitum.

The day hadn't begun auspiciously anyway. I had found all 4 tires of my Mercedes flat. A bunch of high school kids from down below, high on alcohol or who knows what, had come up during the night like Vietcong and gone what they called "coring" again. They not only had let the air out of the tires of every expensive car they could find in the open on campus, Porsches and Jaguars and Saabs and BMWs and so on, but had taken out the valve cores. At home, I had heard, they had jars full of valve cores or necklaces of valve cores to prove how often they had gone coring. And they got my Mercedes. They got my Mercedes every time.

So when I found myself tangled in Margaret and Mildred's spider web, my nervous system came close to the breaking point. I was the one who was going to have to clean up this mess. I was the one who was going to have to remake the beds with other sheets, and then buy more sheets the next day. I have always liked housework, or at least not minded it as much as most people seem to. But this was housework beyond the pale!

I had left the house so neat in the morning! And Margaret and Mildred weren't getting any fun out of watching my reactions when I was tangled up in their spider web. They were hiding someplace where they couldn't see or hear me. They expected me to play hide-and-seek, with me as "it."

Something in me snapped. I wasn't going to play hide-and-seek this time. I wasn't going to take down the spider web. I wasn't going to prepare supper. Let them come creeping out of their hiding places in an hour or whatever. Let them wonder, as I had when I walked into the spider web, what on Earth had happened to their previously dependable, forgiving Universe?

Out into the cold night I went, with no destination in mind save for good old oblivion. I found myself in front of the house of my best friend, Damon Stern, the entertaining professor of History. When he was a boy in Wisconsin, he had learned how to ride a unicycle. He had taught his wife and kids how to ride one, too.

The lights were on, but nobody was home. The family's 4 unicycles were in the front hall and the car was gone. They never got cored. They were smart. They drove one of the last Volkswagen Bugs still running.

I knew where they kept the liquor. I poured myself a couple of stiff shots of bourbon, in lieu of their absent body warmth. I don't think I had had a drink for a month before that.

I got this hot rush in my belly. Out into the night I went again. I was automatically looking for an older woman who would make everything all right by becoming the beast with two backs with me.

A coed would not do, not that a coed would have had anything to do with somebody as old and relatively poor as me. I couldn't even have promised her a better grade than she deserved. There were no grades at Tarkington.

But I wouldn't have wanted a coed in any case. The only sort of woman who excites me is an older one in uncomfortable circumstances, full of doubts not only about herself but about the value of life itself. Although I never met her personally, the late Marilyn Monroe comes to mind, maybe 3 years before she committed suicide.

Cough, cough, cough.

———————————

If there is a Divine Providence, there is also a wicked one, provided you agree that making love to off-balance women you aren't married to is wickedness. My own feeling is that if adultery is wickedness then so is food. Both make me feel so much better afterward.

———————————

Just as a hungry person knows that somewhere not far away somebody is preparing good things to eat, I knew that night that not far away was an older woman in despair. There had to be!

Zuzu Johnson was out of the question. Her husband was home, and she was hosting a dinner party for a couple of grateful parents who were giving the college a language laboratory.

When it was finished, students would be able to sit in sound-proof booths and listen to recordings of any one of more than 100 languages and dialects made by native speakers.

The lights were on in the sculpture studio of Norman Rockwell Hall, the art building, the only structure on campus named after a historical figure rather than the donating family. It was another gift from the Moellenkamps, who may have felt that too much was named after them already.

There was a whirring and rumbling coming from inside the sculpture studio. Somebody was playing with the crane in there, making it run back and forth on its tracks overhead. Whoever it was had to be playing, since nobody ever made a piece of sculpture so big that it could be moved only by the mighty crane.

After the prison break, there was some talk on the part of the convicts of hanging somebody from it, and running him back and forth while he strangled. They had no particular candidate in mind. But then the Niagara Power and Light Company, which was owned by the Unification Church Korean Evangelical Association, shut off all our electricity.

Outside Rockwell Hall that night, I might have been back on a patrol in Vietnam. That is how keen my senses were. That was how quick my mind was to create a whole picture from the slightest clues.

I knew that the sculpture studio was locked up tight after 6:30 P.M., since I had tried the door many times, thinking that I might sometime bring a lover there. I had considered getting a key somehow at the start of the semester and learned from Building and Grounds that only they and that year's Artist in Residence, the sculptress Pamela Ford Hall, were allowed to have keys. This was because of vandalism by either students or Townies in the studio the year before.

They knocked off the noses and fingers of replicas of Greek statues, and defecated in a bucket of wet clay. That sort of thing.

So that had to be Pamela Ford Hall in there making the crane go back and forth. And the crane's restless travels had to represent unhappiness, not any masterpiece she was creating. What use did she have for a crane, or even a wheelbarrow, since she worked exclusively in nearly weightless polyurethane. And she was a recent divorcée without children. And, because she knew my reputation, I'm sure, she had been avoiding me.

I climbed up on the studio's loading dock. I thumped my fist on its enormous sliding door. The door was motor driven. She had only to press a button to let me in.

The crane stopped going back and forth. There was a hopeful sign!

She asked through the door what I wanted.

"I wanted to make sure you were OK in there," I said.

"Who are you to care whether I'm OK or not in here?" she said.

"Gene Hartke," I said.

She opened the door just a crack and stared out at me, but didn't say anything. Then she opened the door wider, and I could see she was holding an uncorked bottle of what would turn out to be blackberry brandy.

"Hello, Soldier," she said.

"Hi," I said very carefully.

And then she said, "What took you so long?"

15

P AMELA sure got me drunk that night, and we made love. And then I spilled my guts about the Vietnam War in front of a bunch of students at the Pahlavi Pavilion. And Kimberley Wilder recorded me.

I had never tasted blackberry brandy before. I never want to taste it again. It did bad things to me. It made me a crybaby about the war. That is something I swore I would never be.

If I could order any drink I wanted now, it would be a Sweet Rob Roy on the Rocks, a Manhattan made with Scotch. That was another drink a woman introduced me to, and it made me laugh instead of cry, and fall in love with the woman who said to try one.

That was in Manila, after the excrement hit the air-conditioning in Saigon. She was Harriet Gummer, the war correspondent from Iowa. She had a son by me without telling me.

His name? Rob Roy.

After we made love, Pamela asked me the same question Harriet had asked me in Manila 15 years earlier. It was something they both had to know. They both asked me if I had killed anybody in the war.

I said to Pamela what I had said to Harriet: "If I were a fighter plane instead of a human being, there would be little pictures of people painted all over me."

I should have gone straight home after saying that. But I went over to the Pavilion instead. I needed a bigger audience for that great line of mine.

So I barged into a group of students sitting in front of the great fireplace in the main lounge. After the prison break, that fireplace would be used for cooking horse meat and dogs. I got between the students and the fire, so there was no way they could ignore me, and I said to them, "If I were a fighter plane instead of a human being, there would be little pictures of people painted all over me."

I went on from there.

***

I was so full of self-pity! That was what I found unbearable when Jason Wilder played back my words to me. I was so drunk that I acted like a victim!

***

The scenes of unspeakable cruelty and stupidity and waste I described that night were no more horrible than ultrarealistic shows about Vietnam, which had become staples of TV entertainment. When I told the students about the severed human head I saw nestled in the guts of a water buffalo, to them, I'm sure, the head might as well have been made of wax, and the guts those of some big animal which may or may not have belonged to a real water buffalo.

What difference could it make whether the head was or was not wax, or whether the guts were or were not those of a water buffalo?

No difference.

***

"Professor Hartke," Jason Wilder said to me gently, reasonably, when the tape had reached its end, "why on Earth would you want to tell such tales to young people who need to love their country?"

I wanted to keep my job so much, and the house which came with it, that my reply was asinine. "I was telling them history," I said, "and I had had a little too much to drink. I don't usually drink that much."

"I'm sure," he said. "I am told that you are a man with many problems, but that alcohol has not appeared among them with any consistency. So let us say that your performance in the Pavilion was a well-intended history lesson of which you accidentally lost control."

"That's what it was, sir," I said.

His balletic hands flitted in time to the logic of his thoughts before he spoke again. He was a fellow pianist. And then he said, "First of all, you were not hired to teach History. Second of all, the students who come to Tarkington need no further instructions in how it feels to be defeated. They would not be here if they themselves had not failed and failed. The Miracle on Lake Mohiga for more than a century now, as I see it, has been to make children who have failed and failed start thinking of victory, stop thinking about the hopelessness of it all."

"There was just that one time," I said, "and I'm sorry."

Cough. One cough.

Wilder said he didn't consider a teacher who was negative about everything a teacher. "I would call a person like that an 'unteacher.' He's somebody who takes things out of young people's heads instead of putting more things in."

"I don't know as I'm negative about everything," I said.

"What's the first thing students see when they walk into the library?" he said.

"Books?" I said.

"All those perpetual-motion machines," he said. "I saw that display, and I read the sign on the wall above it. I had no idea then that you were responsible for the sign."

He was talking about the sign that said "THE COMPLICATED FUTILITY OF IGNORANCE."

"All I knew was that I didn't want my daughter or anybody's child to see a message that negative every time she comes into the library," he said. "And then I found out it was you who was responsible for it."

"What's so negative about it?" I said.

"What could be a more negative word than 'futility'?" he said.

"'Ignorance,'" I said.

"There you are," he said. I had somehow won his argument for him.

"I don't understand," I said.

"Precisely," he said. "You obviously do not understand how easily discouraged the typical Tarkington student is, how sensitive to suggestions that he or she should quit trying to be smart. That's what the word 'futile' means: 'Quit, quit, quit.' "

"And what does 'ignorance' mean?" I said.

"If you put it up on the wall and give it the prominence you have," he said, "it's a nasty echo of what so many Tarkingtonians were hearing before they got here: 'You're dumb, you're dumb, you're dumb.' And of course they aren't dumb."

"I never said they were," I protested.

"You reinforce their low self-esteem without realizing what you are doing," he said. "You also upset them with humor appropriate to a barracks, but certainly not to an institution of higher learning."

"You mean about Yen and fellatio?" I said. "I would never have said it if I'd thought a student could hear me."

"I am talking about the entrance hall of the library again," he said.

"I can't think of what else is in there that might have offended you," I said.

"It wasn't I who was offended," he said. "It was my daughter."

"I give up," I said. I wasn't being impudent. I was abject.

"On the same day Kimberley heard you talk about Yen and fellatio, before classes had even begun," he said, "a senior led her and the other freshmen to the library and solemnly told them that the bell clappers on the wall were petrified penises. That was surely barracks humor the senior had picked up from you."

For once I didn't have to defend myself. Several of the Trustees assured Wilder that telling freshmen that the clappers were penises was a tradition that antedated my arrival on campus by at least 20 years.

But that was the only time they defended me, although 1 of them had been my student, Madelaine Astor, née Peabody, and 5 of them were parents of those I had taught. Madelaine dictated a letter to me afterward, explaining that Jason Wilder had promised to denounce the college in his column and on his TV show if the Trustees did not fire me.

So they dared not come to my assistance.

———————————

She said, too, that since she, like Wilder, was a Roman Catholic, she was shocked to hear me say on tape that Hitler was a Roman Catholic, and that the Nazis painted crosses on their tanks and airplanes because they considered themselves a Christian army. Wilder had played that tape right after I had been cleared of all responsibility for freshmen being told that the clappers were penises.

Once again I was in deep trouble for merely repeating what somebody else had said. It wasn't something my grandfather had said this time, or somebody else who couldn't be hurt by the Trustees, like Paul Slazinger. It was something my best friend Damon Stern had said in a History class only a couple of months before.

If Jason Wilder thought I was an unteacher, he should have heard Damon Stern! Then again, Stern never told the awful truth about supposedly noble human actions in recent times. Everything he debunked had to have transpired before 1950, say.

So I happened to sit in on a class where he talked about Hitler's being a devout Roman Catholic. He said something I hadn't realized before, something I have since discovered most Christians don't want to hear: that the Nazi swastika was intended to be a version of a Christian cross, a cross made out of axes. Stern said that Christians had gone to a lot of trouble denying that the swastika was just another cross, saying it was a primitive symbol from the primordial ooze of the pagan past.

And the Nazis' most valuable military decoration was the Iron Cross.

And the Nazis painted regular crosses on all their tanks and airplanes.

I came out of that class looking sort of dazed, I guess. Who should I run into but Kimberley Wilder?

"What did he say today?" she said.

"Hitler was a Christian," I said. "The swastika was a Christian cross."

She got it on tape.

———————————

I didn't rat on Damon Stern to the Trustees. Tarkington wasn't West Point, where it was an honor to squeal.

———————————

Madelaine agreed with Wilder, too, she said in her letter, that I should not have told my Physics students that the Russians, not the Americans, were the first to make a hydrogen bomb that was portable enough to be used as a weapon. "Even if it's true," she wrote, "which I don't believe, you had no business telling them that."

She said, moreover, that perpetual motion was possible, if only scientists would work harder on it.

She had certainly backslid intellectually since passing her orals for her Associate in the Arts and Sciences Degree.

I used to tell classes that anybody who believed in the possibility of perpetual motion should be boiled alive like a lobster.

I was also a stickler about the Metric System. I was famous for turning my back on students who mentioned feet or pounds or miles to me.

They hated that.

I didn't dare teach like that in the prison across the lake, of course.

Then again, most of the convicts had been in the drug business, and were either Third World people or dealt with Third World people. So the Metric System was old stuff to them.

Rather than rat on Damon Stern about the Nazis' being Christians, I told the Trustees that I had heard it on National Public Radio. I said I was very sorry about having passed it on to a student. "I feel like biting off my tongue," I said.

"What does Hitler have to do with either Physics or Music Appreciation?" said Wilder.

I might have replied that Hitler probably didn't know any more about physics than the Board of Trustees, but that he loved music. Every time a concert hall was bombed, I heard somewhere, he had it rebuilt immediately as a matter of top priority. I think I may actually have learned that from National Public Radio.

I said instead, "If I'd known I upset Kimberley as much as you say I did, I would certainly have apologized. I had no idea, sir. She gave no sign."

What made me weak was the realization that I had been mistaken to think that I was with family there in the Board Room, that all Tarkingtonians and their parents and guardians had come to regard me as an uncle. My goodness—the family secrets I had learned over the years and kept to myself! My lips were sealed. What a faithful old retainer I was! But that was all I was to the Trustees, and probably to the students, too.

I wasn't an uncle. I was a member of the Servant Class.

They were letting me go.

Soldiers are discharged. People in the workplace are fired. Servants are let go.

"Am I being fired?" I asked the Chairman of the Board incredulously.

"I'm sorry, Gene," he said, "but we're going to have to let you go."

The President of the college, Tex Johnson, sitting two chairs away from me, hadn't let out a peep. He looked sick. I surmised mistakenly that he had been scolded for having let me stay on the faculty long enough to get tenure. He was sick about something more personal, which still had a lot to do with Professor Eugene Debs Hartke.

He had been brought in as President from Rollins College down in Winter Park, Florida, where he had been Provost, after Sam Wakefield did the big trick of suicide. Henry "Tex" Johnson held a Bachelor's Degree in Business Administration from Texas Tech in Lubbock, and claimed to be a descendant of a man who had died in the Alamo. Damon Stern, who was always turning up little-known facts of history, told me, incidentally, that the Battle of the Alamo was about slavery. The brave men who died there wanted to secede from Mexico because it was against the law to own slaves in Mexico. They were fighting for the right to own slaves.

Since Tex's wife and I had been lovers, I knew that his ancestors weren't Texans, but Lithuanians. His father, whose name certainly wasn't Johnson, was a Lithuanian second mate on a Russian freighter who jumped ship when it put in for emergency repairs at Corpus Christi. Zuzu told me that Tex's father was not only an illegal immigrant but the nephew of the former Communist boss of Lithuania.

So much for the Alamo.

I turned to him at the Board meeting, and I said, "Tex—for pity sakes, say something! You know darn good and well I'm the best teacher you've got! I don't say that. The students do! Is the whole faculty going to be brought before this Board, or am I the only one? Tex?"

He stared straight ahead. He seemed to have turned to cement. "Tex?" Some leadership!

I put the same question to the Chairman, who had been pauperized by Microsecond Arbitrage but didn't know it yet. "Bob—" I began.

He winced.

I began again, having gotten the message in spades that I was a servant and not a relative: "Mr. Moellenkamp, sir—" I said, "you know darn well, and so does everybody else here, that you can follow the most patriotic, deeply religious American who ever lived with a tape recorder for a year, and then prove that he's a worse traitor than Benedict Arnold, and a worshipper of the Devil. Who doesn't say things in a moment of passion or absentmindedness that he doesn't wish he could take back? So I ask again, am I the only one this was done to, and if so, why?"

He froze.

"Madelaine?" I said to Madelaine Astor, who would later write me such a dumb letter.

She said she did not like it that I had told students that a new Ice Age was on its way, even if I had read it in *The New York Times*. That was another thing I'd said that Wilder had on tape. At least it had something to do with science, and at least it wasn't something I had picked up from Slazinger or Grandfather Wills or Damon Stern. At least it was the real me.

"The students here have enough to worry about," she said. "I know I did."

She went on to say that there had always been people who had tried to become famous by saying that the World was going to end, but the World hadn't ended.

There were nods of agreement all around the table. I don't think there was a soul there who knew anything about science.

"When I was here you were predicting the end of the World," she said, "only it was atomic waste and acid rain that were going to kill us. But here we are. I feel fine. Doesn't everybody else feel fine? So pooh."

She shrugged. "About the rest of it," she said, "I'm sorry I heard about it. It made me sick. If we have to go over it again, I think I'll just leave the room."

Heavens to Betsy! What could she have meant by "the rest of it"? What could it be that they had gone over once, and were going to have to go over again with me there? Hadn't I already heard the worst?

No.

16

"THE REST OF IT" was in a manila folder in front of Jason Wilder. So there is Manila playing a big part in my life again. No Sweet Rob Roys on the Rocks this time.

In the folder was a report by a private detective hired by Wilder to investigate my sex life. It covered only the second semester, and so missed the episode in the sculpture studio. The gumshoe recorded 3 of 7 subsequent trysts with the Artist in Residence, 2 with a woman from a jewelry company taking orders for class rings, and maybe 30 with Zuzu Johnson, the wife of the President. He didn't miss a thing Zuzu and I did during the second semester. There was only 1 misunderstood incident: when I went up into the loft of the stable, where the Lutz Carillon had been stored before there was a tower and where Tex Johnson was crucified 2 years ago. I went up with the aunt of a student. She was an architect who wanted to see the pegged post-and-beam joinery up there. The operative assumed we made love up there. We hadn't.

We made love much later that afternoon, in a toolshed by the stable, in the shadow of Musket Mountain when the Sun goes down.

I wasn't to see the contents of Wilder's folder for another 10 minutes or so. Wilder and a couple of others wanted to go on discussing what really bothered them about me, which was what I had been doing, supposedly, to the students' minds. My sexual promiscuity among older women wasn't of much interest to them, the College President excepted, save as a handy something for which I could be fired without raising the gummy question of whether or not my rights under the First Amendment of the Constitution had been violated.

Adultery was the bullet they would put in my brain, so to speak, after I had been turned to Swiss cheese by the firing squad.

To Tex Johnson, the closet Lithuanian, the contents of the folder were more than a gadget for diddling me out of tenure. They were a worse humiliation for Tex than they were for me.

At least they said that my love affair with his wife was over.

He stood up. He asked to be excused. He said that he would just as soon not be present when the Trustees went over for the second time what Madelaine had called "the rest of it."

He was excused, and was apparently about to leave without saying anything. But then, with one hand on the doorknob, he uttered two words chokingly, which were the title of a novel by Gustave Flaubert. It was about a wife who was bored with her husband, who had an exceedingly silly love affair and then committed suicide.

"*Madame Bovary*," he said. And then he was gone.

He was a cuckold in the present, and crucifixion awaited him in the future. I wonder if his father would have jumped ship in Corpus Christi if he had known what an unhappy end his only son would come to under American Free Enterprise.

I had read *Madame Bovary* at West Point. All cadets in my day had to read it, so that we could demonstrate to cultivated people that we, too, were cultivated, should we ever face that challenge. Jack Patton and I read it at the same time for the same class. I asked him afterward what he thought of it. Predictably, he said he had to laugh like hell.

He said the same thing about *Othello* and *Hamlet* and *Romeo and Juliet*.

I confess that to this day I have come to no firm conclusions about how smart or dumb Jack Patton really was. This leaves me in doubt about the meaning of a birthday present he sent me in Vietnam shortly before the sniper killed him with a beautiful shot in Hué, pronounced "whay." It was a gift-wrapped copy of a stroke magazine called *Black Garterbelt*. But did he send it to me for its pictures of women naked except for black garterbelts, or for a remarkable science fiction story in there, "The Protocols of the Elders of Tralfamadore"?

But more about that later.

I have no idea how many of the Trustees had read *Madame Bovary*. Two of them would have had to have it read aloud to them. So I was not alone in wondering why Tex Johnson would have said, his hand on the doorknob, "*Madame Bovary*."

If I had been Tex, I think I might have gotten off the campus as fast as possible, and maybe drowned my sorrows among the nonacademics at the Black Cat Café. That was where I was going to wind up that afternoon. It would have been funny in retrospect if we had wound up as a couple of sloshed buddies at the Black Cat Café.

Imagine my saying to him or his saying to me, both of us drunk as skunks, "I love you, you old son of a gun. Do you know that?"

One Trustee had it in for me on personal grounds. That was Sydney Stone, who was said to have amassed a fortune of more than $1,000,000,000 in 10 short years, mainly in commissions for arranging sales of American properties to foreigners. His masterpiece, maybe, was the transfer of ownership of my father's former employer, E. I. Du Pont de Nemours & Company, to I. G. Farben in Germany.

"There is much I could probably forgive, if somebody put a gun to my head, Professor Hartke," he said, "but not what you did to my son." He himself was no Tarkingtonian. He was a graduate of the Harvard Business School and the London School of Economics.

"Fred?" I said.

"In case you haven't noticed," he said, "I have only 1 son in Tarkington. I have only 1 son anywhere." Presumably this 1 son, without having to lift a finger, would himself 1 day have $1,000,000,000.

"What did I do to Fred?" I said.

"You know what you did to Fred," he said.

What I had done to Fred was catch him stealing a Tarkington beer mug from the college bookstore. What Fred Stone did was beyond mere stealing. He took the beer mug off the shelf, drank make-believe toasts to me and the cashier, who were the only other people there, and then walked out.

I had just come from a faculty meeting where the campus theft problem had been discussed for the umpteenth time. The manager of the bookstore told us that only one comparable institution had a higher percentage of its merchandise stolen than his, which was the Harvard Coop in Cambridge.

So I followed Fred Stone out to the Quadrangle. He was headed for his Kawasaki motorcycle in the student parking lot. I came up behind him and said quietly, with all possible politeness, "I think you should put that beer mug back where you got it, Fred. Either that or pay for it."

"Oh, yeah?" he said. "Is that what you think?" Then he smashed the mug to smithereens on the rim of the Vonnegut Memorial Fountain. "If that's what you think," he said, "then you're the one who should put it back."

I reported the incident to Tex Johnson, who told me to forget it.

But I was mad. So I wrote a letter about it to the boy's father, but never got an answer until the Board meeting.

"I can never forgive you for accusing my son of theft," the father said. He quoted Shakespeare on behalf of Fred. I was supposed to imagine Fred's saying it to me.

"'Who steals my purse steals trash; 'tis something, nothing,'" he said. "''Twas mine, 'tis his, and has been slave to thousands,'" he went on, "'but he that filches from me my good name robs me of that which not enriches him and makes me poor indeed.'"

"If I was wrong, sir, I apologize," I said.

"Too late," he said.

17

THERE WAS 1 Trustee I was sure was my friend. He would have found what I said on tape funny and interesting. But he wasn't there. His name was Ed Bergeron, and we had had a lot of good talks about the deterioration of the environment and the abuses of trust in the stock market and the banking industry and so on. He could top me for pessimism any day.

His wealth was as old as the Moellenkamps', and was based on ancestral oil fields and coal mines and railroads which he had sold to foreigners in order to devote himself full-time to nature study and conservation. He was President of the Wildlife Rescue Federation, and his photographs of wildlife on the Galápagos Islands had been published in *National Geographic*. The magazine gave him the cover, too, which showed a marine iguana digesting seaweed in the sunshine, right next to a skinny penguin who was no doubt having thoughts about entirely different issues of the day, whatever was going on that day.

Not only was Ed Bergeron my doomsday pal. He was also a veteran of several debates about environmentalism with Jason Wilder on Wilder's TV show. I haven't found a tape of any of those ding-dong head-to-heads in this library, but there used to be 1 at the prison. It would bob up about every 6 months on the TV sets there, which were running all the time.

In it, I remember, Wilder said that the trouble with conservationists was that they never considered the costs in terms of jobs and living standards of eliminating fossil fuels or doing something with garbage other than dumping it in the ocean, and so on.

Ed Bergeron said to him, "Good! Then I can write the epitaph for this once salubrious blue-green orb." He meant the planet.

Wilder gave him his supercilious, vulpine, patronizing, silky debater's grin. "A majority of the scientific community," he said, "would say, if I'm not mistaken, that an epitaph would be premature by several thousand years." That debate took place maybe 6 years before I was fired, which would be back in 1985, and I don't know what scientific community he was talking about. Every kind of scientist, all the way down to chiropractors and podiatrists, was saying we were killing the planet fast.

"You want to hear the epitaph?" said Ed Bergeron.

"If we must," said Wilder, and the grin went on and on. "I have to tell you, though, that you are not the first person to say the game was all over for the human race. I'm sure that even in Egypt before the first pyramid was constructed, there were men who attracted a following by saying, 'It's all over now.' "

"What is different about now as compared with Egypt before the first pyramid was built—" Ed began.

"And before the Chinese invented printing, and before Columbus discovered America," Jason Wilder interjected.

"Exactly," said Bergeron.

"The difference is that we have the misfortune of knowing what's really going on," said Bergeron, "which is no fun at all. And this has given rise to a whole new class of preening, narcissistic quacks like yourself who say in the service of rich and shameless polluters that the state of the atmosphere and the water and the topsoil on which all life depends is as debatable as how many angels can dance on the fuzz of a tennis ball."

He was angry.

When this old tape was played at Athena before the great escape, it kindled considerable interest. I watched it and listened with several students of mine. Afterward one of them said to me, "Who right, Professor—beard or mustache?" Wilder had a mustache. Bergeron had a beard.

"Beard," I said.

That may have been almost the last word I said to a convict before the prison break, before my mother-in-law decided that it was at last time to talk about her big pickerel.

Bergeron's epitaph for the planet, I remember, which he said should be carved in big letters in a wall of the Grand Canyon for the flying-saucer people to find, was this:

WE COULD HAVE SAVED IT,
BUT WE WERE TOO DOGGONE CHEAP.

Only he didn't say "doggone."

But I would never see or hear from Ed Bergeron again. He resigned from the Board soon after I was fired, and so would miss being taken hostage by the convicts. It would have been interesting to hear what he had to say to and about that particular kind of captor. One thing he used to say to me, and to a class of mine he spoke to one time, was that man was the weather now. Man was the tornadoes, man was the hailstones, man was the floods. So he might have said that Scipio was Pompeii, and the escapees were a lava flow.

He didn't resign from the Board on account of my firing. He had at least two personal tragedies, one right on top of the other. A company he inherited made all sorts of products out of asbestos, whose dust proved to be as carcinogenic as any substance yet identified, with the exception of epoxy cement and some of the radioactive stuff accidentally turned loose in the air and aquifers around nuclear weapons factories and power plants. He felt terrible about this, he told me, although he had never laid eyes on any of the factories that made the stuff. He sold them for practically nothing, since the company in Singapore that bought them got all the lawsuits along with the machinery and buildings, and an inventory of finished materials which was huge and unsalable in this country. The people in Singapore did what Ed couldn't bring himself to do, which was to sell all those floor tiles and roofing and so on to emerging nations in Africa.

And then his son Bruce, Tarkington Class of '85, who was a homosexual, joined the Ice Capades as a chorus boy. That was all right with Ed, who understood that some people were born homosexual and that was that. And Bruce was so happy with the ice show. He was not only a good skater but maybe the best male or female dancer at Tarkington. Bruce used to come over to the house and dance with my mother-in-law sometimes, just for the sake of dancing. He said she was the best dance partner he had ever had, and she returned the compliment.

I didn't tell her when, 4 years after he graduated, he was found strangled with his own belt, and with something like 100 stab wounds, in a motel outside of Dubuque. So there was Dubuque again.

18

S HAKESPEARE.

I think William Shakespeare was the wisest human being I ever heard of. To be perfectly frank, though, that's not saying much. We are impossibly conceited animals, and actually dumb as heck. Ask any teacher. You don't even have to ask a teacher. Ask anybody. Dogs and cats are smarter than we are.

If I say that the Trustees of Tarkington College were dummies, and that the people who got us involved in the Vietnam War were dummies, I hope it is understood that I consider myself the biggest dummy of all. Look at where I am now, and how hard I worked to get here and nowhere else. Bingo!

And if I feel that my father was a horse's fundament and my mother was a horse's fundament, what can I be but another horse's fundament? Ask my kids, both legitimate and illegitimate. They know.

I didn't have a Chinaman's chance with the Trustees, if I may be forgiven a racist cliché—not with the sex stuff Wilder had concealed in the folder. When I defended myself against him, I had no idea how well armed he was—a basic situation in the funniest slapstick comedies.

I argued that it was a teacher's duty to speak frankly to students of college age about all sorts of concerns of humankind, not just the subject of a course as stated in the catalogue. "That's how we gain their trust, and encourage them to speak up as well," I said, "and realize that all subjects do not reside in neat little compartments, but are continuous and inseparable from the one big subject we have been put on Earth to study, which is life itself."

I said that the doubts I might have raised in the students' minds about the virtues of the Free Enterprise System, when telling them what my grandfather believed, could in the long run only strengthen their enthusiasm for that system. It made them think up reasons of their own for why Free Enterprise was the only system worth considering. "People are never stronger," I said, "than when they have thought up their own arguments for believing what they believe. They stand on their own 2 feet that way."

"Did you or did you not say that the United States was a crock of doo-doo?" said Wilder.

I had to think a minute. This wasn't something Kimberley had gotten on tape. "What I may have said," I replied, "is that all nations bigger than Denmark are crocks of doo-doo, but that was a joke, of course."

I now stand behind that statement 100 percent. All nations bigger than Denmark are crocks of doo-doo.

Jason Wilder had heard enough. He asked the Trustees to pass the folder from hand to hand down the table to me. He said, "Before you see what's inside, you should know that this Board promised me that its contents would never be mentioned outside this room. It will remain in your sole possession, provided that you submit your resignation immediately."

"My goodness—" I said, "what could be in here? And what made Tex Johnson run out of the room the way he did?"

"The bottom-most document," said Wilder, "was painful for him to read."

"What can it be?" I said. I honestly couldn't imagine how I might have caused Tex pain. When I made love to his wife, I only wanted to make the 2 of us happier. I didn't think of her as somebody's wife. When I make love to a woman, the farthest thing from my mind is whom she may be married to. I can't speak for Zuzu, but I myself had no wish to cause Tex even a little pain. When Zuzu spoke contemptuously of him, I had to remember who he was, and then I stuck up for him.

My first impression of the bottom-most document in the folder is that it was a timetable of some sort, maybe for the bus from Scipio to Rochester, a not very subtle hint that I should get out of town as soon as possible. But then I realized that what was doing all the arriving and departing was me, and that the depot, so to speak, was the home of the College President.

The accuracy of the times and dates was attested to by Terrence W. Steel, Jr., whom I had known simply as Terry. I hadn't known his full name, and believed him to be what he was said to be, a new gardener working for Buildings and Grounds. He was in fact the private detective Wilder hired to get the goods on me. What little he had told me about himself may have been invented by GRIOT™, or much of it could have been true. Who knows? Who cares?

He told me, I remember, that his wife had discovered she was a lesbian, and fell in love with a female junior high school dietitian. Then both women disappeared along with his 3 kids. GRIOT™ could have cooked that up.

The timetable about me and Zuzu was signed by the detective and notarized. I knew the Notary. Everybody did. He was Lyle Hooper, the Fire Chief and owner of the Black Cat Café. He, too, would be killed soon after the prison break. That document with his seal was all I needed to see in order to understand that my tenure was down the toilet.

Wilder said that the rest of the papers in the folder were affidavits gathered by his detective. They attested to my having been a shameless adulterer from the moment I and my family hit Scipio. "I expect you to agree with me," he said, "that your behavior in this valley would fall dead center into even the narrowest definition of moral turpitude."

I put the folder flat on the table to indicate that I had no need to look inside. My gesture was like folding a poker hand. In so doing, I would lay it on top of the school's annual Treasurer's Report, one copy of which had been put at every seat before the meeting. I would inadvertently take the report with me when I left, learning later from it something I hadn't known before. The college had sold all its property in the town below, including the ruins of the brewery and the wagon factory and the carpet mills and the land under the Black Cat Café, to the same Japanese corporation which owned the prison.

And then the Treasurer had put the proceeds of the sale, less real estate commissions and lawyers' fees, into preferred stock in Microsecond Arbitrage.

"This is not a happy moment in my life," said Wilder.

"Nor mine," I said.

"Unfortunately for all of us," he said, "the moving finger writes; and, having writ, moves on."

"You said a mouthful," I said.

Now the Chairman of the Board, Robert Moellenkamp, spoke up. He was illiterate, but legendary among Tarkingtonians, and no doubt back home, too, for his phenomenal memory. Like the father of the founder of the college, his ancestor, he could learn by heart anything that was read out loud to him 3 times or so. I knew several convicts at Athena, also illiterate, who could do that, too.

He wanted to quote Shakespeare now. "I want it on the record," he said, "that this has been an extremely painful episode for me as well." And then he delivered this speech from Shakespeare's *Romeo and Juliet*, in which the dying Mercutio, Romeo's gallant and witty best friend, describes the wound he received in a duel:

"No, 'tis not so deep as a well, nor so wide as a church door; but 'tis enough, 'twill serve: ask for me tomorrow, and you shall find me a grave man. I am peppered, I warrant, for this world. A plague on both your houses!"

The two houses, of course, were the Montagues and the Capulets, the feuding families of Romeo and Juliet, whose nitwit hatred would indirectly cause Mercutio's departure for Paradise.

I have lifted this speech from Bartlett's *Familiar Quotations*. If more people would acknowledge that they got their pearls of wisdom from that book instead of the original, it might clear the air.

If there really had been a Mercutio, and if there really were a Paradise, Mercutio might be hanging out with teenage Vietnam draftee casualties now, talking about what it felt like to die for other people's vanity and foolishness.

19

WHEN I HEARD a few months later, after I had gone to work at Athena, that Robert Moellenkamp had been wiped out and then some by Microsecond Arbitrage, and had had to sell his boats and his horses and his El Greco and all that, I assumed he quit the Board. Tarkington's Trustees were expected to give a lot of money to the college every year. Otherwise why would Lowell Chung's mother, who had to have everything that was said at meetings translated into Chinese, have been tolerated as a member of the Board?

Actually, I don't think Mrs. Chung would have become a member if another Trustee, a Caucasian Tarkington classmate of Moellenkamp's, John W. Fedders, Jr., hadn't grown up in Hong Kong, and so could serve as her interpreter. His father was an importer of ivory and rhinoceros horns, which many Orientals believed to be aphrodisiacs. He also traded, it was suspected, in industrial quantities of opium. Fedders was perhaps the most conceited man I ever saw out of uniform. He thought his fluency in Chinese made him as brilliant as a nuclear physicist, as though 1,000,000,000 other people, including, no doubt, 1,000,000 morons, couldn't speak Chinese.

When I met with the Trustees 2 years ago, and they had become hostages in the stable, I was surprised to see Moellenkamp. He had been allowed to stay on the Board, even though he didn't have a nickel. Mrs. Chung had dropped out by then. Fedders was there. Wilder, as I've said, had since become a Trustee. There were some other new Trustees I didn't know.

All the Trustees survived the ordeal of captivity, with nothing to eat but horse meat roasted over burning furniture in the huge fireplace in the Pavilion, although Fedders would be the worse for an untreated heart attack. While he was going through the worst of it, he spoke Chinese.

I wouldn't be under indictment now if I hadn't paid a compassionate visit to the hostages. They wouldn't have known that I was within 1,000 kilometers of Scipio. But when I appeared to them, seemingly free to come and go as I pleased, and treated with deference by the Black man who was actually guarding me, they jumped to the conclusion that I was the mastermind behind the great escape.

It was a racist conclusion, based on the belief that Black people couldn't mastermind anything. I will say so in court.

In Vietnam, though, I really was the mastermind. Yes, and that still bothers me. During my last year there, when my ammunition was language instead of bullets, I invented justifications for all the killing and dying we were doing which impressed even me! I was a genius of lethal hocus pocus!

You want to know how I used to begin my speeches to fresh troops who hadn't yet been fed into the meat grinder? I squared my shoulders and threw out my chest so they could see all my ribbons, and I roared through a bullhorn, "Men, I want you to listen, and to listen good!"

And they did, they did.

I have been wondering lately how many human beings I actually killed with conventional weaponry. I don't believe it was my conscience which suggested that I do this. It was the list of women I was making, trying to remember all the names and faces and places and dates, which led to the logical question: "Why not list all you've killed?"

So I think I will. It can't be a list of names, since I never knew the name of anybody I killed. It has to be a list of dates and places. If my list of women isn't to include high school or prostitutes, then my list of those whose lives I took shouldn't include possibles and probables, or those killed by artillery or air strikes called in by me, and surely not all those, many of them Americans, who died as an indirect result of all my hocus pocus, all my blah blah blah.

I have long had a sort of ballpark figure in my head. I am quite sure that I killed more people than did my brother-in-law. I hadn't been working as a teacher at Athena very long before it occurred to me that I had almost certainly killed more people than had the mass murderer Alton Darwin or anybody else serving time in there. That didn't trouble me, and still doesn't. I just think it is interesting.

It is like an old movie. Does that mean that something is wrong with me?

My lawyer, a mere stripling, has paid me a call. Since I have no money, the Federal Government is paying him to protect me from injustice. Moreover, I cannot be tortured or otherwise compelled to testify against myself. What a Utopia!

Among my fellow prisoners here, and the 1,000s upon 1,000s of those across the lake, you better believe there's a lot of jubilation about the Bill of Rights.

I told my lawyer about the two lists I am making. How can he help me if I don't tell him everything.

"Why are you making them?" he said.

"To speed things up on Judgment Day," I said.

"I thought you were an Atheist," he said. He was hoping the Prosecuting Attorney wouldn't get wind of that.

"You never know," I said.

"I'm Jewish," he said.

"I know that, and I pity you," I said.

"Why do you pity me?" he said.

I said, "You're trying to get through life with only half a Bible. That's like trying to get from here to San Francisco with a road map that stops at Dubuque, Iowa."

I told him I wanted to be buried with my 2 lists, so that, if there really was going to be a Judgment Day, I could say to the Judge, "Judge, I have found a way to save you some precious time in Eternity. You don't have to look me up in the Book in

Which All Things Are Recorded. Here's a list of my worst sins. Send me straight to Hell, and no argument."

He asked to see the 2 lists, so I showed him what I had written down so far. He was delighted, and especially by their messiness. There were all sorts of marginal notes about this or that woman or this or that corpse.

"The messier the better," he said.

"How so?" I said.

And he said, "Any fair-minded jury looking at them will have to believe that you are in a deeply disturbed mental state, and probably have been for quite some time. They will already believe that all you Vietnam veterans are crazy, because that's their reputation."

"But the lists aren't based on hallucinations," I protested. "I'm not getting them from a radio set the CIA or the flying-saucer people put in my skull while I was sleeping. It all really happened."

"All the same," he said serenely. "All the same, all the same."

20

AFTER Robert Moellenkamp, broke-and-didn't-know-it, said so grandly, "A plague on both your houses!" Jason Wilder commented that he did not feel, in the case under discussion, my case, that 2 houses were involved.

"I don't believe there is 2 of anything involved," he said. "I venture to say that even Mr. Hartke now agrees that this Board cannot conceive of any alternative to accepting his resignation. Am I right, Mr. Hartke?"

I got to my feet. "This is the second worst day of my life," I said. "The first was the day we got kicked out of Vietnam. Shakespeare has been quoted twice so far. It so happens that I can quote him, too. I have always been bad at memorizing, but I had an English teacher in high school who insisted that everyone in her class know his most famous lines by heart. I never expected to speak them as being meaningful to me in real life, but now's the time. Here goes:

" 'To be, or not to be: that is the question: Whether 'tis nobler in the mind to suffer the slings and arrows of outrageous fortune, or to take arms against a sea of troubles, and by opposing end them?

" 'To die: to sleep; no more; and by a sleep to say we end the heart-ache and the thousand natural shocks that flesh is heir to, 'tis a consummation devoutly to be wished.

" 'To die, to sleep; to sleep: perchance to dream: ay, there's the rub; for in that sleep of death what dreams may come when we have shuffled off this mortal coil, must give us pause.' "

There was more to that speech, of course, but that was all the teacher, whose name was Mary Pratt, required us to memorize. Why overdo? It was certainly enough for the occasion, raising as it did the specter of having yet another Vietnam veteran on the faculty killing himself on school property.

I fished the key to the bell tower from my pocket and threw it into the middle of the circular table. The table was so big that somebody was going to have to climb up on it to retrieve the key, or maybe find a long stick somewhere.

"Good luck with the bells," I said. I was out of there.

I departed Samoza Hall by the same route Tex Johnson had taken. I sat down on a bench at the edge of the Quadrangle, across from the library, next to the Senior Walk. It was nice to be outside.

Damon Stern, my best friend on the faculty, happened by and asked me what I was doing there.

I said I was sunning myself. I wouldn't tell anybody I had been fired until I found myself sitting at the bar of the Black Cat Café. So Professor Stern felt free to talk cheerful nonsense. He owned a unicycle, and he could ride it, and he said he was considering riding it in the academic procession to the graduation ceremonies, which were then only about an hour in the future.

"I'm sure there are strong arguments on both sides," I said.

He had grown up in Shelby, Wisconsin, where practically everybody, including grandmothers, could ride a unicycle. The thing was, a circus had gone broke while playing Shelby 60 years earlier and had abandoned a lot of its equipment, including several unicycles. So more and more people there learned how to ride them, and ordered more unicycles for themselves and their families. So Shelby became and remains today, so far as I know, the Unicycling Capital of the World.

"Do it!" I said.

"You've convinced me," he said. He was happy. He was gone, and my thoughts rode the breeze and the sunbeams back to when I was still in uniform, but home from the war, and was offered a job at Tarkington. That happened in a Chinese restaurant on Harvard Square in Cambridge, Massachusetts, where I was dining with my mother-in-law and my wife, both of them still sane, and my two legitimate children, Melanie, 11, and Eugene, Jr., 8. My illegitimate son, Rob Roy, conceived in Manila only 2 weeks before, must have been the size of a BB shot.

I had been ordered to Cambridge in order to take an examination for admission as a graduate student to the Physics

Department of the Massachusetts Institute of Technology. I was to earn a Master's Degree, and then return to West Point as a teacher, but still a soldier, a soldier to the end.

My family, except for the BB, was awaiting me at the Chinese restaurant while I walked there in full uniform, ribbons and all. My hair was cut short on top and shaved down to the skin on the sides and back. People looked at me as though I were a freak. I might as well have been wearing nothing but a black garterbelt.

That was how ridiculous men in uniform had become in academic communities, even though a major part of Harvard's and MIT's income came from research and development having to do with new weaponry. I would have been dead if it weren't for that great gift to civilization from the Chemistry Department of Harvard, which was napalm, or sticky jellied gasoline.

It was near the end of the humiliating walk that somebody said to somebody else behind me, "My goodness! Is it Halloween?"

I did not respond to that insult, did not give some draft-dodging student burst eardrums and a collapsed windpipe to think about. I kept on going because my mind was swamped with much deeper reasons for unhappiness. My wife had moved herself and the kids from Fort Bragg to Baltimore, where she was going to study Physical Therapy at Johns Hopkins University. Her recently widowed mother had moved in with them. Margaret and Mildred had bought a house in Baltimore with money left to them by my father-in-law. It was their house, not mine. I didn't know anybody in Baltimore.

What the heck was I supposed to do in Baltimore? It was exactly as though I had been killed in Vietnam, and now Margaret had to make a new life for herself. And I was a freak to my own children. They, too, looked at me as though I were wearing nothing but a black garterbelt.

And wouldn't my wife and kids be proud of me when I told them that I hadn't been able to answer more than a quarter of the questions on the examination for admission to graduate studies in Physics at MIT?

Welcome home!

As I was about to go into the Chinese restaurant, two pretty girls came out. They, too, showed contempt for me and my haircut and my uniform. So I said to them, "What's the matter? Haven't you ever before seen a man wearing nothing but a black garterbelt?"

Black garterbelts were on my mind, I suppose, because I missed Jack Patton so much. I had survived the war, but he hadn't, and the present he sent me only a few days before he was shot dead, as I said before, was a skin magazine called *Black Garterbelt*.

So there we were in that restaurant, with me on my third Sweet Rob Roy. Margaret and her mother, again acting as though I were 6 feet under in Arlington National Cemetery, did all the ordering. They had it served family style. Nobody asked me how I had done on the exam. Nobody asked me what it was like to be home from the war.

The others gabbled on to each other about all the tourist sights they had seen that day. They hadn't come along to keep me company and give me moral support. They were there to see "Old Ironsides" and the belfry where Paul Revere had waved the lantern, signaling that the British were coming by land, and so on.

Yes, and, speaking of belfries, it was on this same enchanted evening that I was told that my wife, the mother of my children, had a remarkable number of ancestors and collateral relatives with bats in their belfries on her mother's side. This was news to me, and to Margaret, too. We knew that Mildred had grown up in Peru, Indiana. But all she had ever said about Peru was that Cole Porter had been born there, too, and that she had been very glad to get out of there.

Mildred had let us know that her childhood had been unhappy, but that was a long way from saying that she, which meant my wife and kids, too, was from a notorious family of loonies there.

It turned out that my mother-in-law had run into an old friend from her hometown, Peru, Indiana, during the tour of

"Old Ironsides." Now the old friend and his wife were at the table next to ours. When I went to urinate, the old friend came with me, and told me what a hard life Mildred had had in high school, with both her mother and her mother's mother in the State Hospital for the Insane down in Indianapolis.

"Her mother's brother, who she loved so much," he went on, shaking the last droplets from the end of his weenie, "also went nuts in her senior year, and set fires all over town. If I was her, I would have taken off like a scalded cat for Wyoming, too."

As I say, this was news to me.

"Funny thing—" he went on, "it never seemed to hit any of them until they were middle-aged."

"If I'm not laughing," I said, "that's because I got out on the wrong side of the bed today."

No sooner had I returned to our table than a young man passing behind me could not resist the impulse to touch my bristly haircut. I went absolutely ape-poop! He was slight, and had long hair, and wore a peace symbol around his neck. He looked like the singer Bob Dylan. For all I know or care, he may actually have been Bob Dylan. Whoever he was, I knocked him into a waiter carrying a heavily loaded tray.

Chinese food flew everywhere!

Pandemonium!

I ran outside. Everybody and everything was my enemy. I was back in Vietnam!

But a Christ-like figure loomed before me. He was wearing a suit and tie, but he had a long beard, and his eyes were full of love and pity. He seemed to know all about me, and he really did. He was Sam Wakefield, who had resigned his commission as a General, and gone over to the Peace Movement, and become President of Tarkington College.

He said to me what he had said to me so long ago in Cleveland, at the Science Fair: "What's the hurry, Son?"

21

R EMEMBERING my homecoming from Vietnam always
puts me in mind of Bruce Bergeron, a student of mine at
Tarkington. I have already mentioned Bruce. He joined the Ice
Capades as a chorus boy after winning his Associate in the Arts
and Sciences Degree, and was murdered in Dubuque. His father
was President of the Wildlife Rescue Federation.

When I had Bruce in Music Appreciation I played a recording
of Tchaikovsky's *1812 Overture*. I explained to the class that the
composition was about an actual event in history, the defeat of
Napoleon in Russia. I asked the students to think of some major
event in their own lives, and to imagine what kind of music
might best describe it. They were to think about it for a week
before telling anybody about the event or the music. I wanted
their brains to cook and cook with music, with the lid on tight.

The event Bruce Bergeron set to music in his head was getting
stuck between floors in an elevator when he was maybe 6 years
old, on the way with a Haitian nanny to a post-Christmas white
sale at Bloomingdale's department store in New York City. They
were supposed to be going to the American Museum of Natural
History, but the nanny, without permission from her employers, wanted to send some bargain bedding to relatives in Haiti
first.

The elevator got stuck right below the floor where the white
sale was going on. It was an automatic elevator. There was no
operator. It was jammed. When it became obvious that the
elevator was going to stay there, somebody pushed the alarm
button, which the passengers could hear clanging far below.
According to Bruce, this was the first time in his life that he
had ever been in some kind of trouble that grownups couldn't
take care of at once.

There was a 2-way speaker in the elevator, and a woman's
voice came on, telling the people to stay calm. Bruce remembered that she made this particular point: Nobody was to try

to climb out through the trapdoor in the ceiling. If anybody did that, Bloomingdale's could not be responsible for whatever might happen to him or her afterward.

Time went by. More time went by. To little Bruce it seemed that they had been trapped there for a century. It was probably more like 20 minutes.

Little Bruce believed himself to be at the center of a major event in American history. He imagined that not only his parents but the President of the United States must be hearing about it on television. When they were rescued, he thought, bands and cheering crowds would greet him.

Little Bruce expected a banquet and a medal for not panicking, and for not saying he had to go to the bathroom.

———————————

The elevator suddenly jolted upward a few centimeters, stopped. It jolted upward a meter, an aftershock. The doors slithered open, revealing the white sale in progress behind ordinary customers, who were simply waiting for the next elevator, without any idea that there had been something wrong with that one.

They wanted the people in there to get out so that they could get in.

There wasn't even somebody from the management of the store to offer an anxious apology, to make certain that everybody was all right. All the actions relative to freeing the captives had taken place far away—wherever the machinery was, wherever the alarm gong was, wherever the woman was who had told them not to panic or climb out the trapdoor.

That was that.

———————————

The nanny bought some bedding, and then she and little Bruce went on to the American Museum of Natural History. The nanny made him promise not to tell his parents that they had been to Bloomingdale's, too—and he never did.

He still hadn't told them when he spilled the beans in Music Appreciation.

"You know what you have described to perfection?" I asked him.

"No," he said.

I said, "What it was like to come home from the Vietnam War."

22

I READ ABOUT World War II. Civilians and soldiers alike, and even little children, were proud to have played a part in it. It was impossible, seemingly, for any sort of person not to feel a part of that war, if he or she was alive while it was going on. Yes, and the suffering or death of soldiers and sailors and Marines was felt at least a little bit by everyone.

But the Vietnam War belongs exclusively to those of us who fought in it. Nobody else had anything to do with it, supposedly. Everybody else is as pure as the driven snow. We alone are stupid and dirty, having fought such a war. When we lost, it served us right for ever having started it. The night I went temporarily insane in a Chinese restaurant on Harvard Square, everybody was a big success but me.

Before I blew up, Mildred's old friend from Peru, Indiana, spoke as though we were in separate businesses, as though I were a podiatrist, maybe, or a sheet-metal contractor, instead of somebody who had risked his life and sacrificed common sense and decency on his behalf.

As it happened, he himself was in the medical-waste disposal game in Indianapolis. That's a nice business to learn about in a Chinese restaurant, with everybody dangling who knows what from chopsticks.

He said that his workaday problems had as much to do with aesthetics as with toxicity. Those were both his words, "aesthetics" and "toxicity."

He said, "Nobody likes to find a foot or a finger or whatever in a garbage can or a dump, even though it is no more dangerous to public health than the remains of a rib roast."

He asked me if I saw anything on his and his wife's table that I would like to sample, that they had ordered too much.

"No, thank you, sir," I said.

"But telling you that," he said, "is coals to Newcastle."

"How so?" I said. I was trying not to listen to him, and was looking in exactly the wrong place for distraction, which was the face of my mother-in-law. Apparently this potential lunatic with no place else to go had become a permanent part of our household. It was a fait accompli.

"Well—you've been in war," he said. The way he said it, it was clear that he considered the war to have been my war alone. "I mean you people must have had to do a certain amount of cleaning up."

That was when the kid patted my bristles. My brains blew up like a canteen of nitroglycerin.

My lawyer, much encouraged by the 2 lists I am making, and by the fact that I have never masturbated and like to clean house, asked me yesterday why it was that I never swore. He found me washing windows in this library, although nobody had ordered me to do that.

So I told him my maternal grandfather's idea that obscenity and blasphemy gave most people permission not to listen respectfully to whatever was being said.

I repeated an old story Grandfather Wills had taught me, which was about a town where a cannon was fired at noon every day. One day the cannoneer was sick at the last minute and was too incapacitated to fire the cannon.

So at high noon there was silence.

All the people in the town jumped out of their skins when the sun reached its zenith. They asked each other in astonishment, "Good gravy! What was that?"

My lawyer wanted to know what that had to do with my not swearing.

I replied that in an era as foulmouthed as this one, "Good gravy" had the same power to startle as a cannon shot.

There on Harvard Square, back in 1975, Sam Wakefield again made himself the helmsman of my destiny. He told me to stay out on the sidewalk, where I felt safe. I was shaking like a leaf. I wanted to bark like a dog.

He went into the restaurant, and somehow calmed everybody down, and offered to pay for all damages from his own pocket right then and there. He had a very rich wife, Andrea, who would become Tarkington's Dean of Women after he committed suicide. Andrea died 2 years before the prison break, and so is not buried with so many others next to the stable, in the shadow of Musket Mountain when the Sun goes down.

She is buried next to her husband in Bryn Mawr, Pennsylvania. The glacier could still shove the 2 of them into West Virginia or Maryland. Bon Voyage!

Andrea Wakefield was the 2nd person I spoke to after Tarkington fired me. Damon Stern was the first. I am talking about 1991 again. Practically everybody else was eating lobsters. Andrea came up to me after meeting Stern farther down on the Senior Walk.

"I thought you would be in the Pavilion eating lobster," she said.

"Not hungry," I said.

"I can't stand it that they're boiled alive," she said. "You know what Damon Stern just told me?"

"I'm sure it was interesting," I said.

"During the reign of Henry the 8th of England," she said, "counterfeiters were boiled alive."

"Show biz," I said. "Were they boiled alive in public?"

"He didn't say," she said. "And what are you doing here?"

"Enjoying the sunshine," I said.

She believed me. She sat down next to me. She was already wearing her academic gown for the faculty parade to graduation. Her cowl identified her as a graduate of the Sorbonne in Paris, France. In addition to her duties as Dean, dealing with unwanted pregnancies and drug addiction and the like, she also taught French and Italian and oil painting. She was from a genuinely distinguished old Philadelphia family, which had given civilization a remarkable number of educators and lawyers and physicians and artists. She actually may have been what Jason Wilder and several of Tarkington's Trustees believed themselves to be, obviously the most highly evolved creatures on the planet.

She was a lot smarter than her husband.

I always meant to ask her how a Quaker came to marry a professional soldier, but I never did.

Too late now.

Even at her age then, which was about 60, 10 years older than me, Andrea was the best figure skater on the faculty. I think figure skating, if Andrea Wakefield could find the right partner, was eroticism enough for her. General Wakefield couldn't skate for sour apples. The best partner she had on ice at Tarkington, probably, was Bruce Bergeron—the boy who was trapped in an elevator at Bloomingdale's, who became the youth who couldn't get into any college but Tarkington, who became the man who joined the chorus of an ice show and then was murdered by somebody who presumably hated homosexuals, or loved one too much.

Andrea and I had never been lovers. She was too contented and old for me.

"I want you to know I think you're a Saint," said Andrea.

"How so?" I said.

"You're so nice to your wife and mother-in-law."

"It's easier than what I did for Presidents and Generals and Henry Kissinger," I said.

"But this is voluntary," she said.

"So was that," I said. "I was real gung-ho."

"When you realize how many men nowadays dissolve their marriages when they become the least little bit inconvenient or uncomfortable," she said, "all I can think is that you're a Saint."

"They didn't want to come up here, you know," I said. "They were very happy in Baltimore, and Margaret would have become a physical therapist."

"It isn't this valley that made them sick, is it?" she said. "It isn't this valley that made my husband sick."

"It's a clock that made them sick," I said. "It would have struck midnight for both of them, no matter where they were."

"That's how I feel about Sam," she said. "I can't feel guilty."

"Shouldn't," I said.

"When he resigned from the Army and went over to the peace movement," she said, "I think he was trying to stop the clock. Didn't work."

"I miss him," I said.

"Don't let the war kill you, too," she said.

"Don't worry," I said.

"You still haven't found the money?" she said.

She was talking about the money Mildred had gotten for the house in Baltimore. While Mildred was still fairly sane, she deposited it in the Scipio branch of the First National Bank of Rochester. But then she withdrew it in cash when the bank was bought by the Sultan of Brunei, without telling me or Margaret that she had done so. Then she hid it somewhere, but she couldn't remember where.

"I don't even think about it anymore," I said. "The most likely thing is that somebody else found it. It could have been a bunch of kids. It could have been somebody working on the house. Whoever it was sure isn't going to say so."

We were talking about $45,000 and change.

"I know I should give a darn, but somehow I can't give a darn," I said.

"The war did that to you," she said.

"Who knows?" I said.

As we chatted in the sunshine, a powerful motorcycle came to life with a roar in the valley, in the region of the Black Cat Café. Then another one spoke, and yet another.

"Hell's Angels?" she said. "You mean it's really going to happen?"

The joke was that Tex Johnson, the College President, having seen one too many motorcycle movies, believed that the campus might actually be assaulted by Hell's Angels someday. This fantasy was so real to him that he had bought an Israeli sniper's rifle, complete with a telescopic sight, and ammunition for it from a drugstore in Portland, Oregon. He and Zuzu were visiting Zuzu's half sister. That was the same weapon which would eventually get him crucified.

But now Tex's anticipation of an assault by Hell's Angels didn't seem so comical after all. A mighty doomsday chorus of basso profundo 2-wheelers was growing louder and louder and coming closer and closer. There could be no doubt about it! Whoever it was, whatever it was, its destination could only be Tarkington!

23

I T WASN'T HELL'S ANGELS.
It wasn't lower-class people of any kind.

It was a motorcade of highly successful Americans, most on motorcycles, but some in limousines, led by Arthur Clarke, the fun-loving billionaire. He himself was on a motorcycle, and on the saddle behind him, holding on for dear life, her skirt hiked up to her crotch, was Gloria White, the 60-year-old lifelong movie star!

Bringing up the rear were a sound truck and a flatbed carrying a deflated hot-air balloon. When the balloon was inflated at the center of the Quadrangle it would turn out to be shaped like a castle Clarke owned in Ireland!

Cough, cough. Silence. Two more: Cough, cough. There, I'm OK now. Cough. That's it. I really am OK now. Peace.

This wasn't Arthur C. Clarke, the science fiction writer who wrote all the books about humanity's destiny in other parts of the Universe. This was Arthur K. Clarke, the billionaire speculator and publisher of magazines and books about high finance.

Cough. I beg your pardon. A little blood this time. In the immortal words of the Bard of Avon:

"Out, damned spot! out, I say! One; two: why, then, 'tis time to do't. Hell is murky! Fie, my lord, fie! a soldier, and afeared? What need we fear who knows it, when none can call our power to account? Who would have thought the old man to have had so much blood in him?"

Amen. And especial thanks to Bartlett's *Familiar Quotations*.

I read a lot of science fiction when I was in the Army, including Arthur C. Clarke's *Childhood's End*, which I thought was a masterpiece. He was best known for the movie *2001*, the very year in which I am writing and coughing now.

I saw *2001* twice in Vietnam. I remember 2 wounded soldiers in wheelchairs in the front row at 1 of those showings. The whole front row was wheelchairs. The 2 soldiers had had their feet wrecked some way, but seemed to be OK from the knees on up, and they weren't in any pain. They were awaiting transportation back to the States, I guess, where they could be fitted with prostheses. I don't think either of them was older than 18. One was black and 1 was white.

After the lights went up, I heard the black one say to the white one, "You tell *me*: What was that all about?"

The white one said, "I dunno, I dunno. I'll be happy if I can just get back to Cairo, Illinois."

He didn't pronounce it "*ky*-roe." He pronounced it "*kay*-roe."

My mother-in-law from Peru, Indiana, pronounces the name of her hometown "*pee*-roo," not "puh-*roo*."

Old Mildred pronounces the name of another Indiana town, Brazil, as "brazzle."

Arthur K. Clarke was coming to Tarkington to get an honorary Grand Contributor to the Arts and Sciences Degree.

The College was prevented by law from awarding any sort of degree which sounded as though the recipient had done serious work to get it. Paul Slazinger, the former Writer in Residence, I remember, objected to real institutions of higher learning giving honorary degrees with the word "Doctor" in them anywhere. He wanted them to use "Panjandrum" instead.

When the Vietnam War was going on, though, a kid could stay out of it by enrolling at Tarkington. As far as Draft Boards were concerned, Tarkington was as real a college as MIT. This could have been politics.

It must have been politics.

Everybody knew Arthur Clarke was going to get a meaningless certificate. But only Tex Johnson and the campus cops and the Provost had advance warning of the spectacular entrance he planned to make. It was a regular military operation. The motorcycles, and there were about 30 of them, and the balloon had been trucked into the parking lot behind the Black Cat Café at dawn.

And then Clarke and Gloria White and the rest of them, including Henry Kissinger, had been brought down from the Rochester airport in limousines, followed by the sound truck. Kissinger wouldn't ride a motorcycle. Neither would some others, who came all the way to the Quadrangle by limousine.

Just like the people on the motorcycles, though, the people in the limousines wore gold crash helmets decorated with dollar signs.

It's a good thing Tex Johnson knew Clarke was coming by motorcycle, or Tex just might have shot him with the Israeli rifle he had bought in Oregon.

Clarke's big arrival wasn't a half-bad dress rehearsal for Judgment Day. St. John the Divine in the Bible could only imagine such an absolutely knockout show with noise and smoke and gold and lions and eagles and thrones and celebrities and marvels up in the sky and so on. But Arthur K. Clarke had created a real one with modern technology and tons of cash!

The gold-helmeted motorcyclists formed a hollow square on the Quadrangle, facing outward, making their mighty steeds roar and roar.

Workmen in white coveralls began to inflate the balloon.

The sound truck ripped the air to shreds with the recorded racket of a bagpipe band.

Arthur Clarke, astride his bike, was looking in my direction. That was because great pals of his on the Board of Trustees were waving to him from the building right behind me. I found myself deeply offended by his proof that big money could buy big happiness.

I yawned elaborately. I turned my back on him and his show. I walked away as though I had much better things to do than gape at an imbecile.

Thus did I miss seeing the balloon snap its cable and, as unattached as myself, sail over the prison across the lake.

All the prisoners over there could see of the outside world was sky. Some of them in the exercise yard saw a castle up there for just a moment. What on Earth could the explanation be?

"There are more things in heaven and earth, Horatio, than are dreamt of in your philosophy."—Bartlett's *Familiar Quotations*

That empty castle with its mooring snapped, a plaything of the wind, was a lot like me. We were so much alike, in fact, that I myself would pay a surprise visit to the prison before the Sun went down.

If the balloon had been as close to the ground as I was, it would have been blown this way and that at first, before it gained sufficient altitude for the prevailing wind to take it across the lake. What caused me to change course, however, wasn't random gusts but the possibility of running into this person or that one who had the power to make me even more uncomfortable. I particularly did not want to run into Zuzu Johnson or the departing Artist in Residence, Pamela Ford Hall.

But life being what it was, I would of course run into both of them.

I would rather have faced Zuzu than Pamela, since Pamela had gone all to pieces and Zuzu hadn't. But as I say, I would have to face them both.

I wasn't what had shoved Pamela over the edge. It was her 1-woman show in Buffalo a couple of months earlier. What went wrong with it seemed funny to everybody but her, and it was in the papers and on TV. For a couple of days she was the light side of the news, comic relief from reports of the rapid growth of glaciers at the poles and the desert where the Amazon rain forest used to be. And I am sure there was another oil spill. There was always another oil spill.

If Denver and Santa Fe and Le Havre, France, hadn't been evacuated yet because of atomic wastes in their water supplies, they soon would be.

What happened to Pamela's 1-woman show also gave a lot of people an opportunity to jeer at modern art, which only rich people claimed to like.

As I've said, Pamela worked in polyurethane, which is easy to carve and weighs almost nothing, and smells like urine when it's hot. Her figures, moreover, were small, women in full skirts, sitting and hunched over so you couldn't see their faces. A shoebox could have contained any 1 of them.

So they were displayed on pedestals in Buffalo, but they weren't glued down. Wind was not considered a problem, since there were 3 sets of doors between her stuff and the main entrance to the museum, which faced Lake Erie.

The museum, the Hanson Centre for the Arts, was brand-new, a gift to the city from a Rockefeller heir living in Buffalo who had come into a great deal of money from the sale of Rockefeller Center in Manhattan to the Japanese. This was an old lady in a wheelchair. She hadn't stepped on a mine in Vietnam. I think it was just old age that knocked the pins out from under her, and all the waiting for Rockefeller properties to be sold off so she could have some dough for a change.

The press was there because this was the Centre's grand opening. Pamela Ford Hall's first 1-woman show, which she called "Bagladies," was incidental, except that it was mounted in the gallery, where a string quartet was playing and champagne and canapés were being served. This was black-tie.

The donor, Miss Hanson, was the last to arrive. She and her wheelchair were set down on the top step outside. Then all 3 sets of doors between Pam's bagladies and the North Pole were thrown open wide. So all the bagladies were blown off their pedestals. They wound up on the floor, piled up against the hollow baseboards which concealed hot heating pipes.

TV cameras caught everything but the smell of hot polyurethane. What a relief from mundane worries! Who says the news has to be nothing but grim day after day?

24

P AMELA was sulking next to the stable. The stable wasn't in the shadow of Musket Mountain yet. It would be another 7 hours before the Sun went down.

This was years before the prison break, but there were already 2 bodies and 1 human head buried out that way. Everybody knew about the 2 bodies, which had been interred with honors and topped with a tombstone. The head would come as a complete surprise when more graves were dug with a backhoe at the end of the prison break.

Whose head was it?

***

The 2 bodies everybody knew about belonged to Tarkington's first teacher of Botany and German and the flute, the brewmaster Hermann Shultz and his wife Sophia. They died within 1 day of each other during a diphtheria epidemic in 1893. They were in fairly fresh graves the day I was fired, although their joint grave marker was 98 years old. Their bodies and tombstone were moved there to make room for the Pahlavi Pavilion.

The mortician from down in town who took charge of moving the bodies back in 1987 reported that they were remarkably well preserved. He invited me to look, but I told him I was willing to take his word for it.

***

Can you imagine that? After all the corpses I saw in Vietnam, and in many cases created, I was squeamish about looking at 2 more which had absolutely nothing to do with me. I am at a loss for an explanation. Maybe I was thinking like an innocent little boy again.

I have leafed through the Atheist's Bible, Bartlett's *Familiar Quotations*, for some sort of comment on unexpected squeamishness. The best I can do is something Lady Macbeth said to her henpecked husband:

"Fie! a soldier, and afeared?"

Speaking of Atheism, I remember one time when Jack Patton and I went to a sermon in Vietnam delivered by the highest-ranking Chaplain in the Army. He was a General.

The sermon was based on what he claimed was a well-known fact, that there were no Atheists in foxholes.

I asked Jack what he thought of the sermon afterward, and he said, "There's a Chaplain who never visited the front."

The mortician, who is himself now in a covered trench by the stable, was Norman Updike, a descendant of the valley's early Dutch settlers. He went on to tell me with bow-wow cheerfulness back in 1987 that people were generally mistaken about how quickly things rot, turn into good old dirt or fertilizer or dust or whatever. He said scientists had discovered well-preserved meat and vegetables deep in city dumps, thrown away presumably years and years ago. Like Hermann and Sophia Shultz, these theoretically biodegradable works of Nature had failed to rot for want of moisture, which was life itself to worms and fungi and bacteria.

"Even without modern embalming techniques," he said, "ashes to ashes and dust takes much, much longer than most people realize."

"I'm encouraged," I said.

I did not see Pamela Ford Hall by the stable until it was too late for me to head off in the opposite direction. I was distracted from watching out for her and Zuzu by a parent who had fled the bagpipe music on the Quadrangle. He commented that I seemed very depressed about something.

I still hadn't told anybody I had been fired, and I certainly didn't want to share the news with a stranger. So I said I couldn't help being unhappy about the ice caps and the deserts and the busted economy and the race riots and so on.

He told me to cheer up, that 1,000,000,000 Chinese were about to throw off the yoke of Communism. After they did that, he said, they would all want automobiles and tires and gasoline and so forth.

I pointed out that virtually all American industries having to do with automobiles either were owned or had been run out of business by the Japanese.

"And what is to prevent you from doing what I've done?" he said. "It's a free country." He said that his entire portfolio consisted of stocks in Japanese corporations.

Can you imagine what 1,000,000,000 Chinese in automobiles would do to each other and what's left of the atmosphere?

I was so intent on getting away from that typical Ruling Class chowderhead that I did not see Pamela until I was right next to her. She was sitting on the ground drinking blackberry brandy, with her back to the Shultzes' tombstone. She was gazing up at Musket Mountain. She had a serious alcohol problem. I didn't blame myself for that. The worst problem in the life of any alcoholic is alcohol.

The inscription on the grave marker was facing me.

HERMANN SHULTZ
1830–1893
SOPHIA HIMMLER SHULTZ
1841–1893
FREETHINKERS

The diphtheria epidemic that killed so many people in this valley took place when almost all of Tarkington's students were away on vacation.

That was certainly lucky for the students. If school had been in session during the epidemic, many, many of them might have wound up with the Shultzes, first where the Pavilion now stands, and then next to the stable, in the shadow of Musket Mountain when the Sun goes down.

And then the student body got lucky again 2 years ago. They were all away on a recess between semesters when habitual criminals overran this insignificant little country town.

Miracles.

I have looked up who the Freethinkers were. They were members of a short-lived sect, mostly of German descent, who believed, as did my Grandfather Wills, that nothing but sleep awaited good and evil persons alike in the Afterlife, that science had proved all organized religions to be baloney, that God was unknowable, and that the greatest use a person could make of his or her lifetime was to improve the quality of life for all in his or her community.

Hermann and Sophia Shultz weren't the only victims of the diphtheria epidemic. Far from it! But they were the only ones who asked to be buried on the campus, which they said on their deathbeds was holy ground to them.

Pamela wasn't surprised to see me. She was insulated against surprises by alcohol. The first thing she said to me was, "No." I hadn't said anything yet. She thought I had come to make love to her. I could understand why she might think that.

I myself had started thinking that.

And then she said, "This has certainly been the best year of my life, and I want to thank you for being such a big part of it." This was irony. She was being corrosively insincere.

"When are you leaving?" I said.

"Never," she said. "My transmission is shot." She was talking about her 12-year-old Buick 4-door sedan, which she had gotten as part of her divorce settlement from her ex-husband. He used to mock her efforts to become a serious artist, even slapping or kicking her from time to time. So he must have laughed even harder than everybody else when her 1-woman show was blown off its pedestals in Buffalo.

She said a new transmission was going to cost $850 down in town, and that the mechanic wanted to be paid in Yen, and that he hinted that the repairs would cost a lot less if she would go to bed with him. "I don't suppose you ever found out where your mother-in-law hid the money," she said.

"No," I said.

"Maybe I should go looking for it," she said.

"I'm sure somebody else found it, and just isn't saying anything," I said.

"I never asked you to pay for anything before," she said. "How about you buy me a new transmission? Then, when anybody asks me, 'Where did you get that beautiful transmission?' I can answer, 'An old lover gave that to me. He is a very famous war hero, but I am not free to reveal his name.' "

"Who is the mechanic?" I asked.

"The Prince of Wales," she said. "If I go to bed with him, he will not only fix my transmission, he will make me the Queen of England. You never made me Queen of England."

"Was it Whitey VanArsdale?" I said. This was a mechanic down in town who used to tell everybody that he or she had a broken transmission. He did it to me with the car I had before the Mercedes, which was a 1979 Chevy station wagon. I got a second opinion, from a student, actually. The transmission was fine. All I'd wanted in the first place was a grease job. Whitey VanArsdale, too, is now buried next to the stable. He ambushed some convicts and got ambushed right back. His victory lasted 10 minutes, if that. It was, "Bang," and then, a few minutes later, "Bang, bang," right back.

Pamela, sitting on the ground with her back to the tombstone, didn't do to me what Zuzu Johnson would soon do to me, which was to identify me as a major cause of her unhappiness. The closest Pam came to doing that, I guess, was when she said I had never made her the Queen of England. Zuzu's complaint would be that I had never seriously intended to make her my wife, despite all our talk in bed about our running off to Venice, which neither one of us had ever seen. She would open a flower shop there, I promised her, since she was so good at gardening. I would teach English as a second language or help local glassblowers get their wares into American department stores, and so on.

Zuzu was also a pretty good photographer, so I said she would soon be hanging around where the gondolas took on passengers, and selling tourists Polaroid pictures of themselves in gondolas right then and there.

When it came to dreaming up a future for ourselves, we left GRIOT™ in the dust.

I considered those dreams of Venice part of lovemaking, my erotic analogue to Zuzu's perfume. But Zuzu took them seriously. She was all set to go. And I couldn't go because of my family responsibilities.

Pamela knew about my love affair with Zuzu, and all the hocus pocus about Venice. Zuzu told her.

"You know what you ought to say to any woman dumb enough to fall in love with you?" she asked me. Her gaze was on Musket Mountain, not on me.

"No," I said.

And she said, " 'Welcome to Vietnam.' "

She was sitting over the Shultzes in their caskets. I was standing over a severed head which would be dug up by a backhoe in 8 years. The head had been in the ground so long that it was just a skull.

A specialist in Forensic Medicine from the State Police happened to be down here when the skull showed up in the backhoe's scoop, so he had a look at it, told us what he thought. He didn't think it was an Indian, which was my first guess. He said it had belonged to a white woman maybe 20 years old. She hadn't been bludgeoned or shot in the head, so he would have to see the rest of the skeleton before theorizing about what might have killed her.

But the backhoe never brought up another bone.

Decapitation, alone, of course, could have done the job.

He wasn't much interested. He judged from the patina on the skull that its owner had died long before we were born. He was here to examine the bodies of people who had been killed after the prison break, and to make educated guesses about how they had died, by gunshot or whatever.

He was especially fascinated by Tex Johnson's body. He had seen almost everything in his line of work, he told me, but never a man who had been crucified, with spikes through the palms and feet and all.

I wanted him to talk more about the skull, but he changed the subject right back to crucifixion. He sure knew a lot about it.

He told me one thing I'd never realized: that the Jews, not just the Romans, also crucified their idea of criminals from time to time. Live and learn!

How come I'd never heard that?

Darius, King of Persia, he told me, crucified 3,000 people he thought were enemies in Babylon. After the Romans put down the slave revolt led by Spartacus, he said, they crucified 6,000 of the rebels on either side of the Appian Way!

He said that the crucifixion of Tex Johnson was unconventional in several ways besides Tex's being dead or nearly dead when they spiked him to timbers in the stable loft. He hadn't been whipped. There hadn't been a cross-beam for him to carry to his place of execution. There was no sign over his head saying what his crime was. And there was no spike in the upright, whose head would abrade his crotch and hindquarters as he turned this way and that in efforts to become more comfortable.

As I said at the beginning of this book, if I had been a professional soldier back then, I probably would have crucified people without thinking much about it, if ordered to do so.

Or I would have ordered underlings to do it, and told them how to do it, if I had been a high-ranking officer.

I might have taught recruits who had never had anything to do with crucifixions, who maybe had never even seen one before, a new word from the vocabulary of military science of that time. The word was *crurifragium*. I myself learned it from the Medical Examiner, and I found it so interesting that I went and got a pencil and wrote it down.

It is a Latin word for "breaking the legs of a crucified person with an iron rod in order to shorten his time of suffering." But that still didn't make crucifixion a country club.

What kind of an animal would do such a thing? The old me, I think.

The late unicyclist Professor Damon Stern asked me one time if I thought there would be a market for religious figures of Christ riding a unicycle instead of spiked to a cross. It was just a joke. He didn't want an answer, and I didn't give him one. Some other subject must have come up right away.

But I would tell him now, if he hadn't been killed while trying to save the horses, that the most important message of a crucifix, to me anyway, was how unspeakably cruel supposedly sane human beings can be when under orders from a superior authority.

But listen to this: While idly winnowing through old local newspapers here, I think I have discovered whom that probably Caucasian, surely young and female skull belonged to. I want to rush out into the prison yard, formerly the Quadrangle, shouting "Eureka! Eureka!"

My educated guess is that the skull belonged to Letitia Smiley, a reputedly beautiful, dyslexic Tarkington senior who disappeared from the campus in 1922, after winning the traditional Women's Barefoot Race from the bell tower to the President's House and back again. Letitia Smiley was crowned Lilac Queen as her prize, and she burst into tears for reasons nobody could understand. Something obviously was bothering her. People were agreed, I learn from a newspaper of the time, that Letitia Smiley's tears were not happy tears.

One suspicion had to be, although nobody said so for publication, that Miss Smiley was pregnant—possibly by a member of the student body or faculty. I am playing detective now, with nothing but a skull and old newspapers to go on. But at least I have what the police were unable to find back then: what might be proof positive in the hands of a forensic cranial expert that Letitia Smiley was no longer among the living. The morning after she was crowned Lilac Queen, her bed was found to contain a dummy made of rolled-up bath towels. A souvenir football given to her by an admirer at Union College in Schenectady was the dummy's head. On it was painted: "Union 31, Hobart 3."

After that: thin air.

A dentist would be no help in identifying the skull, since whoever owned it never had so much as a single cavity to be filled. Whoever it was had perfect teeth. Who is alive today who could tell us whether or not Letitia Smiley, who herself would be 100 years old now, in the year 2001, had perfect teeth?

That was how a lot of the more mutilated bodies of soldiers in Vietnam were positively identified, by their imperfect teeth.

There is no statute of limitations on murder, the most terrible crime of all, they say. But how old would her killer be by now? If he was who I think he was, he would be 135. I think he was none other than Kensington Barber, the Provost of Tarkington College at the time. He would spend his last days in the State Hospital for the Insane up in Batavia. I think it was he, empowered to make bed checks in both the women's and the men's dormitories, who made the dummy whose head was a football.

I think Letitia Smiley was dead by then.

And it was a matter of public record that it was the Provost who found the dummy.

The medical examiner from the State Police said it was odd that there was no hair still stuck to the skull. He thought it might have been scalped or boiled before it was buried, to make it that much harder to identify. And what have I discovered? That Letitia was famous in her short life for her long golden hair. The newspaper description of the race she won goes on and on about her golden hair.

Yes, and the same story gives Kensington Barber as the sole source of the assertion that Letitia had been deeply troubled by a stormy romance with a much older man down in Scipio. The Provost wished that he or somebody knew the name of the man, so that the police could question him.

In another story, Barber told a reporter that he had planned to take his family to Europe that summer but would stay in Scipio instead, in order to do all he could to clear up the mystery of what had become of Letitia Smiley. Such dedication to duty!

He had a wife and 2 kids, and he sent them to Europe without him. Since the campus was virtually deserted in the summertime, except for the maintenance staff, which took orders from him, he could easily have ensured his own privacy by sending the workmen to another part of the campus while he buried small parts of Letitia, possibly using a post-hole digger.

I have to wonder, too, in light of my own experiences in public-relations hocus pocus and the recent history of my Government, if there weren't a lot of people back in 1922 who could put 2 and 2 together as easily as I have now. For the sake of the reputation of what had become Scipio's principal business, the college, there could have been a massive cover-up.

Kensington Barber would have a nervous breakdown at the end of the summer, and be committed, as I've said, to Batavia. The President of Tarkington at that time, who was Herbert Van Arsdale, no relation to Whitey VanArsdale, the dishonest mechanic, ascribed the Provost's crackup to exhaustion brought on by his tireless efforts to solve the mystery of the disappearance of the golden-haired Lilac Queen.

25

M Y LAWYER found only one thing really interesting in my theory about the Lilac Queen, and that was about the broad purple hair ribbons worn by all the girls in that footrace, right up to the last race before the prison break. The escaped convicts discovered spools and spools of that ribbon in a closet in the office of the Dean of Women. Alton Darwin had them cut it up into armbands as a sort of uniform, a quick way to tell friend from foe. Of course, skin color already did a pretty good job of that.

The significance of the purple armbands, my lawyer says, is that I never put one on. This would help to prove that I was truly neutral.

The convicts didn't create a new flag. They flew the Stars and Stripes from the bell tower. Alton Darwin said they weren't against America. He said, "We *are* America."

So I took my leave of Pamela Ford Hall on the afternoon Tarkington fired me. I would never see her again. The only real favor I ever did for her, I suppose, was to tell her to get a second opinion before letting Whitey VanArsdale sell her a new transmission. She did that, I heard, and it turned out that her old transmission was perfectly OK.

It and the rest of the car took her all the way down to Key West, where the former Writer in Residence Paul Slazinger had settled in, living well on his Genius Grant from the MacArthur Foundation. I hadn't realized that he and she had been an item when they were both at Tarkington, but I guess they were. She certainly never told me about it. At any rate, when I was working over at Athena, I got an announcement of their impending wedding down there, forwarded from Scipio.

But evidently that fell through. I imagine her drinking and her insistence on pursuing an art career, even though she wasn't talented, frightened the old novelist.

Slazinger was no prize himself, of course.

After the prison break, I told the GRIOT™ here all I knew about Pamela, and asked it to guess what might become of her after her breakup with Paul Slazinger. GRIOT™ had her die of cirrhosis of the liver. I gave the machine the same set of facts a second time, and it had her freezing to death in a doorway in Chicago.

The prognosis was not good.

After leaving Pamela, whose basic problem wasn't me but alcohol, I started to climb Musket Mountain, intending to think things out under the water tower. But I was met by Zuzu Jackson, who was coming down. She said she had been under the water tower for hours, trying to think up dreams to replace those we had had of running off to Venice.

She said that maybe she would run off to Venice alone, and take Polaroid pictures of tourists getting in and out of gondolas.

The prognosis for her was a lot better than for Pamela, short-term anyway. At least she wasn't an addict, and at least she wasn't all alone in the world, even if all she had was Tex. And at least she hadn't been held up as an object of public ridicule from coast to coast.

And she could see the humorous side of things. She said, I remember, that the loss of the Venice dream had left her a walking corpse, but that a zombie was an ideal mate for a College President.

She went on like that for a little while, but she didn't cry, and she ran out of steam pretty quick. The last thing she said was that she didn't blame me. "I take full responsibility," she said, speaking over her shoulder as she walked away, "for falling in love with such an obvious jerk."

Fair enough!

I decided not to climb Musket Mountain after all. I went home instead. It would be wiser to think things out in my garage, where other loose cannons from my past were unlikely to interrupt me. But when I got there I found a man from United Parcel Service ringing the bell. I didn't know him. He was new to town, or he wouldn't have asked why all the blinds were drawn. Anybody who had been in Scipio any length of time knew why the blinds were drawn.

Crazy people lived in there.

I told him somebody was sick in there, and asked what I could do for him.

He said he had this big box for me from St. Louis, Missouri.

I said I didn't know anybody in St. Louis, Missouri, and wasn't expecting a big box from anywhere. But he proved to me that it was addressed to me all right, so I said, "OK, let's see it." It turned out to be my old footlocker from Vietnam, which I had left behind when the excrement hit the air-conditioning, when I was ordered to take charge of the evacuation from the roof of the embassy.

Its arrival was not a complete surprise. Several months earlier I had received a notice of its existence in a huge Army warehouse that was indeed on the edge of St. Louis, where all sorts of unclaimed personal property of soldiers was stored, stuff ditched on battlefields or whatever. Some idiot must have put my footlocker on one of the last American planes to flee Vietnam, thus depriving the enemy of my razor, my toothbrush, my socks and underwear, and, as it happened, the late Jack Patton's final birthday present to me, a copy of *Black Garterbelt*. A mere 14 years later, the Army said they had it, and asked me if I wanted it. I said, "Yes." A mere 2 years more went by, and then, suddenly, here it was at my doorstep. Some glaciers move faster than that.

So I had the UPS man help me lug it into the garage. It wasn't very heavy. It was just unwieldy.

The Mercedes was parked out front. I hadn't noticed yet that kids from the town had cored it again. All 4 tires were flat again.

Cough, cough.

The UPS man was really only a boy still. He was so childlike and new to his job that he had to ask me what was inside the box.

"If the Vietnam War was still going on," I said, "it might have been you in there." I meant he might have wound up in a casket.

"I don't get it," he said.

"Never mind," I said. I knocked off the lock and hasp with a hammer. I lifted the lid of what was indeed a sort of casket to me. It contained the remains of the soldier I used to be. On top of everything else, lying flat and face up, was that copy of *Black Garterbelt*.

"Wow," said the kid. He was awed by the woman on the magazine cover. He might have been an Astronaut on his first trip in space.

"Have you ever considered being a soldier?" I asked him. "I think you'd make a good one."

I never saw him again. He could have been fired soon after that, and gone looking for work elsewhere. He certainly wasn't going to last long as a UPS man if he was going to hang around like a kid on Christmas morning until he found out what was inside all the different packages.

I stayed in the garage. I didn't want to go into the house. I didn't want to go outdoors again, either. So I sat down on my footlocker and read "The Protocols of the Elders of Tralfamadore" in *Black Garterbelt*. It was about intelligent threads of energy trillions of light-years long. They wanted mortal, self-reproducing life forms to spread out through the Universe. So several of them, the Elders in the title, held a meeting by intersecting near a planet called Tralfamadore. The author never said why the Elders thought the spread of life was such a hot idea. I don't blame him. I can't think of any strong arguments in favor of it. To me, wanting every habitable planet to be inhabited is like wanting everybody to have athlete's foot.

The Elders agreed at the meeting that the only practical way for life to travel great distances through space was in the form of extremely small and durable plants and animals hitching rides on meteors that ricocheted off their planets.

But no germs tough enough to survive a trip like that had yet evolved anywhere. Life was too easy for them. They were a bunch of creampuffs. Any creature they infected, chemically speaking, was as challenging as so much chicken soup.

There were people on Earth at the time of the meeting, but they were just more hot slop for the germs to swim in. But they had extra-large brains, and some of them could talk. A few could even read and write! So the Elders focused in on them, and wondered if people's brains might not invent survival tests for germs which were truly horrible.

They saw in us a potential for chemical evils on a cosmic scale. Nor did we disappoint them.

What a story!

It so happened, according to this story, that the legend of Adam and Eve was being written down for the first time. A woman was doing it. Until then, that charming bunkum had been passed from generation to generation by word of mouth.

The Elders let her write down most of the origin myth just the way she had heard it, the way everybody told it, until she got very close to the end. Then they took control of her brain and had her write down something which had never been part of the myth before.

It was a speech by God to Adam and Eve, supposedly. This was it, and life would become pure hell for microorganisms soon afterward: "Fill the Earth and subdue it; and have dominion over the fish of the sea and over the birds of the air and over every living thing that moves on the Earth."

Cough.

26

S O THE PEOPLE on Earth thought they had instructions from
the Creator of the Universe Himself to wreck the joint. But
they were going at it too slowly to satisfy the Elders, so the
Elders put it into the people's heads that they themselves were
the life forms that were supposed to spread out through the
Universe. This was a preposterous idea, of course. In the words
of the nameless author: "How could all that meat, needing so
much food and water and oxygen, and with bowel movements
so enormous, expect to survive a trip of any distance whatsoever
through the limitless void of outer space? It was a miracle that
such ravenous and cumbersome giants could make a roundtrip
for a 6-pack to the nearest grocery store."

The Elders, incidentally, had given up on influencing the
humanoids of Tralfamadore, who were right below where they
were meeting. The Tralfamadorians had senses of humor and
so knew themselves for the severely limited lunkers, not to say
crazy lunkers, they really were. They were immune to the kilo-
volts of pride the Elders jazzed their brains with. They laughed
right away when the idea popped up in their heads that they
were the glory of the Universe, and that they were supposed to
colonize other planets with their incomparable magnificence.
They knew exactly how clumsy and dumb they were, even
though they could talk and some of them could read and write
and do math. One author wrote a series of side-splitting satires
about Tralfamadorians arriving on other planets with the intention of spreading enlightenment.

But the people here on Earth, being humorless, found the
same idea quite acceptable.

It appeared to the Elders that the people here would believe
anything about themselves, no matter how preposterous, as
long as it was flattering. To make sure of this, they performed
an experiment. They put the idea into Earthlings' heads that
the whole Universe had been created by one big male animal
who looked just like them. He sat on a throne with a lot of less

fancy thrones all around him. When people died they got to sit on those other thrones forever because they were such close relatives of the Creator.

The people down here just ate that up!

Another thing the Elders liked about Earthlings was that they feared and hated other Earthlings who did not look and talk exactly as they did. They made life a hell for each other as well as for what they called "lower animals." They actually thought of strangers as lower animals. So all the Elders had to do to ensure that germs were going to experience really hard times was to tell us how to make more effective weapons by studying Physics and Chemistry. The Elders lost no time in doing this.

They caused an apple to fall on the head of Isaac Newton.

They made young James Watt prick up his ears when his mother's teakettle sang.

The Elders made us think that the Creator on the big throne hated strangers as much as we did, and that we would be doing Him a big favor if we tried to exterminate them by any and all means possible.

That went over big down here.

So it wasn't long before we had made the deadliest poisons in the Universe, and were stinking up the air and water and topsoil. In the words of the author, and I wish I knew his name, "Germs died by the trillions or failed to reproduce because they could no longer cut the mustard."

But a few survived and even flourished, even though almost all other life forms on Earth perished. And when all other life forms vanished, and this planet became as sterile as the Moon, they hibernated as virtually indestructible spores, capable of waiting as long as necessary for the next lucky hit by a meteor. Thus, at last, did space travel become truly feasible.

If you stop to think about it, what the Elders did was based on a sort of trickle-down theory. Usually when people talk about the trickle-down theory, it has to do with economics. The richer people at the top of a society become, supposedly, the more wealth there is to trickle down to the people below. It never really works out that way, of course, because if there are 2 things people at the top can't stand, they have to be leakage and overflow.

But the Elders' scheme of having the misery of higher animals trickle down to microorganisms worked like a dream.

There was a lot more to the story than that. The author taught me a new term, which was "Finale Rack." This was apparently from the vocabulary of pyrotechnicians, specialists in loud and bright but otherwise harmless nighttime explosions for climaxes of patriotic holidays. A Finale Rack was a piece of milled lumber maybe 3 meters long and 20 centimeters wide and 5 centimeters thick, with all sorts of mortars and rocket launchers nailed to it, linked in series by a single fuse.

When it seemed that a fireworks show was over, that was when the Master Pyrotechnician lit the fuse of the Finale Rack.

That is how the author characterized World War II and the few years that followed it. He called it "the Finale Rack of so-called Human Progress."

If the author was right that the whole point of life on Earth was to make germs shape up so that they would be ready to ship out when the time came, then even the greatest human being in history, Shakespeare or Mozart or Lincoln or Voltaire or whoever, was nothing more than a Petri dish in the truly Grand Scheme of Things.

In the story, the Elders of Tralfamadore were indifferent, to say the least, to all the suffering going on. When 6,000 rebellious slaves were crucified on either side of the Appian Way back in good old 71 B.C., the elders would have been delighted if a crucified person had spit into the face of a Centurion, giving him pneumonia or TB.

If I had to guess when "The Protocols of the Elders of Tralfamadore" was written, I would have to say, "A long, long time ago, after World War II but before the Korean War, which broke out in 1950, when I was 10." There was no mention of Korea as part of the Finale Rack. There was a lot of talk about making the planet a paradise by killing all the bugs and germs, and generating electricity with atomic energy so cheaply that it wouldn't even be metered, and making it possible for everybody to have an automobile that would make him or her mightier than 200 horses and 3 times faster than a cheetah, and incinerating the other half of the planet in case the people there got the idea that it was their sort of intelligence that was supposed to be exported to the rest of the Universe.

The story was very likely pirated from some other publication, so the omission of the author's name may have been intentional. What sort of writer, after all, would submit a work of fiction for possible publication in *Black Garterbelt*?

I did not realize at the time how much that story affected me. Reading it was simply a way of putting off for just a little while my looking for another job and another place to live at the age of 51, with 2 lunatics in tow. But down deep the story was beginning to work like a buffered analgesic. What a relief it was, somehow, to have somebody else confirm what I had come to suspect toward the end of the Vietnam War, and particularly after I saw the head of a human being pillowed in the spilled guts of a water buffalo on the edge of a Cambodian village, that Humanity is going somewhere really nice was a myth for children under 6 years old, like the Tooth Fairy and the Easter Bunny and Santa Claus.

Cough.

I'll tell you one germ that's ready to take off for the belt of Orion or the handle on the Big Dipper or whatever right now, somewhere on Earth, and that's the gonorrhea I brought home from Tegucigalpa, Honduras, back in 1967. For a while there, it looked like I was going to have it for the rest of my life. By now it probably can eat broken glass and razor blades.

The TB germs which make me cough so much now, though, are pussycats. There are several drugs on the market which they have never learned to handle. The most potent of these was ordered for me weeks ago, and should be arriving from Rochester at any time. If any of my germs are thinking of themselves as space cadets, they can forget it. They aren't going anywhere but down the toilet.

Bon voyage!

But listen to this: You know the 2 lists I've been working on, 1 of the women I've made love to, and 1 of the men, women, and children I've killed? It is becoming ever clearer that the lengths of the lists will be virtually identical! What a coincidence! When I started out with my list of lovers, I thought that however many of them there were might serve as my epitaph, a number and nothing more. But by golly if that same number couldn't stand for the people I've killed!

There's another miracle on the order of Tarkington's students being on vacation during the diphtheria epidemic, and then again during the prison break. How much longer can I go on being an Atheist?

"There are more things in heaven and earth . . ."

27

H ERE IS HOW I got a job at the prison across the lake on the same day Tarkington College fired me:

I came out of the garage, having read that germs, not people, were the darlings of the Universe. I got into my Mercedes, intending to go down to the Black Cat Café to pick up gossip, if I could, about anybody who was hiring anybody to do practically any kind of work anywhere in this valley. But all 4 tires went *bloomp*, *bloomp*, *bloomp*.

All 4 tires had been cored by Townies the night before. I got out of the Mercedes and realized that I had to urinate. But I didn't want to do it in my own house. I didn't want to talk to the crazy people in there. How is that for excitement? What germ ever lived a life so rich in challenges and opportunities?

At least nobody was shooting at me, and I wasn't wanted by the police.

So I went into the tall weeds of a vacant lot across the street from and below my house, which was built on a slope. I whipped out my ding-dong and found it was aimed down at a beautiful white Italian racing bicycle lying on its side. The bicycle was so full of magic and innocence, hiding there. It might have been a unicorn.

After urinating elsewhere, I set that perfect artificial animal upright. It was brand-new. It had a seat like a banana. Why had somebody thrown it away? To this day I do not know. Despite our enormous brains and jam-packed libraries, we germ hotels cannot expect to understand absolutely everything. My guess is that some kid from a poor family in the town below came across it while skulking around the campus. He assumed, as would I, that it belonged to some Tarkington student who was superrich, who probably had an expensive car and more beautiful clothes than he could ever wear. So he took it, as would I when my turn came. But he lost his nerve, as I would not, and hid it in the weeds rather than face arrest for grand larceny.

As I would soon find out the hard way, the bike actually belonged to a poor person, a teenage boy who worked in the stable after school, who had scrimped and saved until he could

384

afford to buy as splendid a bicycle as had ever been seen on the campus of Tarkington.

To play with my mistaken scenario of the bike's belonging to a rich kid: It seemed possible to me that some rich kid had so many expensive playthings that he couldn't be bothered with taking care of this one. Maybe it wouldn't fit into the trunk of his Ferrari Gran Turismo. You wouldn't believe all the treasures, diamond earrings, Rolex watches, and on and on, that wound up unclaimed in the college's Lost and Found.

Do I resent rich people? No. The best or worst I can do is notice them. I agree with the great Socialist writer George Orwell, who felt that rich people were poor people with money. I would discover this to be the majority opinion in the prison across the lake as well, although nobody over there had ever heard of George Orwell. Many of the inmates themselves had been poor people with money before they were caught, with the most costly cars and jewelry and watches and clothes. Many, as teenage drug dealers, had no doubt owned bicycles as desirable as the one I found in the weeds in the highlands of Scipio.

When convicts found out that my car was nothing but a 4-door, 6-cylinder Mercedes, they often scorned or pitied me. It was the same with many of the students at Tarkington. I might as well have owned a battered pickup truck.

So I walked that bicycle out of the weeds and onto the steep slope of Clinton Street. I wouldn't have to pedal or turn a corner in order to deliver myself to the front door of the Black Cat Café. I would have to use the brakes, however, and I tested those. If the brakes didn't work, I would go off the end of the dock of the old barge terminal and, alley-oop, straight into Lake Mohiga.

I straddled the banana-shaped saddle, which turned out to be surprisingly considerate of my sensitive crotch and hindquarters. Sailing down a hill on that bicycle in the sunshine wasn't anything like being crucified.

I parked the bike in plain view in front of the Black Cat Café, noting several champagne corks on the sidewalk and in the gutter. In Vietnam they would have been cartridge cases. This was where Arthur K. Clarke had formed up his motorcycle gang for its unopposed assault on Tarkington. The troops and their ladies had first drunk champagne. There were also remains of sandwiches, and I stepped on one, which I think was either cucumber or watercress. I scraped it off on the curbing, left it there for germs. I'll tell you this, though: No germ is going to leave the Solar System eating sissy stuff like that.

Plutonium! Now there's the stuff to put hair on a microbe's chest.

I entered the Black Cat Café for the first time in my life. This was my club now, since I had been busted down to Townie. Maybe, after a few drinks, I'd go back up the hill and let air out of the tires of some of Clarke's motorcycles and limousines.

I bellied up to the bar and said, "Give me a wop." That was what I had heard people down in the town called Budweiser beer, ever since Italians had bought Anheuser-Busch, the company that made Budweiser. The Italians got the St. Louis Cardinals, too, as part of the deal.

"Wop coming up," said the barmaid. She was just the kind of woman I would go for right now, if I didn't have TB. She was in her late 30s, and had had a lot of bad luck recently, and didn't know where to turn next. I knew her story. So did everybody else in town. She and her husband restored an old-time ice cream parlor 2 doors up Clinton Street from the Black Cat Café. But then her husband died because he had inhaled so much paint remover. The germs inside him couldn't have felt too great, either.

Who knows, though? The Elders of Tralfamadore may have had her husband restore the ice cream parlor just so we could have a new strain of germs capable of surviving a passage through a cloud of paint remover in outer space.

Her name was Muriel Peck, and her husband Jerry Peck was a direct descendant of the first President of Tarkington College. His father grew up in this valley, but Jerry was raised in San Diego, California, and then he went to work for an ice cream company out there. The ice cream company was bought by President Mobutu of Zaire, and Jerry was let go. So he came here with Muriel and their 2 kids to discover his roots.

Since he already knew ice cream, it made perfect sense for him to buy the old ice cream parlor. It would have been better for all concerned if he had known a little less about ice cream and a little more about paint remover.

Muriel and I would eventually become lovers, but not until I had been working at Athena Prison for 2 weeks. I finally got nerve enough to ask her, since she and Jerry had both majored in Literature at Swarthmore College, if either of them had ever taken the time to read a label on a can of paint remover.

"Not until it was much too late," she said.

Over at the prison I would encounter a surprising number of convicts who had been damaged not by paint remover but by paint. When they were little they had eaten chips or breathed dust from old lead-based paint. Lead poisoning had made them very stupid. They were all in prison for the dumbest crimes imaginable, and I was never able to teach any of them to read and write.

Thanks to them, do we now have germs which eat lead?

I know we have germs which eat petroleum. What their story is, I do not know. Maybe they're that Honduran gonorrhea.

28

JERRY PECK was in a wheelchair with a tank of oxygen in his lap at the grand opening of the Mohiga Ice Cream Emporium. But he and Muriel had a nice little hit on their hands. Tarkingtonians and Townies alike were pleased by the decor and the luscious ice cream.

After the place had been open for only 6 months, though, a man came in and photographed everything. Then he pulled out a tape and made measurements which he wrote down in a book. The Pecks were flattered, and asked him if he was from an architectural magazine or what. He said that he worked for the architect who was designing the new student recreation center up on the hill, the Pahlavi Pavilion. The Pahlavis wanted it to have an ice cream parlor identical to theirs, right down to the last detail.

So maybe it wasn't paint remover that killed Jerry Peck after all.

The Pavilion also put the valley's only bowling alley out of business. It couldn't survive on the business of Townies alone. So anybody in this area who wanted to bowl and wasn't connected to Tarkington had to go 30 kilometers to the north, to the alleys next to the Meadowdale Cinema Complex, across the highway from the National Guard Armory.

It was a slow time of day at the Black Cat Café. There may have been a few prostitutes in vans in the parking lot out back but none inside.

The owner, Lyle Hooper, who was also Chief of the Volunteer Fire Department and a Notary, was at the other end of the bar, doing some kind of bookkeeping. Until the very end of his life, he would never admit that the availability of prostitutes in his parking lot accounted in large measure for the business he did in liquor and snacks, and for the condom machine in the men's room.

To the Elders of Tralfamadore, of course, that condom machine would represent a threat to their space program.

—————————————

Lyle Hooper surely knew about my sexual exploits, since he had notarized the affidavits in my portfolio. But he never mentioned them to me, or so far as I know to anyone. He was the soul of discretion.

Lyle was probably the best-liked man in this valley. Townies were so fond of him, men and women alike, that I never heard one call the Black Cat Café a whorehouse. Up on the hill, of course, it was called almost nothing else.

The Townies protected the image he had of himself, in spite of State Police raids and visits from the County Health Department, as a family man who ran a place of refreshment whose success depended entirely on the quality of the drinks and snacks he served. This kindly conspiracy protected Lyle's son Charlton, as well. Charlton grew to be 2 meters tall, and was a New York State High School All-Star basketball center in his senior year at Scipio High School, and all he ever had to say about his father was that he ran a restaurant.

Charlton was such a phenomenal basketball player that he was invited to try out for the New York Knickerbockers, which were still owned by Americans back then. He accepted a full scholarship to MIT instead, and became a top scientist running the huge subatomic particle accelerator called "the Supercollider" outside Waxahachie, Texas.

—————————————

As I understand it, the scientists down there forced invisible particles to reveal their secrets by making them go *splat* on photographic plates. That isn't all that different from the way we treated suspected enemy agents in Vietnam sometimes.

Have I already said that I threw one out of a helicopter?

—————————————

The Townies didn't have to protect the sensibilities of Lyle's wife by never saying why the Black Cat Café was so prosperous. She had left him. She discovered in midlife that she was a lesbian, and ran off with the high school's girls' gym teacher to Bermuda, where they gave and probably still give sailing lessons.

I made a pass at her one time at an Annual Town-and-Gown Mixer up on the hill. I knew she was a lesbian before *she* did.

At the very end of his life 2 years ago, though, when Lyle Hooper was a prisoner of the escaped convicts up in the bell tower, he was addressed by his captors as "Pimp." It was, "Hey, Pimp, how you like the view?" and "What you think we ought to do with you, Pimp?" and so on. It was cold and wet up there. Snow or rain blown into the belfry fell down through a myriad of bullet holes in the ceiling. Those had been made from below by escaped convicts when they realized that a sniper was up there among the bells.

There was no electricity. All electric and telephone service had been shut off. When I visited Lyle up there, he knew the story of those holes, knew the sniper had been crucified in the stable loft. He knew that the escaped convicts hadn't decided yet what to do with him. He knew that he had committed what was in their eyes murder pure and simple. He and Whitey VanArsdale had ambushed and killed 3 escaped convicts who were on their way up the old towpath to the head of the lake, to negotiate with the police and politicians and soldiers at the roadblock there. The would-be negotiators were carrying flags of truce, white pillowcases on broomsticks, when Lyle Hooper and Whitey VanArsdale shot them dead.

And then Whitey was himself shot dead almost immediately, but Lyle was taken prisoner.

But what bothered Hooper most when I talked to him up in the bell tower was that his captors called him nothing but "Pimp."

At this point in my story, and in order to simplify the telling, and not to make any political point, let me from now on call the escaped convicts in Scipio what they called themselves, which was "Freedom Fighters."

So Lyle Hooper was without question responsible for the death of 3 Freedom Fighters carrying flags of truce. The Freedom Fighter who was guarding him in the tower when I came to see him, moreover, was the half brother and former partner in the crack business, along with their grandmother, of 1 of the Freedom Fighters he or Whitey had killed.

But all Lyle could talk about was the pain of being called a pimp. To many if not most of the Freedom Fighters, of course, it was no particular insult to call someone a pimp.

Lyle told me that he had been raised by his paternal grandmother, who made him promise to leave the world a better place than when he found it. He said, "Have I done that, Gene?"

I said he had. Since he was facing execution, I certainly wasn't going to tell him that, in my experience anyway, ambushes made the world seem an even worse place than it was before.

"I ran a nice, clean place, raised a wonderful son," he said. "Put out a lot of fires."

It was the Trustees who told the Freedom Fighters that Lyle ran a whorehouse. Otherwise they would have thought he was just a restaurateur and Fire Chief.

Lyle Hooper's mood up there in the bell tower reminded me of my father's mood after he was let go by Barrytron, and he went on a cruise down the Inland Waterway on the East Coast, from City Island in New York City to Palm Beach, Florida. This was on a motor yacht owned by his old college roommate, a man named Fred Handy. Handy had also studied chemical engineering, but then had gone into junk bonds instead. He heard that Father was deeply depressed. He thought the cruise might cheer Dad up.

But all the way to Palm Beach, where Handy had a waterfront estate, down the East River, down Barnegat Bay, up Delaware Bay and down Chesapeake Bay, down the Dismal Swamp Canal, and on and on, the yacht had to nuzzle its way through a shore-to-shore, horizon-to-horizon carpet of bobbing plastic bottles. They had contained brake fluid and laundry bleach and so on.

Father had had a lot to do with the development of those bottles. He knew, too, that they could go on bobbing for 1,000 years. They were nothing to be proud of.

In a way, those bottles called him what the Freedom Fighters called Lyle Hooper.

Lyle's despairing last words as he was led out of the bell tower to be executed in front of Samoza Hall might be an apt epitaph for my father:

OK, I ADMIT IT.
IT REALLY WAS A
WHOREHOUSE.

29

Lyle Hooper's last words, I think we can say with the benefit of hindsight in the year 2001, might serve as an apt epitaph for a plurality of working adults in industrialized nations during the 20th Century. How could they help themselves, when so many of the jobs they or their mates could get had to do with large-scale deceptions, legal thefts from public treasuries, or the wrecking of the food chain, the topsoil, the water, or the atmosphere?

After Lyle Hooper was executed, with a bullet behind the ear, I visited the Trustees in the stable. Tex Johnson was still spiked to the cross-timbers in the loft overhead, and they knew it.

But before I tell about that, I had better finish my story of how I got a job at Athena.

So there I was back in 1991, nursing a Budweiser, or "wop," at the bar of the Black Cat Café. Muriel Peck was telling me how exciting it had been to see all the motorcycles and limousines and celebrities out front. She couldn't believe that she had been that close to Gloria White and Henry Kissinger.

Several of the merry roisterers had come inside to use the toilet or get a drink of water. Arthur K. Clarke had provided everything but water and toilets. So Muriel had dared to ask some of them who they were and what they did.

Three of the people were Black. One Black was an old woman who had just won $57,000,000 in the New York State Lottery, and the other 2 were baseball players who made $3,000,000 a year.

A white man, who kept apart from the rest, and, according to Muriel, didn't seem to know what to make of himself, was a daily book reviewer for *The New York Times*. He had given a rave review to Clarke's autobiography, *Don't Be Ashamed of Money*.

One man who came in to use the toilet, she said, was a famous author of horror stories that had been made into some of the most popular movies of all time. I had in fact read a couple of them in Vietnam, about innocent people getting murdered by walking corpses with axes and knives and so on.

I passed 1 of them on to Jack Patton, I remember, and asked him later what he thought of it. And then I stopped him from answering, saying, "You don't have to tell me, Jack. I already know. It made you want to laugh like hell."

"Not only that, Major Hartke," he replied. "I thought of what his next book should be about."

"What's that?" I asked.

"A B-52," he said. "Gore and guts everywhere."

One user of the toilet, who confessed to Muriel that he had diarrhea, and asked if she had anything behind the bar to stop it, was a retired Astronaut whom she recognized but couldn't name. She had seen him again and again in commercials for a sinus-headache remedy and a retirement community in Cocoa Beach, Florida, near Cape Kennedy.

So Arthur K. Clarke, along with all his other activities, was a whimsical people-collector. He invited people he didn't really know, but who had caught his eye for 1 reason or another, to his parties, and they came, they came. Another one, Muriel told me, was a man who had inherited from his father a painting by Mark Rothko that had just been sold to the Getty Museum in Malibu, California, for $37,000,000, a new record for a painting by an American.

Rothko himself had long since committed suicide.

He had had enough.

He was out of here.

"She's so short," Muriel said to me. "I was so surprised how short she was."

"Who's so short?" I said.

"Gloria White," she said.

I asked her what she thought of Henry Kissinger. She said she loved his voice.

I had seen him up on the Quadrangle. Although I had been an instrument of his geopolitics, I felt no connection between him and me. His face was certainly familiar. He might have been, like Gloria White, somebody who had been in a lot of movies I had seen.

I dreamed about him once here in prison, though. He was a woman. He was a Gypsy fortune-teller who looked into her crystal ball but wouldn't say anything.

I said to Muriel, "You worry me."

"I what?" she said.

"You look tired," I said. "Do you get enough sleep?"

"Yes, thank you," she said.

"Forgive me," I said. "None of my business. It's just that you were so full of life while you were talking about the motorcycle people. When you stopped, it was as though you took off a mask, and you seemed as though you were suddenly all wrung out."

Muriel knew vaguely who I was. She had seen me with Margaret and Mildred in tow at least twice a week during the short time the ice cream parlor was in business. So I did not have to tell her that I, too, practically speaking, was without a mate. And she had seen with her own eyes how kind and patient I was with my worse than useless relatives.

So she was already favorably disposed to me. She trusted me, and responded with undisguised gratitude to my expressions of concern for her happiness.

"If you want to know the truth," she said, "I hardly sleep at all, I worry so much about the children." She had 2 of them. "The way things are going," she said, "I don't see how I can afford to send even 1 of them to college. I'm from a family where everybody went to college and never thought a thing about it. But that's all over now. Neither 1 is an athlete."

We might have become lovers that night, I think, instead of 2 weeks from then, if an ugly mountain of a man hadn't entered raging, demanding to know, "All right, where is he? Where's that kid?"

He was asking about the kid who worked at Tarkington's stable after school, whose bicycle I had stolen. I had left the kid's bike in plain view out front. Every other place of business on Clinton Street was boarded up, from the barge terminal to half-way up the hill. So the only place the boy could be, he thought, was inside the Black Cat Café or, worse, inside one of the vans out back in the parking lot.

———————

I played dumb.

We went outside with him to find out what bicycle he could possibly be talking about. I offered him the theory that the boy was a good boy, and nowhere near the Black Cat Café, and that some bad person had borrowed the bike and left it there. So he put the bike on the back of his beat-up pickup truck, and said he was late for an appointment for a job interview at the prison across the lake.

"What kind of a job?" I asked.

And he said, "They're hiring teachers over there."

I asked if I could come with him.

He said, "Not if you're going to teach what I want to teach. What do you want to teach?"

"Anything you don't want to teach," I said.

"I want to teach shop," he said. "You want to teach shop?"

"No," I said.

"Word of honor?" he said.

"Word of honor," I said.

"OK," he said, "get in, get in."

30

To understand how the lower ranks of guards at Athena in those days felt about White people, and never mind Black people, you have to realize that most of them were recruited from Japan's northernmost island, Hokkaido. On Hokkaido the primitive natives, the Ainus, thought to be very ugly because they were so pallid and hairy, were White people. Genetically speaking, they are just as white as Nancy Reagan. Their ancestors long ago had made the error, when humiliated by superior Asiatic civilizations, of shambling north instead of west to Europe, and eventually, of course, to the Western Hemisphere.

Those White people on Hokkaido had sure missed a lot. They were way behind practically everybody. And when the man who wanted to teach shop and I presented ourselves at the gate to the road that led through the National Forest to the prison, the 2 guards on duty there were fresh from Hokkaido. For all the respect our being Whites inspired in them, we might as well have been a couple of drunk and disorderly Arapahos.

The man who wanted to teach shop said his name was John Donner. On the way over he asked me if I had seen him on the Phil Donahue show on TV. That was a 1-hour show every weekday afternoon, which featured a small group of real people, not actors, who had had the same sort of bad thing happen to them, and had triumphed over it or were barely coping or whatever. There were 2 very similar programs in competition with *Donahue*, and the old novelist Paul Slazinger used to watch all 3 simultaneously, switching back and forth.

I asked him why he did that. He said he didn't want to miss the moment when, suddenly, there was absolutely nothing left to talk about.

I told John Donner that, unfortunately, I couldn't watch any of those shows, since I taught Music Appreciation in the afternoon, and then Martial Arts after that. I asked him what his particular *Donahue* show had been about.

"People who were raised in foster homes and got beat up all the time," he said.

I would see plenty of *Donahue* reruns at the prison, but not Donner's. That show would have been coals to Newcastle at Athena, where practically everybody had been beaten regularly and severely when he was a little kid.

I didn't see Donner on TV over there, but I did see myself a couple of times, or somebody who looked a whole lot like me in the distance, on old footage of the Vietnam War.

I even yelled 1 time at the prison, "There I am! There I am!"

Convicts gathered behind me, looking at the TV and saying, "Where? Where? Where?"

But they were too late. I was gone again.

Where did I go?

Here I am.

31

J OHN DONNER could have been a pathological liar. He could have made that up about being on *Donahue*. There was something very fishy about him. Then again, he could have been living under the Federal Witness Protection Program, with a new name and a fake biography GRIOT™ had written out for him. Statistically speaking, GRIOT™ would have to put it into a biography every so often, I suppose, that the fictitious subject was on *Donahue*.

He claimed that the boy he lived with was his son. But he could have kidnapped that kid whose bike I stole. They had come to town only about 18 months before, and kept to themselves.

I am sure his last name wasn't Donner. I have known several Donners. One was a year behind me at the Academy. Two were unrelated Tarkingtonians. One was a First Sergeant in Vietnam who had his arm blown off by a little boy with a homemade hand grenade. Every one of those Donners knew the story of the infamous Donner Party, which got caught in a blizzard back in 1846 while trying to cross the Sierra Nevada Mountains in wagons to get to California. Their wagons were very likely made right here in Scipio.

I have just looked up the details in the *Encyclopaedia Britannica*, published in Chicago and owned by a mysterious Egyptian arms dealer living in Switzerland. Rule Britannia!

Those who survived the blizzard did so by becoming cannibals. The final tally, and several women and children were eaten, was 47 survivors out of 87 people who had begun the trip.

Now there's a subject for *Donahue*: people who have eaten people.

People who can eat people are the luckiest people in the world.

But when I asked the man who claimed his last name was Donner if he was any relation to the man who led the Donner Party, he didn't know what I was talking about.

Whoever he really was, he and I wound up side by side on a hard bench in the waiting room outside the office of Athena's Warden, Hiroshi Matsumoto.

While we sat there, incidentally, some supplier to the prison was stealing the bicycle from the back of Donner's pickup truck.

A mere detail!

Donner told the truth about 1 thing at least. The Warden was ready to interview applicants for a teaching job. But we were the only 2 applicants. Donner said he heard about the job opening on the National Public Radio station in Rochester. That isn't the sort of station people looking for work are likely to listen to. It is much too sophisticated.

That was the only area station I know of, incidentally, which said it was tragic, not funny, what happened to Pamela Ford Hall's 1-woman show in Buffalo.

There was a Japanese TV set in front of us. There were Japanese TV sets all over the prison. They were like portholes on an ocean liner. The passengers were in a state of suspended animation until the big ship got where it was going. But anytime they wanted, the passengers could look through a porthole and see the real world out there.

Life was like an ocean liner to a lot of people who weren't in prison, too, of course. And their TV sets were portholes through which they could look while doing nothing, to see all the World was doing with no help from them.

Look at it go!

At Athena, though, the TVs showed nothing but very old shows from a large library of tapes 2 doors down from the office of Warden Matsumoto's office.

The tapes weren't played in any particular order. A guard who might not even understand English kept the central VCR stoked with whatever came to hand, just as though the cassettes were charcoal briquettes and the VCR was a hibachi back on Hokkaido.

But this whole scheme was an American invention taken over by the Japanese, like the VCR and the TV sets. Back when races were mixed in prisons, the adopted son of a member of the Board of Directors of the Museum of Broadcasting was sent to Athena for having strangled a girlfriend behind the Metropolitan Museum of Art. So the father had hundreds of tapes of TV shows in the library of the Museum of Broadcasting duplicated and presented to the prison. His dream, apparently, was that the tapes would provide the basis for a course at Athena in Broadcasting, which industry some of the inmates might consider entering after they got out, if they ever got out.

But the course in Broadcasting never materialized. So the tapes were run over and over again as something better than nothing for the convicts to look at while they were serving time.

———————

The adopted son of the donor of the tapes came back into the news briefly at the time the prison populations were being segregated according to race. There was talk of paroling him and a lot of others rather than transferring them to other prisons.

But the parents of the girl he had murdered behind the museum, who were well connected socially, demanded that he serve his full sentence, which, as I recall it, was 99 years. He was adopted, as I say. It came out that his biological father had also been a murderer.

So he now may be on one of the aircraft carriers or missile cruisers in New York Harbor that have been converted into prison ships.

———————

While Donner and I waited to see the Warden, we watched the assassination of President John F. Kennedy. Bingo! The back of his head flew off. His wife, wearing a pillbox hat, crawled out over the trunk of the convertible limousine.

And then the show cut to the police station in Dallas as Lee Harvey Oswald, the ex-Marine who supposedly shot the

President with a mail-order Italian rifle, was shot in the guts by the owner of a local strip joint. Oswald said, "Ow." There, yet again, was that "Ow" heard round the world.

Who says history has to be boring?

———————————

Meanwhile, out in the prison parking lot, somebody who had delivered food or whatever to the prison was taking the bicycle out of Donner's truck and putting it in his own, and taking off. It was like the murder of the Lilac Queen back in 1922, a perfect crime.

Cough.

———————————

There is even talk now of turning our nuclear submarines into jails for persons who, like myself, are awaiting trial. They wouldn't submerge, of course, and the rocket and torpedo tubes and all the electronic equipment would be sold for junk, leaving more space for cells.

If the entire submarine fleet were converted into jails, I've heard, the cells would be filled up at once. When this place stopped being a college and became a prison, it was filled to the brim before you could say "Jack Robinson."

———————————

I was called into the Warden's Office first. When I came back out, with not only a job but a place to live, the TV set was displaying a program I had watched when I was a boy, *Howdy Doody*. Buffalo Bob, the host, was about to be sprayed with seltzer water by Clarabell the Clown.

They were in black and white. That's how old that show was.

I told Donner the Warden wanted to see him, but he didn't seem to know who I was. I felt as though I were trying to wake up a mean drunk. I used to have to do that a lot in Vietnam. A couple of times the mean drunks were Generals. The worst was a visiting Congressman.

I thought I might have to fight Donner before he realized that *Howdy Doody* wasn't the main thing going on.

———————————

Warden Hiroshi Matsumoto was a survivor of the atom-bombing of Hiroshima, when I was 5 and he was 8. When the bomb was dropped, he was playing soccer during school recess. He chased a ball into a ditch at one end of the playing field. He bent over to pick up the ball. There was a flash and wind. When he straightened up, his city was gone. He was alone on a desert, with little spirals of dust dancing here and there. But I would have to know him for more than 2 years before he told me that.

His teachers and schoolmates were executed without trial for the crime of Emperor Worship.

Like St. Joan of Arc, they were burned alive.

———————————

Crucifixion as a mode of execution for the very worst crimi-nals was outlawed by the first Christian Roman Emperor, who was Constantine the Great.

Burning and boiling were still OK.

———————————

If I had had more time to think about it, I might not have applied for a job at Athena, realizing that I would have had to admit that I had served in Vietnam, killing or trying to kill nothing but Orientals. And my interviewer would surely be Oriental.

Yes, and no sooner did Warden Matsumoto hear that I was a West Pointer than he said with terrible heaviness, "Then of course you spent time in Vietnam."

I thought to myself, "Oh oh. There goes the ball game."

I misread him completely, not knowing then that the Japa-nese considered themselves to be as genetically discrete from other Orientals as from me or Donner or Nancy Reagan or the pallid, hairy Ainus, say.

"A soldier does what he is ordered to do," I said. "I never felt good about what I had to do." This wasn't entirely true. I had gotten high as a kite on the fighting now and then. I actually killed a man with my bare hands 1 time. He had tried to kill me. I barked like a dog and laughed afterward, and then threw up.

———————————

My confession that I had served in Vietnam, to my amazement, made Warden Matsumoto feel that we were almost brothers! He came out from behind his desk to take me by the hand
and stare into my eyes. It was an odd experience for me, simply
from the physical standpoint, since he was wearing a surgical
mask and rubber gloves.

"So we both know what it is," he said, "to be shipped to an
alien land on a dangerous mission of vainglorious lunacy!"

32

W HAT AN AFTERNOON!
Only 3 hours before, I had been so at peace in my
bell tower. Now I was inside a maximum-security prison, with
a masked and gloved Japanese national who insisted that the
United States was his Vietnam!

What is more, he had been in the middle of student antiwar
protests over here when the Vietnam War was going on. His
corporation had sent him to the Harvard Business School to
study the minds of the movers and shakers who were screwing
up our economy for their own immediate benefit, taking money
earmarked for research and development and new machinery
and so on, and putting it into monumental retirement plans and
year-end bonuses for themselves.

During our interview, he used all the antiwar rhetoric he had
heard at Harvard in the '60s to denounce his own country's
overseas disaster. We were a quagmire. There was no light at
the end of the tunnel over here, and on and on.

Until that moment, I had not given a thought to the mental
state of members of the ever-growing army of Japanese nation-
als in this country, who had to make a financial go of all the
properties their corporations had bought out from under us.
And it really must have felt to most of them like a war overseas
about Heaven knows what, and especially since, as was my case
in Vietnam, they were color-coded in contrast with the majority
of the native population.

On the subject of color-coding: You might have expected
that a lot of black people would be shot after the prison break,
even though they weren't escaped convicts. The state of mind
of Whites in this valley, certainly, was that any Black male had
to be an escapee.

Shoot first, and ask questions afterward. I sure used to do
that.

But the only person who wasn't an escapee who got shot just
for being black was a nephew of the Mayor of Troy. And he was

only winged. He lost the use of his right hand, but that has since been repaired by the miracle of microsurgery.

He was left-handed anyway.

He was winged when he was where he wasn't supposed to be, where nobody of any race was supposed to be. He was camping in the National Forest, which is against the law. He didn't even know there had been a prison break.

And then: *Bang!*

And here I am capitalizing "Black" and "White" sometimes, and then not capitalizing them, and not feeling right about how the words look either way. That could be because sometimes race seems to matter a tremendous lot, and other times race seems to matter a little less than that. And I keep wanting to say "so-called Black" or "so-called black." My guess is that well over half the inmates at Athena, and now in this prison here, had white or White ancestors. Many appear to be mostly white, but they get no credit for that.

Imagine what that must feel like.

I myself have claimed a black ancestor, since this is a prison for Blacks only, and I don't want to be transferred out of here. I need this library. You can imagine what sorts of libraries they must have on the aircraft carriers and missile cruisers which have been converted into prison ships.

This is home.

My lawyer says I am smart not to want to be transferred, but for other reasons. A transfer might put me back in the news again, and raise a popular clamor for my punishment.

As matters stand now, I am forgotten by the general public, and so, for that matter, is the prison break. The break was big news on TV for only about 10 days.

And then it was displaced as a headliner by a lone White girl. She was the daughter of a gun nut in rural northern California. She wiped out the Prom Committee of her high school with a Chinese hand grenade from World War II.

Her father had one of the World's most complete collections of hand grenades.

Now his collection isn't as complete as it used to be, unless, of course, he had more than 1 Chinese hand grenade from the Finale Rack.

Warden Matsumoto became chattier and chattier during my job interview. Before he was sent to Athena, he said, he ran a hospital-for-profit his corporation had bought in Louisville. He loved the Kentucky Derby. But he hated his job.

I told him I used to go to the horse races in Saigon every chance I got.

He said, "I only wish our Chairman of the Board back in Tokyo could have spent just one hour with me in our emergency room, turning away dying people because they could not afford our services."

"You had a body count in Vietnam, I believe?" he said.

It was true. We were ordered to count how many people we killed so that higher headquarters, all the way back to Washington, D.C., could estimate how much closer, even if it was only a teeny-weeny bit closer, all our efforts were bringing us to victory. There wasn't any other way to keep score.

"So now we count dollars the way you used to count bodies," he said. "What does that bring us closer to? What does it mean? We should do with those dollars what you did with the bodies. Bury and forget them! You were luckier with your bodies than we are with all our dollars."

"How so?" I said.

"All anybody can do with bodies is burn them or bury them," he said. "There isn't any nightmare afterwards, when you have to invest them and make them grow."

"What a clever trap your Ruling Class set for us," he went on. "First the atomic bomb. Now this."

"Trap?" I echoed wonderingly.

"They looted your public and corporate treasuries, and turned your industries over to nincompoops," he said. "Then they had your Government borrow so heavily from us that we had no choice but to send over an Army of Occupation in business suits. Never before has the Ruling Class of a country found a way to stick other countries with all the responsibilities their wealth might imply, and still remain rich beyond the dreams of avarice! No wonder they thought the comatose Ronald Reagan was a great President!"

His point was well taken, it seems to me.

When Jason Wilder and all the rest of the Trustees were hostages in the stable, and I paid them a call, I got the distinct impression that they regarded Americans as foreigners. What nationality that made them is hard to say.

They were all White, and they were all Male, since Lowell Chung's mother had died of tetanus. She died before the doctors could understand what was killing her. None of them had ever seen a case of tetanus before, because practically everybody in this country in the old days had been immunized.

Now that public health programs have pretty much fallen apart, and no foreigners are interested in running them, which is certainly understandable, quite a number of cases of tetanus, and especially among children, are turning up again.

So most doctors know what it looks like now. Mrs. Chung had the misfortune to be a pioneer.

The hostages told me about that. One of the first things I said to them was, "Where is Madam Chung?"

I thought I should reassure the Trustees after the execution of Lyle Hooper. His corpse had been shown to them as a warning, I suppose, against their making any plans for derring-do. That body was surely icing on the cake of terror, so to speak.

The College President, after all, was dangling from spikes in the loft above.

One of the hostages said in a TV interview after he was liberated that he would never forget the sound of Tex Johnson's head bouncing on the steps as Tex was dragged up to the loft feet first. He tried to imitate the sound. He said, "*Bloomp, bloomp, bloomp*," the same sound a flat tire makes.

What a planet!

The hostages expressed pity for Tex, but none for Lyle Hooper, and none for all the other faculty members and Townies who were also dead. The locals were too insignificant for persons on their social level to think about. I don't fault them for this. I think they were being human.

The Vietnam War couldn't have gone on as long as it did, certainly, if it hadn't been human nature to regard persons I didn't know and didn't care to know, even if they were in agony, as insignificant. A few human beings have struggled against this most natural of tendencies, and have expressed pity for unhappy strangers. But, as History shows, as History yells: "They have never been numerous!"

Another flaw in the human character is that everybody wants to build and nobody wants to do maintenance.

And the worst flaw is that we're just plain dumb. Admit it! You think Auschwitz was intelligent?

When I tried to tell the hostages a little about their captors, about their childhoods and mental illnesses, and their not caring if they lived or died, and what prison was like, and so on, Jason Wilder actually closed his eyes and covered his ears. He was being theatrical rather than practical. He didn't cover his ears so well that he couldn't hear me.

Others shook their heads and indicated in other ways that such information was not only tiresome but offensive. It was as though we were in a thunderstorm, and I had begun lecturing on the circulation of electrical charges in clouds, and the formation of raindrops, and the paths chosen by lightning strokes, and what thunder was, and on and on. All they wanted to know was when the storm would stop, so they could go on about their business.

What Warden Matsumoto had said about people like them was accurate. They had managed to convert their wealth, which had originally been in the form of factories or stores or other demanding enterprises, into a form so liquid and abstract, negotiable representations of money on paper, that there were few reminders coming from anywhere that they might be responsible for anyone outside their own circle of friends and relatives.

They didn't rage against the convicts. They were mad at the Government for not making sure that escapes from prison were impossible. The more they ran on like that, the clearer it became that it was their Government, not mine or the convicts' or the Townies'. Its first duty, moreover, was to protect them from the lower classes, not only in this country but everywhere.

Were people on Easy Street ever any different?

Think again about the crucifixions of Jesus and the 2 thieves, and the 6,000 slaves who followed the gladiator Spartacus.

Cough.

My body, as I understand it, is attempting to contain the TB germs inside me in little shells it builds around them. The shells are calcium, the most common element in the walls of many prisons, including Athena. This place is ringed by barbed wire. So was Auschwitz.

If I die of TB, it will be because my body could not build prisons fast enough and strong enough.

Is there a lesson there? Not a cheerful one.

If the Trustees were bad, the convicts were worse. I would be the last person to say otherwise. They were devastators of their own communities with gunfights and robberies and rapes, and the merchandising of brain-busting chemicals and on and on.

But at least they saw what they were doing, whereas people like the Trustees had a lot in common with B-52 bombardiers way up in the stratosphere. They seldom saw the devastation they caused as they moved the huge portion of this country's wealth they controlled from here to there.

Unlike my Socialist grandfather Ben Wills, who was a nobody, I have no reforms to propose. I think any form of government, not just Capitalism, is whatever the people who have all our money, drunk or sober, sane or insane, decide to do today.

Warden Matsumoto was an odd duck. Many of his quirks were no doubt a consequence of his having had an atomic bomb dropped on him in childhood. The buildings and trees and bridges and so on which had seemed so substantial vanished like fantasies.

As I've said, Hiroshima was suddenly a blank tableland with little dust devils spinning here and there.

After the flash, little Hiroshi Matsumoto was the only real thing on the table. He began a long, long walk in search of anything else that was also real. When he reached the edge of the city, he found himself among structures and creatures both real and fantastic, living people with their skins hanging on their exposed muscles and bones like draperies, and so on.

These images about the bombing are all his, by the way. But I wouldn't hear them from him until I had been teaching at the prison and living next door to him by the lake for 2 long years.

Whatever else being atom-bombed had done to him, it had not destroyed his conscience. He had hated turning away poor people from the emergency room at the hospital-for-profit he ran in Louisville. After he took over the prison-for-profit at

Athena, he thought there ought to be some sort of educational program there, even though his corporation's contract with New York State required him to keep the prisoners from escaping and nothing more.

He worked for Sony. He never worked for anybody but Sony.

"New York State," he said, "does not believe that education can rehabilitate the sort of criminal who ends up at Athena or Attica or Sing Sing." Attica and Sing Sing were for Hispanics and Whites respectively, who, like the inmates at Athena, had been convicted of at least 1 murder and 2 other violent crimes. The other 2 were likely to be murders, too.

"I don't believe it, either," he said. "I do know this, though: 10 percent of the people inside these walls still have minds, but there is nothing for those minds to play with. So this place is twice as painful for them as it is for the rest. A good teacher just might be able to give their minds new toys, Math or Astronomy or History, or who knows what, which would make the passage of time just a little bit more bearable. What do you think?"

"You're the boss," I said.

He really was the boss, too. He had made such a financial success of Athena that his corporate superiors allowed him to be completely autonomous. They had contracted with the State to take care of prisoners for only 2 thirds as much money per capita as the State had spent when it owned the place. That was about as much as it would have cost to send a convict to medical school or Tarkington. By importing cheap, young, short-term, nonunion labor, and by getting supplies from the lowest bidders rather than from the Mafia and so on, Hiroshi Matsumoto had cut the per capita cost to less than half of what it used to be.

He didn't miss a trick. When I went to work for him, he had just bought a state-of-the-art crematorium for the prison. Before that, a Mafia-owned crematorium on the outskirts of Rochester, in back of the Meadowdale Cinema Complex, across the highway from the National Guard Armory, had had a monopoly on cremating Athena's unclaimed bodies.

After the Japanese bought Athena, though, the Mob doubled their prices, using the AIDS epidemic as an excuse. They had to take extra precautions, they said. They wanted double even if the prison provided a doctor's certificate guaranteeing that a body was AIDS-free, and the cause of death, as anybody could see, was some sort of knife or garrote or blunt instrument.

———————

There wasn't a Japanese manufacturer of crematoria, so Warden Matsumoto bought one from A. J. Topf und Sohn in Essen, Germany. This was the same outfit that had made the ovens for Auschwitz in its heyday.

The postwar Topf models all had state-of-the-art smoke scrubbers on their smokestacks, so people in Scipio, unlike the people living near Auschwitz, never knew that they had a busy corpse carbonizer in the neighborhood.

We could have been gassing and incinerating convicts over there around the clock, and who would know?

———————

Who would care?

———————

A while back I mentioned that Lowell Chung's mother died of tetanus. I want to say before I forget that tetanus might have a real future in astronautics, since it becomes an extremely rugged spore when life becomes intolerable.

———————

I haven't nominated AIDS viruses as promising intergalactic rock jockeys, since, at their present state of development, they can't survive for long outside a living human body.

Concerted efforts to kill them with new poisons, though, if only partially successful, could change all that.

———————

The Mafia crematorium behind the Meadowdale Cinema Complex has all this valley's prison business again. Some of the convicts who stayed in or near Athena after the great escape, rather than attack Scipio across the ice, felt that at least they could bust up the A. J. Topf und Sohn crematorium.

The Meadowdale Cinema Complex itself has gone belly up, since so few people can afford to own an automobile anymore.

Same thing with the shopping malls.

One thing interesting to me, although I don't know quite what to make of it, is that the Mafia never sells anything to foreigners. While everybody else who has inherited or built a real business can't wait to sell out and take early retirement, the Mafia holds on to everything. Thus does the paving business, for example, remain a strictly American enterprise.

Same thing with wholesale meat and napkins and tablecloths for restaurants.

I told the Warden right up front that I had been canned by Tarkington. I explained that the charges against me for sexual irregularities were a smokescreen. The Trustees were really angry about my having wobbled the students' faith in the intelligence and decency of their country's leadership by telling them the truth about the Vietnam War.

"Nobody on this side of the lake believes there is such a thing in this miserable country," he said.

"Such a thing as what, sir?" I said.

And he said, "Leadership." As for my sexual irregularities, he said, they seemed to be uniformly heterosexual, and there were no women on his side of the lake. He himself was a bachelor, and members of his staff were not allowed to bring their wives with them, if they had them. "So over here," he said, "you would truly be Don Juan in Hell. Do you think that you could stand that?"

I said I could, so he offered me a job on a trial basis. I would start work as soon as possible, offering general education mostly on the primary-school level, not all that different from what I had done at Tarkington. An immediate problem was housing. His staff lived in barracks in the shadows of the prison walls, and he himself had a renovated house down by the water and was the only inhabitant of the ghost town, a ghost hamlet, actually, after which the prison was named: Athena.

If I didn't work out for some reason, he said, he would still need a teacher on the property, who would surely not want to live in the barracks. So he was having another old house in the ghost town made livable, right next to his own. But it wouldn't be ready for occupancy until August. "Do you think the college will let you stay where you are until then, and meanwhile you could commute to work from over there? You have a car?"

"A Mercedes," I said.

"Excellent!" he said. "That will give you something in common with the inmates right away."

"How so?" I said.

"They're practically all former Mercedes owners," he said. This was only a slight exaggeration. He told the truth when he said, "We have one man in here who bought his first Mercedes when he was 15 years old." That was Alton Darwin, whose dying words on the skating rink after the prison break would be, "See the Nigger fly the airplane."

So the college did let us stay in the Scipio house over the summer. There was no summer session at Tarkington. Who would have come to one? And I commuted to the prison every day.

In the old days, before the Japanese took over Athena, the whole staff was commuters from Scipio and Rochester. They were unionized, and it was their unceasing demands for more and more pay and fringe benefits, including compensation for their travel to and from work, that made the State decide to sell the whole shebang to the Japanese.

My salary was what I had been paid by Tarkington. I could keep our Blue Cross–Blue Shield, since the corporation that owned the prison also owned Blue Cross–Blue Shield. No problem!

Cough.

That is another thing the prison break cost me: our Blue Cross–Blue Shield.

33

I T WOULD work out well. When I moved Margaret and Mildred into our new home in the ghost town and pulled down the blinds, it was to them as though we had never left Scipio. There was a surprise present for me on our freshly sodded front lawn, a rowboat. The Warden had found an old boat that had been lying in the weeds behind the ruins of the old Athena Post Office since before I was born, quite possibly. He had had some of his guards fiberglass the outside of it, making it watertight again after all these years.

It looked a lot like the hide-covered Eskimo umiak that used to be in the rotunda outside the Dean of Women's Office here, with the outlines of the ribs showing through the fiberglass.

I know what happened to a lot of college property after the prison break, the GRIOT™ and so on, but I haven't a clue what became of that umiak.

If it hadn't been on display in the rotunda, I and hundreds of Tarkington students and their parents would have gone all the way through life without ever seeing a genuine Eskimo umiak.

I made love to Muriel Peck in that boat. I lay on the bottom, and she sat upright, holding my mother-in-law's fishing rod, pretending to be a perfect lady and all alone.

That was my idea. What a good sport she was!

I don't know what became of the man who claimed his name was John Donner, who wanted to teach shop at Athena, 8 years before the prison break. I do know that the Warden gave him very short shrift during his job interview, since the last things the prison needed inside its walls were chisels and screwdrivers and hacksaws and band saws and ball-peen hammers and so on.

I had to wait for Donner outside the Warden's Office. He was my ticket back to civilization, to my home and family and copy of *Black Garterbelt*. I didn't watch *Howdy Doody* on the little screen. I interested myself in another person, who was waiting to see the Warden. His color-coding alone would have told me that he was a convict, but he was also wearing leg irons and handcuffs, and was seated quietly on a bench facing mine across the corridor, with a masked and rubber-gloved guard on either side of him.

He was reading a cheap-looking booklet. Since he was literate, I thought he might be one of the people I was being hired to divert with knowledge. I was right. His name was Abdullah Akbahr. With my encouragement, he would write several interesting short stories. One, I remember, was supposedly the autobiography of a talking deer in the National Forest who has a terrible time finding anything to eat in winter and gets tangled in barbed wire during the summer months, trying to get at the delicious food on farms. He is shot by a hunter. As he dies he wonders why he was born in the first place. The final sentence of the story was the last thing the deer said on Earth. The hunter was close enough to hear it and was amazed. This was it: "What the blankety-blank was that supposed to be all about?"

———————————

The 3 violent crimes that had gotten Abdullah into Athena were murders in drug wars. He himself would be shot dead with buckshot and slugs after the prison break, while carrying a flag of truce, by Whitey VanArsdale, the mechanic, and Lyle Hooper, the Fire Chief.

"Excuse me," I said to him, "but may I ask what you are reading?"

He displayed the book's cover so I could read it for myself. The title was *The Protocols of the Elders of Zion*.

Cough.

Abdullah was summoned to the Warden's Office, incidentally, because he was 1 of several persons, guards as well as convicts, who claimed to have seen a castle flying over the prison. The Warden wanted to find out if some new hallucinatory drug had been smuggled in, or whether the whole place was finally going insane, or what on Earth was happening.

———————————

The Protocols of the Elders of Zion was an anti-Semitic work first published in Russia about 100 years ago. It purported to be the minutes of a secret meeting of Jews from many countries who planned to cooperate internationally so as to cause wars and revolutions and financial busts and so on, which would leave them owning everything. Its title was parodied by the author of the story in *Black Garterbelt*, and its paranoia, too.

The great American inventor and industrialist Henry Ford thought it was a genuine document. He had it published in this country back when my father was a boy. Now here was a black convict in irons, who had the gift of literacy, who was taking it seriously. It would turn out that there were 100s of copies circulating in the prison, printed in Libya and passed out by the ruling gang at Athena, the Black Brothers of Islam.

That summer I would start a literacy program in the prison, using people like Abdullah Akbahr as proselytizers for reading and writing, going from cell to cell and offering lessons. Thanks to me, 1,000s of former illiterates would be able to read *The Protocols of the Elders of Zion* by the time of the prison break.

I denounced that book, but couldn't keep it from circulating. Who was I to oppose the Black Brothers, who regularly exercised what the State would not, which was the death penalty.

Abdullah Akbahr rattled and clinked his fetters. "This any way to treat a veteran?" he said.

He had been a Marine in Vietnam, so he never had to listen to one of my pep talks. I was strictly Army. I asked him if he had ever heard of an Army officer they called "The Preacher," who was me, of course. I was curious as to how far my fame had spread.

"No," he said. But as I've said, there were other veterans there who had heard of me and knew, among other things, that I had pitched a grenade into the mouth of a tunnel one time, and killed a woman, her mother, and her baby hiding from helicopter gunships which had strafed her village right before we got there.

Unforgettable.

You know who was the Ruling Class that time? Eugene Debs Hartke was the Ruling Class.

Down with the Ruling Class!

John Donner was unhappy on our trip back to Scipio from the prison. I had landed a job, and he hadn't. His son's bicycle had been stolen in the prison parking lot.

The Mexicans have a favorite dish they call "twice-fried beans." Thanks to me, although Donner never found out, that bicycle was now a twice-stolen bicycle. One week later, Donner and the boy dematerialized from this valley as mysteriously as they had materialized, leaving no forwarding address.

Somebody or something must have been catching up with them.

I pitied that boy. But if he is still alive, he, like me, is a grownup now.

Somebody was catching up with me, too, but ever so slowly. I am talking about my illegitimate son out in Dubuque, Iowa. He was only 15 then. He didn't even know my name yet. He had yet to do as much detective work to discover the name and location of his father as I have done to identify the murderer of Letitia Smiley, Tarkington College's 1922 Lilac Queen.

I made the acquaintance of his mother while sitting alone at a bar in Manila, soon after the excrement hit the air-conditioning in Vietnam. I didn't want to talk to anybody of either sex. I was fed up with the human race. I wanted nothing more than to be left strictly alone with my thoughts.

Add those to my growing collection of Famous Last Words.

This reasonably pretty but shopworn woman sat down on a stool next to mine. "Forgive my intrusion on your thoughts," she said, "but somebody told me that you are the man they call

'The Preacher.' " She pointed out a Master Sergeant in a booth with 2 prostitutes who could not have been much over 15 years of age.

"I don't know him," I said.

"He didn't say he knew you," she said. "He's heard you speak. So have a lot of other soldiers I've talked to."

"Somebody had to speak," I said, "or we couldn't have had a war."

"Is that why they call you 'The Preacher'?" she said.

"Who knows," I said, "in a world as full of baloney as this 1 is?" I had been called that as far back as West Point because I never used profanity. During my first 2 years in Vietnam, when the only troops I gave pep talks to were those who served under me, I was called "The Preacher" because it sounded sinister, as though I were a puritanical angel of death. Which I was, I was.

"Would you rather I went away?" she said.

"No," I said, "because I think there is every chance we could wind up in bed together tonight. You look intelligent, so you must be as blue as I am about our nation's great unvictory. I worry about you. I'd like to cheer you up."

What the heck.

It worked.

———————————————

If it ain't broke, don't fix it.

34

I WAS reasonably happy teaching at the prison. I raised the level of literacy by about 20 percent, with each newly literate person teaching yet another one. I wasn't always happy with what they chose to read afterward.

One man told me that literacy made it a lot more fun for him to masturbate.

I did not loaf. I like to teach.

I dared some of the more intelligent prisoners to prove to me that the World was round, to tell me the difference between noise and music, to tell me how physical traits were inherited, to tell me how to determine the height of a guard tower without climbing it, to tell me what was ridiculous about the Greek legend which said that a boy carried a calf around a barn every day, and pretty soon he was a man who could carry a bull around the barn every day, and so on.

I showed them a chart a fundamentalist preacher from downtown Scipio had passed out to Tarkington students at the Pavilion one afternoon. I asked them to examine it for examples of facts tailored to fit a thesis.

Across the top the chart named the leaders of warring nations during the Finale Rack, during World War II. Then, under each name was the leader's birthdate and how many years he lived and when he took office and how many years he served, and then the total of all those numbers, which in each case turned out to be 3,888.

It looked like this:

	CHURCHILL	HITLER	ROOSEVELT	IL DUCE	STALIN	TOJO
BORN	1874	1889	1882	1883	1879	1884
AGE	70	55	62	61	65	60
TOOK OFFICE	1940	1933	1933	1922	1924	1941

	CHURCHILL	HITLER	ROOSEVELT	IL DUCE	STALIN	TOJO
YEARS IN OFFICE	4	11	11	22	20	3

As I say, every column adds up to 3,888.

Whoever invented the chart then pointed out that half that number was 1944, the year the war ended, and that the first letters of the names of the war's leaders spelled the name of the Supreme Ruler of the Universe.

The dumber ones, like the dumber ones at Tarkington, used me as an ambulatory *Guinness Book of World Records*, asking me who the oldest person in the world was, the richest one, the woman who had had the most babies, and so on. By the time of the prison break, I think, 98 percent of the inmates at Athena knew that the greatest age ever attained by a human being whose birthdate was well documented was about 121 years, and that this incomparable survivor, like the Warden and the guards, had been Japanese. Actually, he had fallen 128 days short of reaching 121. His record was a natural foundation for all sorts of jokes at Athena, since so many of the inmates were serving life sentences, or even 2 or 3 life sentences either superimposed or laid end to end.

They knew that the richest man in the world was also Japanese and that, about a century before the college and the prison were founded across the lake from each other, a woman in Russia was giving birth to the last of her 69 children.

The Russian woman who had more babies than anyone gave birth to 16 pairs of twins, 7 sets of triplets, and 4 sets of quadruplets. They all survived, which is more than you can say for the Donner Party.

Hiroshi Matsumoto was the only member of the prison staff with a college education. He did not socialize with the

others, and he took his off-duty meals alone and hiked alone
and fished alone and sailed alone. Neither did he avail himself
of the Japanese clubs in Rochester and Buffalo, or of the lavish
rest-and-recuperation facilities maintained in Manhattan by
the Japanese Army of Occupation in Business Suits. He had
made so much money for his corporation in Louisville and then
Athena, and was so brilliant in his understanding of American
business psychology, that I am sure he could have asked for
and gotten an executive job in the home office. He may have
known more about American black people than anybody else
in Japan, thanks to Athena, and more and more of the businesses his corporation was buying here were dependent on black
labor or at least the goodwill of black neighborhoods. Again
thanks to Athena, he probably knew more than any other Japanese about the largest industry by far in this country, which
was the procurement and distribution of chemicals that, when
introduced into the bloodstream in one way or another, gave
anybody who could afford them undeserved feelings of purpose
and accomplishment.

Only 1 of these chemicals was legal, of course, and was the
basis of the fortune of the family that gave Tarkington its band
uniforms, and the water tower atop Musket Mountain, and an
endowed chair in Business Law, and I don't know what all else.

That mind-bender was alcohol.

In the 8 years we lived next door to him in the ghost town
down by the lake, he never once indicated that he longed to
be back in his homeland. The closest he came to doing that
was when he told me 1 night that the ruins of the locks at the
head of the lake, with huge timbers and boulders tumbled this
way and that, might have been the creation of a great Japanese
gardener.

In the Japanese Army of Occupation he was a high-ranking
officer, the civilian peer of a Brigadier, maybe, or even a Major
General. But he reminded me of several old Master Sergeants
I had known in Vietnam. They would say worse things about
the Army and the war and the Vietnamese than anybody. But I
would go away for a couple of years, and then come back, and
they were all still there, crabbing away. They wouldn't leave

until the Vietnamese either killed them or kicked them out of there.

How they hated home. They were more afraid of home than of the enemy.

———————————

Hiroshi Matsumoto called this valley a "hellhole" and the "anus of the Universe." But he didn't leave it until he was kicked out of here.

I wonder if the Mohiga Valley hadn't become the only home he ever knew after the bombing of Hiroshima. He lives in retirement now in his reconstructed native city, having lost both feet to frostbite after the prison break. Is it possible that he is thinking now what I have thought so often: "What is this place and who are these people, and what am I doing here?"

———————————

The last time I saw him was on the night of the prison break. We had been awakened by the racket of the Jamaicans' assault on the prison. We both came running out onto the street in front of our houses barefoot and in our nightclothes, although the temperature must have been minus 10 degrees centigrade.

The name of our main street in the ghost town was Clinton Street, the name of the main street in Scipio. Can you imagine that: two communities so close geographically, and yet in olden times so separate socially and economically that, with all the street names they might have chosen, they both named their main street Clinton Street?

———————————

The Warden tried to reach the prison on a cordless telephone. He got no answer. His 3 house servants were looking out at us from upstairs windows. They were convicts over 70 years old, serving life sentences without hope of parole, long forgotten by the outside world, and coked to the gills on Thorazine.

My mother-in-law came out on our porch. She called to me, "Tell him about the fish I caught! Tell him about that fish I caught!"

The Warden said to me that a boiler up at the prison must have blown, or maybe the crematorium. It sounded to me like military weaponry, whose voices he had never heard. He hadn't even heard the atomic bomb go off. He had only felt the hot whoosh afterward.

And then all the lights on our side of the lake went off. And then we heard the strains of "The Star-Spangled Banner" floating down from the blacked-out penitentiary.

There was no way that the Warden and I, even with massive doses of LSD, could have imagined what was going on up there. We were faulted afterward for not having alerted Scipio. As far as that goes, Scipio, hearing the explosion and "The Star-Spangled Banner" and all the rest of it across the frozen lake, might have been expected to take some defensive action. But it did not.

Survivors over there I talked to afterward said they had just pulled the covers over their heads and gone to sleep again. What could be more human?

What was happening up there, as I've already said, was a stunningly successful attack on the prison by Jamaicans wearing National Guard uniforms and waving American flags. They had a public-address system mounted atop an armored personnel carrier and were playing the National Anthem. Most of them probably weren't even American citizens!

But what Japanese farm boy, serving a 6-month tour of duty on a dark continent, would be crazy enough to open fire on seeming natives in full battle dress, who were waving flags and playing their hellish music?

No such boy existed. Not that night.

If the Japanese had started shooting, they would have lost their lives like the defenders of the Alamo. And for what?

For Sony?

Hiroshi Matsumoto threw on some clothes! He drove up the hill in his Isuzu jeep!

He was fired upon by the Jamaicans!

He bailed out of his Isuzu! He ran into the National Forest!

He got lost in the pitch blackness. He was wearing sandals and no socks.

It took him 2 days to find his way back out of the forest, which was almost as dark in the daytime as it was at night.

Yes. And gangrene was feasting on his frostbitten feet.

I myself stayed down by the lake.

I sent Mildred and Margaret back to bed.

I heard what must have been the Jamaicans' shots at the Isuzu. Those were their parting shots. After that came silence.

My brain came up with this scenario: An attempted escape had been thwarted, possibly with some loss of life. The explosion at the beginning had been a bomb made by the convicts from nail parings or playing cards or who knows what?

They could make bombs and alcohol out of anything, usually in a toilet.

I misread the silence as good news.

I dreaded a continuation of the shooting, which would have meant to me that the Japanese farm boys had developed a taste for killing with guns, which can suddenly become, for the uninitiated, easy and fun.

I envisioned convicts, in or out of their cells, becoming ducks in a shooting gallery.

I imagined, now that there was silence, that order had been restored, and that an English-speaking Japanese was notifying the Scipio Police Department and the State Police and the County Sheriff about the squashed escape attempt, and probably asking for doctors and ambulances.

Whereas the Japanese had been bamboozled and overwhelmed so quickly that their telephone lines were cut and their radio was smashed before they could get in touch with anyone.

There was a full moon that night, but its rays could not reach the floor of the National Forest.

The Japanese were not hurt. The Jamaicans disarmed them and sent them up the moonlit road to the head of the lake. They told them not to stop running until they got all the way back to Tokyo.

Most of them had never seen Tokyo.

And they did not arrive at the head of the lake hollering bloody murder and flagging down passing cars. They hid up there. If the United States was against them, who could be for them?

I had no gun.

If a few convicts had broken out and were still at large, I thought, and they came down into our ghost town, they would know me and think well of me. I would give them whatever they wanted, food, money, bandages, clothes, the Mercedes.

No matter what I gave them, I thought, since they were color-coded, they would never escape from this valley, from this lily-white cul-de-sac.

There was nothing but White people all the way to Rochester's city-limits sign.

I went to my rowboat, which I had turned upside down for the wintertime. I sat down astride its slick and glossy bow, which was aimed at the old barge terminal of Scipio.

They still had lights over in Scipio, which was a nice boost for my complacency.

There wasn't any excitement over there, despite the noise at the prison. The lights in several houses went off. None went on. Only 1 car was moving. It was going slowly down Clinton Street. It stopped and turned off its lights in the parking lot behind the Black Cat Café.

The little red light atop the water tower on the summit of Musket Mountain winked off and on, off and on. It became a sort of mantra for me, so that I sank even deeper into thoughtless meditation, as though scuba diving in lukewarm bouillon.

Off and on that little light winked, off and on, off and on.

How long did it give me rapture from so far away? Three minutes? Ten minutes? Hard to say.

I was brought back to full wakefulness by a strange transformation in the appearance of the frozen lake to the north of me. It had come alive somehow, but noiselessly.

And then I realized that I was watching 100s of men engaged in a sort of project which I myself had planned and led many times in Vietnam, which was a surprise attack.

It was I who broke the silence. A name tore itself from my lips before I could stop it.

The name? "Muriel!"

35

M URIEL PECK wasn't a barmaid anymore. She was a Full Professor of English at Tarkington, making good use of her Swarthmore education. She was asleep at the time of the surprise attack, all alone in faculty housing, a vine-covered cottage at the top of Clinton Street. Like me, she had sent her 2 kids to expensive boarding schools.

I asked her one time if she ever thought of marrying again. She said, "Didn't you notice? I married you."

She wouldn't have gotten a job at Tarkington if the Trustees hadn't fired me. An English teacher named Dwight Casey hated the head of his department so much that he asked for my old job just to get away from him. So that created a vacancy for Muriel.

If they hadn't fired me, she probably would have left this valley, and would be alive today.

If they hadn't fired me, I would probably be lying where she is, next to the stable, in the shadow of Musket Mountain when the Sun goes down.

Dwight Casey is still alive, I think. His wife came into a great deal of money soon after he replaced me. He quit at the end of the academic year and moved to the south of France.

His wife's family was big in the Mafia. She could have taught but didn't. She had a Master's Degree in Political Science from Rutgers. All he had was a BS in Hotel Management from Cornell.

The Battle of Scipio lasted 5 days. It lasted 2 days longer than the Battle of Gettysburg, at which Elias Tarkington was shot by a Confederate soldier who mistook him for Abraham Lincoln.

On the night of the prison break, I was as helpless a voyeur, once the attack had begun, as Robert E. Lee at Gettysburg or Napoleon Bonaparte at Waterloo.

There was 1 shot fired by someone in Scipio. I will never know who did it. It was some night owl with a loaded gun in easy reach. Whoever did it must have been killed soon afterward, otherwise he would have bragged about what he had done so early in the game.

———————————

Those were good soldiers who crossed the ice. Several of them had been in Vietnam, and so, like me, had had lessons in Military Science on full scholarships from the Government. Others had had plenty of experience with shooting and being shot at, often from early childhood on, and so found a single shot unremarkable. They saved their ammunition until they could see clearly what they were shooting at.

When those seasoned troops went ashore, that was when they commenced firing. They were stingy with their bullets. There would be a *bang*, and then silence for several minutes, and then, when another target appeared, maybe a bleary-eyed householder coming out his front door or peering out a window, with or without a weapon, there would be another *bang* or 2 or 3 *bang*s, and then silence again. The escaped convicts, or Freedom Fighters as they would soon call themselves, had to assume, after all, that many if not most households had firearms, and that their owners had long daydreamed of using them with deadly effect should precisely what was happening happen. The Freedom Fighters had no choice. I would have done the same thing, had I been in their situation.

Bang. Somebody else would jerk backward and downward, like a professional actor on a TV show.

———————————

The biggest flurry of shots came from what I guessed from afar to be the parking lot in back of the Black Cat Café, where the prostitutes parked their vans. The men who visited the vans that late at night had handguns with them, just in case. Better safe than sorry.

———————————

And then I could tell from the sporadic firing that the Freedom Fighters had begun to climb the hill to this college, which was brightly lit all night every night to discourage anybody who might be tempted to do harm up here. From my point of view across the lake, Tarkington might have been mistaken for an emerald-studded Oz or City of God or Camelot.

You can bet I did not go back to sleep that night. I listened and listened for sirens, for helicopters, for the rumble of armored vehicles, for proofs that the forces of law and order would soon put a stop to the violence in the valley with even greater violence. At dawn the valley was as quiet as ever, and the red light on top of the water tower on the summit of Musket Mountain, as though nothing remarkable had happened over there, winked off and on, off and on.

I went next door to the Warden's house. I woke up his 3 servants. They had gone back to bed after the Warden charged up the hill in his Isuzu. These were old, old men, sentenced to life in prison without hope of parole, back when I was a little boy in Midland City. I hadn't even learned to read and write, probably, when they ruined some lives, or were accused of doing so, and were forced to lead lives not worth living as a consequence.

That would certainly teach them a lesson.

At least they hadn't been put into that great invention by a dentist, the electric chair.

"Where there is life there is hope." So says John Gay in the Atheist's Bible. What a starry-eyed optimist!

These 3 old geezers hadn't had a visitor or a phone call or a letter for decades. Under the circumstances, they had no vivid ideas of what they would like to do next, so they were glad to take orders from almost anybody. Other people's ideas of what to do next were like brain transplants. All of a sudden they were full of pep.

So I had them drink a lot of black coffee. Since I was worried about what might have happened to the Warden, they acted worried, too. Otherwise, they wouldn't have. I did not tell them that there had been a mass prison break and that Scipio had been overrun by criminals. Such information would have been useless to them, would have been like more TV. They were supposed to stay where they had been put, no matter what in the real world might be going on.

Those 3 were what psychologists call "other-directed."

I took them over to my house and ordered them to keep the wood fire in the fireplace going, and to feed Margaret and Mildred when they got hungry. There were plenty of canned goods. I didn't have to worry about the perishables in the refrigerator, since the air in the kitchen was already so cold. The stove itself ran on bottled propane, and there was a month's supply of that science fiction miracle.

Imagine that: bottled energy!

Margaret and Mildred, thank goodness, felt neutral about the Warden's zombies, the same way they felt about me. They didn't like them, but they didn't dislike them, either. So everything was falling into place. They would still have a life-support system, even if I went away for several days or got wounded or killed.

I didn't expect to get wounded or killed, except by accident. All the combatants in Scipio would regard me as unthreatening, the Whites because of my color-coding and the Blacks because they knew and liked me.

The issues were clear. They were Black and White.

All the Yellow people had run away.

I had hoped to get away from the house while Margaret and Mildred were fast asleep. But as I passed my boat on my way to the ice, an upstairs window flew open. There my poor old wife was, a scrawny, addled hag. She sensed that something important was happening, I think. Otherwise she wouldn't

have exposed herself to the cold and daylight. Her voice, moreover, which had been rasping and bawdy for years, was liquid
and sweet, just as it had been on our Honeymoon. And she
called me by name. That was another thing she hadn't done for
a long, long time. This was disorienting.

"Gene—" she said.

So I stopped. "Yes, Margaret," I said.

"Where are you going, Gene?" she said.

"I'm going for a walk, Margaret, to get some fresh air," I said.

"You're going to see some woman, aren't you?" she said.

"No, Margaret. Word of Honor I'm not," I said.

"That's all right. I understand," she said.

It was so pathetic! I was so overwhelmed by the pathos, by
the beautiful voice I hadn't heard for so long, by the young
Margaret inside the witch! I cried out in all sincerity, "Oh, Margaret, I love you, I love you!"

Those were the last words she would ever hear me say, for I
would never come back.

She made no reply. She shut the window and pulled down the
opaque black roller blind.

I have not seen her since.

After that side of the lake was recaptured by the 82nd Airborne, she and her mother were put in a steel box on the back
of one of the prison vans and delivered to the insane asylum
in Batavia. They will be fine as long as they have each other.
They might be fine even if they didn't have each other. Who
knows, until somebody or something performs that particular
experiment?

I have not been on that side of the lake since that morning,
and may never go there again, as close as it is. So I will probably
never find out what became of my old footlocker, the coffin
containing the soldier I used to be, and my very rare copy of
Black Garterbelt.

I crossed the lake that morning, as it happens, never to return,
to deliver a particular message to the escaped convicts, with the

idea of saving lives and property. I knew that the students were on vacation. That left nothing but social nobodies, in which category I surely include the college faculty, members of the Servant Class.

To me this low-grade social mix was ominous. In Vietnam, and then in later show-biz attacks on Tripoli and Panama City and so on, it had been perfectly ordinary for our Air Force to blow communities of nobodies, no matter whose side they were on, to Kingdom Come.

It seemed likely to me, should the Government decide to bomb Scipio, that it would be sensible to bomb the prison, too.

And everything would be taken care of, and no argument.

Next problem?

How many Americans knew or cared anyway where or what the Mohiga Valley was, or Laos or Cambodia or Tripoli? Thanks to our great educational system and TV, half of them couldn't even find their own country on a map of the world.

Three-quarters of them couldn't put the cap back on a bottle of whiskey without crossing the threads.

As I expected, I was treated by Scipio's conquerors as a harmless old fool with wisdom. The criminals called me "The Preacher" or "The Professor," just as they had on the other side.

I saw that many of them had tied ribbons around their upper arms as a sort of uniform. So when I came across a man who wasn't wearing a ribbon, I asked him jokingly, "Where's your uniform, Soldier?"

"Preacher," he said, referring to his skin, "I was born in a uniform."

Alton Darwin had set himself up in Tex Johnson's office in Samoza Hall as President of a new nation. He had been drinking. I do not mean to present any of these escapees as rational or capable of redemption. They did not care if they lived or died. Alton Darwin was glad to see me. Then again, he was glad about everything.

I had to advise him, nonetheless, that he could expect to be bombed unless he and the rest of them got out of town right away. I said their best chance to survive was to go back to the prison and fly white flags everywhere. If they did that right away, they might claim that they had nothing to do with all the killings here. The number of people the escapees killed in Scipio, incidentally, was 5 less than the number I myself had killed single-handedly in the war in Vietnam.

So the Battle of Scipio was nothing but a "tempest in a teapot," an expression the Atheist's Bible tells us is proverbial.

I told Alton Darwin that if he and his people didn't want to be bombed and didn't want to return to the prison, they should take whatever food they could find and disperse to the north or west. I told him one thing he already knew, that the floor of the National Forest to the south and east was so dark and lifeless that anyone going in there would probably starve to death or go mad before he found his way back out of there. I told him another thing he already knew, that there would soon be all these white people to the west and north, having the times of their lives hunting escaped convicts instead of deer.

My second point, in fact, was something the convicts had taught me. They all believed that the White people who insisted that it was their Constitutional right to keep military weapons in their homes all looked forward to the day when they could shoot Americans who didn't have what they had, who didn't look like their friends and relatives, in a sort of open-air shooting gallery we used to call in Vietnam a "Free Fire Zone." You could shoot anything that moved, for the good of the greater society, which was always someplace far away, like Paradise.

Alton Darwin heard me out. And then he told me that he thought I was right, that the prison probably would be bombed. But he guaranteed that Scipio would not be bombed, and that it would not be attacked on the ground, either, that the

Government would have to keep its distance and respect the demands he meant to put to it.

"What makes you think that?" I said.

"We have captured a TV celebrity," he said. "They won't let anything happen to him. Too many people will be watching."

"Who?" I said.

And he said, "Jason Wilder."

That was the first I heard that they had taken hostage not only Wilder but the whole Board of Trustees of Tarkington College. I now realize, too, that Alton Darwin would not have known that Wilder was a TV celebrity if old tapes of Wilder's talk show hadn't been run again and again at the prison across the lake. Poor people of any race on the outside never would have watched his show for long, since its basic message was that it was poor people who were making the lives of the rest of us so frightening.

36

"STAR WARS," said Alton Darwin.

He was alluding to Ronald Reagan's dream of having scientists build an invisible dome over this country, with electronics and lasers and so on, which no enemy plane or projectile could ever penetrate. Darwin believed that the social standing of his hostages was an invisible dome over Scipio.

I think he was right, although I have not been able to discover how seriously the Government considered bombing the whole valley back to the Stone Age. Years ago, I might have found out through the Freedom of Information Act. But the Supreme Court closed that peephole.

Darwin and his troops knew the lives of the hostages were valued highly by the Government. They didn't know why, and I am not sure that I do, either. I think that the number of people with money and power had shrunk to the point where it felt like a family. For all the escaped convicts knew about them, they might as well have been aardvarks, or some other improbable animal they had never seen before.

Darwin regretted that I, too, was going to have to stay in Scipio. He couldn't let me go, he said, because I knew too much about his defenses. There were none as far as I could see, but he sounded as though there were trenches and tank traps and mine fields all around us.

Even more hallucinatory was his vision of the future. He was going to restore this valley to its former economic vitality. It would become an all-Black Utopia. All Whites would be resettled elsewhere.

He was going to put glass back into the windows of the factories, and make their roofs weather-tight again. He would get the money to do this and so many other wonderful things by selling the precious hardwoods of the National Forest to the Japanese.

That much of his dream is actually coming true now. The National Forest is now being logged by Mexican laborers using Japanese tools, under the direction of Swedes. The proceeds are expected to pay half of day-before-yesterday's interest on the National Debt.

That last is a joke of mine. I have no idea if any money for the forest will go toward the National Debt, which, the last I heard, was greater than the value of all property in the Western Hemisphere, thanks to compound interest.

Alton Darwin looked me up and down, and then he said with typical sociopathic impulsiveness, "Professor, I can't let you go because I need you."

"What for?" I said. I was scared to death that he was going to make me a General.

"To help with the plans," he said.

"For what?" I said.

"For the glorious future," he said. He told me to go to this library and write out detailed plans for making this valley into the envy of the World.

So that, in fact, is what I mainly did during most of the Battle of Scipio.

It was too dangerous to go outside anyway, with all the bullets flying around.

My best Utopian invention for the ideal Black Republic was "Freedom Fighter Beer." They would get the old brewery going again, supposedly, and make beer pretty much like any other beer, except that it would be called Freedom Fighter Beer. If I say so myself, that is a magical name for beer. I envisioned a time when, all over the world, the bored and downtrodden and weary would be bucking themselves up at least a little bit with Freedom Fighter Beer.

Beer, of course, is actually a depressant. But poor people will never stop hoping otherwise.

Alton Darwin was dead before I could complete my long-range plan. His dying words, as I've said, were, "See the Nigger fly the airplane." But I showed it to the hostages.

"What is this supposed to mean?" said Jason Wilder.

"I want you to see what they've had me doing," I said. "You keep talking as though I could turn you loose, if I wanted. I'm as much a prisoner as you are."

He studied the prospectus, and then he said, "They actually expect to get away with this?"

"No," I said. "They know this is their Alamo."

He arched his famous eyebrows in clownish disbelief. He has always looked to me a lot like the incomparable comedian Stanley Laurel. "It would never have occurred to me to compare the rabid chimpanzees who hold us in durance vile with Davy Crockett and James Bowie and Tex Johnson's great-great-grandfather," he said.

"I was just talking about hopeless situations," I said.

"I certainly hope so," he said.

I might have added, but didn't, that the martyrs at the Alamo had died for the right to own Black slaves. They didn't want to be a part of Mexico anymore because it was against the law in that country to own slaves of any kind.

I don't think Wilder knew that. Not many people in this country do. I certainly never heard that at the Academy. I wouldn't have known that slavery was what the Alamo was all about if Professor Stern the unicyclist hadn't told me so.

No wonder there were so few Black tourists at the Alamo!

Units of the 82nd Airborne, fresh from the South Bronx, had by then retaken the other side of the lake and herded the prisoners back inside the walls. A big problem over there was that almost every toilet in the prison had been smashed. Who knows why?

What was to be done with the huge quantities of excrement produced hour after hour, day after day, by all these burdens on Society?

We still had plenty of toilets on this side of the lake, which is why this place was made an auxiliary prison almost immediately. Time was of the essence, as the lawyers say.

Imagine the same sort of thing happening on a huge rocket ship bound for Betelgeuse.

37

ON THE LAST AFTERNOON of the siege, National Guard units relieved the Airborne troops across the lake. That night, undetected, the paratroops took up positions behind Musket Mountain. Two hours before the next dawn, they came quietly around either side of the mountain, captured the stable, freed the hostages, and then took possession of all of Scipio. They had to kill only 1 person, who was the guard dozing outside the stable. They strangled him with a standard piece of equipment. I had used one just like it in Vietnam. It was a meter of piano wire with a wooden handle at either end.

So that was that.

The defenders were out of ammunition. There were hardly any defenders left anyway. Maybe 10.

———

Again, I don't believe there would have been such delicate microsurgery by the best ground troops available, if it hadn't been for the social prominence of the Trustees.

They were helicoptered to Rochester, where they were shown on TV. They thanked God and the Army. They said they had never lost hope. They said they were tired but happy, and just wanted to get a hot bath and then sleep in a nice clean bed.

———

All National Guardsmen who had been south of the Meadowdale Cinema Complex during the siege got Combat Infantryman's Badges. They were so pleased.

The paratroops already had theirs. When they dressed up for the victory parade, they wore campaign ribbons from Costa Rica and Bimini and El Paso and on and on, and from the Battle of the South Bronx, of course. That battle had had to keep on going without their help.

———

Several nobodies tried to get onto a helicopter with the Trustees. There was room. But the only people allowed aboard were on a list which had come all the way from the White House. I saw the list. Tex and Zuzu Johnson were the only locals named.

I watched the helicopters take off, the happy ending. I was up in the belfry, checking on the damage. I hadn't dared to go up there earlier. Somebody might have taken a shot at me, and it could have been a beautiful shot.

And as the helicopters became specks to the north, I was startled to hear a woman speak. She was right behind me. She was small and was shod in white sneakers and had come up ever so quietly. I wasn't expecting company.

She said, "I wondered what it was like up here. Sure is a mess, but the view is nice, if you like water and soldiers." She sounded tired. We all did.

I turned to look at her. She was Black. I don't mean she was so-called Black. Her skin was very dark. She may not have had any white blood whatsoever. If she had been a man at Athena, skin that color would have put her in the lowest social caste.

She was so small and looked so young I mistook her for a Tarkington student, maybe the dyslexic daughter of some over-thrown Caribbean or African dictator who had absquatulated to the USA with his starving nation's treasury.

Wrong again!

If the college GRIOT™ had still been working, I am sure it couldn't have guessed what she was and what she was doing there. She had lived outside all the statistics on which GRIOT™ based its spookily canny guesses. When GRIOT™ was stumped by somebody who had given statistical expectations as wide a berth as she had, it just sat there and hummed. A little red light came on.

Her name was Helen Dole. She was 26. She was unmarried. She was born in South Korea, and had grown up in what was then West Berlin. She held a Doctorate in Physics from the University of Berlin. Her father had been a Master Sergeant in the Quartermaster Corps of the Regular Army, serving in Korea and then in our Army of Occupation in Berlin. When her father retired after 30 years, to a nice enough little house in a nice enough little neighborhood in Cincinnati, and she saw the horrible squalor and hopelessness into which most black people

were born there, she went back to what had become just plain
Berlin and earned her Doctorate.

She was as badly treated by many people over there as she
would have been over here, but at least she didn't have to think
every day about some nearby black ghetto where life expectancy
was worse than that in what was said to be the poorest country
on the planet, which was Bangladesh.

This Dr. Helen Dole had come to Scipio only the day before
the prison break, to be interviewed by Tex and the Trustees
for, of all things, my old job teaching Physics. She had seen the
opening advertised in *The New York Times*. She had talked to
Tex on the telephone before she came. She wanted to make sure
he knew she was Black. Tex said that was fine, no problem. He
said that the fact that she was both female and black, and held a
Doctorate besides, was absolutely beautiful.

If she had landed the job and signed a contract before Tarkington ceased to be, that would have made her the last of a long
succession of Tarkington Physics teachers, which included me.

But Dr. Dole had blown up at the Board of Trustees instead.
They asked her to promise that she would never, whether in class
or on social occasions, discuss politics or history or economics
or sociology with students. She was to leave those subjects to
the college's experts in those fields.

"I plain blew up," she said to me.

"All they asked of me," she said, "was that I not be a human
being."

"I hope you gave it to them good," I said.

"I did," she said. "I called them a bunch of European planters."

Lowell Chung's mother was no longer on the Board, so all
the faces Dr. Dole saw were indeed of European ancestry.

She asserted that Europeans like them were robbers with guns
who went all over the world stealing other people's land, which
they then called their plantations. And they made the people
they robbed their slaves. She was taking a long view of history, of course. Tarkington's Trustees certainly hadn't roamed
the world on ships, armed to the teeth and looking for lightly

defended real estate. Her point was that they were heirs to the property of such robbers, and to their mode of thinking, even if they had been born poor and had only recently dismantled an essential industry, or cleaned out a savings bank, or earned big commissions by facilitating the sale of beloved American institutions or landmarks to foreigners.

She told the Trustees, who had surely vacationed in the Caribbean, about the Carib Indian chief who was about to be burned at the stake by Spaniards. His crime was his failure to see the beauty of his people's becoming slaves in their own country.

This chief was offered a cross to kiss before a professional soldier or maybe a priest set fire to the kindling and logs piled up above his kneecaps. He asked why he should kiss it, and he was told that the kiss would get him into Paradise, where he would meet God and so on.

He asked if there were more people like the Spaniards up there.

He was told that of course there were.

In that case, he said, he would leave the cross unkissed. He said he didn't want to go to yet another place where people were so cruel.

She told them about Indonesian women who threw their jewelry to Dutch sailors coming ashore with firearms, in the hopes that they would be satisfied by such easily won wealth and go away again.

But the Dutch wanted their land and labor, too.

And they got them, which they called a plantation.

I had heard about that from Damon Stern.

"Now," she said to them, "you are selling this plantation because the soil is exhausted, and the natives are getting sicker and hungrier every day, begging for food and medicine and shelter, all of which are very expensive. The water mains are breaking. The bridges are falling down. So you are taking all your money and getting out of here."

One Trustee, she didn't know which, except that it wasn't Wilder, said that he intended to spend the rest of his life in the United States.

"Even if you stay," she said, "you and your money and your soul are getting out of here."

So she and I, working independently, had noticed the same thing: That even our natives, if they had reached the top or been born at the top, regarded Americans as foreigners. That seems to have been true, too, of people at the top in what used to be the Soviet Union: to them their own ordinary people weren't the kinds of people they understood and liked very much.

"What did Jason Wilder say to that?" I asked her. On TV he was always so quick to snatch any idea tossed his way, cover it with spit, so to speak, and throw it back with a crazy spin which made it uncatchable.

"He just let it lie there for a while," she said.

I could see how he might have been flummoxed by this little black woman who spoke many more languages than he did, who knew 1,000 times more science than he did, and at least as much history and literature and music and art. He had never had anybody like that on his talk show. He may never have had to debate with a person whose destiny GRIOT™ would have described as unpredictable.

He said at last, "I am an American, not a European."

And she said to him, "Then why don't you act like one?"

38

Yes, and now the Japanese are pulling out. Their Army of Occupation in Business Suits is going home. The prison break at Athena was the straw that broke the camel's back, I think, but they were already abandoning properties, simply walking away from them, before that expensive catastrophe.

Why they ever wanted to own a country in such an advanced state of physical and spiritual and intellectual dilapidation is a mystery. Maybe they thought that would be a good way to get revenge for our having dropped not 1 but 2 atomic bombs on them.

So that makes two groups so far who have given up on owning this country of their own free will, mainly, I think, because so many unhappy and increasingly lawless people of all races, who don't own anything, turn out to come along with the properties.

It looks like they will keep Oahu as a sort of memento of their empire's high-water mark, just as the British have kept Bermuda.

Speaking of unhappy poor people of all races, I have often wondered how the Tarkington Board of Trustees would have been treated if Athena had been a White prison instead of a Black one. I think Hispanic convicts would have regarded them as the Blacks did, as aardvarks, as exotic creatures who had nothing to do with life as they had experienced it.

It seems to me that White convicts, though, might have wanted to kill them or at least beat them up for not caring what became of them any more than they cared what became of Blacks and Hispanics.

Dr. Dole went back to Berlin. At least that is where she said she was going.

I asked her where she had hidden during the siege. She said she had crawled into the firebox under an old boiler in the basement of this library. It hadn't been used since before I taught here, but it would have cost a lot of money to move. The school hated to spend money on improvements that didn't show.

So during the siege she was only a few meters away from me while I sat up here and engaged in the wonderful new science of Futurology.

Dr. Dole sure didn't think much of her own country. She ranted on about its sky-high rates of murder and suicide and drug addiction and infant mortality, its low rate of literacy, the fact that it had a higher percentage of its citizens in prison than any other country except for Haiti and South Africa, and didn't know how to manufacture anything anymore, and put less money into research and primary education than Japan or Korea or any country in East or West Europe, and on and on.

"At least we still have freedom of speech," I said.

And she said, "That isn't something somebody else gives you. That's something you have to give yourself."

Before I forget: During her job interview, she asked Jason Wilder where he had gone to college.

He said, "Yale."

"You know what they ought to call that place?" she said.

"No," he said.

And she said, "Plantation Owners' Tech."

When she was living in Berlin, she told me, she had been appalled by how ignorant so many American tourists and soldiers were of geography and history, and the languages and customs of other countries. She asked me, "What makes so many Americans proud of their ignorance? They act as though their ignorance somehow made them charming."

I had been asked the same general question by Alton Darwin when I was working at Athena. A World War II movie was being shown on all the TVs over there. Frank Sinatra had been captured by the Germans, and he was being interrogated by an SS Major who spoke English at least as well as Sinatra, and who played the cello and painted watercolors in his spare time, and who told Sinatra how much he looked forward to getting back, when the war was over, to his first love, which was lepidopterology.

Sinatra didn't know what lepidopterology was. It is the study of moths and butterflies. That had to be explained to him.

And Alton Darwin asked me, "How come in all these movies the Germans and the Japanese are always the smart ones, and the Americans are the dumb ones, and still the Americans win the war?"

Darwin didn't feel personally involved. The American combat soldiers in the movie were all White. That wasn't just White propaganda. That happened to be historically accurate. During the Finale Rack, American military units were segregated according to race. The feeling back then was that Whites would feel like garbage if they had to share quarters and dining facilities and so on with Blacks. That went for civilian life, too. The Black people had their own schools, and they were excluded from most hotels and restaurants and places of entertainment, except onstage, and polling booths.

They were also strung up or burned alive or whatever from time to time, as reminders that their place was at the very bottom of Society. They were thought, when they were given soldier suits, to be lacking in determination and initiative in battle. So they were employed mostly as common laborers or truck drivers behind the Duke Waynes and Frank Sinatras, who did the fearless stuff.

There was one all-Black fighter squadron. To the surprise of many it did quite well.

See the Nigger fly the airplane?

To get back to Alton Darwin's question about why Frank Sinatra deserved to win even though he didn't know anything: I said, "I think he deserves to win because he is like Davy Crockett at the Alamo." The Walt Disney movie about Davy Crockett had been shown over and over again at the prison, so all the convicts knew who Davy Crockett was. And one thing it might be good to bring out at my trial is that I never told the convicts the Mexican General who besieged the Alamo was trying and failing to do what Abraham Lincoln would later do successfully, which was to hold his country together and outlaw slavery.

"How is Sinatra like Davy Crockett?" Alton Darwin asked me.

And I said, "His heart is pure."

Yes, and there is more of my story to tell. But I have just received a piece of news from my lawyer that has knocked the wind out of me. After Vietnam, I thought there was nothing that could ever hit me that hard again. I thought I was used to dead bodies, no matter whose.

Wrong again.

Ah me!

If I tell now who it is that died, and how that person died, died only yesterday, that will seem to complete my story. From a reader's point of view, there would be nothing more to say but this:

THE END

But there is more I want to tell. So I will carry on as though I hadn't heard the news, albeit doggedly. And I write this:

The Lieutenant Colonel who led the assault on Scipio and then kept locals off the helicopters was also a graduate of the Academy, but maybe 2 score and 7 years younger than myself. When I told him my name and he saw my class ring, he realized who I was and what I used to be. He exclaimed, "My Lord, it's the Preacher!"

If it hadn't been for him, I don't know what would have become of me. I guess I would have done what most of the other valley people did, which was to go to Rochester or Buffalo or beyond, looking for any kind of work, minimum wage for sure. The whole area south of the Meadowdale Cinema Complex was and still is under Martial Law.

His name was Harley Wheelock III. He told me he and his wife were infertile, so they adopted twin girl orphans from Peru, South America, not Peru, Indiana. They were cute little Inca girls. But he hardly ever got home anymore, his Division was so busy. He was all set to go home on leave from the South Bronx when he was ordered here to put down the prison break and rescue the hostages.

His father Harley Wheelock II was 3 years ahead of me at the Academy, and died, I already knew, in some kind of accident in Germany, and so never served in Vietnam. I asked Harley III how exactly Harley II had died. He told me his father drowned while trying to rescue a Swedish woman who committed suicide by opening the windows of her Volvo and driving it off a dock and into the Ruhr River at Essen, home, as it happens, of that premier manufacturer of crematoria, A. J. Topf und Sohn.

Small World.

Now Harley III said to me, "You know anything about this excrement hole?" Of course, he himself didn't say "excrement." He had never heard of the Mohiga Valley before he was ordered here. Like most people, he had heard of Athena and Tarkington but had no clear idea where they were.

I replied that the excrement hole was home to me, although I had been born in Delaware and raised in Ohio, and that I expected 1 day to be buried here.

"Where's the Mayor?" he said.

"Dead," I said, "and all the policemen, too, including the campus cops. And the Fire Chief."

"So there isn't any Government?" he said.

"I'd say you're the Government," I said.

He used the Name of Our Savior as an explosive expletive, and then added, "Wherever I go, all of a sudden I am the Government. I'm already the Government in the South Bronx, and I've got to get back there as quick as I can. So I hereby declare you the Mayor of this excrement hole." This time he actually said, "excrement hole," echoing me. "Go down to the City Hall, wherever that is, and start governing."

He was so decisive! He was so loud!

As though the conversation weren't weird enough, he was wearing one of those coal-scuttle helmets the Army started issuing after we lost the Vietnam War, maybe to change our luck.

Make Blacks, Jews, and everybody else look like Nazis, and see how that worked out.

"I can't govern," I protested. "Nobody would pay any attention to me. I would be a joke."

"Good point!" he cried. So loud!

He got the Governor's Office in Albany on the radio. The Governor himself was on his way to Rochester by helicopter, in order to go on TV with the freed hostages. The Governor's Office managed to patch through Harley III's call to the Governor up in the sky. Harley III told the Governor who I was and what the situation was in Scipio.

It didn't take long.

And then Harley III turned to me and said, "Congratulations! You are now a Brigadier General in the National Guard!"

"I've got a family on the other side of the lake," I said. "I've got to go find out how they are."

He was able to tell me how they were. He personally, the day before, had seen Margaret and Mildred loaded into the steel box on the back of a prison van, consigned to the Laughing Academy in Batavia.

"They're fine!" he said. "Your country needs you more than they do now, so, General Hartke, strut your stuff!"

He was so full of energy! It was almost as though his coal-scuttle helmet contained a thunderstorm.

Never an idle moment! No sooner had he persuaded the Governor to make me a Brigadier than he was off to the stable, where captured Freedom Fighters were being forced to dig graves for all the bodies. The weary diggers had every reason to believe that they were digging their own graves. They had seen plenty of movies about the Finale Rack, in which soldiers in coal-scuttle helmets stood around while people in rags dug their own final resting places.

I heard Harley III barking orders at the diggers, telling them to dig deeper and make the sides straighter and so on. I had seen leadership of such a high order exercised in Vietnam, and I myself had exhibited it from time to time, so I am quite certain that Harley III had taken some sort of amphetamine.

———————

There wasn't much for me to govern at first. This place, which had been the sole remaining business of any size in the valley, stood vacant and seemed likely to remain so. Most locals had managed to run away after the prison break. When they came back, though, there was no way to make a living. Those who owned houses or places of business couldn't find anybody to sell them to. They were wiped out.

So most of the civilians I might have governed had soon packed the best of their belongings into cars and trailers, and paid small fortunes to black marketeers for enough gasoline to get them the heck out of here.

———————

I had no troops of my own. Those on my side of the lake were on loan from the commander of the National Guard Division, the 42nd Division, the "Rainbow Division," Lucas Florio. He had his headquarters in Hiroshi Matsumoto's old office at the prison. He wasn't a graduate of West Point, and he was too young to have fought in Vietnam, and his home was in Schenectady, so we had never met before. His troops were all White, with Orientals classified as Honorary White People. The same was true of the 82nd Airborne. There were also Black and Hispanic units somewhere, the theory being, as with the prisons, that people were always more comfortable with those of their own race.

This resegregation, although I never heard any public figure say so, also made the Armed Forces more like a set of golf clubs. You could use this battalion or that one, depending on what color people they were supposed to fight.

The Soviet Union, of course, with its citizenry, including every sort of a human being but a Black or Hispanic, found out the hard way that soldiers wouldn't fight hard at all against people who looked and thought and talked like them.

The Rainbow Division itself began during World War I, as an experiment integrating unlike Americans who weren't Army Regulars. Reserve Divisions activated back then were all identified with specific parts of the country. Then somebody got the idea of putting together a Division composed of draftees and volunteers from all different parts of the country, to prove how well they could get along.

Harmony between White people thought not to like each other very much was what the rainbow represented then. The Rainbow Division did in fact fight about as well as any other one during the War to End Wars, the prelude to the Finale Rack.

Afterward, the experiment complete, the 42nd Division became merely one more National Guard outfit, arbitrarily handed over with its battle ribbons to New York State.

But the symbol of the rainbow lives on in its shoulder patch.

Before I was arrested for insurrection, I myself was a wearer of that rainbow, along with the star of a Brigadier!

39

D URING my first 2 weeks as Military Commander of the Scipio District, all the way to the head of the lake and all the way down to the National Forest, the best thing I did, I think, was to make some of the soldiers firemen. A few had been firemen in civilian life, so I got them to familiarize themselves with the town's firefighting apparatus, which hadn't been hurt during the siege. One real stroke of luck: the fire trucks all had full tanks of gasoline. You would have thought, in a society where everybody from top to bottom was stealing everything that wasn't nailed down, that somebody would have siphoned off that priceless gasoline.

Every so often, in the midst of chaos, you come across an amazing, inexplicable instance of civic responsibility. Maybe the last shred of faith people have is in their firemen.

I also supervised the exhumation of the bodies next to the stable. They had been buried for only a few days, but then the Government, personified by a Coroner and the Medical Examiner from the State Police who knew so much about crucifixions, ordered us to dig them up again. The Government had to fingerprint and photograph them, and describe their dental work, if any, and their obvious wounds, if any, and so on. We didn't have to dig up the Shultzes again, who had already been dug up once, to make room for the Pavilion.

And we hadn't found the young woman's skull yet. The digging hadn't gone deep enough yet to find out what had become of the head of the missing Lilac Queen.

The Government, just those 2 guys from out of town, said we had to bury the bodies much deeper when they were through with them. That was the law.

"We wouldn't want to break the law," I said.

The Coroner was black. I wouldn't have known he was Black if he hadn't told me.

I asked him if he couldn't arrange for the County or the State or somebody to take possession of the bodies until the next-of-kin, if any, could decide what was to be done with them. I hoped they would be taken to Rochester, where they could be embalmed or refrigerated or cremated, or at least buried in decent containers of some kind. They had been buried here in nothing but their clothing.

He said he would look into it, but that I shouldn't get my hopes up. He said the County was broke and the State was broke and the Country was broke and that he was broke. He had lost what little he had in Microsecond Arbitrage.

After the Government left, I faced the problem of what the best way would be to dig much deeper graves. I was reluctant to ask National Guardsmen to do it with shovels. They had been resentful when I had them dig up the bodies and were growing more sullen in any case as it became more and more apparent, even that early in the game, that they might never be allowed to return to civilian life. The glamour of their Combat Infantry-man's Badges was wearing thin.

I couldn't use convict labor from across the lake. That, too, was the law. And then I remembered that the college had a backhoe which ran on diesel fuel, which wasn't a hot item on the black market. So if somebody could find the backhoe, there might still be some fuel in its tank.

A soldier found it, and the tank was full!

Miracle!

Again I ask the question: "How much longer can I go on being an Atheist?"

The tank was full because there was only one diesel auto-mobile in Scipio when the diaspora began. It was a Cadillac General Motors put on the market about the time we got kicked out of Vietnam. It is still here. It was such a lemon that you might as well have tried to go on a Sunday spin in an Egyptian pyramid.

It used to belong to a Tarkington parent. He was coming to his daughter's graduation when it broke down in front of the

Black Cat Café. It had already stopped of its own accord many times between here and New York City. So he went to the hardware store and bought yellow paint and a brush and painted big lemons all over it, and sold it to Lyle Hooper for a dollar.

This was a man who was on the Board of Directors of General Motors!

During the brief time the bodies were all aboveground again, a person showed up with a Toyota hearse and an undertaker from Rochester to claim 1. That was Dr. Charlton Hooper, who had been invited to try out for the New York Knickerbockers basketball team but had chosen to become a Physicist instead. As I've said, he was 2 meters tall.

That's tall!

I asked the undertaker where he had found the gasoline for the trip.

He wouldn't tell me at first, but I kept after him. He finally said, "Try the crematorium in back of the Meadowdale Cinema Complex. Ask for Guido."

I asked Charlton if he had come all the way from Waxahachie, Texas. The last I'd heard, he was running experiments with the enormous atom-smasher, the Supercollider, down there. He said the funds for the Supercollider had dried up, so he had moved to Geneva, New York, not that far away. He was teaching Freshman Physics at Hobart College.

I asked him if there was any way the Supercollider could be turned into a prison.

He said he guessed they could put a bunch of bad guys in there, and throw the switch, and make their hair stand on end and raise their temperatures a couple of degrees centigrade.

About a week after Charlton took his father's body away and we reburied all the others to a legal depth with the backhoe, I was awakened 1 afternoon by a terrible uproar in what had been such a peaceful town. I was living down in the Town Hall back then, and often took naps in the afternoon.

The noise was coming from up here. Chain saws were snarling. There was hammering. It sounded like an army. As far as I knew, there were supposed to be only 4 Guardsmen up here, keeping a fire watch.

The soldier who was stationed in my reception room, to wake me up in case there was something important for me to do, had vanished. He had gone up the hill to discover what on Earth was happening. There had been no warning of any special activity.

So I trudged up Clinton Street all alone. I was wearing civilian shoes and a camouflage suit General Florio had given me, along with 1 of his own stars on each shoulder. That was all I had for a uniform.

When I got to the top of Clinton Street, I found General Florio directing soldiers brought over from his side of the lake. They were turning the Quadrangle into a city of tents. Others constructed a barbed-wire fence around it.

I did not have to ask the meaning of all this. It was obvious that Tarkington College, which had stayed small as the prison across the lake had grown and grown, was itself a prison now.

General Florio turned to me and smiled. "Hello, Warden Hartke," he said.

———

Once all those 10-man tents, which were brought down from the Armory across the highway from the Meadowdale Cinema Complex, were set up on the Quadrangle as though on a checkerboard, it seemed so logical. The surrounding buildings, Samoza Hall, this library, the bookstore, the Pavilion, and so on, with machine-gunners at various windows and doorways, and with barbed wire between them and the tents, served well enough as prison walls.

General Florio said to me, "Company's coming."

———

I remember a lecture Damon Stern gave about his visit with several Tarkington students to Auschwitz, the infamous Nazi extermination camp in Poland during the Finale Rack. Stern used to make extra money taking trips to Europe with students whose parents or guardians didn't want to see them over Christmas or during the summertime. He caught a lot of heck for taking some to Auschwitz. He did it impulsively and without asking permission from anyone. It wasn't on the schedule, and some of the students were very upset afterward.

He said in his lecture that if the fences and gallows and gas chambers were removed from the tidy, tidy checkerboard of streets and old stucco two-story shotgun buildings, it might have made a nice enough junior college for low-income or underachieving people in the area. The buildings had been put up years before World War I, he said, as a comfortable outpost for soldiers of the Austro-Hungarian Empire. Among the many titles of that Emperor, he said, was Duke of Auschwitz.

What General Florio was after on our side of the lake was our sanitary facilities. The prisoners were to use buckets in their tents for toilets, but then these could be emptied into toilets in the surrounding buildings and flushed from there into Scipio's state-of-the-art sewage-disposal plant. Across the lake they were having to bury everything.

And no showers.

We had plenty of showers.

One touching rather than horrible thing about the siege, surely, was how little damage the escaped convicts did to this campus. It was as though they really believed that it was going to be theirs for generations.

This brings to mind another of Damon Stern's lectures, which was about how the brutalized and starving poor people of Petrograd in Russia behaved after they broke into the palace of the Czars in 1917. They got to see for the first time all the treasures inside the palace, and they were so outraged they wanted to wreck them.

But then one man got their attention by firing a gun at the ceiling, and he said, "Comrades! Comrades! This is all ours now! Don't hurt anything!"

They renamed Petrograd "Leningrad." Now it's Petrograd again.

In a way, the escaped convicts were like a neutron bomb. They had no compassion for living things, but they did surprisingly little damage to property.

Damon Stern the unicyclist, on the other hand, laid down his life for living things. They weren't even human beings. They were horses. They weren't even his horses.

His wife and kids got away, and, last I heard, were living in Lackawanna, where they have relatives. That's nice when people have relatives they can run away to.

But Damon Stern is buried deep and close to where he fell, next to the stable, in the shadow of Musket Mountain when the Sun goes down.

———————————

His wife Wanda June came back here after the siege in a pickup truck she said belonged to her half brother. She paid a fortune for enough gas to get here from Lackawanna. I asked her what she was doing for money, and she said she and Damon had put away a lot of Yen in their freezer in a box marked "Brussels sprouts."

Damon woke her up in the middle of the night and told her to get into the Volkswagen with the kids and take off for Rochester with the headlights off. He had heard the explosion across the lake, and seen the silent army crossing the ice to Scipio. The last thing he ever did with Wanda June was hand her the box marked "Brussels sprouts."

———————————

Damon himself, over his wife's objections, stayed behind to spread the alarm. He said he would be along later, by hitching a ride in somebody else's car, or by walking all the way to Rochester on back roads he knew, if he had to. It isn't clear what happened after that. He probably called the local police, although none of them lived to say so. He woke up a lot of people in the immediate neighborhood.

The best conjecture is that he heard gunfire inside the stable and unwisely went to investigate. A Freedom Fighter with an AK-47 was gut-shooting horses for the fun of it. He didn't shoot them in the head.

Damon must have asked him to stop, so the Freedom Fighter shot him, too.

His wife didn't want his body. She said the happiest years of his life had been spent here, so he should stay buried here.

She found all 4 of the family unicycles. That was easy. The soldiers were taking turns trying to ride them. Before that, several of the convicts had also tried to ride them, so far as I know with no success.

So I went back down Clinton Street to the Town Hall, to ponder this latest change in my career, that I was next to be a Warden.

There was a Rolls-Royce Corniche, a convertible coupe, parked out front. Whoever had a car like that had enough Yen or Marks or some other stable currency to buy himself or herself enough black-market gas for a trip from anywhere to anywhere.

My guess was that it was the chariot of some Tarkington student or parent who hoped to recover property left in a dorm suite at the start of the vacation period, a vacation which now, obviously, might never end.

The soldier who was supposed to be my receptionist was back on duty. He had returned to his post after General Florio told him to stop standing around with his thumb in his anus and start stringing barbed wire or erecting tents. He was waiting for me at the front door, and he told me I had a visitor.

So I asked him, "Who is the visitor?"

He said, "It's your son, sir."

I was thunderstruck. "Eugene is here?" I said. Eugene Jr. had told me that he never wanted to see me again as long as he lived. How is that for a life sentence? And he was driving a Rolls-Royce now? Eugene?

"No, sir," he said. "Not Eugene."

"Eugene is the only son I have," I said. "What did he say his name was?"

"He told me, sir," he said, "that he was your son Rob Roy."

That was all the proof I needed that a son of mine did indeed await me in my office: that name, "Rob Roy." "Rob" and "Roy," and I was back in the Philippine Islands again, having just been kicked out of Vietnam. I was back in bed with a voluptuous female war correspondent from *The Des Moines Register*, whose lips were like sofa pillows, telling her that, if I had been a fighter plane, I would have had little pictures of people painted all over me.

I calculated how old he was. He was 23, making him the youngest of my children. He was the baby of the family.

He was in the reception room outside my office. He stood up when I came in. He was exactly as tall as myself. His hair was the same color and texture as mine. He needed a shave, and his potential beard was as black and thick as mine. His eyes were the same color as mine. All 4 of our eyes were greenish amber. We had the same big nose, my father's nose. He was nervous and polite. He was expensively dressed in leisure clothes. If he had been learning-disabled or merely stupid, which he wasn't, he might have had a happy 4 years at Tarkington, especially with that car of his.

I was giddy. I had taken off my overcoat on the way in, so that he could see my General's stars. That was something, anyway. How many boys had a father who was a General?

"How can I help you?" I said.

"I hardly know how to begin," he said.

"I think you've already begun by telling the guard that you were a son of mine," I said. "Was that a joke?"

"Do you think it was a joke?" he asked.

"I don't pretend I was a Saint when I was young and away from home so much," I said. "But I never made love using an alias. I was always easy to find afterward, if somebody wanted to find me badly enough. So, if I did father a child out of wedlock somewhere along the line, that comes as a complete surprise to me. I would have thought the mother, the minute she found out she was pregnant, would have gotten in touch with me."

"I know 1 mother who didn't," he said.

Before I could reply, he blurted words he must have rehearsed en route. "This is going to be a very brief visit," he said. "I am going to be in and out of here before you know it. I'm on my way to Italy, and I never want to see this country ever again, and especially Dubuque."

It would turn out that he had been through an ordeal that lasted much, much longer than the siege of Scipio, and was probably harder on him than Vietnam had been on me. He had been tried for child molestation in Dubuque, Iowa, where he had founded and run a free child-care center at his own expense.

He wasn't married, a strike against him in the eyes of most juries, a character flaw like having served in the Vietnam War.

"I grew up in Dubuque," he would tell me, "and the money I inherited was made in Dubuque." It was a meat-packing fortune.

"I wanted to give something back to Dubuque. With so many single parents raising children on minimum wage, and with so many married couples both working to make enough to feed and clothe their children halfway decently, I thought what Dubuque needed most was a child-care center that was nice and didn't cost anything."

Two weeks after he opened the center, he was arrested for child molestation because several of the children came home with inflamed genitalia.

He was later to prove in court, after smears were taken from the children's lesions, that a fungus was to blame. The fungus was closely related to jock itch, and may actually have been a new strain of jock which had learned how to rise above all the standard remedies for that affliction.

By then, though, he had been held in jail without bail for 3 months, and had to be protected from a lynch mob by the National Guard. Luckily for him, Dubuque, like so many communities, had backed up its police with Armor and Infantry.

After he was acquitted, he had to be transported out of town and deep into Illinois in a buttoned-up tank, or somebody would have killed him.

The judge who acquitted him was killed. He was of Italian ancestry. Somebody sent him a pipe bomb concealed in a huge salami.

But that son of mine did not tell me about any of that until just before he said, "It's time to say, 'Good-bye.' " He prefaced the tale of how he had suffered so with these words: "I hope you understand, the last thing I wanted to do was make any demands on your emotions."

"Try me," I said.

Thinking about our meeting now fills me with a sort of sweetness. He had liked me enough, found me warm enough, to use me as though I were a really good father, if only for a little while.

In the beginning, when we were feeling each other out very gingerly, and I hadn't yet admitted that he was my son, I asked him if "Rob Roy" was the name on his birth certificate, or whether that was a nickname his mother had hung on him.

He said it was the name on his birth certificate.

"And the father on the birth certificate?" I asked.

"It was the name of a soldier who died in Vietnam," he said.

"Do you remember what it was?" I said.

Here came a surprise. It was the name of my brother-in-law, Jack Patton, whom his mother had never met, I'm sure. I must have told her about Jack in Manila, and she'd remembered his name, and that he was unmarried and had died for his country.

I thought to myself, "Good old Jack, wherever you are, it's time to laugh like hell again."

"So what makes you think I'm your father instead of him?" I said. "Your mother finally told you?"

"She wrote me a letter," he said.

"She didn't tell you face to face?" I said.

"She couldn't," he said. "She died of cancer of the pancreas when I was 4 years old."

That was a shock. She sure hadn't lasted long after I made love to her. I've always enjoyed thinking of the women I have made love to as living on and on. I had imagined his mother, game and smart and sporty and funny, with lips like sofa pillows, living on and on.

"She wrote me a letter on her deathbed," he continued, "which was put into the hands of a law firm in Dubuque, not to be opened until after the death of the good man who had married her and adopted me. He died only a year ago."

"Did the letter say why you were named Rob Roy?" I inquired.

"No," he said. "I assumed it must be because she liked the novel by that name by Sir Walter Scott."

"That sounds right," I said. What good would it do him or anybody else to know that he was named for 2 shots of Scotch, 1 shot of sweet vermouth, cracked ice, and a twist of lemon peel?

"How did you find me?" I said.

"At first I didn't think I wanted to find you," he said. "But then 2 weeks ago I thought that we were entitled to see each other once, at least. So I called West Point."

"I haven't had any contact with them for years," I said.

"That's what they told me," he said. "But just before I called they got a call from the Governor of New York, who said he had just made you a Brigadier General. He wanted to make sure he hadn't been made a fool of. He wanted to make sure you were what you were claimed to be."

"Well," I said, and we were still standing in the reception room, "I don't think we need to wait for blood tests to find out whether you are really my son or not. You are the spit and image of me when I was your age.

"You should know that I really loved your mother," I went on.

"That was in her letter, how much in love you were," he said.

"You will have to take my word for it," I said, "that if I had known she was pregnant, I would have behaved honorably. I'm not quite sure what we would have done. We would have worked something out."

I led the way into my office. "Come on in. There are a couple of easy chairs in here. We can close the door."

"No, no, no," he said. "I'm on my way. I just thought we should see each other just one time. We've done that now. It's no big thing."

"I like life to be simple," I said, "but if you went away without another word, that would be much too simple for me, and for you, too, I hope."

So I got him into my office and closed the door, and got us settled in facing easy chairs. We hadn't touched. We never would touch.

"I would offer you coffee," I said, "but nobody in this valley has coffee."

"I've got some in my car," he said.

"I'm sure," I said. "But don't go get it. Never mind, never mind." I cleared my throat. "If you'll pardon my saying so, you seem to be what I have heard called 'fabulously well-to-do.' "

He said that, yes, he was fortunate financially. The Dubuque meat packer who married his mother and adopted him had sold his business to the Shah of Bratpuhr shortly before he died, and had been paid in gold bricks deposited in a bank in Switzerland.

The meat packer's name was Lowell Fenstermaker, so my son's full name was Rob Roy Fenstermaker. Rob Roy said he certainly wasn't going to change his last name to Hartke, that he felt like Fenstermaker and not Hartke.

His stepfather had been very good to him. Rob Roy said that the only thing he didn't like about him was the way he raised calves for veal. The baby animals, scarcely out of the womb, were put in cages so cramped that they could hardly move, to make their muscles nice and tender. When they were big enough their throats were cut, and they had never run or jumped or made friends, or done anything that might have made life a worthwhile experience.

What was their crime?

Rob Roy said that his inherited wealth was at first an embarrassment. He said that until very recently he never would have considered buying a car like the 1 parked outside, or wearing a cashmere jacket and lizard-skin shoes made in Italy. That was what he was wearing in my office. "When nobody else in Dubuque could afford black-market coffee and gasoline, I, too, did without. I used to walk everywhere."

"What happened very recently?" I said.

"I was arrested for molesting little children," he said.

I itched all over with a sudden attack of psychosomatic hives. He told me the whole story.

I said to him, "I thank you for sharing that with me."

The hives went away as quickly as they had come.

I felt wonderful, very happy to have him look me over and think what he would. I had seldom been happy to have my legitimate children look me over and think what they would.

What made the difference? I hate to say so, because my answer is so paltry. But here it is: I had always wanted to be a General, and there I was wearing General's stars.

How embarrassing to be human.

There was this, too: I was no longer encumbered by my wife and mother-in-law. Why did I keep them at home so long, even though it was plain that they were making the lives of my children unbearable?

It could be, I suppose, because somewhere in the back of my mind I believed that there might really be a big book in which all things were written, and that I wanted some impressive proof that I could be compassionate recorded there.

———————————

I asked Rob Roy where he had gone to college.

"Yale," he said.

I told him what Helen Dole said about Yale, that it ought to be called "Plantation Owners' Tech."

"I don't get it," he said.

"I had to ask her to explain it myself," I said. "She said Yale was where plantation owners learned how to get the natives to kill each other instead of them."

"That's a bit strong," he said. And then he asked me if my first wife was still alive.

"I've only had 1," I said. "She's still alive."

"There was a lot about her in Mother's letter," he said.

"Really?" I said. "Like what?"

"About how she was hit by a car the day before you were going to take her to the senior prom. About how she was paralyzed from the waist down, but you still married her, even though she would have to spend the rest of her life in a wheelchair."

If that was in the letter, I must have told his mother that.

———————————

"And your father, is he still alive?" he said.

"No," I said. "The ceiling of a gift shop fell on him at Niagara Falls."

"Did he ever regain his eyesight?" he said.

"Regain his what?" I said. And then I realized that his question was based on some other lie I had told his mother.

"His eyesight," he said.

"No," I said. "Never did."

"I think it's so beautiful," he said, "how he came home from the war blind, and you used to read Shakespeare to him."

"He sure loved Shakespeare," I said.

"So," he said, "I am descended not just from 1 war hero, but 2."

"War hero?" I said.

"I know you would never call yourself that," he said. "But that's what Mother said you were. And you can certainly call your father that. How many Americans shot down 28 German planes in World War II?"

"We could go up to the library and look it up," I said. "They have a very good library here. You can find out anything, if you really try."

"Where is my Uncle Bob buried?" he said.

"Your what?" I said.

"Your brother Bob, my Uncle Bob," he said.

I had never had a brother of any kind. I took a wild guess. "We threw his ashes out of an airplane," I said.

"You have certainly had some bad luck," he said. "Your father comes home blind from the war. Your childhood sweetheart is hit by a car right before the senior prom. Your brother dies of spinal meningitis right after he is invited to try out for the New York Yankees."

"Yes, well, all you can do is play the cards they deal you," I said.

"Have you still got his glove?" he said.

"No," I said. What kind of glove could I have told his mother about when we were both sozzled on Sweet Rob Roys in Manila 24 years ago?

"You carried it all the way through the war, but now it's gone?" he said.

He had to be talking about the nonexistent baseball glove of my nonexistent brother. "Somebody stole it from me after I got home," I said, "thinking it was just another baseball glove, I'm sure. Whoever stole it had no idea how much it meant to me."

He stood. "I really must be going now."

I stood, too.

I shook my head sadly. "It isn't going to be as easy as you think to give up on the country of your birth."

"That's about as meaningful as my astrological sign," he said.

"What is?" I said.

"The country of my birth," he said.

"You might be surprised," I said.

"Well, Dad," he said, "it certainly won't be the first time."

―――――――――――――――――

"Can you tell me who in this valley might have gasoline?" he said. "I'll pay anything."

"Do you have enough gas to make it back to Rochester?" I said.

"Yes," he said.

"Well," I said, "head back the way you came. That's the only way you can get back, so you can't get lost. Right at the Rochester city limits you will see the Meadowdale Cinema Complex. Behind that is a crematorium. Don't look for smoke. It's smokeless."

"A crematorium?" he said.

"That's right, a crematorium," I said. "You drive up to the crematorium, and you ask for Guido. From what I hear, if you've got the money, he's got the gasoline."

"And chocolate bars, do you think?" he said.

"I don't know," I said. "Won't hurt to ask."

40

NOT THAT THERE is any shortage of real child-molesters, child-shooters, child-starvers, child-bombers, child-drowners, child-whippers, child-burners, and child-defenestrators on this happy planet. Turn on the TV. By the luck of the draw, though, my son Rob Roy Fenstermaker does not happen to be one of them.

OK. My story is almost ended.

And here is the news that knocked the wind out of me so recently. When I heard it from my lawyer, I actually said, "Ooof!"

Hiroshi Matsumoto was dead by his own hand in his hometown of Hiroshima! But why would I care so much?

He did it in the wee hours of the morning, Japanese time, of course, while sitting in his motor-driven wheelchair at the base of the monument marking the point of impact of the atomic bomb that was dropped on Hiroshima when we were little boys.

He didn't use a gun or poison. He committed hara-kiri with a knife, disemboweling himself in a ritual of self-loathing once practiced by humiliated members of the ancient caste of professional soldiers, the samurai.

And yet, so far as I am able to determine, he never shirked his duty, never stole anything, and never killed or wounded anyone.

Still waters run deep. R.I.P.

If there really is a big book somewhere, in which all things are written, and which is to be read line by line, omitting nothing, on Judgment Day, let it be recorded that I, when Warden of this place, moved the convicted felons out of the tents on the Quadrangle and into the surrounding buildings. They no longer had to excrete in buckets or, in the middle of the night, have their homes blown down. The buildings, except for this

1, were divided into cement-block cells intended for 2 men, but most holding 5.

The War on Drugs goes on.

I caused 2 more fences to be erected, 1 within the other, enclosing the back of the inner buildings, and with antipersonnel mines sown in between. The machine-gun nests were reinstalled in windows and doorways of the next ring of buildings, Norman Rockwell Hall, the Pahlavi Pavilion, and so on.

It was during my administration that the troops here were Federalized, a step I had recommended. That meant that they were no longer civilians in soldier suits. That meant that they were full-time soldiers, serving at the pleasure of the President. Nobody could say how much longer the War on Drugs might last. Nobody could say when they could go home again.

General Florio himself, accompanied by six MPs with clubs and sidearms, congratulated me on all I had done. He then took back the two stars he had loaned me, and told me that I was under arrest for the crime of insurrection. I had come to like him, and I think he had come to like me. He was simply following orders.

I asked him, as 1 comrade to another, "Does this make any sense to you? Why is this happening?"

It is a question I have asked myself many times since, maybe 5 times today between coughing fits.

His answer to it, the first answer I ever got to it, is probably the best answer I will ever get to it.

"Some ambitious young Prosecutor," he said, "thinks you'll make good TV."

Hiroshi Matsumoto's suicide has hit me so hard, I think, because he was innocent of even the littlest misdemeanors. I doubt that he ever double-parked, even, or ran a red light when nobody else was around. And yet he executed himself in a manner that the most terrible criminal who ever lived would not deserve!

He had no feet anymore, which must have been depressing. But having no feet is no reason for a man to disembowel himself.

It had to have been the atom bomb that was dropped on him during his formative years, and not the absence of feet, that made him feel that life was a crock of doo-doo.

As I have said, he did not tell me that he had been atom-bombed until we had known each other for 2 years or more. He might never have told me about it, in my opinion, if a documentary about the Japanese "Rape of Nanking" hadn't been shown on the prison TVs the day before. This was a program chosen at random from the prison library. A guard who did the choosing couldn't read English well enough to know what the convicts would see next. So there was no censorship.

The Warden had a small TV monitor on his desk, and I knew he watched it from time to time, since he often remarked to me about the inanity of this or that old show, and especially *I Love Lucy*.

The Rape of Nanking was just one more instance of soldiers slaughtering prisoners and unarmed civilians, but it became famous because it was among the first to be well photographed. There were evidently movie cameras everywhere, run by gosh knows whom, and the footage wasn't confiscated afterward.

I had seen some of the footage when I was a cadet, but not as a part of a well-edited documentary, with a baritone voice-over and appropriate music underneath.

The orgy of butchery followed a virtually unopposed attack by the Japanese Army on the Chinese city of Nanking in 1937, long before this country became part of the Finale Rack. Hiroshi Matsumoto had just been born. Prisoners were tied to stakes and used for bayonet practice. Several people in a pit were buried alive. You could see their expressions as the dirt hit their faces.

Their faces disappeared, but the dirt on top kept moving as though there were some sort of burrowing animal, a woodchuck maybe, making a home below.

Unforgettable!

How was that for racism?

The documentary was a big hit in the prison. Alton Darwin said to me, I remember, "If somebody is going to do it, I am going to watch it."

This was 7 years before the prison break.

I didn't know if Hiroshi had seen the show on his monitor or not. I wasn't about to ask. We were not pals.

I was willing to be a pal, if that was part of the job. I believe he moved me in next door to him with the idea that it was time he had a pal. My guess is that he never had had a pal. No sooner had I become his neighbor, I think, than he decided he didn't want a pal after all. That didn't have anything to do with what I was or how I acted. To him, I think, a pal was like a piece of merchandise heavily promoted at Christmas, say. Why junk up his life with such a cumbersome contraption and all its accessories merely because it was advertised?

So he went on hiking alone and boating alone and eating alone, which was OK with me. I had a rich social life across the lake.

But the day after the documentary was shown, late in the afternoon, about suppertime, I was rowing for shore in my fiberglass umiak, headed for the mud beach in front of our 2 houses in the ghost town. I had been fishing. I hadn't been to Scipio. My own 2 great pals over there, Muriel Peck and Damon Stern, were on vacation. They wouldn't be back until Freshman Orientation Week, before the start of the fall semester.

The Warden was waiting for me on the beach, looking out at me in my crazy boat like a mother who had been worried to death about where her little boy had gone. Had I failed to keep a date with him? No. We had never had a date. My best supposition was that Mildred or Margaret had tried to burn 1 of our houses down.

But he said to me as I disembarked, "There is something you should know about me."

There was no pressing reason why I should know anything about him. We didn't work as a team up at the prison. He didn't care what or how I taught up there.

"I was in Hiroshima when it was bombed," he said.

I am sure there was an implied equation there: The bombing of Hiroshima was as unforgivable and as typically human as the Rape of Nanking.

So I heard about his going into a ditch after a ball when he was a schoolboy, about his straightening up to find that nobody was alive but him.

And on and on.

When he was through with that story he said to me, "I thought you should know."

I said earlier that I had a sudden attack of psychosomatic hives when Rob Roy Fenstermaker told me that he had been busted for molesting children. That wasn't my first such attack. The first was when Hiroshi told me about being atom-bombed. I suddenly itched all over, and scratching wouldn't help.

And I said to Hiroshi what I would say to Rob Roy: "I thank you for sharing that with me."

This was an expression, if I am not mistaken, which originated in California.

I was tempted to show Hiroshi "The Protocols of the Elders of Tralfamadore." I'm glad I didn't. I might now be feeling a little bit responsible for his suicide. He might have left a note saying: "The Elders of Tralfamadore win again!"

Only I and the author of that story, if he is still alive, would have known what he meant by that.

The most troubling part of his tale about the vaporization of all he knew and loved had to do with the edge of the area of the blast. There were all these people dying in agony. And he was only a little boy, remember.

That must have been for him like walking down the Appian Way back in 71 B.C., when 6,000 nobodies had just been crucified there. Some little kid or maybe a lot of little kids may have walked down that road back then. What could a little kid say on such an occasion? "Daddy, I think I have to go to the bathroom"?

It so happens that my lawyer is on a first-name basis with our Ambassador to Japan, former Senator Randolph Nakayama of California. They are of different generations, but my lawyer was a roommate of the Senator's son at Reed College out in Portland, Oregon, the town where Tex bought his trusty rifle.

My lawyer told me that both sets of the Senator's racially Japanese grandparents, one set immigrants, the other set native Californians, were put into a concentration camp when this country got into the Finale Rack. The camp, incidentally, was only a few kilometers west of the Donner Pass, named in honor of White cannibals. The feeling back then was that anybody with Japanese genes inside our borders was probably less loyal to the United States Constitution than to Hirohito, the Emperor of Japan.

The Senator's father, however, served in an infantry battalion composed entirely of young Americans of Japanese extraction, which became our most decorated unit taking part in the Italian Campaign during, again, the Finale Rack.

So I asked my lawyer to find out from the Ambassador if Hiroshi had left a note, and if there had been an autopsy performed to determine whether or not the deceased had ingested some foreign substance that might have made hara-kiri easier. I don't know whether to call this friendship or morbid curiosity.

The answer came back that there was no note, and that there had been no autopsy, since the cause of death was so horribly obvious. There was this detail: A little girl who didn't know him was the first person of any age or sex to see what he had chosen to do to himself.

She ran and told her mama.

Back when we were neighbors, I asked the Warden why he never left this valley, why he didn't get away from the prison and me and the ignorant young guards and the bells across the lake and all the rest of it. He had years of leave time he had never used.

He said, "I would only meet more people."

"You don't like any kind of people?" I said. We were talking in a sort of joshing mode, so I could ask him that.

"I wish I had been born a bird instead," he said. "I wish we had all been born birds instead."

He never killed anybody and had the sex life of a calf kept alive for its veal alone.

I have lived more vividly, and I promised to tell at the end of this book the number I would like engraved on my tombstone, a number that represents both my 100-percent-legal military kills and my adulteries.

If people hear of the number at the end and its double significance, some will turn to the end to learn the number in order to decide that it is too small or too big or just about right or whatever without reading the book. But I have devised a lock to thwart them. I have concealed its oddly shaped key in a problem that only those who have read the whole book will have no trouble solving.

So:

Take the year Eugene Debs died.

Subtract the title of the science fiction movie based on a novel by Arthur C. Clarke which I saw twice in Vietnam. Do not panic. This will give you a negative number, but Arabs in olden times taught us how to deal with such.

Add the year of Hitler's birth. There! Everything is nice and positive again. If you have done everything right so far, you should have the year in which Napoleon was banished to Elba and the metronome was invented, neither event, however, discussed in this book.

Add the gestation period of an opossum expressed in days. That isn't in the book, either, so I make you a gift of it. The number is 12. That will bring you to the year in which Thomas Jefferson, the former slave owner, died and James Fenimore Cooper published *The Last of the Mohicans*, which wasn't set in this valley but might as well have been.

Divide by the square root of 4.

Subtract 100 times 9.

Add the greatest number of children known to have come from the womb of just 1 woman, and there you are, by gosh.

Just because some of us can read and write and do a little math, that doesn't mean we deserve to conquer the Universe.

THE END

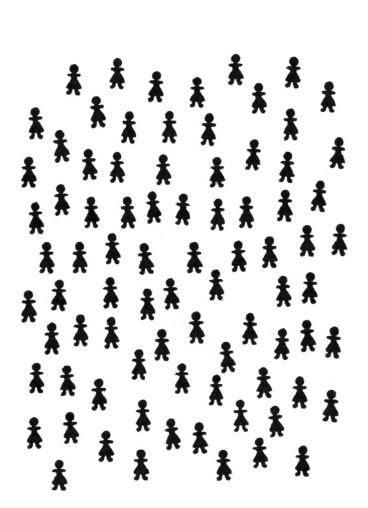

TIMEQUAKE

In memory of Seymour Lawrence,
a romantic and great publisher
of curious tales told with ink
on bleached and flattened wood pulp

All persons, living and dead, are purely coincidental.

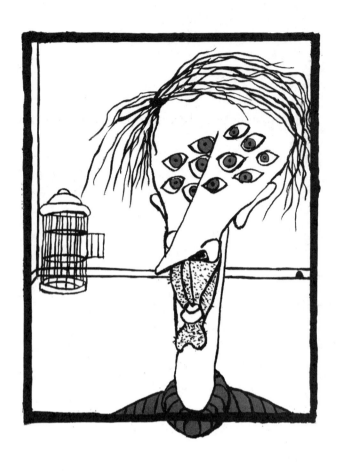

Out-of-print science fiction writer Kilgore Trout in Cohoes, New York, in 1975, having learned of the death of his estranged son, Leon, in a Swedish shipyard, having given his parakeet, "Cyclone Bill," his freedom, and about to become a vagabond.

Prologue

ERNEST HEMINGWAY in 1952 published in *Life* magazine a long short story called *The Old Man and the Sea*. It was about a Cuban fisherman who hadn't caught anything for eighty-four days. The Cuban hooked an enormous marlin. He killed it and lashed it alongside his little boat. Before he could get it to shore, though, sharks bit off all the meat on the skeleton.

I was living in Barnstable Village on Cape Cod when the story appeared. I asked a neighboring commercial fisherman what he thought of it. He said the hero was an idiot. He should have hacked off the best chunks of meat and put them in the bottom of the boat, and left the rest of the carcass for the sharks.

It could be that the sharks Hemingway had in mind were critics who hadn't much liked his first novel in ten years, *Across the River and into the Trees*, published two years earlier. As far as I know, he never said so. But the marlin could have been that novel.

And then I found myself in the winter of 1996 the creator of a novel which did not work, which had no point, which had never wanted to be written in the first place. *Merde!* I had spent nearly a decade on that ungrateful fish, if you will. It wasn't even fit for shark chum.

I had recently turned seventy-three. My mother made it to fifty-two, my father to seventy-two. Hemingway almost made it to sixty-two. I had lived too long! What was I to do?

Answer: Fillet the fish. Throw the rest away.

This I did in the summer and autumn of 1996. Yesterday, November 11th of that year, I turned seventy-four. Seventy-four!

Johannes Brahms quit composing symphonies when he was fifty-five. Enough! My architect father was sick and tired of architecture when he was fifty-five. Enough! American male novelists have done their best work by then. Enough! Fifty-five is a long time ago for me now. Have pity!

My great big fish, which stunk so, was entitled *Timequake*. Let us think of it as *Timequake One*. And let us think of this one, a stew made from its best parts mixed with thoughts and

485

experiences during the past seven months or so, as *Timequake Two.*

Hokay?

The premise of *Timequake One* was that a timequake, a sudden glitch in the space-time continuum, made everybody and everything do exactly what they'd done during a past decade, for good or ill, a second time. It was déjà vu that wouldn't quit for ten long years. You couldn't complain about life's being nothing but old stuff, or ask if just you were going nuts or if *everybody* was going nuts.

There was absolutely nothing you could say during the rerun, if you hadn't said it the first time through the decade. You couldn't even save your own life or that of a loved one, if you had failed to do that the first time through.

I had the timequake zap everybody and everything in an instant from February 13th, 2001, back to February 17th, 1991. Then we all had to get back to 2001 the hard way, minute by minute, hour by hour, year by year, betting on the wrong horse again, marrying the wrong person again, getting the clap again. You name it!

Only when people got back to when the timequake hit did they stop being robots of their pasts. As the old science fiction writer Kilgore Trout said, "Only when free will kicked in again could they stop running obstacle courses of their own construction."

Trout doesn't really exist. He has been my alter ego in several of my other novels. But most of what I have chosen to preserve from *Timequake One* has to do with his adventures and opinions. I have salvaged a few of the thousands of stories he wrote between 1931, when he was fourteen, and 2001, when he died at the age of eighty-four. A hobo for much of his life, he died in luxury in the Ernest Hemingway Suite of the writers' retreat Xanadu in the summer resort village of Point Zion, Rhode Island. That's nice to know.

His very first story, he told me as he was dying, was set in Camelot, the court of King Arthur in Britain: Merlin the Court Magician casts a spell that allows him to equip the Knights of the Round Table with Thompson submachine guns and drums of .45-caliber dumdums.

Sir Galahad, the purest in heart and mind, familiarizes himself with this new virtue-compelling appliance. While doing so, he puts a slug through the Holy Grail and makes a Swiss cheese of Queen Guinevere.

Here is what Trout said when he realized that the ten-year rerun was over, that he and everybody else were suddenly obligated to think of new stuff to do, to be creative again: "Oh, Lordy! I am much too old and experienced to start playing Russian roulette with free will again."

Yes, and I myself was a character in *Timequake One*, making a cameo appearance at a clambake on the beach at the writers' retreat Xanadu in the summer of 2001, six months after the end of the rerun, six months after free will kicked in again.

I was there with several fictitious persons from the book, including Kilgore Trout. I was privileged to hear the old, long-out-of-print science fiction writer describe for us, and then demonstrate, the special place of Earthlings in the cosmic scheme of things.

So now my last book is done, with the exception of this preface. Today is November 12th, 1996, about nine months, I would guess, from its publication date, from its emergence from the birth canal of a printing press. There is no rush. The gestation period for a baby Indian elephant is more than twice that long.

The gestation period for a baby opossum, friends and neighbors, is twelve days.

I have pretended in this book that I will still be alive for the clambake in 2001. In chapter 46, I imagine myself as still alive in 2010. Sometimes I say I'm in 1996, where I really am, and sometimes I say I am in the midst of a rerun following a timequake, without making clear distinctions between the two situations.

I must be nuts.

1

CALL ME JUNIOR. My six grown kids do. Three are adopted nephews, three are my own. They call me Junior behind my back. They think I don't know that.

I say in speeches that a plausible mission of artists is to make people appreciate being alive at least a little bit. I am then asked if I know of any artists who pulled that off. I reply, "The Beatles did."

It appears to me that the most highly evolved Earthling creatures find being alive embarrassing or much worse. Never mind cases of extreme discomfort, such as idealists' being crucified. Two important women in my life, my mother and my only sister, Alice, or Allie, in Heaven now, hated life and said so. Allie would cry out, "I give up! I give up!"

The funniest American of his time, Mark Twain, found life for himself and everybody else so stressful when he was in his seventies, like me, that he wrote as follows: "I have never wanted any released friend of mine restored to life since I reached manhood." That is in an essay on the sudden death of his daughter Jean a few days earlier. Among those he wouldn't have resurrected were Jean, and another daughter, Susy, and his beloved wife, and his best friend, Henry Rogers.

Twain didn't live to see World War One, but still he felt that way.

Jesus said how awful life was, in the Sermon on the Mount: "Blessed are they that mourn," and "Blessed are the meek," and "Blessed are they which do hunger and thirst after righteousness."

Henry David Thoreau said most famously, "The mass of men lead lives of quiet desperation."

So it is not one whit mysterious that we poison the water and air and topsoil, and construct ever more cunning doomsday devices, both industrial and military. Let us be perfectly frank for a change. For practically everybody, the end of the world can't come soon enough.

My father, Kurt Senior, an Indianapolis architect who had cancer, and whose wife had committed suicide some fifteen years earlier, was arrested for running a red light in his hometown. It turned out that he hadn't had a driver's license for twenty years!

You know what he told the arresting officer? "So shoot me," he said.

The African-American jazz pianist Fats Waller had a sentence he used to shout when his playing was absolutely brilliant and hilarious. This was it: "Somebody shoot me while I'm happy!"

That there are such devices as firearms, as easy to operate as cigarette lighters and as cheap as toasters, capable at anybody's whim of killing Father or Fats or Abraham Lincoln or John Lennon or Martin Luther King, Jr., or a woman pushing a baby carriage, should be proof enough for anybody that, to quote the old science fiction writer Kilgore Trout, "being alive is a crock of shit."

2

I MAGINE THIS: A great American university gives up football in the name of sanity. It turns its vacant stadium into a bomb factory. So much for sanity. Shades of Kilgore Trout.

I am speaking of my alma mater, the University of Chicago. In December of 1942, long before I got there, the first chain reaction of uranium on Earth was compelled by scientists underneath the stands of Stagg Field. Their intent was to demonstrate the feasibility of an atomic bomb. We were at war with Germany and Japan.

Fifty-three years later, on August 6th, 1995, there was a gathering in the chapel of my university to commemorate the fiftieth anniversary of the detonation of the first atomic bomb, over the city of Hiroshima, Japan. I was there.

One of the speakers was the physicist Leo Seren. He had participated in the successful experiment under the lifeless sports facility so long ago. Get this: He *apologized* for having done that!

Somebody should have told him that being a physicist, on a planet where the smartest animals hate being alive so much, means never having to say you're sorry.

Now imagine this: A man creates a hydrogen bomb for a paranoid Soviet Union, makes sure it will work, and then wins a Nobel Peace Prize! This real-life character, worthy of a story by Kilgore Trout, was the late physicist Andrei Sakharov.

He won his Nobel in 1975 for demanding a halt to the testing of nuclear weapons. He, of course, had already tested *his*. His wife was a pediatrician! What sort of person could perfect a hydrogen bomb while married to a child-care specialist? What sort of physician would stay with a mate that cracked?

"Anything interesting happen at work today, Honeybunch?"

"Yes. My bomb is going to work just great. And how are you doing with that kid with chicken pox?"

Andrei Sakharov was a sort of saint in 1975, a sort that is no longer celebrated, now that the Cold War is over. He was a *dissident* in the Soviet Union. He called for an end to the development and testing of nuclear weapons, and also for more freedoms for his people. He was kicked out of the USSR's Academy of Sciences. He was exiled from Moscow to a whistlestop on the permafrost.

He was not allowed to go to Oslo to receive his Peace Prize. His pediatrician wife, Elena Bonner, accepted it for him there. But isn't it time for us to ask now if she, or any pediatrician or healer, wasn't more deserving of a Peace Prize than anyone who had a hand in creating an H-bomb for any kind of government anywhere?

Human rights? What could be more indifferent to the rights of any form of life than an H-bomb?

Sakharov was in June of 1987 awarded an honorary doctorate by Staten Island College in New York City. Once again his government wouldn't let him accept in person. So I was asked to do that for him.

All I had to do was deliver a message he had sent. This was it: "Don't give up on nuclear energy." I spoke it like a robot.

I was so polite! But this was one year after this crazy planet's most deadly nuclear calamity so far, at Chernobyl, Ukraine. Children all over northern Europe will be sickened or worse for years to come by that release of radiation. Plenty of work for pediatricians!

More heartening to me than Sakharov's cockamamie exhortation was the behavior of firemen in Schenectady, New York, after Chernobyl. I used to work in Schenectady. The firemen sent a letter to their brother firemen over there, congratulating them on their courage and selflessness while trying to save lives and property.

Hooray for firemen!

Scum of the Earth as some may be in their daily lives, they can all be saints in emergencies.

Hooray for firemen.

3

I N *Timequake One*, Kilgore Trout wrote a story about an atom bomb. Because of the timequake, he had to write it twice. The ten-year rerun following the timequake, remember, made him and me, *and you*, and everybody else, do everything we'd done from February 17th, 1991, to February 13th, 2001, a second time.

Trout didn't mind writing it again. Rerun or not, he could tune out the crock of shit being alive was as long as he was scribbling, head down, with a ballpoint pen on a yellow legal pad.

He called the story "No Laughing Matter." He threw it away before anybody else could see it, and then had to throw it away again during the rerun. At the clambake at the end of *Timequake One*, in the summer of the year 2001, after free will kicked in again, Trout said this about all the stories he had torn to pieces and flushed down toilets, or tossed into trash-strewn vacant lots, or whatever: "Easy come, easy go."

"No Laughing Matter" got its title from what a judge in the story said during a top-secret court-martial of the crew of the American bomber *Joy's Pride*, on the Pacific island of Banalulu, one month after the end of World War Two.

Joy's Pride itself was perfectly OK, and in a hangar there on Banalulu. It was named in honor of the pilot's mother, Joy Peterson, a nurse in obstetrics in a hospital in Corpus Christi, Texas. *Pride* had a double meaning. It meant self-respect. It meant a lion family, too.

Here's the thing: After an atom bomb was dropped on Hiroshima, and then another one was dropped on Nagasaki, *Joy's Pride* was ordered to drop yet another one on Yokohama, on a couple of million "little yellow bastards." The little yellow bastards were called "little yellow bastards" back then. It was wartime. Trout described the third atom bomb like this: "A purple motherfucker as big as a boiler in the basement of a mid-size junior high school."

It was too big to fit inside the bomb bay. It was slung underneath the plane's belly, and cleared the runway by a foot when
Joy's Pride took off into the wild blue yonder.

As the plane neared its target, the pilot mused out loud on
the intercom that his mother, the obstetrics nurse, would be a
celebrity back home after they did what they were about to do.
The bomber *Enola Gay*, and the woman in whose honor it was
named, had become as famous as movie stars after it dropped
its load on Hiroshima. Yokohama was twice as populous as
Hiroshima and Nagasaki combined.

The more the pilot thought about it, though, the surer he
was that his sweet widowed mother could never tell reporters
she was happy that her son's airplane had killed a world's record
number of civilians all at once.

Trout's story reminds me of the time my late great-aunt
Emma Vonnegut said she hated the Chinese. Her late son-in-
law Kerfuit Stewart, who used to own Stewart's Book Store in
Louisville, Kentucky, admonished her that it was *wicked* to hate
that many people all at once.

Whatever.

The crewmen aboard *Joy's Pride*, at any rate, told the pilot on
the intercom that they felt much as he did. They were all alone
up there in the sky. They didn't need a fighter escort, since the
Japanese didn't have any air lanes left. The war was over, except
for the paperwork, arguably the situation even before *Enola Gay*
cremated Hiroshima.

To quote Kilgore Trout: "This wasn't war anymore, and neither had been the obliteration of Nagasaki. This was 'Thanks to
the Yanks for a job well done!' This was *show biz* now."

Trout said in "No Laughing Matter" that the pilot and his
bombardier had felt somewhat godlike on previous missions,
when they had had nothing more than incendiaries and conventional high explosives to drop on people. "But that was godlike
with a little *g*," he wrote. "They identified themselves with minor
deities who only avenged and destroyed. Up there in the sky
all alone, with the purple motherfucker slung underneath their

plane, they felt like the Boss God Himself, who had an option which hadn't been theirs before, which was to be *merciful.*"

Trout himself had been in World War Two, but not as an airman and not in the Pacific. He had been a forward observer for the Army field artillery in Europe, a lieutenant with binoculars and a radio, up with the infantry or even ahead of it. He would tell batteries to the rear where their shrapnel or white phosphorus or whatever might help a lot.

He himself had certainly not been merciful, nor, by his own account, had he ever felt he should have been. I asked him at the clambake in 2001, at the writers' retreat Xanadu, what he'd done during the war, which he called "civilization's second unsuccessful attempt to commit suicide."

He said without a scintilla of regret, "I made sandwiches of German soldiers between an erupting Earth and an exploding sky, and in a blizzard of razor blades."

The pilot of *Joy's Pride* made a U-turn way up in the sky. The purple motherfucker was still slung underneath. The pilot headed back for Banalulu. "He did it," wrote Trout, "because that is what his mother would have wanted him to do."

At the top-secret court-martial afterward, everybody was convulsed with laughter at one point in the proceedings. This caused the chief judge to bang his gavel and declare that what those on trial had done was "no laughing matter." What people found so funny was the prosecutor's description of what people did at the base when *Joy's Pride* came in for a landing with the purple motherfucker only a foot above the tarmac. People jumped out of windows. They peed in their pants.

"There were all kinds of collisions between different kinds of vehicles," wrote Kilgore Trout.

No sooner had the judge restored order, though, than a huge crack opened in the floor of the Pacific Ocean. It swallowed Banalulu, court-martial, *Joy's Pride*, unused atom bomb and all.

4

WHEN the excellent German novelist and graphic artist Günter Grass heard that I was born in 1922, he said to me, "There are no males in Europe your age for you to talk to." He himself was a kid during Kilgore Trout's and my war, as were Elie Wiesel and Jerzy Kosinski and Milos Forman, and on and on. I was lucky to be born over here instead of over there, and white and middle-class, and into a house full of books and pictures, and into a large extended family, which exists no more.

I heard the poet Robert Pinsky give a reading this summer, in which he apologized didactically for having had a much nicer life than normal. I should do that, too.

At least I seized the opportunity this past May to thank my birthplace, as a graduation speaker at Butler University. I said, "If I had it to do all over, I would choose to be born again in a hospital in Indianapolis. I would choose to spend my childhood again at 4365 North Illinois Street, about ten blocks from here, and to again be a product of that city's public schools.

"I would again take courses in bacteriology and qualitative analysis in the summer school of Butler University.

"It was all here for me, just as it has all been for you, the best and the worst of Western Civilization, if you cared to pay attention: music, finance, government, architecture, law and sculpture and painting, history and medicine and athletics and every sort of science, and books, books, books, and teachers and role models.

"People so smart you can't believe it, and people so dumb you can't believe it. People so nice you can't believe it, and people so mean you can't believe it."

I gave advice, too. I said, "My uncle Alex Vonnegut, a Harvard-educated life insurance salesman who lived at 5033 North Pennsylvania Street, taught me something very important. He said that when things were really going well we should be sure to *notice* it.

"He was talking about simple occasions, not great victories: maybe drinking lemonade on a hot afternoon in the shade, or smelling the aroma of a nearby bakery, or fishing and not caring if we catch anything or not, or hearing somebody all alone playing a piano really well in the house next door.

"Uncle Alex urged me to say this out loud during such epiphanies: 'If this isn't nice, what is?' "

Another way I was lucky: for the first thirty-three years of my life, telling short stories with ink on paper was a major American industry. Although I then had a wife and two children, it made good business sense for me to quit my job as a publicity man for General Electric, with health insurance and a retirement plan. I could make more money selling stories to *The Saturday Evening Post* and *Collier's*, weekly magazines full of ads, which published five short stories and an installment of a cliff-hanging serial in every issue.

Those were just the top-paying buyers of what I could produce. There were so many other magazines hungry for fiction that the market for stories was like a pinball machine. When I mailed off a story to my agent, I could be pretty sure somebody would pay me something for it, even though it might be rejected again and again.

But not long after I moved my family from Schenectady, New York, to Cape Cod, television, a much better buy for advertisers than magazines, made playing short story pinball for a living obsolete.

I commuted from the Cape to Boston to work for an industrial advertising agency, and then became a dealer in Saab

automobiles, and then taught high school English in a private school for seriously fucked-up rich kids.

My son the doctor Mark Vonnegut, who wrote a swell book about his going crazy in the 1960s, and then graduated from Harvard Medical School, had an exhibition of his watercolors in Milton, Massachusetts, this summer. A reporter asked him what it had been like to grow up with a famous father.

Mark replied, "When I was growing up, my father was a car salesman who couldn't get a job teaching at Cape Cod Junior College."

5

I STILL think up short stories from time to time, as though there were money in it. The habit dies hard. There used to be fleeting fame in it, too. Highly literate people once talked enthusiastically to one another about a story by Ray Bradbury or J. D. Salinger or John Cheever or John Collier or John O'Hara or Shirley Jackson or Flannery O'Connor or whomever, which had appeared in a magazine in the past few days.

No more.

All I do with short story ideas now is rough them out, credit them to Kilgore Trout, and put them in a novel. Here's the start of another one hacked from the carcass of *Timequake One*, and entitled "The Sisters B-36": "On the matriarchal planet Booboo in the Crab Nebula, there were three sisters whose last name was B-36. It could be only a coincidence that their family name was also that of an Earthling airplane designed to drop bombs on civilian populations with corrupt leaderships. Earth and Booboo were too far apart to ever communicate."

Another coincidence: The written language of Booboo was like English on Earth, in that it consisted of idiosyncratic arrangements in horizontal lines of twenty-six phonetic symbols, ten numbers, and about eight punctuation marks.

All three of the sisters were beautiful, so went Trout's tale, but only two of them were popular, one a picture painter and the other a short story writer. Nobody could stand the third one, who was a scientist. She was so *boring*! All she could talk about was thermodynamics. She was envious. Her secret ambition was to make her two artistic sisters feel, to use a favorite expression of Trout's, "like something the cat drug in."

Trout said Booboolings were among the most adaptable creatures in the local family of galaxies. This was thanks to their great big brains, which could be programmed to do or not do, and feel or not feel, just about anything. You name it!

The programming wasn't done surgically or electrically, or by any other sort of neurological intrusiveness. It was done *socially*, with nothing but talk, talk, talk. Grownups would speak to little Booboolings favorably about presumably appropriate and desirable feelings and deeds. The brains of the youngsters would respond by growing circuits that made civilized pleasures and behavior automatic.

It seemed a good idea, for example, when nothing much was really going on, for Booboolings to be beneficially excited by minimal stimuli, such as idiosyncratic arrangements in horizontal lines of twenty-six phonetic symbols, ten numbers, and eight or so punctuation marks, or dabs of pigment on flat surfaces in frames.

When a little Boobooling was reading a book, a grownup might interrupt to say, depending on what was happening in the book, "Isn't that sad? The little girl's nice little dog has just been run over by a garbage truck. Doesn't that make you want to cry?" Or the grownup might say, about a very different sort of story, "Isn't that funny? When that conceited old rich man stepped on a *nim-nim* peel and fell into an open manhole, didn't that make you practically pop a gut laughing?"

A *nim-nim* was a banana-like fruit on Booboo.

An immature Boobooling taken to an art gallery might be asked about a certain painting whether the woman in it was really smiling or not. Couldn't she be sad about something, and still look that way? Is she married, do you think? Does she have a kid? Is she nice to it? Where do you think she's going next? Does she want to go?

If there was a bowl of fruit in the painting, a grownup might ask, "Don't those *nim-nims* look good enough to eat? Yummy yum yum!"

These examples of Boobooling pedagogy aren't mine. They're Kilgore Trout's.

Thus were the brains of most, but not quite all, Booboolings made to grow circuits, microchips, if you like, which on Earth would be called *imaginations*. Yes, and it was precisely because a vast majority of Booboolings had imaginations that two of the B-36 sisters, the short story writer and the painter, were so beloved.

The bad sister had an imagination, all right, but not in the field of art appreciation. She wouldn't read books or go to art galleries. She spent every spare minute when she was little in the garden of a lunatic asylum next door. The psychos in the garden were believed to be harmless, so her keeping them company was regarded as a laudably compassionate activity. But the nuts taught her thermodynamics and calculus and so on.

When the bad sister was a young woman, she and the nuts worked up designs for television cameras and transmitters and receivers. Then she got money from her very rich mom to manufacture and market these satanic devices, which made imaginations redundant. They were instantly popular because the shows were so attractive and no thinking was involved.

She made a lot of money, but what really pleased her was that her two sisters were starting to feel like something the cat drug in. Young Booboolings didn't see any point in developing imaginations anymore, since all they had to do was turn on a switch and see all kinds of jazzy shit. They would look at a printed page or a painting and wonder how anybody could have gotten his or her rocks off looking at things that simple and dead.

The bad sister's name was Nim-nim. When her parents named her that, they had no idea how unsweet she was going to be. And TV wasn't the half of it! She was as unpopular as ever because she was as boring as ever, so she invented automobiles and computers and barbed wire and flamethrowers and land mines and machine guns and so on. That's how pissed off she was.

New generations of Booboolings grew up without imaginations. Their appetites for diversions from boredom were perfectly satisfied by all the crap Nim-nim was selling them. Why not? What the heck.

Without imaginations, though, they couldn't do what their ancestors had done, which was read interesting, heartwarming stories in the faces of one another. So, according to Kilgore Trout, "Booboolings became among the most merciless creatures in the local family of galaxies."

6

TROUT SAID at the clambake in 2001 that life was undeniably preposterous. "But our brains are big enough to let us adapt to the inevitable pratfalls and buffoonery," he went on, "by means of manmade epiphanies like this one." He meant the clambake on a beach under a starry sky. "If this isn't nice, what is?" he said.

He declared the corn on the cob, steamed in seaweed with lobsters and clams, to be *heavenly*. He added, "And don't all the ladies look like *angels* tonight!" He was feasting on corn on the cob and women as *ideas*. He couldn't eat the corn because the upper plate of his false teeth was insecure. His long-term relationships with women had been disasters. In the only love story he ever attempted, "Kiss Me Again," he had written, "There is no way a beautiful woman can live up to what she looks like for any appreciable length of time."

The moral at the end of that story is this: "Men are jerks. Women are psychotic."

Chief among manmade epiphanies for me have been stage plays. Trout called them "artificial timequakes." He said, "Before Earthlings knew there were such things as timequakes in Nature, they invented them." And it's true. Actors know everything they are going to say and do, and how everything is going to come out in the end, for good or ill, when the curtain goes up on Act One, Scene One. Yet they have no choice but to behave as though the future were a mystery.

Yes, and when the timequake of 2001 zapped us back to 1991, it made ten years of our pasts ten years of our futures, so we could remember everything we had to say and do again when the time came.

Keep this in mind at the start of the next rerun after the next timequake: *The show must go on!*

The artificial timequake that has moved me most so far this year is an old one. It is *Our Town*, by the late Thornton Wilder. I had already watched it with undiminished satisfaction maybe five or six times. And then this spring my thirteen-year-old daughter, dear Lily, was cast as a talking dead person in the graveyard of Grover's Corners in a school production of that innocent, sentimental masterpiece.

The play zapped Lily and her schoolmates from the evening of the performance back to May 7th, 1901! Timequake! They were robots of Thornton Wilder's imaginary past until the curtain came down after the funeral of the heroine Emily in the very last scene. Only then could they live in 1996 again. Only then could they again decide for themselves what to say or do next. Only then could they exercise free will again.

I reflected sadly that night, with Lily pretending to be a dead grownup, that I would be seventy-eight when she graduated from high school, and eighty-two when she graduated from college, and so on. Talk about remembering the future!

What hit me really hard that night, though, was the character Emily's farewell in the last scene, after the mourners have gone back down the hill to their village, having buried her. She says, "Good-by, good-by, world. Good-by, Grover's Corners . . . Mama and Papa. Good-by to clocks ticking . . . and Mama's sunflowers. And food and coffee. And new-ironed dresses and hot baths . . . and sleeping and waking up. Oh, earth, you're too wonderful for anybody to realize you.

"Do any human beings ever realize life while they live it?— every, every minute?"

I myself become a sort of Emily every time I hear that speech. I haven't died yet, but there is a place, as seemingly safe and simple, as learnable, as acceptable as Grover's Corners at the turn of the century, with ticking clocks and Mama and Papa and hot baths and new-ironed clothes and all the rest of it, to which I've already said good-by, good-by, one hell of a long time ago now.

Here's what that was: the first seven years of my life, before the shit hit the fan, first the Great Depression and then World War Two.

They say the first thing to go when you're old is your legs or your eyesight. It isn't true. The first thing to go is parallel parking.

Now I find myself maundering about parts of plays hardly anybody knows or cares about anymore, such as the graveyard scene in *Our Town*, or the poker game in Tennessee Williams's *A Streetcar Named Desire*, or what Willy Loman's wife said after that tragically ordinary, clumsily gallant American committed suicide in Arthur Miller's *Death of a Salesman*.

She said, "Attention must be paid."

In *A Streetcar Named Desire*, Blanche DuBois said as she was taken away to a madhouse, after she was raped by her sister's husband, "I have always depended on the kindness of strangers."

Those speeches, those situations, those people, became emotional and ethical landmarks for me in my early manhood, and remain such in the summer of 1996. That is because I was immobilized in a congregation of rapt fellow human beings in a theater when I first saw and heard them.

They would have made no more impression on me than *Monday Night Football*, had I been alone eating nachos and gazing into the face of a cathode-ray tube.

In the early days of television, when there were only half a dozen channels at most, significant, well-written dramas on a cathode-ray tube could still make us feel like members of an attentive congregation, alone at home as we might be. There was a high probability back then, with so few shows to choose from, that friends and neighbors were watching the same show we were watching, still finding TV a whizbang miracle.

We might even call up a friend that very night, and ask a question to which we already knew the answer: "Did you see *that*? Wow!"

No more.

7

I WOULDN'T HAVE MISSED the Great Depression or my part in World War Two for anything. Trout asserted at the clambake that our war would live forever in show biz, as other wars would not, because of the uniforms of the Nazis.

He commented unfavorably on the camouflage suits our own generals wear nowadays on TV, when they describe our blasting the bejesus out of some Third World country because of petroleum. "I can't imagine," he said, "any part of the world where such garish pajamas would make a soldier less rather than more visible.

"We are evidently preparing," he said, "to fight World War Three in the midst of an enormous Spanish omelet."

He asked what relatives of mine had been wounded in wars. As far as I knew, only one. That was my great-grandfather Peter Lieber, an immigrant who became a brewer in Indianapolis after being wounded in one leg during our Civil War. He was a Freethinker, which is to say a skeptic about conventional religious beliefs, as had been Voltaire and Thomas Jefferson and Benjamin Franklin and so on. And as would be Kilgore Trout and I.

I told Trout that Peter Lieber's Anglo-American company commander gave his men, all Freethinkers from Germany, Christian religious tracts for inspiration. Trout responded by giving his own revision of the Book of Genesis.

Fortunately, I had a tape recorder, which I turned on.

"Please stop eating and pay attention," he said. "This is important." He paused to press the upper plate of his false teeth against the roof of his mouth with the ball of his left thumb. It would come unstuck again every two minutes or so. He was left-handed, as was I until my parents made me switch, and as are my daughters Edith and Lily, or, as we call them affectionately, Edie Bucket and Lolly-boo.

"In the beginning there was absolutely nothing, and I mean *nothing*," he said. "But nothing implies something, just as up implies down and sweet implies sour, as man implies woman and drunk implies sober and happy implies sad. I hate to tell you this, friends and neighbors, but we are teensy-weensy implications in an enormous implication. If you don't like it here, why don't you go back to where you came from?

"The first something to be implied by all the nothing," he said, "was in fact two somethings, who were God and Satan. God was male. Satan was female. They implied each other, and hence were peers in the emerging power structure, which was itself nothing but an implication. Power was implied by weakness."

"God created the heaven and the earth," the old, long-out-of-print science fiction writer went on. "And the earth was without form, and void, and darkness was upon the face of the deep. And the spirit of God moved upon the face of the waters. Satan could have done this herself, but she thought it was stupid, action for the sake of action. What was the point? She didn't say anything at first.

"But Satan began to worry about God when He said, 'Let there be light,' and there was light. She had to wonder, 'What in heck does He think He's doing? How far does He intend to go, and does He expect me to help Him take care of all this crazy stuff?'

"And then the shit really hit the fan. God made man and woman, beautiful little miniatures of Him and her, and turned them loose to see what might become of them. The Garden of Eden," said Trout, "might be considered the prototype for the Colosseum and the Roman Games."

"Satan," he said, "couldn't undo anything God had done. She could at least try to make existence for His little toys less painful. She could see what He couldn't: To be alive was to be either bored or scared stiff. So she filled an apple with all sorts of ideas that might at least relieve the boredom, such as rules for games with cards and dice, and how to fuck, and recipes for beer and wine and whiskey, and pictures of different plants that were smokable, and so on. And instructions on how to make music and sing and dance real crazy, real sexy. And how to spout blasphemy when they stubbed their toes.

"Satan had a serpent give Eve the apple. Eve took a bite and handed it to Adam. He took a bite, and then they fucked."

"I grant you," said Trout, "that some of the ideas in the apple had catastrophic side effects for a minority of those who tried them." Let it be noted here that Trout himself was not an alcoholic, a junkie, a gambler, or a sex fiend. He just wrote.

"All Satan wanted to do was help, and she did in many cases," he concluded. "And her record for promoting nostrums with occasionally dreadful side effects is no worse than that of the most reputable pharmaceutical houses of the present day."

8

SIDE EFFECTS of Satan's booze recipes have played a deleterious part in the lives and deaths of many great American writers. In *Timequake One*, I envisioned a writers' retreat called Xanadu, where each of the four guest suites was named in honor of an American winner of a Nobel Prize for Literature. The Ernest Hemingway and Eugene O'Neill were on the second floor of the mansion. The Sinclair Lewis was on the third. The John Steinbeck was in the carriage house.

Kilgore Trout exclaimed upon arriving at Xanadu, two weeks after free will kicked in again, "All four of your ink-on-paper heroes were certifiable alcoholics!"

Gambling ruined William Saroyan. A combination of booze and gambling did in the journalist Alvin Davis, a much-missed friend of mine. I asked Al one time what was the biggest kick he got from games of chance. He said it came after he had lost all his money in an around-the-clock poker game.

He went back after a few hours with money he had gotten wherever he could get it, from a friend, from hocking something, from a loan-shark. And he sat down at the table and said, "Deal me in."

The late British philosopher Bertrand Russell said he lost friends to one of three addictions: alcohol or religion or chess. Kilgore Trout was hooked on making idiosyncratic arrangements in horizontal lines, with ink on bleached and flattened wood pulp, of twenty-six phonetic symbols, ten numbers, and about eight punctuation marks. He was a black hole to anyone who might imagine that he or she was a friend of his.

I have been married twice, divorced once. Both my wives, Jane and now Jill, have said on occasion that I am much like Trout in that regard.

My mother was addicted to being rich, to servants and unlimited charge accounts, to giving lavish dinner parties, to taking frequent first-class trips to Europe. So one might say she was tormented by withdrawal symptoms all through the Great Depression.

She was *acculturated*!

Acculturated persons are those who find that they are no longer treated as the sort of people they thought they were, because the outside world has changed. An economic misfortune or a new technology, or being conquered by another country or political faction, can do that to people quicker than you can say "Jack Robinson."

As Trout wrote in his "An American Family Marooned on the Planet Pluto": "Nothing wrecks any kind of love more effectively than the discovery that your previously acceptable behavior has become ridiculous." He said in conversation at the 2001 clambake: "If I hadn't learned how to live without a culture and a society, acculturation would have broken my heart a thousand times."

In *Timequake One*, I had Trout discard his "The Sisters B-36" in a lidless wire trash receptacle chained to a fire hydrant in front of the American Academy of Arts and Letters, way-the-hell-and-gone up on West 155th Street in Manhattan, two doors west of Broadway. This was on the afternoon of Christmas Eve, 2000, supposedly fifty-one days before the timequake zapped everybody and everything back to 1991.

The members of the Academy, I said, who were addicted to making old-fashioned art in old-fashioned ways, without computers, were experiencing acculturation. They were like the two artistic sisters on the matriarchal planet Booboo in the Crab Nebula.

There really is an American Academy of Arts and Letters. Its palatial headquarters are where I placed them in *Timequake One*. There really is a fire hydrant out front. There really is a library inside, and an art gallery and reception halls and meeting rooms and staff offices, and a very grand auditorium.

By an act of Congress passed in 1916, the Academy can have no more than 250 members, American citizens, all of whom have distinguished themselves as novelists, dramatists, poets, historians, essayists, critics, composers of music, architects,

painters, or sculptors. Their ranks are regularly diminished by
the Grim Reaper, by death. A task of the survivors is to nomi-
nate and then, by secret ballot, elect persons to fill the vacancies.

Among the Academy's founders were old-fashioned writers such as Henry Adams and William and Henry James, and
Samuel Clemens, and the old-fashioned composer Edward
MacDowell. Their audiences were necessarily small. Their own
brains were all they had to work with.

I said in *Timequake One* that by the year 2000, craftspeople of
their sort had become "as quaint," in the opinion of the general
public, "as contemporary makers in New England tourist towns
of the toy windmills known since colonial times as *whirligigs*."

9

FOUNDERS of the Academy at the turn of the century were contemporaneous with Thomas Alva Edison, inventor of, among other things, sound recordings and motion pictures. Before World War Two, though, these schemes for holding the attention of millions all over the world were only squawking or flickering lampoons of life itself.

The Academy occupied its present home, designed by the firm of McKim, Mead & White, and paid for by the philanthropist Archer Milton Huntington, in 1923. In that year, the American inventor Lee De Forest demonstrated apparatus that made possible the addition of sound to motion pictures.

I had a scene in *Timequake One*, set in the office of Monica Pepper, fictitious Executive Secretary of the Academy, on Christmas Eve, 2000. That was the afternoon on which Kilgore Trout put "The Sisters B-36" in the lidless wire trash receptacle out front, again, fifty-one days before the timequake struck.

Mrs. Pepper, wife of the wheelchair-ridden composer Zoltan Pepper, bore a striking resemblance to my late sister Allie, who hated life so much. Allie died of cancer of the everything way back in 1958, when I was thirty-six and she was forty-one, hounded by bill collectors to the very end. Both women were pretty blondes, which was OK. But they were six-foot-two! Both women were permanently acculturated in adolescence, since nowhere on Earth, save among the Watusis, did it make any sense for a woman to be that tall.

Both women were unlucky. Allie married a nice guy who lost all their money and then some in dumb businesses. Monica Pepper was the reason her husband Zoltan was paralyzed from the waist down. Two years earlier, she had accidentally landed on top of him in a swimming pool out in Aspen, Colorado. At least Allie had to die so deep in debt, and with four sons to raise, only once. After the timequake struck, Monica Pepper would have to swan-dive on top of her husband a second time.

•

Monica and Zoltan were talking in her office at the Academy that Christmas Eve, 2000. Zoltan was crying and laughing simultaneously. They were the same age, forty, which made them baby boomers. They didn't have any kids. Because of her, his ding-dong didn't work anymore. Zoltan was crying and laughing about that, certainly, but mostly about a tone-deaf kid next door, who had composed and orchestrated an acceptable, if derivative, string quartet in the manner of Beethoven, with the help of a new computer program called Wolfgang.

Nothing would do but that the father of the obnoxious kid show Zoltan the sheet music his son's printer had spit out that morning and ask him if it was any good or not.

As though Zoltan weren't sufficiently destabilized emotionally by legs and a ding-dong that didn't work anymore, his older brother Frank, an architect, had committed suicide after a nearly identical blow to his self-respect only a month earlier. Yes, and Frank Pepper would eventually be popped out of his grave by the timequake, so he could blow his brains out while his wife and three kids watched a second time.

Here's the thing: Frank went to the drugstore for condoms or chewing gum or whatever, and the pharmacist told him that his sixteen-year-old daughter had become an architect and was thinking of dropping out of high school because it was such a waste of time. She had designed a recreation center for teenagers in depressed neighborhoods with the help of a new computer program the school had bought for its vocational students, dummies who weren't going to anything but junior colleges. It was called Palladio.

Frank went to a computer store, and asked if he could try out Palladio before buying it. He doubted very much that it could help anyone with his native talent and education. So right there in the store, and in a period of no more than half an hour, Palladio gave him what he had asked it for, working drawings that would enable a contractor to build a three-story parking garage in the manner of Thomas Jefferson.

Frank had made up the craziest assignment he could think of, confident that Palladio would tell him to take his custom elsewhere. But it didn't! It presented him with menu after menu, asking how many cars, and in what city, because of various local building codes, and whether trucks would be allowed to use it, too, and on and on. It even asked about surrounding buildings, and whether Jeffersonian architecture would be in harmony with them. It offered to give him alternative plans in the manner of Michael Graves or I. M. Pei.

It gave him plans for the wiring and plumbing, and ballpark estimates of what it would cost to build in any part of the world he cared to name.

So Frank went home and killed himself the first time.

Laughing and crying there in his wife's office at the Academy on the first of two Christmas Eves, 2000, Zoltan Pepper said this to his pretty but gawky wife: "It used to be said of a man who had suffered a catastrophic setback in his line of work that he had been handed his head on a platter. We are being handed our heads with *tweezers* now."

He was speaking, of course, of microchips.

10

ALLIE DIED in New Jersey. She and her husband, Jim, also a native Hoosier, are buried whole in Crown Hill Cemetery in Indianapolis. So is James Whitcomb Riley, the *Hoosier Poet*, a never-married lush. So is John Dillinger, the beloved bank robber of the 1930s. So are our parents, Kurt and Edith, and Father's kid brother Alex Vonnegut, the Harvard-educated life insurance salesman who said, whenever life was good, "If this isn't nice, what is?" So are two previous generations of our parents' forebears: a brewer, an architect, merchants and musicians, and their wives, of course.

Full house!

John Dillinger, a farm boy, escaped from jail once brandishing a wooden pistol he had whittled from a broken washtub slat. He blackened it with shoe polish! He was so *entertaining*. While on the run, robbing banks and vanishing into the boondocks, Dillinger wrote Henry Ford a fan letter. He thanked the old anti-Semite for making such fast and agile getaway cars!

It was possible to get away from the police back then if you were a better driver with a better car. Talk about *fair play*! Talk about what we say we want for everyone in America: *a level playing field*! And Dillinger robbed only the rich and strong, banks with armed guards, and *in person*.

Dillinger wasn't a simpering, sly swindler. He was an *athlete*.

In the slavering search for subversive literature on the shelves of our public schools, which will never stop, the two most subversive tales of all remain untouched, wholly unsuspected. One is the story of Robin Hood. As ill educated as John Dillinger was, that was surely his inspiration: a *reputable* blueprint for what a real man might *do* with life.

The minds of children in intellectually humble American homes back then weren't swamped with countless stories from TV sets. They heard or read only a few stories, and so could remember them, and maybe learn something from them.

Everywhere in the English-speaking world, one of those was "Cinderella." Another was "The Ugly Duckling." Another was the story of Robin Hood.

And another, as disrespectful of established authority as the story of Robin Hood, which "Cinderella" and "The Ugly Duckling" are not, is the life of Jesus Christ as described in the New Testament.

G-men, under orders from J. Edgar Hoover, the unmarried homosexual director of the FBI, shot Dillinger dead, simply executed him as he came out of a movie theater with a date. He hadn't pulled a gun, or lunged or dived, or tried to run away. He was like anybody else coming out into the real world after a movie, awakening from enchantment. He was killed because he had for too long made G-men, all of whom then wore fedoras, look non compos mentis, like nincompoops.

That was in 1934. I was eleven. Allie was sixteen. Allie wept and raged, and we both reviled Dillinger's date at the movie. This *bitch*, and there was nothing else to call her, tipped off the feds about where Dillinger would be that night. She said she would be wearing an orange dress. The nondescript gink by her side when she came out would be the man the gay director of the FBI had branded Public Enemy Number One.

She was Hungarian. As the old saying goes: "If you have a Hungarian for a friend, you don't need an enemy."

Allie later had her picture taken with Dillinger's big tombstone at Crown Hill, not far from the fence on West Thirty-eighth Street. I myself came upon it from time to time, while shooting crows with a .22 semiautomatic rifle our gun-nut father gave me for my birthday. Crows back then were classified as enemies of mankind. Given half a chance, they would eat our corn.

One kid I knew shot a golden eagle. You should have seen the wingspread!

Allie hated hunting so much that I stopped doing it, and so did Father. As I've written elsewhere, he had become a gun nut and hunter in order to prove that he wasn't effeminate, even though he was in the arts, an architect and a painter and potter.

In public lectures, I myself often say, "If you really want to hurt your parents, and you don't have nerve enough to be a homosexual, the least you can do is go into the arts."

Father supposed he could still demonstrate his manhood by fishing. But then my big brother Bernie spoiled that for him, too, saying it was as though he were smashing up Swiss pocketwatches, or some other exquisitely engineered little pieces of machinery.

I told Kilgore Trout at the clambake in 2001 about how my brother and sister had made Father ashamed of hunting and fishing. He quoted Shakespeare: "How sharper than a serpent's tooth it is to have a thankless child!"

Trout was self-educated, never having finished high school. I was mildly surprised, then, that he could quote Shakespeare. I asked if he had committed a lot of that remarkable author's words to memory. He said, "Yes, dear colleague, including a single sentence which describes life as lived by human beings so completely that no writer after him need ever have written another word."

"Which sentence was that, Mr. Trout?" I asked.

And he said, " 'All the world's a stage, and all the men and women merely players.' "

11

I wrote a letter to an old friend last spring about why I evidently couldn't write publishable fiction anymore, after trying and failing to do that for many years. He is Edward Muir, a poet and advertising man my age living in Scarsdale. In my novel *Cat's Cradle*, I say that anybody whose life keeps tangling up with yours for no logical reason is likely a member of your *karass*, a team God has formed to get something done for Him. Ed Muir is surely a member of my *karass*.

Listen to this: When I was at the University of Chicago after World War Two, Ed was there, although we did not meet. When I went to Schenectady, New York, to be a publicist for the General Electric Company, Ed went there to be a teacher at Union College. When I quit GE and moved to Cape Cod, he showed up there as a recruiter for the Great Books Program. At last we met, and whether in the service of God or not, my first wife Jane and I became leaders of a Great Books group.

And when he took an advertising job in Boston, so did I, not knowing he had done that. When Ed's first marriage broke up, so did mine, and now we're both in New York. My point, though, is as follows: When I sent him a letter about my case of writer's block, he made it look like a poem and returned it.

He left off my salutation and the first few lines, which were in praise of *Reader's Block* by David Markson, who had been his student at Union College. I said David shouldn't thank Fate for letting him write such a good book in a time when large numbers of people could no longer be wowed by a novel, no matter how excellent. Something like that. I don't have a copy of my letter as prose. As a poem, though, this is its appearance:

> *And no thanks to Fate.*
> *When we're gone, there won't be anybody*
> *Sufficiently excited by ink on paper*
> *To realize how good it is.*

I have this ailment not unlike
Ambulatory pneumonia, which might be called
Ambulatory writer's block.

I cover paper with words every day,
But the stories never go anywhere
I find worth going.

Slaughterhouse-Five *has been turned*
Into an opera by a young German,
And will have its premiere in Munich this June.
I'm not going there either.
Not interested.

I am fond of Occam's Razor,
Or the Law of Parsimony, which suggests
That the simplest explanation of a phenomenon
Is usually the most trustworthy.

And I now believe, with David's help,
That writer's block is finding out
How lives of loved ones really ended
Instead of the way we hoped they would end
With the help of our body English.
Fiction is body English.

Whatever.

It was nice of Ed to do that. Another nice story about him is from his days as a road man for Great Books. He is a minor poet, publishing occasionally in *The Atlantic Monthly* and suchlike. His name, though, is nearly identical with that of the major poet Edwin Muir, a Scotsman who died in 1959. Hazily sophisticated people sometimes asked him if he was *the poet*, meaning Edwin.

One time, when Ed told a woman he wasn't *the poet*, she expressed deep disappointment. She said one of her favorite poems was "The Poet Covers His Child." Get a load of this: It was the American Ed Muir who wrote that poem.

12

I WISH I'd written *Our Town*. I wish I'd invented Rollerblades.

I asked A. E. Hotchner, a friend and biographer of the late Ernest Hemingway, if Hemingway had ever shot a human being, not counting himself. Hotchner said, "No."

I asked the late great German novelist Heinrich Böll what the basic flaw was in the German character. He said, "Obedience."

I asked one of my adopted nephews what he thought of my dancing. He said, "Acceptable."

When I took a job in Boston as an advertising copywriter, because I was broke, an account executive asked me what kind of name Vonnegut was. I said, "German." He said, "Germans killed six million of my cousins."

You want to know why I don't have AIDS, why I'm not HIV-positive like so many other people? I don't fuck around. It's as simple as that.

Trout said this was the story on why AIDS and new strains of syph and clap and the blueballs were making the rounds like Avon ladies run amok: On September 1st of 1945, immediately after the end of World War Two, representatives of all the chemical elements held a meeting on the planet Tralfamadore. They were there to protest some of their members' having been incorporated into the bodies of big, sloppy, stinky organisms as cruel and stupid as human beings.

Elements such as Polonium and Ytterbium, which had never been essential parts of human beings, were nonetheless outraged that *any* chemicals should be so misused.

Carbon, although an embarrassed veteran of countless massacres throughout history, focused the attention of the meeting on the public execution of only one man, accused of treason in fifteenth-century England. He was hanged until almost dead. He was revived. His abdomen was slit open.

The executioner pulled out a loop of his intestines. He dangled the loop before the man's face and burned it with a torch here and there. The loop was still attached to the rest of the man's insides. The executioner and his assistants tied a horse to each of his four limbs.

They whipped the horses, which ripped the man into four jagged pieces. These were hung on display from meathooks in a marketplace.

It had been agreed before the meeting was called to order that no one was to tell of terrible things grown-up human beings had done to children, according to Trout. Several delegates threatened to boycott the meeting if they were expected to sit still while listening to tales that sickening. What would be the point?

"What grownups had done to grownups left no doubt that the human race should be exterminated," said Trout. "Rehashing ad nauseam what grownups had done to children would be gilding the lily, so to speak."

Nitrogen wept about its involuntary servitude as parts of Nazi guards and physicians in death camps during World War Two. Potassium told hair-raising stories about the Spanish Inquisition, and Calcium about the Roman Games, and Oxygen about black African slavery.

Sodium said enough was enough, that any further testimony would be coals to Newcastle. It made a motion that all chemicals involved in medical research combine whenever possible to create ever more powerful antibiotics. These in turn would cause disease organisms to evolve new strains that were resistant to them.

In no time, Sodium predicted, every human ailment, including acne and jock itch, would be not only incurable but fatal. "All humans will die," said Sodium, according to Trout. "As they were at the birth of the Universe, all elements will be free of sin again."

Iron and Magnesium seconded Sodium's motion. Phosphorus called for a vote. The motion was passed by acclamation.

13

K ILGORE TROUT was right next door to the American Academy of Arts and Letters on Christmas Eve, 2000, when Zoltan Pepper said to his wife that people were now getting their heads handed to them with tweezers instead of on platters. Trout couldn't hear him. There was a thick masonry wall between them as the paraplegic composer ranted on about the seeming mania for making people compete with machines that were smarter than they were.

Pepper asked this rhetorical question: "Why is it so important that we all be humiliated, with such ingenuity and at such great expense? We never thought we were such hot stuff in the first place."

Trout was sitting on his cot in a shelter for homeless men that was once the Museum of the American Indian. Arguably the most prolific writer of short stories in history, he had been caught by the police in a sweep of the New York Public Library down at Fifth Avenue and Forty-second Street. He and about thirty others who had been living there, what Trout called "sacred cattle," were carted off in a black school bus and deposited in the shelter way-the-hell-and-gone up on West 155th Street.

The Museum of the American Indian had moved the detritus of overwhelmed aborigines, and dioramas of how they lived before the shit hit the fan, into a safer neighborhood downtown, five years before Trout arrived.

He was eighty-four years old now, having passed another milestone on November 11th, 2000. He would die on Labor Day, 2001, still eighty-four. But by then the timequake would have given him and all the rest of us an unexpected *bonus*, if you can call it that, of another ten years.

He would write of the rerun when it was over, in a never-to-be-finished memoir entitled *My Ten Years on Automatic Pilot*: "Listen, if it isn't a timequake dragging us through knothole after knothole, it's something else just as mean and powerful."

•

"This was a man," I said in *Timequake One*, "an only child, whose father, a college professor in Northampton, Massachusetts, murdered his mother when the man was only twelve years old."

I said Trout had been a hobo, throwing away his stories instead of offering them to publications, since the autumn of 1975. I said that was after he received news of the death of his own only child, Leon, a deserter from the United States Marine Corps. Leon, I said, was accidentally decapitated in a shipyard accident in Sweden, where he had been granted political asylum and was working as a welder.

I said Trout was fifty-nine when he hit the road, never to have a home again until he was given, when he was about to die, the Ernest Hemingway Suite at the Rhode Island writers' retreat called Xanadu.

When Trout checked into the former Museum of the American Indian, a former reminder of the most extensive and persistent genocide known to history, "The Sisters B-36" was burning a hole in his pocket, so to speak. He had finished the story at the Public Library downtown, but the police had taken him into custody before he could get rid of it.

So he kept his war-surplus Navy overcoat on when he told the clerk at the shelter that his name was Vincent van Gogh, and that he had no living relatives. Then he went outdoors again, and it was cold enough to freeze the balls off a brass monkey out there, and he put the manuscript into the lidless wire trash receptacle, which was chained and padlocked to a fire hydrant in front of the American Academy of Arts and Letters.

When he got back into the shelter, after an absence of ten minutes, the clerk said to him, "Where have you been? We all sure missed you, Vince." And he told him where his cot was. It was butted up against the companion wall between the shelter and the Academy.

On the Academy side of the wall, hanging over the rosewood desk of Monica Pepper, was a painting of a bleached cow's skull on a desert floor, by Georgia O'Keeffe. On Trout's side, right over the head of his cot, was a poster telling him never to stick his ding-dong into anything without first putting on a condom.

After the timequake hit, and then the rerun was finally over, and free will had kicked in again, Trout and Monica would get to know each other. Her desk, incidentally, had once belonged to the novelist Henry James. Her chair had once belonged to the composer and conductor Leonard Bernstein.

When Trout realized how close his cot had been to her desk during the fifty-one days before the timequake struck, he would remark as follows: "If I'd had a bazooka, I could have blown a hole in the wall between us. If I hadn't killed one or both of us, I could have asked you, 'What's a nice girl like you doing in a place like that?'"

14

A BUM on a cot next to Trout's at the shelter wished him a Merry Christmas. Trout replied, "Ting-a-ling! Ting-a-ling!"

It was only by chance that his reply was appropriate to the holiday, alluding, one might suppose, to the bells of Santa Claus's sleigh on a rooftop. But Trout would have said "Ting-a-ling" to anybody who offered him an empty greeting, such as "How's it goin'?" or "Nice day" or whatever, no matter what the season.

Depending on his body language and tone of voice and social circumstances, he could indeed make it mean "And a merry Christmas to you, too." But it would also mean, like the Hawaiian's *aloha*, "Hello" or "Good-bye." The old science fiction writer could make it mean "Please" or "Thanks" as well, or "Yes" or "No," or "I couldn't agree with you more," or "If your brains were dynamite, there wouldn't be enough to blow your hat off."

I asked him at Xanadu in the summer of 2001 how "Ting-a-ling" had become such a frequent *appoggiatura*, or grace note, in his conversations. He gave me what would later turn out to have been a superficial explanation. "It was something I crowed during the war," he said, "when an artillery barrage I'd called for landed right on target: 'Ting-a-ling! Ting-a-ling!'"

About an hour later, and this was on the afternoon before the clambake, he beckoned me into his suite with a crooked finger. He closed the door behind us. "You really want to know about 'Ting-a-ling'?" he asked me.

I had been satisfied with his first account. Trout was the one who wanted me to hear much more. My innocent question earlier had triggered memories of his ghastly childhood in Northampton. He could exorcise them only by telling what they were.

"My father murdered my mother," said Kilgore Trout, "when I was twelve years old."

•

524

"Her body was in our basement," said Trout, "but all I knew was that she had disappeared. Father swore he had no idea what had become of her. He said, as wife-murderers often do, that maybe she had gone to visit relatives. He killed her that morning, after I left for school.

"He got supper for the two of us that night. Father said he would report her as a missing person to the police the next morning, if we hadn't heard from her by then. He said, 'She has been very tired and nervous lately. Have you noticed that?' "

"He was insane," said Trout. "How insane? He came into my bedroom at midnight. He woke me up. He said he had something important to tell me. It was nothing but a dirty joke, but this poor, sick man had come to believe it a parable about the awful blows that life had dealt him. It was about a fugitive who sought shelter from the police in the home of a woman he knew.

"Her living room had a cathedral ceiling, which is to say it went all the way up to the roof peak, with rustic rafters spanning the air space below." Trout paused. It was as though he were as caught up in the tale as his father must have been.

He went on, there in the suite named in honor of the suicide Ernest Hemingway: "She was a widow, and he stripped himself naked while she went to fetch some of her husband's clothes. But before he could put them on, the police were hammering on the front door with their billy clubs. So the fugitive hid on top of a rafter. When the woman let in the police, though, his oversize testicles hung down in full view."

Trout paused again.

"The police asked the woman where the guy was. The woman said she didn't know what guy they were talking about," said Trout. "One of the cops saw the testicles hanging down from a rafter and asked what they were. She said they were Chinese temple bells. He believed her. He said he'd always wanted to hear Chinese temple bells.

"He gave them a whack with his billy club, but there was no sound. So he hit them again, a lot harder, a whole lot harder. Do you know what the guy on the rafter shrieked?" Trout asked me.

I said I didn't.

"He shrieked, 'TING-A-LING, YOU SON OF A BITCH!' "

15

T HE ACADEMY should have moved its staff and treasures to a safer neighborhood when the Museum of the American Indian did so with its genocide mementos. It was still stuck way-the-hell-and-gone uptown, amid nothing but people with lives not worth living for miles in every direction, because its dwindling and demoralized membership couldn't bestir itself to OK a move.

To be perfectly frank, the only people who cared what became of the Academy were its staff, office workers, cleaning and maintenance people, and armed guards. Nor were most of them enraptured by old-fashioned art practices. They needed the jobs, no matter how pointless the work might be, and so were reminiscent of people during the Great Depression of the 1930s, who celebrated when they got any kind of work at all.

Trout characterized the sort of work he was able to get back then as "cleaning birdshit out of cuckoo clocks."

The Academy's Executive Secretary certainly needed the work. Monica Pepper, who looked so much like my sister Allie, was the sole support of herself and her husband Zoltan, whom she had rendered hors de combat with a swan dive. So she had fortified the building by replacing the wooden front door with half-inch steel armorplate, fitted with a *whoozit*, or peephole, which could also be closed and locked.

She had done all she could to make the place look as abandoned and looted as the ruins of Columbia University two miles to the south. The windows, like the front door, were shuttered with steel, and the shutters were concealed in turn by rough plywood painted black and camouflaged with graffiti, which ran continuously across the whole façade. The staff had done the garish artwork. Monica herself had spray-painted "FUCK ART!" in orange and purple across the steel front door.

It so happened that an African-American armed guard named Dudley Prince was looking out through that door's *whoozit* when Trout put "The Sisters B-36" in the trash receptacle out front. Bums interacting with the receptacle were no novelty, God knows, but Trout, whom Prince mistook for a bag lady rather than a bag gentleman, put on an unusual show out there.

Here's the thing about Trout's appearance from a distance: Instead of trousers, he wore three layers of thermal underwear, revealing the shapes of his calves below the hem of his unisex war-surplus Navy overcoat. Yes, and he wore sandals rather than boots, another seemingly feminine touch, as was his babushka, fashioned from a crib blanket printed with red balloons and blue teddy bears.

Trout was out there talking to and gesturing at the lidless wire basket as though it were an editor in an old-fashioned book-publishing house, and as though his four-page hand-written yellow manuscript were a great novel, sure to sell like hotcakes. He wasn't remotely crazy. He would later say of his performance: "It was the world that had suffered the nervous breakdown. I was just having fun in a nightmare, arguing with an imaginary editor about the advertising budget, and about who should play whom in the movie, and personal appearances on TV shows and so on, perfectly harmless funny stuff."

His behavior was so outré that a genuine bag lady passing by asked him, "Are you OK, honey?"

To which Trout replied with all possible gusto, "Ting-a-ling! Ting-a-ling!"

When Trout returned to the shelter, though, the armed guard Dudley Prince unbolted the steel front door and, motivated by boredom and curiosity, retrieved the manuscript. He wanted to know what it was a bag lady, with every reason to commit suicide, one would think, had deep-sixed so ecstatically.

16

H ERE, for whatever it may be worth, and from *Timequake One*, is Kilgore Trout's explanation of the timequake and its aftershocks, the rerun, excerpted from his unfinished memoir *My Ten Years on Automatic Pilot*:

"The timequake of 2001 was a cosmic charley horse in the sinews of Destiny. At what was in New York City 2:27 P.M. on February 13th of that year, the Universe suffered a crisis in self-confidence. Should it go on expanding indefinitely? What was the point?

"It fibrillated with indecision. Maybe it should have a family reunion back where it all began, and then make a great big BANG again.

"It suddenly shrunk ten years. It zapped me and everybody else back to February 17th, 1991, what was for me 7:51 A.M., and a line outside a blood bank in San Diego, California.

"For reasons best known to itself, though, the Universe canceled the family reunion, for the nonce at least. It resumed expansion. Which faction, if any, cast the deciding votes on whether to expand or shrink, I cannot say. Despite my having lived for eighty-four years, or ninety-four, if you want to count the rerun, many questions about the Universe remain for me unanswered.

"That the rerun lasted ten years, short a mere four days, some are saying now, is proof that there is a God, and that He is on the Decimal System. He has ten fingers and ten toes, just as we do, they say, and uses them when He does arithmetic.

"I have my doubts. I can't help it. That's the way I am. Even if my father, the ornithologist Professor Raymond Trout of Smith College in Northampton, Massachusetts, hadn't murdered my mother, a housewife and poet, I believe I would have been that way. Then again, I have never made a serious study of the different religions, and so am unqualified to comment. About all I know for certain is that devout Muslims do not believe in Santa Claus."

On the first of the two Christmas Eves, 2000, the still religious African-American armed guard Dudley Prince thought

Trout's "The Sisters B-36" just might be a message for the Academy from God Himself. What happened to the planet Booboo, after all, wasn't a whole lot different from what seemed to be happening to his own planet, and especially to his employers, what was left of the American Academy of Arts and Letters, way-the-hell-and-gone up on West 155th Street, two doors west of Broadway.

Trout got to know Prince, just as he got to know Monica Pepper and me, after the rerun ended and free will had kicked in again. Because of what the timequake had done to Prince, he had become as contemptuous of the idea of a wise and just God as my sister Allie had been. Allie opined one time, not just about her life but everybody's life, "If there is a God, He sure hates people. That's all I can say."

When Trout heard about how seriously Prince had taken "The Sisters B-36" on the first Christmas Eve, 2000, about how Prince believed a bag lady had put on such a show while throwing the yellow manuscript pages away to ensure that Prince would wonder what they were and retrieve them, the old science fiction writer commented: "Perfectly understandable, Dudley. For anybody who could believe in God, as you once did, it would be a piece of cake to believe in the planet Booboo."

Get a load of what was going to happen to Dudley Prince, a monumental figure of authority and decency in the uniform of the security company that protected the beleaguered Academy around the clock, a holstered pistol at his hip, only fifty-one days from the first of the two Christmas Eves, 2000: The timequake was going to zap him back into a solitary confinement cell, into *the hole*, within the walls and towers of the New York State Maximum Security Adult Correctional Facility at Athena, sixty miles south of his hometown of Rochester, where he used to own a little video rental store.

To be sure, the timequake had made him ten years younger, but that was no break in his case. It meant he was again serving two consecutive life sentences, without hope of parole, for the rape and murder of a ten-year-old girl of Chinese-American and Italian-American parentage, Kimberly Wang, in a Rochester crack house, of which he was entirely innocent!

•

Granted, at the start of the rerun Dudley Prince could remember, as could the rest of us, everything that was going to happen to him during the next ten years. He knew that in seven years he would be exonerated by DNA tests of dried ejaculate material on the victim's panties. This exculpatory evidence would again be found languishing in a glassine envelope in the walk-in vault of the District Attorney who had framed him in the hopes of being nominated for Governor.

And, oh yes, that same DA would be found wearing cement overshoes on the bottom of Lake Cayuga in just six more years. Prince meanwhile was going to have to earn a High School Equivalency Certificate again, and make Jesus the center of his life again, and on and on.

And then, after he was sprung again, he would have to go on TV talk shows again with other people who had been wrongly incarcerated and then rightly exonerated, to say prison was the luckiest thing that ever happened to him because he found Jesus there.

17

O N EITHER ONE of the two Christmas Eves, 2000, and it didn't matter which, except for people's opinions of what was going on, the ex-jailbird Dudley Prince delivered "The Sisters B-36" to Monica Pepper's office. Her husband Zoltan in his wheelchair was predicting the end of literacy in the not-too-distant future.

"The prophet Mohammed couldn't do it," Zoltan was saying. "Jesus, Mary, and Joseph probably couldn't do it, Mary Magdalen couldn't do it. The Emperor Charlemagne confessed he couldn't do it. It was just too hard! Nobody in the whole Western Hemisphere could do it, not even the sophisticated Mayas and Incas and Aztecs could imagine how to do it, until the Europeans came.

"Most Europeans back then couldn't read and write, either. The few who could were specialists. I promise you, sweetheart, thanks to TV that will very soon be the case again."

And then Dudley Prince said, rerun or not, "Excuse me, but I think maybe somebody is trying to tell us something."

Monica read "The Sisters B-36" quickly, with increasing impatience, and declared it ridiculous. She handed it to her husband. But he got no further than the name of the author before he became electrified. "My God, my God," he exclaimed, "after a quarter of a century of perfect silence, Kilgore Trout has come into my life again!"

Here's the explanation of Zoltan Pepper's reaction: When Zoltan was a high school sophomore in Fort Lauderdale, Florida, he copied a story from one of his father's collection of old science fiction magazines. He submitted it to his English teacher, Mrs. Florence Wilkerson, as his own creation. It was one of the last stories Kilgore Trout would ever submit to a publisher. By the time Zoltan was a sophomore, Trout was a bum.

The plagiarized story was about a planet in another galaxy, where the little green people, each with only one eye in the middle of his or her forehead, could get food only if they could sell goods or services to somebody else. The planet ran out of customers, and nobody could think of anything sensible to do about that. All the little green people starved to death.

Mrs. Wilkerson suspected plagiarism. Zoltan confessed, thinking it was a funny rather than a serious thing he'd done. To him, plagiarism was what Trout would have called a *mopery*, "indecent exposure in the presence of a blind person of the same sex."

Mrs. Wilkerson decided to teach Zoltan a lesson. She had him write, "I STOLE PROPERTY FROM KILGORE TROUT," on the blackboard while the class watched. Then, for the next week, she made him wear a shirt cardboard with the letter P on it, hung on his chest from around his neck, whenever he was in her classroom. She could get the piss sued out of her for doing that to a student nowadays. But then was then, and now is now.

The inspiration for what Mrs. Wilkerson did to young Zoltan Pepper was of course *The Scarlet Letter* by Nathaniel Hawthorne. In that one, a woman has to wear a big A for *adultery* on her bosom because she let a man not her husband ejaculate in her birth canal. She won't tell what his name is. He's a *preacher*!

Since Dudley Prince said it was a bag lady who had put the story in the trash receptacle out front, Zoltan didn't consider the possibility that it had been Trout himself. "It could have been his daughter or granddaughter," he speculated. "Trout himself must have died years ago. I certainly hope so, and may his soul rot in Hell."

But Trout was right next door! He was feeling just great! He was so relieved at having gotten rid of "The Sisters B-36" that he had started another story. He had been completing a story every ten days, on average, since he was fourteen. That was thirty-six a year, say. This one could have been his twenty-five-hundredth! It wasn't set on another planet. It was set in the office of a psychiatrist in St. Paul, Minnesota.

The name of the shrink was the name of the story, too, which was "Dr. Schadenfreude." This doctor had his patients lie on a couch and talk, all right, but they could ramble on only about dumb or crazy things that had happened to total strangers in supermarket tabloids or on TV talk shows.

If a patient accidentally said "I" or "me" or "my" or "myself" or "mine," Dr. Schadenfreude went ape. He leapt out of his overstuffed leather chair. He stamped his feet. He flapped his arms.

He put his livid face directly over the patient. He snarled and barked things like this: "When will you ever learn that nobody cares anything about you, you, you, you boring, insignificant piece of poop? Your whole problem is you think you *matter*! Get over that, or sashay your stuck-up butt the hell out of here!"

18

A BUM on a cot next to Trout's asked him what he was writing. It was the opening paragraph of "Dr. Schadenfreude." Trout said it was a story. The bum said maybe Trout could get some money from the people next door. When Trout heard it was the American Academy of Arts and Letters next door, he said, "It might as well be a Chinese barber college as far as I'm concerned. I don't write literature. Literature is all those la-di-da monkeys next door care about.

"Those artsy-fartsy twerps next door create living, breathing, three-dimensional characters with ink on paper," he went on. "Wonderful! As though the planet weren't already dying because it has three billion too many living, breathing, three-dimensional characters!"

The only people next door, actually, of course, were Monica and Zoltan Pepper, and the three-man day shift of armed guards, headed by Dudley Prince. Monica had given her office and janitorial staffs the day off for last-minute Christmas shopping. As it happened, they were all Christian or agnostic or apostate.

The night shift of armed guards would be entirely Muslim. As Trout would write at Xanadu, in *My Ten Years on Automatic Pilot*: "Muslims do not believe in Santa Claus."

"In my entire career as a writer," said Trout in the former Museum of the American Indian, "I created only one living, breathing, three-dimensional character. I did it with my ding-dong in a birth canal. Ting-a-ling!" He was referring to his son Leon, the deserter from the United States Marines in time of war, subsequently decapitated in a Swedish shipyard.

"If I'd wasted my time creating characters," Trout said, "I would never have gotten around to calling attention to things that really matter: irresistible forces in nature, and cruel inventions, and cockamamie ideals and governments and economies that make heroes and heroines alike feel like something the cat drug in."

•

Trout might have said, and it can be said of me as well, that he created *caricatures* rather than characters. His animus against so-called *mainstream literature*, moreover, wasn't peculiar to him. It was generic among writers of science fiction.

19

S TRICTLY SPEAKING, many of Trout's stories, except for
their unbelievable characters, weren't science fiction at all.
"Dr. Schadenfreude" wasn't, unless one is humorless enough
to regard psychiatry as a science. The one he deposited in the
Academy's trash receptacle after "Dr. Schadenfreude," with the
timequake drawing ever nearer, "Bunker Bingo Party," was a
roman à clef.

That one was set in Adolf Hitler's commodious bombproof
bunker underneath the ruins of Berlin, Germany, at the end of
World War Two in Europe. In that story, Trout calls his war,
and my war, also, "Western Civilization's second unsuccessful
attempt to commit suicide." He did that in conversations, too,
one time adding in my presence, "If at first you don't succeed,
try, try, please try again."

Tanks and infantry of the Soviet Union are only a few hundred yards away from the bunker's iron door up at street level.
"Hitler, trapped below, the most loathsome human being who
ever lived," wrote Trout, "doesn't know whether to shit or go
blind. He is down there with his mistress Eva Braun and a few
close friends, including Joseph Goebbels, his Minister of Propaganda, and Goebbels's wife and kids."

For want of anything else remotely decisive to do, Hitler
proposes marriage to Eva. She accepts!

At this point in the story, Trout asked this rhetorical question, an aside with a paragraph all to itself:

"What the heck?"

Everybody forgets his or her troubles during the marriage
ceremony. After the groom kisses the bride, though, the party
goes flat again. "Goebbels has a clubfoot," Trout wrote. "But
Goebbels has always had a clubfoot. That is not the problem."

Goebbels remembers that his kids have brought the game
of Bingo with them. It was captured intact from American
troops during the Battle of the Bulge some four months earlier.
I myself was captured intact during that battle. Germany, in
order to conserve its resources, has stopped making its own

Bingo games. Because of that, and because the grownups in the bunker have been so busy during the rise of Hitler, and now his fall, the Goebbels kids are the only ones who know how the game is played. They learned from a neighbor kid, whose family owned a prewar Bingo set.

There is this amazing scene in the story: A boy and a girl, explaining the rules of Bingo, become the center of the Universe for Nazis in full regalia, including a gaga Adolf Hitler.

That we have a copy of "Bunker Bingo Party," and copies of the four other stories Trout threw away in front of the Academy before the timequake hit, is due to Dudley Prince. The first time through, when the decade was original material, he continued to believe, as Monica Pepper did not, that a bag lady was using the trash receptacle for a mailbox, knowing he would be watching her crazy dances through the *whoozit* in the steel front door.

Prince retrieved each story and pondered it, hoping to discover some important message from a higher power encoded therein. After work, rerun or not, this was a lonely African-American.

20

IN THE SUMMER of 2001 at Xanadu, Dudley Prince handed
Trout the sheaf of stories, which Trout had expected the
Department of Sanitation to incinerate or bury or drop in
the ocean far offshore before anyone other than himself had
read them. By his own account to me, Trout riffled through
the scruffy pages with distaste, while seated tailor-fashion and
naked on his king-size bed in the Ernest Hemingway Suite. The
day was hot. He was fresh from his Jacuzzi.

But then his gaze fell upon the scene in which two anti-Semitic
children teach Bingo to high-ranking Nazis in their madly theatrical uniforms. In amazed admiration for something brilliant
he himself had written, and Trout had never thought of himself
as worth a hill of beans as a writer, he praised the scene as an
echo of this prophecy from the Book of Isaiah:

"The wolf also shall dwell with the lamb, and the leopard
shall lie down with the kid; and the calf and the young lion and
the fatling together; and a little child shall lead them."

A *fatling* is any young animal fattened for slaughter.

"I read that scene," Trout told me and Monica, "and I asked
myself, 'How the hell did I *do* that?'"

That wasn't the first time I'd heard a person who had done a
remarkable piece of work ask that delightful question. Back in
the 1960s, long, long before the timequake, I had a great big old
house in Barnstable Village on Cape Cod, where my first wife,
Jane Marie Vonnegut, née Cox, and I were raising four boys
and two girls. The ell where I did my writing was falling down.

I had it pulled all the way down and hauled away. I hired my
friend Ted Adler, a skilled man-of-all-work my age, to build
me a new one like the old one. Ted alone built the forms for
the footings. Ted supervised the pouring of concrete from a
ready-mix truck. He personally laid concrete blocks atop the
footings. He framed the superstructure, put on the sheathing
and siding, and shingled the roof and wired the place. He hung

the windows and doors. He nailed up and jointed the Sheetrock inside.

The Sheetrock was the last step. I myself would do the exterior and interior painting. I told Ted I wanted to do at least that much, or he would have done that, too. When he himself had finished, and he had taken all the scraps I didn't want for kindling to the dump, he had me stand next to him outside and look at my new ell from thirty feet away.

And then he asked it: "How the hell did I *do* that?"

That question remains for me in the summer of 1996 one of my three favorite quotations. Two of the three are questions rather than good advice of any kind. The second is Jesus Christ's "Who is it they say I am?"

The third is from my son Mark, pediatrician and watercolorist and sax player. I've already quoted him in another book: "We are here to help each other get through this thing, whatever it is."

One might protest, "My dear Dr. Vonnegut, we can't all be pediatricians."

In "Bunker Bingo Party," the Nazis participate in Bingo, with the Minister of Propaganda, arguably the most effective communicator in history, calling out the coordinates of winning or losing squares on the players' cards. The game proves as analgesic for war criminals in deep doodoo as it continues to be for harmless old biddies at church fairs.

Several of the war criminals wear an Iron Cross, awarded only to Germans who have demonstrated battlefield fearlessness so excessive as to be classifiable as psychopathic. Hitler wears one. He won it as a corporal in Western Civilization's first unsuccessful attempt to commit suicide.

I was a PFC during the second botched effort to end it all. Like Ernest Hemingway, I never shot a human being. Maybe Hitler never did that big trick, either. He didn't get his country's highest decoration for killing a lot of people. He got it for being such a brave messenger. Not everybody on a battlefield is supposed to concentrate on nothing but killing. I myself was an intelligence and reconnaissance scout, going places our side hadn't occupied, looking for enemies. I wasn't supposed to fight them if I found them. I was supposed to stay unnoticed and alive, so I could tell my superiors where they were, and what it looked like they were doing.

It was wintertime, and I myself was awarded my country's second-lowest decoration, a Purple Heart for frostbite.

When I got home from my war, my uncle Dan clapped me on the back, and he bellowed, "You're a *man* now!"

I damn near killed my first German.

To return to Trout's roman à clef: As though there were a God in Heaven after all, it is Der Führer who shouts "BINGO!" Adolf Hitler wins! He says incredulously, in German, of course, "I can't believe it. I've never played this game before, and yet I've won, I've *won*! What can this be but a miracle?" He is a Roman Catholic.

He rises from his chair at the table. His eyes are still fixed on the winning card before him, according to Trout, "as if it were a shred from the Shroud of Turin." This prick asks, "What can this mean but that things aren't as bad as we thought they were?"

Eva Braun spoils the moment by swallowing a capsule of cyanide. Goebbels's wife gave it to her for a wedding present. Frau Goebbels had more capsules than she needed for her immediate family. Trout wrote of Eva Braun, "Her only crime was to have allowed a monster to ejaculate in her birth canal. These things happen to the best of women."

A Communistic 240-millimeter howitzer shell explodes atop the bunker. Flakes of calcimine from the shaken ceiling shower down on the deafened occupants. Hitler himself makes a joke, demonstrating that he still has his sense of humor. "It snows," he says. That is a poetic way of saying, too, it is high time he killed himself, unless he wants to become a caged superstar in a traveling freak show, along with the bearded lady and the geek.

He puts a pistol to his head. Everybody says, "*Nein, nein, nein.*" He convinces everyone that shooting himself is the dignified thing to do. What should his last words be? He says, "How about 'I regret nothing'?"

Goebbels replies that such a statement would be appropriate, but that the Parisian cabaret performer Edith Piaf has made a worldwide reputation by singing those same words in French for decades. "Her sobriquet," says Goebbels, "is 'Little Sparrow.' You don't want to be remembered as a little sparrow, or I miss my guess."

Hitler still hasn't lost his sense of humor. He says, "How about 'BINGO'?"

But he is tired. He puts the pistol to his head again. He says, "I never asked to be born in the first place."

The pistol goes "BANG!"

21

I AM Honorary President of the American Humanist Association, whose headquarters in Amherst, New York, I have never seen. I succeeded the late author and biochemist Dr. Isaac Asimov in that functionless capacity. That we have an organization, a boring business, is to let others know we are numerous. We would prefer to live our lives as Humanists and not talk about it, or think more about it than we think about breathing.

Humanists try to behave decently and honorably without any expectation of rewards or punishments in an afterlife. The creator of the Universe has been to us unknowable so far. We serve as well as we can the highest abstraction of which we have some understanding, which is our community.

Are we enemies of members of organized religions? No. My great war buddy Bernard V. O'Hare, now dead, lost his faith as a Roman Catholic during World War Two. I didn't like that. I thought that was too much to lose.

I had never had faith like that, because I had been raised by interesting and moral people who, like Thomas Jefferson and Benjamin Franklin, were nonetheless skeptics about what preachers said was going on. But I knew Bernie had lost something important and honorable.

Again, I did not like that, did not like it because I liked *him* so much.

I spoke at a Humanist Association memorial service for Dr. Asimov a few years back. I said, "Isaac is up in Heaven now." That was the funniest thing I could have said to an audience of Humanists. I rolled them in the aisles. The room was like the court-martial scene in Trout's "No Laughing Matter," right before the floor of the Pacific Ocean swallowed up the third atomic bomb and *Joy's Pride* and all the rest of it.

When I myself am dead, God forbid, I hope some wag will say about me, "He's up in Heaven now."

•

I like to sleep. I published a new requiem for old music in another book, in which I said it was no bad thing to want sleep for everyone as an afterlife.

I see no need up in the sky for more torture chambers and Bingo games.

Yesterday, Wednesday, July 3rd, 1996, I received a well-written letter from a man who never asked to be born in the first place, and who has been a captive of our nonpareil correctional facilities, first as a juvenile offender and then as an adult offender, for many years. He is about to be released into a world where he has no friends or relatives. Free will is about to kick in again, after a hiatus of a good deal more than a decade. What should he do?

I, Honorary President of the American Humanist Association, wrote back today, "Join a church." I said this because what such a grown-up waif needs more than anything is something like a family.

I couldn't recommend Humanism for such a person. I wouldn't do so for the great majority of the planet's population.

The German philosopher Friedrich Wilhelm Nietzsche, who had syphilis, said that only a person of deep faith could afford the luxury of religious skepticism. Humanists, by and large educated, comfortably middle-class persons with rewarding lives like mine, find rapture enough in secular knowledge and hope. Most people can't.

Voltaire, French author of *Candide*, and therefore the Humanists' Abraham, concealed his contempt for the hierarchy of the Roman Catholic Church from his less educated, simpler-minded, and more frightened employees, because he knew what a stabilizer their religion was for them.

With some trepidation, I told Trout in the summer of 2001 about my advice to the man soon to be expelled from prison. He asked if I had heard from this person again, if I knew what had become of him in the intervening five years, or in the intervening ten years, if we wanted to count the rerun. I hadn't and didn't.

He asked if I myself had ever tried to join a church, just for the hell of it, to find out what that was like. *He* had. The closest I ever came to that, I said, was when my second-wife-to-be, Jill Krementz, and I thought it would be cute, and also ritzy, to be married in the Little Church Around the Corner, a Disneyesque Episcopal house of worship on East Twenty-ninth Street off Fifth Avenue in Manhattan.

"When they found out I was a divorced person," I said, "they prescribed all sorts of penitent services I was to perform before I was clean enough to be married there."

"There you are," said Trout. "Imagine all the chickenshit you'd have to go through if you were an ex-con. And if that poor son of a bitch who wrote you really did find a church to accept him, he could easily be back in prison."

"For what?" I said. "For robbing the poor box?"

"No," said Trout, "for delighting Jesus Christ by shooting dead a doctor coming to work in an abortion mill."

22

I FORGET what I was doing on the afternoon of February 13th, 2001, when the timequake struck. It couldn't have been much. I sure as heck wasn't writing another book. I was seventy-eight, for heaven's sakes! My daughter Lily was eighteen!

Old Kilgore Trout was still writing, though. Seated on his cot at the shelter, where everybody thought his name was Vincent van Gogh, he had just begun a story about a working-class Londoner, Albert Hardy, also the name of the story. Albert Hardy was born in 1896, with his head between his legs, and his genitalia sprouting out of the top of his neck, which looked "like a zucchini."

Albert's parents taught him to walk on his hands and eat with his feet. That was so they could conceal his private parts with trousers. The private parts weren't excessively large like the testicles of the fugitive in Trout's father's Ting-a-ling parable. That wasn't the point.

Monica Pepper was at her desk next door, only feet away, but they still hadn't met. She and Dudley Prince and her husband still believed the depositor of stories in the trash receptacle out front was an old woman, so she couldn't possibly live next door. Their best guess was that she came from the shelter for battered old people over on Convent Avenue, or the detox center in the parish house down at the Cathedral of Saint John the Divine, which was unisex.

Monica's own home, and Zoltan's, was an apartment down in Turtle Bay, a safe neighborhood seven miles away, comfortingly close to the United Nations. She came and went from work in her own chauffeur-driven limousine, which was modified to accommodate Zoltan's wheelchair. The Academy was fabulously well-to-do. Money was not a problem. Thanks to lavish gifts from old-fashioned art lovers in the past, it was richer than several members of the United Nations, including, surely, Mali, Swaziland, and Luxembourg.

Zoltan had the limo that afternoon. He was on his way to pick up Monica. She was awaiting Zoltan's arrival when the timequake struck. He would get as far as ringing the Academy doorbell before he was zapped back to February 17th, 1991. He would be ten years younger and *whole* again!

Talk about getting a reaction from a doorbell!

When the rerun was over, though, and free will kicked in again, everybody and everything were exactly where they had been when the timequake struck. So Zoltan was paraplegic again in a wheelchair, ringing the doorbell again. He didn't realize that it was all of a sudden up to him to decide what his finger was going to do next. His finger, for want of instructions from him or anything else, went on ringing and ringing the doorbell.

That's what it was doing when Zoltan was smacked by a runaway fire truck. The driver of the truck hadn't realized yet that it was up to him to *steer* the thing.

As Trout wrote in *My Ten Years on Automatic Pilot*: "It was free will that did all the damage. The timequake and its aftershocks didn't snap as much as a single strand in a spider's web, unless some other force had snapped that strand the first time through."

Monica was working on the budget for Xanadu when the timequake struck. The endowment of that writers' retreat up in Point Zion, Rhode Island, the Julius King Bowen Foundation, was administered by the Academy. Julius King Bowen, who died before Monica was born, was a never-married white man who made a fortune during the 1920s and early 1930s with stories and lectures about the hilarious, but touching, too, efforts by American black people to imitate successful American white people, so they could be successful, too.

A cast-iron historical marker on the border between Point Zion's public beach and Xanadu said the mansion had been Bowen's home and place of work from 1922 until his death in 1936. It said President Warren G. Harding had proclaimed Bowen "Laughter Laureate of the United States, Master of Darky Dialects, and Heir to the Crown of King of Humor Once Worn by Mark Twain."

•

As Trout would point out to me when I read that marker in
2001: "Warren G. Harding sired an illegitimate daughter by
ejaculating in the birth canal of a stenographer in a broom closet
at the White House."

23

WHEN TROUT was zapped back to a line outside a blood bank in San Diego, California, in 1991, he could remember how his story about the guy with his head between his legs and his ding-dong atop his neck, "Albert Hardy," would end. But he couldn't write that finale for ten years, until free will kicked in again. Albert Hardy would be blown to pieces while a soldier in the Second Battle of the Somme in World War One.

Albert Hardy's dogtags wouldn't be found. His body parts would be reassembled as though he had been like everybody else, with his head atop his neck. He couldn't be given back his ding-dong. To be perfectly frank, his ding-dong wouldn't have been what you might call the subject of an exhaustive search.

Albert Hardy would be buried under an Eternal Flame in France, in the Tomb of the Unknown Soldier, "normal at last."

I myself was zapped back to this house near the tip of Long Island, New York, where I am writing now, halfway through the rerun. In 1991, as now, I was gazing at a list of all I'd published, and wondering, "How the hell did I *do* that?"

I was feeling as I feel now, like whalers Herman Melville described, who didn't talk anymore. They had said absolutely everything they could ever say.

I told Trout in 2001 about a redheaded boyhood friend of mine, David Craig, now a builder in New Orleans, Louisiana, who won a Bronze Star in our war for knocking out a German tank in Normandy. He and a buddy came upon this steel monster parked all alone in a woods. Its engine wasn't running. There wasn't anybody outside. A radio was playing popular music inside.

Dave and his buddy fetched a bazooka. When they got back, the tank was still there. A radio was still playing music inside. They shot the tank with the bazooka. Germans didn't pop out of the turret. The radio stopped playing. That was all. That was it.

Dave and his buddy skedaddled away from there.

Trout said it sounded to him as though my boyhood friend's Bronze Star was well deserved. "He almost certainly killed people as well as a radio," he said, "thus sparing them years of disappointments and tedium in civilian life. He made it possible for them, to quote the English poet A. E. Housman, to 'die in their glory and never be old.'"

Trout paused, secured his upper plate with his left thumb, and then went on: "I could have written a best-seller, if I'd had the patience to create three-dimensional characters. The Bible may be the Greatest Story Ever Told, but the most popular story you can ever tell is about a good-looking couple having a really swell time copulating outside wedlock, and having to quit for one reason or another while doing it is still a novelty."

I was reminded of Steve Adams, one of my sister Allie's three sons my first wife Jane and I adopted after Allie's unlucky husband Jim died in a railroad train that went off an open drawbridge in New Jersey, and then, two days later, Allie died of cancer of the everything.

When Steve came home to Cape Cod for Christmas vacation from his freshman year at Dartmouth, he was close to tears because he had just read, having been forced to do so by a professor, *A Farewell to Arms*, by Ernest Hemingway.

Steve, now a middle-aged comedy writer for movies and TV, was so gorgeously wrecked back then that I was moved to reread what it was that had done this to him. *A Farewell to Arms* turned out to be an attack on the institution of marriage. Hemingway's hero is wounded in war. He and his nurse fall in love. They honeymoon far away from the battlefields, consuming the best food and wine, without having been married first. She gets pregnant, proving, as if it could be doubted, that he is indeed all man.

She and the baby die, so he doesn't have to get a regular job and a house and life insurance and all that crap, and he has such beautiful memories.

I said to Steve, "The tears Hemingway has made you want to shed are tears of *relief*! It looked like the guy was going to have to get married and settle down. But then he didn't have to. Whew! What a close shave!"

Trout said he could think of only one other book that despised matrimony as much as *A Farewell to Arms.*

"Name it," I said.

He said it was a book by Henry David Thoreau, called *Walden.*

"Loved it," I said.

24

I SAY IN LECTURES in 1996 that fifty percent or more of American marriages go bust because most of us no longer have extended families. When you marry somebody now, all you get is one person.

I say that when couples fight, it isn't about money or sex or power. What they're really saying is, "You're not enough people!"

Sigmund Freud said he didn't know what women wanted. I know what women want. They want a whole lot of people to talk to.

I thank Trout for the concept of the *man-woman hour* as a unit of measurement of marital intimacy. This is an hour during which a husband and wife are close enough to be aware of each other, and for one to say something to the other without yelling, if he or she feels like it. Trout says in his story "Golden Wedding" that they needn't feel like saying anything in order to credit themselves with a man-woman hour.

"Golden Wedding" is another story Dudley Prince rescued from the trash receptacle before the timequake. It is about a florist who tries to increase his business by convincing people who both work at home, or who spend long hours together running a Ma-and-Pa joint, that they are entitled to celebrate several wedding anniversaries a year.

He calculates that an average couple with separate places of work logs four man-woman hours each weekday, and sixteen of them on weekends. Being sound asleep with each other doesn't count. This gives him a standard *man-woman week* of thirty-six man-woman hours.

He multiplies that by fifty-two. This gives him, when rounded off, a standard *man-woman year* of eighteen hundred man-woman hours. He advertises that any couple that has accumulated this many man-woman hours is entitled to celebrate an anniversary, and to receive flowers and appropriate presents, even if it took them only twenty weeks to do it!

If couples keep piling up man-woman hours like that, as my wives and I have done in both my marriages, they can easily celebrate their Ruby Anniversary in only twenty years, and their Golden in twenty-five!

I do not propose to discuss my love life. I will say that I still can't get over how women are shaped, and that I will go to my grave wanting to pet their butts and boobs. I will say, too, that lovemaking, if sincere, is one of the best ideas Satan put in the apple she gave to the serpent to give to Eve. The best idea in that apple, though, is making jazz.

25

ALLIE'S HUSBAND Jim Adams really did go off an open drawbridge in a railroad train two days before Allie died in a hospital. Stranger than fiction!

Jim had plunged them deep in debt by manufacturing a toy of his own invention. It was a corked rubber balloon with a blob of permanently malleable clay inside. It was clay with a skin! The face of a clown was printed on the balloon. You could make it open its mouth wide with your fingers, or make its nose protrude or its eyes sink in. Jim called it Putty Puss. Putty Puss never became popular. Moreover, Putty Puss amassed enormous debts for its manufacture and advertising.

Allie and Jim, Indianapolis people in New Jersey, had four boys and no girls. One of the boys was a mewling infant, and none of these people had asked to be born in the first place.

Boys and girls of our family often come into this world, as did Allie, with natural gifts for drawing and painting and sculpting and so on. Jane's and my two daughters, Edith and Nanette, are middle-aged professional artists who have shows and sell pictures. So does our son the doctor Mark. So do I. Allie could have done that, too, if she had been willing to work hard and hustle some. But as I have reported elsewhere, she said, "Just because you're talented, that doesn't mean you have to *do* something with it."

I say in my novel *Bluebeard*, "Beware of gods bearing gifts." I think I had Allie in mind when I wrote that, and Allie in mind again when, in *Timequake One*, I had Monica Pepper spray-paint "FUCK ART!" in orange and purple across the steel front door of the Academy. Allie didn't know there was such an institution as the Academy, I'm almost sure, but she would have been happy to see those words emblazoned anywhere.

Our father the architect was so full of ecstatic baloney about any work of art Allie made when she was growing up, as though she were the new Michelangelo, that she was shamed. She wasn't stupid and she wasn't tasteless. Father, without meaning to do so, rubbed her nose in how limited her gifts were, and so spoiled any modest pleasure that she, not expecting too much, might have found in using them.

Allie may have felt patronized, too, lavishly praised for very little because she was a pretty girl. Only men could become great artists.

When I was ten, and Allie was fifteen, and our big brother Bernie the born scientist was eighteen, I said at supper one night that women weren't even the best cooks or clothing makers. Men were. And Mother dumped a pitcher of water over my head.

But Mother was as full of baloney about Allie's prospects for marrying a rich man, and how important it was for Allie to do so, as Father was about the art she did. During the Great Depression, financial sacrifices were made to send Allie to school with Hoosier heiresses at Tudor Hall, School for Girls, or *Two-Door Hell, Dump for Dames,* four blocks south of Shortridge High School, where she could have received what I received, a free and much richer and more democratic and madly heterosexual education.

The parents of my first wife Jane, Harvey and Riah Cox, did the same thing: sent their only daughter to Tudor Hall, and bought her rich girls' clothes, and maintained for her sake membership in the Woodstock Golf and Country Club they could ill afford, so she could marry a man whose family had money and power.

When the Great Depression and then World War Two were over, the idea that a man from a rich and powerful Indianapolis family would be allowed to marry a woman whose family didn't have a pot to piss in, as long as she had the manners and tastes of a rich girl, turned out to be as dumb as trying to sell balloons with blobs of moistened clay inside.

Business is business.

The best Allie could do for a husband was Jim Adams, a beautiful, charming, funny hunk with no money and no profession, who had served in Army Public Relations during the war. The best Jane could do, and it was a time of panic for unmarried women, was a guy who came home a PFC, who had been flunking all his courses at Cornell when he went off to war, and who didn't have a clue as to what to do next, now that free will had kicked in again.

Get this: Not only did Jane have rich girls' manners and clothes. She was a Phi Beta Kappa from Swarthmore, and had been the outstanding writer there!

I thought maybe I could be some kind of half-assed scientist, since that had been my education.

26

I N THE THIRD EDITION of *The Oxford Dictionary of Quotations*, the English poet Samuel Taylor Coleridge (1772–1834) speaks of "that willing suspension of disbelief for the moment, which constitutes poetic faith." This acceptance of balderdash is essential to the enjoyment of poems, and of novels and short stories, and of dramas, too. Some assertions by writers, however, are simply too preposterous to be believed.

Who, for example, could believe Kilgore Trout when he wrote as follows in *My Ten Years on Automatic Pilot*: "There is a planet in the Solar System where the people are so stupid they didn't catch on for a million years that there was another half to their planet. They didn't figure that out until five hundred years ago! Only five hundred years ago! And yet they are now calling themselves *Homo sapiens*.

"Dumb? You want to talk dumb? The people in one of the halves were so dumb, they didn't have an alphabet! They hadn't invented the wheel yet!"

Give us a break, Mr. Trout.

He appears to be heaping scorn in particular on Native Americans, who have already been adequately penalized, one would think, for their stupidity. According to Noam Chomsky, a professor at the Massachusetts Institute of Technology, where my brother, my father, and my grandfather all earned advanced degrees, but where my maternal uncle Pete Lieber flunked out: "Current estimates suggest that there may have been about 80 million Native Americans in Latin America when Columbus 'discovered' the continent—as we say—and about 12 to 15 million more north of the Rio Grande."

Chomsky continues: "By 1650, about 95 percent of the population of Latin America had been wiped out, and by the time the continental borders of the United States had been established, some 200,000 were left of the indigenous population."

In my opinion, Trout, far from giving yet another high colonic to our aborigines, is raising the question, perhaps too subtly, of whether great discoveries, such as the existence of another hemisphere, or of accessible atomic energy, really make people any happier than they were before.

I myself say atomic energy has made people unhappier than they were before, and that having to live in a two-hemisphere planet has made our aborigines a lot less happy, without making the wheel-and-alphabet people who "discovered" them any fonder of being alive than they were before.

Then again, I am a monopolar depressive descended from monopolar depressives. That's how come I write so good.

Are two hemispheres better than one? I know anecdotal evidence isn't worth a pitcher of warm spit scientifically, but a great-grandfather of mine on my mother's side switched hemispheres in time to be wounded in the leg as a soldier for the Union in our notoriously uncivil Civil War. His name was Peter Lieber. Peter Lieber bought a brewery in Indianapolis, and it prospered. A brew of his won a Gold Medal at the Paris Exposition of 1889. Its secret ingredient was coffee.

But Peter Lieber gave the brewery to his son Albert, my maternal grandfather, and he went back to his original hemisphere. He decided he liked that one better. And I am told there is a photograph often used in our textbooks that supposedly shows immigrants disembarking here, but actually they are getting on a ship to go back to where they came from.

This hemisphere is no bed of roses. My mother committed suicide in this one, and then my brother-in-law went off an open drawbridge in a railroad train.

27

THE FIRST STORY Trout had to rewrite after the timequake zapped him back to 1991, he told me, was called "Dog's Breakfast." It was about a mad scientist named Fleon Sunoco, who was doing research at the National Institutes of Health in Bethesda, Maryland. Dr. Sunoco believed really smart people had little radio receivers in their heads, and were getting their bright ideas from somewhere else.

"The smarties *had to be getting outside help*," Trout said to me at Xanadu. While impersonating the mad Sunoco, Trout himself seemed convinced that there was a great big computer somewhere, which, by means of radio, had told Pythagoras about right triangles, and Newton about gravity, and Darwin about evolution, and Pasteur about germs, and Einstein about relativity, and on and on.

"That computer, wherever it is, whatever it is, while pretending to help us, may actually be trying to *kill* us dummies with too much to think about," said Kilgore Trout.

Trout said he hadn't minded writing "Dog's Breakfast" again, or the three hundred or more stories he redid and threw away before free will kicked in again. "Write or rewrite, it's all the same to me," he said. "At the age of four score and four, I am as amazed and entertained as I was when I was only fourteen, and discovered that if I put the tip of a pen on paper, it would write a story of its own accord.

"Wonder why I tell people that my name is Vincent van Gogh?" he asked. And I had better explain that the real Vincent van Gogh was a Dutchman who painted in the south of France, whose pictures are now numbered among the world's most precious treasures, but who in his own lifetime sold only two of them. "It isn't only because he, like me, took no pride in his appearance and disgusted women, although that surely has to be factored in," said Trout.

"The main thing about van Gogh and me," said Trout, "is that he painted pictures that astonished *him* with their importance, even though nobody else thought they were worth a damn, and

I write stories that astonish *me*, even though nobody else thinks they're worth a damn.

"How lucky can you get?"

Trout was the only appreciative audience he needed for what he was and did. That let him accept the conditions of the rerun as unsurprising. It was just more foolishness in the world outside his own, and no more worthy of his respect than wars or economic collapses or plagues, or tidal waves, or TV stars, or what you will.

He was capable of being such a rational hero in the neighborhood of the Academy the instant free will kicked in again, because, in my opinion, Trout, unlike most of the rest of us, had found no significant differences between life as déjà vu and life as original material.

As for how little he was affected by the rerun, as compared with the hell it had been for most of the rest of us, he wrote in *My Ten Years on Automatic Pilot*: "I didn't need a timequake to teach me being alive was a crock of shit. I already knew that from my childhood and crucifixes and history books."

For the record: Dr. Fleon Sunoco at the NIH, who is independently rich, hires grave robbers to bring him the brains of deceased members of Mensa, a nationwide club for persons with high Intelligence Quotients, or IQs, as determined by standardized tests of verbal and nonverbal skills, tests which pit the testees against the Joe and Jane Sixpacks, against the *Lumpenproletariat*.

His ghouls also bring him brains of people who died in really stupid accidents, crossing busy streets against the light, starting charcoal fires at cookouts with gasoline, and so on, for comparison. So as not to arouse suspicion, they deliver the fresh brains one at a time in buckets stolen from a nearby Kentucky Fried Chicken franchise. Needless to say, Sunoco's supervisors have no idea what he's really doing when he works late night after night.

They *do* notice how much he likes fried chicken, apparently, ordering it by the bucket, and that he never offers anybody else some. They also wonder how he stays so skinny. During regular working hours, he does what he is paid to do, which is develop a birth control pill that takes all the pleasure out of sex, so teen-agers won't copulate.

At night, though, with nobody around, he slices up high-IQ brains, looking for little radios. He doesn't think Mensa members had them inserted surgically. He thinks they were *born* with them, so the receivers have to be made of meat. Sunoco has written in his secret journal: "There is no way an unassisted human brain, which is nothing more than a dog's breakfast, three and a half pounds of blood-soaked sponge, could have written 'Stardust,' let alone Beethoven's Ninth Symphony."

One night he finds an unexplained little snot-colored bump, no larger than a mustard seed, in the inner ear of a Mensa member, who as a junior high schooler had won spelling bee after spelling bee. *Eureka!*

He reexamines the inner ear of a moron who was killed when she was grabbing door handles of fast-moving vehicles while wearing Rollerblades. Neither of her inner ears has a snot-colored bump. *Eureka!*

Sunoco examines fifty more brains, half from people so stupid you couldn't believe it, half from people so smart you couldn't believe it. Only the inner ears of the rocket scientists, so to speak, have bumps. The bumps *have to have been the reason* the smarties were so good at taking IQ tests. An extra piece of tissue that little, and as nothing but tissue, couldn't possibly have been much more help than a pimple. It has to be a radio! And radios like that have to be feeding correct answers to questions, no matter how recondite, to Mensas and Phi Beta Kappas, and to quiz show contestants.

This is a Nobel Prize–type discovery! So, even before he has published, Fleon Sunoco goes out and buys himself a suit of tails for Stockholm.

28

Trout said: "Fleon Sunoco jumped to his death into the National Institutes of Health parking lot. He was wearing his new suit of tails, which would never get to Stockholm.

"He realized that his discovery proved that he didn't deserve credit for making it. He was hoist by his own petard! Anybody who did anything as wonderful as what he had done couldn't possibly have done it with just a human brain, with nothing but the dog's breakfast in his braincase. He could have done it only with outside help."

When free will kicked in after a ten-year hiatus, Trout made the transition from déjà vu to unlimited opportunities almost seamlessly. The rerun brought him back to the point in the space-time continuum when he was again beginning his story about the British soldier whose head was where his ding-dong should have been and whose ding-dong was where his head should have been.

Without warning and silently, the rerun stopped.

This was one heck of a moment for anyone operating a form of self-propelled transportation, or who was a passenger in one, or who stood in the path of one. For ten years, machinery, like people, had been doing whatever it had done the first time through the decade, often with fatal results, to be sure. As Trout wrote in *My Ten Years on Automatic Pilot*: "Rerun or not, modern transportation is a game of inches." The second time through, though, the hiccuping Universe, not humanity, was responsible for any and all fatalities. People might look as though they were steering something, but they weren't really steering. They couldn't steer.

Quoting Trout again: "The horse knew the way home." But when the rerun ended, the horse, which might actually have been anything from a motor scooter to a jumbo jet, didn't know the way home anymore. People were going to have to tell it what to do next, if it wasn't going to be an utterly amoral plaything of Newton's Laws of Motion.

•

Trout, on his cot next door to the Academy, was operating nothing more dangerous or headstrong than a ballpoint pen. When free will kicked in, he simply went on writing. He finished the story. The wings of a narrative, begging to be told, had carried its author over what was for most of us a yawning abyss.

Only after he had completed his own absorbing business, the story, was Trout at liberty to notice what the outside world, or, indeed, the Universe, might be doing now, if anything. And as a man without a culture or a society, he was uniquely free to apply Occam's Razor, or, if you like, the Law of Parsimony, to virtually any situation, to wit: The simplest explanation of a phenomenon is, nine times out of ten, say, truer than a really fancy one.

Trout's ruminations about how he had been able to finish a story whose completion had been so long opposed were uncomplicated by conventional paradigms of what life was all about, and what the Universe can or cannot do, and so on. Thus was the old science fiction writer able to go directly to this simple truth: That everybody had been going through what he had been going through for the past ten years, that he hadn't gone nuts or died and gone to hell, and that the Universe had shrunk a little bit, but had then resumed expansion, making everybody and everything a robot of their own past, and demonstrating, incidentally, that the past was unmalleable and indestructible, to wit:

> *The Moving Finger writes; and, having writ,*
> *Moves on: nor all your Piety nor Wit*
> *Shall lure it back to cancel half a Line,*
> *Nor all your Tears wash out a Word of it.*

And then, on what was the afternoon of February 13th, 2001, in New York City, way-the-hell-and-gone up on West 155th Street, and *everywhere*, free will had all of a sudden kicked in again.

29

I TOO, went from déjà vu to unlimited opportunities in a series , of actions that were continuous. An outside observer might have said I exercised free will the instant it became available. But here's the thing: I had dumped a cup of very hot chicken noodle soup into my lap, and had jumped out of my chair, and was with my bare hands sweeping the scalding broth and noodles from the front of my trousers right before the timequake struck. That's what I had to be doing again at the end of the rerun.

When free will kicked in, I simply kept on trying to get the soup off me before it could seep all the way through to my underwear. Trout said, quite correctly, that my actions had been *reflexes*, and not sufficiently creative to be considered acts of free will.

"If you'd been thinking," he said, "you would have unzipped your pants and dropped them around your ankles, since they were already soaked with soup. No amount of frenzied brushing of the surface of your pants was going to stop the soup from seeping all the way through to your underwear."

Trout was surely among the first people in the whole wide world, and not just way-the-hell-and-gone up on West 155th Street, to realize that free will had kicked in. This was very interesting to him, as it certainly wasn't to many others. Most other people, after the relentless reprise of their mistakes and bad luck and hollow victories during the past ten years, had, in Trout's words, "stopped giving a shit what was going on, or what was liable to happen next." This syndrome would eventually be given a name: *Post-Timequake Apathy*, or *PTA*.

Trout now performed an experiment that many of us had tried to perform at the start of the rerun. He said nonsensical things on purpose, and out loud, like, "Boop-boop-a-doop, dingle-dangle, artsy-fartsy, wah, wah," and so on. We all tried to say things on that order back in the second 1991, hoping to prove we could still say or do whatever we liked, if we tried hard enough. We couldn't, of course. But when Trout tried to say,

"Blue mink bifocals," or whatever, *after* the rerun, of course he could.

No problem!

People in Europe and Africa and Asia were in darkness when free will kicked in. Most of them were in bed or sitting down somewhere. Not nearly as many of them fell down in their hemisphere as fell down in ours, where a clear majority was wide awake.

A person walking in either hemisphere was commonly off balance, leaning in the direction he or she was going, and with most of his or her weight unevenly distributed between his or her feet. When free will kicked in, he or she of course fell down, and stayed down, even in the middle of a street with onrushing traffic, because of Post-Timequake Apathy.

You can imagine what the bottoms of staircases and escalators, in the Western Hemisphere in particular, looked like after free will kicked in.

That's the *New World* for you!

My sister Allie in real life, which for her lasted only forty-one years, God rest her soul, thought falling down was one of the funniest things people could do. I don't mean people who fell on account of strokes or heart attacks or snapped hamstrings or whatever. I am talking about people ten years old or older, of any race and either sex, and in reasonably good physical condition, who, on a day like any other day, all of a sudden fell down.

When Allie was dying for sure, with not long to go, I could still fill her with joy, could give her an *epiphany*, if you like, by talking about somebody falling down. My story couldn't be from the movies or hearsay. It had to be about a rude reminder of the power of gravity that I myself had witnessed.

Only one of my stories was about a professional entertainer. It was from back when I was lucky enough to see the death throes of vaudeville on the stage of the Apollo Theater in Indianapolis. A perfectly wonderful man, my kind of saint, as a regular part of his act at one point fell into the orchestra pit, and then climbed back onto the stage wearing the big bass drum.

All my other stories, which Allie never tired of hearing until she was dead as a doornail, involved *amateurs*.

30

ONE TIME when Allie was maybe fifteen and I was ten, she heard somebody fall down our basement stairs: *Bloompity, bloomp, bloomp*. She thought it was I, so she stood at the top of the stairs laughing her fool head off. This would have been 1932, three years into the Great Depression.

But it wasn't I. It was a guy from the gas company, who had come to read the meter. He came clumping out of the basement all bunged up, and absolutely furious.

Another time, when Allie was sixteen or older, since she was driving a car with me as a passenger, we saw a woman come out of a stopped streetcar horizontally, headfirst and parallel to the pavement. Her heels had caught somehow.

As I've written elsewhere, and said in interviews, Allie and I laughed for years about that woman. She wasn't seriously hurt. She got back on her feet OK.

One thing that only I saw, but which Allie liked to hear about anyhow, was a guy who offered to teach a beautiful woman not his wife how to do the Tango. It was at the tail end of a cocktail party that had pretty much petered out.

I don't think the man's wife was there. I can't imagine he would have made the offer if his wife had been there. He was not a professional dance instructor. There were maybe ten people in all there, including the host and hostess. This was in the days of phonographs. The host and hostess had made the tactical mistake of putting an acetate recording of Tango music on their phonograph.

So this guy, his eyes flashing, his nostrils flaring, took this beautiful woman in his arms, and he fell down.

Yes, and all the people falling down in *Timequake One*, and now in this book, are like "FUCK ART!" spray-painted across the steel front door of the Academy. They are homage to my sister Allie. They are Allie's kind of porno: people deprived of dignified postures by gravity instead of sex.

•

Here is a verse from a song popular during the Great Depression:

> *Papa came home late last night.*
> *Mama said, "Pop, you're tight."*
> *When he tried to find the light,*
> *He faw down and go boom!*

That the impulse to laugh at healthy people who nonetheless fall down is by no means universal, however, was brought to my attention unpleasantly at a performance of *Swan Lake* by the Royal Ballet in London, England. I was in the audience with my daughter Nanny, who was about sixteen then. She is forty-one now, in the summer of 1996. That must have been twenty-five years ago now!

A ballerina, dancing on her toes, went *deedly-deedly-deedly* into the wings as she was supposed to do. But then there was a sound backstage as though she had put her foot in a bucket and then gone down an iron stairway with her foot still in the bucket.

I instantly laughed like hell.

I was the only person to do so.

A similar incident happened at a performance of the Indianapolis Symphony Orchestra when I was a kid. It didn't involve me, though, and it wasn't about laughter. There was this piece of music that was getting louder and louder, and was supposed to stop all of a sudden.

There was this woman in the same row with me, maybe ten seats away. She was talking to a friend during the crescendo, and she had to get louder and louder, too. The music stopped. She shrieked, "I FRY MINE IN BUTTER!"

31

M Y DAUGHTER NANNY and I went to Westminster Abbey
the day after I became a pariah at the Royal Ballet. She
was thunderstruck when she came face to face with the tomb
of Sir Isaac Newton. At her age, and in that same place, my big
brother Bernie, a born scientist who can't draw or paint for sour
apples, would have shit an even bigger brick.

And well might any educated person excrete a sizable chunk
of masonry when contemplating the tremendously truthful
ideas this ordinary mortal, seemingly, uttered, with no more
to go by, as far as we know, than signals from his dog's breakfast, from his three and a half pounds of blood-soaked sponge.
This one naked ape invented differential calculus! He invented
the reflecting telescope! He discovered and explained how a
prism breaks a beam of sunlight into its constituent colors! He
detected and wrote down previously unknown laws governing
motion and gravity and optics!

Give us a break!

"Calling Dr. Fleon Sunoco! Sharpen your microtome. Do we
ever have a *brain* for you!"

My daughter Nanny has a son, Max, who is twelve now, in
1996, halfway through the rerun. He will be seventeen when
Kilgore Trout dies. This past April, Max wrote for school a
really swell report on Sir Isaac Newton, a superman so ordinary
in appearance. It told me something I hadn't known before:
That Newton was advised by those who were his nominal
supervisors to take time out from the hard truths of science to
brush up on theology.

I like to think they did this not because they were foolish,
but to remind him of how comforting and encouraging the
make-believe of religion can be for common folk.

To quote from Kilgore Trout's story "Empire State," which is
about a meteor the size and shape of the Manhattan skyscraper,
approaching Earth point-first at a steady fifty-four miles an
hour: "Science never cheered up anyone. The truth about the
human situation is just too awful."

•

And the truth about that situation all over the world will never be worse than it was during the first couple of hours after the rerun stopped. Oh sure, there were millions of pedestrians lying on the ground because the weight on their feet had been unevenly distributed when free will kicked in. But most of them were pretty much OK, except for those who had been near the tops of escalators or stairways. Most were no worse hurt than the woman Allie and I saw come shooting out of a streetcar headfirst.

The real mayhem was wrought, as I said before, by self-propelled forms of transportation, of which there were none, of course, inside the former Museum of the American Indian. Things stayed peaceful in there, even as the crashing of vehicles and the cries of the injured and dying reached the climax of a crescendo outside.

"I fry mine in butter!" indeed.

The bums, or "sacred cattle," as Trout called them, had been seated or prone or supine when the timequake struck. That was how they were when the rerun ended. How could free will hurt them?

Trout would say of them afterward: "Even before the time-quake, they had exhibited symptoms indistinguishable from those of PTA."

Only Trout jumped to his feet when a berserk fire truck, a hook-and-ladder, smacked the entrance of the Academy with its right front bumper and kept on going. What it did after that had nothing to do with people, and could have nothing to do with people. The sudden reduction of its velocity by its brush with the Academy caused the gaga firepersons aboard to hurtle through the air at the velocity it had reached going downhill from Broadway before it hit. Trout's best guess, based on how far the firepersons flew, was about fifty miles an hour.

Thus slowed and depopulated, the emergency vehicle made a sharp left turn into a cemetery across the street from the Academy. It started up a steep slope. It stopped short of the crest, and then rolled backward. The collision with the Academy had knocked its gearshift into *neutral*!

Momentum alone had carried it up the slope. The mighty motor roared. Its throttle was stuck. But the only opposition it could offer to gravity was the inertia of its own mass. It wasn't connected by the drive shaft to the back wheels anymore!

Listen to this: Gravity dragged the bellowing red monster back down into West 155th Street, and then ass-backward toward the Hudson River.

The rescue vehicle's blow to the Academy was so severe, albeit glancing, that it caused a crystal chandelier to drop to the floor of the foyer.

The fancy light fixture missed the armed guard Dudley Prince by inches. If he hadn't been standing upright, his weight equally distributed between his feet when free will kicked in, he would have fallen prone in the direction he was facing, toward the front door. The chandelier would have *killed* him!

You want to talk about luck? When the timequake struck, Monica Pepper's paraplegic husband was ringing the doorbell. Dudley Prince was about to go to the steel front door. Before he could take a step in that direction, though, a smoke alarm went off in the picture gallery behind him. He froze. Which way to go?

So when free will kicked in, he was on the horns of the same dilemma. The smoke alarm behind him had saved his life!

When Trout learned of the miraculous escape from death by chandelier, thanks to a smoke alarm, he quoted Katharine Lee Bates, speaking rather than singing:

> *O beautiful for spacious skies,*
> *For amber waves of grain,*
> *For purple mountain majesties*
> *Above the fruited plain!*
> *America! America!*
> *God shed his grace on thee*
> *And crown thy good with brotherhood*
> *From sea to shining sea.*

The uniformed ex-convict, thanks to PTA, was a motivationally *kaput* statue when Kilgore Trout scampered in through the entrance, which was no longer blocked, minutes after the harsh rules of free will had been reinstated. Trout was shouting, "Wake up! For God's sake, wake up! Free will! Free will!"

Not only was the steel front door lying flat on the floor, bearing the enigmatic message "UCK AR," so Trout had to lope across it to reach Prince. It was still hinged and locked to the door frame. The door frame itself had let go on impact. It had parted from the surrounding masonry. The door and its hinges and bolts and *whoozit* were to all practical purposes as good as new, their frame had offered so little resistance to the berserk hook-and-ladder.

The contractor who installed the door and frame had cut corners when it came to securing the frame to the masonry. He had been a crook! As Trout would later say of him, and it might have been said of all corner-cutting contractors: "The wonder was that he could sleep at night!"

32

I SAY IN SPEECHES in 1996, halfway through the rerun to 2001, that I became a student in the Anthropology Department of the University of Chicago after World War Two. I say jokingly that I never should have studied that subject, because I can't stand primitive people. They're so *stupid*! The real reason my interest in the study of man as an animal flagged was that my wife Jane Marie Cox Vonnegut, who would die as Jane Marie Cox Yarmolinsky, gave birth to a baby named Mark. We needed bucks.

Jane herself, a Swarthmore Phi Beta Kappa, had won a full scholarship in the university's Russian Department. When she got pregnant with Mark, she resigned the scholarship. We found the head of the Russian Department in the library, I remember, and my wife told this melancholy refugee from Stalinism that she had to quit because she had become infected with progeny.

Even without a computer, I can never forget what he said to Jane: "My dear Mrs. Vonnegut, pregnancy is the *beginning*, not the end, of life."

The point I want to make, though, is that one course I took required me to read and then be ready to discuss *A Study of History* by the English historian Arnold Toynbee, who is up in Heaven now. He wrote about challenges and responses, saying that various civilizations persisted or failed depending on whether or not the challenges they faced were just too much for them. He gave examples.

The same might be said for individuals who would like to behave heroically, and most strikingly in the case of Kilgore Trout on the afternoon and evening of February 13th, 2001, after free will kicked in. If he had been in the area of Times Square, or near the entrance or exit of a major bridge or tunnel, or at an airport, where pilots, as they had learned to do during the rerun, had expected their planes to take off or land safely of their own accord, the challenge would have been too much not only for Trout but for anyone else.

What Trout beheld when he came out of the shelter in response to the crash next door was a horrifying scene all right, but the cast was small. The dead and dying were widely scattered, rather than heaped or enclosed in a burning or crumpled airplane or bus. They were still individuals. Alive or dead, they still had personalities, with stories to read in their faces and clothes.

Vehicular traffic on that stretch of West 155th Street, way-the-hell-and-gone uptown and leading nowhere, was at any time of day virtually nonexistent. This made the roaring hook-and-ladder a solo entertainer, as Trout watched gravity drag it ass-backward in the direction of the Hudson River. He was so free to think about the luckless fire truck in detail, despite the racket coming from busier thoroughfares, that he concluded calmly, as he would tell me at Xanadu, that one of three explanations for its helplessness had to be the right one: Either its gearshift was in reverse or neutral, or the drive shaft had snapped, or the clutch was shot.

He did not panic. His experiences as a forward observer for the artillery had taught him that panic only made things worse. He would say at Xanadu: "In real life, as in Grand Opera, arias only make hopeless situations worse."

True enough, he didn't panic. At the same time, though, he had yet to realize that he alone was ambulatory and wide awake. He had figured out the bare bones of what the Universe itself had done, contracted and then expanded. That was the *easy* part. What was actually happening, except for its actuality, might easily have been the ink-on-paper consequences of a premise for a story he himself had written and torn to pieces, and flushed down a toilet in a bus terminal or whatever, years ago.

Unlike Dudley Prince, Trout hadn't even earned a High School Equivalency Certificate, but he bore at least one surprising resemblance to my big brother Bernie, who has a Ph.D. in physical chemistry from MIT. Bernie and Trout had *both*, since their earliest adolescence, played games in their heads that began with this question: "If such-and-such were the case in our surroundings, what then, what then?"

•

What Trout had failed to extrapolate from the premise of the timequake and rerun, in the relative peace of the far end of West 155th Street, was that everybody for miles around was immobilized, if not by death or serious injury, then by PTA. He wasted precious minutes waiting for the arrival of healthy young ambulance crews and policepersons and more firepersons, and disaster specialists from the Red Cross and the Federal Emergency Management Agency, who would take care of things.

Please remember, for God's sake: He was eighty-fucking-four years old! Since he shaved every day, he was often mistaken for a bag lady rather than a bag gentleman, even without his baby-blanket babushka, and so incapable of inspiring any respect whatsoever. As for his sandals: At least they were tough. They were made of the same material as the brake shoes on the Apollo 11 spacecraft, which had delivered Neil Armstrong to the Moon, where he was the first human being ever to walk on it, in 1969.

The sandals were government surplus from the Vietnam War, the only war we ever lost, and during which Trout's only child Leon had been a deserter. American soldiers on patrol in that conflict wore the sandals over their lightweight jungle boots. They did that because the enemy used to stick spikes pointed upward, and dipped in shit so as to cause serious infections, in paths leading through the jungle.

Trout, so reluctant to play Russian roulette with free will again at his age, and especially with the lives of others at stake, finally realized that, for better or worse, he had better get his ass in gear. But what could he do?

33

MY FATHER often misquoted Shakespeare, but I never saw him read a book.

Yes, and I am here to suggest that the greatest writer in the English language so far was Lancelot Andrewes (1555–1626), and not the Bard of Avon (1564–1616). Poetry was certainly in the air back then. Try this:

> *The Lord is my shepherd; I shall not want.*
> *He maketh me to lie down in green pastures:*
>   *he leadeth me beside the still waters.*
> *He restoreth my soul: he leadeth me in the paths of*
>   *righteousness for his name's sake.*
> *Yea, though I walk through the valley of the shadow*
>   *of death, I will fear no evil: for thou art with*
>   *me; thy rod and thy staff they comfort me.*
> *Thou preparest a table before me in the presence of*
>   *mine enemies: thou anointest my head with*
>   *oil; my cup runneth over.*
> *Surely goodness and mercy shall follow me all the*
>   *days of my life: and I will dwell in the*
>   *house of the Lord for ever.*

Lancelot Andrewes was the chief translator and paraphraser among the scholars who gave us the King James Bible.

Did Kilgore Trout ever write poems? So far as I know, he wrote only one. He did it on the penultimate day of his life. He was fully aware that the Grim Reaper was coming, and coming soon. It is helpful to know that there is a tupelo tree between the mansion and the carriage house at Xanadu.

Wrote Trout:

> *When the tupelo*
> *Goes poop-a-lo,*
> *I'll come back to youp-a-lo.*

34

M Y FIRST WIFE JANE and my sister Allie had mothers who went nuts from time to time. Jane and Allie were graduates of Tudor Hall and had once been two of the prettiest, merriest girls at the Woodstock Golf and Country Club. All male writers, incidentally, no matter how broke or otherwise objectionable, have pretty wives. Somebody should look into this.

Jane and Allie missed the timequake, thank goodness. My guess is that Jane would have found some goodness in the rerun. Allie would not have. Jane was life-loving and optimistic, a scrapper against carcinoma to the very end. Allie's last words expressed relief, and nothing more. They were, as I've recorded elsewhere, "No pain, no pain." I didn't hear her say it, and neither did our big brother Bernie. A male hospital attendant, with a foreign accent, relayed those words to us via telephone.

I don't know what Jane's last words may have been. I've asked. She was Adam Yarmolinsky's wife by then, not mine. Jane evidently slipped away without speaking, not realizing that she wouldn't be coming up for air again. At her funeral, in an Episcopal church in Washington, D.C., Adam said to those gathered that her favorite exclamation was, "I can't wait!"

What Jane anticipated with such joy again and again was some event involving one or more of our six children, now all adults with children of their own: a psychiatric nurse, a comedy writer, a pediatrician, a painter, an airline pilot, and a printmaker.

I did not speak at her Episcopal obsequy. I wasn't up to it. Everything I had to say was for her ears alone, and she was gone. The last conversation we had, we two old friends from Indianapolis, was two weeks before she died. It was on the telephone. She was in Washington, D.C., where the Yarmolinskys had their home. I was in Manhattan, and married, as I still am, to the photographer and writer Jill Krementz.

I don't know which of us initiated the call, whose nickel it was. It could have been either one of us. Whoever it was, it turned out that the point of the call was to say good-bye.

Our son the doctor Mark would say after she died that he himself would never have submitted to all the medical procedures she acquiesced to in order to stay alive as long as she could, to go on saying, her eyes shining, "I can't wait!"

Our last conversation was intimate. Jane asked me, as though I knew, what would determine the exact moment of her death. She may have felt like a character in a book by me. In a sense she was. During our twenty-two years of marriage, I had decided where we were going next, to Chicago, to Schenectady, to Cape Cod. It was my work that determined what we did next. She never had a job. Raising six kids was enough for her.

I told her on the telephone that a sunburned, raffish, bored but not unhappy ten-year-old boy, whom we did not know, would be standing on the gravel slope of the boat-launching ramp at the foot of Scudder's Lane. He would gaze out at nothing in particular, birds, boats, or whatever, in the harbor of Barnstable, Cape Cod.

At the head of Scudder's Lane, on Route 6A, one-tenth of a mile from the boat-launching ramp, is the big old house where we cared for our son and two daughters and three sons of my sister's until they were grownups. Our daughter Edith and her builder husband, John Squibb, and their small sons, Will and Buck, live there now.

I told Jane that this boy, with nothing better to do, would pick up a stone, as boys will. He would arc it over the harbor. When the stone hit the water, she would die.

Jane could believe with all her heart anything that made being alive seem full of white magic. That was her strength. She was raised a Quaker, but stopped going to meetings of Friends after her four happy years at Swarthmore. She became an Episcopalian after marrying Adam, who remained a Jew. She died believing in the Trinity and Heaven and Hell and all the rest of it. I'm so glad. Why? Because I loved her.

35

TELLERS OF STORIES with ink on paper, not that they matter anymore, have been either *swoopers* or *bashers*. Swoopers write a story quickly, higgledy-piggledy, crinkum-crankum, any which way. Then they go over it again painstakingly, fixing everything that is just plain awful or doesn't work. Bashers go one sentence at a time, getting it exactly right before they go on to the next one. When they're done they're done.

I am a basher. Most men are bashers, and most women are swoopers. Again: Somebody should look into this. It may be that writers of either sex are *born* to be swoopers or bashers. I visited Rockefeller University recently, and they are seeking and finding more and more genes that tend to *make us* behave this way or that way, just as a rerun after a timequake would do. Even before that visit, it had appeared to me that Jane's and my children and Allie's and Jim's children, while not alike as grownups, had each become the sort of grownups they practically *had to be*.

All six are OK.

Then again, all six have had countless opportunities to be OK. If you can believe what you read in the papers, or what you hear and see on TV and the Information Superhighway, most people don't.

Writers who are swoopers, it seems to me, find it wonderful that people are funny or tragic or whatever, *worth reporting*, without wondering why or how people are alive in the first place.

Bashers, while ostensibly making sentence after sentence as efficient as possible, may actually be breaking down seeming doors and fences, cutting their ways through seeming barbed-wire entanglements, under fire and in an atmosphere of mustard gas, in search of answers to these eternal questions: "What in heck should we be doing? What in heck is really going on?"

If bashers are unwilling to settle for the basher Voltaire's "*Il faut cultiver notre jardin*," that leaves the politics of human rights, which I am prepared to discuss. I begin with a couple of true stories from the end of Trout's and my war in Europe.

Here's the thing: For a few days after Germany surrendered, on May 7th, 1945, having been directly or indirectly responsible for the deaths of maybe forty million people, there was a pocket of anarchy south of Dresden, near the Czech border, which had yet to be occupied and policed by troops of the Soviet Union. I was in it, and have described it some in my novel *Bluebeard*. Thousands of prisoners of war like myself had been turned loose there, along with death camp survivors with tattooed arms, and lunatics and convicted felons and Gypsies, and who knows what else.

Get this: There were also German troops there, still armed but humbled, and looking for anybody but the Soviet Union to surrender to. My particular war buddy Bernard V. O'Hare and I talked to some of them. O'Hare, having become a lawyer for both the prosecution and the defense in later life, is up in Heaven now. Back then, though, we could both hear the Germans saying that America would now have to do what they had been doing, which was to fight the godless Communists.

We replied that we didn't think so. We expected the USSR to try to become more like the USA, with freedom of speech and religion, and fair trials and honestly elected officials, and so on. We, in turn, would try to do what they claimed to be doing, which was to distribute goods and services and opportunities more fairly: "From each according to his abilities, to each according to his needs." That sort of thing.

Occam's Razor.

And then O'Hare and I, not much more than kids actually, went into an undefended barn there in the springtime countryside. We wanted something to eat, anything to eat. But we found a wounded and obviously dying captain of the notoriously heartless Nazi Schutzstaffel, the SS, in a haymow instead. He might easily, until very recently, have been in charge of tormenting and planning the extinction of some of the death camp survivors not far away.

Like all members of the SS, and like all death camp survivors as well, this captain presumably had a serial number tattooed on his arm. Want to talk about postwar *irony*? There was a lot of that.

He asked O'Hare and me to go away. He would soon be dead, and said he looked forward to being such. As we prepared to depart, not feeling much about him one way or the other, he cleared his throat, signaling that he had something more to say after all. This was the last-words business again. If he had any, who but us could hear them?

"I have just wasted the past ten years of my life," he said.

You want to talk about a timequake?

36

M Y WIFE thinks I think I'm such hot stuff. She's wrong. I don't think I'm such hot stuff.

My hero George Bernard Shaw, socialist, and shrewd and funny playwright, said in his eighties that if he was considered smart, he sure pitied people who were considered dumb. He said that, having lived as long as he had, he was at last sufficiently wise to serve as a reasonably competent office boy.

That's how *I* feel.

When the City of London wanted to give Shaw its Order of Merit, he thanked them for it, but said he had already given it to himself.

I would have accepted it. I would have recognized the opportunity for a world-class joke, but would never allow myself to be funny at the cost of making somebody else feel like something the cat drug in.

Let that be my epitaph.

In the waning summer of 1996, I ask myself if there were ideas I once held that I should now repudiate. I consider the example set by my father's only brother, Uncle Alex, the childless, Harvard-educated Indianapolis insurance salesman. He had me reading high-level socialist writers like Shaw and Norman Thomas and Eugene Debs and John Dos Passos when I was a teenager, along with making model airplanes and jerking off. After World War Two, Uncle Alex became as politically conservative as the Archangel Gabriel.

But I still like what O'Hare and I said to German soldiers right after we were liberated: That America was going to become more socialist, was going to try harder to give everybody work to do, and to ensure that our children, at least, weren't hungry or cold or illiterate or scared to death.

Lotsa luck!

I still quote Eugene Debs (1855–1926), late of Terre Haute, Indiana, five times the Socialist Party's candidate for President, in every speech:

"While there is a lower class I am in it, while there is a criminal element I am of it; while there is a soul in prison, I am not free."

In recent years, I've found it prudent to say before quoting Debs that he is to be taken *seriously*. Otherwise many in the audience will start to laugh. They are being nice, not mean, knowing I like to be funny. But it is also a sign of these times that such a moving echo of the Sermon on the Mount can be perceived as outdated, wholly discredited horsecrap.

Which it is not.

37

K ILGORE TROUT's rugged jungle sandals crunched on crystal fragments from the fallen chandelier as he loped across the face of the fallen steel front door and frame, which said "UCK AR." Since there were crystal shards atop the door and frame instead of underneath them, a forensic scientist would have had to testify in a lawsuit, if one had ever been filed against the crooked contractor, that the crook's handiwork fell first. The chandelier must have dangled for a second or so before letting gravity do to it what gravity apparently would have liked to do to simply *everything*.

The smoke alarm in the picture gallery was still ringing, "presumably," Trout would later say, "continuing to do so of its own free will." He was joking, making fun, as was his wont, of the idea that there had ever been free will for anyone or anything, rerun or not.

The Academy doorbell had clammed up the moment Zoltan Pepper was hit by the fire truck. Trout's words again: "Quoth the doorbell with its silence, 'No comment at this time.' "

Trout himself, as I've said, was nevertheless espousing free will when he entered the Academy, and was invoking the Judeo-Christian deity as well: "Wake up! For God's sake, wake up, wake up! Free will! Free will!"

He would say at Xanadu that even if he had been a hero that afternoon and night, his entering the Academy, "pretending," in his words, "to be Paul Revere in the space-time continuum," had been "an act of sheer cowardice."

He was seeking shelter from the growing din on Broadway, half a block away, and from the sounds of really serious explosions from other parts of the city. A mile and a half to the south, near Grant's Tomb, a massive Department of Sanitation truck, for want of sincere steering, plowed through the lobby of a condominium and into the apartment of the building superintendent. It knocked over his gas range. The ruptured pipe of that major appliance filled the stairwell and elevator shaft of the six-story structure with methane laced with skunk smell. Most of the tenants were on Social Security.

And then KA-BOOM!

"An accident waiting to happen," as Kilgore Trout would say at Xanadu.

The old science fiction writer wanted to galvanize the armed and uniformed Dudley Prince into action, he later confessed, so that he himself wouldn't have to do anything more. "Free will! Free will! Fire! Fire!" he shouted at Prince.

Prince did not move a muscle. He batted his eyes, but those were reflexes, and not free will, like me and the chicken noodle soup. One thing Prince was thinking, by his own account, was that if he moved a muscle, he might find himself in the New York State Maximum Security Adult Correctional Facility at Athena back in 1991 again.

Understandable!

So Trout bypassed Prince for the moment, confessedly still looking out for *numero uno*. A smoke alarm was raising hell. If the building was really on fire, and the fire could not be brought under control, then Trout was going to have to find someplace else where a senior citizen could hunker down until whatever was going on outside died down some.

He found a lit cigar resting on a saucer in the picture gallery. The cigar, although illegal everywhere in New York County, was not yet, and probably never would be, a danger to anyone but itself. Its midpoint was centered in the saucer, so it wasn't going anywhere else as it oxidized. But the smoke alarm was yelling about the end of civilization as we had known it.

Trout, in *My Ten Years on Automatic Pilot*, would synthesize what he should have said to the smoke alarm that afternoon: "Nonsense! Get a grip on yourself, you brainless nervous breakdown."

Here's the spooky part: There wasn't anybody but Trout in the gallery!

Could it be that the American Academy of Arts and Letters was haunted by *poltergeists*?

38

I GOT a good letter today, Friday, August 23rd, 1996, from a young stranger named Jeff Mihalich, one would guess of Serb or Croat descent, who is majoring in physics at the University of Illinois at Urbana. Jeff says he enjoyed his physics course in high school, and got top grades, but "ever since I have had physics at the university I have had much trouble with it. This was a huge blow to me because I was used to doing well in school. I thought there was nothing I couldn't do if I just wanted it bad enough."

My reply will go like this: "You might want to read the picaresque novel *The Adventures of Augie March* by Saul Bellow. The epiphany at the end, as I recall, is that we shouldn't be seeking harrowing challenges, but rather tasks we find natural and interesting, tasks we were apparently born to perform.

"As for the charms of physics: Two of the most entertaining subjects taught in high school or college are *mechanics* and *optics*. Beyond these playful disciplines, however, lie mind games as dependent on native talent as playing the French horn or chess.

"Of native talent itself I say in speeches: 'If you go to a big city, and a university is a big city, you are bound to run into Wolfgang Amadeus Mozart. Stay home, stay home.' "

To put it another way: No matter what a young person thinks he or she is really hot stuff at doing, he or she is sooner or later going to run into somebody in the same field who will cut him or her a new asshole, so to speak.

A boyhood friend of mine, William H. C. "Skip" Failey, who died four months ago and is up in Heaven now, had good reason when a high school sophomore to think of himself as unbeatable at Ping-Pong. I am no slouch at Ping-Pong myself, but I wouldn't play against Skip. He put so much spin on his serve that no matter how I tried to return it, I already knew it would go up my nose or out the window or back to the factory, anywhere but on the table.

When Skip was a junior, though, he played a classmate of ours, Roger Downs. Skip said afterward, "Roger cut me a new asshole."

Thirty-five years after that, I was lecturing at a university in Colorado, and who should be in the audience but Roger Downs! Roger had become a businessperson out that way, and a respected competitor on the Senior Men's Tennis Circuit. So I congratulated him on having given Skip a table tennis lesson so long ago.

Roger was eager to hear anything Skip might have said after that showdown. I said, "Skip said you cut him a new asshole."

Roger was enormously satisfied, as well he might have been.

I did not ask, but the surgical metaphor could not have been unfamiliar to him. Furthermore, life being the Darwinian experiment, or "crock of shit," as Trout liked to call it, Roger himself had surely departed more than one tennis tournament having, like Skip, undergone a colostomy to his self-regard.

More news of this day in August, halfway through the rerun, as yet another autumn draws near: My big brother Bernie, the born scientist who may know more about the electrification of thunderstorms than anyone, has an invariably fatal cancer, too far advanced to be daunted by the Three Horsemen of the Oncologic Apocalypse, Surgery, Chemotherapy, and Radiation.

Bernie still feels fine.

It is much too early to talk about, but when he dies, God forbid, I don't think his ashes should be put in Crown Hill Cemetery with James Whitcomb Riley and John Dillinger, who belonged only to Indiana. Bernie belongs to the World.

Bernie's ashes should be scattered over the dome of a towering thunderhead.

39

So there was Roger Downs of Indianapolis in Colorado. Here am I, of Indianapolis, on the South Fork of Long Island. The ashes of my Indianapolis wife Jane Marie Cox are mixed with the roots of a flowering cherry tree, unmarked, in Barnstable Village, Massachusetts. The branches of that tree can be seen from the ell that Ted Adler rebuilt from scratch, after which he asked, "How the hell did I *do* that?"

The Best Man at Jane's and my wedding in Indianapolis, Benjamin Hitz of Indianapolis, is a widower now in Santa Barbara, California. Ben dated an Indianapolis cousin of mine several times this spring. She is a widow on the seacoast of Maryland, and my sister died in New Jersey, and my brother, although he doesn't feel like it yet, is dying in Albany, New York.

My boyhood pal David Craig, who made a radio in a German tank stop playing popular music during World War Two, is a builder in New Orleans. My cousin Emmy, whose dad told me I was a man at last when I came home from war, and who was my lab partner in physics class at Shortridge High School, lives only about thirty miles east of Dave in Louisiana.

Diaspora!

Why did so many of us bug out of a city built by our ancestors, where our family names were respected, whose streets and speech were so familiar, and where, as I said at Butler University last June, there was indeed the best and worst of Western Civilization?

Adventure!

It may be, too, that we wanted to escape the powerful pull, not of gravity, which is everywhere, but of Crown Hill Cemetery.

Crown Hill got my sister Allie. It didn't get Jane. It won't get my big brother Bernie. It won't get me.

I lectured in 1990 at a university in southern Ohio. They put me up in a motel nearby. When I returned to the motel after my speech, and was having my customary scotch and soda so I would sleep like a baby, which is the way I like to sleep, the bar was congenially populated by obviously local old people who seemed to really like each other. They had a lot to laugh about. They were all comedians.

I asked the bartender who they were. He said they were the fiftieth reunion of the Class of 1940 of Zanesville High School. It sure looked nice. It sure looked right. I was in the Class of 1940 at Shortridge High School, and was then skipping my own reunion.

Those people might have been characters out of *Our Town* by Thornton Wilder, as sweet a play as can ever be.

They and I were so old that we could remember when it didn't matter all that much economically whether you did or didn't go to college. You could still amount to something. And I told my father back then that maybe I didn't want to become a chemist like my big brother Bernie. I could save him a ton of money if I went to work for a newspaper instead.

Understand: I could go to college only if I took the same sorts of courses my brother had. Father and Bernie were agreed on that. Any other sort of higher education was what they both called *ornamental*. They laughed at Uncle Alex the insurance salesman because his education at Harvard had been so *ornamental*.

Father said I had better talk to his close friend Fred Bates Johnson, a lawyer who as a young man had been a reporter for the now defunct Democratic daily *The Indianapolis Times*.

I knew Mr. Johnson pretty well. Father and I used to go hunting for rabbits and birds with him down in Brown County, before Allie cried so much we had to give it up. He asked me there in his office, leaning back in his swivel chair, his eyes slits, how I planned to begin my career as a journalist.

"Well, sir," I said, "I thought maybe I could get a job on *The Culver Citizen* and work there for three or four years. I know the area pretty well." Culver was on Lake Maxincuckee in northern Indiana. We used to have a summer cottage on that lake.

"And then?" he said.

"With that much experience," I said, "I should be able to get a job with a much bigger paper, maybe in Richmond or Kokomo."

"And then?" he said.

"After maybe five years on a paper like that," I said, "I think I'd be ready to take a shot at Indianapolis."

"You'll have to excuse me," he said, "but I have to make a phone call."

"Of course," I said.

He swiveled around so his back was to me when he made the call. He spoke softly, but I wasn't trying to overhear. I figured it was none of my business.

He hung up the phone and swiveled around to face me again. "Congratulations!" he said. "You have a job on *The Indianapolis Times*."

40

I WENT TO COLLEGE in faraway Ithaca, New York, instead of going to work for *The Indianapolis Times*. Ever since, I, like Blanche DuBois in *A Streetcar Named Desire*, have always depended on the kindness of strangers.

I think now, with the clambake at Xanadu only five years away, about a man I might have been, spending his adult life among those he went to high school with, loving and hating, as had his parents and grandparents, a town that was his own.

He's gone!

> *Full fathom five he lies;*
> *Of his bones are coral made:*
> *Those are pearls that were his eyes:*
> *Nothing of him that doth fade,*
> *But doth suffer a sea-change*
> *Into something rich and strange.*

He would have known several jokes I know, like the one Fred Bates Johnson told one time, when he and Father and I, just a kid, and some others, were hunting down in Brown County. According to Fred, a bunch of guys like us went hunting for deer and moose up in Canada. Somebody had to do the cooking, or they would all starve to death.

They drew straws to see who would cook while the others hunted from dawn to dusk. To make the joke more immediate, Fred said it was Father who got the short straw. Father could cook. Mother couldn't. She was proud she couldn't cook, and wouldn't wash dishes and so on. I liked to go over to other kids' houses, where their mothers did those things.

The hunters agreed that anybody who complained about Father's cooking became the cook. So Father prepared worse and worse meals, while the others were having one hell of a good time in the forest. No matter how awful a supper was, though, the hunters pronounced it lip-smacking delicious, clapping Father on the back and so on.

After they marched off one morning, Father found a pile of fresh moose poop outside. He fried it in motor oil. That night he served it as steaming patties.

The first guy to taste one spit it out. He couldn't *help* himself! He spluttered, "Jesus Christ! That tastes like moose poop fried in motor oil!"

But then he added, "But *good*, but *good*!"

I think Mother was raised to be so useless because her father Albert Lieber, the brewer and speculator, believed that America was going to have an aristocracy based on the European model. Proofs of membership in such a caste over there, and so it would be over here, too, he must have reasoned, were wives and daughters who were ornamental.

41

I DON'T THINK I missed the boat when I failed to write a novel about Albert Lieber, and how he was largely responsible for my mother's suicide on Mother's Day Eve, 1944. German-Americans in Indianapolis lack universality. They have never been sympathetically, or even villainously, stereotyped in movies or books or plays. I would have had to explain them from scratch.

Lotsa luck!

The great critic H. L. Mencken, himself a German-American, but living all his life in Baltimore, Maryland, confessed that he had difficulty in concentrating on the novels of Willa Cather. Try as he might, he couldn't really care a whole lot about Czech immigrants in Nebraska.

Same problem.

I will say for the record that my grandfather Albert Lieber's first wife, Alice, née Barus, namesake of my sister Allie, died giving birth to her third child, who was Uncle Rudy. Mother was her first. The middle child was Uncle Pete, who flunked out of MIT, but who nonetheless sired a nuclear scientist, my cousin Albert in Del Mar, California. Cousin Albert reports that he has just gone blind.

It isn't radiation that has made cousin Albert blind. It is something else, which could have happened to anybody, in or out of science. Cousin Albert himself has sired a non-nuclear-type scientist, a computer whiz.

As Kilgore Trout used to exclaim from time to time, "Life goes on!"

The point I want to make is that Mother's father, the brewer, Republican big shot, and neo-aristocratic bon vivant, married a violinist after his first wife died. She turned out to be clinically bughouse. Face it! Some women are! She hated his kids with a passion. She was jealous of his love for them. She wanted to be the whole show. Some women do!

This female bat out of hell, who could play a fiddle like nobody's business, abused Mother and Uncle Pete and Uncle Rudy so ferociously, both physically and mentally, during their formative years, before Grandfather Lieber divorced her, that they never got over it.

If there had been a significant body of potential book-buyers who might care about rich German-Americans in Indianapolis, it would have been a piece of cake for me to bang out a roman-fleuve demonstrating that my grandfather in fact *murdered* my mother, albeit very slowly, by double-crossing her so long ago.

"Ting-a-ling, you son of a bitch!"

Working title: *Gone With the Wind*.

When Mother married my father, a young architect in moderate circumstances, politicians and saloonkeepers and the cream of Indianapolis German-American society gave them a treasure trove of crystal and linens and china and silver, and even some gold.

Scheherazade!

Who could doubt then that even Indiana had its own hereditary aristocracy, with useless possessions to rival those of horses' asses in the other hemisphere?

It all seemed like a lot of junk to my brother and my sister and our father and me during the Great Depression. It is now as widely dispersed as the Class of 1940 of Shortridge High School.

Auf Wiedersehen.

42

I ALWAYS HAD TROUBLE ending short stories in ways that would satisfy a general public. In real life, as during a rerun following a timequake, people don't change, don't learn anything from their mistakes, and don't apologize. In a short story they have to do at least two out of three of those things, or you might as well throw it away in the lidless wire trash receptacle chained and padlocked to the fire hydrant in front of the American Academy of Arts and Letters.

OK, I could handle that. But after I had a character change and/or learn something and/or apologize, that left the cast standing around with their thumbs up their asses. That is no way to tell a reader the show is over.

In my salad days, when I was green in judgment, and never having asked to be born in the first place, I sought the advice of my then literary agent as to how to end stories without killing all the characters. He had been fiction editor of an important magazine, and a story consultant for a Hollywood studio as well.

He said, "Nothing could be simpler, dear boy: The hero mounts his horse and rides off into the sunset."

Many years later, he would kill himself on purpose with a twelve-gauge shotgun.

Another friend and client of his said he couldn't possibly have committed suicide, it was so *out of character*.

I replied, "Even with military training, there is no way a man can accidentally blow his head off with a shotgun."

Many years earlier, so long ago that I was a student at the University of Chicago, I had a conversation with my thesis advisor about the arts in general. At that time, I had no idea that I personally would go into any sort of art.

He said, "You know what artists are?"

I didn't.

"Artists," he said, "are people who say, 'I can't fix my country or my state or my city, or even my marriage. But by golly, I can make this square of canvas, or this eight-and-a-half-by-eleven piece of paper, or this lump of clay, or these twelve bars of music, exactly what they *ought* to be!' "

About five years after that, he did what Hitler's Minister of Propaganda and his wife and their kids did at the end of World War Two. He swallowed potassium cyanide.

I wrote a letter to his widow, saying how much his teachings had meant to me. I did not get an answer. It could be that she was overwhelmed with grief. Then again, she may have been sore as hell at him for taking the easy way out.

This very summer, I asked the novelist William Styron in a Chinese restaurant how many people on the whole planet had what we had, which was lives worth living. Between the two of us, we came up with *seventeen percent*.

The next day I took a walk in midtown Manhattan with a longtime friend, a physician who treats every sort of addict at Bellevue Hospital. Many of his patients are homeless and HIV-positive as well. I told him about Styron's and my figure of seventeen percent. He said it sounded about right to him.

As I have written elsewhere, this man is a saint. I define a saint as a person who behaves decently in an indecent society.

I asked him why half his patients at Bellevue didn't commit suicide. He said the same question had occurred to him. He sometimes asked them, as though it were an unremarkable part of a diagnostic routine, if they had thoughts of self-destruction. He said that they were almost without exception surprised and insulted by the question. An idea *that sick* had never entered their heads!

It was about then that we passed an ex-patient of his who was toting a plastic bag filled with aluminum cans he had gathered. He was one of Kilgore Trout's "sacred cattle," somehow wonderful despite his economic uselessness.

"Hi, Doc," he said.

43

Question: What is the white stuff in bird poop?
Answer: That is bird poop, too.

S O MUCH FOR SCIENCE, and how helpful it can be in these times of environmental calamities. Chernobyl is still hotter than a Hiroshima baby carriage. Our underarm deodorants have eaten holes in the ozone layer.

Art or not?

And just get a load of this: My big brother Bernie, who can't draw for sour apples, and who at his most objectionable used to say he didn't like paintings because they didn't *do* anything, just hung there year after year, has this summer become an artist!

I shit you not! This Ph.D. physical chemist from MIT is now the poor man's Jackson Pollock! He squoozles glurp of various colors and consistencies between two flat sheets of impermeable materials, such as windowpanes or bathroom tiles. He pulls them apart, *et voilà!* This has nothing to do with his cancer. He didn't know he had it yet, and the malignancy was in his lungs and not his brain in any case. He was just farting around one day, a semi-retired old geezer without a wife to ask him what in the name of God he thought he was doing, *et voilà!* Better late than never, that's all I can say.

So he sent me some black-and-white Xeroxes of his squiggly miniatures, mostly dendritic forms, maybe trees or shrubs, maybe mushrooms or umbrellas full of holes, but really quite interesting. Like my ballroom dancing, they were *acceptable.* He has since sent me multi-colored originals, which I like a lot.

The message he sent me along with the Xeroxes, though, wasn't about unexpected happiness. It was an unreconstructed technocrat's challenge to the artsy-fartsy, of which I was a prime exemplar. "Is this art or not?" he asked. He couldn't have put that question so jeeringly fifty years ago, of course, before the founding of the first wholly American school of painting, Abstract Expressionism, and the deification in particular of Jack the Dripper, Jackson Pollock, who also couldn't draw for sour apples.

Bernie said, too, that a very interesting *scientific phenomenon* was involved, having to do, he left me to guess, with how different glurps behave when squoozled this way and that, with nowhere to go but up or down or sideways. If the artsy-fartsy world had no use for his pictures, he seemed to imply, his pictures could still point the way to better lubricants or suntan lotions, or who knows what? The all-new Preparation H!

He would not sign his pictures, he said, or admit publicly that he had made them, or describe how they were made. He plainly expected puffed-up critics to sweat bullets and excrete sizable chunks of masonry when trying to answer his cunningly innocent question: "Art or not?"

I was pleased to reply with an epistle which was frankly vengeful, since he and Father had screwed me out of a liberal arts college education: "Dear Brother: This is almost like telling you about the birds and the bees," I began. "There are many good people who are beneficially stimulated by some, but not all, manmade arrangements of colors and shapes on flat surfaces, essentially *nonsense*.

"You yourself are gratified by some music, arrangements of noises, and again essentially *nonsense*. If I were to kick a bucket down the cellar stairs, and then say to you that the racket I had made was philosophically on a par with *The Magic Flute*, this would not be the beginning of a long and upsetting debate. An utterly satisfactory and complete response on your part would be, 'I like what Mozart did, and I hate what the bucket did.'

"Contemplating a purported work of art is a social activity. Either you have a rewarding time, or you don't. You don't have to say *why* afterward. You don't have to say anything.

"You are a justly revered experimentalist, dear Brother. If you really want to know whether your pictures are, as you say, 'art or not,' you must display them in a public place somewhere, and see if strangers like to look at them. That is the way the game is played. Let me know what happens."

I went on: "People capable of liking some paintings or prints or whatever can rarely do so without knowing something about the artist. Again, the situation is social rather than scientific. Any work of art is half of a conversation between two human beings, and it helps a lot to know who is talking at you. Does he or she have a reputation for seriousness, for religiosity, for suffering, for concupiscence, for rebellion, for sincerity, for jokes?

"There are virtually no respected paintings made by persons about whom we know zilch. We can even surmise quite a bit about the lives of whoever did the paintings in the caverns underneath Lascaux, France.

"I dare to suggest that no picture can attract serious attention without a particular sort of human being attached to it in the viewer's mind. If you are unwilling to claim credit for your pictures, and to say why you hoped others might find them worth examining, there goes the ball game.

"Pictures are famous for their humanness, and not for their pictureness."

I went on: "There is also the matter of craftsmanship. Real picture-lovers like to *play along*, so to speak, to look closely at the surfaces, to see how the illusion was created. If you are unwilling to say how you made your pictures, there goes the ball game a second time.

"Good luck, and love as always," I wrote. And I signed my name.

44

I MYSELF paint pictures on sheets of acetate with black India ink. An artist half my age, Joe Petro III, who lives and works in Lexington, Kentucky, prints them by means of the silk-screen process. I paint a separate acetate sheet, again in opaque black, for each color I want Joe to use. I do not see my pictures, which I have painted in black alone, in color until Joe has printed them, one color at a time.

I make negatives for his positives.

There may be easier, quicker, and cheaper ways to create pictures. They might leave us more time for golf, and for making model airplanes and whacking off. We should look into that. Joe's studio looks like something out of the Middle Ages.

I can't thank Joe enough for having me make negatives for his positives after the little radio in my head stopped receiving messages from wherever it is the bright ideas come from. Art is so *absorbing*.

It is a *sopper-upper*.

Listen: Only three weeks ago at this writing, on September 6th, 1996, Joe and I opened a show of twenty-six of our prints in the 1/1 Gallery in Denver, Colorado. A local microbrewery, Wynkoop, bottled a special beer for the occasion. The label was one of my self-portraits. The name of the beer was Kurt's Mile-High Malt.

You think that wasn't fun? Try this: The beer, at my suggestion, was lightly flavored with coffee. What was so great about that? It tasted really good, for one thing, but it was also an homage to my maternal grandfather Albert Lieber, who was a brewer until he was put out of business by Prohibition in 1920. The secret ingredient in the beer that won a Gold Medal for the Indianapolis

Brewery at the Paris Exposition of 1889 was coffee!

Ting-a-ling!

That still wasn't enough fun out there in Denver? OK, how about the fact that the name of the owner of the Wynkoop Brewing Company, a guy about Joe's age, was John Hickenlooper? So what? Only this: When I went to Cornell University to become a chemist fifty-six years ago, I was made a fraternity brother of a man named John Hickenlooper.

Ting-a-ling?

This was his son! My fraternity brother had died when this son was only seven. I knew more about him than his own son did! I was able to tell this young Denver brewer that his dad, in partnership with another Delta Upsilon brother, John Locke, sold candy and soft drinks and cigarettes out of a big closet at the top of the stairs on the second floor of the fraternity house.

They christened it *Hickenlooper's Lockenbar*. We called it *Lockenlooper's Hickenbar*, and *Barkenhicker's Loopenlock*, and *Lockenbarker's Loopenhick*, and so on.

Happy days! We thought we'd live forever.

Old beer in new bottles. Old jokes in new people.

I told young John Hickenlooper a joke his dad taught me. It worked like this: His dad would say to me, no matter where we were, "Are you a member of the Turtle Club?" I had no choice but to bellow at the top of my lungs, "YOU BET YOUR ASS I AM!"

I could do the same thing to his dad. On some particularly solemn and sacred occasion, such as the swearing in of new fraternity brothers, I might whisper to him, "Are you a member of the Turtle Club?" He would have no choice but to bellow at the top of his lungs, "YOU BET YOUR ASS I AM!"

45

A<small>NOTHER OLD JOKE</small>: "Hello, my name is Spalding. No doubt you've played with my balls." It doesn't work anymore because Spalding is no longer a major manufacturer of athletic equipment, just as Lieber Gold Medal Beer is no longer a popular recreational drug in the Middle West, and just as the Vonnegut Hardware Company is no longer a manufacturer and retailer of durable and eminently practical goods out that way.

The hardware company was put out of business fair and square by livelier competitors. The Indianapolis Brewery was shut down by Article XVIII of the United States Constitution, which declared in 1919 that the manufacture, sale, or transportation of intoxicating liquors was against the law.

The Indianapolis humorist Kin Hubbard said about Prohibition that it was "better than no liquor at all." Intoxicating liquors did not become lawful again until 1933. By then, the bootlegger Al Capone owned Chicago, and Joseph P. Kennedy, father of a murdered-President-to-be, was a multimillionaire.

At the daybreak that followed the opening of Joe Petro III's and my show in Denver, a Sunday, I awoke alone in a room in the oldest hotel there, the Oxford. I knew where I was and how I had gotten there. It wasn't as though I had been drunk as a hooty-owl on Grandfather's beer the night before.

I dressed and stepped outside. Nobody else I could see was up yet. There were no moving vehicles. If free will had chosen to kick in again at that moment, and I had been off balance and so fallen down, nobody would have run over me.

The best thing to be when free will kicks in, probably, is a Mbuti, a Pygmy in a rain forest in Zaire, Africa.

Two hundred yards from my hotel was the husk of what used to be the throbbing heart of the city, its turgid auricles and ventricles. I mean its passenger railroad station. It was completed in 1880. Only two trains a day stop there now.

I myself was antique enough to remember as terrific music the hissing and rolling thunder of steam locomotives, and their mournful whistles, and the metronomic clicks of wheels on joints in the rails, and the apparent rise and fall, thanks to the Doppler effect, of the pitch of warning bells at crossings.

I remembered labor history, too, because the first effective strikes by American working people for better pay, and more respect, and safer working conditions, were called against the railroads. And then against owners of coal mines and steel mills and textile mills, and on and on. Much blood was shed in what appeared to most members of my generation of American writers to be battles as worth fighting as any against a foreign enemy.

The optimism that infused so much of our writing was based on our belief that after Magna Carta, and then the Declaration of Independence, and then the Bill of Rights, and then the Emancipation Proclamation, and then Article XIX of the Constitution, which in 1920 entitled women to vote, some scheme for economic justice could also be devised. That was the logical next step.

And even in 1996, I in speeches propose the following amendments to the Constitution:

Article XXVIII: Every newborn shall be sincerely welcomed and cared for until maturity.

Article XXIX: Every adult who needs it shall be given meaningful work to do, at a living wage.

What we have created instead, as customers and employees and investors, is mountains of paper wealth so enormous that a handful of people in charge of them can take millions and billions for themselves without hurting anyone. Apparently.

Many members of my generation are disappointed.

46

C AN YOU BELIEVE IT? Kilgore Trout, who never even saw
a stage play until he got to Xanadu, not only wrote a play
after he got home from our war, which was World War Two,
but he *copyrighted* it! I have just retrieved it from the memory
banks of the Library of Congress, and it is entitled *The Wrinkled
Old Family Retainer.*

It is like a birthday present from my computer here in the
Sinclair Lewis Suite at Xanadu. Wow! The date yesterday was
November 11th, 2010. I have just turned eighty-eight, or ninety-
eight, if you want to count the rerun. My wife, Monica Pepper
Vonnegut, says eighty-eight is a very lucky number, and so is
ninety-eight. She is heavily into numerology.

My darling daughter Lily will turn twenty-eight on December 15th! Who ever thought I would live to see that day?

The Wrinkled Old Family Retainer is about a wedding. The
bride is *Mirabile Dictu*, a virgin. The groom is *Flagrante Delicto*,
a heartless womanizer.

Sotto Voce, a male guest standing at the fringe of the ceremony,
says out of the corner of his mouth to a guy standing next to
him, "I don't bother with all this. I simply find a woman who
hates me, and I give her a house."

And the other guy says, as the groom is kissing the bride, "All
women are psychotic. All men are jerks."

The eponymous wrinkled old family retainer, crying his
rheumy eyes out behind a potted palm, is *Scrotum*.

Monica is still obsessed by the mystery of who left a cigar
smoldering beneath the smoke alarm in the picture gallery of
the Academy minutes before free will kicked in again. That was
more than nine years ago! Who cares? What difference can
knowing that make? That's like knowing what the white stuff
in bird poop is.

What Kilgore Trout did with that cigar was scrooch it out in
the saucer. He scrooched and scrooched and scrooched it, by his
own admission to Monica and me, as though it were responsible

not only for the yelling of the smoke alarm, but for all the din outside as well.

"The wheel that squeaks the loudest gets the oil," he said.

He realized the absurdity of what he was doing, he said, only when, as he took a painting down from the wall, preparing to hit the alarm with a corner of the frame, the alarm fell silent of its own accord.

He hung up the painting again, and even made sure it was hanging straight. "That seemed somehow important, that the picture was nice and straight," he said, "and evenly spaced from the others. At least I could make that little part of the chaotic Universe exactly as it should be. I was grateful for the opportunity to do that."

He returned to the entrance hall, expecting the armed guard to be awakening from his torpor. But Dudley Prince was still a statue, still convinced that, if he budged, he would find himself back in prison again.

Trout again confronted him, saying, "Wake up! Wake up! You've got free will again, and there's work to do!" And so on.

Nothing.

Trout had an inspiration! Instead of trying to sell the concept of free will, which he himself didn't believe in, he said this: "You've been very sick! Now you're well again. You've been very sick! Now you're well again."

That mantra worked!

Trout could have been a great advertising man. The same has been said of Jesus Christ. The basis of every great advertisement is a *credible promise*. Jesus promised better times in an afterlife. Trout was promising the same thing in the here and now.

Dudley Prince's spiritual rigor mortis began to thaw! Trout hastened his recovery by telling him to snap his fingers and stamp his feet, and stick out his tongue and wiggle his butt, and so on.

Trout, who had never even earned a High School Equivalency Certificate, had nonetheless become a real-life Dr. Frankenstein!

47

U NCLE ALEX VONNEGUT, who said we should exclaim out loud whenever we were accidentally happy, was considered a fool by his wife, Aunt Raye. He certainly started out as a fool when a spanking-new freshman at Harvard. Uncle Alex was asked to explain in an essay why he had come to Harvard all the way from Indianapolis. By his own gleeful account, he wrote, "Because my big brother is at MIT."

He never had a kid, and never owned a gun. He owned a lot of books, though, and kept buying new ones, and giving me those he thought were particularly well done. It was an ordeal for him to find this book or that one, so he could read some particularly magical passage aloud to me. Here's why: His wife Aunt Raye, who was said to be artistic, arranged his library according to the size and color of the volumes, and stairstep style.

So he might say of a collection of essays by his hero H. L. Mencken, "I think it was green, and about *this* high."

His sister, my aunt Irma, said to me one time when I was a grownup, "*All* Vonnegut men are scared to death of women." Her two brothers were sure as heck scared of *her*.

Listen: A Harvard education for my Uncle Alex wasn't the trophy of a micromanaged Darwinian victory over others that it is today. His father, the architect Bernard Vonnegut, sent him there in order that he might become *civilized*, which he did indeed become, although fabulously henpecked, and nothing more than a life insurance salesman.

I am eternally grateful to him, and indirectly to what Harvard used to be, I suppose, for my knack of finding in great books, some of them very funny books, reason enough to feel honored to be alive, no matter what else may be going on.

It now appears that books in the form so beloved by Uncle Alex and me, hinged and unlocked boxes, packed with leaves speckled by ink, are obsolescent. My grandchildren are already doing much of their reading from words projected on the face of a video screen.

Please, please, please wait just a minute!

At the time of their invention, books were devices as crassly practical for storing or transmitting language, albeit fabricated from scarcely modified substances found in forest and field and animals, as the latest Silicon Valley miracles. But by accident, not by cunning calculation, books, because of their weight and texture, and because of their sweetly token resistance to manipulation, involve our hands and eyes, and then our minds and souls, in a spiritual adventure I would be very sorry for my grandchildren not to know about.

48

I T IS PIQUANT to me that one of the greatest poets and one of the greatest playwrights of this century would both deny that they were from the Middle West, specifically from St. Louis, Missouri. I mean T. S. Eliot, who wound up sounding like the Archbishop of Canterbury, and Tennessee Williams, a product of Washington University in St. Louis and the University of Iowa, who wound up sounding like Ashley Wilkes in *Gone With the Wind*.

True enough, Williams was born in Mississippi, but moved to St. Louis when he was seven. And it was he who named himself Tennessee when he was twenty-seven. Before he did that to himself, he was Tom.

Cole Porter was born in Peru, Indiana, pronounced PEE-roo. "Night and Day"? "Begin the Beguine"? Not bad, not bad.

Kilgore Trout was born in a hospital in Bermuda, near where his father, Raymond, was gathering material for a follow-up on his doctoral dissertation on the last of the Bermuda Erns. The sole remaining rookery of those great blue birds, the largest of all pelagic raptors, was on Dead Man's Rock, an otherwise uninhabited lava steeple in the center of the notorious Bermuda Triangle. Trout was in fact conceived on Dead Man's Rock during his parents' honeymoon.

What was particularly interesting about these erns was that the female birds, and not anything people had done, so far as anybody could tell, were to blame for the rapidly dwindling population. In the past, and presumably for thousands of years, the females had hatched their eggs, and tended the young, and finally taught them to fly by kicking them off the top of the steeple.

But when Raymond Trout went there as a doctoral candidate with his bride, he found that the females had taken to bowdlerizing the nurturing process by kicking the eggs off the top of the steeple.

•

Thus did Kilgore Trout's father providentially become a specialist, thanks to the female Bermuda Erns' initiative, or whatever you want to call it, in evolutionary mechanisms governing fates of species, mechanisms other than the Occam's Razor of Darwin's *Natural Selection.*

Nothing would do, then, but that the Trout family, when little Kilgore was nine, spend the summer of 1926 camped on the shore of Disappointment Lake in inland Nova Scotia. The Dalhousie Woodpeckers in that area had quit the brain-rattling business of pecking wood, and were feasting on the plentiful blackflies on the backs of deer and moose instead.

Dalhousies, of course, are the commonest woodpeckers in eastern Canada, mainly, ranging from Newfoundland to Manitoba, and from Hudson Bay to Detroit, Michigan. Only those around Disappointment Lake, however, identical with the rest in plumage and beak size and shape, and so on, had stopped getting at bugs the hard way, digging them out one at a time, from holes the bugs had made or found in tree trunks.

They were first observed gorging on blackflies in 1916, with World War One going on in the other hemisphere. The Disappointment Lake Dalhousies, however, were not subjected to observation year after year before that, or since. This was because the clouds of voracious blackflies, often resembling little tornadoes, according to Trout, made the apostate Dalhousies' habitat virtually uninhabitable by human beings.

So the Trout family spent the summer up there dressed like beekeepers night and day, in gloves, in long-sleeved shirts tied at the wrists, and long pants tied at the ankles, in wide-brimmed hats draped with gauze, to protect their heads and necks, no matter how hellishly hot the weather. Father, mother, and son dragged the camping gear and a heavy motion picture camera and tripod to the marshy campsite while harnessed to a travois.

Dr. Trout expected to film nothing more than ordinary Dalhousies, indistinguishable from other Dalhousies, but pecking at the backs of deer and moose instead of tree trunks. Such simple pictures would have been exciting enough, showing that lower animals were capable of cultural as well as biological evolution. One might have extrapolated from them the supposition that one bird in the flock was a sort of Albert Einstein, so to speak, having theorized and then proved that blackflies were as nutritious as anything that could be dug out of a tree trunk.

Was Dr. Trout ever in for a surprise, though! Not only were these birds obscenely fat, and thus easy prey for predators. They were exploding, too! Spores from a tree fungus growing near Dalhousie nests found an opportunity to become a new disease in the intestinal tracts of the overweight birds, thanks to certain chemicals in the bodies of blackflies.

The new life-style of the fungus inside the birds at one point triggered the sudden release of quantities of carbon dioxide so copious that the birds blew up! One Dalhousie, perhaps the last veteran of the Disappointment Lake experiment, would explode a year later in a park in Detroit, Michigan, setting off the second-worst race riot in the Motor City's history.

49

T ROUT WROTE a story one time about another race riot. It was on a planet twice as big as Earth, orbiting Puke, a star the size of a BB, two billion years ago.

I asked my big brother Bernie in the American Museum of Natural History in New York, and this was long before the period of the rerun, whether he believed in Darwin's theory of evolution. He said he did, and I asked how come, and he said, "Because it's the only game in town."

Bernie's reply is the tag line of yet another joke from long ago, like "Ting-a-ling, you son of a bitch!" It seems a guy is off to play cards, and a friend tells him the game is crooked. The guy says, "Yeah, I know, but it's the only game in town."

I am too lazy to chase down the exact quotation, but the British astronomer Fred Hoyle said something to this effect: That believing in Darwin's theoretical mechanisms of evolution was like believing that a hurricane could blow through a junkyard and build a Boeing 747.

No matter what is doing the creating, I have to say that the giraffe and the rhinoceros are ridiculous.

And so is the human brain, capable, in cahoots with the more sensitive parts of the body, such as the ding-dong, of hating life while pretending to love it, and behaving accordingly: "Somebody shoot me while I'm happy!"

Kilgore Trout, the ornithologist's son, wrote in *My Ten Years on Automatic Pilot*: "The *Fiduciary* is a mythological bird. It has never existed in Nature, never could, never will."

Trout is the only person who ever said a fiduciary was any sort of bird. The noun (from the Latin *fiducia*, confidence, trust) in fact identifies a sort of *Homo sapiens* who will conserve the property, and nowadays especially paper or computer representations of wealth, belonging to other people, including the treasuries of their governments.

He or she or it cannot exist, thanks to the brain and the ding-dong, et cetera. So we have in this summer of 1996, rerun or not, and as always, faithless custodians of capital making themselves multimillionaires and multibillionaires, while playing beanbag with money better spent on creating meaningful jobs and training people to fill them, and raising our young and retiring our old in surroundings of respect and safety.

For Christ's sake, let's help more of our frightened people get through this thing, whatever it is.

Why throw money at problems? That is what money is *for*.

Should the nation's wealth be redistributed? It has been and continues to be redistributed to a few people in a manner strikingly unhelpful.

Let me note that Kilgore Trout and I have never used semicolons. They don't do anything, don't suggest anything. They are transvestite hermaphrodites.

Yes, and any dream of taking better care of our people might as well be a transvestite hermaphrodite without some scheme for giving us all the support and companionship of extended families, within which sharing and compassion are more plausible than in an enormous nation, and a *Fiduciary* may not be as mythical as the *Roc* and the *Phoenix* after all.

50

I AM SO OLD that I can remember when the word *fuck* was thought to be so full of bad magic that no respectable publication would print it. Another old joke: "Don't say 'fuck' in front of the B-A-B-Y."

A word just as full of poison, supposedly, but which could be spoken in polite company, provided the speaker's tone implied fear and loathing, was *Communism*, denoting an activity as commonly and innocently practiced in many primitive societies as fucking.

So it was a particularly elegant commentary on the patriotism and nice-nellyism during the deliberately insane Vietnam War when the satirist Paul Krassner printed red-white-and-blue bumper stickers that said FUCK COMMUNISM!

My novel *Slaughterhouse-Five* was attacked back then for containing the word *motherfucker*. In an early episode, somebody takes a shot at four American soldiers caught behind the German lines. One American snarls at another one, who, as I say, has never fucked anyone, "Get your head down, you dumb motherfucker."

Ever since those words were published, mothers of sons have had to wear chastity belts while doing housework.

I of course understand that the widespread revulsion inspired even now, and perhaps forever, by the word *Communism* is a sane response to the cruelties and stupidities of the dictators of the USSR, who called themselves, hey presto, *Communists*, just as Hitler called himself, hey presto, a *Christian*.

To children of the Great Depression, however, it still seems a mild shame to outlaw from polite thought, because of the crimes of tyrants, a word that in the beginning described for us nothing more than a possibly reasonable alternative to the Wall Street crapshoot.

Yes, and the word *Socialist* was the second S in *USSR*, so good-bye, *Socialism* along with *Communism*, good-bye to the soul of Eugene Debs of Terre Haute, Indiana, where the moon-light's shining bright along the Wabash. From the fields there comes the breath of new-mown hay.

"While there is a soul in prison, I am not free."

The Great Depression was a time for discussing all sorts of alternatives to the Wall Street crapshoot, which had suddenly killed so many businesses, including banks. The crapshoot left millions and millions of Americans without any way to pay for food and shelter and clothing.

So what?

That was almost a century ago, if you want to count the rerun. Forget it! Practically everybody who was alive back then is deader than a mackerel. Happy Socialism to them in the Afterlife!

What matters now is that, on the afternoon of February 13th, 2001, Kilgore Trout roused Dudley Prince from his Post-Timequake Apathy. Trout urged him to speak, to say anything, no matter how nonsensical. Trout suggested he say, "I pledge allegiance to the flag," or whatever, to prove to himself thereby that he was again in charge of his own destiny.

Prince spoke groggily at first. He didn't pledge allegiance, but indicated instead that he was trying to understand every-thing Trout had said to him so far. He said, "You told me I *had* something."

"You were sick, but now you're well, and there's work to do," said Trout.

"Before that," said Prince. "You said I *had* something."

"Forget it," said Trout. "I was all excited. I wasn't making sense."

"I still want to know what you said I *had*," said Prince.

"I said you had free will," said Trout.

"Free will, free will, free will," echoed Prince with wry won-derment. "I always wondered what it was I *had*. Now I got a *name* for it."

"Please forget what I said," said Trout. "There are lives to save!"

"You know what you can do with free will?" said Prince.

"No," said Trout.

"You can stuff it up your ass," said Prince.

51

WHEN I LIKEN TROUT there in the entrance hall of the American Academy of Arts and Letters, awakening Dudley Prince from PTA, to Dr. Frankenstein, I am alluding of course to the antihero of the novel *Frankenstein—or, The Modern Prometheus*, by Mary Wollstonecraft Shelley, second wife of the English poet Percy Bysshe Shelley. In that book, the scientist Frankenstein puts a bunch of body parts from different corpses together in the shape of a man.

Frankenstein jazzes them with electricity. The results in the book are exact opposites of those since achieved in real-life American state penitentiaries with real-life electric chairs. Most people think Frankenstein is the monster. He isn't. Frankenstein is the scientist.

Prometheus in Greek mythology makes the first human beings from mud. He steals fire from Heaven and gives it to them so they can be warm and cook, and not, one would hope, so we could incinerate all the little yellow bastards in Hiroshima and Nagasaki, which are in Japan.

In chapter 2 of this wonderful book of mine, I mention a commemoration in the chapel of the University of Chicago of the fiftieth anniversary of the atom-bombing of Hiroshima. I said at the time that I had to respect the opinion of my friend William Styron that the Hiroshima bomb saved his life. Styron was then a United States Marine, training for an invasion of the Japanese home islands, when that bomb was dropped.

I had to add, though, that I knew a single word that proved our democratic government was capable of committing obscene, gleefully rabid and racist, yahooistic murders of unarmed men, women, and children, murders wholly devoid of military common sense. I said the word. It was a foreign word. That word was *Nagasaki*.

Whatever! That, too, was a long, long time ago, and ten years longer ago than that, if you want to count the rerun. What I find worth exclaiming about right now is the continuing applicability to the human condition, years after free will has ceased to be a novelty, of what jazzed Dudley Prince back to life, of what is now known generally as Kilgore's Creed: "You were sick, but now you're well again, and there's work to do."

Teachers in public schools across the land, I hear, say Kilgore's Creed to students after the students have recited the Pledge of Allegiance and the Lord's Prayer at the beginning of each school day. Teachers say it seems to help.

A friend told me he was at a wedding where the minister said at the climax of the ceremony: "You were sick, but now you're well again, and there's work to do. I now pronounce you man and wife."

Another friend, a biochemist for a cat food company, said she was staying at a hotel in Toronto, Canada, and she asked the front desk to give her a wake-up call in the morning. She answered her phone the next morning, and the operator said, "You were sick, but now you're well again, and there's work to do. It's seven A.M., and the temperature outside is thirty-two degrees Fahrenheit, or zero Celsius."

On the afternoon of February 13th, 2001, alone, and then during the next two weeks or so, Kilgore's Creed did as much to save life on Earth as Einstein's *E equals mc squared* had done to end it two generations earlier.

Trout had Dudley Prince say the magic words to the other two armed guards on the day shift at the Academy. They went into the former Museum of the American Indian, and said them to the catatonic bums in there. A goodly number of the aroused sacred cattle, maybe a third of them, became anti-PTA evangelists in turn. Armed with nothing more than Kilgore's Creed, these ragged veterans of unemployability fanned out through the neighborhood to convert more living statues to lives of usefulness, to helping the injured, or at least getting them the hell indoors somewhere before they froze to death.

"God is in the details," Anonymous tells us in the sixteenth edition of Bartlett's *Familiar Quotations*. The seemingly pipsqueak detail of what became of the armored limousine that delivered Zoltan Pepper to be creamed by the hook-and-ladder as he rang the doorbell of the Academy is a case in point. The

limousine driver, Jerry Rivers, had moved it fifty yards to the
west, toward the Hudson River, after unloading his paraplegic
passenger and his wheelchair on the sidewalk.

That was still part of the rerun. Rerun or not, though, Jerry
wasn't to stay parked in front of the Academy, lest the luxury
vehicle arouse suspicions that the Academy might not be an
abandoned building after all. If that hadn't been the policy, the
limousine would have absorbed the impact of the fire truck, and
possibly but not certainly saved the life of Zoltan Pepper as he
rang the doorbell.

But at what cost? The entrance to the Academy would not
have been broached, giving Kilgore Trout access to Dudley
Prince and the other armed guards. Trout could not have put on
a spare guard's uniform he found in there, which made him look
like an authority figure. He would not have been able to arm
himself with the Academy's bazooka, with which he knocked
out the braying burglar alarms of impacted but unoccupied
parked vehicles.

52

THE AMERICAN ACADEMY OF ARTS AND LETTERS owned a bazooka because the warlords who knocked over Columbia University spearheaded their attack with a tank stolen from the Rainbow Division of the National Guard. They were so audacious that they flew *Old Glory, The Stars and Stripes.*

It is conceivable that the warlords, with whom nobody messes, any more than anybody messes with the ten biggest corporations, consider themselves as American as anyone. "America," wrote Kilgore Trout in *MTYOAP*, "is the interplay of three hundred million Rube Goldberg contraptions invented only yesterday.

"And you better have an extended family," he added, although he himself had done without one between the time he was discharged from the Army, on September 11th, 1945, and March 1st, 2001, the day he and Monica Pepper and Dudley Prince and Jerry Rivers arrived by armored limousine, with an overloaded trailer wallowing behind, at Xanadu.

Rube Goldberg was a newspaper cartoonist during the terminal century of the previous Christian millennium. He drew pictures of absurdly complex and undependable machines, employing treadmills and trapdoors and bells and whistles, and domestic animals in harness and blowtorches and mailmen and light bulbs, and firecrackers and mirrors and radios and Victrolas, and pistols firing blank cartridges, and so on, in order to accomplish some simple task, such as closing a window blind.

Yes, and Trout harped on the human need for extended families, and I still do, because it is so obvious that we, because we are human, need them as much as we need proteins and carbohydrates and fats and vitamins and essential minerals.

I have just read about a teenage father who shook his baby to death because it couldn't control its anal sphincter yet and wouldn't stop crying. In an extended family, there would have been other people around, who would have rescued and comforted the baby, and the father, too.

If the father had been raised in an extended family, he might not have been such an awful father, or maybe not a father at all yet, because he was still too young to be a good one, or because he was too crazy to *ever* be a good one.

I was in southern Nigeria in 1970, at the very end of the Biafran War there, on the Biafran side, the losing side, the mostly Ibo side, long before the rerun. I met an Ibo father of a new baby. He had four hundred relatives! Even with a losing war going on, he and his wife were about to go on a trip, introducing the baby to all its relatives.

When the Biafran army needed replacements, big Ibo families met to decide who should go. In peacetime, the families met to decide who should go to college, often to Cal Tech or Oxford or Harvard, a long way off. And then a whole family chipped in to pay for the travel and tuition and clothing suitable for the climate and dominant society where a kid was going next.

I met the Ibo writer Chinua Achebe over there. He is teaching and writing at Bard College in Annandale-on-Hudson, New York, 12504, over here now. I asked him how the Ibos were now, with Nigeria run by a rapacious junta which regularly hangs its critics for having much too much free will.

Chinua said no Ibos had roles in the government, nor did they want any. He said Ibos survived in modest businesses unlikely to bring them into conflict with the government or its friends, which included representatives of Shell Oil Company.

They must have held many meetings, in which ethics as well as survival schemes were debated.

And they still send their smartest kids off to the best universities far away.

When I celebrate the idea of a family and family values, I don't mean a man and a woman and their kids, new in town, scared to death, and not knowing whether to shit or go blind in the midst of economic and technological and ecological and political chaos. I'm talking about what so many Americans need so frantically: what I had in Indianapolis before World War Two, and what the characters in Thornton Wilder's *Our Town* had, and what the Ibos have.

•

In chapter 45, I proposed two amendments to the Constitution. Here are two more, little enough to expect from life, one would think, like the Bill of Rights:

Article XXX: Every person, upon reaching a statutory age of puberty, shall be declared an adult in a solemn public ritual, during which he or she must welcome his or her new responsibilities in the community, and their attendant dignities.

Article XXXI: Every effort shall be made to make every person feel that he or she will be sorely missed when he or she is gone.

Such essential elements in an ideal diet for a human spirit, of course, can be provided convincingly only by extended families.

53

THE MONSTER in *Frankenstein—or, The Modern Prometheus* turns mean because he finds it so humiliating to be alive and yet so ugly, so *unpopular.* He kills Frankenstein, who, again, is the scientist and not the monster. And let me hasten to say that my big brother Bernie never has been a Frankenstein-style scientist, never has worked nor would have worked on purposely destructive devices of any sort. He hasn't been a Pandora, either, turning loose new poisons or new diseases or whatever.

According to Greek mythology, Pandora was the first woman. She was made by the gods who were angry with Prometheus for making a man out of mud and then stealing fire from them. Making a woman was their *revenge.* They gave Pandora a box. Prometheus begged her not to open it. She opened it. Every evil to which human flesh is heir came out of it.

The last thing to come out of the box was *hope.* It flew away.

I didn't make that depressing story up. Neither did Kilgore Trout. Ancient Greeks did.

This is the point I want to make, though: Frankenstein's monster was unhappy and destructive, whereas the people Trout energized in the neighborhood of the Academy, although most of them wouldn't have won any beauty contests, were by and large cheerful and public-spirited.

I have to say *most of them* wouldn't have won any beauty contests. There was at least one strikingly beautiful woman involved. That was a member of the Academy's office staff. That was Clara Zine. Monica Pepper is certain that Clara Zine was the one who was smoking the cigar that set off the smoke alarm in the picture gallery. When confronted by Monica, Clara Zine swore that in her whole life she had never smoked a cigar, that she hated cigars, and she disappeared.

I have no idea what has become of her.

Clara Zine and Monica were tending the wounded in the former Museum of the American Indian, which Trout had turned into a hospital, when Monica asked Clara about the cigar, and then Clara departed in a huffmobile.

Trout, carrying what had become *his* bazooka, and accompanied by Dudley Prince and the other two armed guards, had thrown out all the bums who were still in the shelter. They did that in order to free up the cots for people with broken limbs or skulls or whatever, who needed and deserved to lie down where it was warm even more than the bums did.

It was triage, such as Kilgore Trout had seen practiced on World War Two battlefields. "I only regret that I have but one life to lose for my country," said the American patriot Nathan Hale. "Fuck the bums!" said the American patriot Kilgore Trout.

It was Jerry Rivers, the chauffeur of the Peppers' stretch limousine, however, who steered his dreamboat around wrecked vehicles and their victims, often driving on sidewalks, to reach the studios of the Columbia Broadcasting System down on West Fifty-second Street. Rivers awakened the staff there with, "You were sick, but now you're well again, and there's work to do." And then he got them to broadcast that same message on both radio and TV from coast to coast.

In order to get them to do that, though, he had to tell them a lie. He said everybody was recovering from a nerve gas attack by persons unknown. So the first version of Kilgore's Creed to reach millions in the nation, and then billions in the world, was this: "This is a CBS exclusive! There has been a nerve gas attack by persons unknown. You were sick, but now you're well again, and there's work to do. Make sure all children and senior citizens are safe indoors."

54

CERTAINLY! Mistakes were made! But Trout's silencing of automobile burglar alarms with his bazooka wasn't one of them. If a manual is to be written about how to behave in urban areas should there be another timequake, and then a rerun, and then free will kicks in again, it should recommend that every neighborhood have a bazooka, and that responsible adults know where it is.

Mistakes? The manual should point out that vehicles themselves *are not responsible* for the damage they cause, whether controlled or not. Punishing automobiles as though they were rebellious slaves in need of a hiding is a waste of time! Scapegoating cars and trucks and buses still in running condition, simply because they are *automobiles*, moreover, deprives rescue workers and refugees of their means of transportation.

As Trout advises in *MTYOAP*: "Beating the daylights out of a stranger's parked Dodge Intrepid may well afford fleeting relief from symptoms of stress. When all is said and done, though, that can only leave the life of its owner even more of a crock of shit than it was before. Do unto others' vehicles as you would have them do unto yours.

"It is pure superstition that a motor vehicle with its ignition turned off can start itself up without the help of a human being," he goes on. "If, after free will kicks in, you *must* yank the ignition keys out of driverless vehicles whose engines aren't running, please, please, please throw the keys into a *mailbox*, and not down a storm sewer or into a trash-strewn vacant lot."

The biggest mistake Trout himself made, probably, was in turning the American Academy of Arts and Letters into a morgue. The steel front door and its frame were tacked up back in place again, to keep the heat inside. It would have made more sense to line up the bodies outside, where the temperature was well below freezing.

And Trout couldn't have been expected to worry about it, way-the-hell-and-gone up there on West 155th, but some awakened member of the Federal Aviation Administration should have realized, after all the crashing at ground level petered out, that there were still planes aloft on automatic pilot. Their crews and passengers, still gaga with untreated PTA, couldn't care doodley what would happen when the fuel ran out.

In ten minutes, or maybe an hour, or maybe three hours or whatever, their heavier-than-air-craft, often six miles up, would *cash in the chips*, would *buy the farm*, for all aboard.

For the Mbuti, the rain forest Pygmies of Zaire, Africa, February 13th, 2001, was in all probability a day neither more nor less amazing than any other day, unless a rogue airplane happened to land on top of one of them after the rerun stopped.

The worst of all aircraft when free will kicks in, of course, are helicopters, or *choppers*, air screws first envisioned by the genius Leonardo da Vinci (1452–1519). Choppers can't glide. Choppers don't want to fly in the first place.

A safer place than a helicopter aloft is a roller coaster or a Ferris wheel.

Yes, and when martial law was established in New York City, the former Museum of the American Indian was turned into a barracks, and Kilgore Trout was relieved of his bazooka, and the Academy's headquarters were requisitioned as an officers' club, and he and Monica Pepper and Dudley Prince and Jerry Rivers took off in the limousine for Xanadu.

Trout, the former hobo, had expensive clothing, including shoes and socks and underwear and cuff links, and matched Louis Vuitton luggage which had belonged to Zoltan Pepper. Everybody agreed that Monica's husband was better off dead. What would he have had to look forward to?

When Trout found Zoltan's flattened and elongated wheelchair in the middle of West 155th Street, he leaned it against a tree and said it was modern art. The two wheels had been squashed together so they looked like one. Trout said it was a six-foot aluminum-and-leather praying mantis, trying to ride a unicycle.

He called it *The Spirit of the Twenty-first Century*.

55

I MET the author Dick Francis at the Kentucky Derby years ago. I knew he had been a champion rider in steeplechases. I said he was a bigger man than I had expected. He replied that it took a big man to "hold a horse together" in a steeplechase. This image of his remained in the forefront of my memory so long, I think, because life itself can seem a lot like that: a matter of holding one's self-respect together, instead of a horse, as one's self-respect is expected to hurdle fences and hedges and water.

My dear thirteen-year-old daughter Lily, having become a pretty adolescent, appears to me, as do most American adolescents, to be holding her self-respect together the best she can in a really scary steeplechase.

I said to the new graduates at Butler University, not much older than Lily, that they were being called *Generation X*, two clicks from the end, but that they were as much *Generation A* as Adam and Eve had been. What malarkey!

Esprit de l'escalier! Better late than never! Only at this very moment in 1996, as I am about to write the next sentence, have I realized how meaningless the image of a Garden of Eden must have been to my young audience, since the world was so densely populated with other secretly frightened people, and so overplanted and rigged with both natural and manmade booby traps.

The next sentence: I should have told them they were like Dick Francis when Dick Francis was young, and astride an animal full of pride and panic, in the starting gate for a steeplechase.

More: If a steed balks again and again at hazards, it is put out to pasture. The self-respects of most middle-class American people my age or older, and still alive, are out to pasture now, not a bad place to be. They munch. They ruminate.

If self-respect breaks a leg, the leg can never heal. Its owner has to shoot it. My mother and Ernest Hemingway and my former literary agent and Jerzy Kosinski and my reluctant thesis advisor at the University of Chicago and Eva Braun all come to mind.

But not Kilgore Trout. His indestructible self-respect is what I loved most about Kilgore Trout. Men loving men can happen, in peacetime as well as war. I also loved my war buddy Bernard V. O'Hare.

Many people fail because their brains, their three-and-a-half-pound blood-soaked sponges, their dogs' breakfasts, don't work well enough. The cause of a failure can be as simple as that. Some people, try as they may, can't cut the mustard! That's that!

I have a male cousin my age who was doing miserably back in Shortridge High School. He was a hulking interior lineman, and very sweet. He brought home an awful report card. His father asked him, "What is the *meaning* of this?" My cousin responded as follows: "Don't you *know*, Father? I'm dumb, I'm *dumb*."

Put this in your pipe and smoke it: My maternal great-uncle Carl Barus was a founder and president of the American Physical Society. A building at Brown University is named in his honor. Uncle Carl Barus was a professor there for many years. I never met him. My big brother did. Until this summer of 1996, Bernie and I had thought of him as a serene contributor to modest but tidy increases in human understanding of the laws of Nature.

Last June, though, I asked Bernie to tell me some specific discoveries, however small, made by our distinguished great-uncle, whose genes Bernie had inherited so outstandingly. Bernie's response was anything but *schnip-schnop*, anything but prompt. Bernie was bemused to realize at such a late date that Uncle Carl, while making a career in physics attractive, had never told him about anything he himself had accomplished.

"I'll have to look him up," said Bernie.

Hold on to your hats!

Listen: Uncle Carl, in 1900 or thereabouts, experimented with the effects of X rays and radioactivity on condensation in a cloud chamber, a wooden cylinder filled with a fog he himself had concocted. He concluded and published as a certainty that ionization was relatively unimportant in condensation.

At about the same time, friends and neighbors, the Scottish physicist Charles Thomson Rees Wilson performed similar experiments with a cloud chamber made of *glass*. The canny Scot proved that ions produced by X rays and radioactivity had a lot to do with condensation. He criticized Uncle Carl for ignoring contamination from the wood walls of his chamber, for his crude method of making clouds, and for not shielding his fog from the electrical field of his X-ray apparatus.

Wilson went on to make paths of electrically charged particles visible to the naked eye by means of his cloud chamber. In 1927, he shared a Nobel Prize for Physics for doing this.

Uncle Carl must have felt like something the cat drug in!

56

A Luddite to the end, as was Kilgore Trout, as was Ned Ludd, the possibly but not certainly fictitious workman who smashed up machinery, supposedly, in Leicestershire, England, at the beginning of the nineteenth century, I persist in pecking away at a manual typewriter. That still leaves me technologically several generations ahead of William Styron and Stephen King, who, like Trout, write with pens on yellow legal pads.

I correct my pages with pen or pencil. I have come into Manhattan on business. I telephone a woman who has been doing my retyping for years and years now. She doesn't have a computer, either. Maybe I should can her. She has moved from the city to a country town. I ask her what the weather is like out that way. I ask if there have been any unusual birds at her bird feeder. I ask if squirrels have found a way to get at it, and so on.

Yes, the squirrels have found a new way to get at the feeder. They can become trapeze artists, if they have to.

She has had back trouble in the past. I ask her how her back is. She says her back is OK. She asks how my daughter Lily is. I say Lily is OK. She asks how old Lily is now, and I say she'll be fourteen in December.

She says, "Fourteen! My gosh, my gosh. It seems like only yesterday she was just a little baby."

I say I have a few more pages for her to type. She says, "Good." I will have to mail them to her, since she doesn't have a fax. Again: Maybe I should can her.

I am still on the third floor of our brownstone in the city, and we don't have an elevator. So down the stairs I go with my pages, *clumpity, clumpity, clumpity.* I get down to the first floor, where my wife has her office. Her favorite reading when she was Lily's age was stories about Nancy Drew, the girl detective.

Nancy Drew is to Jill what Kilgore Trout is to me, so Jill says, "Where are you going?"

I say, "I am going to buy an envelope."

She says, "You are not a poor man. Why don't you buy a thousand envelopes and put them in a closet?" She thinks she is being logical. She has a computer. She has a fax. She has an answering machine on her telephone, so she doesn't miss any important messages. She has a Xerox. She has all that garbage.

I say, "I'll be back real soon."

Out into the world I go! Muggers! Autograph hounds! Junkies! People with real jobs! Maybe an easy lay! United Nations functionaries and diplomats!

Our house is near the UN, so there are all kinds of really foreign-looking people getting in or out of illegally parked limousines, doing the best they can, like all the rest of us, to hold their self-respect together. As I saunter a half-block to the news store on Second Avenue, which also sells stationery, I can feel, if I so choose, because of all the foreigners, like Humphrey Bogart or Peter Lorre in *Casablanca*, the third-greatest movie ever made.

The greatest movie ever, as anybody with half a brain knows, is *My Life as a Dog*. The second-greatest movie ever is *All About Eve*.

There is a chance, moreover, that I will see Katharine Hepburn, a *real* movie star! She lives only one block from us! When I speak to her, and tell her my name, she always says, "Oh yes, you're that friend of my brother's." I do not know her brother.

No such luck today, though, but what the heck. I am a philosopher. I have to be.

Into the news store I go. Relatively poor people, with lives not strikingly worth living, are lined up to buy lottery tickets or other crap. All keep their cool. They pretend they don't know I'm a celebrity.

The store is a Ma-and-Pa joint owned by *Hindus*, honest-to-God *Hindus*! The woman has a teeny-weeny ruby between her eyes. That's worth a trip. Who needs an envelope?

You must remember this, a kiss is still a kiss, a sigh is still a sigh.

I know the Hindus' stock of stationery as well as they do. I didn't study anthropology for nothing. I find one nine-by-twelve manila envelope without assistance, remembering simultaneously a joke about the Chicago Cubs baseball team. The Cubs were supposedly moving to the Philippine Islands, where they would be renamed the Manila Folders. That would have been a good joke about the Boston Red Sox, too.

I take my place at the end of the line, chatting with fellow customers who are buying something other than lottery tickets. The lottery ticket suckers, decorticated by hope and numerology, may as well be victims of Post-Timequake Apathy. You could run them over with an eighteen-wheeler. They wouldn't care.

57

From the news store I go one block south to the Postal Convenience Station, where I am secretly in love with a woman behind the counter. I have already put my pages in the manila envelope. I address it, and then I take my place at the end of another long line. What I need now is postage! Yum, yum, yum!

The woman I love there does not know I love her. You want to talk about poker faces? When her eyes meet mine, she might as well be looking at a cantaloupe!

Because she works sitting down, and because of the counter and the smock she wears, all I have ever seen of her is from the neck up. That's enough! From the neck up she is like a Thanksgiving dinner! I don't mean she looks like a plateful of turkey and sweet potatoes and cranberry sauce. I mean she makes me feel like that is what has just been set before me. Dig in! Dig in!

Unadorned, I believe, her neck and face and ears and hair would still be Thanksgiving dinner. Every day, though, she hangs new dingle-dangles from her ears and around her neck. Sometimes her hair is up, sometimes it's down. Sometimes it's frizzy, sometimes it's straight. What she can't do with just her eyes and lips! One day I'm buying a stamp from Count Dracula's daughter! The next day she's the Virgin Mary.

This time she's Ingrid Bergman in *Stromboli*. But she is a long way off still. There are many addled old poops, no good at counting money anymore, and immigrants talking gibberish, maddeningly imagining it to be English, in line ahead of me.

One time I had my pocket picked in that Postal Convenience Center. Convenient for whom?

I put the waiting time to good use. I learn about stupid bosses and jobs I will never have, and about parts of the world I will never see, and about diseases I hope I will never have, and about different kinds of dogs people have owned, and so on. By means of a computer? No. I do it by means of the lost art of conversation.

I at last have my envelope weighed and stamped by the only woman in the whole wide world who could make me sincerely happy. With her I wouldn't have to *fake* it.

I go home. I have had one heck of a good time. Listen: We are here on Earth to fart around. Don't let anybody tell you any different!

58

I HAVE TAUGHT creative writing during my seventy-three years on automatic pilot, rerun or not. I did it first at the University of Iowa in 1965. After that came Harvard, and then the City College of New York. I don't do it anymore.

I taught how to be sociable with ink on paper. I told my students that when they were writing they should be good dates on blind dates, should show strangers good times. Alternatively, they should run really nice whorehouses, come one, come all, although they were in fact working in perfect solitude. I said I expected them to do this with nothing but idiosyncratic arrangements in horizontal lines of twenty-six phonetic symbols, ten numbers, and maybe eight punctuation marks, because it wasn't anything that hadn't been done before.

In 1996, with movies and TV doing such good jobs of holding the attention of literates and illiterates alike, I have to question the value of my very strange, when you think about it, charm school. There *is* this: Attempted seductions with nothing but words on paper are so *cheap* for would-be ink-stained Don Juans or Cleopatras! They don't have to get a bankable actor or actress to commit to the project, and then a bankable director, and so on, and then raise millions and millions of buckareenies from manic-depressive experts on what most people want.

Still and all, why bother? Here's *my* answer: Many people need desperately to receive this message: "I feel and think much as you do, care about many of the things you care about, although most people don't care about them. You are not alone."

Steve Adams, one of my three adopted nephews, was a successful TV comedy writer in Los Angeles, California, a few years back. His big brother Jim is an ex–Peace Corps guy and now a psychiatric nurse. His kid brother Kurt is a veteran pilot with Continental Airlines, with scrambled eggs on his cap, gold braid on his sleeves. All Steve's kid brother ever wanted to do for a living was fly. A dream came true!

Steve learned the hard way that all his jokes for TV had to be about events that had been made much of by TV itself, and very *recently.* If a joke was about something that hadn't been on TV for a month or more, the watchers wouldn't have a clue, even though the laugh track was laughing, as to what they themselves were supposed to laugh about.

Guess what? TV is an *eraser.*

Having even the immediate past erased may indeed make it more comfortable for most people to get through this thing, whatever it is. Jane, my first wife, won her Phi Beta Kappa key at Swarthmore College over the objections of the History Department. She had written, and then argued in oral examinations, that all that could be learned from history was that history itself was absolutely nonsensical, so study something else, like music.

I agreed with her, and so would have Kilgore Trout. But history still hadn't been erased back then. And when I started out as a writer, I could refer to events and personalities in the past, even the distant past, with a reasonable expectation that a fair number of readers would respond with some emotion, whether positive or negative, when I mentioned them.

Case in point: The murder of the greatest President this country will ever have, Abraham Lincoln, by the twenty-six-year-old ham actor John Wilkes Booth.

That assassination was a major event in *Timequake One.* Who is there left under the age of sixty, and not in a History Department, to give a damn?

59

ELIAS PEMBROKE, a fictitious Rhode Island naval architect
who was Abraham Lincoln's Assistant Secretary of the
Navy during our Civil War, was a character in *Timequake One*.
I said he made significant contributions to the design of the
power train of the ironclad warship *Monitor*, but was neglectful
of his wife, Julia, who fell in love with a dashing young actor
and rakehell named John Wilkes Booth.

Julia wrote love letters to Booth. A tryst was arranged for
April 14th, 1863, two years before Booth shot Lincoln from
behind with a derringer. She went to New York City from
Washington with a chaperone, the alcoholic wife of an admiral,
ostensibly to shop, and to escape the tensions in the besieged
capital. They checked into the hotel where Booth was staying,
and attended his performance that night, as Marc Antony in
Julius Caesar, by William Shakespeare.

As Marc Antony, Booth would speak lines horrifyingly pro-
phetic in his case: "The evil that men do lives after them."

Julia and her chaperone went backstage afterward and congratulated not only John Wilkes, but his brothers, Junius, who
had played Brutus, and Edwin, who had played Cassius. The
three American brothers, with John Wilkes the baby, in combination with their British father, Junius Brutus Booth, consti-
tuted what remains to this day the greatest family of tragedians
in the history of the English-speaking stage.

John Wilkes gallantly kissed the hand of Julia, as though
they had just met, and simultaneously slipped her a packet of
chloral hydrate crystals, which would be the active ingredient
in a Mickey Finn for the chaperone.

Julia had been given to believe by Booth that all she would
receive from him when she came to his hotel room would be a
single glass of champagne, and a single kiss she would cherish
for the rest of her life after the war, back in Rhode Island, a life
that would otherwise be humdrum. *Madame Bovary!*

Little did Julia suspect that Booth would mousetrap her champagne, just as *she* had mousetrapped her chaperone's beddy-bye slug of wartime white lightning, with chloral hydrate.

Ting-a-ling!

Booth knocked her up! She had never had a kid before. Something was wrong with her husband's ding-dong. She was thirty-one! The actor was twenty-four!

Incredible?

Her husband was delighted. She's pregnant? There was nothing wrong with Assistant Secretary of the Navy Elias Pembroke's ding-dong after all! Anchors aweigh!

Julia returned to Pembroke, Rhode Island, a town named in honor of an ancestor of her husband's, to have the kid. She was scared to death that the upper rims of the kid's ears would be like those of John Wilkes Booth, pointed like a devil's, instead of curved. But the kid had normal ears. It was a boy. It was christened *Abraham Lincoln Pembroke*.

That the only descendant of the most egomaniacal and destructive villain in American history should bear that name did not become supremely ironical until, exactly two years from the night Booth ejaculated in Julia's birth canal while she was massively sedated, Booth sent a wad of lead into Lincoln's dog's breakfast, into Lincoln's brain.

At Xanadu in 2001, I asked Kilgore Trout for his ballpark opinion of John Wilkes Booth. He said Booth's performance in Ford's Theater in Washington, D.C., on the night of Good Friday, April 14th, 1865, when he shot Lincoln and then jumped from a theater box to the stage, breaking his leg, was "the sort of thing which is bound to happen whenever an actor creates his own material."

60

JULIA shared her secret with no one. Did she have regrets? Of course she did, but not about love. When she turned fifty, in 1882, she founded as a memorial for her only love affair, however brief and star-crossed, without saying that's what it was, an amateur acting group, the Pembroke Mask and Wig Club.

And Abraham Lincoln Pembroke, ignorant of whose son he actually was, in 1889 founded Indian Head Mills, which became the largest textile mill in New England until 1947, when Abraham Lincoln Pembroke III locked out his striking employees and moved the company to North Carolina. Abraham Lincoln Pembroke IV subsequently sold it to an international conglomerate, which moved it to Indonesia, and he died of drink.

Not an actor in the bunch. Not a murderer in the bunch. No pixie ears.

Before Abraham Lincoln Pembroke III departed the town of Pembroke for North Carolina, he knocked up an unmarried African-American housemaid, Rosemary Smith. He paid her handsomely for her silence. He was gone when his child Frank Smith was born.

Hold on to your hats!

Frank Smith has pointed ears! Frank Smith has to be one of the greatest actors in the history of amateur theatricals! He is half black, half white, and only five feet, ten inches tall. But in the summer of 2001 he gave a stunningly convincing matinee performance in the title role in the Pembroke Mask and Wig Club's production of *Abe Lincoln in Illinois*, by Robert E. Sherwood, with Kilgore Trout doing the sound effects!

The cast party afterward was a clambake on the beach at Xanadu. As in the last scene of *8½*, the motion picture by Federico Fellini, *tout le monde* was there, if not in person, then represented by look-alikes. Monica Pepper resembled my sister Allie. The bakemaster, a local man who is paid to stage such parties in the summertime, resembled my late publisher Seymour Lawrence (1927–1994), who rescued me from certain oblivion, from *smithereens*, by publishing *Slaughterhouse-Five*, and then bringing all my previous books back into print under his umbrella.

Kilgore Trout looked like my father.

The only sound effect Trout had to create backstage was in the last moments of the last scene of the last act of the play, of what Trout himself called "a manmade timequake." He was equipped with an antique steam whistle from the heyday of Indian Head Mills. A plumber, who was a club member and looked a lot like my brother, put the gaily mournful whistle atop a tank of compressed air, with a valve in between. That is what Trout was, too, in all he wrote: *gaily mournful*.

There were of course many club members who had no parts in *Abe Lincoln in Illinois*, who would have liked at least to blow that big brass rooster, once they saw it and then heard it blown by the plumber himself during dress rehearsal. But the club most of all wanted Trout to feel that he was home at last, and a vital member of an extended family.

Not merely the club and the household staff at Xanadu, and the chapters of Alcoholics Anonymous and Gamblers Anonymous, which met in the ballroom there, and the battered women and children and grandparents who had found shelter there, were grateful for his healing and encouraging mantra, which made bad times a coma: *You were sick, but now you're well again, and there's work to do.* The whole world was.

61

I N ORDER that Trout not miss his cue to blow the whistle, which he was terrified of doing, of spoiling *everything* for his family, the plumber who looked like my brother stood behind him and the apparatus, his hands on Trout's old shoulders. He would squeeze those shoulders gently when it was time for Trout's debut in show biz.

The last scene in the play is set in the yards of the railroad station at Springfield, Illinois. The date is February 11th, 1861. Abraham Lincoln, in this instance played by the half-African-American great-great-grandson of John Wilkes Booth, having just been elected President of the United States in its darkest hour, is about to depart his hometown by railroad, for Washington, God help him, District of Columbia.

He says, as indeed Lincoln said: "No one, not in my situation, can appreciate my feelings of sadness at this parting. To this place, and the kindness of you people, I owe everything. I have lived here a quarter of a century, and passed from a young to an old man. Here my children have been born and one is buried. I now leave, not knowing when or whether ever I may return.

"I am called upon to assume the Presidency at a time when eleven of our sovereign states have announced their intention to secede from the Union, when threats of war increase in fierceness from day to day.

"It is a grave duty which I now face. In preparing for it, I have tried to enquire: what great principle or ideal is it that has kept this Union so long together? And I believe that it was not the mere matter of separation of the colonies from the motherland, but that sentiment in the Declaration of Independence which gave liberty to the people of this country and hope to all the world. This sentiment was the fulfillment of an ancient dream, which men have held through all time, that they might one day shake off their chains and find freedom in the brotherhood of life. We gained democracy, and now there is the question of whether it is fit to survive.

"Perhaps we have come to the dreadful day of awakening, and the dream is ended. If so, I am afraid it must be ended forever. I cannot believe that ever again will men have the opportunity we have had. Perhaps we should admit that, and concede that our ideals of liberty and equality are decadent and doomed. I have heard of an eastern monarch who once charged his wise men to invent him a sentence which would be true and appropriate in all times and situations. They presented him the words, 'And this too shall pass away.'

"That is a comforting thought in time of affliction—'And this too shall pass away.' And yet—let us believe that it is not true! Let us live to prove that we can cultivate the natural world that is about us, and the intellectual and moral world that is within us, so that we may secure an individual, social and political prosperity, whose course shall be forward, and which, while the earth endures, shall not pass away. . . .

"I commend you to the care of the Almighty, as I hope that in your prayers you will remember me. . . . Good-bye, my friends and neighbors."

An actor playing the bit part of Kavanaugh, an Army officer, said, "Time to pull out, Mr. President. Better get inside the car."

Lincoln gets into the car as the crowd sings "John Brown's Body."

Another actor, cast as a brakeman, waved his lantern.

That was when Trout was supposed to blow the whistle, and he did.

As the curtain descended, there was a sob backstage. It wasn't in the playbook. It was ad lib. It was about beauty. It came from Kilgore Trout.

62

A NYTHING WE SAID at the cast party, the clambake on the beach, was at first hesitant and apologetic, almost as though English were our second language. We were mourning not only Lincoln, but the death of American *eloquence*.

Another look-alike there was Rosemary Smith, Mask and Wig's costume mistress, and mother of Frank Smith, its superstar. She resembled Ida Young, grandchild of slaves, who worked for us in Indianapolis when I was little. Ida Young, in combination with my uncle Alex, had as much to do with my upbringing as my parents did.

Nobody was a near double for Uncle Alex. He did not like my writing. I dedicated *The Sirens of Titan* to him, and Uncle Alex said, "I suppose the young people will like it." Nobody resembled my aunt Ella Vonnegut Stewart, a first cousin of my father's, either. She and her husband, Kerfuit, owned a book-store in Louisville, Kentucky. They did not stock my books because they found my language obscene. So it was back then, when I was starting out.

Among other departed souls whom I would not summon back to life, if I had had the power to do so, but who were represented by doppelgängers: nine of my teachers at Shortridge High School, and Phoebe Hurty, who hired me in high school to write ad copy about teenage clothing for Block's Department Store, and my first wife Jane, and my mother, and my uncle John Rauch, husband to another of Father's first cousins. Uncle John provided me with a history of my family in America, which I printed in *Palm Sunday*.

Jane's unknowing stand-in, a pert young woman who teaches biochemistry at Rhode Island University, over at Kingston, said within my hearing, and apropos of nothing more than that day's theatrical performance and the setting sun: "I can't *wait* to see what's going to happen next."

Only the dead had doppelgängers at that party back in 2001. Arthur Garvey Ulm, poet and Resident Secretary of Xanadu, an employee of the American Academy of Arts and Letters, was short and had a big nose, like my war buddy Bernard V. O'Hare.

My wife Jill was among the living, thank goodness, and was there in the flesh, as was Knox Burger, a Cornell classmate of mine. After Western Civilization's second unsuccessful suicide attempt, Knox became a fiction editor at *Collier's*, which published five short stories every week. Knox got me a good literary agent, Colonel Kenneth Littauer, the first pilot to strafe a trench during World War One.

Trout opined, in *My Ten Years on Automatic Pilot*, incidentally, that we had better start numbering timequakes the same way we numbered World Wars and Super Bowls.

Colonel Littauer sold a dozen or more of my stories, several to Knox, making it possible for me to quit my job with General Electric and move with Jane and our then two kids to Cape Cod as a free-lance writer. When the magazines went bust because of TV, Knox became an editor of paperback originals. He published three books of mine as such: *The Sirens of Titan*, *Canary in a Cathouse*, and *Mother Night*.

Knox got me started, and he kept me going until he could no longer help me. And then Seymour Lawrence came to my rescue.

Also in the flesh at the clambake were five men half my age who made me want to keep on going in my sunset years because of their interest in my work. They weren't there to see me. They wanted at long last to meet Kilgore Trout. They were Robert Weide, who in this summer of 1996 is making a movie in Montreal of *Mother Night*, and Marc Leeds, who wrote and had published a witty encyclopedia of my life and work, and Asa Pieratt and Jerome Klinkowitz, who have kept my bibliography up-to-date and written essays about me as well, and Joe Petro III, numbered like a World War, who taught me how to silk-screen.

My closest business associate, Don Farber, lawyer and agent, was there with his dear wife, Anne. My closest social pal, Sidney Offit, was there. The critic John Leonard was there, and the academicians Peter Reed and Loree Rackstraw, and the photographer Cliff McCarthy, and other kind strangers too numerous to mention.

The professional actors Kevin McCarthy and Nick Nolte were there.

My children and grandchildren weren't there. That was OK, perfectly understandable. It wasn't my birthday, and I wasn't a guest of honor. The heroes that evening were Frank Smith and Kilgore Trout. My kids and my kids' kids had other fish to fry. Perhaps I should say my kids and my kids' kids had other lobsters and clams and oysters and potatoes and corn on the cob to steam in seaweed.

Whatever!

Get it right! Remember Uncle Carl Barus, and get it right!

63

T HIS IS NOT a Gothic novel. My late friend Borden Deal, a first-rate southern novelist, so southern he asked his publishers not to send review copies north of the Mason-Dixon line, also wrote Gothic novels under a feminine nom de plume. I asked him for a definition of a Gothic novel. He said, "A young woman goes into an old house and gets her pants scared off."

Borden and I were in Vienna, Austria, for a congress of PEN, the international writers' organization founded after World War One, when he told me that. We went on to talk about the German novelist Leopold von Sacher-Masoch, who in print found humiliation and pain so delectable at the end of the previous century. Because of him, modern languages have the word *masochism*.

Borden not only wrote serious novels and Gothics. He wrote country music. He had his guitar back in his hotel room, and was working, he said, on a song called "I Never Waltzed in Vienna." I miss him. I want a look-alike for Borden at the clambake, and two luckless fishermen in a little rowboat right offshore, dead ringers for the saints Stanley Laurel and Oliver Hardy.

So be it.

Borden and I mused about novelists such as Masoch and the Marquis de Sade, who had intentionally or accidentally inspired new words. *Sadism*, of course, is joy while inflicting pain on others. *Sadomasochism* means getting one's rocks off while hurting others, while being hurt by others, or while hurting oneself.

Borden said doing without those words nowadays was like trying to talk about life without words for beer or water.

The only contemporary American writer we could think of who had given us a new word, and surely not because he is a famous pervert, which he isn't, was Joseph Heller. The title of his first novel, *Catch-22*, is defined this way in my *Webster's Collegiate Dictionary*: "A problematic situation for which the only solution is denied by a circumstance inherent in the problem."

Read the book!

I told Borden what Heller said in an interview when he was asked if he feared death. Heller said he had never experienced a root-canal job. Many people he knew had. From what they told him about it, Heller said, he guessed he, too, could stand one, if he had to.

That was how he felt about death, he said.

That puts me in mind of a scene from a play of George Bernard Shaw's, his manmade timequake *Back to Methuselah*. The whole play is ten hours long! The last time it was performed in its entirety was in 1922, the year I was born.

The scene: Adam and Eve, who have been around for a long time now, are waiting at the gate of their prosperous and peaceful and beautiful farm for the annual visit from their landlord, God. During every previous visit, and there have been hundreds of them by now, they could tell Him only that everything was nice and that they were grateful.

This time, though, Adam and Eve are all keyed up, scared but proud. They have something *new* they want to talk to God about. So God shows up, genial, big and hale and hearty, like my grandfather the brewer Albert Lieber. He asks if everything is satisfactory, and thinks He knows the answer, since what He has created is as perfect as He can make it.

Adam and Eve, more in love than they have ever been before, tell Him that they like life all right, but that they would like it even better if they could know that it was going to *end* sometime.

Chicago is a better city than New York because Chicago has alleys. The garbage doesn't pile up on the sidewalks. Delivery vehicles don't block main thoroughfares.

The late American novelist Nelson Algren said to the late Chilean novelist José Donoso, when we were all teaching in the Writers' Workshop at the University of Iowa in 1966: "It must be nice to come from a country that long and narrow."

You think the ancient Romans were smart? Look at how dumb their numbers were. One theory of why they declined and fell is that their plumbing was lead. The root of our word *plumbing* is *plumbum*, the Latin word for "lead." Lead poisoning makes people stupid and lazy.

What's *your* excuse?

I got a sappy letter from a woman a while back. She knew I was sappy, too, which is to say a northern Democrat. She was pregnant, and she wanted to know if it was a mistake to bring an innocent little baby into a world this bad.

I replied that what made being alive almost worthwhile for me was the saints I met, people behaving unselfishly and capably. They turned up in the most unexpected places. Perhaps you, dear reader, are or can become a saint for her sweet child to meet.

I believe in original sin. I also believe in original virtue. Look around!

Xanthippe thought her husband, Socrates, was a fool. Aunt Raye thought Uncle Alex was a fool. Mother thought Father was a fool. My wife thinks I'm a fool.

I'm wild again, beguiled again, a whimpering, simpering child again. Bewitched, bothered, and bewildered am I.

And Kilgore Trout said at the clambake, with Laurel and Hardy in a rowboat only fifty yards offshore, that young people liked movies with a lot of shooting because they showed that dying didn't hurt at all, that people with guns could be thought of as "free-lance anesthetists."

He was so happy! He was so popular! He was all dolled up in the tuxedo and boiled shirt and crimson cummerbund and bow tie that had belonged to Zoltan Pepper. I stood behind him in his suite in order to tie the tie for him, just as my big brother had done for me before I myself could tie a bow tie.

There on the beach, whatever Trout said produced laughter and applause. He couldn't believe it! He said the pyramids and Stonehenge were built in a time of very feeble gravity, when boulders could be tossed around like sofa pillows, and people loved it. They begged for more. He gave them the line from "Kiss Me Again": "There is no way a beautiful woman can live up to what she looks like for any appreciable length of time. Ting-a-ling?" People told him he was as witty as Oscar Wilde!

Understand, the biggest audience this man had had before the clambake was an artillery battery, when he was a forward spotter in Europe during World War Two.

"Ting-a-ling! If this isn't nice, what is?" he exclaimed to us all.

I called back to him from the rear of the crowd: "You've been sick, Mr. Trout, but now you're well again, and there's work to do."

My lecture agent, Janet Cosby, was there.

At ten o'clock the old, long-out-of-print science fiction writer announced it was his bedtime. There was one last thing he wanted to say to us, to his *family*. Like a magician seeking a volunteer from the audience, he asked someone to stand beside him and do what he said. I held up my hand. "Me, please, me," I said.

The crowd fell quiet as I took my place to his right.

"The Universe has expanded so enormously," he said, "with the exception of the minor glitch it put us through, that light is no longer fast enough to make any trips worth taking in even the most unreasonable lengths of time. Once the fastest thing possible, they say, light now belongs in the graveyard of history, like the Pony Express.

"I now ask this human being brave enough to stand next to me to pick two twinkling points of obsolete light in the sky above us. It doesn't matter what they are, except that they must twinkle. If they don't twinkle, they are either planets or satellites. Tonight we are not interested in planets or satellites."

I picked two points of light maybe ten feet apart. One was Polaris. I have no idea what the other one was. For all I knew, it was Puke, Trout's star the size of a BB.

"Do they twinkle?" he said.

"Yes they do," I said.

"Promise?" he said.

"Cross my heart," I said.

"Excellent! Ting-a-ling!" he said. "Now then: Whatever heavenly bodies those two glints represent, it is certain that the Universe has become so rarefied that for light to go from one to the other would take thousands or millions of years. Ting-a-ling?

But I now ask you to look precisely at one, and then precisely at the other."

"OK," I said, "I did it."

"It took a second, do you think?" he said.

"No more," I said.

"Even if you'd taken an hour," he said, "something would have passed between where those two heavenly bodies used to be, at, conservatively speaking, a million times the speed of light."

"What was it?" I said.

"Your awareness," he said. "That is a new quality in the Universe, which exists only because there are human beings. Physicists must from now on, when pondering the secrets of the Cosmos, factor in not only energy and matter and time, but something very new and beautiful, which is *human awareness*."

Trout paused, ensuring with the ball of his left thumb that his upper dental plate would not slip when he said his last words to us that enchanted evening.

All was well with his teeth. This was his finale: "I have thought of a better word than *awareness*," he said. "Let us call it *soul*." He paused.

"Ting-a-ling?" he said.

Epilogue

M Y BIG AND ONLY brother Bernard, a widower for
twenty-five years, died after prolonged bouts with can-
cers, without excruciating pain, on the morning of April 25th,
1997, at the age of eighty-two, now four days ago. He was a
Senior Research Scientist Emeritus, in the Atmospheric Sciences Research Center of the State University of New York at
Albany, and the father of five fine sons.

I was seventy-four. Our sister Alice would have been seventy-
nine. At the time of her humbling death at the age of forty-one,
I said, "What a wonderful old lady Allie would have been." No
such luck.

We were luckier with Bernard. He died the beloved, sweet,
funny, highly intelligent old geezer he deserved to become. He
was enraptured at the very end by a collection of sayings of
Albert Einstein. Example: "The most beautiful thing we can
experience is the mysterious. It is the source of all true art and
science." Another: "Physical concepts are free creations of the
human mind, and are not, however it may seem, uniquely determined by the external world."

Most famously, Einstein is reputed to have said, "I shall
never believe that God plays dice with the world." Bernard was
himself so open-minded about how the universe might be dealt
with that he thought praying would help, possibly, in drastic
situations. When his son Terry had cancer of the throat, Bernie,
ever the experimentalist, prayed for his recovery. Terry indeed
survived.

So it was with silver iodide, too. Bernie wondered if crystals
of that substance, so like crystals of frozen water, might not
teach supercooled droplets in clouds how to turn to ice, to snow.
He tried it. It worked.

He spent the final decade of his professional life attempting
to discredit a very old and widely respected paradigm of whence
came electrical charges in thunderstorms, and where they went,
and what they did and why. He was opposed. The last of the
more than one hundred fifty articles he wrote, to be published

649

posthumously, describes experiments that can demonstrate incontrovertibly whether he was right or wrong.

Either way, he could not lose. However the experiments came out, he would have found the results enormously entertaining. Either way, he would have laughed like hell.

He was funnier than I am in conversation. During the Great Depression, I learned as much about jokes while tagging after him as I did from the comedians in movies and on the radio. I was honored that he found me funny, too. It turned out that he had accumulated a small portfolio of my stuff that had amused him. One item was a letter I had written to our uncle Alex when I was twenty-five. At that time, I had published nothing, had a wife and son, and had just come from Chicago to work as a flack for General Electric in Schenectady, New York.

I got that job because Bernie had become a celebrity in the GE Research Laboratory, in association with Irving Langmuir and Vincent Schaefer, for experiments with cloud seeding, and because the company decided to have regular newspaper people handle its publicity. At Bernie's suggestion, GE hired me away from the Chicago City News Bureau, where I had been a beat reporter. I had worked simultaneously for a master's degree in anthropology at the University of Chicago.

I thought Uncle Alex knew that Bernie and I were at GE then, and that I was in Publicity. He *didn't* know!

And Uncle Alex had seen a syndicated photograph of Bernie, credited to the *Schenectady Gazette*. He wrote to that paper, saying he was "a wee bit proud" of his nephew and would like a copy of the picture. He enclosed a dollar. The Gazette got the picture from GE, and so forwarded the request to my new employer. My new boss, logically enough, handed it on to me.

I replied as follows on blue GE stationery:

GENERAL ⊛ ELECTRIC
COMPANY
GENERAL OFFICE SCHENECTADY, N. Y.

1 River Road
Schenectady 5, N. Y.

November 28, 1947

Mr. Alex Vonnegut
701 Guaranty Building
Indianapolis 4, Indiana

Dear Mr. Vonnegut:

    Mr. Edward Themak, city editor for the SCHENECTADY
GAZETTE, has referred your letter of November 26th to me.

    The photograph of General Electric's Dr. Bernard Vonn-
egut originated from our office. However, we have no more
prints in our files, and the negative is in the hands of
the United States Signal Corps. Moreover, we have a lot
more to do than piddle with penny-ante requests like yours.

    We do have some other photographs of the poor man's
Steinmetz, and I may send them to you in my own sweet time.
But do not rush me. "Wee bit proud," indeed! Ha! Vonnegut!
Ha! This office made your nephew, and we can break him in a
minute -- like a egg shell. So don't get in an uproar if you
don't get the pictures in a week or two.

    Also --. one dollar to the General Electric Company is
as the proverbial fart in a wind storm. Here it is back.
Don't blow it all in one place.

Very truly yours,

Guy Fawkes
Press Section
GENERAL NEWS BUREAU

Guy Fawkes:bc

As you can see, I signed it "Guy Fawkes," a name infamous
in British history.

Uncle Alex was so insulted that he flipped his wig. He took
the letter to a lawyer to find out what legal steps he might take to
compel an abject apology from someone high in the company,
and to make this cost the author his job. He was going to write
to the President of GE, telling him he had an employee who did
not know the value of a dollar.

Before he could take such steps, though, somebody told him
who Guy Fawkes was in history, and where I was, and that the
letter was so hilariously grotesque that it had to be a joke from

me. He wanted to kill me for making such a fool of him. I don't think he ever forgave me, although all I intended was that he be tickled pink.

If he had sent my letter to General Electric, demanding spiritual restitution, I would have been fired. I don't know what would then have become of me and my wife and son. Nor would I ever have come upon the material for my novels *Player Piano* and *Cat's Cradle*, and several short stories.

Uncle Alex gave Bernie the Guy Fawkes letter. Bernie on his deathbed gave it to me. Otherwise, it would have been lost forever. But there it is.

Timequake! I am back in 1947 again, having just come to work for General Electric, and a rerun begins. We all have to do again exactly what we did the first time through, for good or ill.

Extenuating circumstance to be mentioned on Judgment Day: We never asked to be born in the first place.

I was the baby of the family. Now I don't have anybody to show off for anymore.

A woman who knew Bernie for only the last ten days of his life, in the hospice at St. Peter's Hospital in Albany, described his manners while dying as "courtly" and "elegant." What a brother!

What a language.

APPENDIX

A "Special Message"
to readers of the Franklin Library's
signed first edition of "Bluebeard"

To ALL my friends and relatives in Alcoholics Anonymous I say that they were right to become intoxicated. Life without moments of intoxication is not worth a nickel. They simply chose what was for them a deadly poison on which to get drunk.

Good examples of harmless toots are some of the things children do. They get smashed for hours on some strictly limited aspect of the Great Big Everything, the Universe, such as water or snow or mud or colors or rocks, throwing little ones, looking under big ones, or echoes or funny sounds from the voicebox or banging on a drum and so on. Only two people are involved: the child and the Universe. The child does a little something to the Universe, and it does something funny or beautiful or sometimes disappointing or scary or even painful in return. The child teaches the Universe how to be a good playmate, to be nice instead of mean.

And professional picture painters, who are what a lot of this made-up story is about, are people who continue to play children's games with goo and chalks and powdered minerals mixed with oil and dead embers and so on, dabbing, smearing, scrawling, scraping and so on, for all their natural lives. When they were children, though, there was just them and the Universe, with only the Universe dealing in rewards and punishments, as a dominant playmate will. When picture painters become adults, and particularly if other people depend on them for food and shelter and clothing and all that, not forgetting heat in the wintertime, they are likely to allow a third player, with dismaying powers to hold up to ridicule or reward grotesquely or generally behave like a lunatic, to join the game. It is that part of society which does not paint well, usually, but which knows what it likes with a vengeance. That third player is sometimes personified by an actual dictator, such as Hitler or Stalin or Mussolini, or simply by a critic or curator or collector or dealer or creditor, or in-laws.

In any case, since the game goes well only when played by two, the painter and the Great Big Everything, *three's a crowd*.

Vincent van Gogh excluded that third player by having no dependents, by selling no paintings save for a few to his loving brother, and conversing as little as possible. Most painters are not that lucky, if you want to call that luck.

• • •

Most good painters I have known wish that they did not have to sell their pictures. The graphic artist Saul Steinberg said to me with whimsical smugness one time that he got to keep most of his creations, even after he had been paid well for them. Most of them are models for reproductions in books and magazines and poster shops, and need have no public life of their own if Steinberg is to make a living.

Both my daughters make pictures and sell them. But they wish that they could keep them. It is the third player who forces them to put them up for adoption. And that player is full of vehement advice about how to make their pictures more adoptable, how to run a successful baby factory, so to speak.

The younger of those daughters is married to a painter who was poor for a long time, but who is having what is called a success now. What do he and she find most exciting about this new affluence? It means that they can now keep their best pictures for themselves.

My point is this: the most satisfied of all painters is the one who can become intoxicated for hours, days or weeks or years with what his or her hands and eyes can do with art materials, and let the rest of the world go hang.

• • •

And may I say parenthetically that my own means of making a living is essentially clerical, and hence tedious and constipating. Intruders, no matter how ill-natured or stupid or dishonest, are as refreshing as the sudden breakthrough of sunbeams on a cloudy day.

The making of pictures is to writing what laughing gas is to Asian influenza.

• • •

As for the founders of the Abstract Expressionist Movement in this country soon after World War Two: the third player crashed into their privacy suddenly, and especially into that of the shy and dead broke Jackson Pollock, with the bewildering uproar of a raid by the Vice Squad. He was goofing around with spatters and dribbles of paint on canvas on his own time and at his own expense and on the advice of nobody, wondering, as indeed a child might, if the result would be interesting.

And it was.

That was his first master stroke, surely, something of which a child would be wholly incapable: recognizing how enchanting to adult minds pictures made in this fashion might be. His second master stroke was to trust his intuition to control his hands so as to show, now doing this with this and then that with that, how mysteriously whole and satisfying such pictures might be.

Some people were very upset with him, feeling that he was a swindler or a mountebank, although getting really mad at a painting or any work of art makes about as much sense as getting really mad at a banana split. Some of his supporters were at least as disconcerting, declaring that he had made an extraordinary breakthrough in scale with the discovery of penicillin, say. He and some of his painter pals were onto something big, and should keep pushing ahead. Everybody would be watching now.

And this was sensational news in terms of money and fame to come. But it was also hellish noise to a person as shy and innocent as Jackson Pollock of Cody, Wyoming. He died young and drunk and by all reports desperately unhappy—in an automobile crash which was his own fault if not of his own making. I did not know him, but I dare to suggest an epitaph for his stone in Green River Cemetery, to wit:

THREE'S A CROWD.

K.V.

Sagaponack, N.Y.

1987

Four essays on artists

Jackson Pollock

J ACKSON POLLOCK (1912–1956) was a painter who, during his most admired period, beginning in 1947, would spread a canvas on his studio floor and dribble or spatter or pour paint on it—and sometimes get up on a stepladder to look down at what he'd done. He was born in Cody, Wyoming, which is named in honor of a legendary creator of dead animals, "Buffalo Bill" Cody. Buffalo Bill died of old age. Jackson Pollock came east to the state of New York, where he died violently at the age of forty-four, having, as the foremost adventurer in the art movement now known as Abstract Expressionism, done more than any other human being to make his nation, and especially New York City, the unchallenged center of innovative painting in all this world.

Until his time, Americans were admirable for their leadership in only one art form, which was jazz. Like all great jazz musicians, Pollock made himself a champion and connoisseur of the appealing accidents that more-formal artists worked hard to exclude from their performances.

Three years before Pollock killed himself and a young woman he had just met, by driving his car into an embankment on a quiet country road, he had begun to move away in his work from being what one critic called "Jack the Dripper." He was laying on much of the paint with a brush—again. He had started out with a brush, and as an enemy of accidents. Let it be known far and wide, and especially among the philistines, that this man was capable of depicting in photographic detail the crossing of the Delaware by the Father of our Country, if such a tableau had been demanded by the passions of himself and his century. He had been meticulously trained in his craft by, among others, that most exacting American master of representational art, a genius of antimodernism, Thomas Hart Benton.

Pollock was a civilian throughout the Second World War, although in the prime of life. He was rejected for military

service, possibly because of his alcoholism, which he would conquer from time to time. He went without a drink, for example,
from 1948 through 1950.

He continued to paint and teach and study during the war,
when the careers of so many of his American colleagues were
disrupted, and when painters his own age in Europe had been
forbidden by dictators to paint as they pleased and were used as
fodder for cannons and crematoria and so on.

So—while Pollock is notorious for having broken with the
past, he was one of the few young artists who during the war
pondered art history uninterruptedly, and speculated in peace
as to what the future of art might be.

He should be astonishing even to people who do not care
about painting—for this reason: he surrendered his will to his
unconscious as he went about his job. He wrote this in 1947,
eight years after the death of Sigmund Freud: "When I am *in*
my painting, I am not aware of what I'm doing."

It might be said that he painted religious themes during a
time of enthusiasm in the Occident for peace and harmony to be
found, supposedly, in a state that was neither sleep nor wakefulness, to be achieved through meditation.

He was unique among founders of important art movements
in that his colleagues and followers did not lay on paint as he
did. French Impressionists painted a lot alike, and Cubists
painted a lot alike, and were supposed to, since the revolutions
in which they took part were, for all their spiritual implications,
quite narrowly technical.

But Pollock did not animate a school of dribblers. He was
the only one. The artists who felt themselves at least somewhat
in his debt made pictures as madly various as the wildlife of
Africa—Mark Rothko and Willem de Kooning and James
Brooks and Franz Kline and Robert Motherwell and Ad Reinhardt and Barnett Newman, and on and on. Those named, by
the way, were personal friends of Pollock. All vigorous schools
of art, it would seem, start with artificial extended families.

What bonded Pollock's particular family was not agreement
as to what, generally, a picture should look like, but whence
inspiration for pictures should come, hey presto—the unconscious, the part of the mind that was lively, but which caught

no likenesses, which might not even have suspected that there was a world outside the cranium.

Who can count, poring over yellowing journals and manifestos, all the art movements that have given themselves fanfares during this most volatile of all centuries? Almost all of them have died as quickly as do lightning bugs. A few have lived as long as dogs and horses. Abstract Expressionism is exciting more painters than ever, twenty-seven years after Jack the Dripper's death, and, because it celebrates what a part of the brain can do rather than what pictures should look like it promises to outlast elephants and whales, and perhaps even tortoises.

James Brooks, at seventy-seven a dean of the movement, describes in conversation the ideal set of mind for a painter who wishes to link his or her hands to the unconscious, as Pollock did: "I must lay on the first stroke of paint. After that, I insist that the canvas do at least half the work." The canvas, which is to say the unconscious, considers that first stroke, and then it tells the painter's hand how to respond to it—with a shape of a certain color and texture at that point there. And then, if all is going well, the canvas ponders this addition and comes up with further recommendations. The canvas becomes a Ouija board.

Was there ever a more cunning experiment designed to make the unconscious reveal itself? Has any psychological experiment yielded a more delightful suggestion than this one: that there is a part of the mind without ambition or information, which nonetheless is expert on what is beautiful?

Has any theory of artistic inspiration ever urged painters so vehemently, while they worked, to ignore life itself—to ignore life utterly? In the Abstract Expressionist paintings in museums and on the walls of art lovers, and in the vaults of speculators, there is very little to suggest a hand or a face, say, or a table or a bowl of oranges, or a sun or a moon—or a glass of wine.

And could any moralist have called for a more apt reaction by painters to World War II, to the death camps and Hiroshima and all the rest of it, than pictures without persons or artifacts, without even allusions to the blessings of Nature? A full moon, after all, had come to be known as "a bomber's moon." Even an orange could suggest a diseased planet, a disgraced humanity, if someone remembered, as many did, that the commandant of

Auschwitz and his wife and children, under the greasy smoke from the ovens, often had had fresh fruit for breakfast.

An appropriately visceral and soul-deep reaction by painters to Auschwitz and Hiroshima and all the rest of it was going to take place within the borders of this rich and sheltered nation when a young and, by most reports, profoundly unhappy genius from, of all places, Cody, Wyoming, began to treat each canvas as a Ouija board. It had seemed impossible that any real artist could honorably create harmonious pictures for a European and North American civilization whose principal industry had become the manufacture of ruins and cripples and corpses.

But then Jackson Pollock found a way.

1983

Jimmy Ernst

THIS IS ABOUT Jimmy Ernst, born in 1920 in Germany— our dear friend the painter and writer, who was killed instantly by a stroke on February 6, 1984. He was at the peak of his powers, and of his happiness, too, by all outward signs. His stunning autobiography had just been published. In two days he expected to attend the opening of a show here in New York City of his most courageous and personal and successful paintings.

I will say a word about his father. Max Ernst was surely the most famous artist in any field to sire a member of the American Academy and Institute of Arts and Letters. To reverse that equation: Jimmy Ernst is the only son of a great artist, that I can think of anyway, who reached for greatness in the selfsame art. It was as though there had never been a Sigmund Freud.

Conrad Aiken told me one time that sons will indeed compete with capable fathers, but only at those fathers' weakest points. Aiken's father fancied himself a renaissance man, a physician and scholar and athlete and poet and so on. And Aiken himself became a poet because his father's poetry was so bad.

Jimmy Ernst was surely not the only American artist whose mother was suffocated by cyanide in a German gas chamber. The Holocaust is a bond between immigrants to this country,

including those who did so much to make this city the art capital of the world. I am not entitled to say what his best painting
was, although I have my favorite—a triptych, black on black,
executed so meticulously that the paint might have been laid
on by a jeweler using a magnifying glass. I will dare to say that
his spiritual masterpiece was to live without hating anyone—to
forgive no one, since there was no one to forgive.

He elected to work without drawing on this quite customary
source of creative energy, and I will name it again: hate.

The painter James Brooks wrote a letter to me about Jimmy—
in longhand, in pen and ink; which included a phrase that so
efficiently describes the ghost of Jimmy which should now live
on in our heads that I will save it for the end. It was at the very
top of the letter.

Toward the bottom of the letter, Brooks celebrated Jimmy's
famous helpfulness to other painters—his obvious enjoyment
of their work, his bringing them together with institutions that
would show their work, and on and on. He also placed him
in the perspective of very short-term art history, saying: "At
the time Jimmy came to New York from Europe, the abstract-
expressionist movement was ripening—which added to any
difficulties he might be having in adjustment. The Americans
couldn't easily accept his highly detailed, closely finished work,
since they were then glorying in the invention of large, free-
flowing shapes with little attention to detail." There ends the
quotation.

He did not change, of course, and at the time of his death
was widely admired not only by Abstract Expressionists, but by
painters of every kind.

I will now tell you the phrase at the top of James Brooks's
letter. "I think first," said Brooks, "of a deliberately unprotected
psyche."

Again: "I think first of a deliberately unprotected psyche."
Again: "I think first of a deliberately unprotected psyche."
Again: "I think first of a deliberately unprotected psyche."

1984

Saul Steinberg

W HO WAS THE WISEST PERSON I ever met in my entire life? It was a man, but of course it needn't have been. It was the graphic artist Saul Steinberg, who like everybody else I know, is dead now. I could ask him anything, and six seconds would pass, and then he would give me a perfect answer, gruffly, almost a growl. He was born in Romania, in a house where, according to him, "the geese looked in the windows."

I said, "Saul, how should I feel about Picasso?"

Six seconds passed, and then he said, "God put him on Earth to show us what it's like to be *really* rich."

I said, "Saul, I am a novelist, and many of my friends are novelists and good ones, but when we talk I keep feeling we are in two very different businesses. What makes me feel that way?"

Six seconds passed, and then he said, "It's very simple. There are two sorts of artists, one not being in the least superior to the other. But one responds to the history of his or her art so far, and the other responds to life itself."

I said, "Saul, are you *gifted*?"

Six seconds passed, and then he growled, "No, but what you respond to in any work of art is the artist's struggle against his or her limitations."

2004

Origami Express

Author's note on the illustrations for
A Man Without a Country, *by Kurt Vonnegut*

T HE FULL-PAGE, hand-lettered statements scattered throughout this book, "samplers suitable for framing" if you like, are pictures of products of Origami Express, a business partnership between myself and Joe Petro III, with headquarters in Joe's painting and silk-screening studio in Lexington,

Kentucky. I paint or draw pictures, and Joe makes prints of some of them, one by one, color by color, by means of the time-consuming, archaic silk screen process, practiced by almost nobody else any more: squeegeeing inks through cloths and onto paper. This process is so painstaking and tactile, almost balletic, that each print Joe makes is a painting in its own right.

Our partnership's name, Origami Express, is my tribute to the many-layered packages Joe makes for prints he sends for me to sign and number. The logo for Origami, made by Joe, isn't his picture of a picture I sent him, but of a picture by me that he found in my novel *Breakfast of Champions*. It is of a bomb in air, on its way down, with these words written on its side:

GOODBYE
BLUE
MONDAY

I have to have been one of the luckiest persons alive, since I have survived for four score and two years now. I can't begin to count all the times I should have been dead or wished I were. But one of the best things that ever happened to me, a one-in-a-billion opportunity to enjoy myself in perfect innocence, was my meeting Joe.

Here's the thing: Back in 1993, almost eleven years ago now, I was scheduled to lecture on November 1 at Midway College, a women's school on the edge of Lexington. Well in advance of my appearance, a Kentucky artist, Joe Petro III, son of the Kentucky artist Joe Petro II, asked me to do a black-and-white self-portrait, which he could then use in silk-screen posters to be used by the school. So I did and he did. Joe was only thirty-seven back then, and I was a mere spring chicken of only seventy-one, not even twice his age.

When I got down there to speak, and was so happy about the posters, I learned from Joe himself that he painted romantic but scientifically precise pictures of wildlife, from which he made silk screen images. He had majored in zoology at the University of Tennessee. Yes, and some of his pictures were so appealing and informative that they had been used as propaganda by Greenpeace, an organization trying, with scant success so far, to prevent the murder of species, even our own, by the way we live now. And Joe, having shown me the poster and his own work and his studio, said to me in effect, "Why don't we keep on going?"

And so we have, and it seems quite possible in retrospect that Joe Petro III saved my life. I will not explain. I will let it go at that.

We have since collaborated on more than two hundred different images, with Joe making editions, signed and numbered by me, of ten or more of each of them. The "samplers" in this book are not at all representative of our total oeuvre, but are simply very recent *jeux d'esprit*. Most of our stuff has been my knockoffs of Paul Klee and Marcel Duchamp and so on.

And since we first met, Joe has beguiled others into sending him pictures for him to do with what he so much loves to do. Among them are the comedian Jonathan Winters, an art student long ago, and the English artist Ralph Steadman, whose accomplishments include the appropriately harrowing illustrations for Hunter Thompson's *Fear and Loathing* books. And Steadman and I have come to know and like each other on account of Joe.

Yes, and last July (2004) there was an exhibition of Joe's and my stuff, arranged by Joe, at the Indianapolis Art Center in the town of my birth. But there was also a painting by my architect and painter grandfather Bernard Vonnegut, and two by my architect and painter father Kurt Vonnegut, and six apiece by my daughter Edith and my son the doctor Mark.

Ralph Steadman heard about this family show from Joe and sent me a note of congratulation. I wrote him back as follows: "Joe Petro III staged a reunion of four generations of my family in Indianapolis, and he has made you and me feel like first cousins. Is it possible that he is God? We could do worse."

Only kidding, of course.

Are Origami's pictures any good? Well, I asked the now regrettably dead painter Syd Solomon, a most agreeable neighbor on Long Island for many summertimes, how to tell a good picture from a bad one. He gave me the most satisfactory answer I ever expect to hear. He said, "Look at a million pictures, and you can never be mistaken."

I passed this on to my daughter Edith, a professional painter, and she too thought it was pretty good. She said she "could rollerskate through the Louvre, saying, 'Yes, no, no, yes, no, yes,' and so on."

Okay?

2005

A "Special Message"
to readers of the Franklin Library's
signed first edition of "Hocus Pocus"

I TOOK AN MA in anthropology years and years ago at the University of Chicago, and ever since doing that I have regarded history and cultures and societies as characters as vivid as any in fiction, as Madame Bovary or Long John Silver or Leopold Bloom or whom you will. A critic for *The Village Voice* announced in triumph some time back his discovery that I was the only well-known writer who had never created a character, and that the next step should be to unfrock me on that account. He was incorrect, since Eliot Rosewater and Billy Pilgrim and some others of my invention are surely stereophonic and three-dimensional, and as idiosyncratic as you please. But he was onto something nonetheless: In many of my books, including this one, individual human beings are not the main characters.

The biggest character in this one (excluding myself, of course) is imperialism, the capture of other societies' lands and people and treasure by means of state-of-the-art wounding and killing machines, which is to say armies and navies. It can't be said too often that when Christopher Columbus discovered this hemisphere there were already millions upon millions of human beings here, and heavily armed Europeans took it away from them. When executed on a smaller scale, such an enterprise is the felony we call "armed robbery." As might be expected, such violence has not been without its consequences, one of which turns out to be the unwillingness of the richest heirs of the conquerors to take responsibility for what has become an awful lot of complicated property in need of skilled management and exceedingly boring and appallingly expensive maintenance, not to mention an increasingly unhappy and destructive and ailing general population.

But in this book, as in real life this very minute, the richest heirs in what has become the United States have been rescued by foreigners, most famously cash-heavy Japanese, eager to buy the country with paper forms of wealth negotiable almost anywhere and free of the least implication of social or managerial obligations. Heaven! So those heirs, many of whom captured the fruits of the European conquest of this part of the Western Hemisphere only recently, through activities in bad faith on Wall Street or the looting of savings banks, reveal themselves as being no more patriotic about where they live than were the British conquerors of Rhodesia, the Belgian conquerors of the Congo, or the Portuguese conquerors of Mozambique. Or all the different sorts of foreigners who are buying up the USA.

How lucky the richest heirs were, when they grew sick of all they owned, that there were so many foreigners in the position and the mood to buy them out! But guess what else happened: A great empire based on compassion and fair play for all, supposedly ("From each according to his abilities. To each according to his needs"), fell to pieces after seventy years of economic fiascoes, manmade famines, paranoia, xenophobia, an invasion by Nazis, and on and on. So it was possible to argue, and many of the heirs and their fans did and do, that anything which sounded vaguely like the Sermon on the Mount (such as the Eugene Debs quotations at the start of this book) was either communist or socialist, and completely discredited. Compassion for the lower social orders (money), history had now proved, could only work to the detriment of everyone.

I blame British literature for this, and the love for all things British exemplified by Eastern-seaboard prep schools and upper-class clothing establishments, and, most recently, *Masterpiece Theatre* on public television. These all say that imperialists are honorable, brave, brilliant, and charming, and that the lower social orders, whether at home or in the colonies, are parasites. I reply in this book that persons over here who respond favorably to such alien messages are unpatriotic, are un-American.

K.V.

New York, New York

1990

The Last Tasmanian

W HY DID IT go on for so long? I look at maps, and I simply can't believe that it went on for so long. I am speaking of the *non-discovery of America* by Europeans. It went on until 1492! That is practically only the day before yesterday! I ask you: Who *couldn't* have found half of a planet as small and navigable as this one is?

Daredevils have since crossed the Atlantic in rowboats and sailboats no bigger than a sofa, and have been rewarded with yawns and minor mentions in *The Guinness Book of Records*. I think of Europeans before 1492, and I am reminded of my regimental commander during World War II, in which I served as a foot soldier. We used to say of him that he couldn't find his own behind while using both hands.

• • •

About twenty years ago I wrote an essay that was printed by the *New York Times* about how inhospitable the moons and asteroids and other planets in the solar system were, so that we would be wise to quit treating this planet as though, in case we wrecked it, there were plenty of spares out there. Letters from readers poured in, most of them saying that I was the sort of person who would have told Christopher Columbus to stay home. They honestly believed, as nearly as I could tell, that, if it weren't for Columbus, we Europeans still wouldn't know about the Western Hemisphere, and General Motors wouldn't now be laying off seventy thousand workers, and Los Angeles wouldn't be running out of water, and we wouldn't have killed a high-school teacher while trying to put her into orbit, and so on.

• • •

The great graphic artist Saul Steinberg, a native of Romania, now a resident of New York City, thanks to Christopher Columbus and Adolf Hitler, told me once that he could not commit political history to memory—when Caesar lived, when Napoleon lived, and so on—until he related it to what artists were doing at such and such a time. Art history was what he was born to care about. He made art history a spine to which to attach whatever else might have been going on.

My big brother, the physical chemist Dr. Bernard Vonnegut, who studies the electrification of thunderstorms, gives his view of history a spine of scientific insights—Newton's laws of motion and Einstein's E=mc² and so on—to which he attaches kings and generals and politicians and explorers and so on. I myself, as a writer, make a spine of works of literature. But most United States citizens, without such specialized enthusiasms, have been given by their teachers a spine of dates to memorize, most prominent among them 1066, when the Normans invaded England, since we all get English history and attitudes along with the language; and 1492, without which we wouldn't exist; and 1776, when we became a beacon of liberty to the rest of the world, slavery and all; and 1941, December 7, to be exact, when the Japanese, without warning, sank a lot of our fleet at Pearl Harbor in the Hawaiian Islands, on, as Franklin Delano Roosevelt said, "a date which will live in infamy."

But making a spine for history out of memorized dates has the side effect of teaching that human destiny is governed by sudden and explosive events, strictly localized in space and time. The truth is that we are the playthings of systems as complex and turbulent as the weather systems pondered by my big brother Bernard. So the reasonable way to think about Columbus and his toy armada, it seems to me, is that he was part of a system of European explorers, a sort of tropical storm that was bound to hit the outlying islands of the Western Hemisphere, the other half of this little planet, after all, in 1492, give or take, say, thirty years.

•   •   •

We like to pretend that so many important discoveries have been made on a certain day, unexpectedly, by one person rather than by a system seeking such knowledge, I think, because we hope that life is like a lottery, where simply anyone can come up with a winning ticket. Paul of Tarsus, after all, became the leading theologian of Christianity in a flash, while on the road to Damascus, didn't he? Newton, after being hit on the head by an apple, was able to formulate a law of gravity, wasn't he? Darwin, while idly watching finches during a brief stopover on the Galápagos Islands during a voyage around the world, suddenly came up with a theory of evolution, didn't he? Who knows? Tomorrow morning, some absolute nobody, maybe you or I, might fall into an open manhole and return to street level with a concussion and a cancer cure.

Perhaps we are so fond of instant discoveries that I have to say didactically that St. Paul and Newton and Darwin, like Columbus, had long pondered whatever puzzle it was that they eventually solved, or seemed to solve, and that they had plenty of similarly inspired company while trying to solve it.

•   •   •

I said to a Jewish friend recently, Sidney Offit, a novelist who occasionally comments on political matters on TV, that I had heard from somewhere that Christopher Columbus might have been Jewish.

"Oh God," he exclaimed. "I hope not."

"I meant to delight you," I said truthfully. "Why would you hope not?"

"We're in enough trouble already," he said.

Sidney was acknowledging two stressful subjects at once: the Gentile habit of making scapegoats of Jews, of course; and the growing body of opinion here that the behavior of Columbus and so many of the Europeans who came after him toward the Native Americans, the people who had already discovered America, was loathsome, to say the least. Our mutual friend, the historian and ardent conservationist Kirkpatrick Sale, had just published a generally well-received book, *The Conquest of Paradise*, which proved by means of contemporaneous documents that Columbus, far from being a hero, was almost insanely greedy and cruel.

•   •   •

Our friend Kirkpatrick concludes in his book that Europeans came ashore "in what they dimly realized was the land of Paradise . . . but all they ever found was half a world of nature's treasures and nature's people that could be taken, and they took them, never knowing, never learning the true regenerative power there, and that opportunity was lost. Theirs was indeed a conquest of Paradise, but as is inevitable with any war against the world of nature, those who win will have lost—once again lost, and this time perhaps forever."

Wham! All of a sudden Kirkpatrick brings us up to the present day, and how we continue to wreck this place like vandals! The amount of garbage I produce each week is surely a case in point. It is picked up every Tuesday morning in this village with an Indian name on the tip of Long Island. I don't know where they take it. It simply disappears like whatever it was that seemed so important on TV only a few days ago. I am allowed only three cans of garbage a week. Anything more than that I have to get rid of myself somehow, and I already have three full cans of garbage. What to do? The Sunday edition of the *New York Times*, which I will pick up tomorrow morning, is all by itself bulky enough to fill a fourth garbage can.

• • •

Europeans are commonly uncomfortable when I call myself a German. When I accepted a prize in Sicily last year, I said that it was most gratefully received by both an American and a German. Several persons said afterward that they had not realized that I was born in Germany, which, actually, was not my case. If I had been born in Germany instead of Indianapolis, Indiana, in 1922, I would almost certainly have been a corpse on the Russian Front. My parents and grandparents were also born in Indianapolis, the first community in the United States, incidentally, where a white man was hanged for the murder of an Indian. It was my great-grandparents who were the immigrants, all Germans, literate and middle class, the males farmers and businessmen. They arrived too late to see the hanging. Better still, they were too late to have anything to do with the enslavement of black Africans or the extermination of the Indians, horrible achievements by Anglos and Spaniards and Portuguese, and here and there by Dutch and French, and, of course, mercenaries like Columbus.

The worst of the dirty work had been done, so my ancestors could feel as innocent as Adam and Eve as they built their homes and founded their schools and libraries and symphony orchestra, and so on, on fertile land where nobody had ever lived before, or so it seemed. And they were fruitful and multiplied, but continued to think of themselves, as do I, as Germans.

•   •   •

"Behind every great fortune lies a great crime," said Balzac, alluding to European aristocrats who imagined themselves to be descended from anything other than sociopaths. Count Dracula comes to mind. Yes, and the coinage of every Western Hemisphere nation might well be stamped with Balzac's words, to remind even the most recent arrivals here from the other half of the planet, perhaps Vietnamese, that they are legatees of maniacs like Columbus, who slit the noses of Indians, poked out their eyes, cut off their ears, burned them alive, and so on.

And while I and my children and grandchildren are entitled to say, as aftershocks of old atrocities continue to be felt by Indians and blacks, that our family never killed an Indian or owned a black, we can scarcely opine that Germans are gentler, kinder, saner than other Europeans. Would we dare? Does anybody perchance remember World War II? For those who never heard of it and its gruesome preamble, there are movies they can see. Word of honor, it really happened. All of it.

Yes, and Heinrich Himmler, a German chicken farmer Adolf Hitler put in charge of killing Jews and Slavs and homosexuals and Jehovah's Witnesses and Gypsies and so on in industrial quantities, once delivered a touching speech to his underlings, who were doing the tormenting and killing day after day, in which he praised them for sacrificing their humane impulses in order to achieve a greater good.

•   •   •

Another native German Heinrich, Heinrich Böll, a great writer, and I became friends even though we had once been corporals in opposing armies. I asked him once what he believed to be the basic flaw in the character of Germans, and he replied "obedience." When I consider the ghastly orders obeyed by underlings of Columbus, or of Aztec priests supervising human sacrifices, or of senile Chinese bureaucrats wishing to silence unarmed, peaceful protesters in Tiananmen Square only three years ago as I write, I have to wonder if obedience isn't the basic flaw in most of humankind.

•   •   •

And it is Monday now. I mustn't forget: Tuesday in this part of the New World is Garbage Day.

When I was in Sicily, accepting a prize for my book *Galápagos*, which argued that human beings were such terrible animals because their brains were too big, everyone was suddenly talking about a story that had just appeared in the papers and on TV. It said that American troops with bulldozers had buried alive thousands of Iraqi soldiers in tunnels where they were hiding from our shells and bombs and rockets. I answered without hesitation that American soldiers could not be found who would do a thing that heartless.

Wrong again.

• • •

The key words in the previous paragraph are "TV" and "bulldozers." These are manmade devices that, like rockets and artillery and war planes, and like the most expensive individual artifacts ever made by *Homo sapiens*, nuclear submarines, do more to comfort chicken-hearted underlings, should they be ordered to commit atrocities, than any inspirational speech by Columbus or Heinrich Himmler. I myself would not have thought of a bulldozer as such an instrument, had I not been trained during World War II to operate the largest tractors then used by our army, not for bulldozing, as it happened, but for dragging siege howitzers (240 mm) over rough terrain. If a blade had been fixed on the front of one, I might have bulldozed just about anything, with only a dim idea of what all was actually happening up front or underneath, as I sat high in the air, atop a lurching, quaking, roaring, clanking, cosmically insensitive juggernaut.

As for TV: I was about to say that it was a leading personality of our time, but now, still the day before Garbage Day, I am moved to declare it the *only* personality of our time, at least in the USA. I suggest that another date our children might be encouraged to memorize along with 1066, 1492, 1776, and 1941, not that they can remember much of anything anymore, thanks to TV, is 1839. That is when the French physicist Alexandre-Edmond Becquerel, according to the *Encyclopaedia Britannica*, "observed that when two electrodes are immersed in a suitable electrolyte and illuminated by a beam of light, an electromotive force is generated between the electrodes." If light could be turned into electricity, and if electricity could be turned into radio waves, and if radio waves could be turned back into electricity, and if electricity could be turned back into light, hey, presto! TV!

• • •

My adopted son Steve Adams wrote funny stuff for TV out in Los Angeles for a while. He made a lot of money, but he had to quit. He could not stand it anymore that every joke he wrote had to refer to something that had been big news on TV during the past two weeks. Otherwise, his audience wouldn't know what he was having fun with. TV was expected to be a great teacher, but its shows are so well done that it has become the only teacher, and an awful teacher, since there is no way for it to make its students learn by doing something. Worst of all, it keeps saying that whatever it has taught in the past doesn't matter anymore, that it has found something much more entertaining for us to look at.

So the wake of North American TV is something like the wake of a bulldozer, in which everything has been made nice and neat, dead level and lifeless and featureless. But a better analogue of TV's wake in the space-time continuum is a black hole into which even the greatest crimes and stupidities, and indeed whole continents, if need be, can be made to disappear from our consciousness.

• • •

I was trained many years ago by the University of Chicago to be an anthropologist, but I could find no work as such because I did not earn a doctorate. I have since inquired as to what became of my classmates who did go on to attain that rank, given that there weren't any primitive people around anymore. I was told that they had become "urban anthropologists." The slums of the richest nation on Earth are now their deserts, their ice caps, their jungles dark, where everybody but the urban anthropologists, thanks to the Second Amendment of the Constitution of the United States of America, seems to have a firearm. Bullets are flying everywhere.

The Second Amendment, written by the Anglo James Madison, a slave owner, says, "A well-regulated Militia, being necessary to the security of a free State, the right of the people to keep and bear Arms, shall not be infringed." As long as the poor people in this country kill each other, which is what so many of them are doing day after day, the federal government, obviously, is content to regard them, as Columbus might have done, as a well-regulated militia.

•   •   •

And, oh my gosh, I almost forgot! It's Tuesday morning! Today is Garbage Day! I will have to stand on top of the contents of a full-to-the-brim garbage can and jump up and down until I have made room for the Sunday *Times*.

OK, I have done that now. A big problem with garbage out here, aside from where the garbage men are supposed to put it after they have collected it, is created by raccoons (*Procyon lotor*) and opossums (*Didelphis virginiana*), both mammals that are omnivorous, nocturnal, and unbelievably cunning at getting the lids off garbage cans. I have heard that the North and South American continents were once separated by water, long before Columbus got here, long before any sort of human being got here. When a land bridge finally married the two land masses, we got some of their unique animals, and they got some of ours. They got our raccoons and we got their opossums, the only marsupials in the whole New World, incidentally, the worst possible news for garbage cans from Tierra del Fuego to Hudson Bay.

•   •   •

If I were worth my salt as an anthropologist, which I am not and never was, I would be writing now about the intermingling of Christianity and Native American religions instead of opossums and raccoons. But whatever it was that Columbus and so many of the Europeans who encountered Native Americans after him thought they were practicing, couldn't have been inspired by the Christian masterpiece, the Sermon on the Mount.

Kirkpatrick Sale tells of Taino Indians who buried Christian icons in their fields in order to increase the fields' fertility. This was a reverent thing for them to do, but Columbus's brother Bartolomé had the Indians burned alive. On several occasions the Spaniards hanged thirteen Indians at once, with their feet barely touching the ground, in honor of Jesus and the twelve Apostles. And of course the Christian Adolf Hitler back in the Old World, not that long ago, had the men who had conspired to assassinate him hanged from meat hooks by piano wire, with their feet barely touching the ground, and had their comical jigs of death filmed by a professional camera crew.

• • •

Let us give poor old Columbus a rest. He was a human being of his times, and aren't we all? We are all so often bad news for somebody else. AIDS, I read somewhere, was probably brought into this country by a Canadian flight attendant on an international flight. And what had his crime been? Nothing but love, love, love. That's life sometimes. And he is surely as dead as Columbus now. And I'm killing the world with garbage, three cans a week, sort of like Chinese water torture.

Speaking of Chinese tortures: I saw a wood engraving one time of a Chinese woman who had been tied down, and some Chinese men were encouraging a Chinese stallion to copulate with her, which, as a caption explained, would kill her. She must have done something wrong, or this wouldn't have been done to her. Not in so many words, certainly, but she must have asked for it.

And then there was the Christian Croatian Nazi in my time, although I was a mere youth then, who kept a bowl of human eyes on his desk. It was common for visitors to at first mistake them for hard-boiled eggs.

• • •

Tempus fugit! It is the day-after-Garbage Day! My three cans are again as vacant and inviting as was Indiana when my immigrant ancestors, without opposition, picked out their homesites there. I can again give my full attention to my cat Claude, a sensuous white male with one blue eye and one yellow eye, speaking of eyes. There are only the two of us here, in a house which appears on a map drawn in 1740. I have calculated that Claude's and my house is twice as old as the theory that invisible germs can cause disease. A woman who knows a lot about cats, or pretends to, told me that white cats with eyes like Claude's are deaf on the side of the blue eye.

I have yet to devise an experiment that can confirm this, or, alternatively, to demonstrate that the woman is as full of shit as a Christmas turkey. I am sixty-nine years old now, and my father didn't go to the New World in the sky until he was seventy-two, so I still have lots of time in which to experiment on Claude. I will need some apparatus, and there will be a temporary loss of dignity on the part of Claude. But without experimentation on lower animals, this world would be an even worse place than it is today. And Claude tortures mice before he kills them. Like Christopher Columbus, he knows nothing of the Beatitudes.

• • •

This part of Long Island has become a summer resort for some of the wealthiest human beings in history so far, many of them Europeans, particularly Germans. It is known generically as "the Hamptons." The political unit of which Claude and I are part is Southampton, but our village, again, an Indian name, is Sagaponack.

I am out here in the wintertime, with all the rich people generating garbage in Palm Beach and Monte Carlo and so on, because of certain problems with my marriage, which my wife and I hope are only temporary. I think she is Columbus and I am the Indians, and she thinks I am Columbus and she is the Indians. But we are calming down.

• • •

And now is as good a time as any to review my own relationship with what is left of the real Indians, or, as they prefer to be called, Native Americans. One time my wife and I invited a man who we thought was a Native American to the Russian Tea Room, an expensive restaurant in Manhattan, on Thanksgiving Day, the most agreeable of all our national holidays. It commemorates a feast in 1621 given by English invaders of what is now Plymouth, Massachusetts, to which Native Americans came as most welcome guests.

Our guest, while born in New York City, was customarily dressed in bits of costumes of many tribes, Navajo jewelry, Iroquois fringed deerskin, Cree moccasins, and so on, and was much respected as a speaker and writer on Native American affairs, and the writer of excellent novels about who he claimed were his people. He never wore a necktie, and the Russian Tea Room at that time had a rule, since honored in the breach to a fare-thee-well, that all male patrons had to wear ties.

I telephoned the restaurant and received in advance a suspension of the rule, in view of our guest's proud and respectable ethnicity. As I recall, we had blintzes with salmon caviar and sour cream, washed down with Stolichnaya vodka. That was about it. It was nice. But then, a couple of years later, several tribes of indigenes protested that this man, while he had served their cause nobly, was a white man pretending to be a Native American. Who knows? The last time I saw him, he was dressed like a Wall Street broker, but with one turquoise earring, which, since the stone's setting was of fine silver wires, I took to be the handiwork of Zunis, stubbornly superstitious aborigines in faraway New Mexico.

•   •   •

Other contacts I have had with Native Americans haven't been that ambiguous. When I was a youth I spent two summers roaming with friends through Arizona and Colorado and New Mexico, observing if not befriending Hopis and Navajos, and, yes, Zunis. We were fortunate enough to hear some of their songs and see some of their dances, and to have the opportunity to buy their artifacts without having to pay extra to an intervening white entrepreneur or two. But I must say that those people had my sympathy and admiration long before I got close enough to one to touch them and their kids.

Even when I was in the first grade in school in Indianapolis, where there were no Indians, or so few that I never heard about them, I think I knew that Indians were innocent victims of crimes by white men that could never be forgiven by me, by anyone. Almost all of my schoolmates felt the same way, and our teachers did, too. It was so obvious, once we learned that Indians used to have their homes where we lived. If we kept a sharp lookout when we walked through woods or along riverbanks, we could actually find their arrowheads. I myself used to have a collection of maybe twenty or more of those. Why would anybody have departed voluntarily from a region so salubrious?

• • •

As a lifelong Indian lover, I am shocked when I meet white people who live near a lot of Indians and have nothing but contempt for them. They are not numerous, and in my experience have almost all been members of our overtly white-supremacist and social-Darwinist political party, the party of Presidents Ronald Reagan and George Bush, the Republicans.

There is much worse to report: I have read about, but never seen, out-of-print writings by my particular literary hero, Mark Twain, in which he speaks of Indians, of whom he had seen plenty, as though they were subhuman, almost vermin. So again, who knows? Maybe they are like that Chinese woman who was tied down and killed by the penis of a stallion. Whatever the Native Americans got and are still getting, maybe they asked for it.

• • •

I correspond regularly with a Sioux named Leonard Peltier, who is serving two consecutive life sentences with no hope of parole, in the federal prison at Leavenworth, Kansas. He has become famous since it has become ever clearer that he was wrongly convicted for the fatal shooting of one or both agents of the Federal Bureau of Investigation killed on Indian property near Oglala, South Dakota, during a confused shootout in 1975. An Indian was also killed, and there can be no doubt that Indians did some shooting.

My friend Peter Matthiessen, who lives half a mile from here, wrote a book about the incident and its aftermath, *In the Spirit of Crazy Horse*. In it he declares, "The ruthless persecution of Leonard Peltier had less to do with his own actions than with underlying issues of history, racism, and economics, in particular Indian sovereignty claims and growing opposition to massive energy development on treaty lands and the dwindling reservations." In any case, evidence has now been uncovered, including a confession by the man who really did the killing, that Peltier didn't deserve even one life sentence, not even a minor fraction thereof.

Several months ago, it may have been on what was Garbage Day out here, this new evidence was brought to the attention of a federal judge in a petition that Peltier be given a new trial. The judge's decision is pending, but what a prosecutor said was noteworthy for its pigheadedness. He said, in effect, and I don't have his exact words, that if Peltier wasn't guilty of murder, he was sure as heck guilty of something almost as bad.

This rang a bell with me. I had written some about the Italian-American anarchists Nicola Sacco and Bartolomeo Vanzetti, who were electrocuted in Massachusetts for the murder of a payroll guard, in 1927, when I was only five. I knew that one of their prosecutors had said very much the same thing about them, that they were certainly guilty of something terrible, although unspecifiable in court. Again, another man had confessed to the crime, but they went to the "hot seat" anyway. Vanzetti sat down in the chair before he was told it was time to do so, just as though he were in his own living room. I told Peltier in a letter about the similarities between their prosecutors and his, and added what I think is true: The Italians back in the 1920s and earlier seemed as non-white to this country's ruling class as Indians. And so seemed Greeks and Jews and Spaniards and Portuguese.

•   •   •

In a P.S. to the letter I said that Al Capone, the Chicago gangster, was asked if his fellow Italian immigrants should be executed, and he replied, "Yes." When asked why Massachusetts should kill them, Capone said, "They are ungrateful to this wonderful country." That could be true of Leonard Peltier as well. His last name is pronounced "Pelter." The capital of his native state, Pierre, South Dakota, is pronounced "Peer." Very little French is spoken there. Al Capone was sent to prison for not paying income tax.

•   •   •

I apologize for writing as though the United States were the entire Western Hemisphere, and as though Claude were the only cat here, half-deaf or otherwise. But the first rule taught in any creative-writing course, and I think it's a good one, is: "Write what you know about."

• • •

Robert Hughes, an Australian who has become this nation's most intelligent art critic and a historian of his native land as well, has written disapprovingly in *Time* magazine of Kirkpatrick Sale's *The Conquest of Paradise*. He says that, while the heroism of Columbus was a myth pleasing to white supremacists, Sale served the truth no better by making Columbus "like Hitler in a caravel, landing like a virus among the innocent people of the New World."

The smallest state in Hughes's Australia, the island of Tasmania, is the only place on Earth where the entire native population was dead soon after the first white people arrived, and whose genes are no longer to be found even in crossbreeds, since the settlers found Tasmanians so loathsome that they would not have sex with them. It is not certain that the Tasmanians had even domesticated fire.

At the University of Chicago so long ago, one professor suggested to me that the Tasmanians found life so intolerable after the white people came that they stopped having sex with each other.

Contrast, if you will, all that celibacy in the Tasman Sea with this uninhibited frolic in 1493, in the Caribbean: "While I was in the boat I captured a very beautiful Carib woman, whom the said Lord Admiral gave to me . . . I conceived desire to take pleasure . . . but she did not want it and treated me with her fingernails in such a manner that I wished I had never begun. But . . . I took a rope and thrashed her well, for which she raised such unheard of screams that you would not have believed your ears. Finally we came to an agreement in such a manner that I can tell you that she seemed to have been brought up in a school for harlots."

That is an account by an Italian nobleman, and I have lifted it from Sale's book. The Lord Admiral, of course, was Columbus. And one is surely not reminded of Hitler, whom Sale mentions nowhere, since Hitler was virtually as celibate as the last Tasmanian, sexually beyond reproach.

• • •

During the Second World War it was generally believed by Hitler's enemies that he had only one testicle. I confess that I believed it. We will never know, I suppose, who started that rumor. But Russians who took possession of Hitler's charred remains in Berlin counted his testicles, and he had two of them. It is also not true that the Nazis made soap and candles of fat rendered from the corpses of concentration-camp victims. I myself helped to spread that story in a novel, *Mother Night*, and have received enough letters from dispassionate fact-gatherers to persuade me that I had been misleading. Mea culpa.

I once worked for a man who was so stupid he believed that all women menstruated on the same day of the month, that they were all controlled by the moon. I certainly never passed *that* on.

• • •

What I have seen with my own two eyes, though, and can easily see again whenever I please, is a nuclear submarine, under construction or slumbering on the surface of the Thames River at Groton, Connecticut. Several of these things operating in concert, and we have several of them, are capable of killing everybody in the other hemisphere, as though there were dozens of hemispheres instead of only two. Yes, and the Soviet Union, which has had the grace to vote itself out of existence, had the same sort of high-tech, whiz-bang, guilt-free, hemisphere-killing, undersea leviathans. I can't help thinking that it is somehow symbolically significant that, on the five hundredth anniversary of the end of Europe's non-discovery of America, each hemisphere had thought it might become necessary to kill the other one, but had suddenly changed its mind about that.

On this side of the water at least, TV, our great teacher, our endlessly diverting teacher, our only teacher, has had a lot to do with this change of heart, as well as with the elaborate preparations for suicide that preceded it. It has made all our enemies vanish into the black hole in its wake. It is as though they never existed. Until practically the day before yesterday, we were loved by only some countries. Now all countries love us, and we should feel like Marilyn Monroe standing over an air vent in the sidewalk, with her skirt blowing up around her ears, absolutely adorable!

• • •

If it weren't for TV, we might now be, to use one of our many colorful expressions, "standing around with egg on our face," since we are stuck with all this doomsday apparatus that has no sane purpose, and that sopped up so much of our wealth that our bridges and schools and hospitals and so forth are falling down.

To "stand around with egg on one's face," as nearly as I can explain it to somebody who doesn't actually live here, is to display charming embarrassment or perhaps winsome silliness about one's participation in an enterprise that was supposed to be necessary, logical, and all-round wonderful, but that turned out to be the exact opposite. But TV is making the weapons disappear by having us look elsewhere.

To "stand around with egg on one's face" is not to be confused with "standing around with one's thumb up one's fundament," which means not knowing what to do next, as does "not knowing whether to defecate or wind one's watch."

• • •

Robert Hughes's disparagement of my friend Kirkpatrick Sale's book is but a tiny part of a long polemic by him against all who depict European colonists as having been purely evil, and the natives they distressed as having been purely virtuous. But Hughes or anyone else reading Sale's documented account of what Columbus and his men did and what the Tainos and Caribs did upon finding themselves intermingled would be hard put to say what persons of a philosophical turn of mind like to say whenever possible: "There was blame enough for everyone."

Nor does Hughes imply as much. What really bothers him, as near as I can tell, is that historians like Sale, although truthful, encourage large numbers of foolish people of all races to believe that persons of European descent in this hemisphere right now still represent pure evil, and that the descendants of the hideously abused Indians and black slaves are charmingly innocent, or would have been, if only white people had never troubled them.

Sale himself is not that foolish. What he does say in one way or another is that white people over here still hold most of the power, and continue to be slovenly and greedy custodians of an ecological system that might still, with a good deal of effort, become something approaching Paradise.

• • •

Robert Hughes's employer, *Time* magazine, has been publishing once a week since 1923, when I was only one year old. Within my own memory, I can't recall a single issue in which *Time* appeared to be standing around with egg on its face or with its thumb up its fundament. Others could be mistaken, but never *Time*. Its founder, Henry Robinson Luce (1898–1967), declared this to be "The American Century," "America" to him and his readers being the United States. And *Time* continues to be profoundly sympathetic with those at the top of the white power structure here, no matter what a bad job they may be doing, on the grounds, I suppose, that it isn't easy to be on top. But the writers and editors of *Time* today are unlikely to feel in their personal lives the aplomb of their magazine. The enormous corporation of which they are mere particles has gone into debt on a catastrophic scale, in order to enrich a very few of its top executives. It does not appear to have revenues adequate to pay even the interest on its debts.

Several employees of *Time* have been laid off as economy measures, and those remaining are entitled to feel as the Tainos and Caribs should have felt in 1492, when the first Europeans beached their longboat, stepped out on the sand with their firearms and edged weapons at the ready, and began to look around.

I do not mean that those laid off or about to be laid off by *Time* can expect to be enslaved or hanged in batches of thirteen or whatever. But they will surely experience severe acculturation, as will the seventy thousand workers recently laid off by General Motors, and many will feel as lonesome and unwanted on Earth, until they find new jobs, God willing, as did, surely, the last Tasmanian. They, and all the others in Henry Robinson Luce's America who are facing unemployment, are as blameless and powerless as persons caught in an avalanche.

• • •

And when I think of avalanches, or indeed of tremendous, unopposable forces of any sort, I am reminded of an English friend of my big brother and me, John Latham, an atmospheric scientist like my brother, but a poet and humorist as well. He has been working for years on a book of advice for travelers in foreign lands, and one of his chapters tells how you should behave after being hit by an avalanche, in the Himalayas, say. The first rule is do not panic. The second rule is, after you have been buried alive, and all movement of rocks and snow around you has stopped, find out which way is up. John says, as I recall, that this can be done by dangling a pocket watch or a locket at the end of its chain. Yes, and much useful information can be garnered, he says, if you study the behavior of snow fleas that may have been buried with you.

Mark Twain, not long before he died a bitter old man, was writing a book much like John Latham's, pretending to be helpful but actually calling attention to how humbling life, and especially its endings, can be. Twain's was about etiquette. His advice on how to behave at a funeral, I remember, included, "Do not bring your dog." Like Latham, he chose to laugh in agony rather than sob in agony about how irresistible forces, whether physical or economic or biological or political or social or military or historical or technological, can at any time smash our hopes for moderately happy and healthy lives for ourselves and our loved ones to smithereens.

• • •

Robert Hughes and many others like him may dislike histories like *The Conquest of Paradise* because they are tearjerkers, making us sympathize with the miseries of nobodies long gone, like the Carib beauty who was whipped and whipped, or like the last Tasmanian, also a woman, rather than celebrating the grandeur of history when viewed from afar. But when I ask myself now of what that grandeur could possibly consist, I can come up with only one answer: The millions and millions of us who, in spite of all the atrocities, are still OK.

• • •

My first wife, née Jane Marie Cox, now dead of cancer, was such an adept student of literature in college that she was nominated by the English Department for the highest honor, which was election to Phi Beta Kappa, a national society of our most diligent students. Her election was opposed by the History Department, whose wares she had denounced often and vocally as being as void of decency as child pornography. She was in good company of course, as I am able to demonstrate with the help of Bartlett's *Familiar Quotations*: "History is but the record of crimes and misfortunes," Voltaire; "History is a nightmare from which I am trying to awake," James Joyce; and on and on. Jane's champions pointed this out to her enemies, and they prevailed. She became a Phi Beta Kappa.

I knew Jane back then, when she was the focal point of that controversy, and thought her stubborn stand attractive but wrongheaded. Back then, I still believed, as I do not believe nowadays, that the human condition was improving despite such heavy casualties. We are incorrigibly the nastiest of all animals, as our history attests, and that is that.

• • •

I have said almost nothing about those of us in the USA who are the descendants of black African slaves. Well over half of them, as any fool can see, are also variously English or Scottish or Irish or Native Americans. The fact that so many of them are white as well as black is as seldom mentioned in polite conversations by whites as the fact that the crosses on the Nazis' tanks and planes testified that those inside believed themselves, as did Columbus, to be in the service of Jesus of Nazareth.

The people who are called black here, and who call themselves black, are a small and easily defeatable minority, somewhere around ten or twelve percent of us. They have nonetheless made what is perhaps this hemisphere's most consoling and harmlessly exciting contribution to world civilization: jazz. Second to that in making life a little better than it would be without it is, in my opinion, the therapeutic scheme for treating dangerous addictions, the invention by two white men in Akron, Ohio, of what are known as the Principles of Alcoholics Anonymous.

Two other men from Ohio invented the flying machine. But I don't believe we should be grateful to them. Such instruments have made smashing to smithereens the hopes of defenseless individuals, in Iraq, for example, even more of a lark than it was five hundred years ago.

• • •

And thus, with those lugubrious words, I end an idiosyncratic voyage of my own on paper. A kitchen chair set before a typewriter has been my caravel. A white tomcat has been my only crew. I have navigated by means of freely associated words and facts and people, starting with the number 1492. That reminded me somehow of my regimental commander years ago, and he reminded me somehow of the exploration of space, and on and on. I encountered raccoons and opossums on the way, and my first wife Jane, and Jesus and Hitler, and atomic submarines, and a virtuous young woman who was whipped until she behaved as though she had been brought up in a school for harlots, and Kirkpatrick Sale and Robert Hughes, and on and on.

The chance juxtaposing of Sale and Hughes gave me the only trinket worth saving, in my opinion, from the whole crazy trip, a definition of the grandeur Hughes and other good people find in history when viewed from a distance: the millions and millions of us who, in spite of all the atrocities, are still OK. The paying guests in evening clothes at a fund-raising banquet for the New York City Ballet Company in a ballroom at the Waldorf-Astoria Hotel come to mind. And how dare I speak ill of them, since I myself have been among them? I love the ballet.

• • •

I have just received a telephone call from a Canadian friend, a filmmaker who says that the planet can feed only six billion mammals our size, provided that the nourishment is fairly divided among us and delivered at once to anyone about to starve to death.

He has gathered together enough money to make a documentary film about the destruction by *Homo sapiens* of the planet, of "Space Ship Earth," as a life-support system. He asked me to be a consultant, since I had written, among other things, that we were "a new sort of glacier, warm-blooded and clever, unstoppable, about to gobble up everything and then make love—and then double in size again." He wants to wake us up.

•   •   •

His call interrupted my reading of this morning's mail, in which an old girlfriend from eons ago, now in the process of being divorced, sent me a newspaper clipping about a physician in Virginia, a specialist in the treatment of infertility in human beings. For years he had been giving women the benefit of sperm donated supposedly by strikingly healthy and intelligent and presentable young men. In at least eighty of the treatments that resulted in pregnancies carried to term, the donor had been the physician himself! So there is just one man who has added eighty more people to the burdens of the Earth. There aren't that many bears left in all of Germany, I heard on the radio this morning, nor elephants in Mozambique. And his kids are all going to want cars when they're old enough, and they'll reproduce.

A headwaiter in a hotel in Haiti, the scene of the only successful slave revolt in all of history, boasted to me that he had twenty-nine children. "I have very strong sperm," he said. And now corpses of whales are washing up on Long Island in industrial quantities. There could be a connection. Then again, the paint remover and the insecticides I put in my garbage cans last Tuesday could be to blame.

•   •   •

I am sorry not to be more encouraged and encouraging about human destiny in 1992, since I myself, with my reasonably strong sperm, have sired three children, and they have given me seven grandchildren in turn.

I am happy to say that all my descendants, mongrelized with Scottish and English and Irish genes, inhabit safe houses in peaceful neighborhoods, houses full of books and music and love and good things to eat. They are clearly beneficiaries of 1492 and all the rest of history when viewed from afar. But I can't see how that can go on much longer, since both hemispheres are now jam-packed with other people who need at least a thousand calories of nourishment every day. Indeed, starving men, women, and children are so numerous and ubiquitous now that our TV is hard put to show us even a minor fraction of them before making them disappear forever into the black hole in its wake.

As an anthropologist, supposedly, I might be expected to say a little something about the cultures that are vanishing along with the people. But hunger, it seems to me, becomes the whole of anybody's culture before death sets in. As Bertolt Brecht said, "*Erst kommt das Fressen, dann kommt die Moral*," or, freely translated, "As long as we're hungry, all we can think about is food."

I agree with the Roman Catholic Church that all schemes for adjusting the human population to the food supply, short of abstinence exemplified by the last Tasmanians, range from indignity to infanticide. They are also impractical. My adopted son, the progeny of my late sister, served in the Peace Corps in a village on the eastern slope of the Andes in Peru. His mission was to discover what the little-known people there needed most, what a higher civilization might give to them. It turned out they wanted condoms, which are expensive, and which, of course, can be used only once and then must be thrown away. If he had been able to make condoms available, which our government surely would not have approved, they probably would have been tossed after use into a tributary of the Amazon River, coming to rest, at last, with any luck, on the beach at Ipanema, with all the nubile girls in their string bikinis.

So I have no choice but to say that the jig is up.

•   •   •

As consolation, I offer this prayer attributed to the great German-American theologian Reinhold Niebuhr (1892–1971), possibly as early as 1937, in the depths of the planetary economic depression before this one: "God grant me the serenity to accept the things I cannot change, courage to change the things I can, and wisdom to know the difference."

—Sagaponack, 1992

Talk prepared for delivery at
Clowes Memorial Hall, Butler University, Indianapolis, April 27, 2007

T HANK YOU.
 I now stand before you as a role model, courtesy of Mayor Bart Peterson, and God bless him for this occasion.

If this isn't nice, I don't know what is.

And just think of this: In only three years' time, during World War Two, I went from Private to Corporal, a rank once held by both Napoleon and Adolf Hitler.

I am actually Kurt Vonnegut, Junior. And that's what my kids, now in late middle age like me, still call me when talking about me behind my back: "Junior this and Junior that."

But whenever you look at the Ayres clock at the Intersection of South Meridian and Washington Streets, please think of my father, Kurt Vonnegut, Senior, who designed it. As far as that goes, he and his father, Bernard Vonnegut, designed the whole darn building. And he was a founder of The Orchard School and The Children's Museum.

His father, my grandfather the architect Bernard Vonnegut, designed, among other things, The Athenæum, which before the First World War was called "Das Deutsche Haus." I can't imagine why they would have changed the name to "The Athenæum," unless it was to kiss the ass of a bunch of Greek-Americans.

I guess all of you know that I am suing the manufacturer of Pall Mall cigarettes, because their product didn't kill me, and I'm now eighty-four. Listen: I studied anthropology at the University of Chicago after the Second World War, the last one we ever won. And the physical anthropologists, who had studied human skulls going back thousands of years, said we were only supposed to live for thirty-five years or so, because that's how long our teeth lasted without modern dentistry.

Weren't those the good old days: thirty-five years and we were out of here. Talk about intelligent design! Now all the Baby Boomers who can afford dentistry and health insurance, poor bastards, are going to live to be a hundred!

Maybe we should outlaw dentistry. And maybe doctors should quit curing pneumonia, which used to be called "the old people's friend."

But the last thing I want to do tonight is to depress you. So I have thought of something we can all do tonight which will definitely be upbeat. I think we can come up with a statement on which all Americans, Republican or Democrat, rich or poor, straight or gay, can agree, despite our country's being so tragically and ferociously divided.

The first universal American sentiment I came up with was "Sugar is sweet."

And there is certainly nothing new about a tragically and ferociously divided United States of America, and especially here in my native state of Indiana. When I was a kid here, this state had within its borders the national headquarters of the Ku Klux Klan, and the site of the last lynching of an African-American citizen north of the Mason-Dixon Line, Marion, I think.

But it also had, and still has, in Terre Haute, which now boasts a state-of-the-art lethal-injection facility, the birthplace and home of the labor leader Eugene Debs. He lived from 1855 to 1926, and led a nationwide strike against the railroads. He went to prison for a while because he opposed our entry into World War One.

And he ran for President several times, on the Socialist Party ticket, saying things like this: "While there is a lower class, I am in it; while there is a criminal element, I am of it; and while there is a soul in prison, I am not free."

Debs pretty much stole that from Jesus Christ. But it is so hard to be original. Tell me about it!

But all right, what is a statement on which all Americans can agree? "Sugar is sweet," certainly. But since we are on the property of a university, we can surely come up with something which has more cultural heft. And this is my suggestion: "The Mona Lisa, the picture by Leonardo da Vinci, hanging in the Louvre in Paris, France, is a perfect painting."

OK? A show of hands, please. Can't we all agree on that?

OK, take down your hands. I'd say the vote is unanimous, that the Mona Lisa is a perfect painting. The only trouble with that, which is the trouble with practically everything we believe: It isn't true.

Listen: Her nose is tilted to the right, OK? That means the right side of her face is a receding plane, going away from us. OK? But there is no foreshortening of her features on that side, giving the effect of three dimensions. And Leonardo could so easily have done that foreshortening. He was simply too lazy to do it. And if he were Leonardo da Indianapolis, I would be ashamed of him.

No wonder she has such a cockeyed smile.

And somebody might now want to ask me, "Can't you ever be serious?" The answer is, "No."

When I was born at Methodist Hospital on November eleventh, 1922, and this city back then was as racially segregated as professional basketball and football teams are today, the obstetrician spanked my little rear end to start my respiration. But did I cry? No.

I said, "A funny thing happened on the way down the birth canal, Doc. A bum came up to me and said he hadn't had a bite for three days. So I bit him!"

But seriously, my fellow Hoosiers, there's good news and bad news tonight. This is the best of times and the worst of times. So what else is new?

The bad news is that the Martians have landed in Manhattan, and have checked in at the Waldorf-Astoria. The good news is that they only eat homeless people of all colors, and they pee gasoline.

Am I religious? I practice a disorganized religion. I belong to an unholy disorder. We call ourselves "Our Lady of Perpetual Consternation." We are as celibate as fifty percent of the heterosexual Roman Catholic clergy.

Actually—and when I hold up my right hand like this, it means I'm not kidding, that I give my Word of Honor that what I'm about to say is true. So actually, I am honorary President of the American Humanist Association, having succeeded the late, great science fiction writer Isaac Asimov in that utterly functionless capacity. We Humanists behave as well as we can, without any expectation of rewards or punishments in an Afterlife. We serve as best we can the only abstraction with which we have any real familiarity, which is our community.

We don't fear death, and neither should you. You know what Socrates said about death, in Greek, of course? "Death is just one more night."

As a Humanist, I love science. I hate superstition, which could never have given us A-bombs.

I love science, and not only because it has given us the means to trash the planet, and I don't like it here. It has found the answers to two of our biggest questions: How did the Universe begin, and how did we and all other animals get the wonderful bodies we have, with eyes and brains and kidneys and so on?

•

OK. So science sent the Hubble telescope out into space, so it could capture light and the absence thereof, from the very beginning of time. And the telescope really did that. So now we know that there was once absolutely nothing, such a perfect nothing that there wasn't even nothing or once. Can you imagine that? You can't, because there isn't even nothing to imagine.

But then there was this great big BANG! And that's where all this crap came from.

And how did we get our wonderful lungs and eyebrows and teeth and toenails and assholes and so on? By means of millions of years of natural selection. That's when one animal dies and another one copulates. Survival of the fittest!

But look: If you should kill somebody, whether accidentally or on purpose, improving our species, please don't copulate afterwards. That's what causes babies, in case your mother didn't tell you.

And yes, my fellow Hoosiers, and I have never denied being one of you: This is indeed the Apocalypse, the end of everything, as prophesied by Saint John the Divine and Saint Kurt the Vonnegut.

Even as I speak, the very last polar bear may be dying of hunger on account of climate change, on account of us. And I will sure miss the polar bears. Their babies are so warm and cuddly and trusting, just like ours.

Does this old poop have any advice for young people in times of such awful trouble? Well, I'm sure you know that our country is the only so-called advanced nation that still has a death penalty. And torture chambers. I mean, why screw around?

But listen: If anyone here should wind up on a gurney in a lethal-injection facility, maybe the one at Terre Haute, here is

what your last words should be: "This will certainly teach me
a lesson."

If Jesus were alive today, we would kill him with lethal injec-
tion. I call that progress. We would have to kill him for the same
reason he was killed the first time. His ideas are just too liberal.

My advice to writers just starting out? Don't use semicolons!
They are transvestite hermaphrodites, representing exactly
nothing. All they do is suggest you might have gone to college.

So first the Mona Lisa, and now semicolons. I might as well
clinch my reputation as a world-class nutcase by saying something good about Karl Marx, commonly believed in this country, and surely in Indian-no-place, to have been one of the most
evil people who ever lived.
He did invent Communism, which we have long been taught
to hate, because we are so in love with Capitalism, which is what
we call the casinos on Wall Street.

Communism is what Karl Marx hoped could be an economic
scheme for making industrialized nations take as good care of
people, and especially of children and the old and disabled, as
tribes and extended families used to do, before they were dispersed by the Industrial Revolution.
And I think maybe we might be wise to stop bad-mouthing
Communism so much, not because we think it's a good idea,
but because our grandchildren and great-grandchildren are now
in hock up to their eyeballs to the Communist Chinese.
And the Chinese Communists also have a big and superbly
equipped army, something we don't have. We're too cheap. We
just want to nuke everybody.

But there are still plenty of people who will tell you that the
most evil thing about Karl Marx was what he said about religion. He said it was the opium of the lower classes, as though
he thought religion was bad for people, and he wanted to get
rid of it.
But when Marx said that, back in the 1840s, his use of the
word "opium" wasn't simply metaphorical. Back then real

opium was the only painkiller available, for toothaches or cancer of the throat, or whatever. He himself had used it.

As a sincere friend of the downtrodden, he was saying he was glad they had something which could ease their pain at least a little bit, which was religion. He liked religion for doing that, and certainly didn't want to abolish it. OK?

He might have said today as I say tonight, "Religion can be Tylenol for a lot of unhappy people, and I'm so glad it works."

About the Chinese Communists: They are obviously much better at business than we are, and maybe a lot smarter, Communists or not. I mean, look how much better they do in our schools over here. Face it! My son, Mark, a pediatrician, was on the Admissions Committee of the Harvard Medical School a while back, and he said that if they had played the admissions game fairly, half of the entering class would be Asian women.

But back to Karl Marx: How subservient to Jesus, or to a humane God Almighty, were the leaders of this country back in the 1840s, when Marx said such a supposedly evil thing about religion? They had made it perfectly legal to own human slaves, and weren't going to let women vote or hold public office, God forbid, for another eighty years.

I got a letter a while back from a man who had been a captive in the American penal system since he was sixteen years old. He is now forty-two, and about to get out. He asked me what he should do. I told him what Karl Marx would have told him: "Join a church."

And now please note that I have raised my right hand. And that means that I'm not kidding, that whatever I say next I believe to be true. So here goes: The most spiritually splendid American phenomenon of my lifetime wasn't our contribution to the defeat of the Nazis, in which I played such a large part, or Ronald Reagan's overthrow of Godless Communism, in Russia at least.

The most spiritually splendid American phenomenon of my lifetime is how African-American citizens have maintained their dignity and self-respect, despite their having been treated by white Americans, both in and out of government, and simply because of their skin color, as though they were contemptible and loathsome, and even diseased.

Their churches have surely helped them to do that. So there's Karl Marx again. There's Jesus again.

And what gift of America to the rest of the world is actually most appreciated by the rest of the world? It is African-American jazz and its offshoots. What is my definition of jazz? "Safe sex of the highest order."

The two greatest Americans of my lifetime, so far as I know, were Franklin Delano Roosevelt and Martin Luther King, Jr.

I have heard it suggested that Roosevelt wouldn't have had such empathy for the lower classes, would have been just another rich, conceited, ruling-class Ivy League horse's ass, if he himself hadn't been humbled by poliomyelitis, infantile paralysis. All of a sudden his legs didn't work anymore.

What can we do about global warming? We could turn out the lights, I guess, but please don't. I can't think of any way to repair the atmosphere. It's way too late. But there is one thing I can fix, and fix this very night, and right here in Indianapolis. It's the name of another good university you've built since my time. But you've named it "I.U.P.U.I." "I.U.P.U.I."? Have you lost your wits?
    "Hi, I went to Harvard. Where did you go?"
    "I went to I.U.P.U.I."
    With the unlimited powers vested in me by Mayor Peterson for the whole year of 2007, I rename I.U.P.U.I. "Tarkington University."
    "Hi, I went to Harvard. Where did you go?"
    "I went to Tarkington." Ain't that classy?

•

Done and done.

With the passage of time, nobody will know or care who Tarkington was. I mean, who nowadays gives a rat's ass who Butler was? This is Clowes Hall, and I actually knew some real Cloweses. Nice people.

But let me tell you: I would not be standing before you tonight if it hadn't been for the example of the life and works of Booth Tarkington, a native of this city. During his time, 1869 to 1946, which overlapped my own time for twenty-four years, Booth Tarkington became a beautifully successful and respected writer of plays, novels, and short stories. His nickname in the literary world, one I would give anything to have, was "The Gentleman from Indiana."

When I was a kid, I wanted to be like him.

We never met. I wouldn't have known what to say. I would have been gaga with hero worship.

Yes, and by the unlimited powers vested in me by Mayor Peterson for this entire year, I demand that somebody here mount a production in Indianapolis of Booth Tarkington's play *Alice Adams*.

By a sweet coincidence, "Alice Adams" was also the married name of my late sister, a six-foot-tall blond bombshell, who is now in Crown Hill along with our parents and grandparents and great-grandparents, and James Whitcomb Riley, the highest-paid American writer of his time.

You know what my sister Allie used to say? She used to say, "Your parents ruin the first half of your life, and your kids ruin the second half."

James Whitcomb Riley, "The Hoosier Poet," was the highest-paid American writer of his time, 1849 to 1916, because he recited his poetry for money in theaters and lecture halls. That was how delighted by poetry ordinary Americans used to be. Can you imagine?

•

You want to know something the great French writer Jean-Paul Sartre said one time? He said, in French of course, "Hell is other people." He refused to accept a Nobel Prize. I could never be that rude. I was raised right by our African-American cook, whose name was Ida Young.

During the Great Depression, African-American citizens were heard to say this, along with a lot of other stuff, of course: "Things are so bad white folks got to raise their own kids."

But I wasn't raised right by Ida Young alone, a great-grand-child of slaves, who was intelligent, kind and honorable, proud and literate, articulate and thoughtful and pleasing in appearance. Ida Young loved poetry, and used to read poems to me.

I was also raised right by teachers at School 43, "The James Whitcomb Riley School," and then at Shortridge High School. Back then, great public school teachers were local celebrities. Grateful former students, well into adult life, used to visit them, and tell them how they were doing. And I myself used to be a sentimental adult like that.

But long ago now, all my favorite teachers went the way of most of the polar bears.

The very best thing you can be in life is a teacher, provided that you are crazy in love with what you teach, and that your classes consist of eighteen students or fewer. Classes of eighteen students or fewer are a family, and feel and act like one.

When my grade graduated from School 43, with the Great Depression going on, with almost no business or jobs, and with Hitler taking charge of Germany, each of us had to say in writing what we hoped to do when grown-ups to make this a better world.

I said I would cure cancer with chemicals, while working for Eli Lilly.

I have the humorist Paul Krassner to thank for pointing out a big difference between George W. Bush and Hitler: Hitler was elected.

•

I mentioned my only son, Mark Vonnegut, a while back. You know: about Chinese women and Harvard Medical School?

Well, he is not only a pediatrician in the Boston area, but a painter and a saxophonist and a writer. He wrote one heck of a good book called *The Eden Express*. It is about his mental crack-up, padded-cell-and-straitjacket stuff. He had been on the wrestling team as an undergraduate in college. Some maniac!

In his book he tells about how he recovered sufficiently to graduate from Harvard Medical School. *The Eden Express*, by Mark Vonnegut.

But don't borrow it. For God's sake, buy it!

I consider anybody who borrows a book instead of buying it, or lends one, a twerp. When I was a student at Shortridge High School a million years ago, a twerp was defined as a guy who put a set of false teeth up his rear end and bit the buttons off the back seats of taxicabs.

But I hasten to say, should some impressionable young person here tonight, at loose ends and from a dysfunctional family, resolve to take a shot at being a real twerp tomorrow, that there are no longer buttons on the back seats of taxicabs. Times change!

I asked Mark a while back what life was all about, since I didn't have a clue. He said, "Dad, we are here to help each other get through this thing, whatever it is." Whatever it is.

"Whatever it is." Not bad. That one could be a keeper.

And how should we behave during this Apocalypse? We should be unusually kind to one another, certainly. But we should also stop being so serious. Jokes help a lot. And get a dog, if you don't already have one.

I myself just got a dog, and it's a new crossbreed. It's half French poodle and half Chinese shih tzu.

It's a shit-poo.

And I thank you for your attention, and I'm out of here.

CHRONOLOGY

NOTE ON THE TEXTS

NOTES

Chronology

money, at 4365 North Illinois Street, near the intersection with Forty-fifth Street, Indianapolis. After the Great Crash of October, the mortgage payment on the property becomes increasingly difficult to meet.

1931   As the Depression deepens and new construction ceases, Vonnegut, Bohn & Mueller struggles. Father sells investments and heirlooms to keep family solvent, and reluctantly dismisses Ida Young. ("She was humane and wise and gave me decent moral instruction," Vonnegut will later remember. "The compassionate, forgiving aspects of my beliefs come from Ida Young.") Father's younger brother, Alex Vonnegut, a Harvard-educated insurance salesman and bon vivant, becomes Vonnegut's mentor and "ideal grownup friend." ("He taught me something very important: that when things are going well, we should notice it. He urged me to say out loud during such epiphanies, 'If this isn't nice, *what is?*'") Vonnegut is withdrawn from private school and begins fourth grade at James Whitcomb Riley Elementary, P.S. 43.

1934   Father, after years without an architectural commission, closes his office, turns an attic room of the house into an art studio, and begins to paint portraits, still lifes, and landscapes. Mother takes night classes in creative writing and attempts, unsuccessfully, to sell commercial short fiction to women's magazines. Vonnegut, age eleven, takes a strong interest and vicarious pleasure in his parents' artistic pursuits. In September, Grandfather Lieber dies at age seventy-one. The Vonneguts' share of his estate after probate is less than eleven thousand dollars, and mother, grieving, resentful, and obsessively insecure about the family's diminished social position, begins a long struggle with alcohol abuse, insomnia, and depression. ("My mother was addicted to being rich," Vonnegut will later write. "She was tormented by withdrawal symptoms all through the Great Depression.")

1936   Vonnegut enters Shortridge High School, the largest and best equipped free public school in the state of Indiana. Excels in English and public-speaking classes, and, after dedicated application, the sciences. Joins the staff of the Shortridge *Daily Echo*, a four-page broadsheet edited, set up, and printed by students in the school's print shop, and develops the habit of writing regularly, on deadline, for an audience of his peers. (In his junior and senior years, he will be editor and chief writer of the paper's Tuesday edition.) Plays clarinet in school orchestra and marching band, and takes private lessons from Ernst Michaelis, first-chair clarinetist of the Indianapolis Symphony. Forms a book club for two with Uncle Alex and reads, mostly at Alex's suggestion, Robert Louis Stevenson, H. G. Wells, H. L. Mencken, Thorstein Veblen, George Bernard Shaw, and Mark Twain. Other enthusiasms include Ping-Pong, model trains, radio comedy, movies, and jazz, especially Benny Goodman and Artie Shaw. Begins smoking Pall Mall cigarettes, which will become a lifelong habit.

1940   At age eighteen his head is a mop of blond curls and he has attained his adult height of six foot two: "I was a real skinny, narrow-shouldered boy . . . a preposterous kind of flamingo." Graduates from Shortridge High, and, still living with his parents, enrolls at local Butler University. His vague ambition is to study journalism and, ultimately, write for one of Indianapolis's three daily papers.

1941   Disappointed in Butler, transfers to Cornell University, Ithaca, New York, in middle of freshman year. Following his father's orders and his scientist brother's example, shuns "frivolous" classes in the arts and humanities, focusing instead on chemistry and physics. ("I had no talent for science," Vonnegut will remember. "I did badly.") Neglects his studies, taking pleasure only in drilling with ROTC, drinking with his Delta Upsilon brothers, and writing jokes and news for the Cornell *Daily Sun*. In summer, father sells the big brick house and, with proceeds, builds a smaller one in Williams Creek, a new suburban development six miles north of Indianapolis.

1942   Vonnegut writes a regular column, "Well All Right," for the *Daily Sun*—"impudent editorializing" and "college-humor sort of stuff"—and is elected the paper's assistant managing editor. In the middle of the fall semester of his junior year, is placed on academic probation due to poor grades. Contracts viral pneumonia, withdraws from school, and goes home to recover.

1943   Against the pleas of his mother, enlists in the U.S. Army and in March begins basic training at Camp Atterbury, forty miles south of Indianapolis. Takes special classes in manning the 240-millimeter howitzer, the army's largest mobile fieldpiece. In summer joins the Army Specialized Training Program, and is sent first to the Carnegie Institute of Technology, Pittsburgh, and then to the University of Tennessee, Knoxville, for advanced studies in engineering ("thermodynamics, mechanics, the actual use of machine tools. . . . I did badly again").

1944   In March returns to Camp Atterbury and is assigned as private first class to Headquarters Company, 2nd Battalion, 423rd Regiment, 106th Infantry Division. Although he has no infantry training ("bayonets, grenades, and so on") he is made one of the battalion's six scouts. Assigned an "Army buddy," fellow scout Bernard V. O'Hare Jr., a Roman Catholic youth from Shenandoah, Pennsylvania, who will become a friend for life. Secures frequent Sunday passes, enjoying meals at his parents' house and movie dates with Jane Marie Cox, his sometimes high-school sweetheart. On May 14, while Vonnegut is home on a Mother's Day pass, mother, age fifty-five, commits suicide using barbiturates and alcohol. In October the 106th leaves Camp Atterbury and is staged at Camp Myles Standish, Taunton, Massachusetts. The division embarks at New York City on October 17 and, after three weeks' training in England, is deployed in the Ardennes on December 11. The Germans launch a surprise offensive against the American front on December 16, and three days later Vonnegut, O'Hare, and some sixty other infantrymen are separated from their battalion and taken prisoner near Schönberg, on the German-Belgian border. They are marched sixty miles to Limburg and on December 21 are warehoused, sixty men to a forty-man boxcar, on a railroad siding there. After more than a week, the stifling, fetid car is hauled by train to Stalag IV-B, a crowded German P.O.W. camp in Mühlberg, thirty miles north of Dresden.

1945   On New Year's Day the boxcar is opened, and Vonnegut and his fellow-prisoners are provided showers, bunks, and starvation rations of cold potato soup and brown bread. On January 10, Vonnegut, O'Hare, and about one hundred fifty other prisoners are transferred to a Dresden factory where, under observation by armed guards, they manufacture vitamin-enriched barley-malt syrup. Vonnegut, who has rudimentary German learned at home, is elected the group's foreman and interpreter. On February 13–14, the Allied air forces bomb Dresden, destroying much of the city and killing some twenty-five thousand people. Vonnegut, his fellow prisoners, and their guards find safety in the subterranean meat locker of a slaughterhouse. After the raid, the guards put the prisoners to work clearing corpses from basements and air-raid shelters and hauling them to mass funeral pyres in the Old Market. In late April, as U.S. forces advance on Leipzig, the prisoners and their guards evacuate Dresden and march fifty miles southeast toward Hellendorf, a hamlet near the border with Czechoslovakia. There, on the morning after the general surrender of May 7, the Germans abandon the prisoners and flee from the advancing Soviet Army. Vonnegut, O'Hare, and six others steal a horse and wagon and, over the following week, slowly make their way back to Dresden. Outside the city they meet the Soviet Army, which trucks them a hundred miles to the American lines at Halle. From Halle they are flown, on May 22, to Le Havre, France, for rest and recovery at Camp Lucky Strike, a U.S. repatriation facility. ("When I was captured I weighed 180 pounds," Vonnegut later remembered. "When I was liberated, I weighed 132. The Army fed me cheeseburgers and milkshakes and sent me home wearing an overcoat of baby fat.") On April 21, Vonnegut and O'Hare board a Liberty Ship, the SS *Lucretia Mott*, bound for Newport News, Virginia. Vonnegut returns to Camp Atterbury by train and serves three more weeks as a clerical typist; is promoted to corporal, awarded a Purple Heart, then honorably discharged in late July. Marries high-school sweetheart Jane Marie Cox, September 14, and honeymoons at a Vonnegut family cottage on Lake Maxinkuckee. Taking advantage of the G.I. Bill, Vonnegut applies, and in October is accepted, to the Master's program in anthropology at the University of Chicago. The newlyweds rent an inexpensive apartment near the campus, their home for the next two years. Vonnegut finds a part-time job as a police reporter for the City News Bureau, an independent news agency that provides local stories to Chicago's five dailies.

1946   Greatly enjoys his anthropology classes, especially those taught by Robert Redfield, whom Vonnegut will remember as "the most satisfying teacher in my life." Redfield's theory that human beings are hardwired for living in a

"Folk Society"—"a society where everyone knew every-body well, and associations were for life," where "there was little change" and "what one man believed was what all men believed," where every man felt himself to be part of a larger, supportive, coherent whole—quickly becomes cen-tral to Vonnegut's world view. ("We are full of chemicals which require us to belong to folk societies, or failing that, to feel lousy all the time," Vonnegut will later write. "We are chemically engineered to live in folk societies, just as fish are chemically engineered to live in clean water—and there are no folk societies for us anymore.")

1947   Son born, May 11, and named Mark Vonnegut in honor of Mark Twain. Master's thesis, "On the Fluctuations Be-tween Good and Evil in Simple Tales," unanimously re-jected by Chicago's anthropology faculty. Vonnegut leaves the program without a degree, fails to turn his part-time job into full-time newspaper work, and searches in vain for appropriate employment. Through the agency of his brother, Bernard, an atmospheric scientist at General Electric, Vonnegut is interviewed by the public-relations department at GE headquarters, in Schenectady, New York. Accepts position of publicist for research laboratory at ninety dollars a week, and moves with family to the vil-lage of Alplaus, five miles north of the GE complex. Joins the Alplaus Volunteer Fire Department, his window into community life, and reads George Orwell, whose work and moral example become a touchstone.

1949   Vonnegut enjoys the daily company of research scientists and is "easily excited and entertained" by their work, but despises the corporate hierarchy of GE and sees no room for advancement within the PR department. Devotes evenings and weekends to drafting his first short stories, one of which, "Report on the Barnhouse Effect," he submits to Knox Burger, chief fiction editor at *Collier's*, a general-interest mass-circulation magazine which, like its rival *The Saturday Evening Post*, publishes five stories a week. "Knox told me what was wrong with it, and how to fix it," Vonnegut will later remember. "I did what he said, and he bought the story for seven hundred and fifty dollars, six weeks' pay at GE. I wrote another, and he paid nine hundred and fifty. . . ." Daughter, Edith ("Edie") Vonnegut, born December 29.

1950   First published story, "Report on the Barnhouse Effect," in *Collier's*, February 11; it is adapted for NBC radio's *Dimension X* program (broadcast April 22) and chosen for inclusion in Robert A. Heinlein's anthology *Tomorrow, the Stars* (1952). Sells several more stories to *Collier's* and begins planning a satirical novel about a fully automated world where human labor and the dignity of work are rendered obsolete.

1951   Vonnegut rents a summer cottage in Provincetown, Massachusetts, and decides to resign from GE and move his family to Cape Cod. Having saved the equivalent of a year's salary in freelance income, he buys a small house at 10 Barnard Street, Osterville, on the south shore of the Cape, where he finishes his novel, *Player Piano.* At the recommendation of Knox Burger, places the book with New York agents Kenneth Littauer and Max Wilkinson, both formerly of *Collier's.* At Vonnegut's request, they submit it to Charles Scribner's Sons, the house of Hemingway and Fitzgerald, and have a contract by Christmas.

1952   *Player Piano* published in hardcover, August 18, in an edition of 7,600 copies. It receives few but respectful reviews. Continues to write short stories for *Collier's* and, with the help of Littauer & Wilkinson, Inc., begins placing work in *The Saturday Evening Post*, *Cosmopolitan*, and other top-paying magazines.

1953   *Player Piano* reprinted as a July/August selection of the Doubleday Science Fiction Book Club. Vonnegut becomes involved, as an advisor, fundraiser, volunteer, and actor, in the business and artistic affairs of two of Cape Cod's leading amateur theatrical companies, the Orleans Arena Theatre (summer-stock) and the Barnstable Comedy Club (a repertory company staging four plays a year).

1954   After several false starts abandons Prohibition-era social novel, "Upstairs and Downstairs," set in Indianapolis and inspired by the riches-to-rags career of grandfather Albert Lieber. Writes six chapters of a novel about "ice-nine," a synthetic form of ice that will not melt at room temperature, but soon sets the project aside. Second daughter and third child, Nanette ("Nanny") Vonnegut, born October 4. *Player Piano* reprinted in paperback by Bantam Books, under the title *Utopia 14.*

1955   In February, the Vonneguts leave the small house in Oster-
            ville for a large one at 9 Scudder Lane, in nearby West
            Barnstable. With his favorite market for stories failing (*Col-
            lier's* became a biweekly in 1953, and will cease publication
            in January 1957) and without ideas for a new novel, Von-
            negut takes a full-time job as copywriter in an industrial
            advertising agency. Commutes to Boston daily, and holds
            the job for about two years. Dabbles in playwriting, with
            an eye toward providing a show for the Orleans Arena
            Theatre.

1956   In January Vonnegut's father, recently retired from a sec-
            ond career in architecture and living alone in rural Brown
            County, Indiana, informs his family that he is dying of lung
            cancer. Vonnegut visits him a number of times before his
            death, on October 1, at age seventy-two.

1957   Makes stage adaptation of his short story "EPICAC" (*Col-
            lier's*, 1950) for an evening of one-acts at the Barnstable
            Comedy Club. (The cast features eight-year-old Edie Von-
            negut in the role of a talking computer.) With small in-
            heritance from his father, opens and manages Saab Cape
            Cod, the second Saab dealership in the United States, with
            a showroom and garage on Route 6A, just up the street
            from his house. At a Littauer & Wilkinson holiday party
            Vonnegut is asked by Knox Burger, now an editor for Dell
            Books, to write a science-fiction novel for his new line of
            mass-market paperback originals.

1958   Improvises an outline for his paperback novel, conceived
            as a satire on human grandeur in the form of a pulp-fiction
            "space opera." Writes the first draft with unaccustomed
            speed, then painstakingly revises. ("I *swooped* through that
            novel," Vonnegut will later recall. "All the others were
            bashed out, sentence by sentence.") Sister, Alice, a house-
            wife and amateur sculptor, dies of breast cancer in a New-
            ark, New Jersey, hospital, September 16, at age forty-one,
            with both of her brothers nearby. Only one day earlier her
            husband of fifteen years, James Carmalt Adams, had died
            when a commuter train taking him to Manhattan plunged
            off an open drawbridge into Newark Bay. Without hesita-
            tion Kurt and Jane Vonnegut take in Alice's four orphaned
            children—James Jr. (fourteen years old), Steven (eleven),
            Kurt (called "Tiger," nine), and toddler "Peter Boo" (twenty-
            one months). As Jane will later write, "Our tidy little fam-

ily of five had blown up into a wildly improbable gang of nine."

1959   The Vonneguts assume custody of the three older Adams boys, but after a protracted, bitter dispute with a childless Adams cousin, relinquish control of the youngest. (Allowing the boys to be split between distant and unlike households will be, according to Jane, "the most difficult decision" of the Vonneguts' marriage. "Peter Boo" is raised in Birmingham, Alabama, and until his teens will see little of his older brothers.) In October, Vonnegut's second novel, *The Sirens of Titan*, published in paperback by Dell in an edition of 175,000 copies. It is popular with readers but receives no reviews.

1960   *Penelope*, a two-act comedy about a war hero's unheroic homecoming, receives six performances at the Orleans Arena Theatre, September 5–10. *The Sirens of Titan* named a finalist for the Hugo Award for the year's best science-fiction novel, and Houghton Mifflin arranges to print 2,500 hardcover copies to meet demand from libraries. Vonnegut, having failed to make money for himself or his Swedish franchisers, closes Saab Cape Cod.

1961   In the ten years since the appearance of "Report on the Barnhouse Effect," Vonnegut has published more than three-dozen short stories in "slick" magazines and science-fiction pulps. In September Knox Burger, now at Fawcett Gold Medal Books, publishes *Canary in a Cat House*, a paperback collection of twelve of these stories. Burger also signs Vonnegut's third novel, *Mother Night*, the fictional memoirs of a German-American double agent during World War II. Vonnegut publishes "My Name Is Everyone" (*The Saturday Evening Post*, December 16), a short story evoking the backstage life of a community playhouse much like that of the Barnstable Comedy Club.

1962   In February *Mother Night* published as a paperback original by Fawcett Gold Medal in an edition of 175,000 copies. Vonnegut, returning to the "ice-nine" material of 1954, begins a new novel, *Cat's Cradle*, which Littauer sells to Holt, Rinehart & Winston. *Who Am I This Time?*, Vonnegut's stage adaptation of "My Name Is Everyone," presented by the Barnstable Comedy Club. (It will be revived two years later by the Cape Playhouse in Dennis, Massachusetts.)

1963   In June *Cat's Cradle* published in hardcover by Holt. Reviews are few but enthusiastic, and at Christmas Graham Greene, writing in the London *Spectator*, names it one of his three favorite novels of the year. In fall accepts year-long assignment as "the whole English department" at the Hopefield School, in East Sandwich, Massachusetts, a small private high school for students with emotional and learning problems.

1964   Responding to a changing editorial marketplace, stops writing short stories and begins contributing personal essays, book reviews, and other nonfiction pieces to periodicals including *The New York Times Book Review*, *Life*, *Esquire*, and the travel magazine *Venture*.

1965   In March *God Bless You, Mr. Rosewater*, a novel about a so-called fool and his money, published in hardcover by Holt, Rinehart & Winston to many if mixed reviews. Accepts last-minute invitation to teach fiction writing at the Writers' Workshop, Iowa City, on a two-year contract. Accompanied by Edie, who enrolls in nearby University High School, he lives on the first floor of a large brick Victorian house at 800 Van Buren Avenue, next door to the writer Andre Dubus. "I didn't get to know any literary people until [my] two years teaching at Iowa," he will later recall. "There at Iowa I was suddenly friends with Nelson Algren and José Donoso and Vance Bourjaily and Donald Justice ... and was amazed. Suddenly writing seemed very important again. This was better than a transplant of monkey glands for a man my age." Enjoys teaching, and is good at it. His students include Loree Rackstraw, a future English professor and memoirist who becomes a friend and confidante for life. Begins work in earnest on a long-contemplated "Dresden novel," based on his experiences during World War II.

1966   In May is joined in Iowa by Jane and daughter Nanny. *Cat's Cradle* becomes a bestseller, especially among college-age readers, in its Dell paperback edition. *Player Piano* reprinted in hardcover by Holt, Rinehart & Winston, and *Mother Night* reprinted in hardcover by Harper & Row. Agent Kenneth Littauer dies, July, and Max Wilkinson, to Vonnegut's dismay, moves literary agency to Long Island and goes into semiretirement. In fall, Richard Yates rejoins the Iowa faculty and quickly becomes a lifelong friend.

Vonnegut's students for 1966–67 include the young and unpublished John Irving, Gail Godwin, and John Casey. In November, forty-year-old editor-publisher Seymour ("Sam") Lawrence—formerly of the Atlantic Monthly Press and Knopf, now launching his own imprint at Delacorte Press—offers Vonnegut a three-book contract. Vonnegut, with Wilkinson's consent, hires entertainment lawyer Donald C. Farber to handle the contract. (In 1977 Farber will become Vonnegut's sole agent and attorney.)

1967   Prepares first book for Sam Lawrence, a miscellany of previously published short works including eleven of the twelve stories in *Canary in a Cat House*, eleven uncollected and later stories, and two recent nonfiction pieces. To anchor the book with something new and substantial, writes "Welcome to the Monkey House," his first short story in nearly five years and the first not conceived for a magazine. In April awarded a fellowship from the John Simon Guggenheim Foundation, which finances a summer research trip to Dresden in the company of his Army buddy Bernard V. O'Hare. In May, ends two-year stay at the Iowa Writers' Workshop and returns with family to Barnstable to work on his Dresden novel.

1968   Collection *Welcome to the Monkey House* published by Delacorte/Seymour Lawrence, August, to mixed reviews. Vonnegut completes his Dresden novel, and Sam Lawrence, convinced of the book's sales potential, begins buying rights to earlier works for reissue as Delacorte hardcovers and Delta/Dell paperbacks. "Fortitude," a one-act teleplay commissioned by CBS for an unrealized comedy special, reshaped as a closet drama and published in the September issue of *Playboy*.

1969   On March 31, Vonnegut's Dresden novel, *Slaughterhouse-Five*, published by Delacorte/Seymour Lawrence to uniformly good and well-placed reviews, including the cover of *The New York Times Book Review*. The book spends sixteen weeks on the *Times* fiction list, peaking at number four, and creates an audience for his newly issued paperback backlist. Vonnegut begins a lucrative second career as a public speaker, especially on college campuses. Works on a new novel and teases the press with its title, *Breakfast of Champions*. In May, producer Lester M. Goldsmith options *Penelope*, Vonnegut's play of 1960, and begins planning

Off-Broadway premiere for the following fall. Vonnegut
spends most of the summer rewriting the play, giving it the
new title *Happy Birthday, Wanda June*.

1970   In early January, at the invitation of a private American
relief organization, visits the short-lived, war-torn African
republic of Biafra shortly before it surrenders to Nigeria,
from which it was attempting to secede. Publishes account
of the trip, "Biafra: A People Betrayed," in April issue of
McCall's. In May receives an Academy Award in Literature
from the American Academy of Arts and Letters. Interviewed by Harry Reasoner of CBS's *60 Minutes*, television's
most-watched program, for the broadcast of September 15.
(Reasoner introduces him as "the current idol of the country's sensitive and intelligent young people, [who] snap up
his books as fast as they're reissued. . . . His gentle fantasies of peace and his dark humor are as current among
the young as was J. D. Salinger's work in the fifties and
Tolkien's in the sixties.") Accepts invitation to teach creative writing at Harvard University for the academic year
beginning in the fall. Commutes to Cambridge two days a
week from New York City, where, by arrangement with producer Lester Goldsmith, he lives as a "kept playwright" in a
Greenwich Village sublet. With director Michael Kane
and a cast starring Kevin McCarthy and Marsha Mason,
workshops the script of *Happy Birthday, Wanda June*
throughout September, tinkering with the show until its
first curtain. Play opens at the Theatre de Lys, Christopher
Street, on October 7; it receives mixed reviews and runs
forty-seven performances, closing on November 15. The
show moves to the Edison Theater, Broadway, on December 22. During production of *Wanda June* Vonnegut meets
and begins a relationship with the photojournalist Jill Krementz, born 1940.

1971   Son Mark, a self-described hippie and co-founder, with
friends from Swarthmore, of a commune at Lake Powell,
British Columbia, suffers a manic mental breakdown. On
February 14, Vonnegut commits him to the care of Hollywood Psychiatric Hospital in Vancouver, where he makes
a slow but steady recovery. Broadway production of *Wanda
June* closes March 14 after ninety-six performances. In
May, Vonnegut delivers the annual Blashfield Address to
the assembled National Institute of Arts and Letters and

American Academy of Arts and Letters. Awarded Master's degree in anthropology by the University of Chicago, which, at the department chair's suggestion, accepts *Cat's Cradle* in lieu of a formal dissertation. In June, book version of *Wanda June*, with a preface by the author and production photographs by Jill Krementz, published by Delacorte/Seymour Lawrence. Resumes work on *Breakfast of Champions*. In December, Sony Pictures releases film version of *Happy Birthday, Wanda June*, directed by Mark Robson and starring Rod Steiger and Susannah York. ("It was one of the most embarrassing movies ever made," Vonnegut later writes, "and I am happy that it sank like a stone.") Grants WNET-New York and WGBH-Boston the option to develop a ninety-minute made-for-television "revue" based on scenes from his writings. The script, by David O'Dell, is revised by Vonnegut and titled *Between Time and Timbuktu, or Prometheus-5: A Space Fantasy*. Separates from Jane Marie Cox Vonnegut and rents a one-bedroom apartment at 349 East Fifty-fourth Street, between First Avenue and Second Avenue.

1972   On March 13 *Between Time and Timbuktu*, starring William Hickey, Kevin McCarthy, and the comedians Bob and Ray (Bob Elliott and Ray Goulding), broadcast nationally as an installment of public television's *NET Playhouse* series. In October, a book version of the teleplay—"based on materials by Kurt Vonnegut, Jr.," with a preface by the author and photographs by Krementz—published by Delacorte/Seymour Lawrence. On March 15 *Slaughterhouse-Five*, directed by George Roy Hill from a screenplay by Stephen Geller, released by Universal Studios. The film, starring Michael Sacks, Ron Leibman, and Valerie Perrine, delights Vonnegut, who finds the adaptation "flawless." In summer, Vonnegut and Krementz collaborate on an illustrated report from the Republican National Convention in Miami, published as the cover story of the November issue of *Harper's*. "The Big Space Fuck," Vonnegut's widely publicized "farewell" to the short-story form, published in *Again, Dangerous Visions*, an anthology of original science-fiction tales commissioned and edited by Harlan Ellison. Named vice president of PEN American Center, the U.S. branch of the international literary and human-rights organization, and remains active on PEN's behalf for the rest of his life.

1973   In April, *Breakfast of Champions*, embellished with more
        than a hundred felt-tip line drawings by the author, pub-
        lished by Delacorte/Seymour Lawrence to mixed reviews
        but strong sales. It dominates the *New York Times* fiction
        list for twenty-eight weeks, ten weeks in the number-one
        position. In May, speaks against state-sponsored censor-
        ship at the conference of International PEN in Stockholm,
        is inducted into the National Institute of Arts and Letters,
        and receives an honorary doctorate in the humanities from
        Indiana University, Bloomington. In September, begins
        one-year term as Distinguished Professor of English Prose
        at City University of New York, where his colleagues in-
        clude Joseph Heller, who becomes a close friend. In No-
        vember *Slaughterhouse-Five* declared obscene by the school
        board of Drake, North Dakota, which orders thirty-six
        copies of the novel burned in the high-school furnace and
        the teacher who assigned it dismissed; it is the first of more
        than a dozen such incidents of censorship during Von-
        negut's lifetime, all successfully challenged by the American
        Civil Liberties Union. Buys a three-story townhouse,
        built in 1862, at 228 East Forty-eighth Street, between
        Second Avenue and Third Avenue, which he shares with
        Jill Krementz. (The top floor of this whitewashed Turtle
        Bay brownstone becomes his office; the separate basement
        apartment, with its entry under the stoop, becomes her
        photography studio.) In December Jane Marie Cox Von-
        negut reluctantly agrees to a divorce.

1974   *Wampeters, Foma & Granfalloons (Opinions)*, a collection
        of twenty-five previously published short prose pieces,
        brought out by Delacorte/Seymour Lawrence, Septem-
        ber. This, the first of his "autobiographical collages" com-
        bining essays, articles, speeches, book reviews, and other
        writings, is the last of his works to be published by "Kurt
        Vonnegut, Jr."; subsequent works, and all reprints, will be
        published under the name "Kurt Vonnegut." In October
        visits Moscow with Krementz; their guide is Rita Rait, the
        translator of his books into Russian.

1975   Writes *Slapstick*, a comic novel about a brother and sister
        dedicated to wiping out "the peculiarly American disease
        called loneliness." In May begins four-year term as Vice
        President for Literature of the National Institute of Arts
        and Letters. Spends summer in a rented beachfront house

in East Hampton, Long Island, and begins search for a second home in the area. Uncle Alex dies, July 28, at age eighty-six. ("I am eternally grateful to him," Vonnegut writes in a tribute, "for my knack of finding in great books reason enough to feel honored to be alive, no matter what else might be going on.") In October, Mark Vonnegut publishes *The Eden Express*, a memoir of his madness, to good reviews and strong sales. The royalties will pay his way through Harvard Medical School.

1976   *Slapstick* published by Delacorte/Seymour Lawrence, October, to uniformly negative reviews, the worst Vonnegut will ever receive. ("The reviewers . . . actually asked critics who had praised me in the past to now admit in public how wrong they'd been," he later wrote. "I felt as though I were sleeping standing up in a boxcar in Germany again.") Sales, however, are strong: it is on the *New York Times* fiction list for twenty-four weeks, peaking at number four.

1977   At the request of George Plimpton, editor of *The Paris Review*, fashions a long autobiographical article in the form of one of the magazine's "Art of Fiction" interviews. Purchases a second home, a clapboard house dating from the 1740s, at 620 Sagg Main Street, Sagaponack, a village in Southampton, Long Island. Summer neighbors include Plimpton, Nelson Algren, Truman Capote, James Jones, and Irwin Shaw.

1978   Works on a new novel, *Jailbird*, the fictional memoirs of a good man who, through no wrongdoing of his own, becomes embroiled in several of the most shameful episodes in modern American political history.

1979   *Jailbird* published by Delacorte/Seymour Lawrence, September, to good reviews and strong sales. It is on the *New York Times* fiction list for thirty-one weeks, five weeks in the number-one position. In April, commemorates the centenary of the Mark Twain house in Hartford, Connecticut, with a speech in which he says that "we would not be known as a nation with a supple, amusing, and often beautiful language of its own, if it were not for the genius of Mark Twain." Throughout the summer a musical adaptation of *God Bless You, Mr. Rosewater*, with book and lyrics by Howard Ashman and music by Alan Menken, is developed by Ashman's WPA Theater company with Vonnegut's "limited but noisy" involvement. The show, produced by Edie Vonnegut, opens at the Entermedia Theatre, in the East Village, on October 11. Despite good reviews, it closes after only twelve performances, having failed to find a Broadway backer. Vonnegut marries Jill Krementz, November 24, at Christ Church United Methodist, on Sixtieth Street at Park Avenue.

1980   On January 27 Vonnegut, a self-described "Christ-worshiping agnostic," delivers his first sermon, a lecture on human dignity at the First Parish Unitarian Church, Cambridge, Massachusetts. Writes the text for *Sun Moon Star*, a picture story with bold and simple full-color images by the graphic designer Ivan Chermayeff. A retelling of the Nativity as seen through the eyes of the infant Jesus, it is published by Harper & Row as a Christmas gift book. First solo art exhibition, featuring thirty felt-tip drawings on vellum, at the Margo Feiden Galleries, Greenwich Village, October 20–November 15.

1981   *Palm Sunday*, an "autobiographical collage" collecting short nonfiction pieces written between 1974 and 1980, published by Delacorte/Seymour Lawrence, March. The title piece is a sermon given on March 30, 1980, at St. Clement's Episcopal Church on West Forty-sixth Street. Vonnegut's text is John 12:1–8: "For the poor always ye have with you . . ."

1982   Television adaptation of *Who Am I This Time?*, directed by Jonathan Demme and starring Susan Sarandon and Christopher Walken, broadcast on PBS in its *American Playhouse* series, February 2. Hires Janet Cosby, a Washington-based lecture agent, to book his annual speaking tours—two weeks in the spring, two weeks in the fall, a schedule he will keep for most of the next two decades. *Deadeye Dick*, a quickly written novel of guilt, self-punishment, and neutron bombs, published by Delacorte/Seymour Lawrence, October, to mixed reviews. It is on the *New York Times* fiction list for fourteen weeks, peaking at number ten. On December 18, Vonnegut and Krementz adopt a three-day-old girl and name her Lily Vonnegut.

1983   Begins work on a new novel, *Galápagos*, a fantasy about the future of human evolution. Makes further drawings, and begins to take himself seriously as a graphic artist, though he doubts his technique.

1984   In January, unsuccessfully tries to interest art publisher Harry N. Abrams in bringing out a book of his drawings. On the evening of February 13, the thirty-ninth anniversary of the firebombing of Dresden, attempts suicide in his Manhattan home, apparently by overdosing on barbiturates and alcohol. Awakes in St. Vincent's Hospital, Greenwich Village, and is diagnosed, as he writes to a friend, "with acute (all but terminal) depression. . . . I was there for eighteen days, under lock and key. . . . I am no renaissance man, but a manic depressive with a few lopsided gifts." Upon release returns to *Galápagos*, finishing the manuscript by Christmas Day.

1985   *Galápagos* published by Delacorte/Seymour Lawrence, October, to good reviews. It is on the *New York Times* fiction list for seventeen weeks, peaking at number five. Completes working draft of *Make Up Your Mind*, a sex farce for four actors. The play, his first since *Happy Birthday, Wanda June*, is given a staged reading in East Hampton. It is optioned by a Broadway producer but is not produced or published.

1986   Writes *Bluebeard*, the fictional memoirs of a seventy-one-year-old Abstract Expressionist painter whose work is loosely modeled on that of Barnett Newman. On December 19, Jane Marie Cox Vonnegut, now married to law-school professor and Defense Department spokesman Adam Yarmolinsky, dies of ovarian cancer. She leaves behind a memoir of her life with Vonnegut and their six children, published by Houghton Mifflin in October 1987 as *Angels Without Wings*.

1987   *Bluebeard* published by Delacorte Press, October, to mixed reviews. It is on the *New York Times* fiction list for eleven weeks, peaking at number eight.

1988   Works on new novel, *Hocus Pocus*, a commentary on "the way we live now" addressing, among much else, American trends in higher education, crime and punishment, political correctness, social privilege, militarism, intolerance, and globalization.

1989   Sam Lawrence, who has moved from Delacorte to Dutton to Houghton Mifflin, asks Vonnegut to follow, but he declines. Sells *Hocus Pocus* to G. P. Putnam's Sons, where his editor is Faith Sale. In October, at the request of the international humanitarian organization CARE, travels to Mozambique to write about the country's decade-old civil war.

1990 "My Visit to Hell," Vonnegut's report on Mozambique, published in *Parade* magazine, January 7. The report is the journalistic centerpiece of his next "autobiographical collage," the assembling of which becomes a yearlong project. In May, gives anti-war speech in the form of an eye-witness account of the firebombing of Dresden at the National Air and Space Museum, Washington, D.C. Wartime buddy Bernard V. O'Hare, a longtime district attorney in Northampton County, Pennsylvania, dies, June 8. *Hocus Pocus* published by Putnam, September, to good reviews. It is on the *New York Times* fiction list for seven weeks, peaking at number four.

1991 Vonnegut and Krementz start divorce proceedings, and Vonnegut spends time at house in Sagaponack. *Fates Worse Than Death: An Autobiographical Collage of the 1980s* published by Putnam, September. The title piece is a sermon on humility, delivered at the Cathedral of St. John the Divine on May 23, 1982. Vonnegut accepts a commission from the New York Philomusica Ensemble for a new libretto to *L'Histoire du Soldat* (1918), Stravinsky's musical setting of a Russian fairy tale of World War I. Vonnegut bases his text on the case of Private Edward Donald Slovik, who, in 1945, became the first American soldier executed for desertion since the Civil War.

1992 Vonnegut and Krementz drop divorce proceedings. Named Humanist of the Year by the American Humanist Association, and accepts invitation to serve as Honorary President of the association until his death. ("We humanists try to behave as decently, as fairly, and as honorably as we can without any expectation of rewards or punishments in an afterlife," he says in his remarks of acceptance. "The Creator of the Universe has been to us unknowable so far. We serve as best we can the only abstraction with which we have some understanding, which is 'Community.'") Begins writing a new novel, which he claims will be his last.

1993 Sam Schacht, formerly of the Steppenwolf Theater Company, directs *Make Up Your Mind* in a limited Off-Broadway run at the New Group Theater, Forty-second Street, April 20–May 5. On May 6 the Philomusica Ensemble gives the world premiere of *L'Histoire du Soldat/An American Soldier's Tale* at Alice Tully Hall, Lincoln Center. Vonnegut approached by a former GE colleague, now a fundraising consultant in Lexington, Kentucky, to do a benefit reading for his client Midway College. Collaborates with Joe Petro III, an area printmaker, on a collectible limited-edition poster for the November 1st event. Delighted with Petro's result—a hand-pulled silkscreen print adapted from a felt-tip self-portrait—Vonnegut visits the thirty-seven-year-old artist in his Lexington studio. The two soon form a partnership, Origami Express, to produce signed and numbered limited-edition prints adapted from Vonnegut's drawings and calligraphy. This enduring collaboration solves most of Vonnegut's problems with technique, and helps him to become the graphic artist he has longed to be. (In 2004, after producing more than two hundred discrete Origami editions, Vonnegut will write: "One of the best things that ever happened to me, a one-in-a-billion opportunity to enjoy myself in perfect innocence, was my meeting Joe.")

1994   Sam Lawrence dies, January 5, at age sixty-seven. "That anything I have written is in print today is due to the efforts of one publisher," Vonnegut writes in tribute. "When [in 1966] I was broke and completely out of print, Sam bought rights to my books, for peanuts, from publishers who had given up on me. [He] thrust my books back into the myopic public eye and made my reputation." Invited by Daniel Simon, publisher-editor of the newly founded Seven Stories Press, to write an introduction to Nelson Algren's 1942 novel *Never Come Morning.* Struck by Simon's commitment to Algren's work and to publishing books on human rights, social justice, and progressive politics, he becomes an advisory editor to the small independent press.

1995   At the end of the year completes a draft of the novel *Timequake*, a fantasy on the subject of free will concerning "a sudden glitch in the space-time continuum" that, occurring on the eve of the millennium, forces mankind to relive, day by day and mistake by mistake, the entire 1990s. He is unhappy with the book and, to the dismay of Putnam, scraps it and begins again from scratch.

1996   On November 1 *Mother Night*, directed by Keith Gordon from a screenplay by Vonnegut's filmmaker friend Robert B.

Weide, released by Fine Line Features. Vonnegut finds the script "too faithful to the novel" but admires the performance of leading man Nick Nolte. In December completes a second version of *Timequake*—a fictional-autobiographical "stew" made up of excerpts from the earlier *Timequake*, humorous meditations on the creative process, and laments for the passing of the America of his youth.

1997   Brother, Bernard, dies, April 25, at age eighty-three; Vonnegut will write his obituary for year-end issue of *The New York Times Magazine*. *Timequake* published by Putnam, September, to admiring and elegiac reviews. It is on the *New York Times* fiction list for five weeks, peaking at number seven. Vonnegut sells the greater part of his personal and professional papers, including the various drafts of his fourteen published novels, to Lilly Library, Indiana University.

1998   With the news and features staff of WNYC-FM, develops a series of twenty-odd ninety-second radio skits, each a satirical "report on the Afterlife" in which Vonnegut, in a "controlled near-death state" chemically induced by Dr. Jack Kevorkian, interviews Sir Isaac Newton, Mary Shelley, Eugene V. Debs, or some other resident of Paradise. (The best of the skits are revised, expanded, and collected in an eighty-page book, *God Bless You, Dr. Kevorkian*, published in April 1999 by Seven Stories Press.) In October again visits Dresden and the slaughterhouse in which he survived the firebombing of 1945.

1999   Peter J. Reed, of the University of Minnesota, gathers the twenty-three short stories published in magazines in the 1950s and 1960s that did not appear in *Welcome to the Monkey House*, writes a critical preface to the collection, and asks Vonnegut for permission to publish. Vonnegut revises a couple of the less successful stories and writes an autobiographical introduction and "coda" to the volume. *Bagombo Snuff Box: Uncollected Short Fiction* published by Putnam, September, to respectful reviews and mild sales.

2000   On the evening of January 31 Vonnegut is hospitalized for smoke inhalation after successfully containing a fire in the third-floor office of his New York townhouse caused by a smoldering Pall Mall in an overturned ashtray. Pulled from the room by Lily and a neighbor, he lies unconscious for two days in Presbyterian Hospital and is dismissed after three weeks' recuperation. At the suggestion of his daughter Nanny, moves to a studio apartment near her home in Northampton, Massachusetts, where she and her family nurse him back to health. In spring invited by local Smith College to join the English faculty as writer-in-residence for the academic year 2000–01. Works with a handful of student fiction-writers and gives occasional public lectures and readings at the many college campuses throughout Western Massachusetts.

2001   In May begins writing a novel, each chapter a monologue by a famous middle-aged standup comedian who entertains America during the final weeks of mankind. Is shocked and creatively paralyzed by the events of September 11, and sets novel aside for more than a year.

2002   In response to threats posed to the First Amendment by the USA Patriot Act of 2001, lends his celebrity to public-service advertisements for the ACLU, stating "I am an American who knows the importance of being able to read and express any thought without fear." Gives Lilly Library drafts of his early short stories and the very few other literary manuscripts that survived the New York house fire. Writes foreword to the Seven Stories Press reissue of son Mark's *Eden Express*. In fall resumes work on novel, now titled "If God Were Alive Today," which develops as a topical satire on the Bush administration.

2003   In January is interviewed about the coming war in Iraq by Joel Bleifuss, editor of *In These Times*, a biweekly nonprofit news magazine headquartered in Chicago. Discovers easy rapport with Bleifuss, whose politics are "Midwestern progressive" in the tradition of Vonnegut's socialist heroes Eugene V. Debs and Powers Hapgood. Soon becomes a regular columnist and honorary senior editor at *In These Times*, contributing political opinion, personal essays, humor pieces, and drawings. Magazine column cannibalizes material developed for "If God Were Alive Today" and becomes the chief literary project of his remaining years.

2005   In October, *A Man Without a Country*, a collection of columns from *In These Times*, published by Seven Stories Press. A surprise bestseller, it is on the *New York Times* nonfiction list for six weeks, peaking at number nine.

2006   In June says to an interviewer: "Everything I've done is
            in print. I have fulfilled my destiny, such as it is, and have
            nothing more to say. So now I'm writing only little things—
            one line here, two lines there, sometimes a poem. And I do
            art. . . . I have reached what Nietzsche called 'the mel-
            ancholia of everything completed.'"

2007   In mid-March, falls from the steps of his townhouse on
            East Forty-eighth Street and hits his head on the pave-
            ment. Despite aggressive medical treatment, he never re-
            gains consciousness. Dies at Mount Sinai Hospital on the
            evening of April 11, at age eighty-four.

Note on the Texts

This volume collects the three novels that Kurt Vonnegut published from 1987 to 1997: *Bluebeard* (1987), *Hocus Pocus* (1990), and *Timequake* (1997). It also presents, in an appendix, a selection of short nonfiction works that Vonnegut wrote from 1983 to 2007 that are thematically related to these novels.

Bluebeard was Vonnegut's twelfth novel, published when the author was sixty-four. The idea of writing a fictional memoir by an American Abstract Expressionist painter occurred to Vonnegut in 1983, while he was researching a biographical article on Jackson Pollock commissioned by *Esquire* magazine. He began work on the novel in the spring of 1984, in an old potato barn on his summer property in Sagaponack, New York, a structure once used by its former owner, the minimalist artist Frank Stella, as a painting studio. Vonnegut completed *Bluebeard* at his New York City townhouse, at 228 East Forty-eighth Street, in February 1987. The novel was published, in hardcover, by Delacorte Press, New York, on October 6, 1987. Five hundred copies of the first printing were specially bound, signed by the author, and sold by Delacorte as a slipcased "limited first edition." In addition, in the fall of 1987 the Franklin Library, of Franklin Center, Pennsylvania, privately printed a specially designed "deluxe" edition of *Bluebeard* for members of its Signed First Editions Society. A British trade edition, offset from the Delacorte pages, was published in hardcover by Jonathan Cape Ltd, London, on April 28, 1988. Vonnegut did not revise the novel after its first printing, and the text of the 1987 Delacorte Press edition is used here.

Hocus Pocus was written in New York City and Sagaponack from the spring of 1987 to January 1990. The novel was published, in hardcover, by G. P. Putnam's Sons, New York, on September 5, 1990. (An excerpt had appeared before publication, under the title "Hocus Pocus," in the September 1990 number of *Penthouse* magazine.) Two hundred fifty copies of the first printing were specially bound, signed by the author, and sold by Putnam as a slipcased "limited first edition." In addition, in the fall of 1990 the Franklin Library, of Franklin Center, Pennsylvania, privately printed a specially designed "deluxe" edition of *Hocus Pocus* for members of its Signed First Editions Society. A British trade edition, offset from the Putnam pages, was published in hardcover by Jonathan Cape Ltd, London, on October 25, 1990. Vonnegut did not revise the novel after its first printing, and the text of the 1990 Putnam edition is used here.

The artworks that decorate the text of *Hocus Pocus* (the rubber-stamped figures of eighty-two men used on page 222 and, in a slightly altered version, of eighty-two women on page 479; the tombstone template used on page 221 and repeated on pages 366, 392, and 478) are the work of the author.

The first draft of *Timequake*, Vonnegut's last completed novel, was written in New York City and Sagaponack from January 1993 to January 1996. The book was reconceived in February 1996 and completely rewritten between March and December 1996. (Vonnegut gives a detailed account of the writing of *Timequake* in his prologue to the novel, pages 485–87 of the present volume.) *Timequake* was published, in hardcover, by G. P. Putnam's Sons, New York, on September 22, 1997. (An excerpt appeared simultaneously with publication, under the title "Timequake," in the December 1997 number of *Playboy*.) Two hundred twenty-five copies of the first printing were specially bound, signed by the author, and sold by Putnam as a slipcased "limited first edition." In addition, in the fall of 1997 the Easton Press, of Norwalk, Connecticut, privately printed a specially designed "deluxe" edition limited to twelve hundred copies signed by the author. A British trade edition, offset from the Putnam pages, was published in hardcover by Jonathan Cape Ltd, London, on October 16, 1997. Vonnegut did not revise the novel after its first printing, and the text of the 1997 Putnam edition is used here.

The artworks that decorate the text of *Timequake* are from several sources. The image on page 484 is reproduced from a three-color silk-screen print, *Trout in Cohoes*, created in 1997 by Origami Express (Kurt Vonnegut and Joe Petro III), Lexington, Kentucky, in an edition of seventy-seven. It appears here courtesy of Joe Petro III. The image on page 497, a photographic reproduction on the letterhead used by Vonnegut when he was manager of Saab Cape Cod (c. 1957–60), appears courtesy of Joe Petro III. The image on page 596, captioned "*Art or not?*," was created by the author's brother, the late Bernard Vonnegut, and appears courtesy of The Kurt Vonnegut, Jr., Trust. The reproductions of beer labels on pages 599 and 600 appear courtesy of Wynkoop Brewing Company, a division of Breckenridge-Wynkoop LLC, Denver, Colorado, and Studio Pattern, Denver, Colorado. The facsimile letter on page 651 appears courtesy of The Kurt Vonnegut, Jr., Trust.

The publication history of the short nonfiction pieces collected in the Appendix is as follows:

"A 'Special Message' to readers of the Franklin Library's signed first edition of 'Bluebeard'" originally appeared in the Franklin Library's deluxe edition of *Bluebeard* (1987). It was later incorporated into

Chapter 3 of Vonnegut's nonfiction work *Fates Worse Than Death: An Autobiographical Collage of the 1980s*, published in hardcover by G. P. Putnam's Sons, New York, in 1991. The text from the Franklin Library edition of *Bluebeard* is used here.

"Jackson Pollock" originally appeared, as "Jack the Dripper," in the special fiftieth-anniversary number of *Esquire*, December 1983. It was reprinted, as "Jack the Dripper," in *Fifty Who Made the Difference: 50 Great Writers on 50 Great Americans*, a hardcover volume based on the fiftieth-anniversary number of *Esquire* and published by Villard Books/Esquire Press, New York, in September 1984. The essay was later incorporated into Chapter 3 of Vonnegut's nonfiction work *Fates Worse Than Death: An Autobiographical Collage of the 1980s*, published by G. P. Putnam's Sons, New York, in 1991. The text from *Fifty Who Made the Difference* is used here.

"Jimmy Ernst," a tribute composed for the dinner meeting of the American Institute of Arts and Letters on November 13, 1984, was published in *Proceedings of the American Academy and Institute of Arts and Letters*, Second Series, no. 35 (1984). The text of the first printing is used here.

"Saul Steinberg" originally appeared, in somewhat different form, as part of "Requiem for a Dreamer," in *In These Times* magazine, October 15, 2004. It was later incorporated into Chapter 12 of Vonnegut's nonfiction work *A Man Without a Country*, edited by Daniel Simon, published by Seven Stories Press, New York, in 2005. The text from *A Man Without a Country* is used here.

"Origami Express" originally appeared as the author's note on the illustrations in Vonnegut's nonfiction work *A Man Without a Country*, edited by Daniel Simon, published by Seven Stories Press, New York, in 2005. The text of the first printing is used here.

"A 'Special Message' to readers of the Franklin Library's signed first edition of 'Hocus Pocus'" originally appeared in the Franklin Library's deluxe edition of *Hocus Pocus* (1990). It was later incorporated into Chapter 14 of Vonnegut's nonfiction work *Fates Worse Than Death: An Autobiographical Collage of the 1980s*, published by G. P. Putnam's Sons, New York, in 1991. The text from the Franklin Library edition of *Hocus Pocus* is used here.

"The Last Tasmanian" was written and copyrighted by Vonnegut in the fall of 1992. It originally appeared as Episode 7 of *Sucker's Portfolio: A Collection of Previously Unpublished Writings by Kurt Vonnegut*, a digital book whose seven chapters were posthumously edited by The Kurt Vonnegut, Jr., Trust in 2012 in partnership with the editors at Amazon Publishing. From November 12 to December 24, 2012, the chapters were uploaded in weekly installments to Amazon.com, where they were collectively marketed as a Kindle Serial. *Sucker's Portfolio* was published as a paperback original by Amazon Publishing, Las Vegas, Nevada, on March 12, 2013. The text from the paperback edition of *Sucker's Portfolio* is used here.

"Talk prepared for delivery at Clowes Memorial Hall, Butler University, Indianapolis, April 27, 2007," is the text of the thirtieth annual Marian McFadden Memorial Lecture, commissioned from Vonnegut in 2006 by the Indianapolis Public Library Foundation and completed about two weeks before Vonnegut's death on April 11, 2007. (The lecture was delivered on Vonnegut's behalf by his son, Mark.) The text originally appeared, as "Kurt Vonnegut at Clowes Hall, April 27, 2007," in *Armageddon in Retrospect*, a volume of Vonnegut's previously unpublished "writings on war and peace" posthumously edited by The Kurt Vonnegut, Jr., Trust and published, in hardcover, by G. P. Putnam's Sons, New York, in 2008. The text of the first printing is used here.

This volume presents the texts of the original printings chosen for inclusion, but does not attempt to reproduce nontextual features of their typographical design. The texts are presented without change, except for the correction of typographical errors. Spelling, punctuation, and capitalization are often expressive features and are not altered, even when inconsistent or irregular. The following is a list of typographical errors corrected, cited by page and line number: 36. 8, Hovanissian,; 49.3, encourgement; 49.27, Lefébvre-Foinet; 50.5, *audience*.''; 51.19, father; 93.10, Eighty-second; 128.11, Dolly; 150.29, prefectly; 161.30, Ziegfield; 213.7, leaning; 216.14, hand; 248.21, Kop; 323.4, freshmen's; 357.15, some where,; 359.22, afeard?; 494.24, airlanes; 626.12, School He; 637.35, 1926–1993; 640.18, Kavanagh; 641.24, Blocks'; 660.15, that; I; 668.7 (and *passim*), conquerers; 694.18, Humanist Society; 700.32, Krasner.

Notes

In the notes below, the reference numbers denote page and line of this volume (line counts include headings but not section breaks). No note is made for material included in standard desk-reference books. Biblical quotations are keyed to the King James Version. Quotations from Shakespeare are keyed to *The Riverside Shakespeare*, edited by G. Blakemore Evans (Boston: Houghton Mifflin, 1974). For reference to other studies, and for further biographical background than is contained in the Chronology, see William Rodney Allen, editor, *Conversations with Kurt Vonnegut* (Jackson: University Press of Mississippi, 1988); Asa B. Pieratt Jr., Julie Huffman-Klinkowitz, and Jerome Klinkowitz, *Kurt Vonnegut: A Comprehensive Bibliography* (Hamden, Conn.: Archon Books, 1987); Loree Rackstraw, *Love as Always, Kurt: Vonnegut as I Knew Him* (Cambridge, Mass.: Da Capo Press, 2009); John G. Rauch, "An Account of the Ancestry of Kurt Vonnegut, Jr., by an Ancient Friend of the Family," in *Summary* 1:2 (1971); Peter J. Reed and Marc Leeds, editors, *The Vonnegut Chronicles: Interviews and Essays* (Westport, Conn.: Greenwood Press, 1996); Charles J. Shields, *And So It Goes: Kurt Vonnegut: A Life* (New York: Henry Holt and Co., 2011); and Dan Wakefield, editor, *Kurt Vonnegut: Letters* (New York: Delacorte, 2012). See also the major collections of Vonnegut's nonfiction prose: *Wampeters, Foma & Granfalloons (Opinions)* (New York: Delacorte/Seymour Lawrence, 1974); *Palm Sunday: An Autobiographical Collage* (New York: Delacorte/Seymour Lawrence, 1981); *Fates Worse Than Death: An Autobiographical Collage of the 1980s* (New York: Putnam, 1991); and *A Man Without a Country* (New York: Seven Stories Press, 2005). For notes on Vonnegut's recurring fictional persons, places, and things, see Marc Leeds, *The Vonnegut Encyclopedia: Revised and Updated Edition* (New York: Delacorte, 2016).

BLUEBEARD

2.3 Dr. Mark Vonnegut, M.D.] Kurt Vonnegut's son (b. 1947) practices pediatrics in Quincy, Massachusetts.

8.11–12 massacre by the Turkish Empire of about one million of its Armenian citizens] On April 24, 1998, the following open letter, signed by Vonnegut and some 150 other concerned writers and scholars, was published in *The New York Times*:

To Honor the 50th Anniversary of the U.N. Genocide Convention
We Commemorate the Armenian Genocide of 1915
and Condemn the Turkish Government's
Denial of This Crime Against Humanity

On April 24, 1915, the Young Turk government of the Ottoman Empire began a systematic, premeditated genocide of the Armenian people—an unarmed Christian minority living under Turkish rule. More than a million Armenians were exterminated through direct killing, starvation, torture, and forced death marches. Another million fled into permanent exile. Thus an ancient civilization was expunged from its homeland of 2,500 years.

The Armenian Genocide was the most dramatic human rights issue of the time and was reported regularly in newspapers across the U.S. The Armenian Genocide is abundantly documented by Ottoman court-martial records, by hundreds of thousands of documents in the archives of the United States and nations around the world, by eyewitness reports of missionaries and diplomats, by the testimony of survivors, and by eight decades of historical scholarship.

After 83 years the Turkish government continues to deny the genocide of the Armenians by blaming the victims and undermining historical fact with false rhetoric. Books about the genocide are banned in Turkey. The words "Armenian" and "Greek" are nonexistent in Turkish descriptions of ancient or Christian artifacts and monuments in Turkey. Turkey's efforts to sanitize its history now include the funding of chairs in Turkish studies—with strings attached—at American universities.

It is essential to remember that . . .

- When Raphael Lemkin coined the word *genocide* in 1944 he cited the 1915 annihilation of the Armenians as a seminal example of genocide;
- The European Parliament, the Association of Genocide Scholars, the Institute on the Holocaust and Genocide (Jerusalem), and the Institute for the Study of Genocide (NYC) have reaffirmed the extermination of the Armenians by the Turkish government as *genocide* by the definition of the 1948 United Nations Genocide Convention.

Denial of genocide strives to reshape history in order to demonize the victims and rehabilitate the perpetrators. Denial of genocide is the final stage of genocide. It is what Elie Wiesel has called a "double killing." Denial murders the dignity of the survivors and seeks to destroy remembrance of the crime. In a century plagued by genocide, we affirm the moral necessity of remembering.

We denounce as morally and intellectually corrupt the Turkish government's denial of the Armenian genocide. We condemn Turkey's manipulation of the American government and American institutions for the purpose of denying the Armenian genocide. We urge our government officials, scholars, and the media to refrain from using evasive or euphemistic terminology to appease the Turkish government; we ask them to refer to the 1915 annihilation of the Armenians as genocide.

9.33   William Howard Taft]   Taft (1857–1930), a Republican, was President of the United States from 1909 to 1913 and Chief Justice of the Supreme Court from 1921 until his death.

10.4   Charles Warren Fairbanks]   Fairbanks (1852–1918), a Republican, was a U.S. senator from Indiana from 1897 to 1905 and Theodore Roosevelt's vice president from 1905 to 1909.

15.14   Maidstone Inn]   Small hotel, originally a private home of the Civil War era, that has operated since the 1920s on Main Street, East Hampton, New York.

17.8   *Captains Courageous*]   MGM feature film (1937) based on the 1897 novel by Rudyard Kipling. The movie's child protagonist (Freddie Bartholomew), the son of a California railway tycoon, is washed overboard during a steamship trip across the North Atlantic. He is saved from drowning by a Portuguese fisherman (Spencer Tracy), who teaches him his trade and raises him as his own.

18.7–8   *Mesrob Mashtots*]   Or Mesrop Mashtots (362–440 C.E.), Armenian theologian, hymnist, and linguist. St. Mesrop is credited not only with inventing the thirty-six-character Armenian alphabet but also with translating the New Testament into Armenian and establishing the liturgy of the Armenian Apostolic Church.

18.19   *Musa Dagh*]   "Mount Moses": mountain on the Turkish seacoast upon whose slopes the Armenians resisted the genocide of 1915.

18.24   *Vartan Mamigonian*]   Or Vardan Mamikonian (393–451 C.E.), Armenian military leader and martyr of the battle of Avarayr. The ferocity of St. Vardan's resistance is said to have persuaded the Persians to abandon their efforts to convert the Armenian Christians to Zoroastrianism by brute force.

19.18   Jackson Pollock]   American Abstract Expressionist painter (1912–1956). For Vonnegut's brief life of the artist, see pages 658–61 of the present volume.

19.18–19   Mark Rothko]   American Abstract Expressionist painter (1903–1970) whose signature images—typically two soft-edged rectangles of saturated color floating one above the other on a vertical picture plane—were crucial to the development of Minimalism and Color Field painting.

24.3   a line from the writer Truman Capote] In September 1959 the American novelist and journalist Truman Capote (1924–1984), while appearing on the live television talk show *Open End with David Susskind*, was asked about the writing style of Beat novelist Jack Kerouac. "That's not writing," Capote said, "it's *typing*."

28.29   William Saroyan] American writer (1908–1981) whose early autobiographical fiction depicted life among Armenian-immigrant fruit farmers in Fresno, California.

28.30   George Mintouchian] Vonnegut here evokes the fictional lawyer and businessman Harold Mintouchian, who, in Saul Bellow's novel *The Adventures of Augie March* (1953), is Augie's Armenian mentor.

36.24   SHAEF] Supreme Headquarters Allied Expeditionary Forces (1943–45).

41.9–10   Green River Cemetery] Cemetery in East Hampton, New York, which, since the burial of Jackson Pollock there in 1956, has become the resting place of many other midcentury American painters, including James Brooks, Jimmy Ernst, Elaine de Kooning, Lee Krasner, and Ad Reinhardt.

57.2   Marmon touring car] The Marmon Motor Car Company, of Indianapolis, Indiana, made luxury automobiles from 1902 to 1933.

68.15   *Liberty* magazine] Large-circulation American weekly (1924–50) that, like its close competitors *Collier's* (1888–1957) and *The Saturday Evening Post* (1821–1963), published richly illustrated feature stories, celebrity profiles, and popular fiction.

69.9–10   That story . . . was made into the movie *You're Fired*] The Paramount comedy *You're Fired* (1919) was loosely based on "The Halberdier of the Little Rheinschloss," a story by O. Henry published in *Everybody's Magazine* for May 1907.

71.20   Fu Manchu] Fictional criminal mastermind, created in 1912 by the English writer Saxe Rohmer (1883–1959), who figured in a long-running series of pulp stories and novels as well as in films, radio series, and comic strips.

72.11   Booth Tarkington] American storyteller and dramatist (1869–1946) who set most of his work in the American Middle West.

His works include the novels *The Magnificent Ambersons* (1918) and *Alice Adams* (1921), both of which won the Pulitzer Prize, and three collections of comic sketches concerning an eleven-year-old Hoosier named Penrod Schofield.

73.18–19   "'Those who cannot remember the past . . . repeat it.'"] From *Reason in Common Sense* (1905), by the Spanish-American philosopher George Santayana (1863–1952).

84.6–7   Matilda tanks, and Stens and Brens and Enfield rifles]   British weapons of the World War II era. The Matilda was an infantry support tank that saw service in North Africa, 1940–42, and in the South Pacific, 1943–45; the Sten a submachine gun (first manufactured in 1941); the Bren a light machine gun; and the Lee-Enfield a bolt-action, magazine-fed rifle.

85.35   Century Club]   The Century Association, at 7 West Forty-third Street, a private club founded in 1847 for "authors, artists, and amateurs of letters and the fine arts."

90.32   Fort Benjamin Harrison]   Former U.S. Army post (1908–91) in Lawrence, Indiana, a few miles northwest of Indianapolis.

91.32–33   "spit-filled penny whistle of American literature"]   In his introduction to a 1986 reissue of Nelson Algren's novel *Never Come Morning* (1942), Vonnegut wrote that "Algren was bitter about how little he had been paid over the years . . . and especially for the movie rights to what may be his masterpiece, *The Man With the Golden Arm*, which made a huge amount of money as a Frank Sinatra film. Not a scrap of the profits had come to him, and I heard him say one time, 'I am the penny whistle of American literature.'"

93.10   John Harlan]   John M. Harlan (1899–1971) was an associate justice of the United States Supreme Court from 1955 to 1971.

101.10   Booth Tarkington story]   "An Overwhelming Saturday," published in *Cosmopolitan*, November 1913, and then revised, under the title "The Two Families," as Chapter 15 of *Penrod* (1914).

104.14   *Sovereign of the Seas*]   Extreme clipper, built in East Boston in 1852 by Donald McKay, that in 1854 was clocked at 22 knots.

110.21   Madeleine Carroll]   English actress (1906–1987) best remembered as the witty and resourceful blonde handcuffed to Robert Donat in Alfred Hitchcock's *The 39 Steps* (1935).

110.35–36   Battle of Sidi Barrani]   On December 10–11, 1940, British and Indian forces took Sidi Barrani, Egypt, from the Italian 10th

Army, which had occupied the Mediterranean port city since the previous September.

115.29   Syd Solomon]   American abstract painter (1917–2004) who worked mainly in vibrant acrylics on canvas. Vonnegut characterized him, in a 1976 speech, as "a painter of bright weather. . . . neon thunderstorms and the like."

121.6   Cord]   The Cord Corporation, of Connersville, Indiana, made technologically innovative luxury automobiles from 1929 to 1932, and again in 1936–37.

125.35–38   Jim Brooks . . . half the work."]   James Brooks (1906–1992) was an American muralist and Abstract Expressionist painter whose signature works, like Helen Frankenthaler's, employed thinned oils on raw canvas. For Vonnegut's further thoughts on Brooks's remark about "how all the Abstract Expressionists operated," see page 660 of the present volume.

141.4–5   Adolph Gottlieb's "Frozen Sounds Number Seven"]   In 1951–52 Adolph Gottlieb (1903–1974), an American sculptor, printmaker, and Abstract Expressionist painter, created a pair of canvases called "Frozen Sounds" as part of his *Imaginary Landscapes* series (1951–57). Number 1 hangs in the Whitney Museum, Number 2 in the Albright-Knox Art Gallery.

141.18   second Battle of Freeman's Farm]   Fought on October 7, 1777, and also known as the second Battle of Saratoga or the Battle of Bemis Heights.

151.20   Fort Belvoir]   U.S. Army post in Fairfax County, Virginia.

186.36   Conrad Aiken]   Prolific American writer (1889–1973) whose nearly fifty books included some thirty volumes of poetry. His *Selected Poems* won a Pulitzer Prize in 1930 and his *Collected Poems* a National Book Award in 1954.

192.14–15   'These Americans . . . learn to swim.']   In May 1968, during an interview with oral historian Paul Cummings of the Smithsonian Institution, the American painter Nicolas Carone (1917–2010) recorded his memories of walking through the U.S. pavilion at the 1950 Venice Biennale with Giorgio Morandi, Gino Severini, and other Italian artists. There, said Carone, "they saw [a] de Kooning for the first time. [It] was the big *Excavation* picture. And they said it was forced. And they said, 'It's strange about these Americans,'—Morandi said this,—'they dive into the water before they learn to swim.'" Vonnegut encountered this anecdote in Jeffrey Potter's book *To a Violent Grave:*

An Oral Biography of Jackson Pollock (1985), which incorporates excerpts from Carone's Smithsonian interview.

198.21–24   *continuous* paintings on canvas . . . rollers at either end]
Vonnegut here describes a theatrical attraction of the nineteenth century known as the "moving panorama," which was popular first in Great Britain and then, especially in the 1840s and '50s, in the United States. A "panorama-show" was, like a modern motion picture, a ninety-minute to two-hour entertainment consisting of moving images (a continuously scrolling painted canvas, sometimes as long as fifteen hundred feet, viewed by the audience through a large cut-out frame) with narration and musical accompaniment. In the U.S. the most popular form of panorama-show was the travelogue of North America, Europe, or the Holy Land. Very few moving-panorama canvases survive, and none are in the collection of the Museum of the City of New York.

HOCUS POCUS

221.2–9   Eugene Victor Debs . . . I am not free."]   Debs was the president of the American Railway Union (1893–97), a founder of the International Workers of the World (1905), and five-time presidential candidate of the Socialist Party (1900, 1904, 1908, 1912, 1920). He was indicted under the 1917 Espionage Act for inciting disloyalty in the armed forces and obstructing military recruiting after making an antiwar speech at Canton, Ohio, on June 16, 1918, and was convicted on September 12. Before his sentencing on September 14 he made a statement to the court that began: "Your Honor, years ago I recognized my kinship with all living beings, and I made up my mind that I was not one bit better than the meanest of earth. I said then, I say now, that while there is a lower class I am in it; while there is a criminal element, I am of it; while there is a soul in prison, I am not free." Debs was sentenced to ten years in prison and began serving his sentence on April 13, 1919, after the U.S. Supreme Court unanimously upheld his conviction. He was released on December 25, 1921, after President Warren G. Harding commuted his sentence.

238.5   Paul Dresser]   American entertainer and songwriter (1857–1906) whose best-known composition, "On the Banks of the Wabash, Far Away" (1897), became the state song of his native Indiana in 1913.

248.20–21   Keystone Kops]   Uniformed troupe of bungling policemen who starred in several silent slapstick comedies filmed by the Keystone Film Company in 1912–17.

250.26   "Hell is other people."]   *"L'enfer, c'est les autres,"* from *No Exit (Huis Clos,* 1944), one-act play by Jean-Paul Sartre (1905–1980).

260.20   plebe year]   The first year at West Point is a cadet's "plebe" year. It is followed by his "yearling" year, his "cow" year, and then his "firstie" year, the year of his graduation and first assignment as a second lieutenant in the U.S. Army.

271.20   "Work Makes Free,"]   The German motto *"Arbeit macht frei"* ("Work Makes [You] Free") was posted by the Nazis above the entrances to several concentration camps after June 1940.

297.8–9   "From each . . . to each according to his needs."]   Phrase (*"Eder nach seinen Fähigkeiten, jedem nach seinen Bedürfnissen"*) popularized by Karl Marx (1818–1883) in his posthumous polemic *Critique of the Gotha Program (Kritik des Gothaer Programms,* 1875).

301.10   Georges Simenon]   Eric Pace's *New York Times* obituary of the Belgian mystery writer Georges Simenon (1903–1989), published on September 7, 1989, reads, in part: "For many years he was a tireless philanderer, and he provoked varied responses by saying so in his *Intimate Memoirs* (1984). The author Mavis Gallant noted in *The New York Times Book Review* that Mr. Simenon, 'trying to account for his two wrecked marriages and his numerous affairs and thousand-and-one casual encounters (most of his partners were paid),' had written: 'The goal of my endless quest, after all, was not a woman, but "the" woman, the real one, loving and maternal at the same time, without artifices.'"

331.28–32   "'Who steals my purse . . . poor indeed.'"]   *Othello*, III.iii.157–61.

339.6–7   "the moving finger writes; and, having writ, moves on."]   Rubái 545, in *The Rubáiyát of Omar Khayyám*, translated from the eleventh-century Persian by Edward FitzGerald (1859). For the complete rubái (or quatrain), see page 562 of the present volume.

339.22–25   "No, 'tis not so deep . . . A plague on both your houses!"]   *Romeo and Juliet*, III.i.96–100.

345.18–27   "To be, or not to be . . . must give us pause."]   *Hamlet*, III.i.55–67.

359.16   Arthur C. Clarke]   British science-fiction writer and futurist (1917–2008) who wrote the novel *Childhood's End* (1953), cowrote the screenplay for Stanley Kubrick's *2001: A Space Odyssey* (1968), and, in a scientific paper of 1945, posited the idea of geostationary telecommunications satellites.

359.22–26 "Out, damned spot! . . . blood in him?"] *Macbeth*, V.i.35–40.

362.4–5 "There are more things . . . philosophy."] *Hamlet*, I.v.166–67.

364.32 "Fie! a soldier, and afeared?"] *Macbeth*, V.i.36–37.

378.29–31 "Fill the Earth . . . on the Earth."] See Genesis 1:28.

383.27 "There are more things in heaven and earth . . ."] See note 362.4–5.

385.12 rich people were poor people with money] In *Down and Out in Paris and London* (1933), George Orwell wrote that "the mass of the rich and the poor are differentiated by their incomes and nothing else, and the average millionaire is only the average dishwasher dressed in a new suit."

394.23 Mark Rothko] See note 19.18–19.

399.30 People who can eat people] Allusion to "People," song from the Broadway musical *Funny Girl* (1964) by Jule Styne, words by Robert Merrill: "People, / People who need people, / Are the luckiest people in the world . . ."

402.22–23 *Howdy Doody*] *The Howdy Doody Show* was a children's television series broadcast on NBC from 1947 to 1960. The marionette Howdy Doody—a gap-toothed, freckle-faced, redheaded boy from the American rodeo—was voiced by the show's host and creator, "Buffalo Bob" Smith (Robert E. Schmidt). The role of Clarabell the Clown, an antic pantomime character, was created in 1948 by Bob Keeshan, who soon found greater fame as CBS's Captain Kangaroo (1955–84).

432.23 "Where there is life there is hope."] The moral to "The Sick Man and the Angel," in *Fables* (1727), by John Gay (1685–1732).

440.14 durance vile] A long prison sentence.

449.2 A World War II movie] *Von Ryan's Express* (1965), starring Frank Sinatra as USAAF pilot Colonel Joseph L. Ryan, with Wolfgang Preiss as SS Major von Klement. The interrogation scene described by Vonnegut does not appear in the film.

449.31 Duke Wayne] Nickname of American actor John Wayne (1907–1979), an icon of rugged masculinity remembered for his starring roles in Hollywood Westerns.

449.33 All-Black fighter squadron] The 99th Pursuit (later Fighter) Squadron, whose pilots trained at the Tuskegee Institute in

Alabama, flew its first combat mission in June 1943. Three other squadrons began combat missions in February 1944 as part of the all-black 332nd Fighter Group, which the 99th Fighter Squadron joined in July 1944.

TIMEQUAKE

482.1   *Seymour Lawrence*]   American editor and publisher (1927–1994) who, through his imprint Seymour Lawrence Books at Delacorte Press, was Vonnegut's principal publisher from 1968 to 1989.

489.15–22   Mark Twain ... Henry Rogers]   In his essay "The Death of Jean," published posthumously in *Harper's Monthly Magazine* (January 1911), Mark Twain (1835–1910) described the final days of Jane Lampton "Jean" Clemens, the youngest of his three daughters, who died on Christmas Eve, 1909, at the age of twenty-nine. (The essay was reprinted as an appendix to *Mark Twain's Own Autobiography* [1924], edited by Albert Bigelow Paine.) Jean had been predeceased by her sister, Twain's second daughter, Olivia Susan "Susy" Clemens, who died in 1896, at the age of twenty-four. Twain's wife, Olivia Langdon Clemens, died in 1904, at the age of fifty-eight. Henry Huttleston Rogers, who had been Twain's closest friend for sixteen years, died on May 19, 1909, at the age of sixty-nine.

489.29–30   "The mass of men ... desperation."]   Henry David Thoreau (1817–1862), in Chapter 1 of *Walden, or Life in the Woods* (1854).

490.7   Fats Waller]   Thomas Wright "Fats" Waller (1904–1943) was a pianist, singer, songwriter, and comic entertainer. Among his compositions were "Ain't Misbehavin'," "Honeysuckle Rose," and "Jitterbug Waltz."

491.15   Leo Seren]   Seren (1918–2001), who as a Ph.D. candidate in physics at the University of Chicago worked on the Manhattan Project, said to the audience at Rockefeller Chapel, "I regret working on the atomic bomb for all the horror and destruction it caused." He once remarked to an interviewer that if he were ever tried for crimes against humanity, he would plead guilty.

491.24–25   Andrei Sakharov ... Nobel in 1975]   Sakharov (1921–1989) was awarded the Nobel Peace Prize in 1975 for his "strong and uncompromising struggle" for human rights and international cooperation.

491.27–28   pediatrician ... hydrogen bomb]   Sakharov met his second wife, the pediatrician and human rights activist Elena Bonner

(1923–2011), in the fall of 1970, after he had stopped working on nuclear weapons.

492.4–5   whistlestop on the permafrost]   From 1980 through 1986, Sakharov was exiled to Gorky (now Nizhny Novgorod), 250 miles northeast of Moscow, for opposing the Soviet invasion of Afghanistan.

496.3   Günter Grass]   Nobel laureate in literature (1927–2015), best known for his novel *The Tin Drum* (*Die Blechtrommel*, 1959).

496.6   Elie Wiesel and Jerzy Kosinski and Milos Forman]   Wiesel (b. 1928), Romanian-born author of *Night* (1960), an autobiographical work based on upon his and his father's experience in the Auschwitz and Buchenwald concentration camps; Kosinski (1933–1991), Polish-American writer whose novels included *The Painted Bird* (1965), *Steps* (1968), and *Being There* (1971); and Forman (b. 1932), Czech-born American filmmaker who directed *One Flew Over the Cuckoo's Nest* (1975), *Hair* (1979), and *Amadeus* (1984).

496.11   Robert Pinsky]   American poet (b. 1940), who in 1996, when *Timequake* was completed, published *The Figured Wheel: New and Collected Poems*, a finalist for that year's Pulitzer Prize.

496.15–497.7   I said, "If I had to do it all over . . . 'If this isn't nice, what is?'"]   The complete text of this speech, delivered on May 11, 1996, at Butler University, in Indianapolis, Indiana, was published, posthumously, as "Remember Where You Came From," in *If This Isn't Nice, What Is? Advice to the Young from Kurt Vonnegut*, edited by Dan Wakefield (New York: Seven Stories Press, 2014).

498.3–4   a swell book about his going crazy in the 1960s]   *The Eden Express*, a memoir by Mark Vonnegut (New York: Praeger, 1975).

508.13   William Saroyan]   See note 28.29.

508.14   Alvin Davis]   American journalist (1926–1982) and long-time member of the staff of the *New York Post* (1942–62), ending as managing editor. As a reporter, his specialty was crime and human-interest stories. In 1965, Vonnegut dedicated his novel *God Bless You, Mr. Rosewater* to "Alvin Davis, the telepath, the hoodlums' friend."

508.22–23   Bertrand Russell . . . chess.]   See Chapter 11 of *The Conquest of Happiness* (1930), by Bertrand Russell (1872–1970).

511.10   Archer Milton Huntington]   American philanthropist (1870–1955) who, with money inherited from his stepfather, the railroad magnate Collis P. Huntington, was not only a benefactor of the American Academy of Arts and Letters but also the founder of the Hispanic Society of America, New York City, and the Mariners' Museum, Newport News, Virginia.

511.11   Lee De Forest]   American inventor (1873–1961) whose more than eight hundred patents include innovations in radio, telephone, sound-recording, and vacuum-tube technology.

514.4   James Whitcomb Riley]   Writer and wit (1849–1916) whose poems include "Little Orphant Annie," "The Barefoot Boy," and "When the Frost Is on the Punkin."

516.11–12   "How sharper . . . thankless child!"]   *King Lear*, I.iv.288–89.

516.21–22   "'All the world's a stage . . . merely players."]   *As You Like It*, II.vii.139–40.

517.4–5   Edward Muir]   Muir (b. 1922), who used the byline "E. A. Muir," published poetry in *Harper's*, *The Atlantic*, and other magazines from the late 1940s through the 1980s. His poem "The Poet Covers His Child" appeared in *Harper's* for December 1949.

517.25   *Reader's Block*]   Novel (1996) by the American writer David Markson (1927–2010), an acquaintance of Vonnegut's for more than forty years. The first edition carried the following prepublication blurb: "Hypnotic . . . a profoundly rewarding read."—*Kurt Vonnegut*.

518.27   Edwin Muir]   Poet and novelist from the Orkney Islands (1887–1959) who, with his wife, Willa Muir, was also co-translator of works by Hermann Broch, Sholem Asch, and Franz Kafka.

519.3   A. E. Hotchner]   American novelist, playwright, and biographer (b. 1920) perhaps best known for *Papa Hemingway* (1966), a biography that draws on his thirteen-year friendship with Ernest Hemingway.

519.6   Heinrich Böll]   German Nobel laureate (1917–1985) whose novels include *The Clown* (*Ansichten eines Clowns*, 1963) and *The Lost Honor of Katharina Blum* (*Die verlorene Ehre der Katharina Blum*, 1974).

538.16–18   "The wolf . . . a little child shall lead them."]   Isaiah 11:6.

539.13   "Who is it they say I am?"]   See Matthew 16:15, Mark 8:29, Luke 9:18.

539.15–17   "We are here . . . whatever it is."]   See the epigraph to *Bluebeard*, on page 2 of the present volume.

541.3   those same words in French]   *"Non, je ne regrette rien"* ("No, I Regret Nothing"), song (1956) by Charles Dumont, words by Michel

Vaucaire, most strongly associated with the French chanteuse Edith Piaf (1915–1963). Kilgore Trout's use of it here, in 1945, is an anachronism.

542.2–5   American Humanist Association . . . Dr. Isaac Asimov]   In the words of its official literature, the American Humanist Association, an educational and advocacy group founded in 1941, "strive[s] to bring about a progressive society where being good without a god is an accepted and respected way to live life." Science-fiction writer Isaac Asimov was its honorary president from 1985 until his death, in April 1992; Vonnegut was honorary president from May 1992 until his death, in 2007.

542.16   Bernard V. O'Hare]   Vonnegut's "war buddy" and lifelong friend Bernard Vincent O'Hare Jr. (1923–1990) practiced law in central Pennsylvania from 1948 until his death.

543.1   new requiem for old music]   On February 12, 1985, Vonnegut attended the Manhattan premiere of Andrew Lloyd Webber's *Requiem*, a mass for the dead scored for chorus, three soloists, and orchestra. The program notes included both the requiem's original Latin text, based on the mass promulgated by Pope St. Pius V in 1570, and a literal translation into English. Vonnegut found the English text "sadistic and masochistic . . . promising a Paradise indistinguishable from the Spanish Inquisition," and before the concert had ended he had resolved to write a new one. Vonnegut asked John F. Collins, a classics professor at New York University, to translate his text into Latin, which was then set to music by Edgar Dana Grana, a Juilliard-trained composer living in Brooklyn. The Vonnegut/Collins/Grana collaboration, *Stones, Time, and Elements: A Humanist Requiem*, received its world premiere on March 13, 1988, at the Unitarian Universalist Church of Buffalo, New York. A recording of the *Requiem*—performed by the Magic Circle Opera Ensemble and the Manhattan Chamber Orchestra, both under the direction of Richard Auldon Clark—was released by Newport Classic Records in September 1994. Vonnegut's history of his *Requiem* was published as Chapter 6 of *Fates Worse Than Death* (1991), and the texts by Pope St. Pius V, Vonnegut, and Collins were printed in the same volume's Appendix.

543.19–21   The German philosopher . . . skepticism]   See "Skirmishes of an Untimely Man," Chapter 8 of *The Twilight of the Idols* (*Götzendämmerung*, 1889), by Friedrich Nietzsche (1844–1900), translated from the German in 1954 by Walter Kaufmann: "The craving for a strong faith is no proof of a strong faith, but quite the contrary. If one has such a faith, then one can afford the beautiful luxury of skepticism: one is sure enough, firm enough, has ties enough for that."

549.5–6   to 'die . . . and never grow old.'"]   From poem XXIII
("The lads in their hundreds . . .") in *A Shropshire Lad* (1896), by A. E.
Housman (1859–1936).

553.25   "Beware of gods bearing gifts."]   See page 144.3 of the present volume.

556.4–5   "that willing suspension of disbelief . . . poetic faith."]
From Chapter 14 of *Biographia Literaria* (1817), by Samuel Taylor
Coleridge (1772–1834).

556.22   Noam Chomsky]   Chomsky (b. 1928), a prolific writer on
linguistics and on American politics, has been a member of the MIT
faculty since 1955. He is currently Institute Professor of the Department
of Linguistics and Philosophy.

556.26–33   "Current estimates . . . population."]   See "The Manufacture of Consent," an address delivered at the Community Church of
Boston on December 9, 1984, collected in *The Chomsky Reader*, edited
by James Peck (New York: Pantheon, 1987).

560.10   'Stardust']   Popular melody (first recorded as "Star Dust,"
1927) by the American composer, pianist, singer, and entertainer Hoagy
Carmichael (1899–1981). Lyrics were added in 1929 by Mitchell Parish
(1900–1993).

562.26–29   *The Moving Finger writes . . . a Word of it.*]   See note
339.6–7.

567.3–6   *Papa came home . . . boom!*]   From "I Faw Down an' Go
Boom!", song by James Brockman and Leonard Stevens, popularized
by Eddie Cantor in Flo Ziegfeld's 1928 musical revue *Whoopee!*

570.27–34   *O beautiful . . . to shining sea*]   From "America the
Beautiful," patriotic poem by the Cape Cod poet Katharine Lee Bates
(1859–1929), first published, in somewhat different form, as "America,"
in 1895. In 1910, Bates revised "America" to fit the melody of a popular
Episcopal hymn tune ("Materna," 1882, by Newark choirmaster Samuel
A. Ward, 1847–1903) and form the song "America the Beautiful." These
lyrics were later included in Bates's *America the Beautiful and Other
Poems* (New York: Crowell, 1911).

572.21–22   *A Study of History* . . . Arnold Toynbee]   The twelve
volumes of *A Study of History*, a comparative analysis of the rise and fall
of twenty-six civilizations by the British polymath Arnold J. Toynbee
(1889–1975), were published from 1934 to 1961.

575.8–21   *The Lord is my shepherd . . . for ever*]   Psalm 23.

578.35   *"Il faut cultiver notre jardin,"*]   "We must cultivate our garden," the hero's final words in *Candide* (1759), by the French satirist
Voltaire (1694–1778).

579.3–8   For a few days after Germany surrendered . . . described
it some in my novel *Bluebeard*]   See page 152 of the present volume.

579.27–28   "From each . . . to each according to his needs."]   See
note 297.8–9.

581.23   Norman Thomas . . . John Dos Passos]   Thomas (1884–
1968), a Presbyterian minister and six-time presidential candidate of
the American Socialist Party, was the author of several books on ethics
and American politics; Dos Passos (1896–1970), a novelist whose works
included *Manhattan Transfer* (1925) and the trilogy *U.S.A.* (1930–38).

581.33–582.3   I still quote Eugene Debs . . . I am not free."]   See
note 221.2–9.

590.11–16   *Full fathom five . . . rich and strange*]   Cf. "Ariel's Song,"
The Tempest, I.ii.397–402.

597.22–598.27   "Dear Brother . . . love as always,"]   The original of
this letter, dated New York City, October 11, 1995, is printed in *Kurt
Vonnegut: Letters*, edited by Dan Wakefield (2012).

599.3   Joe Petro III]   Petro (b. 1956) is an American printmaker and
sculptor. Vonnegut gives a full account of his collaboration with Petro
on pages 663–66 of the present volume.

602.14   Kin Hubbard]   Frank McKinney "Kin" Hubbard (1868–
1930) was a vernacular humorist from rural Indiana and creator of
the nationally syndicated comic panel *Abe Martin of Brown County*
(1904–30).

611.15–18   Fred Hoyle . . . Boeing 747]   In his book *The Intelligent
Universe: A New View of Creation and Evolution* (1983), the British cos-
mologist Fred Hoyle (1915–2001) disputes the idea of abiogenesis—that
is, the idea that the first cellular organisms arose spontaneously and
inevitably from an inorganic "primordial soup." He writes: "A junkyard
contains all the bits and pieces of a Boeing 747, dismembered and in
disarray. A whirlwind happens to blow through the yard. What is the
chance that after its passage a fully assembled 747, ready to fly, will be
found standing there? So small as to be negligible, even if a tornado
were to blow through enough junkyards to fill the whole Universe."

613.13   Paul Krassner]   American satirist, stand-up comic, and
provocateur (b. 1932) who, as editor of the occasional magazine *The*

Realist (founded 1958), a member of Ken Kesey's Merry Pranksters, and a deviser of Yippie happenings, had a shaping influence on the counterculture of the 1950s and 1960s.

614.4   "While there is a soul in prison, I am not free."]   See note 221.2–9.

619.5–29   I was in southern Nigeria . . . far away]   Vonnegut's account of his journey to southern Nigeria, "Biafra: A People Betrayed," was published in the April 1970 issue of *McCall's* and reprinted in *Wampeters, Foma & Granfalloons* (1974). Chinua Achebe (1930–2013) was the author of, among other books, the novel *Things Fall Apart* (1958) and *There Was a Country: A Personal History of Biafra* (2012).

625.2   Dick Francis]   British steeplechase jockey and writer (1920–2010) who published more than forty mysteries set in the world of thoroughbred horse racing.

625.19   *Esprit de l'escalier!*]   French term for the witticism that comes to one's mind too late, after the moment to use it has passed.

625.35   Jerzy Kosinski]   The Polish-American novelist (see note 496.6) committed suicide on May 3, 1991. He was in poor health, and had recently been accused by critics of plagiarizing the works of several Polish novelists little known in the United States.

626.20   Carl Barus]   Barus (1856–1935), Hazard Professor of Physics at Brown University from 1895 to 1926, was a cofounder of the American Physical Society (1899).

627.4   Charles Thomson Rees Wilson]   Wilson (1869–1959) constructed a prototype cloud chamber in 1896, perfected the mechanism in 1911, and published his classic papers on condensation in 1923.

629.34–35   You must remember this . . . a sigh]   From the popular song "As Time Goes By" (1931), written by Herman Hupfeld (1894–1951) for the Broadway musical *Everybody's Welcome*. The song found lasting popularity when Dooley Wilson, in the role of the singing piano player Sam, performed it at Rick's Café in the Academy Award–winning film *Casablanca* (1942).

631.24   Ingrid Bergman in *Stromboli*]   In Roberto Rossellini's film *Stromboli* (1950), Swedish actress Ingrid Bergman (1915–1982) plays Karin, a beautiful and unhappy Lithuanian woman married to a Sicilian fisherman on the volcanic island of Stromboli.

635.18   "The evil that men do lives after them."]   *Julius Caesar*, III. ii.75.

635.34   *Madame Bovary!*] See Vonnegut's summary of Flaubert's novel on page 329 of the present volume.

637.27   *Abe Lincoln in Illinois*] Drama in three acts (1938) by American playwright Robert E. Sherwood (1896–1955). It was awarded a Pulitzer Prize in 1939, and was adapted by the author for an RKO feature film of 1940.

637.30–31   *8½ . . .* Federico Fellini] In *8½* (1963), by the Italian filmmaker Federico Fellini (1920–1993), an overworked film director struggles to complete his current project, and in his crisis is beset by memories of the most important persons in his life: family, friends, lovers, and artistic colleagues and collaborators. In the final scene, the director's set is crowded with all these many and various persons, some from the past, others from the present, who parade before the camera in surreal juxtaposition, out of time and place.

639.15–640.17   "No one, not in my situation . . . my friends and neighbors."] From Act III, Scene 12 of *Abe Lincoln in Illinois*. In Sherwood's original, Lincoln's speech is one long block of text; Vonnegut has broken it into paragraphs here.

641.13   I dedicated *The Sirens of Titan* to him] The dedication page of Vonnegut's second novel, *The Sirens of Titan* (1959), reads: "For Alex Vonnegut, Special Agent, with love—."

641.23   Phoebe Hurty] The dedication page of Vonnegut's seventh novel, *Breakfast of Champions* (1973), reads: "In Memory of Phoebe Hurty, *who comforted me in Indianapolis—during the Great Depression.*"

641.26–28   John Rauch . . . *Palm Sunday*] The Vonnegut family history by John G. Rauch (1890–1970) was published, as "An Account of the Ancestry of Kurt Vonnegut, Jr., by an Ancient Friend of the Family," in *Summary* 1:2 (1971). Parts of this history were incorporated by Vonnegut into Chapter 2 of his book *Palm Sunday* (1981).

642.4   Knox Burger] Burger (1922–2010), a fiction editor at *Collier's* from 1948 to 1951, acquired Vonnegut's first published story, "Report on the Barnhouse Effect," which appeared in the issue for February 11, 1950. The dedication page of Vonnegut's collection *Welcome to the Monkey House* (1968) reads: "For Knox Burger—Ten days older than I am, he has been a very good father to me."

642.8   Kenneth Littauer] Colonel Littauer (1894–1968) was Vonnegut's literary agent for eighteen years, from 1950 until his, Littauer's, death. He was a fiction editor at *Collier's* from 1928 to 1948, and then a partner, with his friend Max Wilkinson, in Littauer & Wilkinson, Inc.

642.18–19   *The Sirens of Titan, Canary in a Cat House*, and *Mother Night*]   *The Sirens of Titan* was published by Dell Books in 1959, *Canary in a Cat House* (twelve short stories) by Gold Medal Books in 1961, and *Mother Night* by Gold Medal Books in 1962.

642.27   Robert Weide]   Weide (b. 1959) wrote and produced the 1996 film adaptation of *Mother Night*, directed by Keith Gordon.

642.28   Marc Leeds]   Leeds (b. 1954) is the editor of *The Kurt Vonnegut Encyclopedia* (1994, revised and updated 2016), an authorized guide to Vonnegut's fictional universe. In 2008 he became cofounder and first president of the Kurt Vonnegut Society.

642.30   Asa Pieratt and Jerome Klinkowitz]   Pieratt (b. 1938) and Klinkowitz (b. 1943) compiled *Kurt Vonnegut, Jr.: A Descriptive Bibliography* (1974) and, with Julie Huffman-Klinkowitz, its successor, *Kurt Vonnegut: A Comprehensive Bibliography* (1987).

642.34   Don Farber]   Donald C. Farber, Esq., was Vonnegut's agent and close friend after the late 1960s and is sole trustee of The Kurt Vonnegut, Jr., Literary Trust.

642.36   John Leonard]   Leonard (1939–2008), a daily book critic for *The New York Times* and an editor of *The New York Times Book Review*, was an early and stalwart champion of Vonnegut's work.

642.37   Peter Reed and Loree Rackstraw]   Reed (b. 1935), Emeritus Professor of English at the University of Minnesota, is the editor of Vonnegut's *Bagombo Snuff Box: Uncollected Short Fiction* (1999); Rackstraw (b. 1931), a former student of Vonnegut's at the University of Iowa and a longtime professor of English at the University of Northern Iowa, is the author of *Love as Always, Kurt: Vonnegut as I Knew Him* (2009).

643.1   Cliff McCarthy]   Vonnegut's friend Clifford T. McCarthy (1921–2003), a painter and photographer, was a professor of art history at Ohio University from 1958 to 1991.

643.3   Kevin McCarthy and Nick Nolte]   McCarthy (1914–2010) created the role of Harold Ryan in Vonnegut's stage play *Happy Birthday, Wanda June* (1970); Nolte (b. 1941) played Howard W. Campbell Jr. in the film of *Mother Night* (1996).

644.2–5   Borden Deal . . . nom de plume]   Mississippi native Borden Deal (1922–1985) published twenty-one novels and more than a hundred short stories, mostly in popular magazines like *The Saturday Evening Post* and *Collier's*. His best-selling soft-porn novels *He, She*, and *Them* were published under the pen name "Anonymous."

644.11   Leopold von Sacher-Masoch]   Austrian writer (1836–1895) whose works include the novella *Venus in Furs* (*Venus im Pelz*, 1870). The term "Masochism" was coined by psychiatrist Richard von Krafft-Ebing in his book *Psychopathia Sexualis* (1886).

645.9   *Back to Methuselah*]   Shaw's epic play-cycle, written in 1918–20, consists of five parts, the first of which, synopsized here by Vonnegut, is titled "In the Beginning."

645.30–31   Nelson Algren . . . José Donoso]   Chicago-born writer Algren (1909–1981), author of *The Man With the Golden Arm* (1949) and other novels, and the Chilean writer Donoso (1924–1996), author of *The Obscene Bird of Night* (1970), were among Vonnegut's favorite colleagues at the Iowa Writers' Workshop in 1965–67.

646.19–20   I'm wild again . . . am I]   From "Bewitched, Bothered, and Bewildered," song by Richard Rodgers, words by Lorenz Hart, from the Broadway musical *Pal Joey* (1940).

647.10   Janet Cosby]   Cosby (b. 1942), CEO of Speakers Worldwide, Inc., of Bethesda, Maryland, was Vonnegut's exclusive lecture agent after 1982.

649.16–18   "The most beautiful thing . . . science."]   From "What I Believe," published in *The Forum* (October 1930) and reprinted, without title, in *Living Philosophies: A Series of Intimate Credos*, a volume of essays commissioned by *Forum* editor Henry Goddard Leach (1931).

649.18–20   "Physical concepts . . . external world."]   From *The Evolution of Physics*, a book for laypersons by Albert Einstein and Leopold Infeld (1938).

649.21–22   "I shall never believe . . . world."]   Einstein made this remark frequently, in letters and interviews. One of its earliest occurrences is in a 1926 letter to the quantum physicist Max Born, published in *The Einstein–Born Letters*, translated by Irene Born (1971).

650.16–17   Irving Langmuir and Vincent Schaefer]   American chemists long employed by General Electric. Langmuir (1881–1957) invented the gas-filled tungsten lamp, perfected the vacuum tube, and, for his discoveries in surface chemistry, won a 1932 Nobel Prize; Schaefer (1906–1993), with the assistance of Langmuir, proved, in 1946, that clouds could be seeded with dry ice.

APPENDIX

656.8   Saul Steinberg]   Romanian-born graphic artist (1914–1999) who, beginning in 1941, contributed more than twelve hundred witty sui generis drawings to *The New Yorker*.

657.32   Green River Cemetery]   See note 41.9–10.

658.33   Thomas Hart Benton]   Benton (1889–1975), a Missouri-
born painter and muralist whose work depicted the rural life of the
American Middle West, was Pollock's teacher at the Art Students
League, in New York City, from 1930 to 1932, and remained his mentor
and benefactor through 1937.

660.12   James Brooks]   See note 125.35–38.

661.21   Max Ernst]   German artist (1891–1976) who worked in the
Dada and Surrealist styles.

661.27   Conrad Aiken]   See note 186.36.

663.1   Saul Steinberg]   See note 656.8.

664.9–15   The logo for Origami . . . GOODBYE BLUE MON-
DAY]   The drawing, from Chapter 4 of *Breakfast of Champions* (1973),
is reproduced below:

665.16   Jonathan Winters]   Improvisational stand-up comic
(1925–2013) who was trained as a visual artist at Kenyon College and
the Dayton Art Institute. In 1988 Random House published a portfolio
of his paintings under the title *Hang-Ups*.

665.17–19   Ralph Steadman . . . Hunter Thompson]   In 1969
the Welsh cartoonist and illustrator Steadman (b. 1936) embarked
upon a forty-year collaboration with American journalist Thompson
(1937–2005). Together they produced a series of illustrated articles for
Scanlan's Monthly and *Rolling Stone*, and several books, including *Fear
and Loathing in Las Vegas* (1972) and *Fear and Loathing on the Campaign
Trail* (1973).

665.35   Syd Solomon]   See note 115.29.

667.8   A critic for the *Village Voice*]   Book and theater critic Ross
Wetzsteon (1932–1998), in "Nostalgia for the Future," a review of *Slap-*

stick in the issue for September 27, 1976, wrote that "Vonnegut is one of the few major novelists never to have created a major character—other, that is, than himself, the author as protagonist."

667.12   Eliot Rosewater and Billy Pilgrim]   Protagonists of, respectively, *God Bless You, Mr. Rosewater* (1965) and *Slaughterhouse-Five* (1969).

668.14–15   "From each . . . to each according to his needs."]   See note 297.8–9.

669.15–19   I wrote an essay . . . spares out there]   "Excelsior! We Are Going to the Moon! Excelsior!" appeared in *The New York Times Magazine* for July 13, 1969, and was reprinted in *Wampeters, Foma & Granfalloons* (1974).

671.25–27   Kirkpatrick Sale . . . *The Conquest of Paradise*]   The American environmentalist and critic of technology Kirkpatrick Sale (b. 1937) published *The Conquest of Paradise: Christopher Columbus and the Columbian Legacy* in October 1990.

671.31–672.2   "in what they dimly realized . . . perhaps forever."]   From the author's Epilogue, *The Conquest of Paradise* (New York: Knopf, 1990), page 370.

673.1   "Behind every great fortune lies a great crime,"]   Cf. Honoré de Balzac, in *Le Père Goriot* (1835): "*Le secret des grandes fortunes sans cause apparente est un crime oublié, parce qu'il a été proprement fait.*"

673:26   Heinrich Böll]   See note 519.6.

674.35–36   Alexandre-Edmond Becquerel]   Becquerel (1820–1891), a specialist in the physics of light, was the first to observe the photovoltaic effect, sometimes called the Becquerel effect, and to devise a solar cell.

677.25   Christian Croatian Nazi]   In his fictional autobiography *Kaputt* (1944), the Italian journalist Curzio Malaparte (1898–1957) described a wartime interview with the Croatian fascist leader Ante Pavelić (1889–1959) during which Pavelić allegedly showed him a basket filled with human eyeballs.

678.30   a man who we thought was a Native American]   Gregory Markopoulos (or Jay Marks, c. 1942–2001), an Armenian American raised by Greek immigrants who, after 1969, fabricated an eclectic Native American background for himself and published Indian-themed fiction, nonfiction, and children's books under the name Jamake Highwater. He was exposed in 1984 by syndicated columnist Jack Anderson.

680.19–681.9   Leonard Peltier . . . almost as bad]   On November 9, 1992, attorneys representing Peltier (b. 1944), an American Indian activist of Chippewa and Lakota ancestry, appeared before the U.S. Court of Appeals for the Eighth Circuit in an attempt to overturn his conviction for the murder in June 1975 of two FBI agents on the Pine Ridge Reservation in South Dakota. Peltier's appeal was denied on July 9, 1993. As of the publication of this book, all of his subsequent appeals have also been denied, and he remains in federal prison.

680.28–30   Peter Matthiessen . . . *In the Spirit of Crazy Horse*]   American novelist and nonfiction writer Matthiessen (1927–2014) published *In the Spirit of Crazy Horse* in March 1983. An updated second edition appeared in March 1992.

680.30–35   "The ruthless persecution . . . dwindling reservations."]   From Matthiessen's introduction, *In the Spirit of Crazy Horse* (New York: Viking, 1983).

681.10–12   I had written some about . . . Nicola Sacco and Bartolomeo Vanzetti]   See Chapters 18 and 19 of Vonnegut's novel *Jailbird* (1979).

682.4–11   Robert Hughes . . . New World."]   See Hughes, "The Fraying of America," *Time* 139.5 (February 3, 1992), page 46. The article was later incorporated into "Multi-Culti and Its Discontents," Chapter 2 of Hughes's book *Culture of Complaint* (1993).

682.24–33   "While I was in the boat . . . school for harlots."]   From the journal of Michele da Cuneo (1448–1503), an Italian nobleman who accompanied Columbus on his second voyage to the Americas in 1493, as quoted by Kirkpatrick Sale in *The Conquest of Paradise* (page 140). Sale's source was *Journals and Other Documents on the Life and Voyages of Christopher Columbus*, edited and translated by Samuel Eliot Morrison (New York: Heritage Press, 1963).

686.3   John Latham]   Latham, born near Liverpool in 1937 and now living in Colorado, is an independent research scientist specializing in lightning. He is also the author of a novel, five books of poetry, and several plays produced by BBC Radio 4.

686.15–20   Mark Twain . . . "Do not bring your dog."]   An excerpt from Twain's "An Unfinished Burlesque on Books of Etiquette" (c. 1881) was published, posthumously, in *Letters from the Earth*, a volume of his previously uncollected and unpublished writing edited by Bernard DeVoto (1962).

687.9–10   "History is but the record of crimes and misfortunes,"] *"L'histoire n'est que le tableau des crimes et de malheurs,"* from Chapter 10 of Voltaire's *Candide* (1759).

687.10–11   "History is a nightmare from which I am trying to awake,"] James Joyce, *Ulysses* (1922).

687.35–36   two white men in Akron, Ohio] William Griffith Wilson ("Bill W.," 1895–1971), a failed businessman, and Robert Holbrook Smith ("Dr. Bob," 1879–1950), a colorectal surgeon, pseudonymously cofounded Alcoholics Anonymous in 1935.

688.27   Canadian friend] Toronto-based filmmaker Allan King (1930–2009) who, in 1991, had directed an adaptation of Vonnegut's story "All the King's Horses" (1951) for the Showtime television series *Kurt Vonnegut's Monkey House* (1991–93).

689.2–4   "a new sort of glacier . . . double in size again."] From Vonnegut's contribution to a series of "open letters to the next generation" commissioned by Volkswagen and printed as paid advertisements in *Time* magazine in 1987–88. Vonnegut reprinted this letter, published on February 8, 1988, as part of Chapter 11 of *Fates Worse Than Death* (1991).

690.9–11   As Bertolt Brecht said . . . food."] See *Die Dreigroschenoper* (*The Threepenny Opera*, 1928), by Bertolt Brecht (1898–1956). In 1954 the American composer and librettist Marc Blitzstein translated this line as "First feed the face, and then talk right and wrong."

690.29–33   Reinhold Niebuhr . . . the difference."] Niebuhr's Serenity Prayer gained currency through its frequent recitation at Alcoholics Anonymous meetings after 1941.

691.1–3   *Talk prepared for delivery at Clowes Memorial Hall, Butler University, Indianapolis, April 27, 2007*] Vonnegut completed this, the text of the thirtieth annual Marian McFadden Memorial Lecture of the Indianapolis Public Library Foundation, two weeks before his death on April 11, 2007. The lecture was delivered on Vonnegut's behalf by his son, Mark.

691.6   Mayor Bart Peterson] Peterson (b. 1958), the mayor of Indianapolis from 2000 to 2008, had proclaimed 2007 the city's "Year of Vonnegut."

691.14   Ayres clock] Architectural clock with four eight-foot circular faces, designed by Kurt Vonnegut (Sr.) and built in 1936 for the L. S. Ayres department store at One West Washington Street, Indianapolis.

It overhangs the corner of Meridian and Washington streets, which the Ayres Company promoted as "The Crossroads of America."

691.18–19   The Orchard School and the Children's Museum]   The Orchard School, founded in 1922 on the educational principles of John Dewey, is a private elementary school in Indianapolis. The Children's Museum of Indianapolis, founded 1925, is the largest and fourth oldest such institution in the country.

692.32–693.2   "While there is a lower class . . . I am not free."]   See note 221.2–9.

694.18   American Humanist Association]   See note 542.2–5.

694.25–26   "Death is just one more night."]   See section 40 of Plato's *Apology*.

699.8   Booth Tarkington]   See note 72.11.

699.19–20   Booth Tarkington's play *Alice Adams*]   Tarkington's Pulitzer Prize–winning novel *Alice Adams* (1921) was adapted to the stage by his personal secretary and literary assistant, Elizabeth Stanley Trotter (1899–1977), in 1945.

699.23   Crown Hill]   Indianapolis cemetery; see page 514 of the present volume.

699.24   James Whitcomb Riley]   See note 514.4.

700.2–3   "Hell is other people."]   See note 250.26.

700.32   Paul Krassner]   See note 613.13.

701.5   *The Eden Express*]   See note 498.3–4.

701.23–24   "Dad, we are here to help each other . . . whatever it is."]   See the epigraph to *Bluebeard*, on page 2 of the present volume.

THE LIBRARY OF AMERICA SERIES

Library of America fosters appreciation of America's literary heritage by publishing, and keeping permanently in print, authoritative editions of America's best and most significant writing. An independent nonprofit organization, it was founded in 1979 with seed funding from the National Endowment for the Humanities and the Ford Foundation.

This book is set in 10 point ITC Galliard Pro, a face designed for digital composition by Matthew Carter and based on the sixteenth-century face Granjon. The paper is acid-free lightweight opaque that will not turn yellow or brittle with age. The binding is sewn, which allows the book to open easily and lie flat. The binding board is covered in Brillianta, a woven rayon cloth made by Van Heek–Scholco Textielfabrieken, Holland. Composition by Publishers' Design and Production Services, Inc. Printing by Sheridan Grand Rapids, Grand Rapids MI. Binding by Dekker Bookbinding, Wyoming MI. Designed by Bruce Campbell.